Evelyn Hood was born and raised in Paisley. She now lives on the Clyde coast with her husband.

D1337814

EVELYN HOOD OMNIBUS

Knowing Me

A Matter of Mischief

sphere

SPHERE

This omnibus edition first published in Great Britain by
Sphere in 2007
Evelyn Hood Omnibus copyright © Evelyn Hood 2007

Previously published separately:
Knowing Me first published in Great Britain in 2004
by Time Warner Books
Reprinted 2005, 2006
Reprinted by Sphere in 2007
Copyright © Evelyn Hood 2004

A Matter of Mischief first published in Great Britain in 1988
by William Kimber and Co Ltd
Published by Warner Books 1998
Copyright © Evelyn Hood 1988

The moral right of the author has been asserted

A CIP catalogue record for this book is available from the British Library.

ISBN 978-0-7515-4012-9

Papers used by Sphere are natural, recyclable products made from
wood grown in sustainable forests and certified in accordance with
the rules of the Forest Stewardship Council.

Printed and bound in Great Britain by Clays Ltd, St Ives plc
Paper supplied by Hellefoss AS, Norway

Sphere
An imprint of
Little, Brown Book Group
Brettenham House
Lancaster Place
London WC2E 7EN

A Member of the Hachette Livre Group of Companies

www.littlebrown.co.uk
www.evelynhood.co.uk

Knowing Me

Dedicated to June (Robertson) Walls, the twin who generously allowed me to use her story as the basis for this book, to Catherine (Haughey) Stevenson, who shared her childhood memories with me, and to Una, who makes soup.

1

May 1941

From the window of her sister's flat, Chrissie Kemp watched the rain drizzling along the pavement opposite the tenement, overflowing into the gutters to become a miniature river gurgling towards the nearest drain. In defiance of the calendar on the wall, which claimed that they were in the month of May, Wellmeadow Street was wreathed in a wet, grey mist and the room she stood in was growing dark. Soon the blackouts would have to be put up so that the lights could be turned on. At least, she thought, it would deter the Jerries from sending their bombers over tonight. From up there they would see nothing but greyness below. She shivered, and turned towards the room behind her.

At once, her spirits lifted, for it seemed as though the bassinet just in front of her gave out its own special light. It was the most beautiful crib Chrissie had ever seen; a nest made of delicately embroidered white satin with snowy muslin cascading from the beribboned hood to form a protective curtain. It was like the mother-of-pearl interior of a seashell, she thought as she bent over it, and the sleeping baby within was a little princess waiting for her fairy godmothers to come and bestow their wishes.

'She's so beautiful, Doreen!'

'Aye, she's all right.' Doreen Nesbitt reached out and adjusted a fold of muslin, scarcely glancing at the little face on the satin pillow.

'All right?' Chrissie echoed, shocked.

Colour rushed to her sister's face and her voice, when she said, 'All babies look the same at that age,' was defensive.

'I don't know about that. I've never seen a bairn as pretty as this wee one.' Chrissie bent closer to study the baby, who was sleeping on her back, long-lashed eyes closed, rosebud mouth pursed and tiny fists curled into pale pink seashells on either side of a head covered with silky black hair. 'You're so lucky, Doreen, and so's she. There's not many bairns lyin' in bassinets like this at a time of war and rationin'.'

'There wasnae a war on when we first got this cot.' Doreen's voice was suddenly bleak.

'No.' With an effort, Chrissie wrenched her attention from the baby and gave it all to her sister, rounding the crib to lay a hand on Doreen's arm. 'No,' she said again. 'It's not been easy for you, or for Frank. But that's all behind you now, isn't it?'

'Ye think so?'

It was Chrissie's turn to colour. 'I didn't mean . . . of course you'll never forget what happened before. What I meant was, now you've got wee Rachel things'll be much better for the two of you. For the three of you,' she corrected herself, and wished that she had had the sense to keep her mouth shut. It was so easy, these days, to say the wrong thing to Doreen.

'I suppose. We'd best go back to the living room now. I don't want her wakened. It took me long enough to

2

get her to sleep.' Doreen would have moved to the door, but Chrissie held her back, tightening her hold on her sister's arm.

'You're happier now, aren't you? You and Frank?'

'Of course, but that doesnae mean that I have to grin like an idiot all the time. It's hard work, looking after a wee baby. She's not a toy, you know. She can't just be put aside when I get too tired to bother. She cries, and sometimes she's sick all over her clothes, and she's forever dirtyin' her nappy.' Doreen glanced down into the snowy bassinet. 'She might look bonny right now but I'd not be surprised if her nappy's needin' changed already, and I only put a clean one on an hour since. You don't know what it can be like.'

Doreen was right, Chrissie acknowledged silently. What would a spinster know about looking after a tiny baby? Nothing at all, and as far as she was concerned, it wasn't likely that she would ever find out. Doreen was small and slender and had delicate, elfin features with blue eyes and hair the colour and sheen of a chestnut. Chrissie, the elder of the two by eighteen months, was half a head taller than her sister, sturdily built and with a round face. Her hair was more mousy-brown than chestnut, and although her eyes were also blue, they were not as thick-lashed as her sister's.

There must have been fairy godmothers a-plenty at Doreen's christening, but the only gift granted to Chrissie had been a strong sense of duty which had kept her at home to look after their fragile mother and demanding father. Doreen, on the other hand, had been a social butterfly since her early teens, with young men clam-ouring for her attention. It was true that her natural sparkle had faded over the past year or so, but there had been good reason for that. And now that wee Rachel had arrived Chrissie had no doubt that Doreen would quickly regain her zest for life.

The baby stirred and her eyelids fluttered. Then she settled again. Chrissie's arms could still feel the imprint of the little body, so light and yet so solid, and her nostrils still held the milky, talcum-y, baby-soap smell that spoke eloquently of innocent beginnings.

'When will you tell her, Doreen?'

'That's somethin' to be decided on later,' Doreen said. 'Much later.' And then, when her sister started to say something else, 'And it'll be decided between Frank and me. No sense in crossing bridges before we come to them. Come on now, she's best left to sleep.'

Chrissie hesitated. 'She'll be all right now, won't she?'

'Of course she'll be all right! She's one of us, one of the family,' Doreen snapped, and then, as the door opened, 'She's sleeping, Frank, and I don't want her disturbed.'

'I wasnae goin' tae disturb her. I just wanted tae know if you could both do with a cup of tea.' Frank Nesbitt went straight to the bassinet as he spoke, as if he had been pulled towards the sleeping baby by an invisible string.

'Me and Chrissie could, but I doubt *she'd* be interested, so no use in asking her,' his wife said. 'Come on, now.' She swept from the room, but Chrissie and Frank lingered for a moment.

'Doreen's much better now, isn't she?' Chrissie asked her brother-in-law anxiously.

'Oh aye, don't you worry about her. It was hard on her, losin' the wee laddie so sudden, but we're both fine now, thanks to this bonny wee pet.' He stroked the back of one finger over the baby's rounded cheek, his touch as gentle as the brush of a butterfly's wing. 'Everything's perfect now,' he went on, his voice thick with sudden

4

emotion. 'We're lucky, Chrissie, tae get a second chance like this.'

'She's lucky too, to have you and Doreen for parents.'

'I hope she always thinks so. We'll do our best by her.'

'I know you will,' Chrissie said warmly, and then, as the baby stirred again, 'We'd best go through. Doreen'll not be pleased if we wake the wee one.'

'Aye.' Frank wrenched himself away from the bassinet.

As they left the room, Chrissie noticed that he looked back longingly, as though unwilling to spend as much as a minute away from the little girl sleeping soundly in her beautiful muslin-and-lace crib.

2

September 1976

'I can't think why I'm doing this,' Kathleen Ramsay grumbled above the busy whirr of the sewing machine.

'It's because we're friends and friends help each other. I can't manage to get all these costumes done on time on my own,' Rachel told her from the paste table, where she was pinning several pieces of cloth together. Every available surface in her small sewing room was covered with material; it looked, as Kathleen had observed earlier, as though a rainbow had exploded in there.

'I can't think why you've taken this job on,' she said. 'It's not as if Fiona's even in the dratted play, though she should be. From what I saw when we were at the school last week, she's prettier than the girls who were on the stage. And she was prompting without having to look at the book, *and* saying the lines better than the actors could.'

'She'd have loved to be in the play, but Martin put his foot down because she's got her Ordinary Grade exams in May.'

'The play's on at the end of October, well before the O Grades.'

'I know, but he doesn't want her to have any distractions.'

'And as the prompt, she has to attend all the rehearsals anyway. So what's the difference between being in it, and prompting it?'

'The difference is that Martin hasn't realised that.'

'Ah. Will I ever understand men?' Kathleen asked the ceiling, then, returning to her work, 'No, I don't think so.'

Rachel shook out the skirt she had been pinning and held it up for inspection. 'What d'you think?'

'Pretty. Those velvet curtains look better than they ever did on our living room windows. Who's it for?'

'Lady Bracknell.'

'Lady Bracknell . . . I think we did *The Importance of Being Earnest* in teacher training. Isn't she the one who says, "In a suitcase"?'

'A handbag.'

'Oh yes.' Kathleen stopped the machine and snipped the thread. 'Finished; will it do?'

Rachel cast a swift glance at the brocade jacket. 'Lovely. Thanks a million, Kathleen, you've been such a help.'

'Shouldn't the staff be doing this? After all, it's a school production.'

'I volunteered because I like making things. And those long dresses are gorgeous to work with. Look . . .' Rachel laid an open book by the sewing machine. 'Those high necks and gathered waists made women look so graceful. You couldn't help walking well in a long skirt like that.'

'You think so? Chunky women like me must have looked like badly tied bundles of washing in those dresses, poor souls. Give me today's loose tops any day; they cover a multitude of sins. Anything else you want me to do before I go?'

7

'No, you've done enough for one afternoon. I'll sew the buttons and the trimming on that jacket tonight. There's one thing . . . if you have any spare walking sticks or long umbrellas, could you bring them next time? I'm going to cover them with the surplus material from the dresses to make matching parasols.' Rachel consulted the list pinned to a corkboard on the wall. 'Thank goodness the school can run to hiring the men's costumes, and Miss Prism's a governess and wears the same suit and blouse throughout. That just leaves us with one outfit for Cecily and two each for Gwendolen and Lady Bracknell. We've got off to a good start.'

Kathleen got up and stretched her arms above her head. 'It's time I got off now, if you don't mind.'

'Stay for a cup of tea. I'm just about to make one for Dad.'

'Can't, I've got a date with a soup pot.'

'Oh dear. What kind?' Kathleen hated cooking, but found it soothing to make soup whenever she was upset, stressed or angry.

'Watercress and whatever I decide goes with it,' she said now, shrugging into her jacket and patting the pockets. 'It's very calming.'

'To eat, or to make?'

'To make. For one thing, Murdo's not all that keen on watercress soup and for another, he doesn't grow it, so I can enjoy buying heaps of it. It's so annoying,' Kathleen went on, searching through her pockets for a second time, 'to have to use shop-bought vegetables when vegetables are all I can see from my kitchen window. Ah, here they are.' She drew out her car keys.

'Murdo lets you use his vegetables sometimes, doesn't he?'

'Only the rejects. There's something depressing about

8

knowing you're eating produce unfit for showing. And something very depressing about being married to a man whose main passion is growing leeks and carrots. How can anyone be passionate about that sort of thing?'

'At least Murdo has a hobby. I wish Martin had one.'

'He doesn't need one, my pet; you've always got enough for two. Say goodbye to your father for me.'

'Come and say it yourself.'

Kathleen sniffed the air as she went into the hall. 'Better not; I'd only give in and stay for tea and guzzle those home-made scones that smell so good. And if I see your lovely back garden with its nice pretty flowers, I might burst into tears.'

The scones, golden brown and fragrant, were easily transferred by spatula from the well-greased baking tray to the wire cooling tray. Rachel had taken five minutes from her work earlier to make the tea so that it could be left to brew, or 'mash', as her mother always said. Rachel had no idea where the word came from and when she asked, having been interested in words and their origins from childhood, her mother had said shortly, 'I got it from my mother . . . and she raised me to learn without asking bothersome questions.'

The words, 'How can I learn if I don't ask questions?' had immediately jumped to Rachel's lips, but she had had the good sense to swallow them before they could leap into the invisible, and yet clearly understood, space that had always lain between her and her mother. She had decided at the age of seven or eight that if she ever had children she would answer all their questions if she could, and be honest about her ignorance if she could not. And although at times she could understand and sympathise with her own mother's impatience with the 'whys' and 'whats' and 'hows' of childhood, she had more or less stuck to her vow.

She split half a dozen scones, and buttered them, then placed them on a tray and carried it out to the small terrace.

'Tea's ready, Dad!'

There was no answer. The lawn Frank Nesbitt had just finished mowing looked like a smooth green carpet, and the earth in the borders was weed-free and bright with the marigolds and begonias he had raised from seed in his allotment greenhouse. Rachel took her apron off and laid it over the tray to protect its contents before crossing the lawn and walking between the two crab-apple trees.

A small drying green, every bit as smooth as the main lawn, lay beyond the trees. Passing the hutch where Charlie and Lucy, the children's pet guinea pigs, worked busily on a pile of fresh grass cuttings, she ducked beneath the clothes on the washing line and found her father outside the potting-shed-cum-greenhouse. He was squatting on the ground, cleaning the blades of the lawn-mower.

'Your tea's ready, Dad. Leave that and I'll do it later.'

'It's done.' He got to his feet, easing up slowly because his knee joints weren't as supple as they had once been. 'Always look after your tools, lass,' he said, as he always did and always had. 'And—'

'Always make sure the horses are fed and watered before you are,' Rachel finished the familiar sentence for him. 'Though if we had horses when I was little, you managed to keep them well hidden.'

Frank grinned as he hoisted the lawnmower into its usual corner. 'It's what my granddad always said, and he was a right good ploughman. It's a piece of advice worth minding, lass. Your washing'll be dried by now,' he added as they ducked beneath the clothes line. 'I'll fetch the basket and bring it in for you.'

'I'll do it while you wash your hands. The grass looks grand, Dad,' Rachel said as they stepped on to it.

'It's growing fast. I'll mebbe mow it again at the end of next week.'

'Martin can do it.' And if he wouldn't, she would. Martin disliked gardening, possibly because his father, a man who believed that nobody could do anything as well as he himself could, had never allowed either of his sons to help in his large garden; whereas Rachel, who had helped in her father's allotment from the time she could toddle, quite enjoyed it. Like washing dishes and ironing, it set her mind free to roam about and do a bit of serious thinking.

'Martin works hard enough – he deserves some time off. I'm retired, and if I wasn't here, or on my allotment, I'd just be gettin' under your mother's feet. Women can't be doin' with a man about the house all the time, they think we make the place untidy,' Frank said cheerfully, crossing to the table and lifting a corner of the apron to peek beneath it. 'Home-made scones!'

'Wash your hands first, while I bring the laundry in,' Rachel commanded, and he grinned at her and went indoors while she fetched the clothes basket and returned to the drying green.

She drew in deep breaths of mild, grass-scented air as she unpegged Martin's shirts and underpants and the children's T-shirts and shorts and jeans from the clothes line, folding them before dropping them into the basket. Beyond the high wooden fence separating the garden from those of their neighbours she could hear snippets from other lives . . . the murmur of voices too far away to intrude, an occasional trill of laughter, the brisk clip of shears and, two gardens along, the creak of a child's swing. Their own swing would be pressed into action as soon as Graham, their youngest, got home. No matter whether the school day had been a problem or a pleasure, Graham liked to swing it out of his system.

In the kitchen, Frank had washed his hands and was busy cleaning the sink.

'Dad, you don't have to do that!'

'Aye, I do. Your mother would never forgive me if I left a speck of dirt in your nice clean sink.'

'My mother wouldn't know because I'd not tell her.'

'I know you wouldnae, but I'd know.' He reached for the towel and dried his hands. 'Now let's go and eat those scones afore they get cold.'

The terrace was pleasantly shaded by a nearby pussy-willow tree; the shifting pattern thrown by its leaves as a faint breeze whispered through them was soothing to the eye.

'I thought Kathleen would have stayed and had a cup with us,' Frank said as he took a scone.

'She had to get home.' Rachel poured the tea and was pleased to see that it was dark and strong, just the way her father liked it. 'It was good of her to help me with the costumes.'

'Ye're always at somethin',' her father said proudly. 'I've never met a lassie that could do all the things you do. These nice cushions ye've made, and the toys for the children, and their clothes, and now costumes for Fiona's school play . . . ye're a talented woman.'

'I've got too much time on my hands, Dad. To tell the truth, I wondered about going back to teaching, now that Graham's settled in at school, but Martin won't hear of it. He thinks that it's his job as the man of the family to support us.'

Frank looked out over the sun-dappled garden. 'He does that all right, but it takes two – while he's been earnin' the money, you've been turnin' the house intae a wee palace, and raisin' three fine children.'

'Behind every successful man stands a nagging woman,' Rachel joked.

'Don't put yoursel' down, lassie. Ye've never nagged in yer life,' Frank said earnestly. 'Just imagine, me a labourer and your mother a shop lassie . . . and our daughter growin' up with enough brains tae be a school teacher!'

'A primary school teacher . . . and I've not taught for years.'

'Even so.' Frank poured himself another cup of tea and took the last scone from the plate.

They settled into a companionable silence, broken only by an occasional comment. Neither of Rachel's parents was given to chattering, but her mother's silences had always been edgy and awkward, full of unknown, unspoken thoughts, while her father's were restful.

Rachel's mind turned to the costumes she was making for the school play, and when her father finally set down his cup with a contented sigh, brushed some crumbs from the table into the palm of his big, callused hand and said, 'Well, lass, time for me tae go,' she was jerked out of her thoughts of muslins and velvets, silks and brocade.

'Already? Can you not wait until the children get back from school?'

'I'd better not. Your mother wants me to do a few things round the house, and you know how she can be when I'm later than expected.' He stepped down onto the crazy paving path that he had put in two years before and deposited the crumbs carefully on the bird table before collecting the jacket that he had hung neatly on the back of a chair.

'There's some grass caught on it.' Rachel brushed green strands from the material.

'Thank you, lass,' he said, and then, his voice suddenly shy, 'I've never told ye this before, lass, because I didnae know how tae put the words, but I've thanked God every single day for sendin' you tae us.'

'Dad!' To her horror she felt tears stinging the backs of her eyes. She had always got on well with her father, but they had never spoken to each other in that way before.

'Ach, don't mind me, I'm just bein' daft.' His voice was gruff and he made a great business of taking his bicycle clips from his pocket. 'I must be goin' soft in my old age. Goodness knows what your mother would say if she heard me talkin' rubbish like that.'

'It's not rubbish, it's lovely.' Rachel wanted to go to him and hug him, and perhaps kiss his stubbly cheek, but knowing that it would only embarrass him further, she held back, picking up his cap and waiting until he had put the bicycle clips on before handing it to him.

He settled it on his balding head, giving it a final tug, as he always did.

'Tell the bairns and Martin that I was askin' for them,' he said as they walked together round the side of the house to where his bicycle was propped against the wall. Then, correcting himself, '. . . your mother and me were askin' for them.'

'I will. And give Mum my . . . my love.'

'I'll do that.' They went down the short driveway and he wheeled the bicycle onto the pavement, adding as he swung one leg over its crossbar, 'I'll be back next week with manure for those roses. I know where I can get some good stuff.'

'Mind the traffic,' Rachel said, as she always said, and got the answer she always got.

14

'Don't teach your grandmother tae suck eggs, lassie. I was on a bike long afore you were found under a gooseberry bush.'

'I know,' she said, and stayed at the gate to watch him cycle slowly along the road, glancing into each garden he passed. Now that he was retired, Frank's favourite hobby was gardening, and he loved to see what other folk did with the ground they owned.

When he had disappeared round the corner she turned back to the house, thinking longingly of the bike rides they had shared in the past. At first, too young to have a cycle of her own, she had travelled on a special seat behind his saddle, and once she graduated to her first two-wheeler they rode side by side, always with her father between her and the traffic. As she gained skill and confidence their bike runs had become longer, and through her growing years they had travelled all over Renfrewshire and beyond, taking picnics with them and exploring ruined castles, rivers, narrow lanes, and whatever happened to take their fancy. Eventually, school exams and then Jordanhill Teacher Training College and pals and dances and the occasional boyfriend had put a stop to their shared outings. Her father had gone back to cycling on his own, as he had done before she was born.

Occasionally, on pleasant days like today, Rachel thought of getting herself a bicycle and suggesting that they go off on a run together, like old times. One day, she promised herself as she rinsed the mugs and plates and then got the ironing board out, she would do it.

When the basket was filled with neatly ironed and folded clothes Rachel carried it around the house, folding the boys' clothes into drawers in the room they shared, and hanging Martin's shirts on their individual hangers in his wardrobe and her own things in her wardrobe.

Fiona's bedroom, neat as always, came last. A much-thumbed copy of *The Importance of Being Earnest* lay on the bedside table. Fiona, who was good at English, had fallen in love with the play when her class studied it, and when the Drama teacher decided to stage it, the girl had been desperate to take part. But Martin, raised in a house where education was more important than pleasure, had refused to let her audition, and all Fiona's begging, pleading, arguing, coaxing and sulking had failed to move him.

A collection of soft toys perched on Fiona's pillow, leaning against the headboard. Rachel sat on the bed for a moment, picking up the shabbiest, a rag doll with yellow wool pigtails, and round blue eyes, a snub nose and a wide, smiling mouth stitched onto the cloth face.

Raggedy Ann was more than just a toy; she was special. Rachel and Martin had first met in Glasgow, when Rachel, dressed as Raggedy Ann with a home-made yellow wool wig perched on top of her own straight brown bob, was collecting for Rag Day with Kathleen. Embarrassed to find himself surrounded by laughing students wearing fancy dress, Martin had dug deep into the pocket of his neat suit and dropped a handful of change into Rachel's collecting tin.

An hour later, calling in at a coffee shop for a much-needed break, she had seen him again, sitting with an office colleague.

'I like that one,' Kathleen had murmured, indicating his companion with a swift nod of the head. 'Let's sit with them.' And she marched towards the two empty chairs at the table, leaving Rachel with no option but to trail shyly along in her wake. In the time it took to drink a cup of coffee Kathleen and the young man she fancied had arranged to meet again.

'I thought the quiet one might have asked you out,' Kathleen said when they went back outside. 'He liked you; I could tell.'

Rachel blushed. There had been something about the dark-haired young man . . . perhaps it had been the two tiny lines already digging in between his grey eyes, adding maturity to his young face. Her hands had itched to smooth them away. 'Don't be daft, he doesn't even know me!'

'And I don't know George, but I'm going to get to know him,' Kathleen pointed out cheerfully. She and George had only gone out together some half-dozen times before finding other, more interesting partners, but by then Martin had plucked up the courage to invite Rachel out. When they got engaged eighteen months later, Martin gave Rachel the Raggedy Ann doll in memory of the day they had met.

Remembering, she smiled, tucking Ann's woolly hair back and running the ball of her thumb over the beginnings of a split in the seam of the doll's leg. Raggedy Ann had been the most romantic gift – the only romantic gift, to be honest – that Martin had ever given her, and she should have taken better care of the doll. Unfortunately, baby Fiona had insisted on having the rag doll for her own. Her repeated kisses had blurred the colours of Ann's stitched features, while being carried everywhere under Fiona's arm for years had faded her once bright, crisp clothes.

'You need a good tidying up, my girl,' Rachel told the doll, and then hurriedly replaced it on the bed as a yell of 'Mum!' from the kitchen heralded the arrival of six-year-old Graham from school.

By the time he had been persuaded to change out of his school uniform, fortified with a peanut butter sandwich and a glass of milk, and gone off to the back garden to play on the swing, his older brother Ian was home, clamouring for food before going off on his bike.

'Remember to be back for half past five . . . and you'll have to do your homework after dinner,' Rachel called after him as he wheeled his bike out of the gate.

'Uh-huh,' he shouted back; then he was in the saddle and off along the road, legs pumping and head down as he raced to meet his pals.

Five minutes later the front door opened and Fiona called out, as she always did, 'Mu-um! Where are you?'

'In the kitchen,' Rachel shouted back as she always did. She heard footsteps running up the stairs. Fiona's bedroom door opened and closed, and a moment later came the muffled sound of Abba singing 'Waterloo'. Fiona was an avid Abba fan and played their music non-stop.

Another five minutes passed before her daughter arrived in the kitchen, having changed from her school uniform to a T-shirt and shorts, and with her curly shoulder-length hair, brown but with red and gold flecks, caught by an elastic band into a ponytail.

The carrots had been scrubbed and were waiting to be chopped. Fiona started work on them without being asked, wielding the sharp knife with swift efficiency while her tongue rattled along, describing her school day in minute detail.

By the time Martin opened the front door and called, 'Anyone home?' Ian was back home and he and Fiona, squabbling amiably, had set the table.

'We're all here,' Rachel shouted in reply, her heart lifting. It was ridiculous, but after seventeen years of marriage she still loved that moment when Martin called from the hall and she knew that her family were all together again, safe under the one roof. They were the centre of her life, her reason for being. She was so lucky, she thought, while aloud she said, 'Dinner will be ready in ten minutes. How was your day?'

'I've been trying to sort out someone's accounts all day. I've had to bring work home.' He dropped a kiss on her cheek.

'Again?' Martin was always bringing work home, always checking and rechecking and always worrying – about his job as an accountant, his duties as a husband and father, the children's well-being and their futures – anything and everything was grist to his mill.

The little worry lines that had been the first things about him to appeal to her had deepened over the years. She had found out why they were there when she met his parents. Martin's father, now retired, had been a doctor, and his mother a high-powered social worker. Adrian, his older brother, had also gone into medicine and was now in the Flying Doctor service in Australia. Martin was the

19

odd one out in his family, the one who, it seemed, had not quite made the grade.

Perhaps, Rachel thought as she began to realise the truth, that was why she had been attracted to him. He was still struggling to please his parents, while she longed to find a way to gain her mother's approval.

'I just want to check over a few things,' he was saying now.

'Martin, don't you think you should learn to leave work in the office instead of bringing it home?'

'And have more to do when I get in tomorrow morning?'

'But you said you only needed to check it. It's probably fine as it is, and you should be able to relax and enjoy your time away from the office.'

The lines between his eyebrows deepened. 'How can I relax when I'm not sure . . .' he began, and then, as the telephone in the hall began to shrill, he went to the door and called, 'Fiona, get that, will you? It's probably for her in any case,' he added, turning back to the kitchen. 'One of her friends wanting to talk about something or other.'

A distant squawk from somewhere in the house was interpreted by Ian, who appeared in the doorway to announce, 'She says she's in the bathroom.'

'I'll get it,' Graham yelled. Rachel hurriedly turned the gas off beneath the pot of potatoes.

'I'm going,' she called. Graham's offbeat sense of humour, at its best when he was answering the telephone, usually resulted in long explanations to the puzzled people on the other end of the line.

'Rachel? Is that you, Rachel?' She heard her mother's voice even as she lifted the phone from its cradle.

'Yes, Mum, it's me. Sorry I took a wee while to answer, I was in the kitch—'

'I'm at the hospital. The Royal Alexandra.' Doreen's voice was always flat, but now it carried a harsh, strained note. 'Rachel, you have to come at once. It's your dad . . .'

The small chapel at Goudie's funeral parlour in Maxwellton Street was filled with folk wanting to attend Frank Nesbitt's funeral, and when the funeral procession arrived at Woodside Cemetery, where he and his wife had bought a lair for themselves, there were more people waiting by the open grave – former work colleagues, fellow gardeners from the allotments, family friends and neighbours all anxious to pay their final respects to a man who had always been the first to offer help in times of need.

Doreen Nesbitt, a small figure dressed from head to toe in black, clutched at her sister Chrissie's arm as soon as Martin had helped her from the car. When Rachel moved to her other side and tried to put a supportive hand beneath her mother's elbow, Doreen twitched free, muttering, 'I'm not an invalid, I can manage.'

'But Mum—'

'We're fine,' Chrissie whispered, smiling at Rachel. 'You see to the children, love, and I'll look out for your mother.'

It was a beautiful day; the sort of day, Rachel thought as the minister took his place, that her father liked best. A growing day, he would have said. She looked at the gleaming coffin with the small brass plaque that read, 'Frank Nesbitt, 1906–1976', and wondered which he would have preferred if given the choice – to be buried in glorious sunshine, or in grey, weeping rain. In the sunshine, she decided, as Martin, summoned by the minister, stepped forward with the other cord-bearers.

Glancing at her mother, she saw that Doreen's back

was ramrod straight and her eyes were locked on the coffin being lowered into the ground. Rachel herself couldn't bear to watch; instead, she looked at the gravestone already in place at the head of the lair. It had been erected before her birth to mark the grave of her brother, Stuart Kemp Nesbitt, who had died at the age of two months. It had been a long and lonely wait, she thought with a sudden wave of pity for the brother she had never known, but now, at last, he would have his father for company. Her loss was this unknown child's gain.

Looking at her own children, she saw Ian standing erect, hands by his sides and his chin stiff as he watched his father and the other cord-bearers. Graham, standing next to his brother, was trying hard to emulate him, while tears trickled down Fiona's pale cheeks. Rachel reached out an arm to draw her daughter close, and Fiona came willingly, her own arm stealing around Rachel's waist.

She and Fiona would always be like this, Rachel vowed to herself as the coffin disappeared from her sight. They would always be close, the way mothers and daughters should be. Even in childhood, she herself had been more comfortable with her father than with her mother. At times it had been as though Doreen was determined to keep her daughter at arm's length; the hurtful rejection when they first arrived at the cemetery was typical of her.

All her life Rachel had envied friends who had a good relationship with their mothers. Perhaps, she thought, but without much hope, her father's death would finally bring them closer together. She felt her eyes mist, then the warmth of tears on her cheekbones, and wondered if she was weeping for her mother or her father, or perhaps, for herself.

★　★　★

Doreen Nesbitt stooped and picked up a handful of soil to throw onto Frank's coffin. It rattled noisily on the lid and as she stepped back and watched Rachel follow suit, she saw a tiny glistening globe roll down the younger woman's cheek and drop onto the black earth at her feet.

Doreen's eyes were dry, and had been since Frank's death. Crying wasn't her way, and in any case, all the tears in the world wouldn't bring him back, or fill the great aching void that his passing had quarried into the centre of her being. Tears couldn't stop the hurting, and the fear of being alone for the rest of her life.

She wondered if what she now felt meant that she had loved her husband. There had been love in the early days, of course – there always was. Why else would they have got married? But the awareness of love had faded along with the bright gold wedding ring that he had slipped onto her finger at the minister's bidding. Perhaps love had turned to habit, and habits were hard to break.

She wondered if she would be able to survive on her own. Chrissie would say that she still had her family; she still had Rachel and Martin and the children. But Doreen had never felt close to Rachel, even when she was a wee scrap of a thing, almost lost in the beautiful bassinet Doreen had bought and furnished for her firstborn.

Frank and Chrissie both used to say that Rachel looked beautiful in that cradle, but Doreen saw only an interloper. To her mind, the cradle still belonged to the child it was bought for; her son, her Stuart.

Glancing up at the headstone where his name had been carved all those years ago, she remembered the moment when the midwife had laid him in her arms, his damp hair plastered close against his tiny fragile skull. He had looked at her with dark blue eyes, and in that moment she had known that she had been put on earth to adore and cherish and nurture him. She had enfolded him in her love, and two short months later he had been taken from her.

She swallowed hard, oblivious to the rattling of soil on wood as the mourners stepped forward one by one to give their final salute to Frank Nesbitt. Everyone – Frank, Chrissie, even Doreen's parents – had seen Rachel as wee Stuart's replacement. Frank himself, aged by grief over his baby son's death, had begun to change as soon as Rachel arrived. His shoulders had straightened, the sorrow had vanished from his face, the light had returned to his eyes. He had worshipped her and she had worshipped him, and their mutual pleasure in each other had made Doreen feel even more isolated and alone.

Chrissie nudged her elbow gently, and she dragged her eyes from the headstone to see that the mourners were forming a straggling line and the gravediggers, waiting at a discreet distance, were beginning to fidget.

Doreen caught Rachel's eye and beckoned her over to stand beside her. Flanked by Martin and Chrissie, they shook hands, received words of sympathy, and thanked everyone for attending the funeral.

'There's a wee cup of tea waiting at the Brabloch Hotel,' Doreen told each and every one of them. 'You're most welcome to join us there.'

'Are you all right, Mum?' Rachel asked anxiously when the three of them – herself, Doreen and Chrissie – were being driven in the hired car to the Brabloch on Renfrew Road. Martin was bringing the children in his own car.

'As right as I can be, seein' as I've just buried my husband.'

'She's fine, pet, aren't you, Doreen? Bearing up well. Frank would be proud of you,' Chrissie told her sister.

'Why don't you come to stay with us for a wee while?'

Rachel suggested. 'The spare room's all ready, and we'd love to have you. Just until you feel able to go back to Wellmeadow.'

'I'm not goin' back to Wellmeadow. I've decided that I'm goin' to sell the flat and move in with Chrissie,' Doreen said, and Rachel blinked, taken aback.

'Are you sure, Mum?'

'I'm quite sure. Chrissie has a spare room, and we get on well enough together. And that flat's not the same now that Frank's gone from it.'

'Are you sure you don't want to move in with us? We could turn our spare room into a nice bed/sitting room for you,' Rachel suggested, and Doreen's lips pursed slightly.

'You and Martin have enough of a houseful as it is, and I couldnae be doin' with the children runnin' around and playin' their music too loud. I'll be more comfortable with Chrissie. She's my own flesh and blood.'

'I'm your flesh and blood too, Mum.'

Doreen's black-gloved hands gripped each other tightly in her lap. 'You've got your own family to look out for and Chrissie and me understand each other. We'll be fine together.'

'Are you sure, Aunt Chrissie?' Rachel asked when they got out of the car before the Brabloch Hotel. Martin's car had drawn up behind theirs, and as soon as she alighted Doreen had gone to speak to her grandchildren. 'Are you all right about Mum moving in with you?'

'Of course I'm sure, pet.' Chrissie Kemp took her niece's hands in hers. 'We've always got on well together, me and Doreen. And I've got a spare room that's never used.'

'Could we not take her for a week or two, just to give her a chance to think about this? You could do with a rest . . . you've been staying with her ever since . . .' Rachel stopped, swallowed, then went on, 'ever since Dad had his heart attack.'

'She's already made up her mind; you know Doreen, once she says something, that's it. And I don't need a rest. Anyway, you've got enough to do, with the wee ones and Martin to see to. I don't know what Doreen would have done without you two there to arrange the funeral.' Chrissie patted Rachel's hand before releasing it. 'You've done a grand job. Your dad would be proud of you.'

'I just wish she would let me do more for her. I feel as if she's keeping me at arm's length all the time.'

'Och, it's just Doreen's way. She's never been very good at showing her feelings.'

'Don't dawdle about there,' Doreen called to them from the top of the steps. 'They'll not bring the tea and sandwiches out to us, you know.'

She went into the hotel, and they all straggled obediently after her.

Two weeks after the funeral, Doreen asked Rachel to help Chrissie to clear the Wellmeadow flat. 'There's all your father's things to be sorted,' she said over the phone, 'and I don't want to do it myself.'

'Of course I will, Mum.'

'Anything that's good enough to be used can go to the Salvation Army or the WRVS and the rest'll have to be put out,' Doreen went on briskly. 'Chrissie can decide what's best.'

Most daughters would have pointed out that they were more than capable of making decisions, but Rachel, used to such treatment, let the slight pass. 'What about things you want to keep?'

'Chrissie went in with me yesterday and we packed everythin' that I want. One of her neighbours brought his van and took away the new bits of furniture I want to keep. All the rest has to go.'

'Are you sure, Mum? You don't think you should wait a few more weeks before you make a final decision?'

'I'm not in my dotage yet,' Doreen snapped. 'I know what I want. The house is goin' up for sale next week and I can't be doin' with a lot of stuff I don't need clutterin' up my sister's house. Are you willin' to help Chrissie tomorrow or are you not?'

'Of course I'll help her.' Rachel had promised to do a costume fitting for the school play the next day, but it could be put off until another time.

'Fiona wondered if she should give up prompting the play because of Dad, but we thought she should go on with it,' Rachel said the next day, as she and Chrissie went through the tenement close and began to climb the stairs to the flat where she had been raised.

'Of course she mustn't give it up. She's enjoying herself, and Doreen's looking forward to seeing the play. She's determined that everything should get back to normal for you and the children. Cancelling things and moping around isn't going to bring Frank back, is it?'

They had reached the landing, and Chrissie started to fish about in her voluminous bag. 'For goodness' sake, what have I done with those keys? Here, pet, hold this for me . . . and this . . .'

A large wallet filled with receipts and scribbled notes was pushed into Rachel's hands, followed by a pair of gloves, a plastic hood, a bulging and heavy change-purse, a hairbrush, a spectacle case . . . As item after item was handed over and Rachel began to have difficulty holding them all, they both began to giggle like schoolgirls. Finally, just as her niece was about to protest that if she had to take one more thing she would be forced to drop the lot, Chrissie delved down into the very depths of the bag, and produced the keys with a triumphant flourish.

'There we are! I knew I had them all the time!' She selected a key and fitted it into the lock. The door swung open, and Rachel followed her aunt into the square

28

entrance hall. The place still held its mixture of familiar smells – furniture polish, the scent from the big bowl of pot-pourri her mother always kept on the hall table, and the faint tang of pipe tobacco – but now there was something else permeating the stuffy air. Rachel took in a deep breath and recognised it as emptiness. Her father would never again be in this flat, and the flat knew it.

'We'd better open the windows while we're here,' Chrissie said over her shoulder as she began to swing doors wide open to let more light into the hall. 'But we'll have to make sure we close them again before we leave.'

Working as a team, they went right through the flat, sorting and packing and bagging everything. They left the larger of the two bedrooms to the last, for this was where they had the most work to do.

'I'll take the drawers, you start on the wardrobes,' Chrissie said briskly as they entered. 'We'll be done in no time, then we can have a nice cup of tea before we go.'

There were two matching wardrobes, one on each side of the window. Doreen's was almost empty and it didn't take Rachel long to fold and pack the few clothes her mother had rejected. Then she opened the door of her father's wardrobe and saw his second-best brown three-piece suit still hanging neatly on the rail, together with his gardening clothes, a pair of flannels and two jackets, one warm tweed for winter, the other of light wool for summer, both with waistcoats.

Suddenly she was engulfed in the smell of him. The soap he had always used, his favourite hair-oil (she had given him a bottle of it, and of his usual aftershave, every Christmas for as long as she could remember), his usual brand of tobacco, and just a hint of perspiration; they blended together into the aroma unique to Frank Nesbitt.

Rachel gasped, gulped, and felt the tears rush to her eyes. Then she felt herself caught by the shoulders, turned about and swept into her aunt's tight, warm embrace.

'Oh lovey, is it all too much for you?' Chrissie rubbed her back. 'I should have had more sense than to expect you to do this!'

'It's all right.' Rachel's voice was muffled in her aunt's shoulder. 'I'm just being silly, that's all. I know he's gone, but it wasn't until just now that I realised he's not . . . he's not ever coming back!'

'You're not being silly, and where better to cry it all out than here, with nob'dy but me to see you? Come on . . .' Chrissie led her niece to the big bed with its elaborately carved headboard and sat down beside her, drawing Rachel's head onto her shoulder. 'We'll have a good cry together, you and me, for Frank.'

Ten minutes later, as they wiped their eyes and blew their noses, she indicated their reflections in the mirrors set in both wardrobe doors. 'What are we like, eh? The two of us could walk into one of those sad Greek plays and we'd not look out of place. But having a right noisy bawl does you good, doesn't it?'

'It does. Has my mother . . . ?'

'Not a tear, as far as I know. But that's Doreen's way. She bottles things up and always did, even as a bairn.' Chrissie studied her niece, her head to one side. 'How do you manage to look so pretty after a good cry, when I just look like a prune past its prime?'

'You don't.' Rachel gave her eyes a final dab and put her handkerchief away. 'Aunt Chrissie, why did you never get married?'

'Because nob'dy asked me. Anyway, someone had to look after Mother and Father when they began to get older.'

'Would you have liked to be married?'

'Of course I would. If anyone had popped the question I'd have accepted him like a shot, even if he'd had a glass eye and a wooden leg and put his teeth in a tumbler at night. But nob'dy noticed me when Doreen was around. She was always the pretty one.'

'You'd have been a good mother.'

'I'd have liked bairns, that's true,' Chrissie admitted, and then, giving Rachel another hug, 'but I've enjoyed being an auntie, every minute of it.'

'I used to wish . . .' Rachel stopped. Saying aloud that she used to wish that Auntie Chrissie had been her mother seemed too disloyal, especially here in her parents' home. She settled for, 'I used to wish that I had lots of brothers and sisters when I was wee.'

'It would have been nice for me, too, having more bairns to spoil. But you'd plenty of friends, didn't you?'

'Yes, but it's not the same. I'm glad I've got three children of my own. They'll always have each other. They'll always have family.'

'That they will, bless 'em.' Chrissie got to her feet, tucking her handkerchief into her sleeve. 'Come on, we'd best get back to work.'

The big case that had been kept on top of the wardrobe for as long as Rachel could remember was soon filling with neatly folded garments, while a cardboard box held the few pieces of clothing, such as Frank's gardening outfit, that were to be discarded. The shoes he had polished every night before going to bed were put into a separate box, and the drawers and wardrobe were almost empty.

Chrissie made tea, and they drank it while they sat on the bedroom floor, working their way through a large wooden box with an inlaid lid. The box, which held all the Nesbitts' official papers as well as letters and bundles of photographs, had been kept at the bottom of her father's wardrobe for as long as Rachel could remember. Doreen had taken the papers, but the box still held a large tattered envelope packed with photographs.

Chrissie, spilling the pictures out onto the linoleum, gave a little cry of pleased recognition and picked up a brown-tinted photograph of two young women paddling in the sea, skirts held up above their knees. 'Oh my, would you look at this picture of me and your mum – talk about Elsie and Doris Waters! You'll not remember them; they used to be on the radio. Very funny, they were.'

'When was it taken?' Rachel studied the picture. The two girls were holding hands and laughing. Chrissie, the taller and more sturdily built of the two, was easily identified by her beaming smile; Doreen, smaller and slimmer and prettier, seemed to be laughing helplessly into the camera . . . or at the person who held it. Rachel had never seen her mother look so carefree.

'Oh, not long before Doreen and Frank got married. In fact, I think he took the photograph. We went to Troon for the day on his motorbike, me on the pillion and Doreen in the sidecar. We'd a great day.'

'She looks so happy.'

'She was; she laughed all the time in those days. She was daft about Frank,' Chrissie said, her face soft with memories. 'D'you want it?'

Rachel did, but she said, 'Best give it to Mum.'

'She's taken all that she wants, so you might as well have it.' Chrissie put it aside.

Among the photographs rejected by her mother, Rachel found a whole bundle of herself as a child, her mouth serious and her eyes wide, almost anxious. The only time she smiled for the camera, it seemed, was when

32

she was being photographed with her father. 'I'll have them.' She put them aside carefully, trying not to feel too hurt by the knowledge that Doreen had rejected them.

There were more photographs, older records of people Rachel had never seen before. She laid them out on the floor, fanning them like playing cards. 'Who are these people?'

Chrissie came to kneel by her side. 'That's my Granny and Granddad Kemp, and these women are my two aunties, Bess and Janet.' Her finger moved from one brown sepia face to another as she identified relatives, most of whom had died before Rachel was born.

'I'm going to keep the lot of them,' Rachel decided. 'I love old photographs, and Fiona does, too. I'll get you to come over some day and go through them so that I can write their names on the back.' Then, struck by a sudden thought, 'I might even start a family tree. That would be interesting. Which one's Flora?'

'Who, dear?'

'Flora, the one I was named after. Rachel Elizabeth Flora,' Rachel prompted as her aunt looked at her, puzzled. 'You've mentioned Bess, so that must be where my parents got the Elizabeth from. Which one's Flora?'

'I . . . I don't know.' Chrissie's voice was suddenly uncertain. 'I think Doreen and Frank just liked the name.'

'I used to wish that my parents had given me your name as a middle name.'

'Christina? You wouldn't want to be saddled with an old-fashioned name like that!' Chrissie scoffed, though she looked pleased.

'Flora's old-fashioned too.'

'But at least it's light and flowery. We'd better get on or you'll not be home in time for the children coming out of school. This envelope's falling apart,' Chrissie fussed, scrambling to her feet. 'I'll get a bag from the kitchen to put the pictures in.'

She returned in a few minutes, bag in hand, but Rachel stopped her when she started gathering up the photographs.

'Aunt Chrissie, look at these.' Her index finger rested on face after face; a young Doreen and Frank posed self-consciously against the backdrop of a photographer's studio, while Frank's parents were caught walking down a street arm in arm. Frank's two brothers were pictured with the wives and children they had taken off to New Zealand years ago.

'What about them?'

'Look, there's Dad's nose . . . and there, and there. It's a family feature. And look at the way all the men in Mum's family have thick hair that comes down in a sort of widow's peak. Graham and Ian don't have hair like that.'

'They take after their dad's side of the family.'

'And those heavy-lidded eyes. Mum has them, and so do most of her family.' Rachel's wide blue eyes looked up at her aunt. 'But I don't. I don't look like any of these people.'

'You're you, and that's all that matters. Let's have another cup of tea before we go. My throat's parched.'

'It's as if the fairies took the real Rachel and put me into the cot instead. Perhaps I was a changeling.' Rachel smiled up at her aunt. Then, as she saw Chrissie's face, the smile died. 'What is it?'

'I told you, I'm parched.'

'It's more than that. Aunt Chrissie—'

'You're imagining things, love. Come on, help me with the tea and then we'll be on our way.' Chrissie pulled a handkerchief from the cuff of her cardigan and mopped at her face. 'It's still stuffy in here.'

'I'll just gather up the photographs first,' Rachel said, and her aunt left the room without another word.

When Rachel went into the kitchen five minutes later the kettle was belching out steam while Chrissie stood at the sink, staring out of the window at the buildings opposite. When Rachel spoke to her, she jumped and then whirled round, her eyes unnaturally bright.

'Would you look at me, away in a dream and letting the kettle fill the place up with steam. It'll start to loosen the wallpaper if we're not careful. Not that whoever buys the place'll want this wallpaper; folk always prefer to decorate to their own taste when they move into a house. That's why Doreen's decided not to waste time redecorating before it goes on the market . . .'

'Aunt Chrissie, what's wrong?'

'Nothing's wrong,' Chrissie said firmly, reaching out for the kettle. In her agitation, she ignored the padded kettle-holder that always hung by the gas cooker, and let out a squeak of pain as she grasped the metal handle.

'Aunt Chrissie!'

'It's all right . . .' Chrissie reeled back against the sink, cradling her injured hand in its partner. 'It's my own fault, silly old fool that I am!'

Rachel edged her gently but firmly aside and turned on the cold tap. 'Hold your hand under the water,' she instructed as she turned the gas off beneath the kettle, 'while I fetch the first aid box.'

The first aid box was in the sideboard in the living room, where it always was. Rachel took it back into the kitchen and made Chrissie sit down. She patted the injured hand dry, tutting over the puffy red weal scored across its palm, then smeared ointment over it as gently as she could before bandaging it.

'There, how does that feel?'

'Much better, dear, thanks. It was a stupid thing to do,' Chrissie fretted. 'I wasn't thinking. The tea . . .'

'I'll make it. You just sit still.' Rachel chattered on about the children as she heated the teapot, emptied it, spooned in tea leaves from the tin caddy that had been so well handled over the years that the picture painted on it was now unrecognisable, and then added boiling water. She rinsed the cups they had already used, dried them and put in milk and sugar before pouring the tea.

'Extra sugar for you, to help you get over the shock,' she said as she put the cup into Chrissie's undamaged hand.

'I'm not in shock; I just got a wee bit of a fright. And serve me right!'

Rachel studied the older woman's face. It was paler than usual, and her eyes were bright with unshed tears.

'Is the pain still bad? There might be some aspirin in the bathroom cabinet.'

'It's fine; I can scarcely feel it at all. No need to fuss.'

'I'm entitled to fuss. I need to take care of you. After all,' Rachel said cheerfully, 'you're my only aunt and I'd not want to lose you, would I?' Then, as Chrissie's tears suddenly spilled over, 'Oh, Aunt Chrissie, is it hurting badly? I'll phone for a taxi and take you home. Or d'you want to go to the hospital to let them have a look at your hand?'

'No!' Chrissie snatched at the tea towel and buried her face in it. 'It's not the hand I'm crying about, it's the photos, and what you were sayin' about them, and . . .' She raised a red, wet face from the towel. 'It's not my business, but I said to Doreen right from the start that someone should find a way to tell you. Only she kept sayin' it wasn't the right time, and Frank . . . well, he didn't want to upset her, or you, and it wasn't my place to interfere, but I was never happy about it . . .'

The room was warm enough, but now a chill began to creep over Rachel. 'Is it . . . was Dad ill and I didn't know? I'd never have let him work in the garden that day if I'd thought there was anything wrong with his heart!'

'No no, he was as strong as an ox, at least as far as we knew.' Chrissie mopped her face again and then lowered the tea towel to her lap, where she twisted it between both hands. 'Nob'dy expected the heart attack, it came out of the blue.'

'Mum, then . . . is *she* ill?' Rachel began to panic. Even though she and her mother had never been close, the thought of losing both parents was more than she could bear.

'Nob'dy's ill. It's something that happened a long time ago. Mebbe Doreen's right,' Chrissie said desperately. 'Mebbe it was so long ago that it's best forgotten. She'd be so angry with me if she knew that I was talkin' out of turn.'

'She doesn't need to know. It can be just between you and me. Tell me, Aunt Chrissie . . . please!'

'I wish I'd never got myself into this,' Chrissie wailed, and then, clenching both hands on the tea towel, 'You should have been told before this, Rachel! You'd a right to know. A year after Doreen married Frank they'd a wee boy.'

'I know about Stuart, he died when he was just two months old. Mum used to take me to put flowers on his grave every year.'

'He was a bonny baby, the image of Frank, and when he died I thought for a while that the grief of it was goin' to send Doreen out of her mind. She couldnae come to terms with it at all. She was just a shadow of herself,' Chrissie said, pain in her voice and in her face at the memory. 'The best thing, Frank thought, was for them to have another bairn as soon as possible.'

'And that's why they had me — as a replacement.' Rachel nodded. 'My mother never made any secret of it. I always felt that as far as she was concerned, I could never make up for the baby she lost. I've always been second best.'

'Not in Frank's eyes, pet. He doted on you from the first moment he set eyes on you. But Doreen . . . she tried hard to be a good mother, Rachel. She's always done her best by you.'

'There's a difference between loving and doing your best,' Rachel said from the heart. 'I tried to love her, Aunt Chrissie, but all I could do was my best, the same as she was doing with me.'

'It was different for her.' The tears began to roll down Chrissie's cheeks again, and this time she let them drop unheeded from her chin to her agitated hands. 'You see, she carried Stuart for nine months, and she gave birth to him. But you . . . oh, Rachel, pet, you were adopted.'

The walls closed in on Rachel, threatening to fall on her and crush the breath from her body; then they zoomed away again at a frightening pace, so far away that she could scarcely see the pictures on the wall opposite her. Finally, they went back to normal and she realised that the room hadn't changed at all. She had.

'Adopted? Me? You're saying that I'm not their daughter?' She had been too hot only a moment ago, but now she felt like a block of ice. Her fingers were so cold that when Chrissie reached out and took them in her warm grip, Rachel almost expected them to start melting.

'You *are* their daughter. They adopted you and they raised you and you're their daughter!'

'When did I . . . how old was I?'

'Three weeks, just. So you see, you've been with them all your life. You're family, Rachel,' Chrissie said, her voice pleading. 'Almost as much as you'd have been if Doreen had given birth to you herself.'

'Why didn't they just have another baby of their own?'

'Doreen nearly died when wee Stuart was born. The doctor said she might the next time, if she had another baby. She was willing to take the chance, but Frank wouldn't hear of it. That's why they decided to adopt a baby instead.'

'Who . . . where do I come from?' Rachel asked, and then, when Chrissie looked at her, puzzled, 'Who's my real mother?'

'I don't know anything about that side of it, dear. They never told me. Doreen never spoke of it to anyone.'

'But Mu . . . she must know.'

Chrissie's reddened eyes widened in panic. 'Don't ask her, Rachel! Please don't go stirring things up, not just after Frank's funeral. I don't know if she'll remember much about it anyway. Not after all these years.'

'The adoption agency . . .'

'Oh no, there weren't adoption agencies in those days. Frank saw this advertisement in the paper, and—'

'An advertisement?' Rachel almost shrieked. 'I was advertised in the newspapers? Like a second-hand coat, or a puppy nobody wanted?'

'You *were* wanted! Frank and Doreen were desperate for another baby!'

'A replacement for the baby that died . . . *that's* what they wanted.'

'But we all loved you when you arrived. You were such a beautiful baby, Rachel, and you were a real credit to your parents. We decided – Doreen insisted – that nobody was going to make a difference between you and the rest of the family, and we never did.' Chrissie's face was still white, apart from two bright red patches over her cheekbones.

'Why didn't they tell me? They had no right to keep a thing like that from me!'

'They were going to, one day, I know they were . . . and I wish they had, lovey, but Doreen kept saying that it wasn't the right time, and Frank would never have gone against her wishes, you know that. I'm sure he wanted to tell you.'

Suddenly, Rachel had to get out of the flat. 'Is that the time? I have to get home. I'll get a taxi,' she said, and started towards the door.

'Not a taxi . . . I can't let Doreen see me arriving back in a taxi!'

'But your hand . . .'

'It's fine.' Chrissie struggled to her feet. 'I can manage on the bus. What about all the stuff that has to be cleared?'

Rachel put a hand to her head, trying to think clearly. 'I've got a key at home somewhere. I'll ask Kathleen Ramsay to bring me back tomorrow in her car. We'll deliver the clothes and the shoes and everything else to the WRVS and Mum can arrange for someone to collect the furniture she doesn't want.'

She went into the hall and pulled her coat on, then took Chrissie's coat through to the kitchen before returning to the bedroom to pick up the bag of photographs. She desperately needed to get out of the flat where, she now knew, the first nineteen years of her life had been a lie. She had to get out before she suffocated, or started screaming; she wasn't sure which it would be.

'Rachel, you'll not tell Doreen that I told you?' Chrissie ventured as they went through the close. 'I wish I'd cut my tongue out before I'd said a word.'

'It's all right, Auntie Chrissie,' Rachel soothed while an inner voice murmured in her head, She's not your auntie. You've got no right to call her that. *Not any more.* Not now that you know . . .

'It's all right,' she said again. And then, summoning up a smile that was more a stretching of the lips than anything else, she said as they stepped on to the sunny pavement, 'I'm glad you told me.' She put her arm through Chrissie's, guiding her towards the bus stop. 'And I'll not say anything to Mu . . . to her.'

They travelled on the bus together as far as Paisley Cross, where Rachel had to transfer to another bus.

'Are you sure you'll be all right on your own?' she asked anxiously as she got up from her seat.

'I'm fine, and I'm only a few stops from home now,' Chrissie said. 'It's you I'm worried about.'

'No need,' Rachel said, but when the bus carrying Chrissie on to Whitehaugh had gone and she herself had crossed over and started to walk down St Mirren Brae she had to stop and lean against a shop wall for a moment, sucking in long ragged breaths of air.

'Are you all right, dear?' a woman asked, pausing to eye her doubtfully.

'I'm fine, thanks. It was just coming out into the sunlight after being in the shop.'

'It does that to my eyes too,' the woman agreed, and hurried on her way.

Rachel had intended to do some shopping before catching the bus to Thornly Park, the pleasant residential area where she and Martin lived, but she was getting off the bus before she remembered. They would just have to eat out of tins tonight, she decided.

Arriving home, turning her key in the lock and stepping into the house helped to calm her. Here, at least, she knew who she was: Rachel Carswell, wife and mother, with Martin's wedding ring on her finger and stretch marks on her belly to prove it.

'Are you all right?' Martin asked later.

'Yes, fine. Why?'

'You look a bit tense. It can't have been easy, sorting out your father's belongings today.'

'Someone had to do it and I can't expect my . . . my mother to take it on. Aunt Chrissie was helping.'

'Poor old Frank. He was a great guy, I'll miss him,' Martin said, and then added almost casually, 'for one thing, I'm going to have to spend a lot more time in the garden now he's gone.'

'Is that all he meant to you?' she flared at him.

'What?' He looked up, startled by the ragged edge to her voice, and then had the grace to colour slightly under her outraged glare. 'Sorry, I didn't mean to sound uncaring. It just came out wrong. Of course I'll miss him for himself, and so will you. The two of you were very close.'

'Yes, we were. He was a great father.'

'And a terrific grandfather and father-in-law. We'll all miss him.' He gave her a swift hug. 'Tell you what, I'll do some weeding after dinner. We owe it to him to keep the garden the way he left it.'

'You haven't brought work home with you, then?'

'Not today, thank God.'

They both worked in the garden that evening, and when the children had gone to bed and Martin was watching a television programme Rachel took the bag of photographs from her wardrobe, where she had put it when she came back from the flat, into the small, rarely used dining room. She spread them over the table and had been standing there for a long time, studying each face in minute detail, when Martin came looking for her.

'I missed you.' He slipped his arms around her from behind, drawing her close. 'God, my muscles have seized up! It took me several minutes to struggle out of my chair when that programme ended. I'm not used to

43

gardening.' Then, looking down over her shoulder at the table, 'What on earth have you got there?'

'Photographs I brought back from Mum's flat today.'

'You're not keeping them all, are you?'

'I don't suppose there's much point in keeping any of them.'

'You're absolutely right. What's the sense in saving pictures of people you've never met?' He nuzzled her neck. 'You smell nice. New perfume?'

'The same old stuff.'

'I like it. I've always liked it.'

'Martin, look.' She eased herself free so that she could bend over the table. 'These are my father's parents, and there are my parents around about the time they married. And this is my father's brother George, and his other brother Tom, with their children. And these . . .' she pointed at a separate group of photographs, 'are my mother's parents, with my mother as a young woman. And over here are photographs of me when I was young.'

'We'll keep them, of course.'

She caught his hand and drew him to her side. 'If you look closely you'll see that the Nesbitt side of the family all have strong noses. See? Grandfather, my father, his brothers, my cousins. They all have the family nose,' she said, and then, resting her index finger on her own child-hood pictures, 'but I don't have it.'

'My darling, be grateful for small mercies. And small noses.'

'Now if you look at the Kemp side of the family, Mum's side, you'll see that they tend to have thick curly hair. My grandmother had it, and so do my mother and Aunt Chrissie. And the men have widow's peaks, too. But me . . .' She indicated her own brown hair, hanging almost to her shoulders and with just a slight curl at the ends.

'My hair's as straight as a yardstick, and it always was. My mother used to curl it every night in twists of toilet paper.'

She could still remember the way Doreen had rolled her hair up so tightly that it made her scalp sting and brought tears to her eyes. She recalled the discomfort of sleeping on the curlers, and how, when her hair was released in the morning, it fell straight again. She remembered praying every night for curls, and always eating her crusts because Doreen said that that made hair curly.

'You have lovely hair.' He ran both hands down it, lifting it out slightly at the ends and then letting it fall back against her neck.

'That's not the point. The point is that I don't look anything like either side of the family I grew up in. And I never will, because I don't belong.' Saying it directly like that, 'I don't belong,' suddenly sounded so final and so bleak that for a moment she couldn't say any more. She made a pretence of gathering up the photographs in order to hide her face from her husband; and then, when she was able to look at him again, she said, 'Martin, I'm adopted.'

'Adopted?' He started to smile and then, as she looked back at him stonily, the amusement faded. 'You can't be adopted.'

'Why can't I be?'

'Because you've never mentioned it before. You'd have told me; we never keep secrets from each other.'

'I didn't know myself, until Aunt Chrissie told me today.'

'But . . .' He ran a hand through his short dark hair, his eyes confused and the two little lines between his brows deepening. 'Are you telling me that for all these years they've never said a word? How could you not know a thing like that? What about your birth certificate?'

'I have a shortened certificate, remember? I was told that the first one got lost. It was wartime, nothing was ordinary or normal then.'

Martin turned and took a couple of steps towards the door, then swung round and came back to her. 'Chrissie told you? Why? Why today, I mean.'

'It just spilled out. We were looking at these photographs, and I was saying how I didn't look like anyone in them, and about one of my names being Flora, only there were no Floras in the family. I made a joke about the fairies taking the real Rachel out of her cot and replacing her with a changeling, and she got a bit upset. Then she burned her hand on the kettle when it was boiling, and got more upset, and suddenly it all came tumbling out.'

'Good grief,' Martin said, and sat down heavily.

'I've been thinking about it ever since Aunt Chrissie told me, and there are so many things that make sense now. My mother's always been so reserved with me, and sometimes when I was growing up she'd say things that made me wonder at the time.'

'What sort of things?'

'Well . . . the latest was at Dad's funeral, when I tried to take her arm and she only wanted Aunt Chrissie to help her. And when she said she was going to stay at Whitehaugh afterwards, instead of going back to the flat, she said, "Chrissie's my own flesh and blood." She was always saying things like that.'

'It's just the way she is.'

'That what I thought, but now it makes sense.'

'You don't think that Chrissie's got the wrong end of the stick? Or perhaps she was playing some sort of trick on you.'

'Why would she tell me lies? She never has – as far

as I know, she's the only person who's ever told me the truth,' Rachel said bleakly.

'But if it's true, why tell you now?' An angry note crept into his voice. 'Why stir things up at this point in your life?'

'I told you; she got upset when I started talking about not looking like anyone else in the family. She said that she had been worried about me not knowing the truth, but my mother kept saying that it wasn't the time to tell me.'

'All the more reason for Chrissie to bite her tongue now, surely.'

'Martin, what if one of the children fell ill?'

'For heaven's sake, Rachel, what has that got to do with all this?' He waved his hand at the photographs. 'The kids are all perfectly healthy, why should any of them fall ill?'

'But just suppose it happened? Supposing doctors needed medical backgrounds for some reason? I don't have one. I don't have any sort of background. I thought I had, but I don't!'

He bit his lip, thinking hard, then said, 'Fiona has curly hair. She looks like you, everyone says so, but she has curly hair, just like your mother's family.'

'Your mother has curls too. She could have inherited it from your side of the family.'

'Are you going to say anything to Doreen about this?'

'Aunt Chrissie asked me not to.'

'I think she's right. You need to forget about this whole adoption business.'

'How can I just forget a bombshell like that?'

'What else can you do? You can't speak to your mother, and if Chrissie's telling the truth, Doreen's probably the only person who can confirm it.' He gathered her into his arms. 'You're thirty-five years old and you've got a life and a family and that's all that matters. You belong with us . . . the children and me. I think you should try to forget what Chrissie told you.'

'You mean that I should settle for not knowing who I am?' she said into his shoulder as he stroked her back soothingly.

'My darling, you know who you are, and so do I. You're Rachel Carswell, my wife and Fiona and Ian and Graham's mother. You're very special, and you're loved.' He eased her back slightly, so that he could look down at her. 'You don't need to know any more, Rachel, and neither do I. Please, darling, please let's just leave it at that.'

'I can understand what he means,' Kathleen said as the two of them finished packing boxes for the WRVS. 'You're not the only one to feel insecure about being adopted. From what you say, Martin's just as shaky about it as you are.'

'I don't see why. He's got his own family, and he knows where his roots are.' Rachel felt a sudden stab of jealousy twist deep within her as she spoke. 'He's got a wall at his back, but the way I feel at the moment, if I fall backwards, I'll just keep on falling because there's nothing there to stop me.'

'He's worried. He feels threatened.'

'That's just stupid. Nobody's threatening him!'

'He could be scared that if you start trying to find out who your birth parents are, you won't be *you* any longer – not the you that he knows and . . . that sounds ridiculous, doesn't it?' Kathleen added with a snort of laughter. She had wrapped twine round a box of Frank's clothes; now she cut it and tied a neat running knot. 'There, that's another one ready. Have you had any thoughts about trying to find your biological mother?'

'Yes, but I don't have any paperwork, and the only way I can get that is to ask my mother for it. And I promised Aunt Chrissie that I'd keep my mouth shut.'

'So you've reached a dead end, and that might not be a bad idea. From what you say, Martin would prefer it if you just forgot about the entire business. I suppose,' Kathleen said slowly, 'he wants everything to go on the way it always has, and you to go on being you.' Then, with a brisk change of tone, 'Now then, we've got all the clothes boxed, and the bedding, and the towels and so on. And the cutlery and dishes and kitchen stuff. The WRVS are going to be very happy with this little lot. Ready to start loading the car? Just think of all the exercise we're going to get, carrying this lot down the stairs in relays.'

Ever the dutiful daughter, Rachel went to Whitehaugh the following day to report to her mother.

'The WRVS are very grateful for all the things you donated, and I'll see to the business of getting the furniture uplifted if you want.'

'I can do that myself, with Chrissie's help. We've got more free time than you have. Sit down,' Doreen ordered, 'and I'll make us a cup for tea. Chrissie's out, and I want to talk to you.'

'Do you have any coffee?'

'It's not good for you. Tea's better, so we'll have tea.' Doreen bustled into the small kitchen, leaving Rachel in the bright, comfortable living room.

'Are you settling in all right?' she asked, raising her voice slightly in order to be heard. The kitchen led off the living room, and her mother had left the door open.

'Well enough. We got rid of most of the furniture in Chrissie's spare room so that I could put a few bits of my own in there. And the neighbours seem a decent enough lot. Quiet folk, thank goodness. No noisy children playing loud music and kickin' footballs about.'

Chrissie's upper flat was one of four in a block, two on the ground floor, and two above, each accessed by a side door and an interior flight of stairs.

'When are you going to have the flat valued? I could—'

'It's been done. The lawyer doesnae think I'll have much trouble selling it.' Doreen brought a tray in, saying when Rachel sprang to her feet and tried to take it from her, 'I can manage . . . we'll just drop the whole lot if we both try to carry it. If you want to make yourself useful, away into the kitchen and bring the teapot through. And the milk jug.'

Doing as she was told, Rachel marvelled at how easily her mother could turn her from a thirty-five-year-old woman, capable of running a home and raising a family, to a clumsy, hesitant schoolgirl, with just a few terse words.

'You can pour the tea out while you've got the pot,' Doreen said when her daughter emerged from the kitchen. And then, as Rachel settled the teapot on its three-legged wrought-iron stand after filling both cups, she said, 'Chrissie told me what she did.'

'What did she do?'

'She spoke out of place. She told you things it wasnae her business to tell you or anyone else.'

Rachel felt crimson heat flood over her face. 'You mean, about me being adopted?'

'She'd no right!' Doreen's voice was suddenly harsh.

'It wasn't her fault. I was just looking at some old photographs and saying that I didn't look like any of the family and it all . . . it just slipped out. I wasn't going to say anything to you, she knew that. She didn't need to tell you.'

'Of course she did. Chrissie's as honest as the day's long and she knows when she's done wrong. She couldnae hold herself back from confessin' to me.'

'I hardly think that confessing is the right word,' Rachel said sharply, and then, as her mother simply looked at her in silence, 'I just wish that you and Dad had told me yourselves, a long time ago.'

'Would it have made any difference to your life?'

'I should have been told. Who else knows about it?'

'Of the folk that are still alive, you mean?'

'I doubt if there's much gossiping in a cemetery,' Rachel snapped, and then, instantly ashamed of herself, 'I'm sorry, I didn't think.'

'No, you didn't,' Doreen snapped back at her. She helped herself to milk and sugar, stirred her tea for about half a minute, then said, 'Only Chrissie knows, and your father's brothers and their wives, and they've probably forgotten about it long since. It all happened years ago; you were better off not knowing.'

'But who am I?'

Doreen's head came up swiftly. 'That's a daft question! You know fine who you are. You're my daughter.'

'But—'

'I've got papers to prove it. D'you think your daddy and me stole you, or bought you, or whatever?' Doreen's voice rose and her eyes were fierce. 'We got the adoption paper, Frank made sure of that. The woman signed it and someone in authority witnessed it. Everything was done according to the law and the law says that you're our daughter, so there's nothin' more to be said on the subject.'

Rachel knew from Doreen's tone of voice that she was treading on dangerous ground, but she persisted. 'Aunt Chrissie said that there was a newspaper advertisement – that I was advertised in the papers.'

'That's the way things were done in those days. There was a war on,' Doreen said, as though that explained and excused everything.

'You said you had papers signed and witnessed. Can I see them?'

'Why would you want to do that?'

'Everyone's got a right to see their own papers,' Rachel argued, and then, when Doreen said nothing, 'My birth certificate, for one. You said that it was lost and that's why I had a shortened certificate.'

'I don't know what happened to that, if we ever had it. It wasn't among the papers Frank had. The certificate you got's perfectly legal – and so are you. Can you not be content with that?' Doreen made it sound as though Rachel was being deliberately difficult.

'But I don't just want to be legal, I want to belong!'

'Of course you belong! Have you said anythin' to Martin about this?'

'I told him what Aunt Chrissie told me. He had a right to know,' Rachel insisted as she saw the older woman's thin lips tighten. 'He's my husband.'

'And what does he think you should do?'

'He . . . he wants me to forget about it,' Rachel admitted, and triumph flashed into her mother's face.

'There, you see? Listen to him, Rachel. Martin's a clever man; he's got a good job. He knows what's best.'

'But even if you don't have my birth certificate, there's still the paperwork from the adoption. I'd like to see that,' Rachel pressed on as Doreen's lips tightened and her chin went up.

'Your father saw to all those things. I'd nothin' to do with them.'

'But you've still got the papers, surely?' Rachel asked, recalling the wooden box kept in the bottom of her father's wardrobe. It had been empty apart from the packet of old photographs. And then, as her mother said nothing, 'If you don't know where they are, I suppose I can get copies from somewhere . . . the Registrar's Office in Edinburgh, or some place like that.'

'You're not thinkin' of tryin' to trace your real mother, are you? For goodness' sake, lassie, even if she's still alive, you don't know what you'd be stirring up. She might be a terrible woman – she rid herself of you fast enough, didn't she? What sort of mother would do that?'

Rachel's hands clenched in her lap. 'She might have had a good reason. Didn't you meet her? Who gave me to you?'

'She did,' Doreen admitted.

'Where?'

'At the Clyde Street bus stop in Glasgow.'

'She just handed me over to complete strangers at a bus stop?' Rachel felt as though she were moving into some weird Alice in Wonderland existence. All at once being found under a gooseberry bush, the very first explanation her mother had given to young Rachel's questions about where babies came from, seemed quite proper and desirable.

'That's the way things were done then. There was a war on,' Doreen said again.

'What was she like?'

'How can I be expected to remember that? It was well over thirty years ago. She was just a woman,' Doreen said as Rachel kept quiet, waiting. 'Plainly dressed, quite ordinary.'

'Young?' Rachel had some picture in her mind of a teenager who had fallen pregnant to a serviceman. For all she knew, she might be part Polish or French or American or . . . the list was endless.

'If I'd known that one day you were goin' to cross-question me like this I'd have taken your daddy's Box Brownie camera with me and got her to pose for her picture,' Doreen said with a flash of irritation. Then, rising to her feet, 'Wait a minute.'

Left alone in the room, Rachel went over to peer at herself in the mirror. The face she had always known – oval and neat-featured, framed with straight brown hair – looked back at her. Her blue eyes looked even more uncertain than usual and her cheeks were flushed. As far as she knew, French and American and Polish people looked much the same as British people.

'Here.' Doreen was back, holding out a folded sheet of paper. 'It's the official adoption paper that we signed after we got you. That's the only thing I found in the box in the wardrobe.'

The document was yellowed with age, and Rachel had to unfold it carefully for fear of tearing it. It was a form, filled out in beautiful copperplate handwriting and with an official seal at the bottom of the page. Rachel's eyes raced greedily over line after line, snatching at phrases. *Rachel Elizabeth Flora . . . father unknown . . . consent given by mother . . .* Then came the information she had been hoping for. *Miss Flora McCrimmon Moodie of . . . Glasgow . . . mother of said child . . .*

'Flora,' Rachel said. 'She gave me her name.'

'Aye, you were named when you came to us. We were-nae bothered about choosin' other names,' Doreen said, not seeming to realise how cruel her casual tone was. 'So we just left you as you were.'

Rachel bit her lip, then looked down at the paper again . . . *do hereby state that I understand the nature and effect of the adoption order . . . and that the effect . . . will be permanently to deprive me of my parental rights.*

Next came the affidavit from the public official over-seeing the adoption. *I . . . have satisfied myself that Flora McCrimmon Moodie, in giving her consent to the proposed adoption, understands that the effect of the adoption will be permanently to deprive her of her parental rights.* This was followed by signatures, and a date in May 1941.

'Are you satisfied now?' Doreen broke the silence just as Rachel was beginning to read the form again, more carefully.

'Can I keep this?'

Doreen shrugged. 'I've no use for it,' she said, and then, sudden apprehension in her eyes, 'You're not goin' to try to find your real mother, are you?'

'I don't know what I want to do. I'll need to think about it.'

'Leave it be, lassie,' Doreen urged, leaning forward in her chair. 'It all happened a long time ago and a lot of water's flowed beneath the bridge since then. You were a lot better off with me and Frank, believe me. She didnae want you – remember that. And goodness knows what trouble you might be causin' for Martin and those bairns of yours if you go diggin' up the past. Think of them if you'll not think of me. Think of your daddy. He'd not want you to go lookin' for a stranger that just gave you away when you were a tiny wee thing.'

'I'd better get back home.' The paper in Rachel's hands sprang naturally back into its folds, and she tucked it away in her bag.

'Aye, best go. Chrissie'll be back soon, and I don't want her to know what we've been talkin' about. She knows too much as it is,' Doreen said, and almost hustled her daughter out of the house, leaving the two cups of tea untouched.

'Speak to Martin before you do anything daft,' was her parting shot. 'He's the man of the hoose, he'll know best.'

Rachel stood at the bus stop in Glasgow Road without seeing the passing traffic or the shops and tenements. She was remembering little things that Doreen had said over the years, remarks that, although puzzling, had been shrugged off, forgotten.

Only they hadn't really been forgotten, they had been tucked away in her subconscious, and now they were resurfacing in a steady stream, one after another, to be studied and wondered about. Many of them made complete sense to her now, in the light of Chrissie's bombshell. Some left her wondering whether Doreen had meant them to be as hurtful as they now seemed, or whether, suffering the pain of her newfound knowledge, she was reading more into them than had been meant.

Her first instinct had been to tell Martin what her mother had said, and to show him the adoption paper. But in the short walk from Chrissie's flat to Glasgow Road she had changed her mind. He would probably agree with Doreen, and urge her to forget the whole business.

So when someone tapped her on the shoulder and asked, a trifle impatiently, 'Excuse me, dear, but are you getting on this bus?' she shook her head and stepped back to let the rest of the queue board. Then she waited for a bus that would take her to the west end of the town.

It arrived a few minutes later and she paid her fare, then stared out of the window, wishing that her father had still been alive. She could have done with some of his sensible advice. But if he had been, she thought as her stop approached, she and Chrissie would never have had to sort out the family photographs, and her aunt would not have blurted out the secret that had been kept from Rachel all her life. Nothing would have changed . . . and that thought made her wish even harder that Frank were still alive.

'Are you all right, dear?' the conductress asked as she blundered off the bus. Rachel glanced up, saw the woman through a mist of tears, and blinked them away. 'I'm fine, thanks.'

She only had minutes to wait before a Lounsdale bus came along, and within another half-hour she was drinking a cup of coffee in the living room of Kathleen's neat bungalow in Corsebar Drive, while her friend studied the paper Doreen had handed over.

'So . . . Martin wants you to let sleeping dogs lie, and your mother says the same. But clearly, you're all for nudging the dogs with your toe, which is why you've come to me. And to be honest, I don't know what to say.'

'At least you'll listen instead of just telling me what I should do. The thing is, Kathleen, I don't feel like me any more. Who am I? Where do I come from? We all need roots. I don't feel that I belong anywhere any more. And I know that that's silly,' Rachel said swiftly as her friend started to speak, 'but it's true.' Then she jumped as someone knocked loudly on the back door. 'Who's that?'

'It's just Murdo's gardener, looking for his money. Won't be a minute.'

'You have a gardener?' Rachel asked when Kathleen returned.

'No, I don't have a gardener; Murdo has. He's too busy to give his precious vegetables the tender loving care they need, so now he pays a man to do a bit of cherishing while he's at work.' Kathleen poured more coffee for them both. 'He did hint that I should do it, since I'm at home during the day, but then he realised that letting me loose among his beloved plants would not be a good idea. Which reminds me . . . why don't you take some soup home for the family? The freezer's getting a bit full.'

'What is it?'

'Carrot and coriander; or potato and leek if you prefer. All prime shop-bought vegetables,' Kathleen added. 'None of your home-grown rubbish.'

'Carrot and coriander sounds lovely. Did you notice that she gave me her name? My real mother, I mean. So at least I know now where the Flora comes from. It always seemed to me to be an unusual name to pick out of the blue.'

'Is that why you're not happy about letting the matter drop in order to please Martin and your mother?'

'She might have cared more than they seem to think. That might be why she gave me her name.'

Kathleen flipped at the adoption paper with the tip of one finger. 'The final decision has to be yours.'

'I know, and even that confuses me. I feel as if I'm at a fork in the road and there aren't any signposts.' Rachel took a sip of her coffee and put the cup down again. 'And I can't turn back, because the road behind me, the road that used to be my life, has disappeared. It's like one of these children's stories, Kathleen. All my life I've been leaving a trail of breadcrumbs or string or whatever behind me, and I've just looked round and discovered that it's gone and I won't be able to find my way back.'

'I think you should pitch your tent at the fork in the road and give yourself time to decide which direction you want to take. Don't rush into anything.'

'That makes sense. I've got a lot of decisions to make – I've been thinking of going back to teaching.'

'What on earth for?'

'I feel restless now that Graham's settled into school. I need to have something to do.'

'You're always doing things – sewing, embroidery, making costumes for this school play. And isn't looking after a house and three kids enough?' Kathleen demanded. 'I've no notion to teach again; I enjoy being a kept woman, and I've only got Murdo to look after – when he's home. Even then he spends most of his time in the garden. My one big fear is that one day he'll decide to give up his job and go in for market gardening. If he does that I shall have no option but to leave him – which might not be a bad idea,' she added thoughtfully. 'I'd love the chance to put some romance back into my life.'

'You don't mean that.'

'Don't be so sure, my dear. What does Martin say to you going back to the classroom? I bet he's against it.'

'Why should you think that?'

'Because your Martin is the sort of man who thinks that it's his place to support his family. Sweet, but just a tad old-fashioned,' Kathleen said placidly. 'Man the hunter, woman the cave-cleaner. Only instead of wielding clubs, the Martins of this world go out into the jungle armed with briefcases. Just teasing,' she added hastily as Rachel began to protest. 'But am I right, or am I right?'

'You're right, but I've been wondering about putting my name down as a relief teacher.'

'If I were you I'd have a good long think about going back to work, love. Pitch your tent on that decision too. Be sure that it's what you want.'

'I have to do something, Kathleen. I can't just sit around the house waiting to grow old.'

Kathleen grinned. 'You'd have a long wait. And you don't have to sit around – there's always coffee chats with me. And shopping.'

The Scottish Registry Office in Edinburgh exuded an almost eerie sense of timelessness, as well it might since it contained details of every single person who had been born or married in Scotland since the sixteenth century.

The central room where Rachel stood was the full height of the imposing building. Galleries linked by stairs like fire escapes were ranged around the walls, each one holding shelves stacked with volumes full of certificates.

All these people, Rachel thought in awe, staring up at row upon of row of galleries. Everyone she knew and had ever known was recorded here – their births, marriages and deaths. She and Martin and the children were here, and would be for evermore.

Death records were only available from the nineteenth century, she had been informed when she booked an appointment, but it was a birth certificate she needed to see – a birth registered in 1941. And after twenty minutes spent leafing through one of the huge books listing every birth for that year, she found herself looking at her own name. It was the final entry on the right-hand page and her hand was already easing the corner up, preparatory to turning to the next page, when she noticed the words, *Rachel Elizabeth Flora Moodie*.

Her heart gave a double flip and then started to beat fast as she stared at the name. The date was right, and the surname was the one she had first seen on the adoption paper.

'Make a note of the entry number and take it to the desk,' she had been told when she was ushered in. She scribbled the number on the small notepad she had brought with her, and closed the book. A glance at her watch told her that it was almost noon. She would have to be home in three hours' time. Her knees trembled as she made her way to the desk, where she had to wait in line to be served.

She had said nothing to Martin about her conversation with Doreen; she knew that he would agree with the older woman's views, but the adoption paper that was hidden away in the bedroom drawer had kept nagging at her. It was like the short story about the man who committed murder and was then driven mad by the sound of his victim's heart still beating. Try as she might to forget what had happened, she knew that she must try to find out what she could about her natural mother. And so, after a great deal of soul-searching, she now stood in the Registry Office.

It had been hard, that morning, to behave as though it was just a normal day, and as she dashed to the bedroom to change from her everyday sweater and trousers into a blouse and skirt, guilt niggled at her. She knew that if Martin had realised what she was planning he would have talked her out of it. But once she was on the Edinburgh train the guilt gave way to nervous anticipation. She felt like an explorer moving into unknown territory.

Her name was called and a guide escorted her to the

narrow metal staircase leading up to the galleries. 'No problem, love,' he said when she gave the number of the certificate she wanted to see. 'Up here.'

Following him up the stairs and along the first gallery she was glad that she had decided to wear low-heeled shoes instead of the high heels she usually wore with her best outfit. The galleries were also of metal, floored in a lacy pattern; nobody wearing high heels could have walked on them without getting caught in the holes.

They went up more stairs, and after one swift glance down at the counter below – further below than she had realised – Rachel kept her eyes firmly fixed on her guide's back, almost bumping into him when he stopped and said, 'Here we are.'

He ran a hand along a row of volumes, selected one, turned the pages with practised skill, and pointed at the page. 'That what you're looking for?'

She nodded, and swallowed hard before asking, 'Can I . . . can I note down what it says?'

'If you've got a pencil. We can't let anyone use pens in here, just in case they try to deface the records. Here . . .' He put the book down on one of the small lecterns placed at intervals along the gallery and stood back. 'Take your time, love.'

'Thank you.' She scribbled the information into her little notepad, writing small in order to get it all onto two pages. *Rachel Elizabeth Flora Moodie, born April 28th 1941, mother Flora McCrimmon Moodie, Clerkess. Father unknown.* The address on the certificate was the same as the address on the adoption paper that Doreen had given her.

'Thank you,' she said when she had finished, and the man nodded and said as he put the book back on the shelf, 'You do know that you can get a copy of the certificate?'

63

'Can I?'

'Just tell them the number at the desk and pay the fee, and they'll send it on to you. It takes about a week.'

As the train covered the miles between Edinburgh and Glasgow, Rachel read and reread the notes she had scribbled down. *Flora McCrimmon Moodie, Clerkess.* Who was she? Where was she? Was she still alive? At least the two stark words, *Father unknown,* answered the puzzle as to why Flora McCrimmon Moodie, clerkess, had given her three-week-old infant away.

They reached Queen Street station. Rachel caught the bus that transported passengers between the Queen Street and Glasgow Central railway stations, arriving at Central just in time to catch a train that would take her back to Paisley. She settled into a seat, then leaned her head against the headrest and closed her eyes, trying to summon her real mother from the shadows. Young . . . probably still in her teens, and pregnant. Perhaps her parents had thrown her out when they discovered she was carrying a child. How could an unmarried girl afford to keep and raise an illegitimate baby, especially during the uncertainty and turmoil of a worldwide war?

Unable to see much beyond the picture of a pathetic little figure with a pale, featureless face and a shawl around her bowed head, she gave up on Flora and turned to wondering about her unknown father. Perhaps he had been a mere lad himself; someone who, on the verge of going off to fight for his country, had sought comfort in the arms of his young sweetheart. Had he survived the war, or had he died on some far-flung battlefield, or trapped in a torpedoed, sinking ship? Had he known of Rachel's imminent arrival?

She had reached the stage of wondering if he had been an older man who had taken advantage of Flora's youth

64

and innocent naivety when the train began to slow down and she opened her eyes to discover that they were approaching Paisley's Gilmour Street station.

Just as well, she thought as she tucked her notebook back into her bag and prepared to alight. Another ten minutes of daydreaming and she would have turned her real parents into the Little Match Girl and the Unknown Warrior.

The certificate was delivered exactly one week later. Rachel, who had been listening every morning for the post to arrive so that she could get to it before anyone else, happened to be going through the hall when three envelopes shot through the letter box and landed on the mat. One was for Martin, one from Fiona's French pen pal and the third envelope, official-looking and addressed to Rachel herself, she thrust into a drawer in the hall table just as Martin said from the top of the stairs, 'Did I hear the post arriving?'

'One for you, but it looks like a bill. And one for Fiona.' Rachel blessed the Fates for these letters. She would have been in a pickle if the envelope from the Registry Office had arrived on its own.

He came downstairs, fastening his shirtsleeves, and took the proffered envelope. 'The electricity bill, and the car insurance'll be in next. More money going out,' he grumbled, and went ahead of her into the kitchen.

The wait until Martin and the children had gone to office and school seemed endless. As soon as she had the house to herself Rachel fetched the envelope from its hiding place, slit it open, and poured herself another cup of tea.

Sitting at the kitchen table with the birth certificate and adoption paper spread out before her, she tried hard to picture Flora McCrimmon Moodie, but as before, all she could come up with was a mental image of a shy, frightened teenager who once again changed into the Little Match Girl, with a long ragged skirt and bare feet blue with cold.

Rachel gave up speculating about her unknown mother, and studied the address, which was the same as the one on the adoption paper. Then the words *Father Unknown* seemed to leap out of the page at her.

That, perhaps, was the hardest part of the blow that had been dealt to her. She had never really felt like her mother's daughter, and now she knew why; but Frank Nesbitt had been a warm, caring father, and it hurt to know that he too had been deceiving her. Until recently she had been safe in the knowledge that her father had loved her, and now she found herself confronting the idea of another man, faceless and nameless; a man who might not even have known of her existence.

Music from the radio on the kitchen counter formed pleasant background noise to the daily ritual of getting the family off to school and work, before washing the dishes and starting her own day. Very often, Rachel was scarcely aware of it, but now, right on cue, it started playing Fiona's favourite group, Abba, singing 'Knowing Me, Knowing You'.

Rachel gave a hysterical giggle. The song could have been written for her – a woman who for years thought she knew exactly who she was, but now had no idea of her background or parentage, or why her unknown mother had decided to give her away.

'I wish I did know me,' she told the radio. And then, as the Swedish group brought their poignant song to an end, tears came to her eyes without warning. It was as though she had been doubly bereaved, first by losing the only father she had known, and then by losing her own identity. She wanted her father; she needed him, and he was no longer there. Alone in the house, free to do as she pleased, she put her head down on to her folded arms, and gave herself up to a howling, snivelling, tear-dripping and thoroughly childlike bout of misery.

Kathleen was right, Rachel decided, cleansed and refreshed by her therapeutic bout of weeping. Best to pitch her tent and say nothing to Martin about her visit to the Registry Office until she had had a chance to think things over.

She made the beds, put on the washing, and went out to the shops before settling down to getting more work done on the costumes for *The Importance of Being Earnest*.

The day rushed by in a whirl of planning, cutting and stitching, and she was so busy trying to recreate the beautiful Edwardian clothes pictured in her reference books that everything else was swept from her mind.

The boys came home, and after giving them something to eat, making sure they fed the guinea pigs, and seeing them both settled in the garden, Graham on his beloved swing and Ian with his Space Hopper, Rachel peeled potatoes and chopped carrots for their dinner, then returned to her sewing machine. Above its whirring she heard Fiona's usual shout of 'Mum, where are you?'

'In here,' she called back, and then heard her daughter running upstairs. Almost at once, Abba began to blare out from the music centre that had been the girl's fifteenth birthday present.

The music stopped in mid-song five minutes later, then Fiona came back downstairs and into the sewing room.

'Mum?'

'Hello, dear,' Rachel said absently, concentrating on a tricky bit of pinning. 'How was school today?'

'Mum, what's this?' Fiona dropped a sheet of paper in front of her mother.

'Fiona, I'm trying to . . .' Rachel began, and then her eye fell on the paper. When the pin she was about to push through the fabric in her hand missed the mark and jabbed into her finger she scarcely registered the sudden pain.

'Where did you get that?'

'In one of your drawers. I was borrowing a sanitary towel and I found it underneath them. And this, too.' Fiona laid the birth certificate beside the adoption paper. 'Mum, what are they?'

'Nothing.' Rachel, reaching for the paper, suddenly noticed the bead of bright red blood welling up on the ball of her thumb. She snatched her hand back before it touched the material she was working on, and put it to her mouth. 'Nothing important,' she said indistinctly.

'If it's not important, why hide it in that drawer?'

'Perhaps I wanted to keep it away from nosy snoopers!'

Fiona pressed both hands to her stomach. 'I wasn't snooping. I've had the most terrible cramps all afternoon and I was looking for a sanitary towel.' She picked up the certificate and peered at it. 'It's official looking, and the handwriting's so old-fashioned. May 1941 . . . it's ancient! Mum, this is about some baby being adopted.'

'It has nothing to do with you.'

'I know that, I wasn't born until 1961 and this is twenty years before th . . . Rachel? Mum,' her voice was suddenly sharp, her eyes widening, 'it's you! You were the baby!'

There was no sense in denying it; clearly the girl wasn't going to let the matter go. 'Yes,' Rachel said reluctantly. 'Yes, it's me. But it all happened a long time ago and I was only a few weeks old . . .'

'When did Gran and Grandpa tell you?' Fiona's eyes were bright with interest. 'It must be exciting, discovering that your parents aren't really your parents.'

'No,' Rachel said flatly. 'No, it's not.'

'There's an adopted girl in my class, Cecily Dawson. She thinks it gives her an air of mystery. She can pretend that her real parents could have been anything – nobility, or famous actors, or gypsies; it depends on the mood she's in. The rest of us are dead jealous. Why didn't you tell me, Mum?'

'Because I didn't know myself, until a few weeks ago.'

'Gran didn't tell you? Why did she wait so long?'

'Auntie Chrissie told me, and it came out by accident.'

'Oh, poor Mum! It must have been a terrible shock!'

'As a matter of fact . . .' Rachel tried to sound flippant, but her voice began to shake, ruining the effect, so that she finished with a miserable, 'it was.'

'I'll make you a cup of coffee, and then you can tell me all about it,' Fiona said, and rushed off to the kitchen.

By the time her daughter returned with the coffee and a glass of milk and two chocolate wafer biscuits, Rachel had pulled herself together and was able to give a brief outline of all that had happened since her father's death. Fiona listened, her vivid blue eyes round with astonishment and excitement.

'Does Gran know that you know?' she asked when the story came to an end.

'Yes, and she's not very happy about it.'

'Why didn't she and Grandpa tell you earlier?'

'Apparently they meant to, but then time went on and it didn't seem to be important. She's got a point, I suppose.'

Fiona thought about it, pulling a strand of her curly hair straight so that she could chew on the end of it, as she always did when concentrating. 'I don't agree,' she said at last. 'I think it *is* important. People have the right to know who they are.'

'Do you really think so?'

'I've just said it, haven't I?' Fiona pointed out. 'Does Dad know?'

'Of course. I wouldn't keep something like this from him.'

'What does he think you should do about it?'

'Do about it? It's a bit late to do anything, isn't it?'

'Not really. Your real mother and father might still be alive. You might have brothers and sisters. Mum . . .' Fiona took a gulp of milk and began to get enthusiastic, 'you could have a whole family you know nothing about. I could have aunts and uncles and cousins and—'

'And they might be people we wouldn't like.'

'Surely you're not going to leave it at this?' Fiona thumped the papers, which were still lying on top of the material her mother had been working on. 'You have to find this Flora McCrimmon Moodie. She's the only one who can tell you who you really are.'

'I *know* who I am. Fiona, your grandmother and your father both think that I should just let matters stay as they are, and they're probably right.'

'But you can't! It's not just you . . . I want to know about my background too. And what about the boys?'

Rachel began to panic. 'Fiona, you've not to say a word to either of your brothers, do you hear me?'

'All right, I won't. But for fifteen years I've been thinking that Gran and Grandpa Nesbitt were my real grandparents, and now you're telling me that they're not. If I have another gran and another grandpa I want to meet them. I want to know what they look like, and what sort of lives they've lived!' And then, with a little skip of excitement, 'This is just like the play we're rehearsing at

70

school! Jack Worthing didn't know who his real parents were either.'

'It's nothing like *The Importance of Being Earnest.* I wasn't found in a handbag in Victoria station, for a start,' Rachel protested, and then suddenly remembered that her real mother had handed her over to her adoptive parents at a Glasgow bus stop. Perhaps her story wasn't so different from Jack Worthing's . . . other than the fact that he was a fictional character in a play, while she was a real person in a very real and very difficult situation.

'How can I find anything out after all this time?' she asked aloud, and her daughter's index finger – the nail freshly painted dark red, Rachel noticed – stabbed down on the birth certificate.

'We could start with this address. She might still be living there.'

'I doubt it, not after thirty-five years.'

'Lots of people stay at the same address for most of their lives. Look at Gran, she must have lived in Wellmeadow Street since before you were born and if Grandpa hadn't died she'd still be there. Even if this Flora's not at that address any more, there might be a neighbour who remembers her. We won't know until we go and ask, will we?'

'We?'

'Of course, we. Tomorrow,' Fiona said. 'We could go tomorrow.'

'You've got school tomorrow.'

'Saturday, then. Dad'll be here on Saturday to look after the boys.'

'Fiona, your father would prefer if it I did nothing about this adoption business. He doesn't even know that I went to Edinburgh to look for my real birth certificate. Why do you think I hid it away in that drawer?'

'We won't tell him then. We'll say we're going shopping. And if we do manage to find Flora McCrimmon Moodie, or anything about her,' Fiona added, forestalling the argument that had jumped to Rachel's lips, '*then* we can decide whether or not to say anything to him.'

'Fiona . . . !'

'*Please* say yes, Mum!' the girl begged. 'It would be great to have an adventure together, just the two of us.' Then, craftily, 'If you say yes, I promise not to say a word about this to Dad or the boys.'

'You've already promised that.'

'And I meant it,' Fiona assured her, her eyes suddenly sapphire pools of innocence. 'But there's always the danger of the wrong word slipping out before I have time to think. If you agree that we can go to Glasgow tomorrow, I promise that I'll work extra hard at keeping a brake on my tongue.'

'Fiona, that's blackmail.'

'I know,' Fiona said cheerfully, 'but it'll be fun. Let's do it!'

8

The tenement buildings lining both sides of the street named in Rachel's birth certificate and adoption paper were old, tired and shabby. Litter clustered around doorways and lay in heaps in the gutters; children freed from school for the weekend cycled up and down the road or sped along the pavements on roller skates to the annoyance of women returning home, head-scarfed and weighed down by shopping bags.

A handful of boys played football in the street while little girls bounced balls against the tenement walls, or wielded skipping ropes. Dolls' prams were parked by several closes.

The women, and even the children, seemed to have taken on the colourless look of the street they lived in, and Fiona, with her head of tawny curls, her fresh, clear skin and her red wool jacket and ankle-length patchwork skirt, looked like a bird of paradise that had strayed from its usual haunts. Oblivious to the attention she was attracting, she marched along the street on her clumpy, fashionable shoes, counting numbers.

'There it is. Come on . . .'

Rachel's stomach, which had been fluttering ever since they had boarded the bus to Glasgow, suddenly started to turn somersaults. 'I don't know if I want to.'

'Why not?'

'What if she's still living there? What will I say?'

'You don't need to say anything. Leave it to me.' Fiona took command with ease. 'I'll say . . . I'll say that a friend who lives in England asked us to make enquiries.'

'What if she asks for this friend's name and address?'

'I'll make something up. Come on, Mum,' Fiona said impatiently, snatching at Rachel's hand and pulling her across the road. 'We've come this far; you can't just turn and walk away!'

The close was dark, and most of the flats lacked nameplates. Tutting her exasperation, Fiona dragged Rachel from door to door, checking the two ground-floor flats before heading up the first flight of stairs. They could hear music being played in one of the upper flats, and as her daughter peered closely at the nameplate, her nose almost against the door, Rachel fully expected it to fly open. But it didn't, and they went up to the top flight without seeing anyone.

'No luck,' Fiona said, disappointed, and knocked on the final door.

'Fiona . . .'

'Ssshh, someone's coming. Leave this to me, Mum.' Fiona's eyes sparkled in the gloom of the landing. 'Isn't this fun? It's like being a detective!'

The door opened to reveal an old man with braces over an armless vest. 'Aye, whit d'ye want? If ye're collectin' for somethin', the wife's no' in. She sees tae all that.'

Fiona beamed on him. 'Good morning. We're looking for Flora Moodie.'

'Who?'

'Flora Moodie. We think she might live in this building.'

'Woodie, ye say?' He slid his thumbs inside his braces and ran his hands up and down them, pulling them away from his scrawny chest.

'Moodie. Flora Moodie.'

'I don't know that name, hen, but she might live here right enough. It's the wife that knows all that sort of thing and she's no' in.'

'Is your wife coming home soon?'

'Ye'd have tae ask her that, hen, she's the one that knows that sort of thing. She's no' in, though.'

'Well, thanks all the same. Sorry to bother you. I'll ask one of the other neighbours,' Fiona said, and collapsed in giggles when the door had closed.

'Come on, it's not worth the bother.' Rachel made for the stairs, anxious to escape into the street, but Fiona was having none of it.

'Mum, we've come this far, let's do the job properly.' She marched across to the door on the other side of the landing and rapped firmly on it. 'We're going to try them all,' she said, and then, as the door opened, 'Good morning . . .'

Some flats were empty and others contained harassed young mothers with squalling babies propped on their hips, or children who rapped out, 'My Mammy's no' at hame,' before slamming the door in Fiona's face. One very deaf old woman was convinced that they had come from 'the Social' and kept insisting in a panicky voice that she didn't need any help.

'I think she does, poor soul,' Fiona said as they trailed down the last flight of stairs. 'You don't think *she's* Flora Moodie, do you, Mum?'

'Of course not,' Rachel said firmly, while her stomach began churning again. What if her real mother was a sad old woman like the one they had just spoken to? What if she were alone in the world and desperately in need of assistance? What could she, Rachel, do about it? Would Martin be willing to help?

They were soon back in the close, where Fiona knocked on one of the two remaining doors. A gust of hot steam belched out at them as the door opened.

'Aye, what is it?' The woman was drying her hands on a towel. Her face was flushed with heat and the front of her wrap-around apron was damp. Machinery rumbled and clanked in the depths of the flat behind her.

'Good morning,' Fiona said for what seemed like the umpteenth time.

'No offence, hen, but if ye're sellin' religion, I've no' time for it the now. I'm in the middle of my washin'.'

'We're not selling anything, we're looking for a woman called Flora Moodie. Do you happen to know her?'

'Moodie?' The woman deliberated, frowning. 'I don't know the name. Is she supposed tae live here?'

'She was living in this building during the war,' Fiona said. 'But she must have moved. We thought a neighbour might know about her. Have you lived here long?'

'Twenty year,' the woman said, and then, as the noise from behind her grew louder, 'Wait a minute.' She turned and yelled into the steamy darkness of the small hall, 'Elsie, see tae that bloody washin' machine, will ye, afore it floods the kitchen again. It's no workin' right,' she explained, turning back to her callers. 'We were better off when we had wash-hooses with boilers and mangles in them. It's damn near soaked me already, but his dunga-rees have tae be cleaned for the first shift on Monday so I've just got tae go on strugglin' with it. There wasnae

76

anyone cried Moodie livin' here when I moved in.'

'D'you think the people across there might know about her?' Fiona indicated the opposite flat.

'No, hen, they're a young couple, not long in. They scarce know anyone who's livin' in the place now, let alone durin' the war. Sorry,' the woman said, and then, on the point of closing the door, she opened it again. 'Wait a minute, I've just minded. I thought that name rang a bell somewhere in my heid. Moodie, aye.'

'You remember her? Was she here when you moved in?' Rachel asked, her heart beginning to thump.

'No, she was long gone by then, but I was brought up in the tenement next door. I just moved here when I got married. Moodie . . . aye, I think I do mind folk with that name. There was a lassie about ten year older than me. Awful quiet, she was. The parents an' all; the three of them kept themselves tae themselves. But they moved out long afore I moved in.'

'Your own parents wouldn't know more about them, would they?' Fiona suggested.

'My parents are long dead. It was my granny that raised us. She might be able tae help ye, but she gets a bit wandered at times. That's why it's handy tae be livin' in the next close tae her. It means I can keep an eye on her.'

'Do you think she would mind if we called in?' Fiona asked eagerly.

'Och no, she likes tae see folk. But if this isnae one of her good days you'll no' get much out of her. Ground floor, name of MacKellar. I'll have tae go,' the woman added as the thrumming of machinery grew louder and a wail of despair wafted through the hall. 'By the sound of it that damned washin' machine's got our Elsie pinned intae the corner again.'

★　★　★

'Perhaps we should just go home,' Rachel suggested as they emerged from the close. 'If that old woman's having a bad day we'll only be a bother to her.'

'You heard what her granddaughter said – she likes visitors. And maybe this is one of her good days. Come on, Mum,' Fiona coaxed, 'this is our best lead yet and we've gone too far to turn back now. Ground floor, she said, so it must be this way, since the building on that side's got a shop on the ground floor.' She had clumped along the pavement, her patchwork skirt swinging round her calves, and was entering the close before Rachel had time to argue with her.

The woman who eventually answered the door was very small and very old, but her eyes, Rachel was relieved to see, were bright and shrewd. Clearly, this was a good day.

'If ye're collectin', I've already gave tae the Salvation Army when I was out at the shops,' she said briskly. 'So yez're out of luck.'

'We're not collecting, Mrs MacKellar,' Fiona assured her. 'Your granddaughter sent us round. She said you might be able to help us.'

'I don't think so, pet. I'm sorry, but I'd tae give up bein' a cleaner when the arthritis got too bad.'

Rachel stepped forward. 'We're trying to find out what happened to the Moodies who used to live in the tenement next door. Your granddaughter said that you might remember them.'

'Moodie . . . Moodie. Oh aye, of course I mind the Moodies.' The woman swung the door open. 'Come in, I've just put the kettle on.'

Fiona moved forward eagerly, but Rachel put a restraining hand on her arm. 'We don't want to be a bother.'

'I'd soon tell ye if ye were. Come on in, I cannae stand for too long at a time now. That door there,' the woman said as they went past her, and Rachel followed her daughter into a spotless kitchen where a large black cat sprawled on the rug before the fire lifted its head and looked at them with sleepy green eyes.

'Oh, aren't you lovely?' Fiona swooped forward to crouch down and stroke the glossy ebony fur. 'What's his name?'

'Jackie. He's a lazy bugger, that one. Sit down, hen.' Mrs MacKellar busied herself at the stove. 'If he'd his way of it he'd spend the whole day afore that fire, wouldn't ye, Jackie?'

She chattered on while she made tea and poured it into pretty floral cups produced from a glass-fronted corner cabinet. Biscuits and shortbread were laid out on a plate and sugar, milk, spoons, plates and napkins were all produced with surprising speed before Mrs MacKellar, pouring the tea, said, 'Now then, what was it ye wanted tae know about the Moodies?'

'I think they might have been related to my father,' Rachel said swiftly as Fiona opened her mouth to speak. 'He died several months ago and I found their name and address in among his papers. I thought I should let them know that he'd gone.'

'Did he live round here? What was his name? Wash yer hands in the sink there, lassie, afore ye have a biscuit,' Mrs MacKellar added to Fiona. 'Jackie's a clean cat, but ye never know what ye can catch. I cannae abide tae see folk clappin' animals an' then shovin' food intae their mouths without washin' their hands.'

'My father never lived in Glasgow himself . . .' Rachel sidestepped the need to give the old woman any names. 'But I think he had cousins in the city.'

'So his family werenae what ye'd call close? It could have been the Moodies, then,' Mrs MacKellar mused. 'They were awful quiet folk, the sort that liked tae keep themselves tae themselves. A decent enough couple, mind. I never in my life saw the man drunk, and Mrs Moodie never missed her turn at washin' the stairs. This was always a nice respectable street, but there were special times like New Year an' the war endin', when we'd all get together for a bit of a celebration. Not the Moodies, though. Never the Moodies; not that the rest of us thought any the less of them for that. Everyone's got the right tae follow their own way.'

Fiona had washed and dried her hands, and now she settled in a chair and accepted a cup of tea and a piece of shortbread, asking, 'What happened to them?'

'The Moodies? They died years ago, hen. First her, and then him, and then the flat was sold. It's changed hands a few times since then.'

'Did they have any family?' Rachel probed.

'Fam'ly. Let me think.' Mrs MacKellar drank some tea, and then set the cup back on its saucer. 'Jist the one . . . a lassie. What was her name, now? Freda? No, Flora. Does that ring a bell with ye?'

'It does,' Rachel said, her stomach churning again, while Fiona chimed in with, 'D'you know what happened to her?'

'She was a bit of a mystery, as I mind,' the woman said, leaning forward and lowering her voice. 'She left home early on in the war . . . war work, her mother said, but then she came back again for a while.'

'Why was that?' Fiona asked, bright-eyed.

'Nob'dy knew. She scarcely came out of the flat. I mind meetin' her mother in the street and sayin' that I'd not seen Flora for a while. She said the lassie had taken ill – I think she said Flora'd been workin' on a farm – and she'd been sent home tae be nursed.' She pursed her mouth. 'There were those who said Flora'd got intae trouble, but if she did, I never saw her or her mother out pushin' a pram, though there was another lassie livin' in the flat by then, a niece who'd been bombed out of her own place and brought her wee bairn tae stay with her auntie. Her husband was in the Navy, Mrs Moodie said. It must have been a tight squeeze, but that's what happened durin' the war. Ye just made the best o' things. Anyway, Flora went back to her war work and her cousin was rehoused. The thing was, Flora never came home after the war was over. At least, not as far as I mind.'

'Did you not ask her mother where she was?'

'Oh no, hen. Askin' the once was neighbourly, but askin' twice would have been pryin'. Some of the more nosy neighbours said that she'd met up with some Yank or a Pole or a Frenchie or a Canadian, and married him and gone back tae his country after the war. But I don't see that happenin' tae Flora Moodie. She wasnae that sort of lassie,' Mrs MacKellar said thoughtfully, passing the biscuits round again. 'Never even had a boyfriend before the war. I never saw her as much as talkin' tae a man, let alone walking arm in arm with one. She was as quiet as her mammy and her daddy, and she wasnae what ye'd call a looker. That's why I can't believe that she'd a bairn. But then again, it takes all sorts, doesn't it?'

'Where did she work?'

'She'd an office job somewhere, but I've no notion of where it was,' the old woman said. 'Would ye like some more tea, hen?'

'We could try the tenements on either side, and across the road,' Fiona suggested when they were back on the pavement.

81

'No, I think we've done all we can. You heard Mrs MacKellar – the Moodies kept themselves to themselves. They don't sound like the kind of people who would keep in touch with former neighbours.'

'D'you think she fell in love with a soldier or a sailor or an airman, and eloped with him?'

'I doubt it, somehow. If she'd got married why would she have given me up for adoption?'

'Perhaps your father was killed. Perhaps he died in action before you were born. He might not even have known that he had a daughter, poor man.' Fiona's imagination was beginning to run riot. 'Or he might have been an American, suddenly posted back home, leaving poor Flora on her own with a baby to look after and no money. So she had to hand you over to strangers for your own good.'

'If she was a respectable war widow, why didn't she keep me? We could both have stayed with her parents.'

'Perhaps they disapproved of her whirlwind romance with a foreigner and told her never to darken their door again.'

'What makes you think that my father was foreign?'

'There were lots of foreign men about during the war, weren't there? Wouldn't it be great, Mum, if you were the daughter of an American or a Frenchman?'

'The Americans weren't in the war in 1940.'

'A Canadian, then. Perhaps—'

'Let's get into town and do some shopping. That's what your father thinks we're here for. He'll ask questions if we don't buy anything.'

'We could always say we couldn't find anything we wanted.' Fiona eyed the next close as they passed it. 'I'm enjoying being a detective. I might make it my career.'

'No you won't. Your Dad gave me some money and

told me to let you choose something nice to wear,' Rachel said, and Fiona immediately took the bait.

'Oh goodie,' she said, quickening her step. 'Let's go and have a nice lunch, then we can hit the shops!'

'There you are! Guess what?' Fiona, fresh from an after-school rehearsal, burst out of the back door and took the two steps from the patio to the lawn in a flying leap. 'Janet Dickinson's broken her ankle!'

'Poor Janet Dickinson, whoever she is. I don't see why her bad luck should be an occasion for celebrating,' Martin said, and went on hoeing the border round the lawn.

'I'm not celebrating . . . well, not about her broken ankle at any rate. I'm pleased because Janet was playing Gwendolen in *The Importance of Being Earnest*, only now she can't because she tripped over a paving stone or something last night and broke her ankle, and she'll be in plaster for a month so she can't be in the play. So Miss Beattie's asked me to be Gwendolen instead. Isn't that great, Mum?'

'Now wait a minute, Fiona. We'd already agreed that you weren't going to take on any extra work because you have to concentrate on passing your exams in May.'

'But the play's going to be over by the end of October; I'll still have ages left between then and May.'

'You've got your preliminaries in February.'

All Fiona's joy had evaporated. 'I can study and be in the play at the same time. Honestly, I can manage it! Can't I, Mum?' she asked Rachel, who was pruning roses.

'Don't try to appeal to your mother, Fiona, because she agrees with me on this one. Don't you, Rachel?' Martin said, then swept on before she could reply. 'I've told you before that these exams represent the key to a place in a good university.'

'But I already know the lines, Dad. I'm the prompt, remember?'

'I know we agreed to let you do that, and right now,' Martin said levelly, 'I'm wondering if that wasn't a mistake.'

'But Dad—'

'Isn't it time you went and washed your hands? We've already had to keep dinner back until you came home. Your brothers are starving.' He indicated Graham bouncing happily up and down the paved path on his orange Space Hopper, and Ian cleaning his bike.

The girl bit her lip, then turned and walked slowly back into the house, her shoulders slumped.

'Martin . . .'

'You know what we've always said, Rachel . . . let them win the little battles while we concentrate on the big ones. We agreed to her being prompt because she likes this play so much. And as far as I'm concerned, that's what she is – the prompt.'

Fiona was silent all though dinner, pushing her food around the plate with her fork and scarcely eating anything, but when the meal ended she got to her feet and started gathering the plates together.

'I'll do that.'

'It's all right, Mum. I'll wash up, too.'

'What about your homework?' Martin asked.

'I'll have plenty of time for that afterwards.'

Twenty minutes later she put her head round the living room door. 'That's the washing-up done.'

'Thanks, love.'

'You're welcome, Mum.' Fiona came into the room. 'Dad . . .'

'No, Fiona,' he said without taking his eyes from the television screen.

'You don't know what I was going to say.'

'Let me guess. Could it have been about you taking on that part in the school play? Because if so, the answer's still the same.'

'What if I promised to—'

85

'No, Fiona. Now, don't you have some homework to catch up on?'

'You're . . . mean!' Fiona stormed, and then, throwing out her arms to encompass both parents, 'You're both so mean!'

'Just sensible,' Martin said levelly, and she rushed out, slamming the door hard behind her.

'What's up with her now?' Graham wanted to know, while Ian sighed heavily and rolled his eyes heavenwards.

'Nothing,' Martin said as his daughter's feet thundered up the stairs. 'Haven't you two got homework to do as well?'

'Did it when we got home,' Ian said smugly, and he and Graham settled back down on the rug to watch television.

'So you decided to go down the road that led to the Registry Office and this mysterious birth mother of yours?' Kathleen said as she manoeuvred her small car into a space in the school car park.

'I did, although much good it did me. The road led to a dead end. But at least Fiona enjoyed herself. She's thinking of becoming a detective when she leaves school. Or an actress. Poor Martin's finally beginning to find out what being the parent of a teenager is like. And we've still got it all ahead of us with the boys.'

Kathleen had opened the boot of the car. 'You take this,' she instructed, pushing a large cardboard box into Rachel's arms, 'and I'll take the suitcase. Did they say that the hats and shoes would be here for today?'

'Yes. Someone in the drama club Miss Beattie goes to runs a costumier's shop in Glasgow, and she's fetched the accessories from there so that we can have a look through them and pick out the ones that suit. Open that door for me, will you? I've got both hands full.'

'What did your last slave die of?' Kathleen puffed, setting the bulging suitcase down and opening the door.

'Overwork. I'll get the next door.'

'Isn't it strange how schools always smell the same?' Kathleen mused as they crossed the large foyer. 'Chalk, and wet coats, and last week's school dinners. That smell always gives me an irresistible urge to tuck my hanky into my knicker elastic.'

'Me too.' Rachel nudged the swing door open with her backside then managed to hold it with one foot until Kathleen had squeezed herself and the suitcase through.

'. . . *may be regarded as a misfortune*,' the uniformed girl sitting on the stage was declaiming loudly. '*To lose both looks like* . . .' Her voice faltered as she and the boy standing before her turned to look at the newcomers.

'. . . *carelessness*,' Rachel heard her daughter say from the shelter of the wings.

'I know!' the girl on the stage said. 'I was just—'

'Keep going until I tell you to stop!' Lizbeth Beattie jumped up from the auditorium, where she had been sitting at a table. 'And leave me to deal with visitors.' Then, as her chastened actors pulled themselves together, she hurried along the length of the hall. 'Mrs Carswell, and Mrs . . .'

'Ramsay.'

'Oh yes. Thank you for coming. How are you getting on with the costumes?'

'Almost finished.' Rachel carried the box over to a row of tables against a side wall, put it down on top of the tables and began to unpack it. 'This could be the final fitting. Did you get the hats and bags and shoes?'

'All here.' Lizbeth Beattie pointed to a collection of boxes nearby. 'My friend says that we can keep what we need until after the show, as long as I return the unwanted items. You don't mind if we carry on rehearsing while you're fitting the costumes, do you? With the play going on in four weeks, we're a bit short of time. I'm running Lady Bracknell and Jack Worthing through their scene at the moment, so you can have Cecily just now, then Lady Bracknell once she comes offstage.' Then, as Kathleen and Rachel began to lay the costumes out, 'Oh, they look beautiful! I can't tell you how grateful I am to you both for doing this. There's little enough money for drama productions, and what we do have goes to the school drama group. This play was my own idea, so I can't really expect the school to fund all of the expense.'

'It's been a pleasure to work on the costumes,' Rachel assured her.

'I'll send Cecily . . . Anne, that is . . . over. She can change in that walk-in cupboard over in the corner,' Lizbeth said, and then, before hurrying back to her duties, 'I wonder, Mrs Carswell, if I could have a word with you before you go?'

'Of course. You're not in a hurry, are you, Kathleen?' Rachel asked as the teacher stopped to speak to a girl who had been sitting watching the rehearsal. The girl nodded, got to her feet and headed their way.

'Absolutely not. And here, if I'm not mistaken, comes our Cecily.'

As they pinned the girl's costume on and tried to match a hat with it, Lizbeth Beattie put the young actors through their paces, pulling them up short each time they made a mistake, making them go over and over lines until they came easily, and working hard to teach her Scottish-born pupils how to ease their native burr into Wilde's elegant English prose. Every now and again, when an awkward silence fell, Fiona's clear voice rang out from the wings.

The girl playing Lady Bracknell left the stage and came over for her fitting. Rachel was hunting for a suitable hat when she suddenly realised that she was hearing Fiona more often than before. Glancing up, she saw her daughter on the stage, script in hand. '*Few parents nowadays,*' she was saying sweetly, '*pay any regard to what their children say to them.*'

The words reminded Rachel uncomfortably of the scene between Fiona and her father the night before. As she worked, she found time to glance up at the stage again and saw that this morning's mutinous anger had gone completely. Now Fiona was smiling, teasing, drifting gracefully about the stage and elegantly wafting a paper fan. Even though she wore her school uniform and her hair was fastened back in a ponytail, she was no longer Fiona Carswell, but the Honourable Gwendolen Fairfax, elegant and coolly self-possessed.

The rehearsal was brought to an end by a bell announcing the morning break.

'Thank you, everyone,' Lizbeth told her assembled cast. 'You've done very well and you deserve a rest. Off you go . . . and keep working on those lines,' she called after them as they scampered off. Then, to Kathleen and Rachel, 'I'll show you to my room, and fetch some tea for the three of us. There's coffee if you prefer it, but believe me, the tea tastes better.'

In the classroom, Kathleen browsed through a pile of books, exclaiming each time she came across an old favourite, while Rachel stood by the window, looking out on the busy playground. Lizbeth was back with a tray in no time.

'I managed to get hold of a few biscuits as well.' She put the tray down on her desk and drew two chairs forward. 'Sorry I didn't have more time to look at the costumes, but the rehearsal was going well and I didn't want to stop them. Were the hats any good?'

'I think we've got what we want.' Rachel accepted a biscuit. 'Can I take them away with me? I want to alter them a bit – trim them with feathers, flowers and ribbons to suit the costumes – but they'll all be changed back to the way they are now before they're returned to your costumier friend.'

'Fine.'

'And tell the cast that they'll need to be responsible for supplying their own gloves. Elbow-length evening gloves for the girls to match their outfits, and white for all the men. The shoes are more difficult, but the stage is quite high, so I don't think that they will be easily seen. They need to get as close to the real thing as they can, though. I'll send you some sketches as a guide.'

Lizbeth had picked up a notepad and was scribbling busily. 'Is that all?'

Rachel glanced over at Kathleen, who shrugged and helped herself to another biscuit. 'I think so. I'll give the drawings to Fiona, together with notes of anything else that comes to mind. We want to get the costumes completed quite soon, so that the girls can start wearing them. I think you'll find that once they're in long skirts they'll really begin to act the part.'

'That would be very helpful. Robbie McNaughton – the boy who's playing Jack Worthing – is going to do the illustration for the front of the programmes, and we'll need that quite soon. He's a talented young artist, and he hopes to go to art school when he leaves school in July. His brother runs a small printing business, and he's offered to do the programmes and tickets at cost price.' The young woman smiled at her visitors. 'We're very fortunate in this school when it comes to supportive families. And talking of acting the part . . .' she went on swiftly, 'I was wondering if you and your husband could possibly change your minds, Mrs Carswell, and let Fiona take over the part of Gwendolen.'

'I'm afraid that my . . . we feel that with this being the year she sits her Ordinary Grade exams, she has enough to do as it is.'

'I can appreciate that, but as you must have seen for yourself when she stood in for Janet this morning, she's very good; better, to be honest, than anyone else in the school. Even if I did get one of the girls from the drama club,' the teacher rushed on, 'I doubt she would be able to learn the lines and moves in the time we have left. Fiona almost knows the lines off by heart, and she's already attending rehearsals.'

'You would need to get a new prompt.'

'That would be a lot easier than getting a new Gwendolen, believe me. I could take on the job myself, if it comes to that. Oh please, Mrs Carswell! I know that I'm being impertinent, asking you this favour after all you're already doing for us, but the students have worked really hard at the rehearsals, and I would hate to have to cancel the production.'

'Surely it wouldn't come to that?'

'It might.' Lizbeth Beattie bit her lip, and Rachel realised that the young woman was close to tears.

'Fiona was certainly very good,' Kathleen put in, and Rachel glared at her.

'Well . . . I'll speak to my husband, but to be honest, I don't hold out much hope,' she said.

When Rachel and Kathleen were loading the costumes back into the car, together with the hats they had chosen, Rachel asked, 'Why did you have to side with her about Fiona playing Gwendolen? Why couldn't you have sided with me?'

'For one thing, that teacher's right; Fiona played that part today as if it had been written for her, and they're unlikely to get anyone half as good in the few weeks they have left. And for another, you can see that she loves being on the stage. As her godmother,' Kathleen said loftily, 'I feel duty bound to put her happiness before yours and Martin's.'

'If I had known that being godmother meant that you would side with her against me, I would never have asked you to do it.'

'Too late now.' Kathleen opened the driver's door. 'Do you want a lift home, or are you planning to ride home on your high horse? And there's another thing,' she went on as the car turned out of the school gates. 'She and that lad playing Jack – Robbie, did the teacher say his name was? – look great together. She's got a crush on him.'

'Nonsense.'

'She has,' Kathleen insisted. 'She positively glowed when they were sharing that scene, and I doubt if it could all have been an act. Go on, Rachel, talk Martin into letting her play the part. It'll be over in a few weeks' time; why not let the lassie enjoy herself while she has the chance?'

'Mum—' Fiona started as soon as she arrived home.

'Before you start trying to coax me . . . don't.'

'Did Miss Beattie speak to you?'

'Oh yes. She's very civil that way.'

'Mum, you know that that's not what I meant. Stop teasing!'

'Yes, she spoke to me, and I'm going to speak to your father. But I'm not making any promises, Fiona. If his mind's definitely made up, I'll not be able to change it.'

'But you'll try?'

'I'll try, and if I fail you're just going to have to accept it with good grace. That's part of growing up. And another thing . . . I don't want you moping and scowling around the house when he comes home. It won't help at all. Understand?'

'Yes Mum.' Rachel was peeling apples; now Fiona's slim hand slipped into her line of vision, caught hold of a long piece of peel, and then withdrew. 'Can I just ask you one thing? How did I do on the stage today?'

'You were terrific.'

'Will you tell Dad that?'

'Possibly.'

'And what did you think of Robbie?'

'That's two things.'

'Isn't he great?'

'He's good,' Rachel acknowledged, glancing sideways at her daughter's face and realising that Kathleen was right. The very mention of the boy's name had brought a delicate flush to Fiona's cheeks and stars to her eyes.

'Thank God Fiona's gone back to normal.' Martin sat on the side of the bed to pull his socks off. 'I hate seeing her sulking. She's always been such a cheerful kid.'

Rachel, already in bed, drew her feet up so that she could prop the book she was reading against the slope of her thighs and said casually, 'Kathleen and I were at the rehearsal today. We took the costumes along for a fitting.'

'How's it getting on?' He turned the overhead light out and slid into bed. It was amazing how after all those years she still thrilled to the way her side of the mattress dipped slightly as it adjusted to the weight of his solid body. The comfort and pleasure of knowing that there was a man, her man and nobody else's, in her bed always gave her a secret tingle of pleasure.

'It looked really good, even though they were all wearing school uniform. Miss Beattie's fantastic with them;

you can see that she cares one hundred percent about her students.'

'Good for her.' Martin said, and opened his own book.

'Unfortunately, the play might not be going on, now that that girl's broken her ankle. Fiona stood in for her today.'

'Ah, so that's where this conversation's going. Rachel, we've decided . . .'

'She was right, Martin, when she said that she already knew the lines. She knows everyone's lines. She loves that play, and she can act . . . you should see her. Well, you will see her, if we agree to let her go ahead.'

He had turned a page. Now he turned it back again. 'We? It sounds as though *you've* already agreed.'

'I said that we had both told Fiona that she couldn't be in the play, but Miss Beattie says that nobody else could learn the lines and moves in time. And the students are all working really hard at it, Martin.' She closed her book and turned to face him. 'It would be a tragedy if it had to be scrapped.'

'And if it is, it'll be my fault, won't it? I'll be the big bad villain of the piece.'

She reached out to turn his face towards hers. 'There is no villain in *The Importance of Being Earnest*. And you couldn't be a villain even if you tried.'

'I'm sure I could. Don't do that,' he said as she traced the outline of his lips with the tip of her finger. 'You know what it does to me.'

'That's why I'm doing it.'

'You think you can win me round, don't you?' he said, reaching out to stroke her arm. 'You think you can make me change my mind.'

'Nobody could ever make you do something against your own will. You're a very strong-willed man, Martin

Carswell.' She let her hand drift up the side of his face to tug gently at the hair above his ear. 'And I'm only a weak . . . helpless . . . woman.'

'I'm halfway through a chapter. I want to know what happens next.'

'I could show you what happens next,' she said, and with a resigned sigh he put the book aside and put out the bedside light before turning to slide his hand up to her shoulder and under the broad strap of her nightdress.

Much later, as they were both drifting off to sleep in a delicious tangle of limbs, he murmured into the darkness, 'I suppose it wouldn't do any harm to let Fiona play that part.'

'No harm at all, in my opinion. It might even encourage her to work harder once it's over.'

'Your responsibility, mind you. If this ends in tears, the blame falls fairly and squarely on you.'

'Yes, Martin. Can we tell her tomorrow morning?'

'I suppose so.'

Rachel squirmed round so that she could kiss him. 'You're a lovely man, Martin Carswell!'

'I know,' he said.

'I'm going to have to take in the costumes I've made for Gwendolen. Janet's a bigger girl than Fiona.'

'Serves you right.' She felt his warm body relax, and within a few minutes he had started to snore lightly against her shoulder.

The girl originally playing the part of Gwendolen had dark hair, and for the first scene in the play, Rachel had made her a cream, waist-length bolero jacket to wear over a sleeveless, high-necked cotton dress. The jacket and dress were both trimmed with brown ribbon, but now she decided to replace it with blue, to match Fiona's eyes. For the second scene, set in a country house, she had opted for a more casual cotton dress in a jaunty blue and gold pseudo-tartan design, which caught on the left hip with a bow. Both dresses needed taking in slightly, but otherwise they were perfect for Fiona's colouring.

For the cream outfit, Rachel had chosen a small straw hat that tipped over one eye and could be covered with artificial flowers. A plain Eton straw set off the second outfit, with a band of the same material as the dress.

They had a fitting when Fiona returned from school. She swished about the house, much to the amusement of her brothers, practising going up and down stairs in the long skirts.

'We don't have stairs in the play, but I need to know what it feels like to use them, if I'm to look right when I walk about the stage,' she said as Rachel helped her out of the cream dress. 'Mum, they're perfect. I'm going to feel so good wearing them. And thank you, thank you . . .' she threw her arms about Rachel, 'for talking Dad into letting me be Gwendolen.'

'You can repay me by working really hard and doing well in your exams.' Rachel shook the dress out and put it on a hanger. 'I'll take the brown ribbon off tonight, and sew on the blue. I've got a pair of cream party shoes some-where – I think they might fit you. I'll have a look for them later.'

'Robbie was thinking that he might draw me for the programme, in one of my costumes.'

'That would be nice.'

'That's what I thought. D'you think he could come over on Saturday afternoon to do it? We don't have much time left,' Fiona hurried on, twiddling with a strand of hair, 'so it needs to be soon.'

'Saturday. That should be all right.'

'Thanks, I'll tell him tonight.'

'Tonight?' Rachel asked, and her daughter blushed.

'I'll probably be going to Cardosi's with Amy and Beth for a coffee. Sometimes there are other people there from school.'

'Oh . . . right. Remember that you have to be home by half past nine, and do your homework before you go out.'

'Okay,' Fiona said, and danced out, humming an Abba song.

10

'I think Fiona's got a bit of a crush on a boy,' Rachel said to Martin that night.

'Nonsense, she's too young to have a boyfriend.'

'She's nearly sixteen, Martin, and a very attractive girl. And I didn't say she had a boyfriend, I just said she had a crush.'

He looked up from his newspaper. 'She wouldn't start going out with anyone without telling us, would she?'

'Why should she tell us? I didn't tell my parents about you, at first.'

'That's different. You were at college by then, and your parents were a bit old-fashioned about that sort of thing.'

Rabbie Burns was right, Rachel thought. People very often lacked the power to see themselves as others saw them.

'Actually, I wanted to be sure of my own feelings about you before I said anything to them. You might have been a one-date ship that was just passing by.'

'Did you really think that that's all I might have been to you?'

'How was I to know, at first?' To tell the truth, which

she had no intention of doing, she had been so taken with him at first sight that she was convinced that she would soon lose him to some prettier, more glamorous and self-assured girl. Marrying Martin had been the most wonderful thing that had ever happened to her, and still was.

'This boy, is he in her class?'

'He's older, but he's in the play.'

'How old?'

'He's in Sixth Year, I think. He's planning to go to Art College next year. He seems to be quite talented; as a matter of fact, he's designing the programme for the play, and—'

'Sixth Year? That makes him at least two years older than Fiona. I don't like the sound of it, Rachel. She's got her entire future ahead of her; if she doesn't do well at school she'll miss out on the chance to get into a decent university. She can't afford to be distracted by boyfriends just now. What if—'

'You're over-reacting, and I wish I'd never mentioned it. I just meant that I got the impression that she liked him, that's all.'

'Oh,' he said, and then, after a brief silence, 'You can't blame me for worrying about my only daughter.'

'Do as I plan to do, Martin,' Rachel said. 'Don't start worrying until you've something to worry about.'

'There's always something to worry about when you're responsible for children,' he said gloomily.

He had arranged to take the boys to the park for a kick about game of football on Saturday afternoon. That meant that he would be out when Robbie arrived, and probably wouldn't come back until teatime, by which time the boy would have left. It was just as well, Rachel thought, and decided to say nothing to him about the visit. Then she felt a twinge of guilt. She and Martin had never kept secrets from each other, but now she seemed to be breaking their unwritten rule with depressing frequency. He still didn't know about her visit to the Registry Office in Edinburgh, or about the morning she and Fiona had spent in Glasgow trying to trace her birth mother.

But then again, Martin was a worrier, and always had been. So she tried to ease her own guilt by telling herself that silence was sometimes the kindest thing.

'Mum!' Fiona came dashing down the staircase. 'He's here! It's Robbie!'

'You didn't tell me he has a motorbike.' Rachel, in her sewing room, had been drawn to the window by the sound of the machine roaring along the normally quiet road. She had been stunned when its helmeted, leather-suited rider slowed to turn through the gateway.

'Oh yes. He's eighteen, old enough to ride one. I'll let him in,' Fiona added, throwing open the front door.

Thank heavens Martin's already left, Rachel thought. He had never cared for motorbikes and had already said on more than one occasion that he hoped his sons would never join the craze for them.

'Mum, this is Robbie.'

'Hello,' Rachel said. 'I saw you at the rehearsal the other day, but we didn't actually meet.'

'Hello, Mrs Carswell.' The boy carried a crash helmet, which he hurriedly tucked beneath his left arm before extending his right hand. His handshake was firm, his grin disarming and his manner businesslike. He set the helmet down on an empty chair, then unzipped his jacket and brought out a small sketchpad and a pack of half-sized coloured pencils.

'These are the dresses, Robbie.' Fiona indicated them, hanging side by side.

'Nice. The cream, I think. What about the hats? Yes,' he swept on when Rachel held out the little straw, now covered with small flowers. 'That will be great. You'll need to pin your hair up, Fee, it'll suit the hat better that way.'

'I'll put them on. Can you come up and give me a hand, Mum?'

'And I'll wash my hands and tidy my hair,' Robbie said cheerfully. 'That helmet always musses it up.'

'He's nice, isn't he?' Fiona said as Rachel buttoned her into the dress.

'I've only just met him, but yes, he seems very nice.'

Fiona, who normally let her slender body drop onto seats, settled herself gracefully on the stool in front of her dressing table mirror and arranged her long skirt carefully before using both hands to sweep back her mane of curly russet hair. With a competent twist of the wrists she twirled it into a loose knot at the back of her head.

'Hand me that dish, will you?' she said, and Rachel did as she was asked, then watched her daughter stab the pins in her hair, marvelling at the skill of today's teenagers. She herself had never been any good at doing her own hair, which was why she was content to keep it in a simple style.

'Nice,' Robbie approved when the three of them were reunited in the sewing room. 'Now the hat should go just . . .' He took it from Rachel and placed it on Fiona's head, tipped slightly over her right eye. '. . . just there. I'll hold it in place while you pin it, Fee.'

The side of one hand rested lightly against Fiona's cheekbone, and Rachel saw a faint tremor flicker across her daughter's face as she worked with the hat pins. It came as a shock to recognise it as the tremor she herself

101

still experienced at times, when Martin touched her. For an instant, the words, But she's too young! She's still a child! flared through her mind.

'That's great. Now stand like this, with both hands on the parasol, but don't lean on it, keep your shoulders straight. And dip your head slightly. That's it. Now look at me, and try not to move.' Robbie picked up his sketchpad and a soft lead pencil, completely unaware of the effect he was having on the two women in the room. 'You look great in that outfit.'

'Really?' Fiona glowed with pleasure.

'I like the ribbon, it brings out the colour of your eyes,' the boy said. Then, as he began to sketch with swift, sure strokes, he added almost absent-mindedly, 'You've got really beautiful eyes, Fee.'

He was so intent on his work, and Fiona was so intent on him, that neither of them noticed Rachel leaving the room. In the kitchen she ran the tap until the water was as cold as it could be, then drank down an entire tumblerful without stopping. After that she opened the back door and drew in several deep breaths before returning to the sewing room, where Robbie was now working with the coloured crayons.

When he had finished he held the sketchpad out to her. 'It's just a rough sketch at the moment, but I think it'll work.'

Rachel glanced at the sketch and then found herself unable to speak. Robbie had caught exactly what she herself had seen – a beautiful, elegant young woman peeping out from beneath the tilted brim of her pretty hat at a future that, her vivid blue eyes said with assurance, was going to be both exciting and wonderful.

'Mum?' she heard Fiona say, her voice suddenly uncertain. 'Don't you like it?'

Rachel glanced up to see that the two young people were standing side by side, watching her anxiously. Although broad-shouldered, Robbie was of average height, little more than six inches taller than Fiona, and yet he seemed to loom over her protectively. They looked as though they belonged together; like two halves of a whole, Rachel thought uneasily.

'It's . . . it's marvellous.' She handed the pad back to its owner. 'You're good.'

His fair skin flushed with pleasure at the compliment, and his hazel eyes were suddenly shy. 'Not really, but I hope I will be, one day. With the proper training.'

'Fiona said that you were going to Art College?'

'I'm hoping to be accepted for Glasgow Art School next year. I'm trying to put a portfolio together at the moment. You need to build up a good portfolio if you want to get a place there.'

'What area are you interested in?'

'I'd like to go into advertising eventually.'

'Would you like a coffee? I've got some home-made pancakes with raspberry jam.' Martin wouldn't be back for ages; there was still plenty of time.

When he grinned, Robbie's hazel eyes crinkled appealingly at the outer corners. 'That sounds great.'

'Can I go over one of the scenes with Robbie now?' Fiona begged. 'I've got a bit of catching up to do.'

'Get changed first. I'll give you a call when the coffee's ready.'

Rachel returned to the living room just as Robbie was saying fervently, '*I have never loved anyone in the world but you.*' Fiona was sitting on the edge of the sofa, Robbie on one knee before her.

'Almost finished, Mum,' Fiona hissed, and then, her voice

suddenly altered, '*Yes, but men often propose for practise . . .*'

She rose and walked across the room straight-backed and moving with small, graceful steps, as though she was still wearing the long-skirted gown instead of her denim trousers and a light blouse. Turning to face Robbie, she swept through the speech to its end without hesitation, then finished with a brisk, 'And that's where Lady Bracknell comes in. Coffee time!'

Robbie talked about his older brother's printing business while he ate his way through several of the pancakes Rachel had put out.

'He and Maggie have done really well. I help when I can, with deliveries and doing a bit of design. I'll be of more help when I've started my art course.'

'Is your brother interested in art too?'

'Not really. Thanks,' he said when Rachel offered more coffee. 'It was our father's business originally. Fraser wanted to be an engineer, but our mother died when I was young, and then my dad took ill about eight or nine years ago, just as Fraser was leaving school. So he had to help out with the business. When Dad died, he just kept it going. Maggie — that's Fraser's wife — looks after the books. I'd have been willing to go in as well, but Fraser wanted me to try for art school.'

'You don't have any parents?' Fiona asked, shocked. 'I didn't know that!'

He grinned across the table at her. 'It's okay, I wasn't brought up in an orphanage or anything like that. We still live in the house we were born in. There's plenty of room for the three of us.' Then, as the front doorbell began to ring insistently, 'Sounds like an urgent summons.'

'It's my brother Graham,' Fiona said in disgust. 'He always does that.'

Rachel hurried across the hall and threw the front door open. 'Graham, do you have to keep your finger on the bell like that?'

'Yep.' He blew into the hall like a small tornado. 'I'm starving!' He rushed into the kitchen and then stopped short in the doorway, the sight of a stranger bringing on a bout of sudden shyness.

'Hello,' Rachel heard Robbie say as Ian rushed in from the garden.

'Mum! There's a smashing motorbike outside our house!'

'I know. It belongs to a friend of Fiona's. He's in the kitchen.'

As Ian went to investigate, Martin arrived. 'Rachel, what the blazes is that bike doing there?'

'Ssshh! One of the boys from the play came to rehearse with Fiona. He's in the kitchen,' she said, low-voiced, closing the door.

Robbie got to his feet as they went in. 'Hello, sir.'

He stuck out his hand, and Martin had no option but to take it.

'Sorry, I didn't catch the name . . . ?'

'This is Robbie McNaughton, Daddy,' Fiona said proudly. 'He's Jack Worthing in the school play.'

'Ah. I take it that you're the owner of the motorbike in our front garden?'

'That's right, sir. I hope it wasn't in your way.'

'No, I just . . . What on earth have you done to your hair, Fiona?'

'Robbie's been sketching me in one of the dresses I'll be wearing in the play. I'm going to be on the front of the programmes. I had to pin my hair up.' She pirouetted before him. 'D'you like it?'

'That style's too old for you. Put it back the way it should be.'

'I think I might wear it like this when I leave school,' Fiona said, even as she took the pins out and allowed her hair to fall about her face.

'That won't be for a few years yet.'

She went pink. 'Dad . . . !'

'I'd better be going now and let you have your dinner in peace,' Robbie said swiftly.

'Stay and have dinner with us,' Fiona suggested. 'He can, can't he, Mum? Dad?'

Graham and Ian beamed, while Martin gulped noticeably before saying, 'Of course – if he wants to.'

'Thank you, sir, but Maggie will be expecting me home,' Robbie said, and the boys' faces fell.

'I wanted to ask you all about your bike,' Ian said, while Graham added sadly, 'We don't know anyone with a bike like that.'

'You can ask questions on the way out, if you want, and have a look at it before I go,' Robbie suggested, and it was Fiona's turn to look disappointed.

'Maggie?' Martin asked when he and his wife were alone. 'Who's Maggie? His wife?'

'He's too young to have a wife. Maggie's married to his brother.'

The penny dropped. 'That's the boy you mentioned the other night. The one she's fallen for!'

'The boy I think she's got a crush on, I said.'

'And I said that she was too young, and she's got her future to think of. And he's got a motorbike!'

'As far as I know, owning a motorbike isn't against the law. You're home early.'

'Too early, apparently,' Martin said as Fiona came hurrying in, her face flushed.

'Dad, did you *have* to treat me like that in front of Robbie?'

'Like what?'

'Telling me I'm too young to put my hair up. I'm nearly sixteen!'

'Too young to have boyfriends with motorbikes.'

Her flush deepened. 'He's not my boyfriend, he's just someone in the play. You practically threw him out of the house.'

'I did no such thing. I said he could stay for dinner, didn't I?'

'It was the way you said it; as if you didn't want him to.'

'I did not Fiona,' he said when she stared at him, silent and mutinous, 'you're standing on the threshold of the rest of your life. You need to concentrate on preparing for your future.'

'Trying for university, you mean. What if I don't make it, Dad?'

'Of course you will. You're an intelligent girl. You were the brightest toddler I had ever seen.'

'Dad, I was probably the *first* toddler you had ever seen, and I'm not all that brainy.'

'Nonsense! You've always done well in your exams.'

'I get average marks. Ian and Graham will probably turn out to be miles more intelligent than I am.'

'If they are, I'll be over the moon,' Martin said, signalling the end of the discussion by picking up his newspaper.

'You're being too hard on her,' Rachel protested when their daughter had gone upstairs. 'He's a nice, sensible young man, and they were only rehearsing bits of the play.'

'Did you see that motorbike he owns? D'you really want Fiona to go charging about the town on that?'

'As far as I know, she doesn't intend to.'

'She'd better not,' Martin said.

★   ★   ★

For her sixteenth birthday on October 15th, Fiona opted for a meal and a night at the pictures with a group of her closest friends. Costly, but peaceful, Rachel and Martin agreed, and paid the money willingly.

'Can you believe it, Rachel . . . our daughter, sixteen!' Martin marvelled. 'Where has the time gone? It just seems like yesterday that you went into labour. Remember?'

'You think I could ever forget?' They hadn't had a car then, so Martin, shaking so hard that he could scarcely operate the telephone, had phoned for an ambulance.

'I couldn't get you into hospital quick enough,' he said now. 'I was convinced that you'd have the baby there and then and that I'd have to deliver it.'

'That's what I thought too. Thank goodness we were both wrong. Remember how tiny she was, and how scared we were of doing the wrong thing? Remember sitting, looking at her asleep when she was six weeks old, being amazed at having managed to keep her alive for six whole weeks?'

'Talk about greenhorns. Still, we've done all right as parents,' Martin said smugly.

'The costumes look terrific, though I say it myself,' Kathleen murmured in Rachel's ear.

'Especially considering they were mostly made up of bits and pieces,' Rachel murmured back, and then settled down to concentrate on the play. The Fiona Supporters' Club, as Kathleen termed it, took up the best part of a row of seats; apart from Kathleen, Rachel and Martin, Graham and Ian were there, having promised, cross-their-hearts-and-hope-to-die, to sit quietly and refrain from sniggering when their sister appeared on stage.

Doreen and Chrissie were also there, Doreen having brushed aside Rachel's explanation that nobody would expect her to attend with a brusque, 'What are you talking about? Why shouldn't I want to go and see my granddaughter acting in a real live play?'

'I just thought, with Dad . . .'

'Sittin' in the house mopin' won't bring him back,' Doreen pointed out, 'apart from the fact that he'd not want me to carry on like that. Anyway, Chrissie can't wait to see Fiona on the stage and she'd never forgive me if I refused to go with her. And before you say anythin' about wee Graham's birthday party at the end of the month – me and Chrissie'll be there too, helping with the food the way we usually do. Life has tae go on, Rachel.'

Murdo Ramsay was supposed to be there as well, but Kathleen had arrived on her own, and in a grumpy mood.

'Working late,' she snapped when she had located the others in the hall. 'That blasted job of his is taking over his life – apart from the bit that's devoted to his blasted vegetables.'

'My husband used to grow lovely vegetables in his allotment,' Doreen pointed out. 'It's a healthy hobby, Kathleen. An outdoor activity that puts fresh vegetables on the table. I saved a fortune at the greengrocer's when my Frank was alive.'

'You were lucky. Murdo only grows his for exhibiting at shows. Oh well,' Kathleen said, settling into her seat, 'let's stop talking about greens and enjoy the evening.'

Lizbeth Beattie had done an excellent job. Oscar Wilde's fast-paced and elegant drawing room comedy caught the audience's attention from the moment the curtain rose, and the well-rehearsed cast threw themselves into their roles with an enthusiasm that was infectious.

As Fiona's first entrance drew near, Rachel's stomach began to twist itself into a knot. Fiona had had so little time to rehearse – what if she made a wrong move, lost her cue and brought the play to a standstill? Memories of her own drama experiences at school and teacher-training college came sweeping back to haunt her, and her heart began to beat faster.

Then Fiona swept onto the stage in Lady Bracknell's wake, a vision of loveliness in the cream cotton dress and bolero, the beflowered little straw hat perched elegantly over one eye, and suddenly she was no longer Fiona Carswell, but Gwendolen Fairfax, saying sweetly in a clear, confident voice, '*I am always smart! Am I not, Mr Worthing?*'

Martin's hand reached out to find and squeeze Rachel's. They smiled at each other, proud parental smiles, and Rachel relaxed into her seat and began to enjoy the performance.

'Isn't she beautiful? Isn't she clever?' Chrissie enthused at the first interval. 'And the costumes are so pretty!' While Doreen, quietly glowing with pride, said, 'Aye, well, she's a clever lassie, Fiona. She can turn her hand to anythin' she puts her mind to. I'll have a cup of tea with two sugars and plenty of milk, Martin. Chrissie and me can find a table while you're fetchin' it. Come with us, boys.'

During the interval they shamelessly eavesdropped on the comments of the people milling around them, hearing nothing but praise. Then as they took their seats for the final performance, a voice from the row behind said clearly, 'The play's well cast, isn't it? Lady Bracknell's giving a very convincing performance, and that young couple playing Gwendolen and Jack work so well together.'

'There's a definite chemistry there,' another voice agreed, and Kathleen nudged Rachel's arm, while at the same time, Martin, sitting on her other side, went tense. A swift side-long glance showed that his mouth had suddenly tightened and his brows were drawn together in a disapproving scowl.

Fiona's face was radiant when she rushed up to her family after the performance. 'Did you like it? Was it all right?'

'It was better than all right,' Kathleen pronounced, while Chrissie, eyes bright, said, 'It was brilliant! You were brilliant, pet!'

'Honest? What did you think?' Fiona asked her parents anxiously.

'A marvellous performance, darling, and you were terrific,' Rachel said warmly.

'I don't know if the girl who was supposed to play the part could have done as well as you did,' Martin assured his daughter.

'Oh, thanks, Daddy! Miss Beattie's pleased.'

'Well she may be,' Doreen said severely. 'You've all worked very hard. And you looked lovely on that stage, pet.'

'Glad it wasn't me who had to do all that kissing,' Ian smirked. He dropped a loud, extravagant kiss on the back of his own hand, and Graham went into yelps of laughter, which ceased suddenly when Martin snapped, 'Behave yourselves!'

Robbie McNaughton was at the other side of the hall, talking to a young man and woman. The brother and sister-in-law, Rachel guessed; the man had Robbie's curly fair hair and snub nose, while the girl was small, slender and dark. As Rachel glanced at them, the girl reached up to put her arms around Robbie's neck and kissed him on the cheek.

'Better get changed, Fiona,' Martin was saying. 'School tomorrow, so we don't want to be too late home.'

'Okay, won't be a minute,' she assured them, and skipped off, stopping to speak to Robbie's small group. The dark girl, beaming, kissed her, and so did Robbie's brother. Clearly, Rachel thought, there was no need for introductions. Fiona knew these people already, and knew them well.

Glancing at Martin, she was relieved to see that he was

too busy talking to Kathleen, who was to take Doreen and Chrissie home in her car, to notice the friendly little meeting by the exit.

'So how are things?' Kathleen asked on the phone the next morning.

'It was hell trying to get the boys up and dressed and fed in time for school, but we made it. Martin's threatening that that's the last time they'll be allowed to stay up late until they reach their twenty-first birthdays, but Fiona's still on an adrenalin rush; she was up and out with no effort at all. Thank goodness the play has another two nights to run – it'll give her a chance to work off all that suppressed energy.'

'Good. But I was actually asking about the costumes. Is there any further work to be done? No ripped hems, or buttons coming off?'

'None at all. I had a quick word with Miss Beattie after you left last night, and she's delighted with everything.'

'She deserves to be, and so does Fiona, bless her. It's true what that woman behind us in the hall said – she and the lad playing the part of Ernest or whatever he was called were dynamite together.'

'They were just enthusiastic about the play.'

'It was more than that. He's quite gorgeous, and I was right when I said that she had more than just a passing interest in him.'

'Just don't say that in front of Martin, please! He's got a real bee in his bonnet about her having nothing to do with boyfriends until she's passed all her school exams and landed her university degree – with Honours, no doubt.'

'Men can be so narrow-minded, can't they?' There was an all-too-familiar bitter note in Kathleen's voice.

'Was Murdo late getting home last night?'

'Oh no, he was back before me. In bed, fast asleep, snoring like a pig. I've a good mind to report the minister who married us to the Trades Descriptions people. For richer or poorer, in sickness and in health my foot,' Kathleen snorted. 'If he'd been honest, and asked if I would take this man for snoring instead of making intelligent conversation and vegetables instead of pretty flowers, I could have said no and saved us both a lot of bother.'

'It can't be that bad!'

'D'you know something, Rachel?' Kathleen said, suddenly serious. 'I'm beginning to think that it is. Must dash – the gardener's due in about twenty minutes and I want to steal a few things before he gets here. A carrot here, an onion there, and then I tidy up the earth and hope he won't notice. He's an awful clype, that man. Murdo pays him too well.'

'Soup again?'

'Courgette and mushroom, I think. With perhaps a dash of wine. There's a slightly autumnal nip in the air. Or is it just me?' Kathleen said, and hung up.

'Dad, I deserve that after-show party! I've worked hard for it, and I can't be the only member of the cast who isn't there!'

'I'm not saying that you can't go, I'm just saying that you can't stay out till all hours.'

'But the play doesn't finish until almost ten o'clock,' Fiona argued. 'Then we have to get changed, wipe our make-up off and take the set down and put it away before the party can even begin!'

'She's right, Martin, you can't possibly insist on her being home for a certain time . . . within reason,' Rachel added, anxious to see both sides of the argument.

'And tomorrow's Saturday,' Fiona pointed out. 'I can have a long lie if I need one. Not that I will.'

'So I have to stay up and wait for a phone call summoning me to the school to fetch you, then?'

'Of course not. The teachers are going to take us home in their cars. It's all taken care of, Dad, honest!'

'Oh, very well.' Martin gave in. 'But just this once, mind. Don't think you can get away with staying out to all hours every time there's a party.'

'I won't. Thanks, Dad, you're the best father in the world,' Fiona said, giving him a bear hug.

'She'll be all right,' Rachel said that evening. 'She'll be fine.'

'Did I say she wouldn't be?'

'You've been looking at the clock every two minutes. It's driving me mad.'

'No, I'm . . .' Martin began, and then glanced at the clock. 'Well, maybe I am,' he conceded as she started to laugh. 'It's a big responsibility, parenting a teenager, especially a girl as pretty as Fiona. She looked so grown up on that stage, Rachel, but she's still a child.'

'She's old enough to get married. We live in Scotland, remember?' Rachel added as he looked at her, appalled.

'Good God, don't make me worry more than I already am!'

'I'm her parent too, and I think she should get a little bit of slack now and again.'

'Give them enough rope and what do they do? Hang themselves.'

'Nonsense. Our daughter is sensible and she's at the age where we have to learn to trust her.'

'Humph,' he said, and returned to his newspaper.

At midnight she persuaded him to go upstairs to bed.

'We'll leave the light on and we'll probably still be awake when she comes home.'

'I certainly will be.' He drew the bedroom curtain back and peered out of the window. 'No sign of a car yet.'

Rachel climbed into bed and opened her book. 'It'll be along soon,' she said calmly.

Half an hour later Martin was still shifting and twitching at her side, making the bed bounce and distracting her from her reading – not that she could concentrate on the words, though she would never have admitted it to him.

He turned over and peered at the bedside clock. 'My God – twenty to one!'

'She'll be . . . Listen,' Rachel said. 'I can hear something now. A car engine.'

'Is it?' Martin lifted his head from the pillow, then bounced upright in the bed. 'No, by God, it's a blasted motorcycle!'

'Martin, don't you dare go downstairs and make a scene,' Rachel said swiftly as he bounded out of bed. 'Don't humiliate her in front of someone else.'

'It'll be that Robbie fellow. You don't really think she's going to be allowed to invite him in for milk and biscuits at this hour, do you?'

'I don't see why not.' The motorbike engine cut out and blessed silence fell. Martin was out of bed now, and over at the window.

'Don't spy on them!' Rachel hurriedly switched off the bedside lamp so that the young couple outside wouldn't realise that they were being watched.

'I'm a father, I'm entitled to spy. Oh . . . she's coming in on her own.'

They strained their ears, and heard the front door open, then close. The motorbike started up again, and within a minute its roar had dwindled and given way to silence.

'I wonder if she's locked the door?'

'She has,' Rachel said through her teeth. 'Just get back into bed and let's get some sleep!'

Since Graham had been born on October 31st – Hallowe'en – his birthday parties always featured fancy dress, dooking for apples, and trying to eat sticky buns suspended from lengths of string, as well as the traditional cake, candles and presents.

This year his seventh birthday fell on a Sunday, and by mid-afternoon a dozen small, active and noisy boys and girls, all in fancy dress, were rampaging around the garden while Rachel, Martin, Chrissie and Doreen surveyed the scant remains of the food that had taken hours to prepare.

'It's the nearest I've been to a Biblical plague of locusts,' Martin said in awe. 'Perhaps worse. At least the locusts in the Bible weren't dressed as ghosts and scarecrows and assorted monsters from *Dr Who*.' Then, as the phone rang, 'Now what?'

'Don't worry, I'll see to it.' Rachel hurried to the hall, pleased to have an excuse to get away from the wreckage and noise.

'Rachel, it's me,' Kathleen said. 'Have you seen today's *Sunday Mail*?'

'I've not had a chance, but I think Martin managed to sneak a quick look this morning. We're in the thick of Graham's birthday party at the moment.'

'So you've not seen the Personals?'

'Mum, Dad wants you,' Ian shouted from the kitchen.

'Just coming! Sorry, Kathleen, did I deafen you? I never look at the Personals; nor does Martin.'

'I think you should today,' Kathleen said. 'But do it

quietly, on your own. I have to go now; we're off to visit friends and Murdo's fidgeting in the car. I'll phone you tomorrow to find out what you think.'

Rachel replaced the receiver and went into the living room, where the *Sunday Mail* lay on the small table by the window. Turning to the Personal section, she ran her finger down the column of small print, and then stopped as her own name jumped out of the page at her. *Rachel Elizabeth Flora, please telephone . . .* she read.

Then came a telephone number. There was nothing to indicate who had inserted the notice, or why.

She was still staring at it when Doreen said from behind her, 'What on earth are you doing in here, reading the paper, when you've got all those children trampling about your garden?'

Rachel jumped, and closed the newspaper. 'Just snatching a quiet moment.'

'They've decided that they're thirsty now. Each and every one of them.'

'There's juice in the fridge. Can Martin not see to it?'

'Why should he?' Doreen asked sharply. 'You're the wee lad's mother.'

'Who was that on the phone?' Martin wanted to know when Rachel returned to the kitchen.

'Kathleen. She wants me to cut an article from the *Sunday Mail* for her.'

'Oh? What's it about?' Chrissie wanted to know. Fortunately Rachel was saved from answering by her mother.

'Could she not buy a copy for herself? Some people have no consideration.' Doreen fussed around the kitchen, opening one cupboard after another, then reaching up on tiptoe to take glasses from a high shelf. 'Does she not realise that you've got a birthday party on your hands today?'

'Not those glasses, Mum, I bought plastic tumblers for safety's sake. They're in that cupboard over there.'

'It's all right, I've got them.' Chrissie produced the tumblers and a large tray, and proceeded to organise the drinks. 'I'll pour, and you and Rachel can take them out to the garden, Martin. They can have their drinks on the terrace, then it won't matter if anything gets spilled.'

'If?' Doreen snorted. 'We'll be lucky if half that juice gets as far as their mouths. Thank goodness the weather's decent. I shudder to think what it would be like if they were all indoors instead of outside.'

Rachel seized the first tray and carried it outside. She watched the children streaming towards her, their voices ringing through the air, but all she could think of was the few words she had just read . . . please telephone . . . please telephone . . . please telephone . . . please telephone . . .

When the birthday guests had gone home and calm had returned to the Carswell household, Martin settled down with the Sunday papers. Rachel watched him like a hawk, convinced that at any moment he would turn a page and see her name in print, but he read the *Sunday Mail*, commenting from time to time on some item or another, glanced with his usual disinterest at the Personals page, and moved on to the sports section.

Kathleen phoned on Monday morning. 'Did you see it?' she wanted to know. 'Have you tried the number?'

'No, and I don't know if I'm going to. It might not even be for me.'

'How many Rachel Elizabeth Floras do you know?'

'How many Kathleen Annes do *you* know?' Rachel countered.

'One, at least, but my names are more commonly used than yours. Aren't you in the least bit curious?'

'Yes, but . . . I don't know what I might be letting myself in for.'

'Perhaps someone's left you a fortune.'

'I doubt it.'

'Have you said anything to Martin?'

'No.'

'Are you going to?'

'I'm not sure,' Rachel said, and heard a sigh drift down the line. Then Kathleen said, 'It's so unfair . . . here I am, longing for some excitement in my life and getting nothing, while an interesting and mysterious door creaks open in your life and you don't want to do anything about it.'

'What happened to the idea of me pitching my tent and taking time to think things over before I act?'

'I've gone off camping,' Kathleen said, and then, 'D'you want me to call the number for you?'

'Don't you dare! Leave it with me,' Rachel said. 'I'll think about it.'

Chrissie rang half an hour later. 'Rachel, did you see yesterday's *Sunday*—'

'The *Sunday Mail*? Yes, I saw it.'

'Have you phoned?'

Rachel leaned her forehead against the cool glass covering a painting she and Martin had bought in the early days of their marriage. 'No, and I haven't told Martin either,' she said; then, struck by a terrible thought, 'Mum hasn't seen it, has she?'

'I saw it before she read the paper. She always reads the Personals, so I tore that page out and told her I'd spilled tea all over it. She wasn't very pleased with me.'

'What do you think I should do, Aunt Chrissie?'

'I really don't know what to say, dear. You'll have to follow your own instincts,' Chrissie said. And then, hurriedly, 'I'll have to go, I can hear Doreen's key in the lock.'

12

Rachel picked up the phone several times that day and then put it back into its cradle. Once she had made contact with the person who was apparently looking for her, there might be no going back. Martin would be furious if she did it without telling him, but if she did tell him, he would almost certainly try to talk her out of it.

Finally, taking a deep breath, she dialled the number.

The telephone on the other end of the line rang three times without being answered, giving Rachel long enough to wonder if it was an old-fashioned phone, or a modern one. Red, white, black, or blue? And what sort of room or hall or, perhaps, kitchen was it in? She would let it ring six times, she decided as it began the fourth double ring. Six should be enough. Or perhaps . . .

Suddenly her nerve went. She reached out to the cradle to break the connection with a swift, decisive stab of the finger, just as the ringing stopped and a woman's voice said breathlessly, 'I've not found it yet, you'll have to give me a bit more time. I'll phone you back as soon as I lay hands on it, all right?'

'Hello?' The phone was suddenly slippery against Rachel's palm.

'Anna?'

'Er . . . no.'

'Oh, sorry. You must think I'm a right idiot!' The woman's laugh was warm and genuine. 'My friend lost an earring when she was here last night and I've been down the back of every seat in the living room looking for the damned thing. Sorry about that. What can I do for you?'

'I don't know if you . . .' Rachel moistened her lips and wished that she had had time to hang up. Just one second would have made all the difference!

'I saw a notice,' she said. 'In the *Sunday Mail*.'

'Oh my goodness!' The disembodied voice was suddenly quick with interest. 'Is it really you? Are you Rachel Elizabeth Flora?'

'That's my name, but I don't know if I'm the person you're looking for.'

'Were you born Rachel Elizabeth Flora Moodie in Glasgow on April 28th, 1941?'

'Yes.' Rachel's stomach began to churn.

'And adopted soon after that?'

'Yes, but . . .'

'Then you're the one,' the woman said, her laughter bubbling up again. This time, it was excited rather than amused. 'Oh, Rachel, this is wonderful! Thank you, thank you, thank you so much for calling me!'

'But . . . I don't understand. Why did you put the notice into the paper?' A sudden thought struck Rachel. 'Are you my mother?'

'Your mother?' The laugh rang out again. 'No, of course not. I'm your younger sister. I'm Cara . . . Catherine.'

'Sister? I have a sister?' It was fortunate that there was a chair near the phone; if she hadn't been able to fall onto it, Rachel would have ended up on the floor.

'Didn't you know?'

'How could I know?'

'You've never tried to find out anything about your background? You've not been to the Registry Office in Edinburgh?'

'Yes, I went there, but I didn't find out much.'

'Oh dear, this must be a bit of a shock to you, then. Can we meet? I live in Barrhead, where are you?'

'Paisley, but I don't know—'

'So we're quite near to each other! Isn't that amazing? Oh please say you'll meet me, Rachel – I'm longing to find out all about you and tell you all about myself. Please?' the voice wheedled. 'Could you be in Cochran's tea room at ten o'clock tomorrow morning?'

'I . . . I suppose I could.'

'That's wonderful! It's going to be lovely to meet you after all those years apart. Have you still got the newspaper with the notice in it?'

'Yes.'

'Good, you bring your copy and I'll bring mine. Whoever gets there first can put hers on the table, where it's easily seen. Although we might recognise each other straight away, of course. I don't know if we're identical or not. It isn't always like that, is it? Better take the newspapers, just in case.'

'Wait a minute,' Rachel interrupted, confused. 'What isn't always like that? Why should we be identical?'

'Don't tell me you don't know?'

'Know what?'

'We're not just sisters, Rachel – we're twins!'

'Is there something wrong?' Martin asked as soon as he came home.

'No. Why should there be?'

'You look different, somehow.'

Of course I'm different. I'm a twin now. The words sprang to her lips, but she managed to swallow them back and say instead, 'I can't think why.'

'There isn't anything wrong with one of the children, is there?' His voice was suddenly sharp with anxiety.

'Nothing's wrong with any of us.' Apart from the rather surprising fact that when you went to work this morning I was just me, and now I'm a twin.

'That's all right, then,' Martin said. 'What's for dinner?'

Too twitchy to settle down and read, or to watch television, Rachel spent the first part of the evening ironing and then went into her sewing room to finish off a blouse she was making for herself, before organising the boys' bedtime routine.

Fiona had gone to the pictures with her two best friends. When the boys had had their supper and gone off to bed, Rachel, her mind made up, went into the living room and laid the *Sunday Mail*, open at the advertisement, on the arm of Martin's chair.

'Look.'

He cast a swift glance at the newspaper. 'It's all right, I've finished with it. You can put it out if you want.'

'Have you read this page? Have you read this notice I marked?' She pointed to it, and he gave it a cursory glance, and then looked again before picking up the paper and reading the few circled words carefully.

'It's a joke. Must be. Something Kathleen's dreamed up.'

'It has nothing to do with Kathleen, though she was the one who spotted it first and told me about it.'

124

'It's probably meant for someone else.'

'With the same Christian name as me? And the same two middle names as me?'

'It can't possibly be for you! People like us don't get mentioned in the newspapers.'

'Ah, but I'm not people like us, am I? I don't know what sort of people I am. Remember?' she said, and he groaned.

'Not that adoption stuff again. I thought you'd put that behind you.'

'So did I, until I saw this notice.'

'I hope you're not thinking of ringing that number, Rachel – you don't know what can of worms it might open up.'

'I did ring it, this afternoon.' At the memory of the conversation she had had, her knees went weak again. She backed up to the sofa and sat down. 'Martin, I spoke to my sister.'

'Sister?'

'My twin sister. Her name's Cara and she lives in Barrhead.'

'My God. Are you sure?'

'As sure as I can be. She knew all about me . . . my full name, and my date of . . . *our* date of birth,' she corrected herself. 'And I'm meeting her tomorrow morning in Cochran's tea room. I couldn't go ahead with that without telling you first.'

'My God,' he said again. And then, struggling out of his comfortable armchair, 'I think I need a drink.'

'Imagine . . . me, a twin!' Rachel said an hour later, for the umpteenth time. She and Martin were sitting in the living room, a bottle of sherry on the coffee table between them. 'I have a twin!'

'So that woman on the phone claims.' He still looked shell-shocked.

'Why would she lie?'

'I don't know,' Martin said. 'Blackmail? Or perhaps she's a con-woman, or someone with a mental problem.'

'She didn't sound as if she had a mental problem. She sounded . . . nice. I wonder if she looks like me?' She reached for the bottle.

'Are you sure you want another drink? You've already had three glasses of the stuff, and it's not meant to be downed like that.' Martin wasn't a drinker, and it worried him to see his wife making so free with the sherry that was only kept for visitors, and would normally be expected to last the best part of a year. His own glass had barely been touched.

'It's all we have in the house, and yes, I'm quite sure.' Rachel filled her glass, splashing a little on the table. 'Oops,' she said, giggling and dipping a finger into the puddle. Martin, who hated mess, got up and went into the kitchen to fetch a cloth.

'If you ask me, you've had enough,' he said severely as he mopped at the spilled sherry. 'You know you can't hold your drink.'

'I might not be able to hold it, but I certainly need it. It's not every day a woman of my age turns into a twin.' She took a large, defiant slurp of sherry. 'D'you think she looks like me?'

'How should I know?'

Rachel set her glass down carefully and got to her feet. She swayed across the room to the mirror on the wall, peering into its depths at her straight brown hair, its long bob framing her face, and at her solemn blue eyes set in an unremarkable face. Her Aunt Chrissie and her father had often told her what a pretty child

126

she had been, but she had never believed them.

'Imagine someone living in Barrhead, looking exactly like me. Or perhaps not like me, but a bit like me. What d'they call twins who aren't identical?'

'I can't remember.'

Rachel frowned at her reflection, then said, 'Whatever it is, it means that they're not identical. I wonder if we're alike in other ways. Wouldn't it be amazing if she was married to a Martin and they had a Fiona and an Ian and a Graham?'

'It would be incredible. Rachel, are you quite sure you want to meet this woman?'

'Of course I am.' Moving carefully, she walked back to the table and sat down. 'Perhaps she knows who my . . . *our* mother is. Perhaps she's met her.'

'And perhaps she'll turn out to be someone you don't like and can't get rid of.'

'How can you not like your own sib . . . sibling?'

'Easily,' said Martin. 'I never liked Adrian all that much, and he didn't like me. I think it was a relief to both of us when he and Leonie moved to Australia.'

'That was different. Adrian always struck me as a bit of a cold fish, whereas my sister,' Rachel said, and then, rolling the words round her tongue with relish, 'my *twin sister* Cara sounded very nice.'

She drained her glass again, and Martin reached out to take her hand in his as it moved towards the sherry bottle.

'Fiona'll be in at any moment. Shall I make some coffee?'

'All right. D'you think I should tell Fiona about speaking to Cara on the phone?'

'I don't think you should tell anyone just yet,' he said firmly, raising her to her feet and edging her towards the door. 'Let's keep it our secret until you've met this woman and decided whether or not you want to see her again.'

Martin was already up when Rachel woke the next morning. She could hear his voice mingling with the boys' voices downstairs. For a moment she lay still, drowsily wondering why she felt so excited. Then she remembered – today she was going to meet her sister. Her twin sister.

She stretched luxuriously, smiling to herself, as Martin came into the bedroom. 'You're awake at last. How do you feel?'

'Lovely.' She gave him a dreamy smile. 'What's the time?'

'Quarter past eight.'

'What?' She shot upright in bed, then clutched at her head and groaned.

'Hangover?' he asked.

'No, just a mild headache. It'll clear up.'

When the room had stopped spinning Rachel got out of bed and pushed her feet into slippers, then shrugged herself into her housecoat and made for the bathroom which, for once and for a mercy, was empty.

After a swift tepid shower she returned to the bedroom and dressed hurriedly before going down to the kitchen, where her family were all eating their way through bowls of cereal. It was fortunate that the Carswells never had a cooked breakfast during the week; Rachel was not sure if her stomach could have coped with the smell of bacon and eggs.

When he was leaving the house Martin drew her into the hall with him. 'Are you still set on going to meet this woman?' he asked, low-voiced.

'Yes, I am.'

'Are you quite sure?'

'Yes, I'm quite sure that I'm going.'

'No, I meant . . . are you quite sure you're doing the right thing?'

'You think I should just let her turn up and sit there by herself until she realises that I'm not coming?'

'I didn't mean it like that. I just wonder if you're making a wise decision.'

'Martin, I'm going. Wish me luck.'

He dropped a kiss on the tip of her nose. 'Good luck – if that's what you want,' he said, and then, 'If you need me, just ring and I'll come running.'

'You look different,' Fiona said when her mother returned to the kitchen.

'In what way?' Rachel asked nervously, thinking of the sherry she had so freely indulged in the night before. Visions of red noses, trembling hands and heavy pouches under eyes came to mind. She picked up Martin's cup and saucer and was pleased to see that if her hands were trembling, it was imperceptible.

'Excited,' Fiona was saying. 'Sparkly – as if you've got a secret.'

'Have you, Mum?' Ian asked. Suddenly Rachel was the centre of attention.

'No, I haven't,' she lied. Martin was right; best not to say anything to the children until after she had met Cara.

'Are you sure?' Fiona probed.

'Go on, Mum,' Graham chimed in. Then, excitedly, 'Is it a puppy? Have you and Dad decided to buy a puppy?'

'Or is it a holiday?' Fiona probed. 'Somewhere fantastic, like snorkelling in Australia?'

'It's nothing at all.'

'Not a holiday? I've always wanted to go to the Algarve. Wouldn't it be great?'

'We have no plans to go to the Algarve.'

'Perhaps she's having another baby,' Ian suggested.

'Oh, no! Are you, Mum? What am I going to say to my friends?' Fiona wailed, tears springing to her blue eyes. 'You're too old to have another baby!'

'For goodness' sake, I am not having a baby, or a puppy, or a holiday in Australia or Portugal or anywhere else. And have you looked at the clock lately?' Rachel snapped. 'If you don't all leave now you're going to be late for school!'

The tea room on the top floor of Cochran's emporium was half-full when she got there. Of the only two women sitting at tables on their own, one was elderly, while the other, young and smartly dressed in a tailored suit and crisp white blouse, studied an open folder while sipping a cup of coffee. She had placed a newspaper on her table, but it was the *Glasgow Herald*, folded and still in pristine condition.

Rachel chose a table in the far corner, where she had a clear view of the door, and ordered a cup of tea. Waiting for it to arrive, she fished her crumpled copy of the *Sunday Mail* from her bag and put it on the table with the front-page banner facing the room, so that it could be clearly read by anyone approaching her.

When the waitress arrived with her tea she was still alone. After five minutes of watching the door and jumping nervously every time anyone walked into the tea room, she could stand the suspense no longer, and fell to studying the menu, line by line.

She was halfway down the list of biscuits, scones and cakes when a voice said, 'Rachel?'

13

It was like looking in one of those fairground mirrors that blurred and altered the usual reflection. Or, Rachel thought in that first astonished moment, like seeing herself as she might have been. The woman standing before her was generously built, while Rachel was slim. She too had brown hair, but in her case it was an untidy mop of curls framing a face slightly fuller than Rachel's. Curly hair, Rachel thought, stunned, her twin had curly hair! Her eyes were blue like Rachel's, but while Rachel's eyes tended to be timid, almost fawn-like, this woman's sparkled with life.

'It is Rachel, isn't it? Please say you're you?' she begged.

'Cara?' The word came out as a squeak.

'Oh good, you're the only person in here that I want to be related to.' Cara scattered several bags over two of the four chairs, unwound the large scarf she had been wearing over her shoulders like a cape and dropped it on top of the bags, then hauled out the only empty chair left and sat down. 'Isn't this wonderful? Imagine not meeting your own twin sister until you're in your thirties. What an adventure! What are you drinking?' she swept on as the waitress arrived, pad and pencil at the ready.

'Er . . . tea.'

'Coffee for me,' Cara said. 'And another cup of tea for you, Rachel? And cakes . . . cream cakes.'

'I don't usually—'

'I do, and anyway, this is a celebration. We should really be ordering champagne and caviar.'

'We don't do champagne,' the waitress said in a shocked voice. 'Or caviar either.'

'In that case we'll have a plate of your creamiest cakes, dear. That way we can have a choice. Oh, and better put two of each kind on the plate because being sisters, we might share the same taste in cakes.'

'Yes madam,' the girl said, looking thoroughly confused. As she scuttled off, Cara turned her attention to Rachel.

'Well now, look at you! You're gorgeous!' she said, and then, with a spurt of laughter, 'We could pose for a before-and-after poster. You're the way I might look if I gave up smoking and chocolates and drink. Do you smoke or drink?'

'I don't like the taste of tobacco. We have wine on special occasions.' And lots of sherry on very special occasions.

'Angus never waits for special occasions. I can't blame him for enjoying a few drinks after work; he works bloody hard, poor man. And he doesn't like to drink alone.'

'Angus is your husband?'

'Mmm. We met at a dance just after I left school and we got married when I was seventeen. What about you?'

'I married Martin when I was nineteen.'

'What does he do?'

'He's an accountant.'

'Oh, posh! Angus is a landscape gardener. He was working for the Council when we first married, but he started up his own business five years ago. Now . . . children. Do you have children?' Cara wanted to know, her eyes bright with interest.

'Three – two boys and a girl. She's the oldest.'

'Lucky you! We only had one . . . a little girl.' Suddenly the vitality was wiped from Cara's face, and her eyes filled with sad memories. 'We called her Alice. She died when she was nine.'

'Oh Cara! What happened?'

'A lorry driver carrying bales of hay took a bend too quickly and shed his load. Alice was out on her bike, and the whole lot came down on her. It all happened within seconds, thank goodness. She didn't suffer, they said.'

'I'm so sorry.'

'Oh well, you know what they say . . . God only takes the best. And that was my Alice, all right. The very best.'

The waitress arrived with their order, and by the time the tea and coffee had been served and a large plate of cakes had been placed on the table, Cara was sparkling again. She selected a cream bun and deftly split it in two halves, spreading the cream equally between them.

'How did you find out that we were twins?' Rachel asked, taking a meringue.

'Easy . . . we were born on the same day. I found our birth certificates in the Registry Office in Edinburgh.'

'But I went there about six weeks ago, after I discovered that I was adopted, and I only saw my name in the register. Yours wasn't there.'

'Oh, but it was. Everyone's listed in those books. You found yours at the bottom of a page, didn't you?' Cara said, and when Rachel nodded, the other woman shot a triumphant grin across the table. 'Exactly . . . so once you'd found it, there was no need for you to turn the page, was there? But I was at the top of the next page because I'm the younger twin. You're twenty-seven minutes older than I am.' Then, while Rachel silently digested this, 'Did you say that you only started to look for your birth registration a few weeks ago? What took you so long?'

'I didn't know until then that I was adopted. My aunt told me after my father died in September.'

'Oh, my dear, what a shock you must have got! Why did nobody tell you earlier?'

'My mother said that they just didn't find the right time.'

'Golly.' Cara licked cream from her fingers, wiped her mouth with her napkin, and selected another cake. 'I've always known. I'm going to need more coffee. Tea?' she asked, turning to signal to the waitress.

'When you say that you've always known . . . ?' Rachel probed tentatively once Cara had given their order.

'Ever since I can remember. My mam and da told me when I was little that my real mother had given me to them as a present because they couldn't have babies of their own. It made perfect sense to me,' Cara said. 'My da had had mumps when he was a lad, and when they'd been married for eight years without any sign of a baby they decided that the mumps had done for him. And then they saw the advertisement in the *Glasgow Evening Times*.'

'I wonder why she advertised us separately?'

'To save money, of course. One advert would do for the two of us,' Cara explained when Rachel frowned. 'And she probably thought that nob'dy would want twins. Whatever the reason, she didn't get around to mentioning to Mam and Da or, apparently, to your parents, that there were two of us.'

'It doesn't seem right to split twins up like that.'

134

'Thanks, love,' Cara said as the waitress arrived with fresh tea and coffee. 'The poor soul was probably desperate to get us off her hands,' she went on when the girl had departed with the used cups.

'So when did you start trying to find out if you had any family of your own?'

'Funnily enough, it must have been around about the same time as you. I wonder if it was some sort of twin thing,' Cara said with interest. 'You know how they say that sometimes twins know what the other one's thinking. I might have sensed that you were starting to wonder about your real background. Or p'raps it was just coincidence that you discovered the truth not long after my mam died. I wouldn't have wanted to do anything while she was alive, in case she felt that I was putting her nose out of joint. She came to live with us a few years ago, and she died last year. That was when I began to wonder if my other mother was still around. I talked about it so much that Angus told me to shut up or do something about it. That's when I went to the Registry Office in Edinburgh – about two months ago, it would be – and discovered that I was a twin.'

She giggled, then said, 'I couldn't get back home fast enough to tell Angus that I was a twin. He said bloody hell, not two like me! Wait till he sees you . . . he'll be impressed.'

'Did you go to Flora Moodie's address?'

Cara shook her curly head. 'I started with you; I've not done anything about her. I kept thinking about having a twin sister, and about trying to find you. And then I thought, well, it's worth a try, though she's probably moved to England or gone abroad. So I advertised, and here we are. At last,' she finished happily. 'Better late than never.'

'Fiona – my daughter – and I went to the address on

the adoption paper, but only one person remembered Flora Moodie, and she had no idea what happened to her. She might still be alive.'

Cara shrugged. 'She could be anywhere. Married, mebbe, with a whole brood of legitimate kids. We might have lots of half-brothers and half-sisters.'

'I wish we'd been kept together. I never liked being an only child, did you?'

'I never got the chance to find out. I was eighteen months old when Mam and Da discovered that our George was on the way, and they'd been wrong about the mumps. Mam was in her mid-thirties then . . . about the same age we are now. Then Aileen was born, and then Denise.' Cara gave the broad grin that Rachel was already getting to know, a grin that lit up her entire face and made her eyes sparkle amid their laughter lines. 'They both said it was my doing. My da said it was as if they were constipated and I was the big dose of syrup of figs that got everything into working order, but Mam said I was like a fairy waving a magic wand. She even made me a fairy costume. It was lovely – a yellow silk bodice with a tulle skirt and tissue paper wings. I'll never forget it.'

She heaved a nostalgic sigh, then reached for the last cake on the plate and went on briskly, 'Goodness knows how many more kids they might have had if my poor da hadn't been killed in an accident at work. He worked on the railways. And there was my mam with four kids – me and three of her own – and precious little money coming in to keep us all.'

'Were you living in Barrhead then?'

'No, I was born and raised in Govan. Mam went out to work as a skivvy at some big houses because that was the only sort of work she knew, while I looked after the wee ones.'

'How old were you?'

Cara considered, then said, 'I must have been eight by then. A neighbour saw to the wee ones while I was at school, and I took over when I got home.'

'It must have been terrible for you!'

'Not really. They were good kids and we only lived in a room and kitchen, so there wasn't a lot of cleaning to do. And the neighbours looked out for us when my mam wasn't there. She was a lovely woman, but hard work and worry made her old before her time.' Again, sadness touched her animated face, and then she shook it off and said briskly, 'So you didn't have any brothers or sisters?'

'My parents had had a little boy who died not long after he was born. I think they only adopted me because my mother couldn't stop grieving for him. I never really took his place. It might have been better for her if they'd adopted a boy instead of a girl.'

'Is she still alive?'

'Oh yes. She wasn't happy about me finding out that I was adopted,' Rachel admitted. 'And she doesn't know anything about you.'

'Are you going to tell her?'

'I suppose I'll have to, now.' Rachel's heart sank at the prospect.

'How does your husband feel about us meeting like this? You've told him, haven't you?'

'Yes, Martin knows.'

'And he's not very happy about it either,' Cara guessed shrewdly.

'He's got . . . reservations.'

'I can understand that. I could be anyone,' Cara said airily. 'A lush, a hanger-on looking for sympathy and money . . . you name it. But fortunately for him, I'm very happy with my own life. I just wanted to know if I'd any blood kin in the world.'

'And your husband – Angus – was all right about it?'

'Oh yes.' Cara scooped a stray drop of cream from the empty plate and licked it from the tip of a finger. 'My Angus never lets anything bother him.'

'I wonder who our father was? The war was on . . . he might have been a serviceman. Perhaps he'd been killed.'

'It's more likely that our mother didn't even know who he was.'

'She lived with her parents, the neighbour said. I can understand why she had to find good homes for us,' Rachel said. 'A teenager, with nobody to turn to, forced to give away her babies . . .'

'Teenager? She was a full-grown woman, my mam said, and as plain as a pikestaff. She couldn't hand me over quick enough. Mam took a dislike to her because of that. She'd been desperate for a baby of her own all those years, and she couldn't believe that anyone could give away their own flesh and blood as easy as our mother did. I reckon we were both better off without her than we might have been with her. Hang on . . .'

Cara delved into her handbag and produced a photograph. 'That's me and Angus at a dinner dance last year,' she said, and then, as Rachel studied the picture, which showed a broadly smiling, groomed Cara on the arm of a well-built man with long curly fair hair, 'Did you bring any pictures of your kids? And your husband, of course.'

Rachel had remembered to stuff some photographs in her bag before leaving the house. Now Cara went through them slowly, exclaiming over each one. 'I like your dress in this one, did you make it yourself? Your Martin looks quite like that man in *Jaws*, did you see that film? I thought it was great. You know, the man who warned everyone about the great white shark but they didn't believe him at first. Oh, what a sweet wee boy!'

'Not so sweet in the flesh. That's Graham, my youngest. He's just turned seven. And that's Ian; he's ten. He's more serious than Graham.'

'He looks a bit serious. It's nice to have them all diff . . .' Cara was beginning, when she gave a sudden gasp. 'Oh, my God.'

Rachel looked up to see that the colour had drained from the other woman's face. 'What's the matter? Are you feeling ill?'

She looked round the busy tea room nervously, remembering the way Cara had wolfed down the cream cakes.

'It's . . . Fiona, did you say?' Cara looked up, her eyes huge in her pale face. 'Rachel, she's the image of my Alice. I don't know what Angus is going to say when he sees her. He adored Alice.' She was silent for a moment, her head bent over the photograph, then said shakily, 'I've just realised . . . we're twins, and our daughters look just like each other.' She looked up, smiling, though her eyes were moist. 'We've a family likeness!'

'So we have!' Rachel was stunned. Since finding out that she was adopted she had agonised over the realisation that she couldn't say that her children had her mother's colouring, or her father's chin. Now, she had a family resemblance that was hers alone – not Martin's, or her adoptive parents', but hers. 'So we have,' she said again.

'Isn't it exciting?' Cara said, and they grinned at each other across the table. Then Cara, back to her cheerful self, said, 'We've got so much to catch up on! What did you do when you grew up?'

'Became a primary school teacher and then married Martin.'

'A teacher!' Cara looked impressed. 'You must be clever.'

'Not very. And I wasn't a teacher for very long. I was still in college when I married Martin, then Fiona arrived just before our first anniversary.'

'My God, you weren't much more than a baby yourself then! I might have married young, but I was twenty-three when Alice was born.'

'I completed my teacher training after Fiona arrived – my parents looked after her when I was in college. Then I went to work because Martin wasn't earning much. He was going to night school and studying all the time so that he could get his qualifications as quickly as possible. Once he was earning enough to support us I gave up work and had our sons. I've stayed at home ever since, but now that Graham's settled in school I'm thinking of going back to teaching.'

'Tell me something . . . do you like needlework and materials and colours?'

'I used to make all my own clothes, and the children's too, when they were younger. And a friend and I have just finished making costumes for Fiona's school play. They did *The Importance of Being Earnest*. She played the part of Gwendolen in it,' Rachel said proudly.

'That's amazing! I love sewing too. I made all of Alice's clothes. She was the best-dressed wee girl in the street.'

'Do you think we got that talent for sewing from our birth mother?'

'Maybe, but I always put it down to us being so poor when I was a kid. My mam and my da only just managed to keep themselves and their own three kids as well as me on what my da earned. After he died, God rest the man, Ma had a real struggle to pay the rent and keep us fed.' She gave a reminiscent chuckle. 'Many's the time we all hid under the table when the man from the Prudential came round for his money. But the thing that got me was not being able to dress the wee ones well. Aileen was so bonny – she was like a china doll and it broke my heart to see her dressed in cast-offs. I mind one day a lady we didn't even know came to the door when Aileen was only weeks old and gave my mam a bag filled with beautiful clothes that her baby had grown out of. Aileen grew out of them fast enough too, and then she had to go back to the bits and pieces Ma bought from second-hand shops, but it was lovely seeing her well-dressed for a wee while. That lady's kindness made me decide that when I was grown up I'd buy all the muslins and silks and lace and ribbons that I could afford and I'd make pretty clothes for babies. And that's what I do.'

'You have a shop?'

'No, no . . . I used to work in a shop before I was married, but that was a grocery store. I make the clothes at home and I give them to hospitals or to women like my mam who can't afford to buy nice things for their wee ones. I don't need the money,' Cara said. 'My Angus isn't rich but he earns enough to keep the two of us comfortable. And what more do we want?'

Then, glancing at her watch. 'My God, is that the time? I'll have to go. He's coming home at twelve today, and I don't want him to find an empty table.'

'Here, let me help you.' As Cara shrugged on her coat, Rachel began gathering the motley collection of bags together.

'Thanks.' Cara took them, threading her fingers skilfully through the maze of handles. 'Are you going to the loo? Good, you can look after my bags while I'm in. Those cubicles are so small that there's scarcely room in them for all of me, let alone my shopping,' she tossed

141

over her shoulder as she sailed through the tea room.

In the Ladies' toilet she handed her purchases back to Rachel before disappearing into the only empty cubicle.

'When are we going to see each other again?' Cara's voice inquired through the door. 'When can you come to our house? I want to meet my new niece and nephews and brother-in-law. And Angus is dying to meet you.'

Rachel's stomach gave an uneasy flutter. 'Can I phone you once I've sorted out a date with Martin?'

'Sure. You need to give him time to get used to the idea. Why don't you bring your mother too?'

'I think I'd best leave Mum out of it for the moment,'

'Okay.' The cistern flushed and after a moment the door lock clicked and Cara came out just as the cistern in the other cubicle was flushed. 'I'll take your bag while you're in,' she said. 'There's no hook to hang it on and these doors have a space at the bottom. Thieves could reach in and grab it.'

'In Cochran's? This is one of the most respectable shops in the town,' Rachel was saying as the other cubicle door opened and a woman emerged. Her smart black costume and the name badge pinned to one lapel showed that she was an employee. She shot a frosty glance at Cara, and then bent over a washbasin.

'The thieves know that too,' Cara said blithely. 'And if one of them got your bag you couldn't chase after them with your knickers round your ankles, could you?'

'If there isn't a hook on the back of the door, I loop the strap round my ankle.'

'I'd a friend who did that, and some cheeky wee sneak still managed to get it off her. Reached in under the door and grabbed it. Broke her ankle, too.'

The other woman had finished drying her hands. Now she directed a second, even frostier look at both of them before leaving, her silvery, immaculately coiffed head in the air.

'Snooty-looking bitch, isn't she?' Cara said conversationally just before the door closed. 'Did you see that look she gave us? She must be having a bad day.' She relieved Rachel of the smart leather bag Martin had bought her for her last birthday.

'In you go.'

As they sank down towards the ground floor in the lift five minutes later Rachel said tentatively, 'About us coming to visit you – how will Angus feel about seeing Fiona, since she looks so like your own daughter?'

'I'll get him ready for the shock of it. I know that once I tell him, he'll be longing to see her. Could I keep the photographs, to let him see them?'

'Of course.' Rachel took them from her bag and handed them over.

'And you have this one to show Martin and the children,' Cara said. As they left the shop and stepped out onto the pavement she added, 'So you'll phone and let me know when you can bring your family to Barrhead?'

'Yes, I will.'

'Make it soon,' Cara said, stretching across her parcels in order to dab a kiss on Rachel's cheek.

As she did her shopping and caught the bus home, the words, 'I have a sister. I have a sister!' ran through Rachel's head in a continuous loop. All at once, 'sister' was the most wonderful word in the English vocabulary.

She left the bus and walked the short distance to the house, her feet keeping in step with the rhythm of the phrase, and when she was finally behind her own closed door she announced aloud to the empty house, 'I have a sister! I have a twin sister!'

Then she dropped the shopping bags on to the floor and stared into the hall mirror, trying hard to imagine Cara's round, cheerful face reflected beside her own neat, serious features, and Cara's mop of curly hair brushing her own straight pageboy.

Her newly discovered twin looked like a blurred version of herself, but Cara's strong personality was nothing like Rachel's quiet, almost timid reserve. Cara the extrovert, Rachel the introvert. Gathering up her shopping bags and carrying them into the kitchen, Rachel wondered if, had she been raised by Cara's adoptive parents rather than her own, she might have been as confident and outgoing as her twin.

She began to unpack the shopping and put it away, then found herself sitting at the kitchen table, chin in hand, smiling like an idiot at the opposite wall. A twin! Throughout all the years of growing up she had felt oddly out of things. Now she was half of a complete unit formed by herself and Cara.

She abandoned the half-unpacked shopping and hurried into the hall. She had to tell someone what had happened!

Kathleen wasn't at home, and after letting the phone ring twelve times Rachel gave up and tried her aunt's number.

'Aunt Chrissie? Is Mum there?'

'She's gone to get her hair done. Has something happened?' Chrissie asked. 'Did you phone that number?'

'Yes I did, and Aunt Chrissie, I have a sister! And she's not just a sister, she's a twin, and we've just had tea in Cochran's.'

'Did you say . . . a twin sister?'

'Yes, and I'm the oldest . . . older,' Rachel corrected herself. Once a teacher, always a teacher.

'But Doreen never said you were a twin!'

'She didn't know. Cara – that's her name – found out when she went to the Registry Office and saw our two names.'

'What's she like?' Chrissie asked eagerly.

'I can't wait for you to meet her, Aunt Chrissie. You'll like her.'

'Does she look like you?'

'In a blurred sort of way. She says we're a set of before-and-after pictures.' Rachel giggled, feeling as though she had just had several gin and tonics, instead of tea and cream cakes. 'I'm the after.'

'I can't wait to . . . I think that's your mother coming home, I'll have to go,' Chrissie said hurriedly, and hung up.

'So what's she like?' Martin asked. Homework, with its ever-attendant groans and complaints, had been done and the boys were out on their bikes, while music throbbed from Fiona's bedroom. It was the first time they had been alone and free to talk.

'You mean, my twin sister? Martin, she's terrific. She's lively and funny and . . . she's just the sort of sister I've always wanted.'

'Ah.'

'You've been hoping that I wouldn't like her, haven't you?'

'No, of course not.'

'Yes you have. You're worried in case me having a sister's going to change things for us. As if that could ever happen!'

'It might. You're not an only child any more, Rachel. You're not Doreen's daughter. Not . . .'

He stopped suddenly, and it was left to Rachel to finish the sentence. 'Not the person you married?'

'Since you put it like that, yes.'

'That's just daft. Meeting Cara isn't going to change me, it's just answered a lot of questions that I've been carrying around in my head all these years without realising it.'

They were in the kitchen, Rachel sorting through a pile of clothes to be ironed while Martin was trying to repair a clock. Now she left the ironing and went to fetch the photograph that Cara had given her. 'There, that's her and her husband Angus.'

He studied it for several moments, then said, 'They both look a bit florid, don't they?'

'What do you mean, florid?'

'Well . . . larger than life. What does he do?'

146

'Angus has his own landscape gardening business.'

'Ah, that would account for him looking florid.' Martin gave a bark of laughter at his own wit.

'Never mind him – what d'you think of Cara?'

'She's nothing like you.'

'She is! She's got the same colour hair, only hers is quite curly, while mine's as straight as a stick. And our eyes are the same colour, though not as deep a blue as Fiona's, and she has a lovely smile. And she laughs a lot. She could be me if I had lived a different life, or perhaps I mean that I could be her,' Rachel tried to explain, and knew by the look he threw her that he didn't understand a word of what she had just said.

'Martin, she had a daughter called Alice who died in a road accident, and Cara says she was the image of our Fiona. I took photographs of you and me and the children, and she got quite a shock when she saw Fiona. Don't you see what that means? Fiona's like my side of the family!'

'Elementary, my dear Watson,' he said, and then, as she stared at him, uncomprehending, 'Fiona's always had your looks, hasn't she?'

'I suppose so, but now there's a real, official family resemblance.'

'You really think that this Cara looks like your twin?'

'We're not identical, but we do look like sisters. It was so strange, seeing her at first. Like looking in a distorting mirror. She's heavier than me and her face is rounder and she's more of an extrovert than I am. Much more. But we both love needlework. She makes baby clothes. She's got two brothers and a sister, but she's the only one who was adopted.'

'Have you arranged to see her again?'

'She wants us to visit her and her husband in Barrhead.'

'Do we have to?'

'Martin, I want to! And surely you'd like to meet Cara?'

He frowned down at the pieces of clock spread over the table. 'It could be upsetting for the children, meeting a bunch of strangers claiming to be long-lost relatives.'

'Cara *is* my family, and there are just the two of them – her and her husband. Alice was their only child.'

'All the more reason for them to want to take over your children.'

'Don't be so silly!' Rachel began to get angry. 'She's not like that.'

'You're sure of that, are you? After just one meeting? And what about your mother? Are you going to tell her?'

'I suppose I'll have to, since I want to see more of Cara.'

'She's going to be very upset about this.'

'Not as upset as you seem to be.'

'I am not upset,' he said tightly. 'I just think that you might be making a mistake, throwing your life open to a woman you scarcely know.'

'Martin, she's my sister!'

'Sister?' Fiona said with bright-eyed interest from the kitchen doorway. She padded across the room silently on bare feet. 'Mum, what did you just say about a sister?'

'Now you've done it,' Martin said to his wife, and left the room.

'What's wrong with him?' Fiona wanted to know, and then, without waiting for a reply, 'Mum, what did you mean when you said that to Dad about your sister? What sister?'

She listened, wide-eyed, to the story of the newspaper advertisement, the telephone call, and that morning's meeting at Cochran's, then asked excitedly, 'When can we meet her?'

'She wants it to be soon but I think your father's going to have to take time to get used to the idea of me having a twin sister.'

'Then we'll go without him. Imagine . . .' Fiona jigged about the kitchen in her excitement, '. . . I have an Aunt Cara and an Uncle Angus! Perhaps she'll want us to call her Auntie. Auntie Cara.' She grinned at Rachel, who suddenly realised that her daughter had Cara's warm smile. 'It's exciting, isn't it?'

'It's a bit scary, too, to suddenly come face to face with a sister I didn't know I had. Even more scary when she's a twin.'

'I wish I had a twin, or even a sister.'

'Dream on,' Rachel said firmly. 'It's not going to happen now.'

The back door flew open and the boys surged in, demanding something to eat before bedtime. Rachel, putting toast beneath the grill and heating milk for cocoa, turned to make a 'say nothing' face at Fiona, but it was too late. The girl was already blurting out, 'Guess what? Mum's got a twin sister!'

'A twin sister? You've gone completely doolally now,' Ian scoffed, while Graham gaped, his lower jaw sagging.

'It's true, ask her.'

'Tell her, Mum – people your age don't suddenly get twins,' Ian said, and then, as Rachel glared at Fiona, his voice became uncertain. 'Do they? Does Gran know?'

'Nobody knows except us, and I knew first.' Fiona stuck her tongue out at him.

'How can Gran have twins and not know about it?'

'Because Mum's adopted.'

'What does that mean?' Graham wanted to know.

'It means that I had another mother, only she couldn't look after me, so she gave me to Gran and Grandpa when I was little,' Rachel said carefully. She hadn't expected to be plunged into this situation without any warning.

'But Mum didn't know that she was a twin. Nobody

knew, until now. We have an Auntie Cara,' Fiona said, 'and she's married to an Uncle Angus, and we're going to visit them.'

'When?' Graham asked, while Ian wanted to know, 'Where?'

'Barrhead, and soon, perhaps.' Rachel turned the toast and spooned cocoa powder into four mugs. 'You'll like her. She's nice.'

'Does she look like another you?'

'No, Ian, she doesn't. Twins don't always look like each other.'

'Does she have any children we could play with?'

'No, but she's looking forward to meeting you. I gave her some photographs so that she could see what you all looked like. Graham, love, don't suck your thumb. You're not a baby now.'

Graham, who had been staring at his mother, removed the thumb from his mouth, said, 'Are we adopted too?' and put it back. His eyes were round with anxiety. 'Do we have other mothers?'

'No, of course you're not adopted. None of you are. You're our own children.'

'Adoption's not like measles or red hair, silly,' Fiona jeered. 'You don't catch it or inherit it.'

'Silly yourself,' Graham snapped at her just as Martin returned.

'Dad . . . Dad!' Ian leapt at him. 'Did you know that Mum was adopted and she's got a twin who doesn't look like her?'

'Yes, I know.' Martin gave Rachel an accusatory glare, then crossed to the stove and pulled out the grill pan. 'Does nobody else in this house have any sense of smell?' he asked, thrusting the pan, with its two black and smoking pieces of toast, towards her.

'I realise that you have every right to tell the children the truth about your background, but couldn't you have waited until we had discussed it and decided together how to go about it?' he said later, in the privacy of their bedroom.

'You were there when Fiona found out. It wasn't anyone's fault. We just didn't hear her coming downstairs.'

'You didn't need to tell the boys, though.'

'I didn't; she did.'

'Now you're going to have to tell your mother.'

'I'd rather wait until we've all met Cara and her husband.'

'Looking for my support, are you?'

'I have a right to expect it. After all,' Rachel said sharply, 'we are married, and I'd support you if the shoe was on the other foot.'

'Are you certain of that?'

'Of course I am. Being adopted isn't a disease.'

'I didn't say it was.'

'But you're behaving as though it could be!' Rachel rarely lost her temper, and her sharp tone surprised them both. For a moment there was silence as they climbed into bed. Then Martin said, 'It's just a bit of a shock, that's all.'

'All the more reason for us to meet Cara and Angus. Once we get to know them, life can get back to normal.'

'What if they're the clingy type who want to live in our pockets?'

'They're not. Cara's got sisters and a brother already, remember. She's not looking for a new family.'

'And neither should you be.' Before going to sleep every night, Martin thumped and banged his pillow into shape. Tonight he was being particularly vicious. 'You've got your family. You've got us.'

'I know that, and I wouldn't change any of you.'

'Good. That's all right then.'

'Does that mean that I can phone Cara and arrange a visit to Barrhead?'

'I suppose so.'

'Fine.' She opened her book and settled down to read it. Half an hour later, not having absorbed a word of it, she put the light out.

For once, Martin didn't turn over and wrap a long, warm arm about her.

'Wow!' Ian said as the car drew up before a long, low bungalow fronted by an immaculate front garden. The lawn was of bowling-green perfection, edged on three sides with rosebushes still in bloom despite it being early November. On the fourth side, on the other side of the low stone wall separating the house from the road, was a neat, fully planted rockery.

Crazy-paving driveways on either side of the garden led to a garage at one side of the house and to large wooden double doors at the other, with *Angus Longmuir, Landscape Gardening* painted on them in bold white letters. The paved driveways met along the front of the house as a terrace.

'Wow!' Ian said again, and then, as a chorus of barks rang out from behind the double doors at one side of the house, Graham yelped, 'They've got a dog! Dogs, even!'

'Oh, look at that cat. Isn't he beautiful?' Fiona jumped from the car as a large tortoiseshell that had been sunning itself on the front wall raised its head and stared at them, and then sat up and yawned, displaying a rose-pink mouth filled with sharp white teeth. 'Hello, darling,' Fiona cooed, scooping the animal into her arms. 'What's your name, then?'

As the rest of the family got out of the car the front

door opened and Cara emerged, waving. 'You found us, then?' she called.

'After a hunt,' Martin said under his breath, while Rachel called back, 'Yes, of course.'

'Some people have trouble, with us being off the beaten track. Come in, come in!' She walked down the driveway to meet them, her long bright red Indian muslin skirt and multi-coloured boat-necked, full-sleeved blouse rippling about her lush body. 'Rachel, it's lovely to see you again!' She enveloped Rachel in a warm and fragrant hug, and then turned to the rest of the family. 'And here are your sons. They're gorgeous!'

Graham and Ian huddled close to their father, fearing more hugs, but Cara contented herself with a pat on each head and a cheerful, 'Hello, I'm your Auntie Cara!' before holding her hand out to Martin. 'Hello, brother-in-law. You must be finding this very confusing.'

'A little,' he admitted.

'And no wonder. My Angus thinks it's weird. Folk don't find brothers and sisters late in life, he says. Better late than never, I say.' She gave a peal of laughter, which died in her throat as she came face to face with Fiona, still carrying the cat.

'Who's this?' the girl asked.

'Desdemona, but we call her Dessy.' Cara's voice was suddenly uncertain. 'Oh, my darling girl, you're so beautiful!'

'Thanks,' Fiona said awkwardly, while the boys sniggered. Their amusement brought Cara back to the present.

'Come into the house. You'll have to take us as you find us,' she said over her shoulder as she led the way. 'I never seem to get time to tidy the place.'

'It looks immaculate,' Rachel assured her.

'Oh, that's just the outside. It has to look good from

153

the outside to impress Angus's clients,' Cara explained. 'It wouldn't do to have the place looking like *The Darling Buds of May*. Have you read that book?'

'Yes,' Fiona said at once. 'I liked it.'

'So did I. I've read it several times. Well, here we are. Welcome to our humble abode.'

The difference between the neat frontage and the inside of the house was marked. The square entrance hall boasted two folded wooden chairs, an umbrella stand filled with walking sticks and umbrellas, and a low cupboard holding a telephone and a stack of phone books – some of them, Rachel noticed as they passed, were well out of date. A large old-fashioned wooden wardrobe against one wall appeared to serve as a cloakroom; it was so full that the doors swung open, unable to close.

The living room was also cluttered. There were three large comfortable chairs, a three-seater sofa, and two bookcases crammed with books. A sewing table complete with sewing machine stood beneath one of the two wide windows, and a low, broad-shelved bookcase by its side held wool, material, and two sewing-boxes. There were two large dog baskets, each with its own blanket, and every available surface was covered with books and magazines and catalogues.

'Sit down,' Cara invited with a sweep of an arm. 'Just toss stuff off the chairs. Better not sit on that one, Martin,' she added hurriedly as he approached one of the armchairs. 'It's probably covered with dog hairs. The chair by the window might be better.'

'You have a dog?' Ian asked eagerly.

'Two of 'em. Henry belongs to Angus. He's supposed to be the guard dog, but he loves people so that makes him a bit of a washout. Still, he's got a good hefty bark. And Muffin's mine; he's a Westie. They're out the back.

154

Come and meet them,' Cara invited. 'Angus is out there too.'

The Carswells trooped after her, through a door at the back of the hall, into a large untidy kitchen and then through a door leading to a yard filled with small machinery, stacks of folded sacks and piles of paving stones. A long building running parallel to the house was mainly shed, but about a third of it was a greenhouse. *Angus Longmuir, Landscape Gardening* was painted on the doors of an open-bed van parked facing the big double gates.

'Angus!' Cara yelled as she stepped into the yard, and then, as two dogs, one large, with a furry coat in shades of black and brown and the other a small white West Highland Terrier, came racing to meet them, 'Now behave yourselves, you two! No jumping up.'

The dogs, both wriggling with excitement, wove their way in and out of the group, the large animal's tail whipping painfully against their legs.

'Can we play with them?' Graham begged. Martin's 'No!' was drowned out by Cara's hearty 'Yes, of course. Just give them a slap if they annoy you. The kitchen door's unfastened, come in when you get fed up. Angus!' she bellowed again.

This time a muffled reply came from the shed.

'They're here! Come and meet them!'

The voice said something else and she shrugged and turned to lead Rachel and Martin back into the kitchen, where she began to fill the kettle at the sink. 'He'll be here in a minute or two. He's got quite a big job starting tomorrow, so he's busy gathering everything together.'

'Does he work on his own?' Rachel asked. Martin was too busy anxiously watching his sons with the dogs through the window to talk.

'He's got a lad, and a part-time man who comes in

when he's needed. They'll be here tomorrow.' Cara put the kettle on the electric stove and took a tin of biscuits from beside the bread bin. 'There's a plate in that cupboard behind you, Rachel, would you put these on it?'

She herself produced a tray piled with sandwiches, then reached into the cupboard again and brought out a large chocolate cake. 'I hope chocolate's all right,' she said, cutting it into generous slices. 'I was going to make a lemon sponge but then I thought, children prefer chocolate, don't they?'

'They love it. The cake looks marvellous. Do you do a lot of baking?' Rachel felt as though she was chattering like a fool, but she was trying to make up for Martin's silence.

'Oh yes, Angus wouldn't have married me otherwise. He's got a very sweet tooth. Too sweet, as you'll see when he finally comes out of that shed. I sometimes wonder if I should put us both on a diet, but he works hard and sugar's good for energy, isn't it? At least, that's my excuse.' Cara's loud, hearty laugh rang out, and Rachel could have sworn that Martin winced.

'I've set the tray, Martin,' Cara swept on, 'so could you be a lamb and carry it through? You take the biscuits and the cake, Rachel, and I'll bring the teapot.'

As Martin disappeared through the door, edging sideways to accommodate the big tray, she winked at Rachel and murmured, 'He's a quiet one, isn't he?'

'I think he's finding all this hard to take in.'

'Poor lamb, I'm not surprised. He'll be all right,' Cara said comfortably, pouring boiling water into the teapot. 'I never asked if you would prefer coffee, but I forgot to buy some. So tea it must be.'

Fiona had remained in the living room with Dessy the cat when the rest of them went outside. When Rachel and Cara went back into the room she and Martin were standing by the mantelpiece, staring down at the framed picture in Fiona's hand.

'Mum,' she said, puzzled, 'look, Mum, it's me. I thought you didn't know your . . . Auntie Cara until now?'

The room suddenly went quiet for a few seconds, and then Cara, using her elbow to sweep some magazines that were on a table to the floor so that she could set the teapot on it, straightened and went to stand by the girl. 'It's not you, my love,' she said quietly. 'It's Alice, my daughter.'

'But . . . she looks just like me! We could be twins. Couldn't we, Mum?' Fiona thrust the photograph at Rachel. 'Look,' she said excitedly, 'we're more like each other than you and Auntie Cara.' The name slipped from her tongue as though she had been saying it all her life.

Rachel looked down at the likeness. It was of a little girl about seven or eight years of age, on a swing, long slender legs stuck straight out and sandalled feet held neatly together as she prepared to scythe through the air on the downward swoop. Long, brown curly hair flew out around her neat little face, sunlight catching the red and gold tints in it. She was laughing at the camera, her eyes scrunched up so that they couldn't be seen clearly. It was exactly the way Fiona laughed, Rachel realised, a lump coming to her throat.

Glancing at Martin, she saw that he looked as though someone had punched him in the stomach. She knew exactly how he felt.

'What colour were her eyes?' she asked quietly.

'Blue. A really beautiful, strong blue, just like yours, my love,' Cara said to Fiona. 'People used to stop in the street to admire them when she was a baby in her pram. I said to your mum when she showed me your picture the other day that you and my Alice could have been twins.'

'How old is she now? Where is she?' Fiona looked around the room eagerly, as though expecting to find the girl hiding in a corner.

'She died, love, about a year after this was taken. She'd have been twelve now.'

'Oh no! That's terrible . . . she looks so alive,' Fiona said, almost in a whisper.

'Of course she is. Folk don't really die if you keep them alive in your head,' Cara said, and then, holding out her hand to the girl, 'Come and see her room . . .'

Fiona took the proffered hand as though, Rachel thought with a sudden stab of jealousy, she had known this new aunt all her life. Glancing at Martin, she caught a flash of the same unreasonable resentment in his face.

'There's a newspaper buried somewhere on that coffee table, Martin,' Cara said over her shoulder as she led Fiona from the room. 'Angus'll be here in a minute. Come on, Rachel.'

Before following the other two, Rachel placed the photograph gently back on the mantelpiece. 'Are you all right?' she asked her husband.

'I'm . . .' he cleared his throat, then said, 'I'm fine.'

'It was just a bit of a shock, wasn't it? Seeing someone who looked so like our Fiona.'

'Yes. It's . . . uncomfortable. Weird.'

'It must have been even more of a shock to Cara, seeing someone who looks just like her Alice.'

'Where did she say the newspaper was?' Martin looked with fastidious distaste at the pile of magazines and brochures on the coffee table.

Rachel followed the sound of voices and found Fiona and Cara in a bedroom that seemed to be filled with sunshine. The walls were daffodil yellow, and the ruffled curtains were in a light, creamy material splashed with yellow flowers. The few pieces of furniture were white, decorated with big coloured transfers. A teddy bear, several cloth dolls and a big fluffy toy dog lolled on the bed's patchwork quilt.

'We've left it just as it was,' Cara was saying as she went in. 'We'll have to change it one day, but there's no hurry.'

Fiona's eyes were on the dolls that were propped against the pillows. 'Can I lift them?' Her voice was hushed.

'Of course, that's what they're there for. I try to give them a cuddle every day.' Cara watched, smiling, as the girl scooped the dolls into her arms and sat down on a low rocking chair. 'It'll be good for them to be hugged by someone else, for a change.'

'Look, Mum, aren't their clothes pretty? And they've got such sweet faces!'

Cara touched one of the dolls which was dressed in a school uniform. 'This was made for her first day at school, and I made this baby doll with the gap-toothed grin because Alice fell when she was four, and lost a front tooth. She cried and cried – not because it hurt, but because she didn't think she was pretty any more. The doll made her laugh again.'

'I've got a Raggedy Ann . . . well, it's Mum's really. She got it from Dad because she was dressed as Raggedy Ann the first time they met.'

'Really?' Cara asked, delighted.

'It was Rag Day, and I was at college,' Rachel explained hastily.

'And Martin fell in love with you. What a lovely, romantic story! This . . .' Cara ran a hand over the quilt, 'was what I really wanted to show you. It's a remembrance quilt – that means that I made it from Alice's clothes,' she explained to Fiona. 'This flowery bit's her favourite dress, and this comes from a dress I made for a school play. This bit was a skirt and that came from another dress.'

Fiona listened, wide-eyed, as her newfound aunt went over almost every patch on the quilt, touching each one as she gave its history, then said wistfully, 'I wish she was still here; I'd have loved to have a cousin who looked like me. I bet she'd have liked Abba, too.'

'She probably would. Are they your favourite group?'

'They're brilliant.'

'You know that they're coming to Glasgow in February?'

'Oh yes! I'm trying to coax Dad to let me go to see them,' Fiona said. 'But he hasn't said yes yet. Sometimes he behaves as if I'm still a child.'

'That's what fathers are like, sometimes,' Cara said, while Rachel held her tongue; she and Martin were planning to buy tickets for the family, and give Fiona hers on Christmas Day. 'They forget that their children are growing up. He'll come round eventually.'

'I suppose so,' the girl said; then, stroking the quilt, 'It must take a lot of patience to make something like this!'

'Not if you love sewing the way I do. This is what I do in my spare time.' Cara opened a deep drawer and began to bring out tiny clothes, white and blue and pink, yellow and patterned. She spread them on the bed – rompers, suits, dresses, knitted jackets and bootees, coats and hats.

'You made all these?' Rachel marvelled.

'I love working with pretty things. I made most of the clothes for my nieces and nephews, and for anyone who needs them. This,' Cara said, bringing out an exquisite christening robe, trimmed with lace and beautifully embroidered on yoke and hem, 'is for a young woman in my church. She's expecting her fifth next month and she can't afford to buy pretty clothes for the wee mite. She'll have some of these other things too.'

'They're beautiful!' Fiona crooned, stroking a pretty smocked dress.

'We didn't have much money when I was your age.' Cara sat down on the bed. 'We either wore hand-me-downs or clothes my mother got cheap. It didn't matter what they looked like, or even if they fitted properly; as long as we were decently covered they were all right. I swore that when I grew up I would wear pretty clothes.' She looked down at her Indian muslin blouse, and rearranged her full red skirt. 'And lots of colours, even underneath. I remember one time my mother bought half a dozen pairs of knickers for me at a stall. Two pairs navy, two pairs pink, two pairs green. They were thick and boiling hot in the summer, and they had long legs that went right down to my knees. I was fourteen, and I thought they would never wear out.' She gave a sudden giggle at the memory. 'It was horrible when we had gym at school – I had to roll the legs up to try to make them look a bit

161

smarter, but when I did that I looked as if I was wearing tyres round my thighs. They used to cut off my circulation. Did you ever have to wear knickers like that, Rachel?'

'Mine were thick, and they were navy because that was the school regulations, but they didn't have long legs.'

'You were lucky,' Cara said with feeling. 'They'd be elastic, though. When the elastic broke it was always in the waist, wasn't it? Never the legs, where nobody would notice. You could feel them working their way down – remember that, Rachel? – and you would have to go up a close and take them off and push them into your schoolbag, because you knew that you wouldn't make it home before they went all the way and appeared under the hem of your skirt. Then,' she added to Fiona, who was doubled up with laughter, 'you worried the rest of the way home in case you had an accident. My mother would have died of shame if I'd been found dead in the street without any knickers on.'

'You're making it up!'

'Cross my heart, it's true, every word of it. And we had to wear liberty bodices, didn't we, Rachel?'

'What's a liberty bodice?'

'It had nothing to do with liberty, I can tell you that,' Cara said with all her heart. 'They were horrible long-sleeved vests.'

'And they had rubber buttons down the front that got stickier every time the vests were washed,' Rachel remembered.

'That's right. And the stickier they got, the more difficult it was to force them through the buttonholes. My God,' Cara said, wiping tears of mirth from her eyes, 'why did we put up with such misery?' Then, as voices were heard in the hall, 'I think that's my Angus just come in. And your boys too, by the sound of it. Come on, we'd best be getting back. Poor Martin will be wondering if he's ever going to get his tea.'

Ian, Graham, and two over-excited dogs were rushing around the living room while Martin, Rachel saw with a stab of pity, was almost cowering in his chair.

'I thought I heard Angus,' Cara said.

'You did,' said a voice from behind them. 'I was changing out of my boots in the kitchen.'

Rachel turned, and only just managed to suppress a gasp. Angus Longmuir was a bear of a man. He stood a good six feet tall, and seemed to be about six feet wide as well. His checked, short-sleeved shirt strained to remain buttoned over his broad chest.

'Rachel, this is Angus,' Cara said, and then, proudly, 'Angus, this is my sister, Rachel.'

'So we meet at last, Rachel. Sorry I wasn't here to greet you, I had some work to finish.' His deep voice was easy on the ear and his hand, as it swallowed hers, was strong, warm and hard. He exuded a masculine smell of sweat and something else . . . peat? Grass cuttings? She couldn't be certain which, but it was a smell of the outdoors, and it reminded her of her father.

Looking up what seemed to be a cliff formed by his chest and shoulders, she was surprised to find herself gazing into bright green eyes framed by lashes so long and thick that they were almost feminine. His broad, weather-beaten face was framed by a tumble of fair hair, which fell almost to his shoulders, and his smile was both sweet and charming. He was not particularly good-looking, but there was something about him that set Rachel's heart fluttering and weakened her knees in a way that had never happened before, other than with Martin. She had never in her life met such a naturally sexy man, she realised, and blushed at the thought.

He grinned down at her; a just-between-the-two-of-us sort of grin, as though he could read her mind and was amused by her thoughts. If he hadn't released her hand in order to push the big dog out of the way, Rachel herself would never have remembered to let go.

'You've met the boys already. This is my brother-in-law, Martin,' Cara went on, seemingly unaware of the turmoil within Rachel.

Martin struggled to his feet. He was reasonably tall, though not quite six feet, and lean rather than muscular, but he was dwarfed by Angus. Not just by the man's size, Rachel realised, looking at the two of them together, but by Angus Longmuir's sheer presence.

'And this is Fiona, Rachel's daughter. Didn't I say she was like our Alice?'

As Angus turned and looked at Fiona, Rachel got the same sensation she had felt when looking at the photographs of his dead daughter. It was as though time had stopped for a few seconds. He began to say something and then halted, before trying again. 'Aye, you did say, but I'd no idea they were so alike . . .'

'I've just been looking at her picture. I thought it was me when I was younger.' Fiona's voice shook a little. 'It's . . . it's almost as if I had a twin too, just like Mum.'

'Aye, it is. For minute there I thought . . .' Angus stopped again, then said, 'It's a family resemblance, all right.'

Fiona's pretty face lit up. 'It's nice to know that I look like my Mum's family.'

'Nice for us, too, love. Now then, you must all be starving,' Cara swept on briskly. 'Angus, tell those dogs to settle down, they won't heed me when you're around.'

A word from their master sent both dogs slinking off to their baskets.

'D'you play golf, Martin?'

'No, I don't.'

'A Scotsman who doesnae play golf?'

'I don't have the time,' Martin said tightly. 'I work very long hours.'

'So does Angus, but even so, I'm a golf widow whenever he gets the chance to slip away with his cronies,' Cara said placidly. 'Who likes milk in their tea?'

'Milk? Angus scoffed. 'Tea? You'll have a beer, Martin?'

'I'm driving. Tea would be fine.'

'Not at all, tea's a lassie's drink. If you don't like beer, I've got cider in the fridge,' Angus said heartily, and disappeared for a moment, returning with a bottle of beer, a bottle of cider, and two glasses. When he had given Martin the cider and a glass he took his own drink over to the fireplace, where he stood tall and strong with feet apart.

His legs, clad in faded blue jeans, looked as thick and steady as tree trunks, Rachel thought, then blushed again, and averted her eyes.

The children chattered like budgies all the way home, but Martin scarcely said a word. Now and again Rachel shot sidelong glances at him, but he was concentrating on his driving and his expression gave nothing away.

It wasn't until they were getting ready for bed that night that he said, 'Your new family isn't what I had expected. Not like you at all.'

'Not like Mum and Dad, you mean. They were the ones who brought me up. They were the ones who taught me to be the person I am.'

'And God bless them for that.' He was sitting on the edge of the bed, taking his socks off. Now he began to smooth them out before hanging them over the back of the bedside chair. After that, she knew, he would go through the same process with his trousers. Martin was a creature of habit.

She wondered, fleetingly, if Angus Longmuir was a creature of habit, but felt that he was more likely to strip his clothes off and let them drop where they would. Did he wear pyjamas, or . . . ?

'Fiona took to Cara, didn't she?'

'Yes, she did, but I think you found her a bit much.'

'She's nice enough, but . . .' He stopped, socks in hand, staring into space as though trying to marshal his thoughts.

'D'you think we look like sisters?'

'Not like twins.'

'I didn't say twins, I said sisters.' Rachel ached for him to say yes. She so wanted to look like someone for the first time in her life.

'You do in a way,' he said at last, and her heart gave a sudden joyous leap. 'You've got the same colouring, and there's something else I can't put my finger on. Perhaps it's the way you both laugh, or the way you turn your heads. I didn't have much time to study the two of you; I was too busy trying to keep out of the way of that damned dog – the big one. His tail stung like a whip. Animals that size shouldn't be allowed into the house.' He had taken his trousers off and now he examined his legs carefully. 'I could have sworn I'd be covered with bruises.'

'I can't see any.' Rachel put down her hairbrush and went to hug him. There was something endearing about Martin in his shirt tail; there always had been.

He returned the hug absent-mindedly, then said, as she went back to the dressing table, 'Seeing you and your . . . you and Cara together's like looking at two paintings of the same person. You're the watercolour, while she's more of a lush oil painting.'

166

'Lush?'

'You know, those old paintings of curvy Mother Earth women.'

'Oh,' Rachel said flatly.

'I prefer the watercolour look myself,' he assured her, climbing into bed.

'Most men would go for lush.' Angus would definitely go for lush.

'Not me.' He put on the reading glasses he had recently acquired and opened his book. 'In fact, I wish you hadn't been in such a hurry to invite them over here.'

'We have to return their hospitality, Martin.'

'Eventually, yes, but it didn't have to be in two weeks' time. We're not going to keep seeing them on a regular basis, are we?'

'I want to see Cara. We've got a lot to catch up on.'

'Fair enough, but I don't need to be involved every time, do I?'

'No, not if you don't want to. What did you think of Angus?' she asked, after a pause.

'Not our type at all,' Martin said firmly. 'Are you going to tell your mother about today's visit?'

Rachel switched out the overhead light and got into bed. 'I suppose I'll have to.'

'When?'

'Soon,' Rachel said, and opened her own book.

Should she invite her mother to the house, or suggest a shopping trip in Glasgow or lunch somewhere in Paisley and tell her there, or go to see her at Aunt Chrissie's? The question was already nagging at Rachel when she woke in the morning.

'If I were you, I'd tell her at your aunt's,' Kathleen advised when Rachel phoned to report on their visit to

Barrhead. 'It's bound to be a bit of a shock, so best to hear it in familiar surroundings.'

'You really think so?'

'Look at it another way; if she goes for you with the poker, your aunt can pull her off and there won't be anyone else there to see it. So it won't get into the *Paisley Daily Express*. Your mother's the type who would die of shame if she ever saw her own name printed in the newspapers.'

'Kathleen, it's not funny!'

'Who's being funny?' Kathleen wanted to know. 'Bite the bullet, Rachel. Get it over with. By the way, when am I going to meet Cara?'

'Soon. The three of us could meet up for a coffee if you like.'

'I can't wait.'

'Just let me get this business of telling my mother over first.'

'Oh hello, dear, your mother's in the bathroom, but if you hold on, I'll give her a shout.'

'No! I mean, don't disturb her, Aunt Chrissie.' Without thinking, Rachel lowered her voice. 'I was just wondering if you're both going to be at home today.'

'Doreen will be. I thought I might do a bit of shopping.' Chrissie, too, spoke quietly. 'That would leave you both to have a nice chat in peace.'

'I'd rather you were there too.'

'Is it about . . . ?'

'Yes. We visited them yesterday – Cara and her husband.'

'Really?' Chrissie's voice was excited. 'Did you enjoy yourselves?'

'Yes. At least, I did, and so did the children. I'm not so sure about Martin. It's all come as a bit of a shock to him. Aunt Chrissie, it's time I told Mum about Cara. What if one of the children blurted something out in front of her?'

'Are you sure you want me to be there when you do it?' Chrissie asked nervously.

'Yes, please.'

'I'll have to act surprised. She'd be furious if she knew

that I knew. I mean, she's your mother and I'm only your aunt.'

'I wish it was the other way round!' It was a cry from the heart. If Doreen could only be more like her warm-hearted, easy-going sister it would be so much easier to break the news to her.

'Do you, lovey?' Chrissie's voice was suddenly filled with sunshine. 'Oh, so do I, sometimes!'

'They're coming to see us the week after next. I was hoping that you and Mum might come over as well.'

'I'd love to, but I don't know if . . . I'll have to go, dear. Eleven o'clock, then?' Chrissie said hurriedly. 'And stay for lunch.'

'You should have let me know, and made her wait until I got to the phone,' Doreen said sharply.

'It was just a quick call to ask if she could come over later this morning.'

'So she still remembers us, does she?'

'Doreen, she's a busy young woman—'

'Too busy to spare the time to have a word with me on the telephone?'

'She's got the three children and Martin and the house to look after.'

Doreen Nesbitt shuffled over to the fireside chair that had become hers, and picked up her knitting. 'The last time I saw Rachel she was talking about going back to teaching. As if Martin doesn't earn enough to keep them all comfortably. There's no need for her to go out to work at all.'

'I think she just likes to be doing something.'

'Does she not have enough to do with looking after her family? Not to mention me. Surely I'm entitled to a bit of consideration now and again?

170

'And she said that she was just about to go out,' Chrissie improvised swiftly. 'It was just a quick call to ask if she could come over to see us – you – later on this morning.'

'I spent most of my life raising her and keeping the house nice for Frank.' Doreen hung onto the grievance like a dog clinging to a bone. 'That's what women did in my day, and I don't see why they have to change.'

'I'll go and see what we have in for lunch,' Chrissie said, and hurried to the refuge of her little kitchen.

Doreen opened the door to her daughter as the wall clock in Chrissie's hall chimed eleven times. 'I saw you coming up the road. How long have you got?'

'I have to be home for Graham coming in at three,' Rachel said to her mother's back as she followed her along the hall. 'I brought you a cherry cake from the City Bakeries.'

'We've got plenty of cake . . . but the City Bakeries do a good cherry cake,' Doreen conceded. 'Here she is, Chrissie. Take your coat off, then, while I make the tea and slice the cake.'

'Is it not a bit late for tea? We'll be eating in an hour.'

'We can eat a bit later. Rachel's been travelling; she needs a cup of tea.'

'You make it sound as if I've come from Outer Mongolia, Mum!'

'Mebbe that's because you visit so rarely that I feel as if you must live somewhere far away, like Outer Mongolia,' Doreen said pointedly, and disappeared into the kitchen.

'Take no notice, pet,' Chrissie mouthed at her niece's stricken face. 'It's just her way,' then she said aloud, 'Give me your coat, dear. It's beginning to get really cold out, isn't it? Winter's coming over the horizon.'

'Sometimes,' Rachel nodded towards the half-open kitchen door, 'I feel as if it's arrived already.'

Aware of Doreen shuffling around the kitchen, the two of them made polite conversation about the weather and how the children were doing at school.

'And how's Martin?' Chrissie wanted to know when she returned from hanging her niece's coat in the hall.

'He's fine,' Rachel said clearly, and then mimed, pointing at the kitchen, 'How is she today?'

'That's good. There's a bit of a sniffle going about, I just wondered if he'd caught it from anyone in his office,' Chrissie replied, while her hands flipped to and fro in a gesture that meant, 'so so'.

'I'm looking forward to my tea,' Rachel said, adding meaningfully, 'And a nice chat, afterwards.'

'Yes, tea first.' Chrissie's head nodded vigorous agreement. No point in spoiling their cup of tea.

On her way to Whitehaugh Rachel had turned over several opening sentences in her mind, memorising each one carefully and then almost immediately discarding it in favour of something new. But when it came time to make her announcement every one of them vanished from her head and without quite meaning to, she suddenly heard herself cutting into Doreen's story about the yappy wee dog belonging to the woman down the road with, 'Mum, you know this business about me being adopted?'

Doreen's voice stopped as though someone had snipped it off with a pair of sharp scissors. She picked up her teaspoon and began to stir tea round in her half-empty cup before finally saying, 'I thought that was over and done with, and not to be spoken of again.'

'I thought it was over with too, but now I've found my sister.'

'What sister? You never had a sister!'

'I do have one, and I've found her.'

Doreen's face flushed. 'You went behind my back when I advised you to leave things be?'

'Now Doreen—'

'You keep out of this, Chrissie, it's between Rachel and me!' Doreen clattered the teaspoon into the saucer. 'You went behind my back!' she said again.

'I'm a grown woman, Mum. I don't need your permission.'

Doreen placed the saucer very carefully back on the table. 'You knew you'd not get it, more like.'

'That's true. And that's why I haven't told you about this before.'

'You could have let well alone like I said you should.'

'It's not as easy as that, Mum.'

Doreen gave a disbelieving sniff. 'Never could keep your nose out of things, could you?' she said, her fingers running over the buttons on her cardigan as if they were a rosary. 'Questions, questions, questions, ever since you were old enough to string three words together.'

'I have a right to find out more about myself.'

'Do I not have any rights? Who was it that raised you and fed you and sat up at night with you when you had the croup? *Me*, that's who, not that woman who birthed you and then handed you away in Clyde Street as if you were nothing more than a parcel of fish!'

'Doreen, that's a cruel thing to say to the lassie!'

'I don't know what you're sitting there for, Chrissie,' Doreen told her sister coldly. 'This matter's between me and my . . . between me and Rachel.'

'Stay here, Aunt Chrissie,' Rachel ordered as her aunt began to get up. 'I want you to stay. You're entitled to hear what I have to say.'

'She's entitled to listen to our own private business,

you're entitled to look for a woman who didn't even want you — it seems that everyone's got rights except me.'

'That's not true, Mum.' Rachel had never in all her life spoken so firmly to her mother. Every organ in her body was trembling with fright, but her voice was still under control, and so she forged on. 'Why d'you think I'm telling you all this? It's because I know that you've got rights. And I've not found my real mother. I don't know anything about her.'

'So why are you upsetting me like this?'

'I said at the beginning: I've found a sister. My twin sister.'

Doreen's mouth fell open and her fingers stilled on the buttons of her cardigan. The flush disappeared and her eyelids began to flutter as though something was being waved around in front of them.

'Doreen, are you all right?' Chrissie asked anxiously. 'D'you want a drink of water?'

'Leave me be,' Doreen said in a half-whisper. 'Twin, did you say? You've got a twin sister?'

'Yes, and she lives in Barrhead.'

'She never said. She never told us you were a twin.'

'I know. It was the same with the folk who adopted Cara. Her name's Catherine,' Rachel explained to the two women, 'but she calls herself Cara. She was the one who found out about us when she went to the Registry Office in Edinburgh. She's the one who got in touch with me.'

'How?' Doreen wanted to know.

Much to her own surprise, a wry laugh found its way to Rachel's lips. 'The same way you found me — through a newspaper advertisement.'

'Are you going to see her?'

'I've already seen her. We met in Cochran's tea room two weeks ago.'

'Two weeks? You've known about her for two weeks?'

'And we visited her and her husband in Barrhead yesterday. He's a landscape gardener with his own business.'

'Who's we?'

'Me and Martin and the children.'

'You took my grandchildren to visit this woman who claims to be your sister?' Even Doreen's lips were bloodless now.

'She's their aunt. And she really is my twin sister, Mum. She's not making it up.'

'Does she look like you, Rachel?' Chrissie broke in, unable to keep silent any longer; then she subsided as her sister snapped, 'Chrissie!'

'She does in a way. We've got the same colouring, but she's more . . .' Rachel sought for the words, 'more curvy than me. And her hair's curlier. And she laughs a lot.'

'I suppose you'll be seeing her again?'

'The week after next, when they come to our house. I was hoping that you'd come too, Mum.'

'Me? Why should I want to meet this . . . this woman? She's got nothing to do with me!'

'She's Rachel's flesh and blood, Doreen,' Chrissie ventured.

'But not mine.' It wasn't the harsh note in Doreen's voice that made Rachel wince. Chrissie saw the involuntary movement.

'Doreen, she's your own daughter's twin. Surely you'll want to meet her, even if it's only for Rachel's sake?'

'As Rachel says, she's *entitled* . . .' Doreen emphasised the word, '. . . to meet up with this newfound sister of hers, if that's what she wants. But I'm under no obligation.'

'I'd like you to be there,' Rachel lied.

'I'd not want to get in the way of you getting to know your new relatives.'

'Doreen, that's not fair. Rachel's trying to be honest with you—'

'Will you be quiet, Chrissie!' Doreen almost shouted, and then, to Rachel, 'I'm just glad that your father isn't here to see what you're doin' to me, and to his memory. He'd be turnin' in his grave if he knew!'

'Mum, listen; there's no need for you to get upset. You'd like Cara, I'm sure you would. Why don't you come along? And you too, Aunt Chrissie.'

'Chrissie can do whatever she pleases, of course. She always has. As for myself . . .' Doreen clambered to her feet stiffly, as though her joints had all locked. 'If you don't mind, I'm going to have a lie down. All this deceit's given me a sore head.'

'Mum!' Rachel said, while at the same time her aunt pleaded, 'Doreen . . .'

But Doreen ignored them both, walking out of the room and closing the door very quietly behind her.

'Should I follow her?' Rachel wondered as they heard her bedroom door close.

'I think she's best left alone for now, love. It's all come as a bit of a shock.'

'Perhaps I could have put it better.'

'It would have been a shock even if you'd wrapped it up in pretty paper and tied it with a big pink ribbon. Doreen's not very good at dealing with things she's not used to,' Chrissie said. 'She never did like the unexpected, even as a wee lassie. I mind thinking once that our Doreen would promise to do anything, even throw herself off a cliff, as long as it wasn't until next year or even next month. But as always, when it came to the time she said she'd do whatever it was, she'd change her mind. After

176

she married Frank she relied on him to shelter her from the surprises . . . and he did, bless him. He protected her from the world as much as he could. And now we're all the family she's got left, Rachel pet, and she's scared that she's going to lose you.'

'She'll not lose me!'

'I know that, and you know it, but Doreen doesn't. If I were you, pet, I'd just enjoy your sister's visit, and leave the next move to Doreen.'

'I don't suppose you could come to meet her and her husband?'

'I'd love to, Rachel,' Chrissie said. 'But I can't go behind your mother's back. Not the way she's feeling right now. Mebbe later, when things have settled down a bit.'

'I suppose I'd best go now.'

'But you've not had your lunch!'

'I doubt if any of the three of us could eat a bite if I stayed. It's all right, Aunt Chrissie; I'll come and have lunch with you another day, when Mum's come round to the idea of me having a sister we knew nothing about.'

In the hall, Chrissie helped her niece on with her coat while the two of them, aware of the silent listener behind Doreen's closed bedroom door, chatted about the weather and the previous night's television programmes.

When she was ready to go, Rachel hesitated, and then knocked lightly on her mother's door. 'I'm going now, Mum. I'll come back to see you next week. Look after yourself.'

There was no reply. She hugged Chrissie tightly, and went.

From behind her bedroom curtains, Doreen Nesbitt watched her daughter walk down the road. She was poised to dart back out of sight if need be, but Rachel, head down and shoulders bowed as though they carried the weight of the world, didn't turn to look back at the house.

When the younger woman had disappeared from sight, Doreen began to pace around the room, arms wrapped tightly about her thin body and her lips fluttering as though forming swift, soundless words. She hadn't been so frightened since the night Frank had died . . . Frank, her strength and her support. He would have known how to deal with this latest bombshell. He would have shown her how to react, and he would have been there, standing by her, helping her to come to terms with this terrible new situation.

Blood was thicker than water, everyone knew that. Family came first. It was true that she and Rachel had never been wholly at ease with each other, and Doreen had to admit, in her heart of hearts, that the fault was probably hers. Even so, since Frank's death the knowledge that the child she had tended from babyhood was close at hand, willing to give any help that Doreen might need, had brought a little warmth to the cold loneliness that was sudden widowhood.

But now everything had changed. Now, Doreen felt as if she had opened a door, expecting to see a familiar room on the other side, and found instead a great gaping hole in the floor, with only darkness awaiting her far below.

And she felt very, very frightened.

17

Cara and Angus Longmuir arrived at the Carswells' house in a shabby Triumph Herald with a lived-in look.

'It's so tidy!' Cara enthused almost as soon as she stepped into the entrance hall. And then, turning slowly so that she could take everything in, 'D'you know something? I used to dream about a nice house like this when I was a little girl living in a tenement and sharing a bed with my sisters. I always thought that I should have been born into a lovely house like this. And now . . .' she stopped circling and laughed at Rachel, her arms still spread, 'I find my long-lost twin living in my dream house.'

'I was raised in a tenement too, and you already live in a lovely house,' Rachel protested, embarrassed.

'Pay no attention to the daft woman, she's always going on about something or other,' Angus said, adding amiably to his wife, 'and our place would be just as smart as this if you bothered to keep it tidy. Any pets?' he asked, and then, when Rachel said that they only had the children's guinea pigs in the back garden, 'That explains it then. No tails knocking things over and no hairs on the furniture.'

'I couldn't live without my dogs and my cat,' Cara confided. 'Hello, Martin.'

'You found your way then?' he said from halfway down the stairs.

'No problem. Hello, my pet,' she added as Fiona appeared behind her father. 'Don't you look lovely?' Then, as Fiona, in flared trousers and an off-the-shoulder peasant blouse that her father disapproved of, beamed her pleasure at the compliment, 'Where are the boys?'

'In the back garden.'

'Through there, is it?' Cara asked, and breezed into the kitchen. Angus followed, after thrusting an unwrapped bottle of wine into Rachel's hands. With Fiona in tow, the two of them disappeared out of the back door.

'This isn't a visit, it's an invasion,' Martin muttered, joining Rachel in the hall.

'Ssshh!'

By the time they reached the kitchen Cara, Angus and Fiona were out on the patio with the boys. The hutch door was open and Cara nursed one of the guinea pigs while Graham held the other.

'I remember a guinea pig we had once,' Cara was saying as Rachel stepped through the French windows, 'Queenie, she was called, because she queened it over the rest of them. She was daft about grass, and every time we as much as took the lawnmower out of the garden shed she was at the front of her hutch, squeaking like mad because she knew she was going to get a good feed. She would end up buried in grass, eating her way out as happy as Larry . . .'

'Show me your garden, Rachel,' Angus commanded, setting off across the lawn. She trailed after him as he walked down towards the red brick wall at the end, hands stuffed into the pockets of his brown cord trousers, tossing comments over his shoulder as he went.

'That border could be a bit wider. It would look good with some hefty clumps of growth like lupins and clarkia and sweet william . . .' And then, as they walked between the crab apple trees, 'Do they earn their keep?'

'I like the blossom, and I make jelly from the apples.'

'Hmm.' He strode across the drying green and nodded at the japonica. 'I suppose you like that blossom too. Make quince jelly, do you?'

'I've never got around to it. The trees were here when we bought the house,' she said, but he had already plunged into the shed.

'You do the gardening, right?' he said when she went to stand in the doorway. 'Martin doesn't look to me like a man who likes to get his hands dirty.'

'We do it between us. Martin's kept very busy at the office, and he often brings work home with him,' she said defensively. 'I've got more spare time than he has.'

'Your tools need tidying up. And these blades should be oiled before the winter comes in.'

As he passed her on his way out of the shed she was again aware of his musky male smell. Martin never smelled like that, but then again, Martin was particular about using both after-shave and deodorant, and he worked in an office, while Angus did hard, manual out-of-doors work.

He stood, feet apart and legs rigid, studying the wall at the bottom of the garden, before stepping forward to run a hand across the bricks. Then he squinted up at the sky, noting where the sun was. 'You could grow fruit trees against this wall. Pity not to make proper use of it.'

'The shed cuts out some of the light.'

'Move it.'

'Where to?'

'Dig up the crab apple trees and put the shed and the compost heap there. Get rid of that japonica and you could plant fruit trees and have a vegetable patch here too. Grow your own lettuce and kale and turnips and onions and leeks. I'll do it for you,' he offered, turning to stride back to the house. 'At a discount, seeing you're family.'

She stepped back swiftly as he made to brush past her. 'I like it as it is.'

'You can't like this!' Angus waved a hand at the crab apple trees, the japonica, and the shed where her father had spent so many happy hours.

'I do like it. All of it.' She began to get angry. 'My father gave us that shed as a house-warming present. He planned the garden for us, and he came every week and mowed the lawn and dug the flowerbeds. He grew the flowers from seed.'

'He sounds like the sort of man I'd enjoy talking to.'

'He would have been, but he's dead now. He organised this garden and looked after it and I want to keep it the way he left it . . .' Rachel said passionately, and then had to stop as her voice had started wobbling.

'God! Women!' Angus said from above her head. 'Sentimental creatures, every one of 'em.'

'Better than being unsentimental bastards,' she fired back at him, and began to march back to the house.

'Hey . . .' He caught hold of her arm and swung her back to face him. 'Come here, woman.'

To her astonishment she was enfolded in a strong, warm embrace, her nose pressed against his green, open-necked shirt.

'There now,' he soothed, patting her back. 'No need to get into a tizzy.'

His shirt smelled as though it had been washed and then hung outside to dry in the fresh air. Rachel's face was jammed against the top button, which meant that once she had managed to blink the mist of angry tears away she had a close-up view of the thick golden hairs curling across his tanned chest. She drew back sharply, and as she did so, sunlight glinted from a gold chain looped around the strong pillar of his throat.

'Okay, okay, you win. It's your garden,' Angus said. 'Cara's always saying that I charge in where angels would run for their lives.'

He was so close that she had to tilt her head back to look up at him. He was grinning down at her, his eyes just as green as she remembered from their first meeting, his lashes just as long and thick. The tips of them glittered in the sunlight, like the gold chain. His mouth was wide and generous, his breath warm against her cheek. Her heart started to pound again. This is ridiculous! she thought angrily. This man wasn't her type, and yet there was something about him . . . She had never come face to face with sheer male magnetism before, and it confused her utterly.

She pulled herself free of him. 'Cara's right. I don't know how she puts up with you.'

'She's crazy about me,' he said easily. 'That's how.' And then, teasing, 'Are you crazy about Martin, Rachel? Do you shiver all over when he touches you?'

The boys came crashing through the garden towards them. 'Mum, Mum!' Graham was shouting. 'Look, Mum, look what Auntie Cara and Uncle Angus brought us!' He pushed a toy car into her hand, while Graham, close behind him, yelled, 'And I got a motorcycle, look! Thanks, Uncle Angus!'

'Yeah, thanks!' Ian echoed.

'They look expensive; you shouldn't have spent so much money,' Rachel said to Angus as they followed her sons back to the terrace, where Martin leaned against the door frame with arms folded, watching their approach.

The guinea pigs were back in their hutch, and Cara and Fiona were sitting on the garden chairs.

'Och, it's nothing. Money should always be used to make people happy, and kids are for enjoying, and spoiling. And I've got a little something for you right here, young lady,' he added to Fiona as they reached the patio.

'For me?'

'You didn't think we'd miss you out? Just because you're not a kid any longer . . .'

'Don't tease her, Angus,' Cara said sternly. 'Just give them to her.'

'Okay.' He took an envelope from the pocket of his cords, and handed it over. Fiona slit it open with a thumb, took out two slips of pasteboard, glanced at them, and then suddenly gave an ear-piercing scream that made Martin jump, set a dog two gardens away barking, and brought the boys puffing back from the end of the garden to investigate.

'Look, Mum! Look what Auntie Cara and Uncle Angus gave me! Dad, look!' She held up the two slips of pasteboard. 'It's two tickets to Abba's concert in Glasgow! I can't believe it!' Her eyes shone like stars and she clutched the tickets as though they were the most precious things she had ever seen. 'Oh, thank you!'

She threw herself at Cara, and then ran to Angus, who caught her up in his arms and whirled her round, laughing.

'You're quite pleased, then?' he said when he had set her down again.

'Pleased? I can't wait!'

'It's kind of you, Cara,' Rachel said, since Martin was silent.

'It's nothing. I happened to be in Glasgow the other day and I saw the queue of people waiting for tickets. I remembered that Fiona said she loved Abba, so I just joined the queue.'

'It was all her idea; I'm a Beatles man myself,' Angus said.

'They're all right, but they're not Abba,' Fiona said; and then, doubt creeping into her voice, 'I can go, Dad, can't I?'

'Why shouldn't you be able to go, honey?' Cara wanted to know.

'Dad worries about big concerts crowded with people. He doesn't think they're very safe.'

'Ah, but you won't be on your own. There are two tickets . . . I was hoping that you might ask me to go with you. We'll be able to look after each other, Martin, so you don't need to worry.'

'Okay, Dad?'

'Of course,' Martin said. 'Want a beer, Angus?' He had stocked up the fridge beforehand.

'Now you're talking!'

'D'you want to come up to my room, Auntie Cara, to see my Abba posters and my albums?'

'I most certainly do! Lead the way.'

'And I'll put the kettle on,' Rachel said.

The bedroom door was ajar, and as she went upstairs to tell them that tea was ready, Rachel could hear Fiona's light voice saying, 'Some of the fashions are mad. Look at this page; how can anyone look good in that?'

'You'd look wonderful in anything. Oh, Fiona, I'm so envious!' Cara said. 'I wish I'd looked half as pretty at your age. I bet all the boys are after you.'

There was a pause as long as a heartbeat before Fiona said, 'They're too busy thinking about football to bother with girls.'

'Och, come on! I wasn't anything special, but I had boyfriends right from the time I was twelve.'

'Twelve? Did your parents let you have boyfriends at that age?'

'My da was dead by then, God rest him, and my mam, bless her, didn't know. I changed boyfriends faster than I changed my mind. Don't tell me that a pretty lassie like you hasn't got someone special in her life?'

'Well . . .' Fiona said, 'there's Robbie.'

'Fiona, you're not still seeing that boy, are you?' Rachel said from the doorway. 'I thought you promised your father that you'd concentrate on your schoolwork.'

'I didn't promise – he told me that that was what I had to do. I only see Robbie now and then, at week-ends and sometimes in the evenings,' the girl protested.

'What's wrong with this lad, then?' Cara asked, and when nobody answered, she probed, 'Is he in your class at school, pet?'

'He's a bit older than me.'

'Two years older.'

Fiona shot her mother an exasperated look, and then turned back to Cara. 'He's going to Art School next year. We were in the school play together, *The Importance of Being Earnest*. Mum made the costumes. Here we are . . .'

She tossed aside the teenage magazine she had been thumbing through and got to her feet in one easy, almost fluid movement to take a group photograph from the top of the cupboard. She sat on the bed beside Cara, who was cuddling Raggedy Ann. 'That's him, and that's me. Robbie played Jack Worthing, and I was Gwendolen Fairfax.'

'I wish I'd seen the play. The costumes are beautiful, Rachel. And Robbie's a real looker, isn't he? You'll have to bring him to Barrhead some time, I'd love to meet him.'

'I'd like that. Dad won't let me invite him here,' the girl pouted.

'Only because you need to concentrate on your studying if you want to get to university,' Rachel interceded swiftly as Cara's eyebrows rose. 'He just wants you to do well, without any distractions.'

'I keep telling you, I'm not clever enough for university,' Fiona said hotly. Cara glanced at her, then at Rachel, who said, 'Tea's ready.'

'Good.' Cara put the cloth doll back against the pillows and made for the door. 'I'm parched. Last one downstairs is a daffodil.'

'They're great,' Ian said later as they waved their visitors off.

'I'm glad you found Auntie Cara, Mum.' Graham slid a hand into Rachel's and leaned against her side, while Fiona said, 'I love those bright colours she wears. She's like a sunny day, all by herself. Or a rainbow.'

Martin said nothing, while Rachel found herself thinking about Angus. He was so unlike Martin, and so totally unlike the sort of man she would ever want. And yet there was something about him . . .

'Mum,' Fiona said when Rachel went into her room to say goodnight. 'You'll not tell Dad about me seeing Robbie, will you? He'll only make a fuss and try to keep me in every weekend.'

'You make him sound like an ogre, and he's not.' Rachel sat on the edge of the bed. Fiona, propped against her pillows, her knees drawn up to her chin, smelled of soap and toothpaste. Her face looked freshly scrubbed and her lovely bronze hair was tied back with a piece of ribbon.

She looked so young and vulnerable that Rachel's heart twisted within her ribcage. She was just as bad as Martin – she would have given anything at that moment to turn the clock back to when her daughter had been a five-year-old, safe and secure within the charmed circle of her parents' love.

'Please, Mum?'

'I hate keeping secrets from your father.'

Fiona glanced up from beneath her long eyelashes. 'Did you ever tell him about us going to Glasgow to try to find your birth mother?'

'No, but—'

'There you are then, it's not wrong to keep *little* secrets, is it? Sometimes the only way we can protect people, and keep them happy, is to keep secrets from them,' Fiona said with a maturity that belied her childish looks. 'And we both know that Dad would be happier not knowing about Robbie.'

'I noticed at the play that you seemed to know his family. You've been to his home, haven't you?'

Fiona flushed slightly, then gathered up one of her soft toys and plucked at its fur. 'I had to catch up with the play, and I couldn't bring him here for extra rehearsals. You can see that, can't you? How could we rehearse with Dad keeping an eye on our every move?'

'I suppose . . .' Rachel stopped, then said, 'He seems to be a nice boy.'

'He is! D'you think I'd waste my time with someone who wasn't worth seeing?' Fiona asked indignantly.

'I'm sorry,' Rachel said that night.

'What about?' Martin looked up from his magazine.

'About the Abba tickets Cara bought for Fiona.'

'Oh, that.' The two words were tipped with barbed

wire. 'We'll just have to think of something else to give Fiona for Christmas.'

'Perhaps we should have got them as soon as the ticket office opened, and given them to her there and then.'

'What you mean is, I should have gone and got the damned tickets when they first went up for sale.'

'I didn't say that. And Cara wasn't to know what we'd planned. I should have told her.'

'You think so? I thought,' Martin said, returning to his reading, 'she would have known instinctively about our plans, being your twin.'

'I'm bored,' Cara trilled down the phone ten days later. 'And one of Angus's golfing pals has invited us to his daughter's wedding. So . . . want to go shopping with your sister tomorrow?'

'I'm supposed to be meeting a friend for lunch in Glasgow.'

'Even better . . . unless the two of you would prefer to be alone?' There was a sudden note of uncertainty in Cara's voice.

'Of course not. It's Kathleen . . . I did tell you that the three of us would get together, and this would be the perfect chance. She'd love to meet you.'

'Good. What train are you getting?'

'I'd thought the 12.15, but if you want, we can go up earlier and do some shopping before we meet Kathleen.'

'Ten o'clock at Gilmour Street station?'

'I'll be there.'

'You don't fancy asking your mother along, do you?'

'She hates shopping in Glasgow,' Rachel said swiftly. 'Especially with me.'

'I didn't say that!'

'You didn't need to,' Cara said. 'See you tomorrow, sis.'

'We just have to give your mum all the time she needs to get used to the idea of me coming into your life,' Cara said as the train sped along the track between Paisley and Glasgow.

'I don't know if she'll ever get used to it. She's not like your mother, Cara.'

'Ah, but mine was one in a million. I wish you could have met her.'

'Mine was never really comfortable as a mother. Not as my mother, at any rate. I wasn't the child she'd lost; I was just the cuckoo in the nest.'

'No you weren't. Baby cuckoos push the other eggs out of the nest. You didn't kill her poor little boy, did you?'

'No, but even so . . .' Rachel said, and then, with a sudden lift of heart, 'My father was different. He really cared. We had some wonderful times together.'

'I feel sorry for your mum,' Cara said thoughtfully. 'You're all she's got now, then suddenly there I am, smack in the middle of her only daughter's life. If anyone's a cuckoo in the nest it's me, I'll bet that the way she sees it *I'm* pushing *her* out.'

'But it doesn't have to be one or the other of you! Why can't she see that I can be a sister and a daughter at the same time?'

'She's too scared to see anything right now. Be kind to her,' Cara said, suddenly serious. 'Nurture her and fuss over her. Let her see that you still care.'

'It's not easy to nurture my mother. How can you hug a thistle?'

'Let it know that you care about it and it'll stop jagging you,' Cara advised. 'Now then, where should we go first?'

18

Cara proved to be easy to shop for, and an hour after setting foot in the first shop they had both approved of a white cotton dress patterned with streaks of yellow and navy. The neck was scooped, the sleeves short, and a loose, gathered sash of the same material was caught in a knot at one side. The nineteen-twenties look about it gave Cara an unexpected air of elegance and style.

When Rachel said so, Cara grinned and said, 'You mean, it covers my generous proportions.' Then, taking another look at herself in the full-length mirror, 'But it is nice, isn't it? And it feels lovely on.' She gave an experimental twirl and the flared skirt drifted around her legs. She had lovely slender ankles, Rachel suddenly noticed, and small feet.

'What should I wear with it?' Cara was asking.

'A stole – a navy one. With navy shoes and gloves and a navy bag.' Rachel glanced at her watch. 'We'll look for the accessories after lunch. Could you keep this dress aside for us?' she asked the saleswoman.

'Yes please.' Cara gave the woman her warm smile. 'This is definitely the one I want. We'll be back mid-afternoon.'

★　★　★

By the time their first course had arrived, Cara and Kathleen were getting on like a house on fire.

'And thank goodness for that,' Cara said, picking up her soup spoon. 'Isn't it horrible when you meet your friend's friend, and you're daggers drawn from first glance? You can't think why anyone with the taste to like you chose to like this other person too.'

'And the person in the middle feels like the prize in a tug-of-war,' Kathleen agreed, buttering a roll. 'The way I see it, we're all made up of different sections and some friends only see one section while other friends see another. I have friends from my student and teaching days, like Rachel, and friends from my knitting bee, and friends I've had since I was a schoolgirl, and they all know a different me.' She tasted the soup. 'Quite nice, but not as good as mine.'

'You cook?'

'No, I just make soup.'

'So you only like making soup?' Cara tried to make sense of the conversation while Rachel sat back and watched, amused.

'I don't really *like* making it, but it seems to help. It scratches an itch,' Kathleen explained. 'I suppose you could say that I find it soothing.'

'Oh, put her out of her misery, for goodness' sake,' Rachel interrupted as Cara looked even more confused. 'Kathleen's husband uses the whole of their garden to grow his prize vegetables, but he won't let her use any of them in the kitchen, so she has to buy from the shops.'

'While every time I look out of my kitchen window, all I see is vegetables,' Kathleen added. 'Rows of carrots, cabbages, leeks, turnips, onions . . . not to mention the greenhouse he bought to mark our fifth anniversary. It's bursting with cucumbers and tomatoes and courgettes and goodness knows what else, depending on the season. And in the living room we have a glass-fronted cabinet filled with the trophies he's won.'

'And that's why you make soup?'

'It seems to calm me,' Kathleen explained. 'I would rather do something useful and more pleasurable, like embroidery, or playing bingo, or having an affair; but no, I make soup. Pots of it. I think it must have something to do with all those vegetables surrounding my house. Sometimes I feel as if I'm living in that science fiction story – what's it called? *The Day of the Triffids*.'

'He does let you use some of them, Kathleen,' Rachel reminded her.

'Yes, but only because they're not good enough to put into the horticultural shows. Do you have any idea what it does to a woman's soul, knowing that she's only allowed to work with rejects? I'd go out there and dig them all up if it wasn't for the fact that I hate manual labour.'

'That's not a problem; my husband's a landscape gardener. Give him the contract,' Cara said brightly, and Kathleen sighed.

'It's tempting, but even if I went ahead with the idea, Murdo would probably just start replanting.'

After they left Kathleen, Rachel and Cara found the perfect accessories for the dress, even to the hat – a smart navy straw bowler trimmed with a pale blue ribbon fastening in a bow at the back. Back at the dress shop, Cara raided the bags she and Rachel had amassed before disappearing into the cubicle with the dress and the accessories.

'What d'you think?' she asked when she finally emerged. 'Will I do?'

'Angus won't know you. You look so . . . elegant!'

'Inside this homely wee housewife, Rachel, is a glamorous model, struggling to get out. Now then, just let me get out of all this finery and we'll do some more shopping.'

'What for? You've got everything you need.'

'This time it's for you. I insist,' Cara said firmly as Rachel began to protest. 'I want to get you something as a thank-you for your help.'

'It's just not me,' Rachel protested half an hour later, staring into the full-length mirror.

'It *is* you; it's just that you've never tried wearing that sort of thing before. You look terrific, honestly. Martin will love it.'

'I'm not so sure.' Rachel studied the floaty turquoise silk dress doubtfully. The sleeves were caught just below the elbows with ribbon and the square-necked bodice was high-waisted, with the gathered skirt flaring from just below the bust line. It was very feminine, and quite unlike the tailored clothes she usually wore.

'It does look very nice, madam,' the shop assistant said. 'You have the figure to carry it off.'

'We'll take it. Yes we will,' Cara insisted. 'Don't argue . . . presents should be accepted gracefully.'

As they settled into the train at Central Station, their purchases piled on the seat opposite, she said, 'Angus is working in your part of the town. We've arranged for me to go back to yours with you so that he can pick me up at about half past four. Is that okay? It'll give me a chance to see the kids again.'

'Fine.' Martin would be home at about five-thirty; Cara and Angus would probably be back in Barrhead by then, Rachel estimated.

While Cara put the kettle on, Rachel went upstairs to exchange her high-heeled shoes for the comfortable

194

sandals she usually wore around the house. The doorbell rang as she was coming downstairs.

'We've been for a walk,' her mother started as soon as the door opened. 'We went to the Cross and then up Canal Street and into George Street and we thought we'd look in on you before we walked back to the house.' Then, as Rachel stood transfixed, not knowing what to do or to say for the best, 'Are you not going to ask us in, then?'

'Mebbe we came at a bad time,' Chrissie put in.

'No, it's just that . . .'

'Hullo,' Cara said, appearing by Rachel's side.

The two women standing on the doorstep looked at her, and then back at Rachel. Then they looked at Cara again, and Rachel could see the dawning realisation in both pairs of eyes.

'Oh my dear,' Chrissie finally broke the silence, 'you look so like our Rachel!'

'Do I really?' Cara asked in delight. 'I hope so, she's much prettier than me. Are you Rachel's mum?'

'I'm Chrissie Kemp, her auntie.'

'So you must be Mrs Nesbitt. I'm so pleased to meet you.' Cara held a hand out to Doreen, who took an involuntary step back and would have tumbled off the edge of the step if Chrissie hadn't caught her arm.

'Chrissie, I think we should be getting back home.'

'Mum!'

'Come on, Doreen,' Chrissie said swiftly, after a glance at Rachel's stricken face. 'We dropped by in the hope of getting a nice cup of tea and I'm not going until we get one.' She put a hand beneath her sister's elbow and eased her forward.

'I've just put the kettle on.' Cara was still beaming, although she had let her outstretched hand fall back to her side. She turned and walked to the kitchen, and once Doreen had been eased into the hall and the front door shut, Chrissie followed her, leaving Doreen and Rachel alone.

'How could you?' Doreen hissed. 'How could you let me come here when that . . . that *woman's* in your house?'

'I didn't know you were coming, Mum. We've been shopping in Glasgow and she came back for a cup of tea. If I'd known . . . come and have some tea, please.'

'I've no option now, have I, since your auntie's decided to fawn all over the woman?' Doreen snapped, allowing herself to be drawn into the kitchen, where Chrissie was showing Cara where Rachel kept the cups and sugar and biscuits.

Doreen was like the spectre at a feast. She moved her chair to an uncomfortable spot at one corner of the kitchen table and left the other three to talk. Her thin mouth was so pursed that it was a wonder, Rachel thought, that she managed to get anything into it. As it was, she drank her tea in tiny sips and ate her biscuit in minute pieces, which she broke off with her fingers.

Cara worked hard at drawing her into the conversation, congratulating her on her three lovely grandchildren, and on Rachel and Martin, their home and even their garden, as though Doreen had achieved it all by herself. The older woman replied briefly, in the clipped accent that she kept especially for people she didn't like.

It didn't help when all three children arrived home from school and, finding Cara in the house, greeted her warmly. She hugged and kissed them and then said, 'And have you not got a big hug for your grandma?'

It was difficult to know who was more horrified by the suggestion, the children or Doreen, who, as Rachel well knew, was not a toucher. But after a panicky glance at Rachel, who gave them the smallest of nods, they duti-fully hugged their grandmother, who bore the embraces in an awkward and embarrassed way.

And then, just as Rachel was beginning to think that at least things could not get any worse, Angus Longmuir arrived, scorning the front door and walking round to the back of the house where the two boys, playing in the back garden, welcomed him with shrieks of pleasure.

He came up onto the terrace and stood in the door-way, almost filling it. 'I'll not shake hands,' he said when Rachel introduced her mother and aunt, 'and I'll not come in, Rachel, because I've been digging all afternoon and I'm filthy. I'll have a biscuit or two, though.' He held out a huge paw, engrained with dirt. 'Just put several there,' he said, and when she did so they disappeared into his mouth, reminding her of an automated money bank she had had as a child; a clown that, at the press of a lever, conveyed pennies put into his hand to his mouth.

'Coming?' he asked his wife, spraying biscuit crumbs as he spoke. 'I'm starving!'

'And I've been out shopping for that wedding so we'll have to get fish and chips on the way home.'

'Suits me. I'd offer you a lift, ladies,' Angus added to Chrissie and Doreen, 'but I've got the lad in the van, and the back's full of sacks of rubbish.'

'So that's your sister,' Doreen said when the Longmuirs had gone.

'She seems very nice,' Chrissie said hurriedly. 'And she looks very like you, Rachel.'

'I didn't see it myself. She's a lot fatter than Rachel. She's let herself go.'

'There are a lot of similarities, though. You have the

same colour hair, and eyes, and there's something about the way you both move, and smile.'

'She wasn't a teacher, was she?' Doreen observed, and when Rachel said that Cara had worked in a shop, 'I thought as much. No proper education.'

'Just because she was a shop assistant it doesn't mean that she couldn't have done other things. Her father died young and her mother had to raise the family on her own. They had several children after they adopted Cara,' Rachel added as her mother opened her mouth to speak. 'There wasn't the money to let her go to college after school.'

'Her husband's a right common man.'

'He has his own business. He's a landscape gardener.'

'That explains a lot,' Doreen said darkly. 'And I don't think you should let her make such a fuss of your children, Rachel. They'll start expecting it.'

'I see no harm in that,' Rachel snapped, and then, as her mother drew in an outraged breath, 'Martin will be in soon. Why don't the two of you stay for a meal, then he'll drive you home.'

But Doreen claimed that she could feel one of her headaches coming on, and as soon as Martin arrived she was on her feet and ready to leave. While he drove the two women back to Whitehaugh, Rachel started cooking.

'Gran looked as if she'd been sucking a lemon,' Fiona said later, when she and Rachel were washing the dishes. 'She doesn't like Auntie Cara, does she?'

'She hasn't had time to get to know her.'

'She's not Gran's sort of person though. Too outspoken. That's what I like about her – she's real. Not like Gran at all. Not like any of us.'

Martin, who had just come into the kitchen, asked, 'What do you mean by that?'

'She says what she thinks. We're always supposed to say what we think other people want to hear.'

'That's not true, Fiona!'

'Come off it, Mum, you know I'm right. Gran brought you up to be polite and never say anything that might offend people, even though they don't mind offending you. And you were brought up the same way, Dad. So the two of you raised us like that because it's the only way you know. We all behave as if our belly buttons are fastened to our backsides.'

'Fiona!' Martin roared. 'That's a disgusting thing to say! Where did you hear that?'

'Uncle Angus said it.'

'He said that about me and your father?'

'No, of course not, he said it about someone he was doing work for. But I know what he means – prim and proper people who don't want to let anyone know what they're really thinking. We're all like that, especially Gran.'

'That's utter rubbish,' Martin said.

'I don't think so.' Fiona shook the tea towel out and hung it on its hook. 'I'm going upstairs to do my homework.'

'I warned you that this could happen,' Martin said as soon as he and his wife were alone.

'What could happen?'

'Rachel, they're just not our sort of people.'

'Perhaps it's us who aren't their sort of people,' Rachel pointed out, and he glared at her and then walked out of the room, his back stiff with outrage.

From the back, Rachel thought with a spurt of impish amusement, he looked as if his belly button was fastened to his backside.

★ ★ ★

'I've got a great idea,' Cara said as soon as Rachel lifted the receiver. She never introduced herself with the usual 'It's me,' or even 'Hello,' but started talking as soon as the person she was calling answered the phone. It was a habit that had thrown Rachel at first, but now she liked it, because it was yet another of the special things that belonged exclusively to Cara. Her sister, her twin.

'What is it?' she asked cautiously.

'Let's spend Christmas Day together. Wouldn't that be wonderful, Rachel? You, me, Angus and Martin and my new nephews and niece, all having Christmas dinner together. We could have it here, in our house. *Please* say yes,' she begged as Rachel's mind started to go into overdrive. 'We'll be thirty-six years old next year and we've never once spent Christmas Day together!'

What would Martin say? Rachel knew very well what he would say, but at the same time, Cara was right, it would be lovely to celebrate Christmas with her. 'It sounds great,' she said, adding, 'but you and Angus must come to us rather than our tribe filling your house.'

'We always like to fill the house with people on Christmas Day, so it's no bother; but if you'd rather have it at yours that's fine, as long as you let us bring the starter and the pudding.'

'What about your family?'

'You're my family!'

'Your other family, I mean. Your brother and sisters.'

'We've already arranged to see them on Christmas Eve instead. It's Denise's turn to have everyone this year, and they didn't mind changing the day just this once. You'll have to meet them some time, but for now, they all understand me wanting to share this first Christmas Day with you.'

'The only thing is, we always have Mum and Da . . .

Mum and Aunt Chrissie over here for Christmas Day.'

'Good, that will give me the chance to change your mother's mind.'

'About what?'

'Rachel, you're so diplomatic; that's one of the things I like about you. Why don't you just come out and tell the truth? Your mother doesn't like me,' Cara said, on a ripple of laughter.

'No, no, she just takes a while to get to know people.'

'There you go, being diplomatic again. When we accidentally met each other in your house she looked at me as if I was a bad smell under her nose. But she'll come round, given time,' Cara predicted confidently. Then, her voice suddenly taking on a wheedling note, 'You *must* say yes, Rachel!'

'I'll have to speak to Martin . . .'

'Of course you do, but tell him it's really important to both of us. Be nice to him, extra nice. Do whatever you have to do, but get him to agree,' Cara trilled over the telephone line. 'Please, Rachel!'

'But I like the way we spend Christmas Day!' Martin protested, his face falling into what Rachel secretly thought of as his little boy look – mulish and sullen. 'It's peaceful, and familiar.'

'It might be a good idea to do something less familiar now and again.'

'I don't see why we should.'

'It would only be this once, Martin.'

'Until next year,' he snorted in disbelief.

'Just this once, I promise. I'll be thirty-six years old next year and I've never spent Christmas with my sister.' Rachel shamelessly borrowed Cara's tactic.

'You've told the children already, haven't you? You've

got them on your side before you even spoke to me.'

'They don't know a thing about it. I wanted your agreement before I said anything.'

'And what about your mother, and Chrissie?'

'They'll be coming too, the same as always,' Rachel said. Martin stared at her and then gave a great hoot of laughter.

'You seriously think that your mother's going to spend Christmas Day with people she took a dislike to even before she met them by accident?'

'I'm willing to work on her. She'll agree, if she cares about me at all,' Rachel said, and then wondered bleakly if Doreen really did care enough to agree.

'Good luck, mate!'

'Does that mean you're willing?'

'If your mother is, then so am I. But not a word to the kids until it's all settled. I'd hate them to be disappointed.'

19

'No!'

'Mum, Cara and Angus are really nice when you get to know them,' Rachel coaxed. 'And it would just be this once.'

'It's important to Rachel, Doreen,' Chrissie put in. 'She's not long met Cara and it's understandable that they'd want to spend their first Christmas together.'

'She's known me all her life and apparently she's not that bothered about spending it with *me*,' Doreen snapped at her sister. Rachel's anxious expression when she first came into the house had warned her that her visitor was on some difficult errand, and so she had opted to perch on the edge of one of the straight-backed armless dining chairs, shoulders back and elbows digging into her sides.

'Mum, of course we're all going to spend Christmas together. It'll be just the same as always, except that this year Cara and Angus will be with us as well.'

'The trouble with you, Rachel, is that you're gullible. Oh, I know you were clever enough to become a school-teacher, but you still trust everyone you meet. You don't know how to judge faces and you never have. You're like your father,' Doreen swept on. 'He was just the same; as trusting as a newborn bairn.'

'And what's wrong with that?' Chrissie wanted to know.

Her sister shot her a steely glance. 'It's dangerous, that's what's wrong with it.'

'Are you saying that Cara and Angus aren't to be trusted, Mum?'

'I'm sayin' that we don't know them well enough yet. *You* don't know them well enough, for all that the two of you make such a fuss about being blood kin.'

'Mum . . .'

'I'll make the tea,' Chrissie said, rising. 'You'll both be ready for a cup.'

'I'm not bothered.'

'Don't be daft, Doreen, you know we always have a cup of tea at this time of the morning. And there's the nice jam sponge Rachel brought, too.'

'I brought Scotch pies as well,' Rachel said as Chrissie went into the kitchen. 'I thought we could have them for our lunch.'

'So you're stayin' on, are you?'

'If that's all right. Listen, Mum . . .' Rachel glanced at the kitchen door and lowered her voice, 'the children have seen a nice navy blue cardigan in my catalogue and they want to club together to buy it for Auntie Chrissie. D'you think she'd like that for her Christmas present?'

'What's it like?'

'Mohair, three-quarter length with two big pockets and a tie belt. And a V-neck. Warm, and smart at the same time. She could wear it under a coat in the cold weather, or on its own over a blouse or a jumper in the spring. It was Fiona who saw it, but the boys like it too. What d'you think?'

'It sounds all right. Tell them to go ahead and buy it . . . if they can afford it.'

'I'll order it and they can pay it off weekly. Now that Christmas is on the horizon Ian and Graham are becoming very helpful,' Rachel said. 'I got them to sweep up the last of the leaves in the garden yesterday on the promise of ten pence each, then when they'd finished, the two of them disappeared without a word. I thought they'd gone off on their bikes, but it turns out that they were away offering to sweep the neighbours' leaves for twenty pence a time.'

'The wee monkeys!'

'That's what I thought, but then they said that it was so's they could buy Christmas presents.' It was a relief to see Doreen's grim face crack into a smile at the mention of her grandchildren, and a relief to get away from the prickly subject of Christmas Day. 'Martin was quite pleased when he heard about it. He's got them putting the extra money into a wee bank, and he's going to calculate the interest and add it in when it's time for them to do their Christmas shopping.'

When they had finished their tea Doreen carried the tray into the kitchen.

'I'll just rinse these things out and put them on the drainer.'

'I'll help you, Mum.' Rachel was getting to her feet when Chrissie put a hand on her arm.

'You'll probably want to wash your hands first.'

'I'll do that in the kitchen.'

'You'll do it in the bathroom,' Chrissie muttered, her eyebrows signalling busily. 'There's some nice-smelling soap in the bathroom. And take your time. Rinse twice. We're not in a hurry.'

'Oh, right.' Taking the hint, Rachel went off to the

bathroom, while Chrissie went to the kitchen, where her sister was busy at the sink.

'Any harder and you'll wash the pattern off the good china,' she said mildly, taking up the tea towel.

'This is the way I always wash the dishes.'

'Doreen, about Christmas—'

'I'm not going to Rachel's if that woman's there!'

'Just this once wouldn't hurt you, surely.'

'Mebbe not, but it'll be just this once again next year, and the year after that . . .'

'It must be nice, given our age, to feel that you can afford to look so far ahead,' Chrissie said dryly, but Doreen paid no attention.

'And then it'll become a habit and I'll just be dropped and forgotten.'

'Is that what's bothering you? You're worried about Rachel dropping you because she's found her sister? She's your daughter, Doreen – you of all folk should know that she'd never do such a thing to you. Never in a thousand years!'

'She's my *adopted* daughter, not my *flesh and blood* daughter. That means I've got no call on her loyalty,' Doreen sniffed, attacking a saucer as though it had committed a terrible crime.

'Honestly, Doreen, sometimes you can be awful childish! You and Frank have raised that lassie since she was just weeks old. What is it the Jesuits say? If they get a child within its first seven years they can mould it for life.'

'Me and Frank were never Jesuits, as you well know, Chrissie Kemp.'

'The saying still applies. Rachel's your daughter and always will be.'

'That woman would like fine to get her all to herself.'

206

'Folk can be shared by a whole lot of other folk; they don't need to belong to just one person like a . . . a toothbrush.' Chrissie felt her anger beginning to rise. 'And I'll tell you something else, Doreen – the best way to get rid of someone is to try to hang on to them. The more you make Rachel feel as if she has to choose between you and her sister, the more she'll feel the need to be free of you. So think on, and remember that we're only talking about one Christmas, not the rest of our lives.'

'I'll not enjoy it!'

'If you ask me, neither will Martin, for he doesnae like change. Men can be very set in their ways. But he cares for Rachel, and I think he'll have the sense to put up with Cara and her husband for her sake.'

Doreen, emptying the sink and rinsing the suds away, said nothing, but when the three of them were back in the living room she announced grudgingly, 'I've been thinkin', Rachel – if havin' this woman over to your house on Christmas Day means that much to you, I'll go along with it – but just this once, mind.'

'Oh Mum, that's grand!'

'Though I don't know why you should want me and Chrissie to be there. We might like to have a quiet day on our own for once, have you never thought of that?'

'*I* certainly hadn't.' Chrissie glared at her sister. Nobody had asked her opinion, but if the truth were known, she was desperate to get to know Rachel's new sister and brother-in-law better.

'As if Christmas would be Christmas without you and Auntie Chrissie! We'd be lost without the two of you.'

Doreen shot her daughter a startled glance, and then, realising that the comment was genuinely meant, she let her rigid muscles relax for the first time in over an hour.

★　★　★

'I don't want to get up,' Martin groaned into his pillow.

'Of course you do.' Rachel snuggled against his warm back and kissed his ear lobe. 'Merry Christmas, my darling.'

'Hunh!'

'Martin, you love Christmas.' She slid out of bed and reached for her dressing gown.

'I *used* to love Christmas. Now it just means filling the house with people we have nothing in common with.'

Don't start today of all days on a bad note, Rachel warned herself, while she said lightly, 'You and Angus have one thing in common; you're married to sisters.'

'That doesn't make us blood brothers and it never will.'

'Whether it does or not, they're coming, and so are Mum and Aunt Chrissie, and I've got loads of things to do if we're going to sit down to our dinner at two o'clock.'

'Dad!' The door burst open and Graham rushed in, followed closely by Ian. The dressing gowns that Rachel had left at the bottom of their beds the night before to ensure that they didn't get a chill in the morning had been dragged on any old way, and both boys already had chocolate smears around their mouths. 'Dad, come and help me set up my Scalextric . . . *pleeeeaaase*?'

He clambered on to the bed and Ian followed suit. As Martin let out a howl of protest, Rachel, satisfied that there was no chance of him drifting back to sleep, went off to claim first shot at the bathroom.

'I've never seen that outfit before, have I?' Martin asked several hours later as the two of them got ready to receive their visitors.

Rachel was combing her hair and trying to get used to her reflection in the mirror. She glanced down at the turquoise dress with a carefully casual air.

'I bought it a few weeks ago. What d'you think?'

208

'A bit bright, isn't it? Not the sort of thing you usually wear.'

'I just felt like having a change. Something different for Christmas.'

'It's certainly different,' he said, and then, just as her heart had begun to sink, 'but you look good in it.' And then, coming up behind her and putting his arms around her, 'And it feels good, too.'

'Mum,' Fiona squealed when Rachel went downstairs. 'You look great!'

'You think so? It's not too fancy, is it?'

'It's lovely – you suit it,' her daughter pronounced. 'You should wear that colour more often,' while Ian whistled at the sight of his mother, and Graham, trying to follow suit, spluttered chocolate all over himself and had to be mopped down.

Cara and Angus were due to arrive at noon, and Martin had arranged to collect Doreen and Chrissie at about the same time. At half past eleven he and Rachel, who wore a large apron over her new turquoise dress, were busy in the kitchen while Fiona set the seldom-used table in the dining room, when the back door opened and Cara swept in, followed by Angus, both loaded down with brightly wrapped parcels. Both were wearing Father Christmas hats.

'Merry Christmas, everyone! Quick, Martin, take these before they fall! Merry Christmas, Sis!' Cara sang as Martin rushed to obey. As soon as her arms were free she wrapped them around Rachel, enveloping her in a cloud of perfume and something alcoholic – sherry? Her cheek was cold and soft against Rachel's, and the hug almost crushed the breath out of her. 'Isn't this wonderful, being together for Christmas?' she squealed when they finally drew apart.

'Wonderful,' Rachel just had time to say breathlessly before Angus, who had dropped his parcels on the table, almost into the bowl of brandy butter Rachel had been preparing, advanced on her, beaming and waving a generous clump of real mistletoe above his head.

'Merry Christmas, new sister-in-law,' he boomed, sweeping her into an embrace. Laughing, determined to be a good sport about everything, she tilted her head to one side so that he could kiss her cheek, but instead, his mouth deftly found hers and fixed on it.

The kiss was long – too long for the occasion, and, even worse, it was a very good kiss. When he finally released her and stepped back Rachel was tingling from head to toe. Then she saw Martin's tight, angry face, and the tingling stopped as though someone had turned off a tap.

'Martin . . .' she said feebly, but he ignored her, reaching out for the mistletoe.

'My turn, I think,' he said, and spun round to hold it over Cara's head. She melted willingly into his embrace while Angus, grinning, looped an arm about Rachel's shoulders as they watched.

'That's what Christmas is all about,' he said. Then Graham arrived and started yelling, 'They're here! Auntie Cara and Uncle Angus are here!' and Martin finally released Cara as the other two came rushing into the kitchen.

'My little loves!' Cara deposited hugs and kisses all round. 'Let's put our parcels under the tree, shall we? When do we get to open them, Rachel?'

'After dinner.'

'So no guessing, and no shaking. Come on, lead me to the tree. And I'm dying for a drink,' Cara said as she disappeared through the door with the boys jumping and leaping and chattering around her like pet dogs welcoming a beloved owner home.

'There's sherry and port and—' Martin began, and was interrupted by Angus.

'I brought this.' He waved a bottle in the air. 'It's the finest malt you've ever tasted. I get it from a friend who works in a distillery. Wait till you taste it, Martin. Glasses, Rachel,' he ordered, opening the bottle.

'I'm just leaving to pick up Rachel's mother and aunt. I don't drink and drive,' Martin told him stiffly.

'Quite right, mate. That's why I got a teetotal pal to drop us off. He's picking us up again this evening. You can have a glass when you come back, then.'

'Not whisky. It makes me sick.'

'Does it?' Angus stared in amazement, then said sympathetically, 'That's a bugger, isn't it? A Scotsman who can't drink whisky! Poor sod!'

Rachel had put three glasses on the table, and now Angus filled them with a generous hand. Martin eyed them, and then glared at Rachel.

'I'll have lemonade with mine,' she said defiantly.

'No you won't; I'll not allow you to sully this wonderful whisky with lemonade, woman,' Angus told her. 'That's as bad as buying mink and diamonds for a whore. Here . . .' He handed her a glass. 'Let's drink to developing friendships.'

'Shouldn't you be looking after Cara?' Martin, hovering by the back door, directed the question pointedly at his wife, reluctant to leave her alone with Angus.

As though on cue, Cara arrived. 'Rachel, let's have a look at you.' Deftly, she unfastened the apron and whipped it off. 'You look fantastic, doesn't she, Angus? Oh, good,' she added, spotting the whisky. 'This one mine?'

'It certainly is. See you, Martin.' Angus tossed the words over his shoulder, and Martin left, directing a final glare at his wife.

When he ushered Doreen and Chrissie into the house forty minutes later, Angus and the boys were sprawled over the living room floor playing with Graham's new Scalextric, while Fiona, Cara and Rachel were working in the kitchen. It was beginning to feel like a proper family Christmas, Rachel thought, mellowed by the glass of neat whisky and comforted by Cara's unfailing cheerfulness and incredible competence.

Then, going into the hall to greet her mother and aunt, she caught sight of Doreen's set features, and the whisky-induced glow vanished like water from a duck's back.

Wisely, Cara left Doreen alone at first, and then began to talk to her during the meal, first of all with a brief comment here and there, then a question leading into a short discussion. Rachel, who had never known how to cope with her mother, watched in astonishment as Doreen gradually thawed.

During the Queen's Christmas address on television Cara and Doreen sat together on the sofa, drinking in every word and then discussing Her Majesty's outfit and choice of jewellery when it was over. Then they began to talk about their favourite Royals.

'She's daft about them,' Angus said from the armchair where he lolled in comfort, full of food and with a glass of wine in his hand. 'She keeps a scrapbook. She's forever pasting pictures into it.'

'I was brought up on pictures of the Royal family,' Cara said placidly. 'My ma loved them. She enjoyed seeing them in their beautiful clothes and their jewels and their lovely homes. It just rubbed off on me, I suppose.'

'You'd have thought,' Angus contributed, 'that it would have been more likely to turn the old woman bolshie, seeing that family with everything when she'd nothing.'

'Not at all. She loved being part of a country that has a real Royal family. And I feel the same way.'

'Exactly,' Doreen said, nodding vigorously. Chrissie, catching Rachel's eye, winked at her.

'Look at our middle names,' Cara went on, 'mine, and Rachel's. She's got Elizabeth Flora, and my middle names are Margaret Rose. It's obvious that we were named for the two little Princesses, so our birth mother must have been a Royalist too.'

'Really? I never thought of that!' Doreen was impressed. 'Did you know you'd been called after the present Queen, Rachel?'

'How could I know that, Mum?'

'I should have realised.' Doreen preened a little. 'Elizabeth . . . of course!'

Cara gained the final seal of approval with her gift to Doreen – a cameo brooch.

'It's not new, mind,' she said as Doreen exclaimed over it. 'I found it in a second-hand shop that sells really nice old jewellery. Proper jewellery, not fakes. Here, let me.' She took the brooch from its box and deftly pinned it to the lapel of Doreen's grey jacket. 'It looks just right on you. You've got that air of natural dignity that sets off a cameo brooch to perfection.'

She and Angus had given both boys boxed games, while Fiona's parcel held a cloth doll dressed in a loose flower-patterned shirt and flared blue trousers embroidered round the hems. A blue bandanna, also embroidered, was tied round her fair curls, and there was a cheeky grin on her pretty face.

'She's beautiful! Did you make her yourself, Auntie Cara?'

'I did indeed.'

'Give it here, Fiona.' Doreen held out her hands, and

when the doll had been put into them she examined it carefully. 'You made all of it, Cara?'

'I like doing that sort of thing. My mother was a great needlewoman and I learned from her. She had to be clever with a needle because she couldn't afford to buy us much in the way of clothes and toys. Every Christmas she made me a lovely rag doll with brown curly hair. My best friend Margy was jealous because my dolls always had hair just like mine . . .' Cara brushed a hand against her curly mop . . . 'and I was jealous of her because her dolls had china faces and they looked like real babies.'

Fiona, who had settled on the floor beside the sofa, was gazing at her newfound aunt, fascinated by her story. She gave a peal of delighted laughter when Cara finished with, 'It took years for me to realise that every time my mum cut my hair she kept it, and then glued it onto the dolls' heads.'

'How did you know what to choose for Mum?' Rachel asked as the sisters made coffee in the kitchen later.

'I just thought from what you said about her that she was the sort of person who would appreciate a nice cameo brooch. I like her,' Cara added, cutting the home-made Christmas cake she had brought into generous wedges.

'Really?'

'No need to sound so surprised.'

'It's just that I've always found her a bit . . . prickly.'

'Defensive, I'd say. She's not very sure of herself or of other people, poor love. It's just a case of knowing how to handle her.'

'You've certainly managed to do that. You've got her eating out of your hand.'

Cara winked. 'Animals, men and mothers . . . just let them be and pay no heed to them, and when they're ready, they'll come to you.'

20

Doreen and Chrissie opted to leave early in the evening.

'I'll see you two again some time,' Martin said to Cara and Angus as he prepared to drive the two older women home.

'We'll still be here when you get back,' Angus assured him. 'The evening's young.'

Watching Martin, Rachel hoped that she was the only person who realised what a struggle he had to conceal his disappointment.

It was almost midnight when Angus finally phoned the man who had agreed to drive them home.

'About New Year,' he began as he and Cara settled down with one more drink for the road.

'We're going to spend it with my parents in the Lake District,' Martin said swiftly.

'Are we?' The words were out of Rachel's mouth before she could stop them.

'It was meant to be a surprise, darling. I was going to tell you tomorrow. We're driving down on New Year's Eve and coming back on January the second.' He settled back in his chair and smirked – there was no other word for it, Rachel thought – at Angus. 'So how are you two planning to bring in the New Year?'

'Oh, we'll have a houseful of folk, same as always.' Cara beamed at the prospect. 'We have open house every year. Pity you couldn't come, but there's always next time, isn't there?'

It was almost one in the morning before they finally left.

'Promise me one thing,' Martin said as he and Rachel were finally on their own. 'We have next Christmas to ourselves.'

'And next New Year too? You might have told me, Martin. When was this arranged?'

'Last week. I had a feeling that Angus and Cara would try to hijack New Year the way they hijacked Christmas, so I phoned Mum and said we were coming down.'

'How did she feel about that?' Martin's parents liked to have a regular routine in their lives, and didn't care for surprises or upheavals.

'Fine. She was fine. We're all going to have a peaceful, ordered New Year and I for one am looking forward to it.'

'Today wasn't so bad.'

'You certainly seemed to enjoy that kiss Angus gave you when he came in.'

Rachel, reaching under the pillow for her nightdress, felt a sudden warmth sweep over her at the memory. She kept her face averted and her voice neutral as she said, 'Everyone kisses everyone else at Christmas.'

'That wasn't a Christmas kiss, that was a proper kiss.'

'Don't be daft! Anyway, what about the way you kissed Cara?'

'That was just to show that husband of hers that two could play the same game.'

Rachel retrieved the nightdress and straightened, turning to face him. 'So you didn't enjoy it?'

'As a matter of fact, I did. She's all woman, your sister.'

'How nice for you.'

'I'm sure you think that her husband's all man.'

'Actually I didn't enjoy it much,' Rachel said carefully, well aware of the minefield he was drawing her into.

'But I'm going to a Hogmanay party at Alma's,' Fiona protested when Martin broke the news of the trip to the Lake District.

'And now you're going to have a nice family New Year with your grandparents instead.'

'But we never go there for New Year!'

'All the more reason to go this time. Come to think of it . . .' Martin shot a glance at Rachel . . . 'we might make it a regular New Year thing. I'm sure my parents would love that. A family gathering.'

'Can we take our Christmas presents with us?' Ian asked.

'One each, as long as it isn't too big or too noisy. So no Scalextric.'

'But Dad, I was looking forward to that Hogmanay party,' Fiona whined. 'It'll be the first proper party I've ever been to.'

'There's always next year.'

'That's a whole year away!'

'Hang on a minute, Fiona, while I work that one out.' Martin stared at the ceiling, brow wrinkled in thought, then said, 'By George, you're right. So now you've got a whole year to get ready for the your first proper Hogmanay party.'

'It's not fair! Why can't I stay here on my own?'

'Because I want us all to bring in the New Year together – the four of us, and my parents.'

217

There was a pause while Martin returned to his book and Fiona stared at him, chewing her lower lip and fiddling with a lock of hair. Then she said, 'Gran and Auntie Chrissie could keep an eye on me, if that's what's worrying you.'

'Nothing's worrying me, Fiona. I'm sitting here, worry-free, enjoying a good read and looking forward to a family New Year in the Lake District, with everyone having a good time and enjoying each other's company,' he added, putting stress on each of the final words.

'It's not fair!' Fiona stormed.

'Realising that nothing's fair is part of growing up,' her father called after her as she marched from the kitchen.

She was back five minutes later. 'I've phoned Alma and she's spoken to her mum, and she says I can stay with them instead of going to the Lake District.'

'I'm sure that Alma's mother will have enough to do over New Year without having to cope with a lodger into the bargain.'

'Auntie Cara and Uncle Angus – I could stay with them.' Fiona suddenly brightened. 'They'd love to have me, I know they would. Auntie Cara said that I could visit them any time I wanted.'

Martin slapped the flat of his hand down on the book he had been trying to read, and Rachel jumped at the sudden noise and almost put the darning needle through her finger. 'Fiona, this entire family is going to the Lake District and that's that.'

'But Dad!'

'Subject closed. And if Alma's still on the other end of that phone, get back into the hall and finish your conversation. Phone calls cost money.'

'Martin, at her age it's only natural that she should want to spend more time with her friends,' Rachel said when Fiona had returned to the hall.

'And it's only natural that I should want to spend New Year with my parents. After all, your family were here for Christmas . . . all of them. Which reminds me . . . do you know what Graham said to me a week or two ago? He said that he'd had a real "pigeroonie" of a day at school.'

'What?' Rachel started to laugh. 'Where did he get that from?'

'Your sister, where else? It's not funny, Rachel. I want my children to grow up knowing how to express themselves properly.'

The laughter died almost as swiftly as it had arisen. 'Is this Lake District notion of yours a way of getting back at me because of Cara?'

'Of course not.' Martin closed his book and put it aside. 'I think I'll go and have a bath.'

'Don't take too long about it. I fancy a bath myself, when you're finished. It's been a real pigeroonie of a day,' Rachel said to his departing back.

Fiona flounced back into the living room as soon as her father had gone upstairs. 'Mum, can't you get him to change his mind?'

'Your dad's right, Fiona, it would be nice for us to see in the New Year with Granny and Grandpa Carswell. We've never done that before.'

'Does it *have* to be the New Year that I've been invited to a proper party for the first time?'

'There'll be other times, darling.'

'But I wanted it to be *this* time,' Fiona wailed, her face crumpling. 'Dad's a . . . a Neanderthal!' she sobbed, then spun round and ran from the room.

'*Definitely* a pigeroonie of a day,' Rachel said aloud to the empty room.

* * *

'I might have known it,' Martin fumed. 'She's been sulking around the place with a face like a wet weekend ever since I told her that we were going away. She's staying out deliberately, just to worry us.'

It was the evening before they were due to drive down to the Lake District, and Fiona, out with her friends, was late home. It had been a good half-hour beyond the usual time for her return before Rachel and Martin, both busy getting organised for an early-morning start, had realised that she still hadn't come in.

'She's only thirty minutes late, Martin. We can't treat her as if she's still a toddler.'

'We can if she insists on behaving like one. I don't know . . . she used to be such an easy, obedient child. What's gone wrong?'

'Nothing's gone wrong,' Rachel argued, though she was feeling just as uneasy as he was. Fiona never stayed out later than half past ten, and she knew that they had to be up early the next day. 'She's a teenager, that's all. And from what I've heard, a lot of girls her age are much more rebellious than our Fiona.'

'Who's she with?'

'Alma, I suppose, and Beth, and the usual crowd. They've probably gone to Cardosi's the same as they always do after they've been at the pictures or whatever. They've got talking over a coffee and forgotten the time. Where are you going?'

'To fetch the phone book. I'm going to phone this Cardosi's to see if she's there.'

'They won't know who you're talking about.'

'I'm sure they will, since she seems to spend more time there than in her own home. And if I can't run her to ground there, I'm going to start phoning round all her friends.'

Rachel followed him into the hall, where he was thumbing through the phone book. 'Martin, you'll only embarrass her.'

'That wouldn't be a bad thing. What if she's lying in some alley, or worse? Would you fret about me embarrassing her by trying to find her then?'

'Don't be silly,' Rachel said sharply, though the picture his words painted sent a stab of panic through her. 'You're being over-protective. Fathers always are with daughters.'

'That's because daughters are female and females are . . . ah!' Martin had found the number he wanted. He dialled, and then waited with growing impatience.

'Damn it, isn't anyone going to answer the phone? Answer it!' he yelped at the receiver, shaking it.

'They're busy. It's a very popular place.'

'I know one person who might not be going there again,' Martin said grimly. 'Not if I have anything to . . . Hello? Now listen carefully, please. I'm looking for a young girl . . .'

'Martin!' Rachel said, horrified, just as a key rattled in the lock and the front door opened.

'Never mind, she's here.' Martin dropped the receiver back into its cradle as Fiona came in. 'Where have you been? It's after eleven!'

'Sorry. We got talking.'

'Ten-thirty, that's when you're supposed to be home.'

'But that's only during term time, Dad. There's no school tomorrow.'

'No, but we're planning to leave early to try to beat the holiday traffic. I told you that before you went out.'

'That's all right; it won't take me a minute to pack. I'll do it before I go to bed.'

'Fiona, it's difficult enough to get you up in the mornings when you've had a full night's sleep!'

'I'll get up in time, okay?'

'Don't you shout at me, young lady.'

Fiona threw her arms out in a gesture of helplessness, then said quietly, and with an obvious effort, 'Dad, I'm sorry I'm late and I promise you that I'll be packed and up in time to leave early tomorrow morning. All right?'

'She can't say more than that, Martin. And if we're going to stand here arguing, then nobody's going to be able to get up and out early.'

'Oh, have it your own way,' he said, and stomped upstairs. Mother and daughter looked at each other.

'What's wrong with him these days?' Fiona wanted to know.

'I think he's just got a lot on his mind. And he worries about you when you're late in.'

'There's no need. I'm fine. I'd better go and get that packing done before I go to bed.'

'Fancy a mug of cocoa first? And a crumpet? I've got raspberry jam,' Rachel said, knowing that her daughter could never refuse raspberry jam.

There was something different about Fiona. Rachel had sensed it when the girl first came into the house, but in the kitchen, where the light was brighter, she could see it. Her daughter's blue eyes were brighter than usual and there was an air of excitement about her.

'Where were you tonight?' Rachel asked casually as she heated milk for the cocoa. 'The cinema?'

'Just walking about, and talking.' Fiona was giving all her attention to spreading jam on the crumpets.

'Who with?'

'Alma and the rest of them. D'you want your crumpet folded, or rolled up.'

'Rolled, of course.'

'Mum, can I ask you something?'

222

'Go ahead.'

'Are you and Dad . . . are things all right?'

Rachel almost spilled the mugs of cocoa she was setting on the kitchen table. 'Of course everything's all right. What makes you ask a thing like that?'

Fiona flushed. 'It's just that something's changed. Things have been different since you and Auntie Cara found each other.'

'That's nonsense.'

Fiona put the plates down by the mugs and drew a chair in to the table. 'I'm not a child, Mum; you know that, even if Dad doesn't yet. He's scared that now you've found a twin sister you didn't know you had, the rest of us won't matter so much to you.'

'That's nonsense!' Rachel said again. Then, as her daughter said nothing, but just kept on looking at her, 'Is that what you and the boys think too?'

'I don't.' Fiona took a bite of crumpet, then said, 'And I'm sure Ian and Graham don't. We all like Auntie Cara and Uncle Angus. But Dad . . . it's different with him, isn't it? You chose each other, and for all these years you didn't really have anyone else but each other, did you?'

'And you and Ian and Graham, and your two Grans and Grandpas, and Auntie Chrissie.' Rachel pushed a piece of kitchen paper across the table. 'We had lots of people, and you've got jam on your chin.'

Scorning the towel, Fiona felt around with the tip of a finger until she located the jam. She wiped it from her chin and then licked her finger. 'What I mean is, we're the younger generation and they're the older generation. The only people you and Dad had in your own generation were each other, apart from friends. Then suddenly you have a twin sister, and it's great for you, it really is, Mum . . . but I think Dad's scared because now he's

223

having to share you. And he's scared in case Auntie Cara gets a bigger share of you than he does.'

'I'm not a piece of cake. People can be shared over and over again without anyone having to get less.'

'Dad doesn't seem to understand that. Between you and me,' Fiona said solemnly, 'I think he's feeling a bit insecure.'

'If you're right, then that's all the more reason for us all to behave as though going to the Lake District with him tomorrow is what we really want. Right?'

The girl sighed. 'Right,' she agreed reluctantly, popping the last bite of crumpet into her mouth and washing it down with the rest of her cocoa.

'See you tomorrow then, all bright and happy. Off you go and I'll clear this lot up.'

''Night, Mum.' Fiona gave her a hug, and went to the door, where she hesitated. 'Mum?'

'What?'

'Just . . . sorry about being late and worrying you both.'

'That's all right, pet. We weren't all that worried,' Rachel lied. 'We know we can trust you to be sensible.'

Fiona had taken hold of the door handle; now she released it and turned round again. 'Mum . . .'

'Yes?'

'Nothing. See you in the morning.'

21

The New Year visit to the senior Carswells was not a success. It rained all the time and the boys, unable to get out much, were restless. Although Martin's parents were kind in their own way, they were old-fashioned, of the view that children should be seen and not heard, and unused to sharing their immaculate home and their comfortable lives with so many people at one time.

Rachel and Martin had great difficulty in keeping the two boys occupied as quietly as possible, and Fiona was so mopey that her grandmother became concerned.

'Are you sure she's not ill?' she asked Rachel. 'Girls going through . . . I mean, girls of her age sometimes suffer from all sorts of problems.'

'She's fine. Fiona was always quieter than the boys.'

'But not as quiet as she is at the moment, dear.'

'She's sulking, Mother,' Martin said. 'She wanted to go to a friend's Hogmanay party and she couldn't, that's all. Pay no attention.'

'If I were you, Rachel,' her mother-in-law said, 'I would put her onto a spoonful of malt and cod liver oil every morning. It's very bracing and energising. That's what I gave my children. It'll have her back to her usual sunny little self in no time.'

As soon as they arrived back home, the boys, who had been sniping at each other all the way from the Lake District, rushed to their shared bedroom to play, while Fiona settled down to phone her friend Alma. Martin, who had scarcely said a word during the journey, followed Rachel into the kitchen.

'Coffee or tea?'

'Coffee, and make it strong. It was a disaster, wasn't it?'

'What was?'

'For God's sake, Rachel,' he said irritably, 'don't be so condescending! I'm talking about the visit. It was a bloody disaster.'

'You couldn't help the rain, nobody could. The kids were quite well behaved, really, and your parents did their best, but . . .'

'But they're not Cara and Angus, is that what you were going to say? You're right there. Cara would have thrown the door open and invited Ian and Graham to run in and out at will and make mud pies and splash in puddles. She'd have laughed at muddy footprints in her kitchen and found all sorts of fun things for everyone to do. As for Angus – he'd have got out the whisky and encouraged me to drink myself into oblivion. And that wouldn't have been a bad thing, come to think of it.'

'Of course they wouldn't have done any of those things!'

'They'd certainly have found some way of making a wet holiday in the country a lot more exciting than we did.'

'Mum . . .' Fiona said from the doorway. 'Is it all right if I go over to Alma's for a few hours?'

'Why not? Have some pleasure for a while. You've earned it. Everyone's earned it but me.'

'Martin! On you go, love. Be back for ten-thirty.'

'Okay.' Fiona hesitated, looking from one of her parents to the other, then asked diffidently, 'Are you all right?'

'Of course we are. Dad's just tired from all that driving. Off you go, and wish Alma and her parents a Happy New Year from us.

'She's worried about us,' Rachel said when the girl had gone.

'Worried? Why should she be?'

'Because things aren't the way they used to be. She's worried in case we've stopped caring for each other.'

'What?' Martin was shocked. 'But that's nonsense! We love each other, and the kids. Don't we?'

'Of course we do. I told her that.'

'It's just that . . . you've changed.'

The kettle had boiled. He spooned coffee and sugar into a mug, filled it with water, then went to the fridge. 'Blast, no milk.'

'Here you are.' Rachel took a bottle from the bag she had carried in from the car. 'Your mother gave us bread and milk before we left, remember?' Then, as he took the bottle from her, 'Tell me how I've changed.'

'You're not the person I married, for one thing. I married Rachel Elizabeth Flora Nesbitt, only child of Doreen and Frank Nesbitt. And then one day she suddenly turned into Rachel Elizabeth Flora Moodie, twin sister to Cara, father unknown and mother vanished.'

Rachel winced at the stark description. 'That doesn't make me a different person.'

'How can you say that? Oh, damn it!' Martin had poured a large dollop of milk into the mug, more than it could hold, and now hot milky coffee splashed over his hand.

'It's all right, I'll see to it.' Rachel snatched up a cloth and began dabbing at him. 'It's not burned, is it?'

'No, it's not.' He pulled his hand away and picked up the mug, moving to the other side of the kitchen. 'If you had to find a long-lost sister, why couldn't it have been someone more like you?'

'What's wrong with Cara?'

'Her husband, for one thing.'

'Angus is a decent, hard-working man.'

'He's a loud-mouthed oaf. And that wasn't just a Christmas kiss he gave you. It was more than that.'

'You're surely not jealous of Angus?' Rachel asked in amazement.

'Have I got anything to be jealous about? Sisters – twins – probably go for the same type of man.'

'No, they don't,' Rachel said firmly.

Martin banged the mug down on the counter. 'I'm going to have a bath,' he said.

'The water hasn't had a chance to heat up yet.'

'Then I shall have a cold bath,' he growled, and walked out of the room. Rachel sighed, then went to phone Doreen, who would be waiting for a report on their trip.

'My mother used to tell me that we should never let the sun go down on our wrath,' Rachel said as they sat side by side in bed, reading.

It had been a wretched evening. The boys had appeared downstairs briefly, to eat, then hurried back to their bedroom, where they were rediscovering the Christmas presents they had been forced to leave behind when they went to the Lake District, and with Fiona at her friend's house, there hadn't even been the usual throb of pop music from her room. Rachel and Martin had scarcely exchanged more than a few words.

Now, he turned a page of his book. 'Which mother would that be?'

'The only mother I have.' Her patience suddenly snapped. 'The only mother I have ever had and ever will have, damn you!' She slapped the book out of his hand so hard that it flew across the room, hit the wardrobe, and fell to the floor to lie spread-eagled on the carpet. They both stared at it, open-mouthed.

Rachel was horrified – she had never in her life done anything as violent before. Then, when Martin said plaintively, 'Now I've lost my place,' the humour of the situation caught her by the throat.

She started to laugh, and once she had started she couldn't stop. After a while Martin joined in, and they ended up leaning against each other as the laughter faded into helpless giggling.

'I haven't laughed like that in ages,' Rachel gasped when the roars of mirth finally petered out. She mopped her streaming eyes on the edge of the sheet.

'Nor me. We should do it more often. But next time . . .' Martin turned his head and kissed the angle of her jaw, '*I* get to hit *your* book across the room.'

'Sorry about that.'

'It's all right.' His lips moved to her ear lobe, then down the side of her neck in a series of soft little kisses that sent a tingle of excited anticipation through her. 'I wasn't enjoying it anyway,' he said, his voice muffled in the hollow between her neck and her shoulder.

'We should vow never to quarrel again,' she said as he hooked the strap of her nightgown with a practised finger, drawing it over the curve of her shoulder.

'I agree.' He turned away to switch off his bedside lamp. She did the same, and then moved into his waiting arms.

'Martin?'

'Mmm?'

'Is Cara more kissable than I am?'

'Let me check.' He kissed her, then said, 'Point system?'

'Point system.'

'She's six out of ten. You're thirty-three out of ten.'

'Good. Angus isn't very special either.'

'I knew that already,' Martin said smugly, sliding the strap off her other shoulder.

They made love with the easy enjoyment of two people who belonged together. At last, sated and drowsy, they curled up together and soon they were both asleep.

'Oh good,' Kathleen said when Rachel phoned to tell her that she had been asked to help with the costumes for the school production of *The Boyfriend*. 'Beads and fringes and 1920s pizzazz. Count me in. Is Fiona taking part?'

'She'd love to, but with her mock exams in February and the real thing in May, she's got enough on her hands.'

'Poor kid; I thought schooldays were supposed to be the happiest days of their lives?'

'They're too weighed down with studying for exams, then sitting exams, to be happy. But at least she's got the Abba concert to look forward to. Only another two weeks to go.'

'Is that handsome young man who played opposite her last time going to be in *The Boyfriend*?'

'Robbie McNaughton? I don't know. Are you free to visit the school next Wednesday? Lizbeth Beattie wants to talk to us about the costumes.'

The cast were already rehearsing when they went into the hall, and almost at once Rachel spotted Robbie on the stage. Later, passing by when she and Kathleen were talking to Lizbeth, he smiled and waved to her.

When they were finished, they drove in Kathleen's

little car from the school to Paisley Cross, where they had arranged to meet Cara in Cochran's tea room for morning coffee.

She arrived just after they had found a table. 'Thank goodness for you two,' she said, dropping into a chair. 'I've got the January blues. If I had my way I would make it illegal to have New Year's Day a week after Christmas. I'd have it at the end of January instead. That way we could enjoy Christmas, and then wind down a bit instead of having to rush into Ne'erday. And all through January we would have the New Year festivities to look forward to. Don't you think that would be much better than waking up on the first day of January knowing that we have the three worst months in the year stretching ahead of us with nothing to feel good about?'

'If we had Ne'erday at the end of January, it would only be a week after Burns' Night,' Kathleen pointed out.

'You're right. What about having Burns' Night and New Year at the same time? Then everyone could join in and have fun, instead of just the Rabbie fans.'

'I'd go along with that.' Kathleen signalled the waitress and gave their order. 'Cara for Scottish Prime Minister,' she said when they were alone again.

'God no, I'd hate to be a Prime Minister. But you can make me Minister for Enjoyment if you like.'

'That's an idea. Why don't we have a Minister for Enjoyment? We have ministers for everything else.'

'I'll vote for that. There isn't much for Angus to do at this time of year apart from planning ahead, so he's around the house almost all the time just now. Oh thanks, dear. I wouldn't mind that,' Cara said, spooning sugar into her coffee, 'but every time I settle down with a magazine and a box of chocs, he decides that he wants a cup of tea, or that he's hungry. And the place is covered with catalogues and sketches of gardens he'll be doing once the weather improves.'

'You could help us with the costumes for *The Boyfriend* if you like,' Kathleen suggested. 'There's enough work for three.'

'No thanks. I'll help out if needed but I prefer to work on smaller things, like baby clothes. I get bored easily.'

'I thought I might spring clean the boys' room, but just one look inside put me right off,' Rachel confessed, 'so I shut the door and tiptoed away. Perhaps when a nice sunny spring day comes along I'll be able to drum up enough enthusiasm to actually go into the room and strip it to the bone.'

'If you never go inside, does that mean that they make their own beds, and change them?' Kathleen wanted to know.

'Good grief, no! If I left it to those two, the bedclothes would probably end up crawling down the stairs by themselves, begging to be put into the washing machine. I've perfected a way of reaching, making and changing their beds by touch and instinct alone – it's a mother thing,' Rachel added modestly when Kathleen looked impressed.

'I'll come over some time and help you to turn out their room if you want,' Cara offered. 'I don't mind that sort of work.'

'It's good of you, but I'd rather leave it until the better weather comes along. I just don't have the energy or the inclination at the moment,' Rachel said, then rushed on to talk about the materials she and Kathleen would need to buy for the costumes they had just agreed to make.

Ever since she and Martin had quarrelled after the disastrous New Year visit to his parents, she had worked hard at making sure that it wouldn't happen again – hence the coffee meetings. They meant that she could spend time with Cara, without Martin having to be involved.

Cara invited Fiona to her house for tea on the day of the Abba concert, and offered to take her back to Barrhead for the night afterwards.

'The weather's a bit doubtful,' she explained to Rachel. 'Angus is picking us up after the concert, and if it's snowing, which it probably will be, it would be easier to drive straight back home instead of having to call in at your house first.' It made sense, as even Martin had to agree when February 12th turned out to be snowy.

Fiona arrived home the following day, cheeks glowing with excitement and eyes like stars, desperate to share every minute of the evening with her mother. She followed Rachel around the house, chattering like a budgie, and even stood outside the locked bathroom door at one point, talking through the panels.

She described in minute detail the packed theatre, the electric atmosphere, and the excitement when the backing group came onstage. 'Then the theatre went dark and then lights began to flash round and round, and there was this noise like a helicopter landing, and it got louder and louder, and then suddenly there they were, the four of them, running onto the stage and going straight into the first song. And Mum, they were so beautiful, and so *fabulous!*'

She listed every single song and everything that had happened, even to the moment when she emerged from the theatre, dazed and ecstatic, into the lamp-lit Glasgow street outside the Apollo Theatre.

'And the snow was coming down, and guess what, Mum? There was this huge lorry thing – Robbie said it was called a pantechnicon – waiting outside the theatre;

I mean, you could almost have put our whole house into it! And right across the side of it was "Abba", in huge letters.' She drew the letters out in the air with one finger. 'It was so *fabulous!*'

'What did you just say, Fiona?' Rachel had been folding one of Martin's newly ironed shirts, but now she put it down slowly.

'I said that "Abba" was written across the side of the pantechnicon, just the one word in enormous letters. It was really classy!'

'No, before that. You said that Robbie told you what the big lorry was called.'

Fiona gave a slight gasp. Her blue eyes widened, then fell away from her mother's. 'No I didn't.'

'Yes, you did.'

'Then it was an accident. I meant Auntie Cara told me what it was called.'

'Fiona, was Robbie McNaughton at the concert with you last night?'

The girl bit her lip, stabbed at the carpet with the toe of one shoe, and finally nodded.

'Oh, Fiona! You know what your father said . . .'

'It's not fair! Auntie Cara's the only one who understands,' Fiona burst out.

'So she wasn't at the concert with you?'

Again, Fiona shook her head. 'It was just me and Robbie, but she met us outside afterwards, and took us back to Barrhead for some supper. Then Uncle Angus took Robbie home while I told Auntie Cara all about the concert so's she'd know what to say if you and Dad asked her.'

'How could she do this? She knows that your father thinks you're too young for boyfriends, and that we want you to concentrate on your exams. She had absolutely no right to go behind our backs!'

'She was just trying to make me happy. She knows I like Robbie and she can't understand why we shouldn't see each other.'

'Have you two been meeting at Cara's house?'

'Once or twice. But mostly in Cardosi's,' Fiona added hurriedly, 'with the others.'

'But your father said—'

'What does he know about it? What does he know about anything?' Her fists clenched, and tears sprang to her eyes. 'What does he know about loving someone? He doesn't care about my happiness, and Auntie Cara does! I want to go and live with her and Uncle Angus!' And she ran from the room and up the stairs.

Almost as soon as her daughter's bedroom door slammed shut overhead Rachel was dialling Cara's number.

'Rachel, nice to hear from you,' Cara said happily. 'Has Fiona been telling you about last night? It was fantastic, with all those kids going mad with excitement, and the music, and the way they used the lighting. I've never seen lights like that before. Rachel, I wish you could have been there.'

'That's funny,' Rachel said coldly. 'I was just about to say the same to you.'

There was a slight pause, and then Cara said tentatively, 'You were going to say that you wished you had been there?'

'No, I wish that *you* had been at the Apollo with my daughter. I really, really do, Cara. After all, that was what we had arranged, what Martin and I thought was happening.'

'She *told* you?'

'Robbie McNaughton's name slipped out in all the excitement.'

'Oh. I don't suppose there's much use in me telling you that I suddenly came down with this bug, and Robbie agreed to step in at the last minute?'

'No use at all. I trusted you, Cara. Martin trusted you.'

'For goodness' sake, Rachel, Fiona's not a little girl any more and Robbie's a pleasant, intelligent, caring young man. Fiona could do a lot worse, believe me. Why should they have to meet in secret?'

'Robbie's two years older than she is . . .'

'And Angus is five years older than me. It's no big deal.'

Rachel glared at the receiver and then put it back to her ear. 'And Martin wants her to concentrate on her exams. They're important.'

'Oh, phooey to Martin, it's high time he stopped playing the Victorian father. Rachel, whether you and Martin like it or not, your daughter's a young woman now, with her future in front of her, and her own ideas about what she wants to do with it. It's her life, not Martin's. Does he know — do either of you know, come to that — that she would rather go to commercial college and learn how to do shorthand and touch typing than struggle to get a university degree? Do you really care about what Fiona wants, or it is only what Martin wants for her that matters?'

'That's not fair, Cara. Of course he's not going to force her to do something against her own wishes. He just wants her to have as many options available as possible. If she's clever enough to gain a university place, then it would make sense for her to think about it very seriously. And if she doesn't manage it, then I'm sure that Martin would be happy to see her going to commercial college.'

'How generous of him.'

Rachel realised from the bite in her sister's voice that

the conversation was going nowhere. 'Cara, I want you to promise me that you won't do anything like that behind our backs again.'

'I have nothing planned.'

'And you won't encourage any more meetings between Fiona and Robbie McNaughton?'

'How would it be if I just didn't *tell* you about any meetings between them? If I know about the meetings, that is, which I probably wouldn't.'

'That's not enough, Cara. You have to do as I ask!'

There was a pause before Cara, her tone slightly subdued, said, 'You're right. And I will.'

'Thank you.'

'Don't mention it,' Cara said, and then, cheerfully, 'how are you fixed for coffee on Tuesday morning?'

Replacing the receiver a moment later, Rachel bit her lip. She suspected that Cara had given in too quickly, probably for the sake of peace.

She was going to have to keep a closer eye on the relationship between Fiona and her sister.

22

The remainder of February passed by fairly calmly, much to Rachel's relief, and then March arrived, bringing with it the hope that the worst of the winter was finally over. Once the excitement of the Abba concert died down Fiona became very quiet, and Rachel started to worry about her.

'She doesn't seem all that interested in anything at the moment,' she fretted to Martin. Then, glancing at the ceiling, as Abba began to soar into 'Dancing Queen' yet again, 'And she's not eating properly.'

'Exam nerves. Everyone gets them.'

'Yesterday I caught her struggling up the stairs with that little coffee table, and when I asked where she was taking it she looked at it as if she'd never seen it before and said she thought it was a book. D'you think I should take her to the doctor?'

'Exams,' Martin said again. 'Don't you remember what it was like when you were going through them? I certainly do. I once tried to walk through a closed door because I was too busy going over possible maths questions to notice. I got a lump the size of a hen's egg on my forehead.'

'Perhaps we're putting too much pressure on her. Perhaps she's not university material,' Rachel said nervously, recalling what Cara had said.

'We won't know that until she gets the result of the exams, will we?' he said patiently, as though explaining something for the umpteenth time to someone of limited intelligence. 'She did quite well in the mock exams, and I'm confident that she can do even better in the real thing.'

'If she's not eating properly in a week's time,' Rachel said, 'I'm going to take her to the doctor, just in case.'

'No, you're not!' Fiona said a week later, when her mother broached the subject.

'But you're not your usual self, love, and Dad and I are worried about you. Don't do that,' Rachel begged as Fiona grabbed a lock of hair and started chewing the end of it. 'It's very bad for your hair.'

'It's my hair. And I don't need to see the doctor, honest.'

'Then I'm going to get you a tonic. I think you're studying too hard.'

'I have to, if I'm going to pass my exams,' Fiona argued. 'I'll be late for school if I don't go now.' She made for the door, and then hesitated. 'Mum . . . ?'

'Yes?'

'Nothing,' Fiona said, and went out.

A few days later she came home from school earlier than usual. Rachel, pinning box pleats on a skirt for *The Boyfriend*, went into the hall when she heard the front door open.

Fiona was hovering at the foot of the stairs.

'What are you doing home at this hour?'

'I don't feel well.'

She didn't look well; her face was pinched and her eyes huge. Rachel put a hand on her forehead.

'You don't seem to have a temperature. D'you have a headache, or a sore throat?' Then, when Fiona shook her head to both questions, 'It's not your time of the month, is it?'

Tears suddenly flooded Fiona's eyes, but again she shook her head.

'Look, love, why don't you go upstairs and get into bed, and I'll bring a hot drink up. All right?'

'Tomato soup.' It was Fiona's favourite, and the only food she was interested in when she was under the weather.

'All right, tomato soup. Off you go.' Rachel watched her daughter mount the stairs, her shoulders slumped and her feet dragging from step to step as though she didn't have the energy to lift them high enough, and then went into the kitchen. She had a container of Kathleen's home-made tomato soup in the freezer compartment of the refrigerator, but it would take too long to defrost and heat it. Instead, she opened a tin, and while it heated she toasted a slice of bread and cut it into fingers. When the soup was steaming hot she poured it into two mugs and assembled everything on a tray.

Fiona was on her bed instead of in it, fully dressed and sitting with her knees drawn up to her chin and her arms clasped around them.

'I brought some for myself as well.' Rachel kept her voice determinedly cheerful. 'Aunt Kathleen was here this morning, working on *The Boyfriend* costumes with me, and I just kept on working after she left. So I haven't had my lunch yet. Why didn't you get comfy in bed?'

'I don't need to go to bed. I'm not ill.' Fiona reached out for her soup, but instead of drinking from the mug she nursed it in both hands, holding it just beneath her chin so that the steam wreathed around her face.

'You've not looked well for a while now. When we've had our soup I'm going to phone the surgery and arrange an appointment. I'm free tomorrow morning; I could take you then.'

'I'm old enough to go to the doctor on my own. I don't need to be taken by my mother.'

'It's the exams, isn't it? You're worrying about them.'

The girl shook her head so vigorously that her long curly hair, so like Cara's, whipped about her face. 'I'm not worrying about the exams. I don't need to worry, because I'm not going to sit them.'

'Of course you're going to sit them!'

Fiona set her mug carefully on the bedside table and picked up Raggedy Ann from her usual place on the bed. 'I'm not, Mum. There's no point.'

'What are you talking about? You did quite well in your mocks, and when we went to the last Parents' Evening all your teachers told us that you've got every chance of passing the O Grade exams. Even if you don't get good marks, at least you've tried. Think what your father's going to say,' Rachel appealed when her daughter said nothing.

Fiona shrugged, and shot her a smile that was more a cynical twist of the lips than anything else. Then, head bent over the rag doll, 'He's going to have more to worry about than that.'

'What do you mean?'

'I mean,' Fiona said, 'that I'm not going to sit the exams because I'm not going to university. Not for a while at any rate, and probably not ever. I'm going to get married.'

'What?'

'I'm old enough. I don't need anyone's permission to get married.'

'Don't be ridiculous! People don't just get married on a whim!'

'They do when they're pregnant,' Fiona said, and then she lowered her face down on to the floppy rag doll's yellow wool hair, and burst into tears.

'But you can't be pregnant.' Rachel could only just hear her own voice through the ringing sound that had started in her head. 'That's just silly.'

'Mum, I am!' Raggedy Ann's head, arms and legs twitched and flopped agitatedly. Fiona's face couldn't be seen at all, and it was as though the wet muffled voice came from the doll itself.

'We'll go to the doctor. I'll phone now and insist on getting an appointment this afternoon. You'll feel better once you know—'

'I've been to the doctor already. I went two days ago.'

'And what did he say?'

'He said,' Fiona roared, tossing the doll down, 'that I'm *pregnant*! That's what I'm trying to *tell* you!'

'It's Robbie McNaughton's, isn't it?'

Fiona stopped crying long enough to glare at her mother through wet red eyes. 'Of course it is! D'you think I make a habit of this with every boy in Paisley?' she asked irritably, and then, as Rachel moved to sit on the bed, the tears began to flow again. 'Oh, Mum!'

'It's all right, darling. We'll work it out, I promise.' But how could they do that, Rachel wondered, rocking her sobbing daughter. This wasn't a scratched knee or a minor disappointment. If Fiona was right – and Rachel was beginning to realise that the girl knew exactly what she was talking about – it was a mind-numbing, life-changing event, something that would affect all of them, not just Fiona. At least the ringing noise in her head was easing away, making it easier for her to think.

'Does Robbie know?' she asked when her daughter had finally cried herself empty.

'Of c-course he kn-nows.' Fiona clambered down from the bed and went to her dressing table. She picked up an open box of tissues and climbed slowly back on to the bed. 'And he wants to marry me and I want to marry him, and we're going to keep this baby, so don't start talking about terminations!' She hauled a handful of tissues from the box and used them to mop her eyes, blow her nose and wipe her face before adding, 'It's all decided. You and Daddy can't stop me.'

Daddy! What was Martin going to say? What was her mother going to say, Rachel thought, panic mounting. What would Martin's parents say?

'Robbie wanted to come and tell you about the baby himself, but I said to wait until I'd decided the best time to do it. Then this morning at school it all just got too much.' Fiona helped herself to another handful of tissues. 'I just wanted to come home!'

'Of course you did.'

'I've run out of tissues.'

'I'll bring some more,' Rachel said, and then, as the back door banged and Graham shouted, 'Mu-um? from the hall, she jumped up and collected the two mugs. 'Why don't you get into bed and have a sleep? I'll tell the boys you're not feeling well and they've to leave you in peace.'

'Could you bring me a cup of tea and something to eat? I'm starving. It's horrible not being able to eat in the mornings.'

'I know,' Rachel said with feeling. 'But it usually goes away after the first three months.' Then, as she reached the door, 'Er . . . how long . . . ?'

'Nearly three months,' Fiona said.

As she went downstairs to where the boys were arguing amiably in the kitchen, Rachel's mind counted swiftly back. Three months – some time around Christmas and New Year? Then it hit her; the night Fiona had been upset because she had to go to the Lake District for New Year instead of celebrating with her friends. The night she had worried them by staying out late. The night she must have run to Robbie for comfort.

The night, perhaps, when her parents had, without realising it, thrown her into his arms.

When Rachel took a tray upstairs half an hour later Fiona was in bed with Raggedy Ann tucked in beside her. Her eyes were dry but her face was still swollen; she looked so young and so vulnerable that Rachel's heart almost broke. Her daughter, her firstborn, was still a child. She shouldn't have to face what lay ahead of her.

But now that the secret was out, Fiona herself had made a miraculous recovery. She bounced up in bed, almost back to her old self. 'Thanks, Mum.'

'I brought a new box of tissues too.'

'I don't think I'll need them now that I've had that cry. It's been desperate to get out ever since I saw the doctor.' She started to eat as Rachel collected the snowdrift of used tissues.

'You should have told me before.'

'I couldn't find the right time. But at least you know now,' the girl said with the relieved air of someone who has finally handed over a burden.

'How long have you been worrying about this?'

'Not all that long. I kept thinking that it was just the strain of studying and worrying about getting good exam results that had made me late.'

'Fiona, you and Robbie are too young to get married. I know it's legal at your age,' Rachel added swiftly as her daughter began to argue, 'but think of the practical side

244

of it. You're still at school, and he's going to Art College. What are you going to live on? Babies cost money, you know. There are clothes, and nappies, and all sorts of things.'

'Robbie's going to wait for another year now. I wish he didn't have to, but he's made up his mind. He'll get a job, and so will I, after the baby's born,' Fiona said proudly through a mouthful of tuna sandwich, 'and then I can support us while he goes to college. Lots of women do that nowadays.'

'But . . .' Rachel started, and then bit back the words, *you're not a woman*.

'Don't worry, Mum, we'll be all right. We really, truly love each other. It's not just a silly crush.'

'Fiona, how are we going to tell your father?'

'I'll think of something.'

'Best leave it to me. You've been through enough.'

'Mu-um!' A familiar roar came wafting up from the hall.

'I'd better go and see what Graham wants. Try to have a nap. I'll bring up some dinner later, and I'll make sure nobody disturbs you.'

'Thanks.' Fiona took a final mouthful of sandwich and a final gulp of tea before relinquishing the tray. 'Crying makes you sleepy,' she said. Then, as Rachel opened the door, 'Mum?'

'Yes, love?'

'I'm sorry, Mum, I really am.'

'Don't worry about it,' Rachel said, and went out.

No sense in both of us worrying about it, she thought as she went downstairs. But how on earth was she going to tell Martin? And her mother? Her stomach churned at the very thought of Doreen's reaction to the news.

* * *

Martin's first reaction, when he heard that Fiona wasn't well, was to want to go up to her room.

'I'd leave her for now,' Rachel said hastily. 'She's sleeping, and that's the best thing for her. I said I'd take some food up later.'

'If she's not better by the morning you'd best send for the doctor,' he said firmly, then, 'there isn't anything you want to see on television tonight, is there?'

If only life was as simple as that, Rachel thought, while aloud she said, 'No, nothing.'

'Good. There's a football match I'd like to see. I've been looking forward to watching it all day.'

'When are we going to tell Daddy?' Fiona asked when her mother took a tray to her room. The sleep had done her good; she was sitting up in bed, her eyes clear and her hair tousled about her face. She looked heart-wrenchingly young.

'Tonight, when the boys have gone to bed.'

'I'll phone Robbie and get him to come over.'

'No, not yet,' Rachel said swiftly. 'I think it should just be the three of us at first. Your dad's going to get a shock, Fiona,' she rushed on when the girl started to argue, 'and if Robbie's here, he'll only start blaming him. We need to decide what to do for the best first.'

'Robbie and I have already decided, Mum. I told you—'

'I know you have, but we still need to talk it over. There might be another way out of this . . . situation.'

'All right, but it's my place to tell Dad,' Fiona insisted. 'I'll come down once the boys have gone to bed.'

When she had made sure that Graham and Ian were settled for the night Rachel looked in on her daughter, only to find that she had fallen asleep again, her arms wrapped about Raggedy Ann. She looked so peaceful that Rachel hadn't the heart to waken her. Instead, she went down to the living room, where Martin was absorbed in the football game on television.

'Martin, can I have a word?'

'Can it wait until later?' he asked without looking away from the screen.

'Now. It has to be now.'

'Surely it can keep for another hour or so!' His voice was irritated, his eyes still on the screen.

'Well yes, I suppose it can keep for about six months, but not a minute longer than that,' she said, and waited, wondering if he had heard what she'd just said. He had.

'What d'you mean, six months?'

'I mean that that's when our daughter's going to have a baby.'

Unfortunately, someone on the small screen scored a goal just as she spoke. Martin jumped forward in his chair, beaming, and then, as the roar of the crowd abated and the game continued, he fell back into the chair and said, his voice dazed, 'What did you just say?'

'I said . . .' she crossed to the set and turned it off, then spoke into the sudden silence, '. . . that our daughter's pregnant and she's going to have a baby in about six months and we should really have a talk about it. Tonight, if possible.'

'Oh my God!' Martin clutched at the arms of the chair. 'It's not true. It can't be true. Not Fiona. She's too young.'

'She's sixteen, Martin. Old enough to get married.'

'Yes, but only in law. She's still a schoolgirl, a child. I won't have her getting married . . . she's got too much to do with her life!' Then, as Rachel said nothing, 'You're serious, aren't you?'

'I wish to God I was joking. Of course I'm serious.'

'Whose is it?'

'Robbie McNaughton's.'

'But I told her to stop seeing him until after her exams!'

'Sometimes girls of sixteen don't listen to their fathers. Sometimes they follow their own inclinations.'

'Oh my God,' Martin said again. He got up and went to the window, peering out as though worried in case some of the neighbours had overheard. Then he spun round to face Rachel. 'Where did we go wrong?'

'I don't think we did. It's just one of those things.'

'It's not just one of those things at all!' Disbelief and horror were giving way to anger. 'It's Fiona we're talking about here. Our daughter. She's only sixteen and she's going to have a baby!'

'I know; I just told you that, Martin.'

'How long have you known?'

'Since she came home early from school this afternoon.'

'Why didn't you phone me? I'd have come home at once if you'd just phoned me!'

'You're always busy at work, and in any case, what she needed this afternoon was a good cry. She was in a terrible state, Martin.'

'I don't feel too chipper myself.' He ran a hand through his short dark hair. 'What are my parents going to say about this? And your mother – what's she going to say? And what about the exams?'

'I thought that that would be your main worry,' Fiona said from the doorway. She came into the room, wrapped in a fluffy dressing gown, looking from one to the other of her parents. 'Mum, I said that I wanted to tell Daddy myself.'

'You were sleeping, darling. I didn't want to disturb you.'

'For God's sake, Fiona,' Martin burst out, 'you're only sixteen!'

'Old enough to get married, and that's what we're going to do, so you don't have to worry about me. Robbie will look after me,' the girl said with touching dignity.

'Oh, really? And how does he plan to do that? What are you going to live on? Where are you going to stay? And another thing – do you have any idea of how much it costs to raise a child?' Martin stormed.

'We can live with his brother and sister-in-law. Their house is big enough. And Robbie's going to put college off for another year and get a job. Then next year I'll get a job so that he can go to Art School. When that happens, we'll have his student grant. We'll manage.'

'So you're going to throw away your chance of university, but you'll work to support him so that *he* can go to Art School? What d'you call that, Fiona? I'd say that it's

Women's Lib gone mad!' His voice was thick with sarcasm, and she flushed angrily.

'I want Robbie to do that course because he's really good, everyone says so. He needs to go further if he's got me and the baby to support. But it's different for me. I kept trying to tell you, Daddy, that I don't think I'm clever enough for university, but you wouldn't listen. Oh, I might get there if I work really hard and do well in my exams, but I'd probably have to struggle to keep up, and I don't want to struggle and then fail; I want to be a success at something I know I can do well.'

'And what do you see yourself doing well, tell me that? A shop assistant? An office girl?'

'I'm going to night school as soon as I can to study shorthand and typing and bookkeeping. I already do them at school and I enjoy them,' Fiona said calmly. Suddenly, she seemed to have grown up. It was as though impending motherhood had created a protective shield around her, Rachel thought, amazed. Instead of crying and shaking, she was standing up to her father.

'You deserve better than that!'

'What's wrong with being a good secretary or a good bookkeeper, or the best shorthand typist in the pool? What's wrong with being a wife and mother?'

'Nothing, for grown-ups!'

'As far as the law's concerned I *am* a grown-up. And this isn't just a whim, Daddy. I love Robbie and he loves me. Okay, we should have waited until he got through college and I finished school, but there's no sense in crying over spilt milk.'

'This is a lot more serious than spilt milk, young lady. In a year's time,' Martin said angrily, 'you might have gone off this boyfriend of yours and fallen for someone else. Or he'll have decided that you're too young and immature for him, and found someone of his own age. Have you thought of that?'

'Yes, and I know – we both know – that it won't happen.'

'You really think so? Well, I'll tell you something else that won't happen. You're not going to get married, that's what won't happen! I'm not going to stand by and—'

'Martin, please,' Rachel interceded. 'Fiona's trying to deal with this situation in a sensible way and we should be helping her. We need to sit down, the three of us, and talk about what to do next.'

He ran his fingers through his hair again, this time leaving it ruffled and spiky, the way it sometimes looked first thing in the morning. 'What on earth possessed you to do something so stupid, Fiona? We trusted you!'

'Maybe it was because I was tired of you and Mum quarrelling all the time!'

'Quarrelling? We don't quarrel!'

'You might not yell at each other like some parents do, but nothing's the same any more,' Fiona burst out. 'You're angry and upset all the time. You're angry with Mum because she wants to go on seeing Auntie Cara. You don't approve of her, or of Uncle Angus, and you wouldn't let me see Robbie when all we wanted was to be able to enjoy being with each other. D'you really want to know how it happened?'

'Fiona—'

'Remember last New Year?' the girl swept on, ignoring Rachel. 'When you decided that we had to spend it in the Lake District as a family, and you refused to let me see the new year in with my own friends? Remember the night I was out late? Well, I was with Robbie, and I was upset about having to go away, and he was so kind and gentle, and . . .' She hesitated, bit her lip, then said,

'Well, it just happened. I needed someone to care about me that night, and Robbie cared. I'm sorry to have let you down, but if you'd only been a bit less bossy and a bit more understanding it might not have happened. You just want everything to go on the way it was, Daddy, with Mum stuck at home looking after all of us, with no sister for her to talk to and laugh with, and me being your little girl until I suddenly turn into your clever university student daughter. You want to dip us all in bronze the way they do with baby shoes, so that you can keep us on the mantelpiece and we'll never change. That can't happen, Dad. Things *do* change, and people get older and fall in love and start to lead their own lives. You're always saying that people should take responsibility for their actions. Well, that's what I'm doing. This baby is mine and Robbie's. It's our responsibility, and we'll sort it!'

There was a short silence before Martin said ominously, 'I want a word with that young man!'

'And he wants to talk to you. I phoned him when I came downstairs just now, and he was going to come over at once, but I said no. I thought we needed some time on our own first,' Fiona said. 'He's coming over tomorrow afternoon, and his brother's coming with him so that we can all talk reasonably about the future. Our future, Daddy. Mine and Robbie's and our baby's.'

'We'll work it through together,' Rachel said when Fiona had gone back to bed. 'It'll be all right.'

'All right? You heard what she said about us quarrelling all the time. We never used to quarrel – not until you discovered that you were adopted. That's when everything started to go wrong. If Chrissie had kept her mouth shut, this appalling situation would never have happened.'

'How do we know that?' Rachel reeled under the sudden attack.

'You've been too busy thinking about your mysterious biological mother and welcoming Cara into your life – into *our* lives – to keep an eye on our children.'

'Cara has nothing to do with Fiona getting pregnant.'

'So you agree with Fiona that somehow, it's all my fault?'

'Of course I don't think that, and neither does Fiona. She's just upset – and frightened.'

'I've never been comfortable with the way Cara fusses over the girl. She lost her own daughter, and she and that husband of hers would love to have ours to take her place.'

'Martin, that's nonsense!'

'Haven't you noticed that they can scarcely take their eyes off her? They make more fuss of her than they do of the boys.'

'If they do, it's because she looks so like Alice. You've seen the photographs – they were the image of each other.'

'I wouldn't be in the least bit surprised if it turned out that Cara had encouraged Fiona to go on seeing this boy behind our backs,' Martin said hotly. Then, as Rachel opened her mouth to argue, only to shut it again, remembering the Abba concert, he pounced. 'I'm right, aren't I? I can see it in your face.'

'There's nothing to see.' Rachel fought back the impulse to throw herself at him and give him a good shaking. 'Fiona was right in one thing at least. We're quarrelling again.'

'No we're not. I don't quarrel,' he said loftily. 'I'm merely pointing out that you have to accept some responsibility for the mess our daughter's in now.'

'And you don't think that you could be just as responsible? You heard what she said earlier, Martin; sometimes you're too strict with her. You need to give her more freedom.'

He gave a short, angry laugh. 'You mean like letting her stay out later at night? She stayed out late that night, didn't she? And she came home pregnant! Remember telling me a while back that you thought that Fiona had a crush on someone? And when I said she was too young for that sort of thing you said, "Don't start worrying until you've something to worry about," didn't you? Well, Rachel, I took your advice. And do you know what? I've just bloody well started to worry. Only it's too late now, isn't it?'

For a long moment Rachel stared at him in silence. Suddenly the Martin she knew and loved, the Martin who should have worked with her to help their daughter through the crisis that had arisen, had changed.

'I wasn't pregnant when *we* got married,' she said at last. 'Isn't that strange?'

'That's because I had self-control, and respect for you and your parents. It's not strange at all.'

'No, I mean it's strange because I didn't *have* to marry you. I wonder why I bothered,' Rachel said, and walked out of the room.

Rachel and Martin scarcely spoke to each other in the morning. The boys, aware that there was something wrong, were subdued throughout breakfast, darting swift looks at their parents and then at each other. 'Is Fiona not going to school today?' Graham asked when his father had gone to phone his office.

'She's still not very well. Better for her to stay in bed today.'

'Daddy's going to be late for work.' Ian nodded at the wall clock.

'He's staying at home too.'

'Has he got the same as Fiona?' Graham wanted to know, and Rachel had to turn a sudden, hysterical hoot of laughter into a cough.

'No, he just has some other things to see too,' she said, and then, as Martin came back into the kitchen, 'Off you go, the pair of you, and get ready. Is it all right?' she asked her husband when the boys had gone. 'Can they manage without you for the day?'

'They'll just have to,' he said. 'We've got more important things than work to sort out today.'

At exactly one-thirty that afternoon a small, aged car came rattling along the road and turned in at the driveway. Fiona must have been watching out for it, because as soon as it began to turn in at the gate Martin and Rachel, waiting apprehensively in the living room, heard her dash down the stairs and out into the front garden to welcome the three people emerging from it.

'At least he didn't arrive on that dratted motorbike,' Martin muttered, stepping swiftly back from the window in case any of the new arrivals noticed him watching.

'They couldn't all have fitted on the bike.'

'He might have a sidecar for all we know.'

'Should we go into the hall?' Rachel wondered.

'Stay where you are. Let them come to us.'

'Martin . . .' she was beginning when the door opened and Fiona led the McNaughtons in.

'Mum, Dad, you know Robbie . . .'

'We do indeed,' Martin said coldly. Undaunted, Robbie advanced.

'Good afternoon, sir,' he said, and Martin had no option

but to shake his outstretched hand. One up to Robbie, Rachel thought, amused. It was true what they said – attack was definitely the best form of defence.

'And this is his sister-in-law, Maggie, and his b-brother Fraser.' Fiona's voice was taut with nerves, and she gasped slightly over the sentence. Robbie went over to put an arm around her shoulders. She smiled up at him gratefully and Martin tensed, though Rachel could have kissed the boy.

She remembered Maggie and Fraser from the glimpse she had had in the school hall after the performance of *The Importance of Being Earnest*. Maggie, small, slim and dark-haired, was clearly nervous; when she shook hands with Rachel her fingers were icy-cold, and a quick glance showed that the nails were bitten down. Fraser was calmer, with an air of steely resolve. He had his younger brother's curly fair hair, hazel eyes and sturdy build, though he was a few inches taller than Robbie. He looked as though he was too young to be married, let alone running his own business, but his approach to the meeting turned out to be very adult and businesslike.

'Mr Carswell . . . Mrs Carswell, I'm happy to meet you both, but extremely sorry that it's under these circumstances. I'm not proud of my brother right now, and I can assure you that he knows it.'

Martin's eyes had been on Robbie since the moment he had walked into the room. 'You're two years older than my daughter,' he burst out angrily. 'Old enough to know better. How dare you—'

'Dad, no! Robbie's not the only one to blame! If anyone is, it's me. I led him on . . .'

'Fee—'

'I did,' she insisted, turning on him. 'I was unhappy and upset and I . . . it was my fault!'

'But I should have had more sense, Fee. Your father's quite right; I'm older than you and that makes me more responsible.'

'I'm glad to know that you're aware of the gravity of your actions, at least.'

'Dad! If you don't stop talking to Robbie like that I'm going to walk out of this house here and now.' The tears were flowing unchecked down Fiona's ashen face. 'And you'll never see me again!'

'Ssshh, Fee . . .' Robbie drew her into the crook of one arm, fishing with his free hand for a handkerchief and then using it to mop her face gently. 'Don't cry.'

Glancing at her husband, Rachel saw naked anguish in his face as he watched his daughter being comforted by another man.

'Martin,' she said, 'what's done is done. The problem we have to face right now is what we're going to do about it.'

'You're right, Mrs Carswell,' Fraser McNaughton said. 'That's why we're here. Recriminations aren't going to solve anything. We have to decide what to do next.'

'It's *our* problem, and we've already decided, haven't we, Robbie?' Fiona broke free and took a step forward to face her father, dashing the last of her tears away with the palms of both hands. 'We're going to get married as soon as we can, and if it's all right with Fraser and Maggie we'll live in their house until we can get a place of our own.'

'You know you'd always be welcome, Fiona,' Maggie put in, smiling at the girl; and then, to Rachel, 'It's a big house; there's plenty of room for the four of us and a baby. Right, Fraser?'

'Of course they're welcome—'

'Just a minute,' Martin snapped, and Rachel could tell

from the tone of his voice that he felt as though the meeting was being taken out of his hands. 'I'm not happy about the idea of these two rushing into marriage. Fiona needs . . . they both need time to think about it.'

'We don't have much time, and we've thought about it already, Dad. It's what we both want.' Fiona had seated herself on one of the armchairs and Robbie had drawn a straight-backed chair up by her side. They sat close together, hands loosely linked on the arm of her chair.

'It's not what *I* want.'

'It's not your . . .' Fiona subsided as Robbie's fingers squeezed hers.

'Let's listen to what everyone else has to say first, Fee,' he said firmly. 'We know how we feel, but this is their chance to tell us how they feel.'

'Speaking for myself,' Rachel said brightly, 'I feel like having a cup of tea.'

'I'll help you,' Maggie offered, jumping to her feet, and then, when they had escaped to the kitchen, 'Poor kids, as if they're not having a tough enough time without having to be subjected to this heavy-handed parenting bit.'

'I agree, it's almost barbaric. But at the same time, it has to be talked through. There are sandwiches in the fridge, they just need unwrapping.' Rachel filled the kettle. 'And you'll find a cake in the box over there.'

Maggie nodded and set to work, her small hands moving deftly as she arranged sandwiches and then began to slice the sponge cake. 'You've got a lovely home, Mrs Carswell,' she said as she worked.

'It was quite run down when we first bought it. It's taken a while to get things the way we like them.'

'Ours is old-fashioned; Mr and Mrs McNaughton bought it when they were first married, and Fraser and

Robbie grew up in it. It still has the same furniture, and it needs a lot of work now, not to mention redecorating, but we never seem to have the time to get round to it .... or the money. All our money goes into building up the business. Fraser says that one day the business will pay for the work needed on the house; I don't know how long it'll take,' Maggie said with a trace of despair in her voice, 'but you've got to have faith, haven't you?'

'Your husband's young to be running his own business. He must be very ambitious.'

'Oh, he is, and he's twenty-six; older than he looks. Funnily enough, we met while we were both at school, just like Fiona and Robbie. Only Fraser was in the John Neilson and I was at Camphill. It was an inter-schools sports event, and as soon as I set eyes on him I thought he was dreamy. He still is, as far as I'm concerned.' When the girl smiled, her sharp-featured little face was suddenly quite pretty. 'I've known Robbie since he started secondary school. He's a very caring person, just like Fraser. I'd trust Fraser with my life – and Robbie, too. Anything else I can do?'

'You'll find napkins in that drawer.'

'Oh yes . . . they're pretty. I know Robbie's behaved badly, Mrs Carswell . . .'

'Call me Rachel, please.' It made Rachel feel old to be called Mrs Carswell by this capable young woman.

Maggie's dark head ducked in quick acknowledgement. 'Rachel . . .' she said awkwardly, then rushed on, 'Fraser's furious with him. He's given the poor lad a hard time ever since he heard the news yesterday. But I can promise you that Robbie won't let Fiona down. He really does love her, and Fraser and I think the world of her.'

'Did you know Robbie's parents?'

'Not his mother, she died before Fraser and I met. I

259

knew his dad, though. He was a nice man. He died about six years ago, just before we got married, and left the house to both of his sons. So it made sense for us to live in it. Fraser and I were lucky that way; at least we didn't have to start our married lives on a mortgage. I wish I'd met Mrs McNaughton,' the girl added wistfully. 'She looks so nice in her photographs . . . beautiful, too. I seem to be unlucky where mums are concerned. I never knew my own.'

'Why not?'

'She died when I was born, and my dad married someone else quite soon after, and went to live in Australia. My aunt brought me up, but only because she was ashamed of her brother abandoning me and she thought that it was her duty to take me in. To be honest,' the girl added almost shyly, 'that's why I'd rather see Robbie and Fiona keeping this kid, young as they are themselves. At least he or she would have parents. And I'm sure they would be good parents.'

'Did Fiona tell you that I was adopted?'

'Yes, she did. I hope you don't mind her saying. It was unfair, not telling you until you were grown up, but at least you had a mum and a dad.'

'Yes, I did.'

'Right,' Maggie said briskly, 'that's everything. Have you got a tray?'

They returned to the living room to find Fraser and Martin holding a stilted conversation about the printing business while Robbie and Fiona listened silently, their fingers still entwined. Fiona looked miserable, Rachel noticed, and her heart ached for her daughter.

Once tea and coffee had been poured, plates and napkins handed out and sandwiches passed round, Martin blurted out, as though he could no longer suppress the words, 'I don't want my daughter to get married.'

'Dad! You've no right—'

'I have every right, Fiona. I've supported you from birth and I've cared for you – and cared *about* you – every single day of my life since then. After sixteen years of that I'm not going to stand by and watch you throw away your chances of a good future.'

'But I'll have a good future with Robbie, and our baby!'

'And what if you realise too late that you've made a mistake?'

'Isn't it a bit late for that?' She gave a mirthless laugh, then added, 'And if you mean that you want us to get rid of this baby you can forget it, because we're not doing that; are we, Robbie?'

'No way!'

'I have no right to ask such a thing. Nobody has. But I am suggesting that you wait for another six months at least before committing yourself to marriage.'

Again, as Fiona started to speak, Robbie silenced her with a squeeze of his hand. 'Wait until after the baby's born, you mean?' the boy asked.

'Yes, that's exactly what I mean. I want you to go on living here, Fiona, and to go back to school and sit your exams. I suppose that would be all right, given her condition?' Martin asked his wife, and Rachel nodded.

'Of course. Fiona's perfectly fit and the baby's not due for a good six months yet.'

'Take your Ordinary Grade exams and then you can leave school in July,' Martin went on, and found an unexpected ally in Robbie.

'Your father's right, Fee. You've been working hard for those exams, and you ought to go ahead and sit them.'

She thought for a moment, then asked, 'Can Robbie live here too?'

'I would prefer it if things stayed as they are at present, with you and Robbie living with your own families. You can still see each other,' Martin added swiftly as Fiona's eyes began to fill with tears. 'Perhaps I was wrong to stop you before. I won't do that any more. But after all the studying you've already put in, I just want to see how the exams turn out. If you get good grades they might be of use to you in a few years' time. Surely you owe us that, Fiona?'

She dashed the moisture from her eyes with the back of her free hand. 'If I do what you want you'll end up with an illegitimate grandchild. What would the neighbours say? And Gran, and Grandma and Grandpa Carswell?'

Martin's face reddened, but he said levelly, 'I'd rather have an illegitimate grandchild than a grandchild who has to watch his or her parents split up because they'd married too young, and too quickly. I want you both to have time to think things through, and if you're still determined to get married to each other after the child's born I won't stand in your way, because at least I'll know then that you've had time to make your minds up.'

'And what happens if we decide against it? I only said *if*, Fiona,' Robbie added quickly as she turned to look at him, her eyes wide with horror.

Martin drew a deep breath and looked at Rachel. 'Then I suppose we'll have another mouth to feed,' he said, and she nodded agreement.

'But it's not *fair*—' Fiona was starting, when Robbie put a hand on her arm.

'Hang on, Fee. What do you think, Fraser?'

His brother had been watching intently, absorbing every word. Now, after a moment's deliberation, he gave a faint shrug of the shoulders. 'I'd say it's a sensible idea, Rob. You're both young, and perhaps you do need time to get used to what's happening to you.'

'Mrs Carswell?'

'I agree with my husband,' Rachel said simply, and Martin shot a small, tight smile in her direction.

'Maggie?'

She smiled at the young couple. 'I don't think either of you will change your minds, but a bit of breathing space might not be a bad thing.'

'Fiona?' Robbie prompted, and when she remained silent, he added, 'I think we owe it to our families to go along with the idea.'

She gave a long, deep sigh before saying slowly, as though the words were being dragged from her one by one, 'You promise that you won't stop me from seeing Robbie?'

'We promise,' Rachel said.

'He can come to the house? Dad?' Fiona said when Martin didn't reply immediately. 'Can Robbie come here to see me?'

'Yes, he can.' Now it was Martin's turn to sound as though each word was being hauled from between his lips.

'Then I suppose,' she said reluctantly, tears beginning to thicken her voice and glitter in her eyes, 'I have to agree.' Then, fiercely, her grip tightening on Robbie's hand, 'But it won't make any difference to the way we feel about each other, I promise you that!'

'Thank you, Martin,' Rachel said when the McNaughtons had gone and Fiona was in her room, Abba blaring from the music centre. It sounded so normal, and yet, Rachel knew, life in the Carswell household would never be the same again.

'What are you thanking me for?'

'You handled the meeting really well.'

'I was just making the best of a bad job. At least they've agreed to put off the decision about getting married.'

'I think they'll go ahead with it, eventually. Fiona's mad about Robbie, and he seems to be a decent young man.'

'It's not the way I'd hoped it would be. Look at the commitments and responsibilities she's having to take on at her age.'

'She'll manage. And we'll be there to help her.'

'Help her?' he echoed, his voice harsh. 'If we'd brought her up to know right from wrong none of us would have had to go through today's fiasco.'

'How can you say that? We've both been good parents. It's the world that's changing. Young people nowadays expect more freedom.'

'Instead of expecting it they should be earning the right to it. As far as I'm concerned, Fiona and this boyfriend of hers have proved that they weren't fit to be left alone.'

'According to Fiona, it only happened once, and I believe her. She's not a liar, Martin.'

He got to his feet. 'I'm going to mow the lawn. No sense in letting my day off work go to waste entirely.'

'Will you be here for the boys coming home? I have to do some shopping.'

'I'm not going anywhere,' he said, then turned at the door on his way out to say, 'I wish to God he'd stop calling her Fee. Her name is Fiona!'

'Here she comes, at last,' Cara said, and then, as Kathleen wove her way through the tables towards them, 'My God, I've seen a happier face on a gargoyle!'

'Coffee,' Kathleen snapped at a passing waitress, throwing herself into a chair. 'Black!'

'You're not having a good day,' Cara guessed.

'Damned right I'm not!' Kathleen seized a meringue from the plate and bit into it. 'He's only gone and arranged to spend three months in the Middle East!'

'Murdo?'

'Who else? Blast,' Kathleen barked as she showered herself with meringue crumbs.

'Are you going with him?'

'Me?' She stopped in the middle of brushing herself down to give Rachel a malevolent glare. 'Of course I'm not going! Why on earth would he include me in his little jaunt to the sunshine? Someone has to stay home to keep an eye on the garden, and what else are wives for?'

'When did you hear about this?' Rachel was sorry for her friend, but at the same time, it was a welcome relief to think of someone else's problems for a while.

'Last night, when he came home full of the news, and looking like a dog with two tails.'

'I've always wondered why a dog should be excited about having two tails,' Cara mused. 'You'd think the extra one would be a nuisance.'

Kathleen ignored her. 'Apparently he's always wanted to go to the Middle East. He didn't even bother discussing it with me.' Her coffee arrived and she started shovelling brown sugar into it. 'He's leaving in July.'

'No chance of talking him out of it?'

'You know Murdo, Rachel – once his mind's made up nothing can change it. I tried pointing out that he wouldn't be able to have a drink for three months, but that wasn't much of a weapon, given that he only ever has one beer on a Saturday evening. He's not even fretting about all the vaccinations and injections he's going to need . . . and this is the man who insists on going to the Casualty Department if he gets stung by a wasp!'

Kathleen had finished the meringue, and now the area of table around her plate looked as though it had been hit by a snowstorm. 'Why,' she demanded to know, seizing a napkin and starting to scoop crumbs into the palm of one hand, 'do meringues have to be so messy?'

'That's part of their charm. Rachel was just telling me about Fiona's pregnancy.'

'Fiona's what?' Kathleen yelped, tossing meringue crumbs all over the floor. Several other morning-coffee drinkers turned to stare at their table.

'Oh good, that saves me from having to pay to have

a notice in the *Paisley Daily Express*. Thanks, Cara.' Rachel glared at her twin.

'Sorry, I thought Kathleen would know, being your best friend.'

'I know now. Who, when, how?'

'Robbie McNaughton, that lad who played opposite her in *The Importance of Being Earnest* . . .' It all seemed so long ago, now. 'Due round about the end of September, and as for how – get a book out of the library, Kathleen.'

'Does Martin know?'

'Oh yes, Martin knows. We've had the two-family get-together and everything.'

'How has he taken the news?'

'Not well, but he's doing his best to cope.' In as few sentences as possible, Rachel sketched in events so far, ending with, 'So that's how things stand at the moment; Fiona's agreed to stay at home and finish the school year, and if the two of them are still determined to get married after the baby arrives, so be it. We were all very civilised, though I doubt if Martin could have kept his hands off Robbie if his brother and sister-in-law hadn't been there.'

'I like Robbie,' Cara announced. 'A very nice young man, and mature for his age. He'll make a wonderful father. He and Fiona really care for each other, you know, it's not just a schoolgirl crush. Angus likes him, and my Angus is a good judge of character.' And then, struck by a sudden thought, 'If they're looking for somewhere to live once they're married, there's room in our house and we'd love to have them. It would be so nice to have a baby in the house again.'

'Robbie's brother says that they can stay in the family home if necessary.'

'And at least Martin's accepted the situation,' Kathleen put in.

'He's accepted that our daughter is pregnant and that we have to do what's best for her, but he's not happy about it. He seems to think that I could have prevented it, though I can't for the life of me see how.'

'He's looking for someone or something to blame. It's what a lot of men do,' Kathleen said. 'If you ask me, it's a throwback to childhood. You know, the "I didn't break the vase, Mr Nobody did it" syndrome. Like the scapegoats Royalty used to have, who had to take the punishment when their masters misbehaved. Blaming someone else gives Martin the chance to step back a little so that he can think things through. It will pass, once he comes to accept what's happened.'

'We'll all have to learn to accept it.'

'Especially poor little Fiona. Just keep concentrating on her, and let Martin come round in his own good time. Where is she now? At home?'

'Back at school. We had her two best friends over to the house first so that she could tell them about the baby and they were so excited about it that she cheered up quite quickly. And I had a word with the head teacher. The school's being really helpful, so we don't have any worries on that score.'

'Why don't Angus and I drive over this evening?' Cara suggested. 'A family discussion might help Martin to—'

'No!' Rachel said, and then, hurriedly, 'I mean, we've done so much talking since last week. Now we both feel the need to have some breathing space, so that we can mull over what's already been said.'

'You know where we are if you change your mind. And if you ever need a shoulder to cry on, we're here.'

'Do the boys know about the baby?' Kathleen asked.

'Not yet, but they know something's up; I can tell

by the way they look at us. We'll have to tell them eventually.'

'Quite soon, I'd say. If Fiona's going to stay on at school until the summer, word will probably start to get around, and you don't want it to reach either of the boys from someone else.'

'It seems to me,' Cara said, 'that you both need a bit of cheering up, and I know the very thing – a birthday party for me and Rachel.' And then, when Rachel gave her a blank stare, 'For our thirty-sixth birthdays next week.'

'Good heavens, I'd forgotten all about that.'

'Well I haven't. It's the perfect chance for you to meet my brother and sisters and their families. You too, Kathleen, and Murdo.'

'Do I have to bring him?'

'Absolutely, I'm dying to meet him. And we'll invite Robbie too.'

'I don't know if Martin . . .'

'Robbie's family now. Martin will have to get used to having him around.'

'No, I meant that I don't think either of us is in the mood for a party right now.'

'All the more reason to have one,' Cara said robustly. Our house, a week on Saturday.'

'Does Angus know about this?'

'I've just thought of it myself, but he'll love the idea.'

Although Cara's adoptive brother and sisters looked nothing like her, they shared her zest and enthusiasm for life. Just being in their company on the evening of the birthday party cheered Rachel up, and made her feel that no problem was insurmountable.

Cara had baked a huge cake and decorated the entire

house with flags and balloons. There was even a trampoline on the lawn for Graham, Ian, and Cara's other nephews and nieces.

'Enjoying yourself?' Rachel dared to ask Martin when they met up halfway through the evening.

'It's better than I expected it to be.'

'Who's that you were talking to?'

'The tall man over by the buffet? He's married to one of Cara's sisters. He works for a company in the same building as ours. I've seen him around but we've never actually spoken to each other before.'

'It's a small world.'

'Mmm.' He nodded at Fiona and Robbie. 'They look as though they're enjoying themselves.'

'She's glowing, isn't she?'

'That's because she doesn't know yet what parenthood's all about. But she will.'

'She'll always have us to turn to. We'll see her through this, won't we?'

'Do we have an option?'

'It'll be all right, Martin,' she said. 'Really it will,' and suddenly his hand caught at hers, gripping it hard.

'I'm so damned scared, Rachel. I'm . . . I'm not very good at handling the unexpected.'

'Do what I do and take each day as it comes.'

'I suppose the next step will be to tell the boys.'

'D'you want me to do that?'

'It's something we should do together. Quite soon.'

'Tomorrow?'

'You don't think that's too soon?'

'Better get it over with.'

'I suppose so. D'you want anything from the buffet? I'll fetch it,' he said when she nodded and began to get up. He started towards the laden tables at the other side of the room, then turned back and dropped a kiss on her cheek. 'Happy birthday.'

'You said that this morning.'

'It doesn't hurt to say it again.'

The room was crowded, and everyone seemed to be talking at the same time. Fiona and Robbie, hand-in-hand, were deep in conversation with one of Cara's sisters, while Kathleen was talking to Angus. He loomed over her, standing close, as he always did with women. As Rachel glanced across at them he seized a bottle from the mantelshelf and tipped more drink into both their glasses.

'Happy birthday, Rachel.' Murdo Ramsay appeared from the crowd and settled on the floor by her chair. 'Did you hear about me going to Saudi?'

'Kathleen told me.'

'Great, isn't it? I can't wait.'

'It's a pity you can't take her with you.'

'Oh, she'd just get bored. I'm going to be kept pretty busy. It's not a holiday, you know, it's going to be bloody hard work. I was speaking to your brother-in-law – the landscape gardener.'

'Angus.'

'That's the one. I thought he might be able to give me a few tips about making the most of the space I have in the back garden. Make room for more vegetables. He's coming to have a look at it when I get back from Saudi. Autumn'll be coming in then; it'll be the right time to start reorganising,' Murdo said comfortably. 'I've been reading up on the Middle East, since I'm going to be living there for a while. Did you know . . . ?'

'A baby?' Ian squeaked. 'Why does she want a baby when she's still at school?'

'It's just the way things turned out,' Rachel said.

'What things?' Graham wanted to know.

'All sorts of things.'

'So when's she getting this baby, then?'

'Probably at the end of September.'

Graham stared at his mother, his eyes going blank, which meant that his seven-year-old brain was busily calculating. 'It's not going to get in the way of my birthday, is it?'

'I don't see why it should.'

'We can still have Hallowe'en, and a fancy-dress birthday party?'

'Of course,' Martin assured him, and Graham's shoulders slumped with relief.

'I suppose that's all right, then. If she's sure she wants a baby.'

'She is.'

'Is it a secret?' Ian wanted to know.

'Yes,' his father said quickly.

'Why?'

'Because . . . Rachel, why is it a secret?'

'Because it isn't going to happen for ages yet. You can tell people nearer the time.'

'Okay,' Ian said. 'Can I go out on my bike now?'

'Yes, on you go.'

'I think I might be a Dalek next Hallowe'en,' Graham said thoughtfully. 'That gives you plenty of time to make my costume, doesn't it, Mum?'

'I'll start work on it as soon as I've finished with the costumes for *The Boyfriend*,' Rachel promised, and then, when she and Martin were alone, 'That wasn't too hard, was it?'

'They took it very well.'

'Children can be really practical at times.'

'Yes,' he said, and then sighed. 'Our parents next. I'm not sure they'll be as easy as Graham and Ian.'

'Why don't we wait until the term's finished before we tell them?' Rachel suggested. 'Fiona's not showing yet, and it might be best to let her get the exams over and done with in peace. It's not something we'd want to write to your parents about, or tell them on the phone. Better to wait until we visit your folks in July. And I can tell Mum either just before then, or as soon as we get home.'

'You're right,' he said with relief. 'I'm going to get some work done in the garden.'

Rachel went to her sewing room, where she found a certain comfort in cutting and pinning and stitching. Sheer cowardice had been behind the suggestion that they delay the confrontation with her mother and Martin's parents. Her in-laws, she knew from experience, would react exactly as Martin had. They would be confused and bewildered, more likely to dwell on the fact that the unplanned pregnancy should never have happened rather than dealing with the fact that it had. They would be shocked, upset, distressed, and of no help or support at all for their son and his family.

Her own mother would be just as bad. She had seen Doreen several times since Fiona's announcement, had almost blurted the news out more than once, but had drawn back at the last minute. She shuddered, and tried to blank out her thoughts by concentrating on the bright cloth whirling through the sewing machine. If only life could be a frothy, light-hearted musical, ending on a happy note!

Fiona coped well with the exams. 'I don't know if it's because I know that I don't have to worry so much about getting good pass marks,' she said happily when she returned from sitting the final paper, 'or whether I'm smarter than I thought I was. Probably the first one, because it's great not to be nervous and worried all the time.' Then, throwing her arms round Rachel's waist and giving her an impulsive hug, 'And you and Daddy have been fantastic about everything. You've no idea how much that helps. Whatever happens, I'll make it up to you as soon as I can.'

'That's what parents are for.' Rachel returned the hug. 'You don't owe us anything.'

Now that her secret was shared, the girl was blooming. By the time the exams were over she was beginning to put on weight, but it suited her, and the loose clothing she liked to wear when out of school uniform hid her slightly increased waistline effectively.

Martin was making a real effort to treat his daughter as he always had, and to be civil to Robbie when he visited the house, but Rachel was concerned about him.

He had changed; although in front of the children he did his best to be the same as always, when he and Rachel were on their own he was quiet and withdrawn. It was as though he had surrounded himself with barriers that she could not break down, no matter how hard she tried.

She knew that he was bewildered and finding it hard to cope with Fiona's pregnancy, and she longed for a return to the days when they had been able to talk about problems and solve them together. But in the past, she realised sadly, they had never had to deal with anything as momentous as the changes they had had to cope with over the past eight months.

This realisation led to further fears that the marriage she had always looked on as rock-solid might not, after all, be so safe and secure. Was it going to be strong enough to cope with what still lay ahead?

'Of course it is,' Kathleen said robustly when Rachel confided her worries. 'You and Martin go together like . . .'

'Book-ends?'

'I was going to say like Darby and Joan, meaning that I have every confidence that you'll stay together for the rest of your lives. This is just a hiccup, believe me.'

'I wish I felt as sure as you do. I think Cara's part of the problem,' Rachel admitted. 'The other day she brought round some really exquisite baby clothes she'd made, and of course, Fiona was thrilled. The two of them had little jackets and gowns and rompers spread out all over the living room, and then Martin suddenly jumped to his feet and went out without a word and got into the car and drove away. He was gone for two hours. It's not like him to do a thing like that.'

'It's more likely to be the sight of his daughter fussing over baby clothes that unsettled him, rather than Cara being there. If I were you I'd let him work things through on his own. He'll come round,' Kathleen prophesied.

'Perhaps he'll loosen up when we go on holiday.'

'The usual ten days in Berwick-upon-Tweed?'

'It's what we enjoy most. Then,' Rachel said, her heart sinking, 'the usual three days with Martin's parents in the Lake District. And that's when we'll have to tell them about Fiona.'

'Wasn't Martin's father a doctor? I imagine that he'll know as soon as he sets eyes on her,' Kathleen said dryly.

Rachel stared at her, horrified. 'I never thought of that! Perhaps I should suggest bringing the children back here after Berwick and letting Martin go to see his parents on his own.'

'Have a word with him. And why not take some of my leek and potato soup home with you,' Kathleen added as Rachel got to her feet. 'It's comforting as well as nourishing. It'll do you, Martin and Fiona the world of good.'

Rachel followed her into the kitchen, and stared in awe at the large freezer, stacked with labelled containers. 'You and Murdo can't possibly eat it all!'

'I give most of it away to friends and neighbours. It's the only way I can make room for the next batch.'

'Wouldn't it be easier to stop making so much?' A large pot was bubbling gently on the stove, and the kitchen was filled with a tempting aroma.

Kathleen found the labelled container she had been looking for, and closed the freezer door. 'I daren't stop,' she confessed. 'Chopping and dicing comforts me. It's my idea of a security blanket.' Then, with a wicked gleam in her brown eyes, 'I think it might have something to do with the satisfaction of wielding a sharp knife. Besides, there's a sense of unease deep down; a feeling that if I give up the soup-making, I might turn to the bottle instead.'

'Wine-making?'

'Drinking wine made by someone else, I meant.'

'Don't be daft!'

'Oh, I don't know. I used to wake up in the middle of the night, picturing my future self: an old crone pushing my shopping trolley home from the greengrocer's, with folk pointing at me and whispering, "It's the mad vegetable lady!" while Murdo spends his retirement trying to grow the largest marrow ever seen in captivity.'

'It won't come to that.'

'Do you know,' Kathleen said, 'I don't believe it will, after all. For I have a plan!'

'What sort of plan?'

Kathleen smiled enigmatically. 'Wait and see,' she said. 'All may be revealed sooner than you think.'

Rachel broached the subject of the forthcoming family holiday that evening, and was stunned when Martin said, 'I've already thought about that. In fact, I've cancelled our booking at Berwick.'

'Cancelled it? But surely this year of all years we need to get away as a family.'

'Fiona will probably prefer to stay at home, near Robbie. And you're busy with the costumes for this school show.'

'It'll be over well before the holidays. What about the boys? They love going away for the summer holidays. And you need the break.'

'You might as well know that I've decided to spend a week with my parents instead of the usual few days, and I'm taking the boys with me. My folks are all right about it,' he rushed on when she began to speak. 'I've already discussed it with them. As for breaking our news to them – I think it would be best if I do that on my own.'

'When did you arrange all this?'

'Two days ago,' Martin said, not quite meeting her eyes. 'On the phone, from the office.'

'But you know that the boys get bored easily. They could be a handful, Martin.'

'I'm going to take them out and about – there are a lot of places to visit in the Lake District, boat trips and so on. My parents are sending me some brochures so that I can book ahead. It'll be good for the three of us to spend some time together,' he continued. 'And for you and Fiona to get a break from us.'

'Martin, is this because you're ashamed of Fiona?'

He stared at her, open-mouthed, then flushed slightly. 'Of course not!'

'You think your parents will be embarrassed to have her in their house. For goodness' sake, Martin, your father was a family doctor; I'm sure he's seen teenage pregnancies before.'

'But never his own granddaughter!'

'If you're right . . .' Rachel said icily, 'if the sight of our daughter embarrasses and offends her grandparents . . .'

'I didn't say they'd be offended!'

'. . . then I would certainly prefer Fiona to stay at home, with me,' she finished, and walked out of the room and upstairs, where she had a good cry in the bathroom.

The boys were quite happy with the new arrangement, especially when Martin trotted out a list of the various places he was going to take them to. Fiona was pleased to be staying at home, near her beloved Robbie, but Rachel felt as though she had been abandoned, and not just by Martin.

Although she liked Robbie, it was quite hard to see

278

how swiftly he had become the centre of her young daughter's life. The boy looked at Fiona as though she were a goddess and he her most ardent worshipper, while she seemed to light up from within whenever he appeared.

Seeing them together, Rachel remembered what it felt like to be so passionately, so totally in love. It had happened between her and Martin, and no doubt between Romeo and Juliet and Tristan and Isolde and every young couple who had fallen in love throughout time immemorial. But this was the first time it had happened to her daughter.

From the moment of her birth Fiona had been dependent on her parents for security and nourishment and unconditional love, and now that she had found someone else to provide all those essential things, it was almost as though she were turning her back on them. With each visit Robbie made to the house, Rachel could see her firstborn moving a little further away from her; walking swiftly and eagerly, without a backward glance, into another room, another life where she, Rachel, was no longer needed.

She felt so alone. She had never needed Martin as much as she needed him now, but his invisible self-imposed barriers held fast, and she didn't know how to break them down.

The Boyfriend was a success, and the costumes well praised. Robbie, again, turned in a superb performance. The school term came to an end, and all too soon Rachel and Fiona were standing at the gate, watching Martin and the boys set off on their trip to Cumbria. Graham and Ian waved frantically from the open windows right up until the moment the car turned the corner and disappeared from view.

'To be honest, I'm quite glad not to be going to see

Grandma and Grandpa this year.' Fiona entwined her arm with her mother's as they went back into the garden. 'There's never anything to do there.'

'The house is going to seem very quiet with those two away.'

'Just you and me for a whole week. It'll be nice, won't it?'

'Yes. Yes, it will,' Rachel said, squeezing her daughter's arm against her side. 'Let's make the most of every minute of it!' She paused to inspect the rose bushes lining the short driveway, envisaging a trip to the shops, lunch out, and a mother-and-daughter bonding session.

'Actually, Mum, I said I might go over to the print shop today and help Robbie and Maggie. You don't mind, do you?'

What happened to just the two of us? Rachel wondered. Aloud, she said, 'I'd thought we might go shopping together.'

'We will, tomorrow or the day after, but I promised to see Maggie today.'

'On you go, dear. I've got plenty to do here.'

'Thanks. I'll go and phone her.'

Watching her daughter go into the house, Rachel noticed with a pang that the girl was beginning to adopt the flat-footed, leaning-back waddle of pregnancy.

She sighed, and returned to her study of the rose-bushes. As she had suspected, they had greenfly. She fetched the watering can from the garden shed and began to fill it with soapy water at the kitchen sink, while from Fiona's room came the sound of some group – for once, not Abba – singing 'Under the Moon of Love'.

When the roses had been doused she returned to the house, meeting Fiona on her way out.

'Maggie said to go over for lunch, and I'll probably stay there for dinner too. Back this evening, okay?' A quick hug, and she was gone. The house was silent again, and Rachel was alone. More alone, it seemed, than she had been since meeting Martin.

She picked up the phone and dialled Kathleen's number.

'I wondered if you fancied a nice lunch somewhere?'

'Can't manage today, I'm afraid.' Kathleen sounded breathless and excited. 'Murdo left yesterday, and I've decided to do some redecorating while he's out of the way.'

'Can I help?'

'No, everything's under control.' Rachel heard the double chime of a doorbell in the background, then Kathleen said, 'Oops, the decorator's arrived to talk over some ideas. Must dash. I'll be in touch.' Then came a click as she hung up.

Rachel went into the sewing room to tidy away the debris left over from *The Boyfriend*, and ended up staring out of the window, arms folded. The silence surrounding her was so strong that it almost hurt her ears. No Abba, no yells of 'Mu-um!' For the first time since she and Martin had become serious about each other, nobody needed her.

Without warning, her own mother came into her mind. Although she had never been a loving or demonstrative parent, Doreen Nesbitt had tended Rachel from the time she was three weeks old. She had fed her, bathed her, dressed her and had administered iodine and sticking plaster hundreds of times to skinned hands and knees. She had spent hours sewing name labels on school uniforms and covering school books with brown paper or, on occasion, with bits of left-over wallpaper. Rachel could still remember the pleasure of opening her schoolbag and laying an exercise book, freshly covered with floral or striped wallpaper, on her desk.

Doreen had nursed her through the night the time she went down with croup, and had made fancy dress costumes, brushed hair and clipped nails. And despite all that hard work and all that nurturing – not to mention all those covered schoolbooks – Doreen had lost her only daughter not just once, when Rachel met and married Martin, but a second time, when Rachel was reunited with Cara, her blood kin.

Cara had come into her life not long after Doreen lost the husband who had supported and sustained her for forty years. The man who, at one time, must have made the young Doreen glow with the same joy that Rachel knew so well. The joy that now shone from Fiona's eyes.

Blood kin. The words rang in Rachel's head. It had been easy for her to say that Cara's arrival posed no threat to her adoptive mother; but now, looking at it from Doreen's point of view, she could see why the older woman had been so difficult, and so set against meeting Cara. There was a big difference between adoptive relations and blood kin. Now, when she felt alone and unhappy, Rachel began to see Doreen Nesbitt as a woman instead of just a mother.

She went into the hall and dialled the familiar number. 'Aunt Chrissie, it's me. I want to invite Mum over for lunch. I need to see her on her own if you don't mind. She'll tell you why when she gets back.'

'She doesn't need to,' Chrissie said. 'Whatever it is, pet, if it's between the two of you, it's not my business.'

'Believe me, she'll tell you. And she'll probably need you.'

'There's nothing wrong, is there?' Chrissie's voice took on a sudden sharp edge. 'Nobody's ill?'

'No, it's just . . . is Mum there?'

'I'll call her,' Chrissie said, and there was a slight tapping noise as the receiver was laid down on the hall table, followed by, 'Doreen? It's Rachel, she wants to speak to you.'

Almost at once, Rachel heard her mother's flat voice. 'Yes, Rachel?'

'Mum, I was wondering if you'd like to come over for lunch.'

'Today?' Doreen asked, surprised. 'It's nearly eleven o'clock already.'

'I know, but there's something I want to . . . I *need* to talk to you about.'

'When do you want us over?'

'Just you, Mum. And whenever you're ready. Please?'

'Oh. All right, I'll just get changed and then catch the first bus,' Doreen said, and hung up.

The next hour seemed to drag by, but when the doorbell rang Rachel's stomach started doing somersaults. She hadn't had enough time to think of how she was going to break the news, she thought, panicking at the sight of Doreen's small, neat figure, topped by the fur turban she wore every time she went outside the door.

'Hello, Mum, take your coat off and come into the kitchen. I'm just finishing the salad.'

Doreen hung her coat up carefully, but kept her hat on as she always did. 'This place is quiet,' she said, eyeing the table set for two. 'Where's everyone gone?'

'Fiona's out, and Martin and the boys left for his parents' house this morning.'

Doreen, reorganising the place settings to her own satisfaction, whipped round to stare at her daughter. 'They've gone off without you and Fiona? I thought you were all going to Berwick next week.'

'Martin felt that it would be good for him and the

boys to have some time on their own this year. Sit down, Mum. I've got some home-made soup, and I thought you might like a chicken salad.'

'Me and Chrissie usually just have a sandwich in the middle of the day.'

'So do I, but since we don't often get time to ourselves like this, I decided to make a proper lunch, for once.'

'I'll not be able to eat my tea later. Chrissie's bought a steak pie and we're doing fried potatoes.'

'You don't have to eat a lot just now. Leave plenty of room for the pie.' As Rachel set her mother's soup bowl before her, she saw that her hands were shaking slightly. If Doreen noticed, she said nothing.

They ate in silence, apart from the occasional comment on the weather and the previous evening's television programmes. It wasn't until they had started on their salad that Doreen said, 'Well, out with it. You've not asked me here just for a meal, have you? And Martin's never gone off to his mother's on his own before, so I know there's somethin' up. You might as well tell me. I hope you're not thinkin' of gettin' a divorce, for I'll not stand for that.'

'It's not a divorce, Mum, it's Fiona.'

Doreen, about to put a forkful of salad into her mouth, stopped short. 'What's wrong with the lassie? She's not ill, is she?'

'Not ill, but . . . oh Mum!' All of the careful speeches vanished, and Rachel heard her own voice rise to a child-ish wail. 'Mum, she's going to have a baby!'

'Oh my God!' Doreen yelped, and the fork fell from her hand to the table, scattering chicken salad all over the place. The colour had drained from her face; suddenly she looked so old that Rachel was reminded of pictures she had once seen of an Egyptian mummy stripped of its bandages. She jumped up, visions of her mother

284

collapsing and dying from shock rushing through her head.

'Mum, are you all right?'

'My God,' Doreen said. 'My-god-my-god-my-god-my-god . . .'

'Mum?' Rachel wondered if she should slap Doreen to bring her out of whatever she had fallen into; but settled for clutching the older woman's shoulders and shaking her hard enough to dislodge the fur turban and send it reeling towards the back of her mother's head.

'For goodness' sake, lassie!' Doreen wrenched herself free, one arm flying out to sweep half the table's contents to the floor, then jumped to her feet, frantically hauling hatpins from the dangling fur turban. 'One minute you give me the shock of my life and the next ye're attackin' me. Look at this mess!'

'I'm sorry, I . . .' Rachel began, aghast, and then, as the tears began to spill down her face without warning, 'Oh, Mum!' she said. 'Mum!' And she threw her arms around the older woman.

'Imagine lettin' yerself get intae such a state.' Doreen, hatless, put a mug of tea down in front of her daughter, and then added, peering down at Rachel, huddled in her chair, 'You look like somethin' the cat dragged in. Wait a minute . . .'

She took a tea towel from its hook, wet the corner under the tap, squeezed the excess moisture out, and ordered, 'Look up, lassie.'

Rachel did as she was told, closing her eyes as Doreen began to wipe the tears from her face, each firm sweep of the damp cloth bringing back comforting memories of childhood.

'There,' Doreen said at last, and then, as she began to dry her daughter's face with the other end of the towel, 'So when's this bairn due, then?'

'Th-the end of Sep-tember,' Rachel hiccuped.

'What took ye so long? Why didn't ye tell me about this months ago?'

'I didn't know how t-to. I didn't know how you'd t-take it.'

'It's no' a case of takin' it, it's a case of workin' through it. What's done's done and now we've got to deal with the consequences. Drink your tea before it gets cold.'

Rachel lifted the mug and sipped, then screwed her face up. 'It's too sweet.'

'I put plenty of sugar in it. It's good for shock.'

'It's not me that's had the shock, it's you. I already knew.'

'But it wasn't me that fell apart, was it?' There was just a touch of triumph in Doreen's voice. 'Drink it up, now, it'll do you good.' She sat down and splashed a generous dollop of milk into her own mug before saying briskly, 'What we've got to do now is sort things out for poor wee Fiona. Now then, who's the father, and is he goin' tae stand by her?'

'He's called Robbie McNaughton.'

'How old?'

'Eighteen. He played opposite Fiona in *The Importance of Being Earnest*. Remember?'

Doreen screwed her face up in thought, and then nodded. 'A good-lookin' lad. So them fallin' in love on the stage wasnae all actin'? No wonder they did so well.'

'They want to get married, Mum.'

Doreen clicked her tongue. 'Fiona's too young for that.'

'Legally, she's of age.'

'Never mind what the law says. I'm her gran, not the law, and I say the lassie's too young.'

'That's what Martin thinks. He's talked them into waiting until after the baby's born, so's they have more time to think about it.'

'He's probably right. September, you said? Time me and Chrissie started knittin'. I used tae be a dab hand at matinee jackets, d'ye mind? I like knittin' baby clothes; they're done before ye've got the chance tae get bored. How's the lassie copin'?'

'She's fine, now that we know about it. Putting on a bit of weight, but not a lot.'

287

'She might be like you – you never showed much. Is that why Martin's taken the boys off tae his mother's on his own?' Doreen asked shrewdly. 'Have you two fallen out over this?'

'No, he just felt that he'd like to tell his mother and father in his own way. And I don't think he wanted Fiona to be there when he did it. He's taking it hard, Mum,' Rachel confessed.

'Of course he is. Men cannae deal with things they don't expect. They like life to be safe and as regular as clockwork. Give him time. It'll be all right for me tae tell Chrissie?'

'Of course.'

'And I think you should bring Fiona to Whitehaugh for her tea tomorrow night, just so's she can see that everythin's all right as far as her gran and her Auntie Chrissie are concerned.'

'Robbie's supposed to be coming over for dinner tomorrow.'

'You mean for his tea?' said Doreen, who had a light dinner in the middle of the day, and a large tea at night.

'Yes, for his tea,' Rachel agreed meekly.

'Oh,' Doreen said, and then, after taking a moment to gather her thoughts, 'You'd best bring him with you, then. It's time me and Chrissie met him.'

'Are you sure?'

'I wouldnae suggest it if I wasnae sure. You'll bring him.' It was an order rather than a request.

'I will.' Rachel forced down another mouthful of the sweet milky tea and then said, 'Thanks, Mum.'

'What for?'

'For being so good about it. I've been giving you a hard time lately, what with Cara and everything. And now this. I'm sorry, I really am.'

'Ach, it's all part and parcel of raisin' bairns. Mebbe I should have listened to Frank, and told ye sooner about yer own . . . circumstances. Sometimes,' Doreen said to her half-empty mug, 'we do things the wrong way because we're scared tae try the right way.'

'Like me, waiting all this time to tell you about Fiona,' Rachel said, and her mother gave her a rare and surprisingly warm smile before saying briskly, 'We'll say no more about that. There's no sense in cryin' over spilled milk.'

'Talking of spilled milk . . .' Rachel began to ease herself slightly from the chair. 'I think I might be sitting on a piece of tomato.'

'Do you know what Kathleen's up to?' Cara said as soon as she realised that Rachel was on the other end of the phone.

'No, what?'

'She's only decided to dig up her back garden while Murdo's out of the way.'

'What? All those vegetables?'

'All of them. Not that she's doing it herself; she's given the job to Angus. He's over there now. And she's giving him the greenhouse.'

'Murdo's greenhouse? But she told me two days ago that she was going to get the decorators in . . .' Rachel began, and then stopped suddenly. 'No, wait a minute – she said that she was redecorating. The decorator arrived at the door when she was on the phone to me. I thought she was talking about the house, not the garden.'

'She might be doing the house as well, for all I know, but Angus never mentioned painters or paper hangers.'

'When did she arrange this with him?'

'At our birthday party, apparently.'

'But Murdo told me at the party that Angus was going

to help him to rearrange the garden in the autumn, when he comes back from Saudi.'

'I know; Angus told me. But after he'd talked to Murdo, Kathleen came over and offered him more money to work for her instead, with a bonus if he started the work as soon as Murdo left. Angus says it makes sense as a businessman to go with the highest bidder. She must have money of her own to throw around.'

'I think they have a joint bank account.'

'You mean she's using her husband's money to have her husband's vegetable garden dug up? What a woman!' Cara chortled.

'He'll kill her when he comes back! We'll have to go over there, Cara.'

'Not me. I'd love to, but since my Angus is making money out of this scheme of hers, I'd better keep out of it. Phone and tell me all about it when you've been there. How's Fiona?'

'Blooming. She looks as though she hasn't a care in the world.'

'That's because her secret's out, she's got a lovely young man in her life, and two very supportive parents. Has she not even had any morning sickness?'

'Not now she's past the first three months.'

'Lucky lass. Did you have it?'

'All the time.'

'Me too.'

'Cara, I told my mother.'

'And?'

'She was wonderful. As solid as a rock. She and Chrissie have started knitting already, and last night Fiona and Robbie and I were invited for our tea. Mum couldn't have been nicer to them both.'

'There you are then. We never know how other people

are going to react, do we? With any luck, Martin's having an easy time of it with his parents, too.'

'Somehow,' Rachel said, 'I doubt it.'

'To tell the truth, so do I. I like my brother-in-law, Rachel, but as you know, I think he can be a bit stuffy. I'm assuming that he inherited it from his parents?'

'I'm afraid so.'

'Poor sod,' said Cara.

Angus Longmuir's van was parked outside the Ramsays' bungalow, and as Rachel neared the house she heard the sound of machinery, and glimpsed a small mechanical digger churning up part of the back garden.

A delicious smell wafted out as soon as the front door opened. 'Rachel! This is a nice surprise,' Kathleen beamed. 'Come on in.'

'Is this a bad time? Are you busy?'

'Rushed off my feet, but I'm pleased to see you.' She was wrapped in a long apron and her normally tidy fair hair curled in damp wisps around her flushed face. 'You don't mind sitting in the kitchen, do you?'

'Kathleen, what are you up to?'

'Redecorating. I said I would, didn't I?' Kathleen tossed the words over her shoulder as she led the way through the hall. 'I'm making the most of Murdo's absence.'

Every surface in the roomy kitchen was covered with boxes and bowls and trays, all heaped with vegetables. The rich red of beetroot glowed from two bowls, the draining board was piled with young carrots, onions, turnips and beans, and a chopping board held a partly dissected parsnip. Three pots bubbled and steamed on the stove.

Rachel went to the window, and found herself gazing out at a scene of destruction. The entire back garden had gone; in its place was a choppy sea of newly turned earth.

The digger was busy churning up even more earth.

'Kathleen Ramsay, what have you done?'

'Struck a blow for womankind.' Kathleen shot her a sparkling smile. 'It came to me when I met your new brother-in-law at your birthday party. Isn't it lucky that he's a landscape gardener? He even agreed to fit this job in at short notice so that I could get it all done while Murdo was out of the way. And he's going to pave the whole area and plant out containers for me. It's going to look great, Rachel. At last, I can sit outside and enjoy the view. Look . . .' Kathleen indicated a dish on the Welsh dresser. 'Asparagus. I didn't even know Murdo was growing asparagus.'

'He's going to kill you when he comes home!'

'No he won't, and even if he tries . . .' Kathleen, who had returned to her task of dicing the parsnip, flourished the sharp knife at Rachel, a daredevil gleam in her eyes, . . . 'it'll be worth it.'

'What are you going to do with all these vegetables?'

'Make soup, what else? Denise – Cara's sister Denise – knows someone who owns two soup and sandwich lunch places, and they're taking all the soup I can make. Isn't that great? You wouldn't mind slicing those leeks for me while you're here, would you? There's a knife in that drawer.'

'How can you possibly cook all these at one time?'

'I'll manage, and anyway, that's only half of what Angus brought in. Fortunately, Denise loves to cook, so she's taken the rest of the vegetables to her house. We'll manage between us. Unfortunately, a lot of the produce is being harvested too early,' Kathleen added, chopping vigorously. 'Trust Murdo to get things wrong. If he had gone abroad in the autumn when everything was ready to gather in I'd have had a lot more to work with. But even so, we've got plenty. You've no idea how I feel right now, Rachel. I've been reborn – I feel as though I've only just found out what living is really like. This must be the way you felt when you found Cara.'

The back door burst open. 'Kathleen, sweetheart, how about some more tea?' Angus Longmuir suggested. 'Me and the lad are parched.'

The day was warm, and his working clothes consisted of shorts and a grubby vest. His sturdy legs and muscular arms were lightly tanned and his face and unruly hair were damp with sweat. He brought into the kitchen with him the smell of fresh air, newly turned earth, perspiration and, above all, sheer maleness. Just looking at him made Rachel feel strangely uneasy, as though she was breaking some unknown rule and bound to be caught.

'Hi, Rachel,' he said casually, producing a battered packet of cigarettes from the pocket of his shorts. 'Anyone got any matches?'

'Here.' Kathleen, already fussing with the kettle, tossed the box over and he caught it easily, lit his cigarette and then leaned against the dresser as though he owned the place.

'So what d'you think, Rachel?' He gestured towards the open door.

'I think Murdo's going to go mad when he finds out what you're up to.'

'He'll be okay. You wait and see, I'll turn this garden into a little paradise. He'll like it.'

'He told me at our birthday party that you were going to advise him on ways to improve the garden when he came back home, so that he could fit in more vegetables,' Rachel said, and he winked at her.

'We did chat about that, but then the lovely Kathleen got hold of me. She's real businesswoman, Rachel. She made me an offer I couldn't refuse.' The gold chain about his powerful neck glittered as he scratched one shoulder. 'As for Murdo, I happen to know of a very nice allotment that's looking for a new owner. He'll be able to grow a lot more there than he ever could here.' He sniffed the air appreciatively. 'That smells good, Kathleen. Any chance of a plateful of that soup for me and the lad in an hour's time?'

'Of course.' Kathleen had set a tray with biscuits and two mugs. Now, she added a filled teapot and turned, the tray in her hands. 'Here you are. This should keep the two of you going until then.'

'Thanks.' He stuck the cigarette in his mouth, narrowing his green eyes against the smoke, and took the tray from her. 'You're a darlin' woman,' he said easily, and Kathleen giggled.

'You sounded just like a schoolgirl then,' Rachel said when Angus had taken the tray away and they were alone again. Kathleen grinned, swept a lock of hair out of her eyes, and got back to work.

'D'you know, there's something about that man that reminds me of all those lovely teenage dreams I used to have. Which is strange, since the men in my dreams weren't anything like Angus. They were much more sophisticated and worldly than he is. I think he's very . . . how can I put it?' She paused, knife in hand, considering, then came out with, 'Sexy, that's it. Don't you think so?'

'Absolutely not,' Rachel said firmly. 'He's not my type at all.'

'Nor mine, and that's what makes it all the more surprising.'

'You're not . . . falling for him, are you?' Rachel asked nervously, and Kathleen gave a hoot of amusement.

'Good lord no! Even if I did find him that attractive, which I don't, he's your brother-in-law. It would be like stealing from a friend. He's just fun to have around,' she said.

As soon as Martin had switched off the engine both boys were out of the car and hurtling towards the house, where Rachel waited to greet them.

'Did you have a lovely time?'

'Great,' Ian said, dropping his rucksack in the hall and dashing past her into the kitchen. 'I'm starving! What's for tea?'

'Sausage and chips.' Rachel fielded Graham on his way past, managing to get in a hug and a kiss on the cheek before he wriggled free. 'How are Grandma and Grandpa?'

'All right, but they don't have proper sausages, and no black pudding. Can we have that too?'

'If you want.'

'Are the guinea pigs all right? Did you and Fiona look after them properly?'

'No, we worked them like slaves all the time and unfortunately, they just faded away.'

'Liar,' Graham said amiably, then, 'I'll just go and let them know I'm back.'

'Take your things upstairs first . . .' Rachel began, and

then gave up as her younger son dashed heedlessly into the kitchen on his way to the back door.

'Hi,' Martin said, dumping the two suitcases in the porch.

'Hello. Good holiday?'

'Fine. How are things here?' He hugged her, but the barriers, she realised in dismay, were still in place.

'Hi, Dad,' Fiona called cheerfully from halfway up the stairs. She wore a long, loose, short-sleeved muslin blouse over a patterned cotton skirt and her curly hair danced around her face and on her shoulders. She looked well . . . and so young, Rachel thought with a pang.

Martin looked up at his daughter, a grin spreading over his face. 'Hi, how're you?'

'Couldn't be better. Mum and I did some shopping, and we went to Gran's, and Robbie came with us. Gran liked him, and he thinks she's great. But we missed you and the boys, didn't we, Mum?' She came down the last few steps with a rush, and went straight into her father's arms.

'Shopping, did you say? I suppose you spent all my money.'

'Most of it. I got a fantastic jacket, Dad. Wait till you see it.' She linked arms with him and together they went into the kitchen, with Rachel following on behind.

'How did your parents take the news?' Rachel asked as she helped Martin to unpack.

'They weren't very happy – but we couldn't expect otherwise, could we?' He settled a jacket carefully on its hanger and opened the wardrobe door. 'It's not something they've ever had to face before.'

'None of us have, including Fiona.'

'They said that if there was anything they can do to help, we just have to let them know.'

'That was good of them.'

'They meant it,' he said sharply.

'I'm sure they did, but since they live hundreds of miles away, I don't see us having to call on them for assistance. Unless you want to send Fiona to the Lake District to have the baby.'

'That's a daft idea.'

'It's what folk used to do with unmarried mothers – send them to distant relatives or friends so that the neighbours wouldn't gossip. In fact,' Rachel took a neatly folded shirt from the case and shook it out carefully before putting it on a hanger, 'I once read that it was such common practice that every time a girl went on a long visit the neighbours assumed she was pregnant.'

'I imagine that our neighbours know that already.'

'As a matter of fact, they do. Mrs Milligan asked me just yesterday what Fiona was going to do now that she's left school, and when I said that she was planning on going to college once the baby was born, she didn't even bat an eyelid.'

'I suppose that makes things easier for us.'

'I think so. Didn't you change your underwear while you were away? This lot's all clean. It's even ironed.'

'My mother laundered everything before we left, to save you the bother.'

'That was kind of her. Are they very upset, Martin?'

'A bit, but they'll come to terms with it eventually,' he said, and then, clearly anxious to change the subject, 'What about your mother?'

'Actually, she shocked me more than I shocked her.' Rachel put his clean socks, washed and neatly rolled, into his sock drawer. 'She's been marvellous. She's knitting jackets already, and so's Chrissie. That's one good thing – between the two of them and Cara, we won't have to buy any baby clothes. And Fiona's doing really well,

Martin. She's started working on her bookkeeping and shorthand already.'

'Good,' he said, with forced cheerfulness.

Kathleen's back garden had been transformed. Crazy paving replaced the vegetable beds, with curving lines leading the eye to gravelled areas holding large containers massed with bright flowers and trailing greenery. A large half-moon gravel patch at the end of the garden, where Murdo Ramsay had once grown prize-winning onions, held a long wrought-iron seat flanked on either side by miniature rose trees in containers.

'Isn't it lovely?' Kathleen said dreamily. She and Carla and Rachel were sitting on the terraced area close to the house wall, sipping glasses of wine and relaxing in the tranquillity of the view before them. 'I could just sit here for ever, admiring it.'

'You're still making soup.' Rachel sniffed the air. An enticing smell of mixed vegetable soup drifted out from the open kitchen window to mingle with the fragrance of the new plants and bushes. 'I thought you only made soup when you needed to calm down.'

'Which means that I don't need to make it at all, now,' her friend agreed. 'But I've discovered that I still enjoy it for its own sake, and Denise's contact wants us to go on supplying him. So now we're buying the vegetables in bulk from a market gardener Angus knows. The income's very useful. And while the soup of the day's simmering, I can come out here and soothe my soul in my beautiful garden.'

'Have you told Murdo yet?'

'Sod Murdo,' Kathleen said placidly. 'He's so busy telling me on the phone about the marvellous time he's having in Saudi that he never even bothers to ask how I'm managing to fill in my time.'

'He doesn't even ask about his leeks and onions and all the rest of them?'

'Oh yes, he asks after them every time he calls.' Kathleen took another sip of wine. 'And I tell him that it all looks fine to me. Which it does. Don't you agree?'

'It certainly does. My Angus,' Cara said complacently, 'is a miracle worker.'

'Oh, he is,' Kathleen agreed. Rachel, sitting between them, looked from her friend to her twin, then back again. Both Kathleen and Cara were contemplating the garden, both smiling, both supremely content with their lot.

She felt like a thorn between two roses.

'Mrs Carswell?' The richly rounded voice on the telephone was unknown to Rachel. 'My name is Amanda Duncan, and I have a stage costume shop in Glasgow. I got your name and telephone number from a friend, Lizbeth Beattie. She's a teacher at your daughter's school,' she added as Rachel desperately tried to remember why the name was so familiar.

'Oh yes, of course.'

'I hope you don't mind me approaching you out of the blue, so to speak, but Liz told me how helpful you were with the costumes for *The Importance of Being Earnest* – I saw one of the performances, by the way, it was very good, and the costumes were excellent. You're a needle-woman of high standard.'

'Not really. A friend helped, and we only did the girls' costumes.'

'Even so . . . the thing is, as well as hiring clothes for professional and amateur productions, I'm frequently approached by people looking for outfits for fancy dress events. I've just lost one of the seamstresses I use to repair and make costumes, and I'm looking for someone to step into her shoes, so to speak. Liz suggested that you might be willing to work for me.'

'I'm afraid I—'

'I'm not expecting you to come into Glasgow every day; you could work from home as and when needed.'

'Even so, I'm afraid that I have my hands full right now,' Rachel apologised. 'I have three children and things are a bit hectic at the moment.'

'Oh. Are you sure you can't help me out, even with a little work?'

'I'm sorry, but I really can't manage it.'

'That's a pity,' the woman said, and then, with a rueful laugh, 'This isn't my lucky day, it seems. Before I dialled your number I tried a really superb seamstress I used to work with – Flora McCrimmon, her name is – but she's hung up her needle, so to speak. Seems to be happier running a wee bed-and-breakfast place in Largs. I've never really taken to the place myself, but—'

'Did you say Flora McCrimmon?' Rachel interrupted rudely. 'Not Flora Moodie?'

'No, McCrimmon. D'you know her?'

The telephone receiver had become slippery, and Rachel had to clutch it tightly to make sure that it didn't slide right out of her hand. 'Do you have her telephone number, by any chance? I . . . my husband and I were just talking about taking the children away for a few days at the end of the term,' she improvised wildly, scrabbling with her free hand for a pen and then trying to turn the notepad, covered with scribbles from previous phone conversations, to a fresh page.

When the number had been written down and the call ended she tore the page from the telephone pad and carried it into the kitchen, where she read it several times. Then she slipped it into her bag, zipping it in securely.

★   ★   ★

Martin was working late that evening. When she and the children had eaten, Rachel phoned Cara.

'Can I come over for a wee while? There's something I want to talk to you about.'

'Of course. Angus is having a night out with some of his mates – I could get him to drop me off at your place if you'd rather.'

Rachel listened to the noise of the boys racing about the house. The school term had started, and they were working off some of the energy they had built up during a day spent penned in their classrooms.

'I'll come to you; we'll get peace to talk in your house. You're sure I'm not disturbing you?'

'Golly, no. I was just going to catch up on some read-ing.'

'Mum!' Fiona hissed, jiggling at the arm that held the receiver.

'See you soon,' Rachel said, and hung up. 'What is it?'

'I said I'd phone Robbie before seven, and it's almost seven now.'

'Could you keep an eye on the boys for me?' Rachel asked as her daughter dialled. 'I've put your father's dinner in the oven on a low heat; tell him I've gone to see Cara and I'll not be long.'

'Okay.' Fiona was listening intently to the ringing of the far-away phone; then her eyes lit up. 'Hello . . .' she said in the special, soft voice she always used when she was speaking to Robbie.

Rachel fetched her coat and bag and told the boys to behave themselves for Fiona. The girl was still talking on the phone when she left the house and hurried to the bus stop.

'This is a nice surprise,' Cara said when they were settled in the untidy living room, the dogs at their feet. 'Angus won't be home much before midnight, and there's nothing worth watching on the telly. How are things at home?'

'Not too bad. The boys are back at school, and thank goodness for that,' Rachel said from the bottom of her heart. 'I don't know why they make summer holidays so long!'

'You *should* know, since you used to be a teacher. It's for the sake of the staff, not the kids and their parents.'

'Oh yes, I forgot the luxury of having all those weeks off work. But now that I see it from the parents' point of view I realise that it isn't such a good idea. Fiona's enrolled in a correspondence course – at Robbie's suggestion – so that she can go on with her studying. And Martin managed to get a second-hand typewriter for her so that she can keep up with her typing.'

'You don't think she's taking on too much?' Cara asked anxiously. 'Remember her condition.'

'Oh, she's as fit as a flea, and she seems to be enjoying studying,' Rachel said, and then laughed. 'Martin thinks that it might be good for the baby; help it to be clever in later life.'

'Trust your Martin,'

'Cara, I got a phone call today from a woman in Glasgow . . .' Rachel launched into her story and Cara listened, open-mouthed.

'Largs!' she said five minutes later. 'To think that the three of us have been living fairly close to each other without realising it.'

'I never thought of trying the phone book before.'

'I did,' Cara said. 'I contacted every Moodie in the book, but none of them knew Flora. Perhaps that's why she took on her middle name – so that she couldn't be traced. Rachel, you clever girl – you've found our mother!'

'We can't be sure that it's her.'

'It's got to be!' Cara jumped to her feet and began to pace the floor. The two dogs had wakened as soon as she moved, and now they trotted at her heels, staring up at her face, puzzled by the back and forth movements. 'It *must* be our mother!' Let me see the phone number.'

Rachel handed it over and her sister studied it carefully, as though it held some sort of cryptic clue. She wished that she had settled in another chair, but didn't like to move. The larger of the two dogs seemed unable to walk around without swishing its feathery tail, and each time it passed her chair she received a painful whack on the leg.

'We must phone her,' Cara announced. She started towards the telephone, then stopped as Rachel yelled, 'No!'

Startled, the West Highland terrier began to bark and the big dog joined in after a moment's bewildered hesitation, rushing to the window to rear up with his big paws on the sill, baying threats to any would-be intruders.

'Shut up, Muffin, you stupid mutt! You too, Henry. Behave yourselves. Basket!' Cara ordered, and then, as both dogs ignored her, '*I said BASKET!* Why on earth not?' she went on, lowering her voice a few decibels as the chastened dogs crept into their beds. 'It's what we want, isn't it − to find our mother?'

'I'm not so sure any more.' Rachel's mouth was suddenly dry, and her stomach felt as though it housed an entire Amazonian forest full of large butterflies. She gulped down a mouthful of cooling tea. 'It's probably not her; it's probably some completely different woman called Flora McCrimmon.'

She held her hand out for the piece of paper, and was

303

glad when Cara gave it up without an argument. She zipped it back into her bag, safe from danger. 'I have to go. Martin must be home by now. Let's sleep on this, and talk about it again some other time.'

Abba's 'Waterloo' was belting out from upstairs when she let herself into the house, and Martin and the boys were in the living room, watching a documentary about aircraft.

'Was your dinner all right? Not dried up?'

'It was fine. Where were you?'

'I went over to see Cara. Didn't Fiona tell you?'

'She said you said Kathleen.'

'No, Cara. She was on the phone to Robbie when I told her; she was too busy listening to him to listen to me.' She settled down in a chair and picked up her book.

'Was Angus there?'

'He was out with friends.' Rachel removed the old envelope she was using as a bookmark. There were at least a dozen proper bookmarks scattered around the house, but she never could find one when she needed it.

'I phoned Kathleen,' Martin said, 'to ask if you wanted me to drive over to fetch you.'

'And she said that I wasn't there. Because I was at Cara's.' Rachel had had to leave the book at an interesting bit, and she was impatient to get back to it.

'Eventually. She took a while to answer the phone, and when she did, she sounded all hot and bothered.'

And Angus was out for the evening, Rachel suddenly realised. She must have jumped, because her elbow knocked the envelope off the arm of her chair. As she lunged for it, her paperback book snapped shut and she only just stopped it from falling too.

'Blast and bother, now I'll have to find my place again! I hate the way paperbacks do that. Kathleen was probably in the kitchen, making soup,' she went on once she had restored order. 'That's all she seems to do these days.'

'She certainly didn't want to talk. Just said that you weren't there, and I said fine, and we hung up.'

'Pity you didn't think to phone Cara next. Barrhead's two bus journeys from here. I can walk home from Kathleen's house.'

'I did phone, after I spoke to Kathleen, but Cara said you'd just left.' Martin yawned, and went back to watching television while Rachel stared unseeingly at her book, wondering what had been going on.

28

Kathleen phoned the next morning, not long after Martin had gone to work.

'Murdo came home last night.'

'I thought he was coming back next week?'

'So did I, but he decided to surprise me. Though he was the one who got the surprise,' Kathleen said, her voice bubbling over with amusement. 'He rushed in the front door, gave me a quick kiss in the passing – I swear that if it had been my cleaning lady standing there instead of me, he'd have kissed her instead, without even noticing his mistake – then shot out of the back door and fell over one of my flower containers.'

'What happened?'

'He bruised his shin and skinned his hand. Just missed landing on another container.'

'I mean, what happened when he saw the garden?'

'Oh, that. He almost went into orbit. It was so funny, Rachel! He was hopping around on one leg, turning the air blue. It took a few minutes before he actually noticed the patio and all the other changes Angus had made. Then he started saying, "What? Where?" over and over again.

That's when Martin phoned. I was laughing so much that I could scarcely speak to him,' Kathleen said with another gurgle of amusement. 'When Murdo had calmed down a bit, I just told him that things had changed and if he didn't like what I had done, I was all set to leave.'

'Did he believe you?'

'Fortunately I had already packed a weekend case ready for his return next week. He believed me when he saw it sitting in the hall cupboard. So after I had cleaned his scraped hand and put some arnica on his shin to ease the bruising, I drove him to the allotment I've rented for him. I'd even got Angus to lay it out so that he can start his autumn planting right away. Must go,' Kathleen said hurriedly. 'I think he's awake. I only came down to put some breakfast on a tray. We're going to have a lazy morning.'

'Poor Murdo must be exhausted, after his long journey home.'

'And other activities,' Kathleen said smugly. 'Talk to you soon.'

Rachel had no sooner returned to the kitchen and started to peel apples for that evening's dinner than the phone summoned her back to the hall.

'Rachel, I thought you'd never get off the phone!'

'It was Kathleen; Mur—'

'I've spoken to her!'

'Spoken to who?'

'Who d'you think? Flora McCrimmon Moodie, that's who.'

Rachel's stomach seemed to clench itself like a fist. 'But we agreed to sleep on it and talk about it again before we decided anything!'

'I did sleep on it, and then this morning I decided to

go for it. I knew you'd not be happy about it, but I couldn't just let it go at that without checking out that phone number.'

'You didn't have the phone number.'

'I memorised it from your bit of paper, and this morning I looked up Flora McCrimmon in the phone book, and there was the same number. Eureka!' Cara crowed. 'I've booked the two of us in next Tuesday. You can manage then, can't you?'

'What?'

'I said, I've booked us in for three nights, starting next Tuesday. She sounds a bit crabbit on the phone, or mebbe it was more brisk than crabbit,' Cara said thoughtfully. 'But I'm not sure that we're going to like her.'

Rachel blinked at the potato peeler she had forgotten to leave in the kitchen. 'You didn't tell her who you are, did you?'

'Of course not. What do you take me for – an idiot? We don't know if we're going to like her, so the last thing we want to do is tell her the truth at this early stage. Anyway, I'm sure that if I had said something like, "Your abandoned twin daughters want to book in so that they can confront you," she would have told me in no uncertain terms that there was no room at the inn. The B & B, I mean. I just said that my sister and I needed a few days' holiday. I booked a twin room, is that all right?'

'Cara, I can't just drop everything and go to Largs.'

'Why not?'

'There's the boys, and Martin, and Fiona not having long to go now, and . . .' Rachel's mind scurried about her skull like a frantic squirrel, trying to find reasons not to go to Largs.

'Fiona's not due for about two weeks, and you said yourself last night that she's absolutely fine. And I'm sure your mum would love to help out for a few days. Doreen needs to be needed, Rachel. And Martin could manage without you for a short while, couldn't he? He's a big boy now. We could wait until Tuesday evening, if you want; it doesn't take long to get to Largs. Then back by Friday afternoon. That means you'll just be away Wednesday and Thursday, and the three nights.'

'Let me think it over. I'll phone you tomorrow morning, okay?'

'I'm going, whether you come with me or not. But I really, *really* want you to be there too,' Cara said. 'First thing tomorrow, mind.'

'Mum?' Fiona said from the bottom of the stairs. 'Are you all right?'

'What? Yes, I'm fine.'

'Then why are you standing there staring at that potato peeler as if it's about to turn into a snake and bite you?'

'I was just . . . that was your Auntie Cara on the phone. She wants me to go to Largs with her next Tuesday to Friday.'

'Why?' Fiona followed Rachel into the kitchen. 'What's happening in Largs?'

'She just fancies some time by the seaside, and she'd like me to go along for company.'

'I hope you said yes. It would do you good, Mum.'

'How can I leave you at a time like this? Not to mention the boys and your father.'

'Oh, phooey.' Fiona patted the bump beneath her loose dress. 'The baby's not due for just over two weeks, and the district nurse says that first babies are usually late.'

'She's right, but babies don't seem to know about the rules. Sometimes they come early.'

'Mum, I'm absolutely fine,' Fiona insisted, taking the peeler from her mother and picking up an apple. 'If

309

anything happens, which it won't, Largs isn't far away. And you need a break, away from here and away from us.'

'I'll see what your father thinks,' Rachel said.

'Largs? Why Largs?'

'It's reasonably close if I happen to be needed here, which I won't be, and Cara thought it might do the two of us good to get away for a few days. After all,' Rachel pointed out, 'I haven't had a holiday this year.' Then as Martin, leafing through the television programme guide, said nothing, she said swiftly, 'And I didn't mean that to sound the way it did. It's only going to be for three days, and Mum says she'll stay here while I'm away, so you won't have to worry about looking after the children.'

'So it's all been settled.'

'Just as you settled everything before you got around to telling me that you were taking the boys to the Lake District,' she pointed out, then felt ashamed of herself when he flushed guiltily.

'Martin, I won't go if you don't want me to.' She waited, hoping that he would ask her to stay. Being needed by Martin was more important than finding a mother she had never known.

'You should go,' he said, and switched the television set on for the evening news. 'I'm sure we can manage for a few days and as you say, you haven't had a break this year.'

Tuesday turned out to be one of those days when every plan Rachel made went wrong. When she should have been ready to go, she was still packing, while Martin was shaving in the bathroom before collecting Doreen from Chrissie's flat.

'I'll be back on Friday,' she said when he came into

the bedroom. 'And you've got the phone number. Just phone if you need me and I can be home in no time.'

'We'll manage.' He picked up his tie. 'It'll probably be good for you to get a bit of breathing space.'

'Martin . . .' she began, then ran to the window as she heard a car door slam. Angus was taking a small suitcase from the boot. He brought it to where Cara was getting out of the passenger seat, kissed her, then got back into the car. As he drove off he tooted the horn and flourished a big hand from the open window, while Cara blew extravagant kisses in return.

'Cara's here already!' Rachel darted back to where her case lay open on the bed. 'Martin, could you let her in and tell her that I won't be a moment?'

'I'm not in the mood for Angus,' he grumbled.

'He's gone, it's just Cara. Please, Martin!'

'Oh, all right.' He picked up his jacket and left the room.

'Rachel's upstairs, finishing her packing,' he said at the open door.

'We're not in a big hurry. I'll leave this here.' Cara put her small suitcase down in the porch before following him into the house. 'Can I phone for a taxi?'

'Help yourself,' he said shortly and went into the living room, where he stood, hands dug into trouser pockets, listening to the sound of her voice in the hall. For some unknown reason, the doll that Cara had made for Fiona was lolling on one of the armchairs. Martin stared at the bright patterned shirt and the flared trousers and the pert grin on the pretty little face. Being a teenager should have been about happiness and friendships and looking forward to the future, not unplanned pregnancy and the sudden burden of adult responsibility. Knowing that the carefree days were over for his little Fiona hurt him so much that he couldn't even talk to Rachel about it. And not being able to talk freely to Rachel was like having an arm cut off. He had never been more unhappy in his life.

Cara's rich, warm laugh rang out, and he wondered what she was laughing at and whom she was laughing with. Only Cara could turn a taxi booking into a social occasion. He didn't turn when she came into the room.

'Ten minutes, they reckon,' she said to his back. 'That gives us plenty of time to get to the station. The house is very quiet, where is everyone?'

'The boys are at a friend's house and Fiona's with Robbie – as usual. I'm just about to go and fetch Doreen. That's why I can't give the two of you a lift,' he added.

'That's all right. I met Fiona in the town this morning; she's looking marvellous, isn't she?'

Martin swallowed to ease his dry throat and stared hard at the blue bandanna tied round the doll's curly hair.

'As marvellous as she can be, under the circumstances.'

Cara put a hand on his arm. 'She'll be all right, Martin.'

'You think so?'

'I know so. Whenever things are bad for me I always tell myself that a year from now I'll be able to look back and say, oh, so *that's* how it worked itself out.'

He swung round to face her. 'And what if we look back in a year's time and find that everything went wrong?'

'Why should it? Robbie and Fiona are going to be all right together, trust me.'

'It's not just Fiona, though. There's Rachel as well.'

'What's wrong with Rachel?'

'She's . . . different now.'

'Of course she isn't.'

'What do you know about the way she used to be? You were strangers up until a few months ago,' he said, and then added sarcastically, 'Oh sorry, I forgot – you're twins, from the same womb, the same seed. Two halves of the same person. That means that you each know every thought the other has, every emotion, every twinge. I wonder if you felt each other's birth pangs? You probably did.'

'Don't be daft.' Cara leaned back against the sideboard, arms folded. 'We don't share any of that mystic twin stuff, and even if we *had* grown up together I could never in a million years know Rachel in the way that you do. Husbands and partners are more special than twins. You and Rachel know each other better than anyone else ever could, and that's the way it'll always be with the two of you.'

'I used to think so. Now I'm not so sure. Sometimes,' he said awkwardly, 'I wish Rachel could be more like you. More . . . oh, I don't know.'

'If Rachel was like me you'd never have married her.'

'That's not true.'

'You and I both married the right people and we wouldn't be happy with anyone else.'

Her confidence stung the wounds festering deep within Martin. 'Does that mean that you haven't noticed the way Angus flirts with your sister whenever they're together?' he said spitefully.

'Angus does that with every woman he meets.' Cara's voice was calm. 'He thinks he's irresistible to women. It's harmless. It doesn't mean anything.'

'Doesn't it? I've a feeling that Kathleen Ramsay might be getting more for her money than a new-look garden.'

Cara studied him, a slight smile curving her full lips. 'My Angus can behave like a big kid at times, but that's all right by me because I need a bit of danger in my life, and he supplies it. That's why I love him, and that's why I know that we would never be unfaithful to each other.'

'If you believe that, you'll believe—'

'Martin,' Cara said levelly, 'I do believe it.' Her blue

eyes were suddenly holding his, wide and clear and honest – just like Rachel's gaze, he realised. 'That's where Rachel and I are very alike,' she said. 'We both believe in trust and fidelity. Neither of us would have married a man we couldn't trust with our lives and our futures. Angus is perfect for me, and you're perfect for Rachel. And believe me, she knows it.'

Her eyes were unwavering, and finally he was forced to look away. 'I'd better go,' he muttered. 'Doreen will be wondering where I've got to.'

Rachel found her twin alone in the living room, flicking through a magazine. 'Sorry I wasn't ready when you arrived.' She looked round the room. 'Where's Martin?'

'He had to leave to collect your mum,' Cara said, and then, as the bleat of a horn signalled the taxi's arrival, 'Well, here we go.'

'Did Martin say anything to you before he went?' Rachel wanted to know as they were driven to the railway station.

'Just the usual hello and how are you stuff. And he said to tell you goodbye, and to have a nice time,' Cara lied as she saw her sister's teeth nibbling at her lower lip. Then, giving Rachel's arm an excited squeeze, 'Just think – our very first trip to the seaside together. We should have brought buckets and spades. Tell you what; we'll buy them there. And do a boat trip too. Let's do the whole kids' holiday thing. We owe it to ourselves.'

The guest house was stone built and semi-detached, with a small neat garden at the front and a *No Vacancies* sign in the window.

'You did book us in, didn't you?' Rachel asked, eyeing it.

'Yes I did. Pity we don't have a sea view, but it's not that far to the front. Come on . . .' Cara opened the gate and began to lead the way up the stone-flagged path. 'And not a word about who we are until we've had a chance to decide how we feel about her.'

'If it really is her,' Rachel said to her sister's back. 'But even if it is, we don't want to start opening doors that should perhaps stay closed.'

'You never know; she might be delighted to see her long-lost babies again.' Cara pressed the doorbell and for a brief moment Rachel contemplated flight. She might just make it to the corner of the road before the door opened. She could call Martin from a phone box and ask him to come at once and take her home . . .

The door opened. 'Hi,' said a young man, and then, seeing their suitcases, 'You must be Mrs Longmuir and Mrs Carswell? Now which is which . . . no, don't tell me, let me guess. I'm usually good at this sort of thing.' His beautiful dark brown eyes seemed to caress Rachel's face, and she felt a strange sensation, almost like a teenage giggle, bubble up in her throat. 'Mrs Carswell, and . . .' the warm gaze passed from her to Cara, 'Mrs Longmuir. Right?'

'We'd prefer Cara – that's me – and Rachel.'

'Danny.' His smile deepened to reveal a dimple in one cheek. 'Let me take your cases. You're in the front room,' he went on as he led the way up the carpeted stairs. 'It's our largest. You're the only guests and so you get the best.'

Cara, following him, turned and glanced down at Rachel, raising her eyebrows and shaping her mouth into an 'O' of astonishment and delight. Then she said demurely, 'We thought the place must be full. You have a *No Vacancies* sign in your window.'

'It's been a busy season, but now we're more or less closed for the winter. Your booking came just in time. A day later and we'd have had to turn you down. Here we are.' He set down one of the cases on the upper landing and opened a door to reveal a spacious, comfortable room. Putting the cases down to one side of the door, Danny switched on the overhead light before stepping aside to let the sisters enter.

The curtains, already drawn across the bay window, matched the floral spreads on the twin beds, and the fitted carpet was a deep rose pink.

'Lots of drawer space, and a big wardrobe,' Danny pointed out. 'The bathroom's just next door, and there's a payphone on the wall opposite your door. You've got the entire floor to yourselves; our quarters are downstairs.'

'You're our landlord, are you?' Cara asked, and he shook his head, showing even white teeth in an amused grin.

'I just help out. I expect you're parched after your journey. We were about to have a cup of tea; why don't you join us in the lounge when you're ready?' He gave them another of his lovely warm smiles. 'It's just below this room.'

'Wow!' Cara said as the door closed behind him. 'Gorgeous, or what?'

'He looks a bit like Byron.'

'Clark Gable, I thought. In his prime, of course. And Danny's definitely in *his* prime. What d'you think?' Cara dropped down onto one of the beds, her eyes bright with curiosity. 'The daily help?'

'He said, "*Our* quarters are downstairs." It sounds to me as though he lives in. Oh, Cara . . . if she's our mother, you don't think he might be our brother?'

'What? I hope not! Fancy fancying your brother!'

'He's too young to be her husband. He could be younger than we are.'

'There's only one way to find out.' Cara jumped up. 'Let's get tidied up and then go downstairs for that cup of tea.'

29

They had been so intent on Danny on the way to their room that they hadn't taken any notice of their surroundings, or seen, as they followed him up the staircase, the mass of photographs that were covering the walls. It was Cara who stopped on the way down and said, 'Isn't that Johnny Ray? And this one's Frankie Vaughan.'

'And that's Jimmy Logan – they're all famous people.' Rachel peered at one of the framed pictures. '"For Dear Flora, With Love, Norman Wisdom." And look there, and there. Every one's a famous person. She must have written away for them.'

'Got them signed in person, lovey. Met every one of 'em.' The woman in the hall below was dressed in such bright clothes that it was a wonder they hadn't noticed her straight away. Her long loose tunic, worn over bright green silk trousers, was a mass of diamond shapes in all the colours of the rainbow, and her unnaturally red hair, a riot of curls, glowed in the electric light.

'Come on in, then,' she ordered, throwing open a door. 'Danny's just bringing the tea.'

In the lounge, every available surface except the large

coffee table was covered with more framed and signed photographs.

'Sit down,' the woman invited, a sweep of her arm taking in the two sofas and three armchairs. 'Anywhere you like.'

She herself chose a high-backed chair. The long, blue velvet curtains had already been drawn and the room was lit by several table lamps and standard lamps, one of which, by the woman's chair, made the rings she wore on every finger sparkle, and illuminated a heavily made-up face with bright red lips and so much blue eyeshadow that each time she looked down it was as though twin shutters had been dropped over her eyes.

'Been to Largs before?' She took a silver cigarette box from a nearby occasional table, and then offered it to each of them. When they shook their heads, she selected one for herself.

'Lots of times,' Cara said breezily. 'I live in Barrhead, and Rachel's in Paisley. We're sisters.'

'Oh yes?' Their hostess took an elaborate lighter from the table.

'We just fancied a few days away. A chance to catch up with each other. You're the owner of the place, I take it? Mrs . . . McCrimmon, is that right?'

'Miss, dear.' Their hostess lit her cigarette, took a deep drag, and blew out a long plume of smoke before saying, 'I never married. Never found the need. Call me Flora, everyone does.'

'I'm Catherine, but everyone calls me Cara. And this is my sister Rachel.'

Flora McCrimmon acknowledged the names with a brief, disinterested nod of the head. 'This is the residents' lounge; you're welcome to use it if you want. There's a radio in the corner, and the television. And magazines and some books that folk have left behind. The dining room

318

where you'll have your breakfast is across the hall. And here's the tea, at last,' she ended as a rattling sound from the hall heralded the arrival of Danny, pushing a trolley.

'Sorry, Flo, I forgot to switch the kettle on. It's new,' he explained to the sisters as he manoeuvred the trolley into position beside Flora's chair. 'I'm not used to it yet.'

'Silly poppet.' She reached up and patted his cheek as he began to pour the tea. 'He's not good with machinery, are you, my angel?'

'Not at all. I nearly flooded the kitchen last week.' He lifted long slender fingers to sweep back a lock of black hair that was falling into one eye. 'I forgot to make sure the washing machine door was properly closed. To tell you the truth, I don't know why she bothers to put up with me.'

'You have your uses,' Flora said almost coyly, and he laughed and winked at Rachel, who blushed.

'Did you say that you knew all the people in these photographs?' Cara asked.

'We weren't bosom buddies, but yes, love, I've met each and every one of 'em in my time.'

'Were you on the stage?'

Flora gave a husky smoker's laugh. 'Not me, though Danny was. He's a dancer. And a lovely mover.'

'*Was* a dancer,' Danny corrected her. 'Before Flora set eyes on me and made me change my ways.'

'For the better – and he's still a lovely mover. No, dear, I was a dresser.'

'Really? In London?'

'Glasgow. You name it, I worked there. The Pavilion, the King's, the Metropole, the Empire, the Alhambra, the Empress. And I met the best because only the best came to Glasgow. Pure gold, all of 'em. Stage folk are lovely to work with. Those were the days, eh, Danny?'

'Maybe they were good times for you, Flo, but not much fun for me. Dancing's hard on the joints. Give me Largs and life with my lovely Flo any time.' Danny reached out to take the older woman's red-tipped hand, kissing it with a romantic flourish. She giggled.

'He's a character, isn't he? More tea, anyone?'

'What d'you think?' Cara asked as soon as they were back in their room with the door safely shut behind them.

'I can't believe that that's our mother. She must be the wrong Flora McCrimmon.'

'I'm talking about Danny.' Cara started tugging out the bedclothes that had been securely tucked in along both sides and the bottom of her bed. 'I hate the way people make beds hospital-style in these places. Sleeping in one of those makes me feel like an Egyptian mummy. How are you expected to get into them at night? Post yourself through the slot at the top?' She worked her way along the bottom of the bed and started up the other side. 'Gorgeous, isn't he? She's right, he is a lovely mover. Poetry in motion! And what about those long muscular legs!'

'You don't think he's . . . you know.'

'With those come-to-bed eyes? Not a chance!'

'Most dancers are.'

'Phooey, that's just a rumour put about by jealous men who lead dull lives and can't dance for toffee.' Cara had finished pulling her bed to pieces; now she kicked her shoes off and flopped down on top of the quilt, wriggling herself into a comfortable position. 'Mmmm, that's better.'

'P'raps he's her husband like we thought at first.'

'Neither of them wears rings . . . well, not wedding rings, anyway. Did you see all those rings on her hands? And she said that she's never married. Never felt the

320

need.' Cara's voice was heavy with meaning. 'They're living together.'

'But he's years and years younger than she is!'

'So what? Our mum got lucky.'

'She's not even attractive, Cara.'

'Perhaps she has a beautiful nature, or hidden depths. Perhaps he's so grateful that she rescued him from a future of sore joints and unemployment that he would do anything for her. You can see that he adores her. It takes all sorts.'

'I can't believe that that woman's our mother,' Rachel said again.

'Remember when we first met in Cochran's tea room and we were surprised because we found out that we both loved sewing? She worked as a dresser in theatres; that means she must be handy with a needle. That's the woman we both inherited our skills from.'

'It could be a coincidence. And I certainly didn't inherit anything else from her.'

'I did.' Cara ran a hand through her curly mop. 'I've got her curls – and so had Alice, and your Fiona. Our dad must have had straight hair.'

'She's so . . . different from anyone I've ever known.'

'What did you expect?' Cara moved onto her back and raised one leg in the air, keeping the knee straight.

'Someone more . . . motherly, I suppose.'

'If she'd been the motherly sort she would have kept us. I think she's fascinating.' Grunting slightly with the effort, Cara lowered her leg slowly, then began to raise the other one. 'She's larger than life. I like the idea of having a mother like nobody else's. Angus will adore her.'

'You're not going to tell her who we are, are you?'

'Why not? We came to see what she was like, and it doesn't seem fair to just go away again without telling her.'

'But we don't know how she'll react. She might want to get to know us. She might want to visit us!'

'I hope she does.'

Rachel tried to picture Flora McCrimmon, with her rings and her rainbow clothes and her heavy make-up and blue-shutter eyelids, being introduced to Martin as his other mother-in-law. He was finding Cara difficult enough to take. And what would he think of Danny?

'Imagine our mother meeting all those famous people!' Cara propped her raised hips on her hands and started bicycling her legs in the air. 'She's had such an exciting life!' After only a dozen brisk revolutions she stopped cycling, and stretched her arms above her head. 'Enough of the exercising. I think the sea air's getting to me already. Time for bed. Let's go to the cinema tomorrow evening.'

'What's on?'

'Who cares?' Cara said blithely, sitting up and reaching for her bag. 'Let's just go anyway. We've never been to the pictures together before.' Producing her purse, she added, 'I promised to phone Angus before I go to bed.'

Rachel, cleaning her teeth in the bathroom, could hear Cara's animated murmur in the hall, punctuated by bursts of laughter. When she emerged, her twin was making elaborate kissing noises into the receiver.

'You'll be wanting to phone Martin,' she said when she hung up.

'It's a bit late.'

'Go on, you know you're longing to hear his voice. Go on!' Cara insisted, and then, as she went into the bedroom, 'I've left some change by the phone in case you need it.'

'Of course we're all right,' Martin said a moment later. 'We're all managing very well.'

'Did the boys do their homework?'

'Yes, and your mother's settled in.'

'I miss you.'

There was a brief pause before he said briskly, 'We all miss you, too.'

'I meant—'

'You'll be back home in less than seventy-two hours.'

'Yes,' she said. 'So I will.' And wondered if he was counting the time spent apart.

Cara was in bed when she went back to the room. 'That was a quick phone call.'

'Martin didn't seem inclined to talk.' Rachel unbuttoned her dressing gown. 'I think he blames me for what's happened with Fiona.'

'I know it takes two to make a baby, but the girl's mother isn't usually one of them.'

'It's not just Fiona, it's . . .' She stopped short.

'It's me, I know that. He married an only child, not a twin.'

'He married me, and I'm still me!' It came out as a childish wail.

'I suppose that us coming here for a few days hasn't helped.'

'Perhaps it's going to help me. Perhaps I needed time to think things through. Perhaps,' Rachel said slowly, 'this is my chance to find out exactly who I am.'

'You're you – always were and always will be.'

'I wish Martin thought that.'

'He does. Give him time,' Cara said; then, as Rachel drew back the bedclothes, 'Put the light out, will you, and open the curtains a bit. I hate dark rooms.'

When the room was lit only by a shaft of pale light slipping in between the parted curtains she said sleepily, 'I'm glad she hasn't put any of her celebrity photos up in this room. I don't fancy being watched by all those famous people when I'm getting dressed and undressed.'

'Nor me.' Rachel got into bed and drew the blankets over her shoulder.

'I'd not mind Clark Gable,' Cara said after a long silence. 'Or that gorgeous Danny.' She yawned, and less than two minutes later Rachel heard her twin's breathing become slower and heavier until finally it turned into small, soft snores.

She watched as the wardrobe and the chest of drawers began to stand out as unfamiliar shapes in the gloom, homesick for her own bed and her familiar bedroom, and the children and, most of all, Martin's solid, warm body beside hers. She wondered, bleakly, whether he was missing her as much as she was missing him.

'I wouldn't mind a nightcap myself,' Doreen said from the kitchen doorway, and then as Martin jumped, sloshing whisky over the rim of his glass, 'You don't need to look so guilty about it. A man's entitled to a drink in his own house.'

'I thought everyone was in bed.' He licked whisky from his hand as his mother-in-law fetched a cloth from the draining board. Her grey hair was as neat as ever, and she wore a dark blue chenille dressing gown, long-sleeved and buttoned to the throat.

'I couldn't sleep. Never can, the first night in a strange bed.' She mopped at the small puddle on the table and then rinsed the cloth, repeating, 'I wouldn't mind a nightcap myself.'

'Whisky?'

Doreen wrinkled her nose in distaste as she hung the cloth on a tap to dry. 'Can't bear the stuff. D'you have any sherry?'

'We always have sherry.'

'I thought so. You're sherry people, you and Rachel.'

'It's in the cabinet in the living room,' Martin said, unsure of just what she meant.

'Bring it in here; we can talk better in the kitchen.' Doreen settled herself at the table, adding to her son-in-law's retreating back, 'You might as well bring the bottle.'

At her first sip she grimaced and went into a brief fit of coughing.

'Is it too dry? It's all we've got, but there's port if you'd rather.'

'No, no.' Doreen patted her mouth with a handkerchief taken from the pocket of her dressing gown, coughed once more, then said, 'The first mouthful always takes me that way. I'll be fine now.' She took a generous swig from the glass before setting it down. 'Though that's more than I can say for you. You look as if you've lost a fortune and found a single sock instead. Was that our Rachel on the phone a minute ago?'

'Yes.'

'She's all right?'

'Oh, *she's* all right.' He sipped some whisky before adding bitterly, 'It's not as if she's alone. She's with Cara, God's in his heaven and all's well with the world.'

'Funny, isn't it, how different those two are, considering they're twins. I suppose it's to do with their upbringing.'

'What d'you make of Cara?'

Doreen took a couple of sips from her glass while she considered the question. 'She's all right. Quite nice, once you get to know her. Her heart's in the right place, even if her dress sense is all over the shop.'

'She's . . .' Martin searched for the right words. 'They're like two reflections in the one mirror. They're alike and yet they're different.' He emptied his glass and immediately refilled it without seeming to notice what he was doing. Then, as Doreen remained silent, he said, 'When I look at Cara, I can't help wondering if that's what Rachel might have been if they'd grown up together. Might still become,' he added. 'I feel as if I don't know her any more; not the real Rachel. It frightens me, but at the same time—' He stopped abruptly.

'At the same time there's a part of you that wouldn't mind if she was a bit more like Cara.'

'No!'

'Aye there is,' Doreen challenged. 'And I know that because I've thought it myself, God help me. There were times when I've wished our Rachel had a bit more gumption in her, even though I know fine that it was probably me that stopped her havin' it in the first place. So go on and say it. There's nob'dy here but me to hear you.'

He bit his lip, stared down into his half-full glass, and then finally muttered, shame-faced, 'I suppose you're right.'

'At least you're bein' honest.' Doreen pushed her empty glass towards him, nodding at the sherry bottle. 'To tell you the truth, Martin, when our Rachel first brought you home I thought you were a right stuffed shirt.'

'Thanks very much.'

'A bit more,' she instructed, nodding approval when he filled her glass almost to the brim. 'Now don't get me wrong, we were both pleased when she met you, me and her dad, because you were a sensible hard-working lad and we could see that you were going to do well. But there was no spark to you. Mind you, when I met your parents I realised why. They're not exactly a barrel of laughs, are they?'

'They never were.'

'And neither were me and Frank, I'll admit that. What we wanted most was to see Rachel well settled with someone who'd look after her, and you filled that bill, all right. But the thing is, she's never sowed any wild oats. Not so much as a single oat as far as I know. What about you?'

'I suppose not.'

'Exactly. Now Cara, on the other hand, and that husband of hers – if you ask me, they've sown every oat. P'raps going off with Cara this week'll give Rachel the chance tae sow an oat or two.'

'That's what I'm worried about.'

'For goodness' sake, laddie, she's in Largs for three nights, not Monte Carlo for the yachting season. All I meant was that she might be the better for having the chance to talk everythin' out with Cara. How much mischief can she get up to, when she's just a few miles away and for only three nights?'

'It's not that. I'm frightened in case . . . I don't know why I'm frightened,' he finished lamely. 'I just am.'

'If it's any consolation, this whole business about her findin' Cara frightened me too, until I realised that there was no need.'

'You think not? It's changed her already.'

'Mebbe a wee bit, but not much.' Doreen eyed him shrewdly over the rim of her glass. 'Mebbe it's changed you too. Have you not thought of that?'

'Me? Why should I change?'

'Exactly!' She set the glass down so that she could wag a finger at him. The sherry, Martin noticed, had brought colour to her cheeks and a new brightness to her eyes, not to mention strength to her voice. 'You're puttin' all the blame for what's gone wrong on Rachel, when some of it might lie with you.'

'All right, so none of us are the same as we were before, and we never will be. It's not just Cara, it's what's happened to Fiona as well.'

'Tut, laddie, you're not the first parents that's happened to and you'll not be the last. Everything'll work out, Martin, but only if you and Rachel can see it through together. Now then . . .' Doreen put down her empty glass and began to rise from the table, then sat down again, suddenly. 'Come round here and give me a hand, will you? It's time I got tae my bed. I'll certainly sleep now,' she added as Martin heaved her to her feet and eased her into the hall and up the stairs.

30

'We thought we might take the ferry over to Cumbrae later,' Rachel told Danny, who was serving breakfast. 'But it looks a bit cloudy.'

'The sun'll be shining by noon.'

'Do you always believe what the weather man says?' Cara asked cheekily, and he grinned.

'Never bother with them. I'm a gardener – in my spare time – so I've learned to read the signs. Wait until tomorrow and you'll find yourselves cycling round the island in the rain.'

'I think my cycling days are over,' Cara said with a snort of laughter. 'It's been so long ago that I don't think I could remember how.'

'Once learned, never forgotten. It keeps you fit.'

'And what is it that keeps you fit?' she wanted to know, eyeing his lean body.

He grinned. 'Gardening,' he said, and then, arching one beautifully curved black eyebrow, 'among other things. Talking of gardening, it's time I was off.'

'Can I have more coffee first?' Cara held up her cup and asked, as Danny filled it, 'How long have the two of you been here?'

'Oh, it must be seven years now. I'll leave the coffee pot, shall I? Shout if you need anything, Flo's in the kitchen.'

Five minutes later he passed by the window, wheeling a bicycle down the path and out of the gate.

'P'raps I *will* hire a bike over on Cumbrae,' Cara said thoughtfully. 'It certainly keeps Danny in good shape.' And then, glancing across the table, 'You're very quiet this morning.'

'I've been thinking; let's tell her.' Rachel jerked her head in the direction of the kitchen. 'I'm getting tired of trying to keep things on a level keel, Cara. Martin and I have never kept secrets from each other, but here I am in Largs, when I should be at home with him and Fiona and the boys – and I haven't told him why we're here. Maybe it's time to get everything out in the open, once and for all!'

'Hang on . . .' Cara was beginning, when Flora McCrimmon brought in an empty tray.

'It's going to be a fine day,' she said as she began to stack their empty plates.

'That's what Danny said, too. We'd been thinking of putting off our trip to Cumbrae until tomorrow,' Cara said, 'but he thought today would be better.'

'He's not often wrong, my Danny. He's gone out early this morning to make the most of the good weather. More toast, or coffee?'

'No thanks,' Cara said.

'Did you know that we're twins?' tumbled from Rachel's mouth before she knew that she was going to say it.

The woman stared at her, puzzled, then said, 'No, just that you're sisters.'

'Rachel . . .'

'Twins don't always look like each other. We didn't even know each other until last year. We were brought up by different people, you see. We were born in Glasgow, on

April 28th, 1941. Our mother advertised us in the news-papers as one baby and so we went to different families. The funny thing is,' Rachel continued as Flora's bewildered stare gradually began to be replaced by dawning realisation, 'we both have copies of our birth certificates, and our adoption papers, and our real mother has almost the same name as you. Only she was called Flora McCrimmon *Moodie*. Isn't that a coincidence?'

'Christ,' Flora said, clawing a chair out from under the other table and sinking into it. 'Sweet Mary, Mother of God!'

'Or you could say, sweet Flora, mother of Rachel Elizabeth Flora and Catherine Margaret Rose,' Rachel suggested, and then sagged back into her chair, exhausted, breathless, and stunned by what she had just done.

'How did you find me?' Flora asked in a weak voice.

'Rachel happened to speak to someone who knew you. It came as a shock to both of us when the woman mentioned your name. So we decided to come to Largs to see you for ourselves.'

'What the hell did you do that for? You're grown women now, too old for pocket money and hair ribbons and bedtime stories.' Flora McCrimmon began to rally. 'If it's a mother you're looking for, you can forget it. I've never been the motherly type and I'm too old to start now!'

'We don't want anything,' Rachel said. 'Except to know who we are, and why you didn't want us.'

'For heaven's sake, why should you start raking up all that stuff now? I haven't given either of you as much as a thought since the day I handed you over. I walked away,' Flora said fiercely, 'and that was it – you were out of my life and I was out of yours. And that's the way I like it!'

'We've got a right to find out more about our back-ground!' Rachel insisted, and Cara reached across the table to put a hand over her sister's.

'We need to know. It's not happened to you, so you won't understand, but being adopted, not having blood kin of your own, can be difficult.'

'You've got each other now. That should be blood kin enough.'

'Just tell us something about yourself and our father and we'll go away and never bother you again. We both promise you that, don't we, Rachel?'

'Yes, we do.'

'I need some coffee.' Flora stood up. 'I'll make some fresh,' she said before blundering from the room.

'D'you not think we should have found a more gentle way to break it to her?' Cara asked in a low voice.

'I don't see how else we could have done it.' Out of habit, Rachel began to load the tray. 'Hand me that cutlery, will you?' she said, and then, when the table was empty and the tray full, 'Come on, we'd better go and find her.'

'You don't think she's run out of the back door?' Cara asked, following her along the hall.

'I wouldn't put it past her. She's already disappeared from our lives once. Open the door for me.'

The kitchen was roomy and surprisingly cosy, with big windows giving a view of a well-kept garden. Vases of fresh flowers stood on the window sill and on the round table in the middle of the room. Flora, working with a large percolator, nodded at one end of the kitchen counter as they came in. 'Fetch three mugs from that shelf, and put the tray down beside the sink.'

When she had poured coffee for the three of them she delved into a cupboard and produced a half-bottle of whisky. She splashed a generous dram into one of the mugs, and then lifted the bottle, eyebrows raised.

'Not for us, it's too early in the morning,' Cara said hurriedly.

'This isn't a normal morning. You think I drink this stuff every day?'

'I'll have some,' Rachel said. 'And so will you, Cara. She's right, it's not a normal morning.'

'By rights,' Flora said when the coffee had been topped up, 'I should send the two of you packing. I don't need this sort of upset, not at my age.'

'You can add the cost of the whisky to our bill,' Rachel told her crisply. For the first time since Chrissie had told her the truth about herself she felt as though she was in control. 'But I have to warn you that if you don't make this visit worth our while I, for one, won't be paying my bill.'

'Is she always such a vindictive little madam?' Flora asked Cara.

'Don't ask me, I haven't know her all that long. So . . . tell us about our father.'

Rachel took a mouthful of the coffee and whisky mixture and felt it travel all the way down from her mouth to her stomach. It was quite a pleasant feeling. 'You wouldn't happen to have a photograph, would you?' she asked hopefully.

'I most certainly would not!'

'D'you even know who he was? I mean,' Rachel added hurriedly as the older woman's eyes widened with outrage, 'it was wartime, and Glasgow must have been full of soldiers and sailors and airmen. Lots of girls made mistakes in those days.'

'It wasn't like that at all. If you must know, he was my boss at work. Oh, I can see that I won't get rid of the pair of you until I tell you everything I know,' Flora said. 'But not a word to Danny. He knows nothing of my life before we met at the Metropole, and that's the way I want things to stay.'

333

'Not a word to Danny,' they both promised fervently, and waited while she took a long swallow from her mug, then lit a cigarette. She sucked smoke into her lungs, coughed for several minutes, then said, 'All right. I was an only child and my parents were middle-aged when I was born. I think I was a bit of a surprise to them, to be honest. They were good religious folk, so it was church and Sunday School every Sunday, and then when I left school they found me a job in an office. Even then I never got the chance to go dancing, or to go to the pictures with the other girls, let alone meet boys. I was desperate to go to the pictures. I used to buy magazines and sneak them into the house and read them under the bedclothes at night. You know, magazines with pictures of film stars like Claudette Colbert and Douglas Fairbanks and Myrna Loy. But I never got to see them on the screen.'

Cara tutted. 'That's terrible! I don't know what I'd have done without my weekly visit to the pictures when I was growing up.'

'It was their way of looking out for me, I suppose. Poor souls, they should never have had me,' Flora said, and then, glaring at her daughters, 'Just as I should never have had you two!'

'Well, you did,' Rachel said coolly. 'So tell us more about our father.'

Bit by bit, easing the memories from her, they reached the truth. World War Two had started and thirty-one-year-old Flora had no option but to take up war work.

'I decided on the Land Army, mainly because my mother and father had the vapours at the thought of me joining one of the other groups and having to mix with men. And munitions didn't attract me. There were a few of us going from the office, so they had a bit of a do for us. It was the first time I'd tasted alcohol. Very nice it was too.' Flora topped up her half-empty cup from the whisky bottle. 'When they all left I stayed behind to tidy up – that's the sort of person I was, always cleaning up after other folk. Then my boss came back for something he'd forgotten, and one thing led to another.' She stubbed out her cigarette, and then took another from the pack on the table.

'He'd had a skinful too; otherwise he'd never have looked at me. But that night he did, and I didn't know what was going to happen to me, what with going away from home, and the war. And I wanted to know what it was like, this love thing that the other girls kept whispering about and giggling over. So I let him. He was respectable, and good-looking. Brown hair – a bit like yours,' she said to Rachel, 'and really lovely blue eyes. I like men with lovely eyes. He looked a bit like a film star and some of the other girls fancied him like mad. Married, of course, with a family.'

'What did you think about . . . you know?' Cara asked, and the woman shrugged.

'A big fuss about nothing at all, if you really want my opinion. I went off to work on some farm out by Stirling, and forgot about it. You could have knocked me down with a feather when I discovered I was expecting. I thought I was just homesick; it was the farmer's wife who realised I'd a bun in the oven. Two buns, as it turned out. So . . .' She blew a plume of smoke into the air. 'I had to go home and tell my parents. My God, that was a day and a half! I could have gone into a hostel – looking back, I know that I should have done it that way – but they insisted on doing their duty by me, even though they hated every minute of it. So did I. I was kept indoors most of the time, for fear of the neighbours finding out. I only got out for a wee walk late at night when the place was quiet. It was worse than being in the jail. It was a relief when you two finally arrived.'

'How did you and your parents keep it all a secret? You

lived in a tenement – surely they would hear us crying?' Rachel wanted to know.

'My cousin Betty had been bombed out of her house so she'd brought her wee boy to stay with my parents. At least she was someone to talk to – my Ma and Dad could scarcely bring themselves to say a word to me. But her kid was a right wee whinger. He never stopped howling.' Flora paused to light a fresh cigarette from the stub of the one she was finishing. 'You were both quiet bairns, right from the start, and any noise you did make was drowned out by his caterwaulin'. Betty and Ma delivered the two of you; I never saw a midwife, let alone a doctor. Luckily it was a straightforward birth, though you could have knocked the lot of us down with the one wee feather when we realised it was twins.'

She took in a lungful of smoke and let it out in a long feathery plume. 'My parents couldn't wait to get rid of all three of us, and I couldn't get out of the place fast enough. When you were just days old they managed to get us away to an old aunt of my father's. That was a barrel of laughs, I can tell you! I couldn't wait to get shot of you two and get back to bein' a Land Girl.'

'So you advertised us in the papers as if you were selling a second-hand coat.' Rachel found it hard to keep the note of bitter betrayal from her voice.

'I couldnae keep you, could I? And even if I'd had any maternal feelings – which I didn't,' Flora added emphatically, glaring across the table at the two of them, 'that whinin' brat of Betty's would have changed my mind long before you arrived, I can tell you that for nothin'!'

'Why let us be separated? Why not advertise us as twins?'

'Who'd want to be lumbered with two babies? I certainly didn't. So I just advertised one kid, and the first two couples to reply seemed decent enough. And that was that.'

'You just went on as if nothing had happened?'

'That's the funny thing, you two being born did make a difference,' Flora said, brightening up. 'Once the war was over I didn't fancy the idea of going back home to let my parents treat me like a fallen woman for the rest of their lives, and there was no way I was going back to that office. My boss never knew about you two, but I couldn't have looked him in the face again. So . . .' the word drifted out on another great plume of smoke, 'I decided that this was my chance to start doing what I wanted, instead of what other folk thought I should do. And what I wanted was glamour. I'd always been good with a needle, so I dropped my surname and took on my middle name instead, and got myself a job at the Pavilion, sewing costumes. And it just went on from there. In a way, I suppose that having you two turned out to be a good thing after all.'

'And have you got any more children scattered around the country?' Rachel wanted to know.

'God no! Once bitten. There was never anyone else,' Flora said firmly, stubbing out her cigarette, 'until my Danny came along.'

'Did you see the way her face softened when she mentioned Danny?' Cara asked as the two of them walked along the esplanade towards the pier. 'I think he's the only person she's really cared about in her entire life.'

'There's one good thing to come out of this – at least she doesn't want to have anything to do with us, so I don't have to introduce her to Martin. I'm sure he'd much rather have Doreen as a mother-in-law than Flora.'

'Look, there's Nardini's.' Cara pointed across the road at the famous tea room and ice cream parlour. 'Let's go in and have an ice cream before we catch the ferry.'

The skies were still clouded, and there was a cold edge

to the wind. Rachel, who was beginning to feel chilled to the bone, shuddered and drew her headscarf closer round her ears. 'Do they do hot Bovril?'

'They do everything, but you can get hot Bovril at home, so we're having ice cream.' Cara began to pull her across the road. 'Come on!'

'I think Flora's fascinating,' she said five minutes later when they were seated at one of the delicate little tables with two large glass dishes of ice cream before them. She had chosen chocolate sauce, and Rachel, denied her hot drink, had opted for raspberry sauce. 'Angus would love her. Perhaps we'll come down next summer for a weekend, just so that he can see her. At least we've found our mother.'

'I'm not sure that I like being the product of a quick session on an office desk.' Rachel was so repelled by the picture in her mind that without thinking she heaped her spoon with ice cream and put the lot into her mouth instead of eating it a little at a time. Her entire mouth froze immediately, and then her teeth started to ache. She felt as though she had just tried to take a huge bite out of an iceberg.

'Better than being the product of a few minutes in a dark close with someone she didn't know,' Cara was saying, oblivious to her sister's suffering. At last, the ice cream warmed, melted, and slid down Rachel's throat. The pain in her teeth subsided and the world came back into focus again.

'Let's take the ferry over to Cumbrae, then hire bikes and cycle round the island,' Cara went on cheerfully. 'Let's pretend that we're teenagers for an afternoon. Let's eat, drink and be merry, for tomorrow we go home and life goes back to normal.'

They arrived back on the mainland late in the afternoon, saddle-sore and drunk on sea air.

'That,' Rachel said as they went down the gangplank, 'was the best afternoon I've ever had.'

'Danny was right, wasn't he? Once you learn to ride a bicycle you never forget – though I had my doubts that time I found myself heading off the road and onto the rocks.'

'That was before you got your sea legs. Your pedal feet, I should say.'

'Just think of the fun we might have had if we'd grown up together.'

'There's still plenty of time,' Rachel said. She hadn't felt so light-hearted since before Fiona had announced that she was pregnant. The short break and the knowledge that she had confronted her birth mother and found out the truth about her beginnings had definitely done her good. She had made up her mind, as she stood on the ferry's deck watching Largs draw closer, that when she got home she was going to sit down with Martin, and put things right between them.

'We should do this once a year,' she said. 'We should have a weekend away somewhere different every time, just the two of us.'

'I'll drink to that. And talking of drink, let's find somewhere nice and have ourselves a high tea. Fish and chips!'

Rachel ran her hands through her wind-tousled hair. 'I need to go back to the guest house first. I want to get washed and changed before I even begin to think about food.'

They were just approaching the house, arm in arm and planning their next outing, when a voice yelled, 'Mum?' and they turned to see Fiona hurrying clumsily in their wake.

'Fiona? What are you doing here?'

'I was in Paisley and a Largs bus came along, and I just jumped on,' the girl said breathlessly. 'I'm so glad I found you . . .' She caught at Rachel's arm. 'The bus was a bit bumpy and I think I've got a bit of a stitch.'

'Does your father know you're here?'

'I told you; I just took a sudden notion to see you. I'll phone him from here and get a bus . . . Ohh!' Fiona said, clutching at Cara with her free hand.

'Are you all right, pet?'

'Rachel.' Cara nodded at the ground. Fiona was wearing a long loose dress with a scooped neckline and a mid-calf hemline. Now water was splashing down her ankles to puddle on the paving stones.

'Come on.' Rachel put her free arm around her daughter. 'Open the door, Cara, we've got to get her inside.'

'It can't be the baby, Mum,' Fiona protested as Rachel half carried her up the path. 'It's too early for that. It was just the bus ride . . .'

'I think that bumpy bus ride's wakened the baby up.'

'What?'

'Your waters have broken, Fiona.' They had reached the door, which Cara was holding open.

'What are we going to do? Take her up to our room?'

'She's best down here,' Rachel said as Flora McCrimmon appeared from the kitchen, Danny at her heels.

'What's going on? Who's this?'

'My daughter, and she's not well.'

'Your daughter? I'm a granny?' Flora yelped, forgetting that Danny stood just behind her, while Fiona said shrilly, 'But I can't have the baby in Largs; I'll have to get back home!'

'She's havin' a baby?' Flora's voice rose a half-octave, and Fiona again chimed in with, 'Granny? Is this . . . ?' Then she doubled up with pain.

'She needs to lie down. Is there somewhere I can take her?'

'There's our room.' Danny, who had been staring from one face to another, trying to make sense of what he was hearing, sprang into action. 'Here, let me.' He pushed Flora aside and lifted Fiona as easily as if she were a child. The three women flocked after him as he carried her into a room at the end of the hall.

'Stop!' Flora shrieked, as he was about to lay the girl down on the large four-poster bed. She nipped past him and began to haul off the flounce-edged white rose-patterned quilt and the pink sheet and blankets beneath it. 'Give me the folded towel by the wash-basin in the alcove,' she ordered Rachel. 'We'll put it under her.'

'Have you got a rubber sheet, or a raincoat, even?' Cara suggested.

'The very thing. Danny, go upstairs and get that waterproof sheet from the cupboard in the wee bedroom.'

'Do I put this lassie down first, or d'you want me to take her upstairs with me?' he asked with amazing patience.

'I forgot. Wait there.' Flora hurried out while Rachel wet a face cloth – white, with pink roses on it to match the quilt, she noticed despite her agitation – at the washbasin and used it to wipe the sweat from her daughter's brow.

'It's all right, darling, we'll just lie you down and get you comfy.'

'Mum, are you sure that this is the baby coming?' The girl's beautiful blue eyes were huge with apprehension.

'It looks like it, but don't worry, we'll get you into hospital in no time at all.'

Flora arrived back clutching the waterproof sheet. 'It's a good thing we had this,' she said breathlessly as Cara helped her to put it in place and tuck the pink sheet over it. 'It's handy – you get all sorts sleeping in your beds when you run a guest house. You can put her down now, Danny.'

Despite his own slim build and Fiona's bulk, the young man had been standing holding the girl as though she weighed no more than before pregnancy. Now he laid her down gently, and stepped back.

'Want me to boil water? That's what folk usually do when a baby's coming, isn't it?'

'I doubt if we'll need it, since she'll be in the hospital in no time; but there's no harm in doing it anyway,' Rachel said. 'Phone for the ambulance first.'

'Will do.' He left them to attend to Fiona, who was clinging to the bed head with one hand and reaching for Rachel with the other. 'Mum . . . !' she whimpered through clenched teeth.

'The contractions are coming awful close together, are they not?' Rachel heard Cara murmur from behind her as she consoled her daughter and tried to tolerate the pain in her fingers. She had had no idea that Fiona had such a strong grip.

Almost on cue, Danny tapped on the door and then opened it a little. 'The hospital want to know the time between contractions,' he said through the small space.

'Not enough,' Cara told him. 'Five minutes at the most. I don't think there's going to be time to get her to hospital.'

'But it's a first baby,' Rachel said desperately. 'They usually take ages.'

'You two were helluva quick,' Flora said from the other side of the bed, adding, 'thank God.'

'So were Fiona and the boys,' Rachel admitted.

'And my Alice.'

'How many kids have you two had?'

'Rachel's had three and I had one.'

'My God. When I got up this mornin' I was a happy single woman. Now look at me,' Flora lamented. 'A mother twice over and four times a granny!'

'And a great-grandchild on the way,' Cara pointed out heartlessly.

'I'll never forgive you two for this! Danny might never forgive me!'

As the contraction began to ease Rachel sank onto a chair provided by Cara and concentrated on mopping Fiona's sweating face while Flora and Cara stripped the girl's clothes off and covered her with the big fluffy towel.

'Why won't Danny forgive you?' Fiona asked weakly.

'Because until you arrived ten minutes ago he didn't know I was even a mother! He's my lover. She might as well know the truth of it,' Flora said defensively as Rachel frowned across the bed at her. 'Why should I be the only one to get all the shocks?'

'He's nice,' Fiona said. 'He's kind.'

'He's gorgeous, pet, but you keep your beautiful blue eyes off him,' Flora told her briskly. 'He's mine. And by the looks of you, you've got a man of your own anyway.'

'Robbie. I wish he was here, Mum.' Two big tears suddenly appeared at the corners of Fiona's eyes, and slid down the sides of her face. 'I want Robbie!'

'You'll see him soon enough, lassie.' Flora took a clean handkerchief from a bedside drawer and wiped the tears away. 'And I'm sure you'd rather he saw you all prettied up afterwards, instead of the way you are now. Listen, I've got a lovely nightdress, I've never even worn it. We'll put it on you later. It'll knock your Robbie's eyes out, I'm tellin' you!'

Danny tapped on the door again. 'They say that there isn't time to get her to the hospital, but they're sending someone. They wanted to know if there was anyone responsible with her and I said there were three of you.'

'He makes us sound like the three witches in Macbeth,' Flora mumbled from the chest of drawers, where she was rooting about. Fiona giggled and then tensed as the next contraction arrived.

'Mu-um . . . !' This time it was longer, and stronger, and when it was over, Cara, who had been standing at the foot of the bed, edged up until she was by Rachel's side.

'I think it's well on its way,' she whispered, and Rachel nodded.

'There, isn't that bonny?' Flora shook out the night-dress and held it where Fiona could admire it at close quarters. It was thigh-length, made of muslin, and as was to be expected of someone who had opted to sleep in this very feminine bedroom, it was sprigged with rose-buds and had rose pink ribbons threaded through the smocking at the bodice.

'It's lovely,' the girl murmured.

'You're going to look a picture in it, pet, you really

344

are. And you're going to feel like a million dollars – it'll be great to be thin again, I can tell you.'

'Are you really my grandmother?'

'I suppose I am. But my name's Flora,' the woman said firmly. 'Or Flo if you'd prefer it. Call me Granny and I'll paper two walls with you.'

'What about some nice music?' Cara asked, nodding at the record player in one corner. 'My Alice was born at home and Angus played my favourite records. It helped to keep my mind off what was happening.'

'Is there any Abba?' Fiona said hopefully.

'Can't see any.' Cara was hurriedly shuffling through records.

'Try this.' Flora slotted a record into place on the player. 'I like this one.' She started clicking her fingers as 'In the Summertime' filled the room.

'I don't think that's the right sort of music,' Rachel protested. 'She needs something soothing at a time like this.'

'But I like it, Mum.'

'Good for you, pet.' Now Flora was jigging around the room in time to the music, her bright loose top swinging around her ample body. 'You listen hard, now; and sing along when you can. The "*uh!*" bits are perfect for pushing.'

The door opened yet again. 'There's a Martin on the phone,' Danny said. 'He wants to speak to Rachel.'

'On you go,' Cara said. 'We'll take good care of her.'

'Don't be long,' Fiona called after her mother as she left the room. 'And tell Dad I'm fine, and not to worry.'

The assurance had come too late; Martin sounded frantic with worry.

'Fiona's disappeared. Doreen thought she was at Robbie's, but I've just phoned them to find out why she didn't come back for her dinner, and they've not seen her all day. Should I phone the hospital first, or the police?'

'She's here. She decided to hop on a Largs bus and now—'

'In Largs? Well, you can just tell her to hop on another bus and get back here.'

'Martin, listen, she's—'

'This isn't a hotel, you know, it's her home and she can't just swan off whenever she pleases without a word to anyone.'

'Martin—'

'Doreen's cooked a meal for her and she doesn't even bother to—'

'*Martin!*' Rachel yelled, at the end of her tether, and Danny, who was busy fussing with pots on the cooker, jumped and spun round to stare at her.

'For pity's sake, Rachel, you almost burst my eardrum there!'

'Martin, shut up and listen. Fiona's gone into labour.'

'She can't have. The baby's not due for a good two weeks yet and you said that first babies are usually late.'

'This one can't have been told the rules, then, because it's on its way right now.'

'I'm coming down. Now.'

'Oh yes,' Rachel said. 'Please come, Martin, we need you. And bring Robbie, Fiona's asking for him.'

'Where is he?'

'How do I know?' She rummaged through the chaos that was her mind at that moment. 'Phone Maggie – the number's in our personal address book under "McNaughton",' she added before he had the chance to ask. 'Tell her what's happening. She'll let him know that you're on the way to pick him up.' Then, as she heard her name being called, 'I have to get back to Fiona . . .'

'Wait, I don't know the address, just the phone number. How do I get to the Bed and Breakfast?'

Rachel thrust the receiver at Danny. 'Tell him how to get here.'

As she left the room she heard Danny clear his throat and say, 'Hi, I'm Danny. We haven't met, but . . .'

The next contraction was longer and stronger, and when it was finally over and Fiona had slumped back against the pillow, exhausted and panting, Cara said, 'I think the next one might do it. Do you know about pushing, Fiona?'

'They told us at the antenatal clinic.'

'It's as if you're constipated, dear, and you're trying to use the toilet,' Flora said briskly. 'Just rest for now, and get your strength up. I'll get some towels to wrap the wee thing in when it arrives.'

'Mum,' Fiona wailed, 'I don't know if I can go on! I want to change my mind. I want to forget all about it!'

'Didn't we all,' Flora muttered.

Rachel stroked the sweat-soaked hair from her daughter's face and soothed, 'You'll manage, darling. We'll all help you, and it's almost over.'

'Was that Dad on the phone?'

'Yes, and he's on his way here,' Rachel said as another song started on the record player.

'"Sugar Baby Love",' Fiona said, smiling. 'Robbie likes the Rubettes.'

'Me too,' Flora agreed, hands and shoulders going.

Fiona turned her head on the pillow and looked around the bedroom. 'This is very pretty. Did you decorate it yourself?'

Flora hummed along with the singers, then, 'I did it with Danny's help. The bed you're lying on was once in a play, you know.'

'On the stage?'

Flora nodded. 'The stage of the King's Theatre in

Glasgow, no less, not long before I retired. It was used in one of those farces where folk keep popping out of different doors and getting mixed up about who's who. I managed to buy it when I retired.'

'Flora was a theatre dresser,' Cara said, and the girl's eyes widened.

'Really? That's terrific. Where did you work?'

'All over. The Alhambra, the Empire and the Empress too. And the Pavilion and the Metropole. I've got signed pictures of all the stars that played Glasgow.'

'Can I see them?'

'Before you go home,' Flora promised, then, 'How old are you, pet?'

'Sixteen.'

'Sixteen! For a moment Flora cupped the girl's face with a ring-laden hand. 'You're young tae be going through this, aren't you?'

'Old enough to get into this situation,' Fiona said with a tremulous smile.

'He sounds like a nice lad, though, your Robbie.'

'He is. He's special,' Fiona said, and then her eyes darkened and her face began to screw up again.

This time Flora took hold of one hand while Rachel held the other and Cara, at the foot of the bed, urged, 'Push, love.'

'I'm . . . trying!'

'You're nearly there,' Cara reported. 'Push! Keep pushing!'

'Have you ever delivered a baby before?' Flora wanted to know as Fiona's face turned dark red with effort.

'I've helped my mam with neighbours, and I helped to deliver her youngest. Have you ever delivered a baby?' Cara asked almost belligerently.

'Once, in the theatre when an understudy went into

labour. Wee minx – nobody even realised she was carrying until it started. The baby was born in a clothes basket, just like in the Judy Garland song,' Flora said. 'Ruined the costumes, of course. Poor little basket.'

'Never mind the basket,' Cara said, 'what about the poor little baby?'

'It's the baby I was talking about,' Flora said.

'Uh-HUH!' Fiona, in the opening throes of another contraction, gave a sudden harsh bark of laughter. It turned into an attack of helpless, hysterical giggles, and she was still giggling when her baby slid into the world to the cheerful accompaniment of 'Gimme Dat Ding' from the record player.

32

November 1977

'Mu-um!' The heartfelt wail floated all the way down the stairs and through the hall to the kitchen.

'Better go up and see what Fiona wants, Rachel,' Doreen advised. 'Chrissie and me can finish things here.'

'Are you sure?' Rachel cast a quick glance over the kitchen table, which was loaded with food. 'D'you think we've got enough?'

'Enough for a regiment and a bit more left over,' Chrissie said. 'Go on now, we'll soon have to leave for the church.' Then, as another wail came from upstairs, 'Go and find out what's ailing the lassie!'

Rachel's foot was on the first stair when Graham came dashing down, resplendent in his new suit. 'Fiona wants you. She can't get Alex into his christening clothes,' he said importantly. 'He's wriggling too much.'

'Where's Ian?'

'In the bedroom, trying to get his tie right. Then he's going to do mine.'

'Ask your dad to help you.'

'He's still away collecting those people from the railway station. Have you forgotten?' he asked kindly, and then heaved a world-weary sigh and shook his head. He and Ian were taking their positions as uncles very seriously, even to the point of agreeing to wear suits for the christening.

'Oh yes, so he is. Go back to the bedroom and I'll send Robbie in to help you.'

In Fiona's bedroom, she and Robbie were trying without much success to coax two-month-old Alex into the christening gown Cara had made for him.

'Mum, every time I think I've won, he squirms again and I've lost,' Fiona wailed. 'And just look what he's done to his lovely wee bonnet!' She held it out to show a red stain on the white fur trimming. 'I was trying it on him and I lifted him up to let him see himself in the mirror, and he threw his head back and got my lipstick all over the fur!'

'Try dabbing it with talcum powder while I dress him. Not you, Robbie, I need you to go and help the boys with their ties. Now then, Alexander Robert . . .' Rachel advanced on her grandson as Robbie went to do her bidding and Fiona seized the tin of baby powder. 'I don't want any more of your shenanigans. This is your big day and you're going to get lots of admiration, so you'd better behave yourself.'

She captured a plump arm and fed it into a sleeve, then settled the gown around the baby's shoulders before sitting down on the bed and lifting him on to her knee. Talking to him all the time, she fastened the tiny buttons up the front of the bodice. 'There now, all done. How's the bonnet?'

'It's looking a bit better, but anyone who looks closely can still see the pink splodge. Oh, Alex,' Fiona lamented, 'could you not have waited until after your big moment before you did that?'

'It looks fine.' Rachel slipped the fur-trimmed satin bonnet over the bald little head, tied the ribbons, and held him up for inspection. 'What do you think?'

'Doesn't he look gorgeous?' Fiona took her son into her arms. 'Mum, I can't believe that he's mine!'

'Believe it. He's yours and he's going to be yours for years and years, so get used to it.' And make the most of it, Rachel thought, because the next sixteen years are going to go by in a flash.

She found a clean bib to tie round Alex's neck before Fiona settled him on the bed, packing her stuffed toys around him to make certain he was in no danger of rolling off.

'And you'd better stay there and behave yourself, young man,' Rachel told him, 'or it'll be off to bed early tonight with no supper. Understand?'

He gave her a wide gummy grin to show that he found the prospect attractive, and waved a chubby hand at Raggedy Ann, who was keeping guard over him. Outside, a car door slammed.

'Is that your dad back from the station with Flora and Danny? I'd better get downstairs quickly before Mum and Flora come face to face.'

'It's all right,' Fiona reported from the window, 'it's just Uncle Angus and Auntie Cara. Dad's not back yet.'

Almost at once they heard quick footsteps on the stairs, then Cara burst into the room. 'We've borrowed my brother-in-law's estate car, so we've got room for everyone we're taking, not to mention a car that looks respectable enough for Thornly Park. Where is he? There you are, my wee lamb! Oh, doesn't he look lovely?'

'Thanks to you, Auntie Cara. The gown's beautiful!'

'Och, it was a pleasure. And you look beautiful too, my pet.' Cara hugged Fiona, then held her back at arm's length to inspect the brown, crimson and gold patterned skirt and jacket.

'She's taken to motherhood like a duck to water,' she said when Fiona had taken the baby downstairs, escorted by Robbie, Ian and Graham. 'She looks so happy, and so does Robbie. I can't wait for the wedding!'

'They've decided to wait until the spring, so we've got her and Alex for a while yet. We're all going to the Lake District for a few days next week to let Martin's parents see the baby, since they weren't able to come to the christening.'

'Where's Martin?'

'Gone to fetch Flora and Danny from the station.'

'You should have phoned; we could have done that on our way here.'

'He needed to get out of the way for a wee while,' Rachel said. 'He adores wee Alex – we all do – but he's still finding it hard to adjust to what's happened.' She bit her lip, then confessed, 'He's still not the same Martin he used to be.'

'And you're not the same Rachel you used to be. Nothing's the same; the boys are wearing proper suits and looking very grown-up, Fiona's become a mother, and Doreen's mellowed.'

'Is that a car at the gate?' Rachel rushed to the window. 'It's Martin. We'd better get downstairs before Flora and Doreen come face to face!'

Cara halted her at the door, a hand on her arm. 'Everything will be all right, Rachel.'

'I hope so,' Rachel said, and ran down the stairs just as Flora, tulle floating in all directions, swept through the door like a ship in full sail and Doreen and Chrissie arrived from the kitchen to meet the newcomers.

Danny charmed both Doreen and Chrissie, especially when he fussed over the baby and Fiona, but Flora, who announced at once that she was gasping for a smoke and hurried out into the back garden to have one, was another matter.

'She's not the way I remember her at all,' Doreen said when the others had gone into the living room and she and Rachel and Cara were in the dining room, unpacking the christening cake. 'The woman we met in Clyde Street when we went to collect you was quite respectable. Now look at her — talk about mutton dressed as lamb! Now I can see where you inherited your nature from, Cara.'

'Mum!'

'You're absolutely right, Doreen.' Cara was unruffled. 'I'm more like my birth mother than Rachel is.'

'Upbringing counts far more than inheritance.'

'Mum, now you're insulting Cara's adoptive mother!' Rachel protested.

Cara just grinned and said, 'Perhaps Rachel would have been the demure one even if we'd both been raised by Flora.'

'And what about that young man? Who's he?'

'I told you, Mum, Danny's her companion.'

Doreen gave a significant sniff. 'We all know what sort of companion, don't we?'

'We do, and good for Flora, say I. Oh, look at that!' Cara breathed as the cake was lifted from the box.

'It's beautiful, isn't it, Mum?'

'Very nice,' Doreen approved. 'Set it there, in the middle of the table, Rachel. Careful, now. That's it. Well now, hadn't we better be getting the rest of them organised to go to the church?'

'Just a minute, Doreen. Your new christening hat's lovely,' Cara said, 'but d'you mind if I try tilting it just a wee bit to the left . . . there! Don't you think that's better?'

Doreen hurried to the hall mirror, then returned, frowning. 'I'm not sure about the shade – it's not what I'm used to.'

'It looks really elegant, Mum, and it brings out the colour of your eyes.'

'It's fantastic,' Cara said emphatically. 'You're going to look wonderful in the photographs.'

'Me? You don't want an old biddy like me in the christening pictures.'

'Of course we do. It's a special occasion. Angus has brought his camera and as Alex's great-grandmother, you've got to be in the pictures. It's going to be a four-generation group, isn't that exciting?'

Martin put his head round the door. 'If we don't leave for the church now, we'll be late. Fiona and Robbie and the wee fellow with me and Rachel, and the rest of you with Angus.'

'Oh . . . oh!' Doreen started panicking. 'What about Robbie's brother and his wife? They're not here yet! We can't have a christening without the godparents!'

'It's all right, Mum, they're going to meet us at the church. Got your bag? And a clean handkerchief?' Talk about role reversal! Rachel thought as she ushered her mother out into the hall, where the others were gathering. She could well remember Doreen saying exactly the same thing to her during her early school days. No doubt Fiona's turn would come one day. It was a depressing thought.

Then all depressing thoughts fled as Robbie came into the hall carrying his small son, all dressed up in his christening robe and fine woollen shawl – also made by Cara – and the fur-trimmed bonnet. Fiona came behind them, pink with excitement and pride.

★　★　★

355

When Martin's car arrived back from the church, Angus was already waiting in the driveway to open the rear door and pluck the baby from Fiona's knee. 'Who was a good boy, then?' he grinned, tucking Alex into the crook of an arm. 'Who's his uncle's clever laddie?'

'Don't shoogle him, Uncle Angus!' Fiona shot out of the car like a bullet from a gun. 'He'll be sick on *you* next!' She drew the shawl more closely round her little son to protect him against the November wind. 'I was so embarrassed when he did that to the minister. And to the lovely gown you made for him, Auntie Cara!'

'It'll wash. And you have to admit it was nice the way he kept talking back to the minister all through the service.'

'If he'd only kept it to talking back, instead of vomiting all over the poor man!'

'It wasn't that much,' Rachel soothed. 'And he didn't cry once.'

'No, but I thought the minister was going to, when Alex decorated his gown.' Angus's grin widened and he poked a big finger at the baby's cheek and crooned again, 'Who's a clever boy?'

'Inside now,' Cara ordered. 'It's too cold for him out here and you'll need to get your photographs, Angus, before Fiona changes him out of that gown.'

'Ten minutes,' Fiona warned, heading for the front door, 'and then he'll be yelling for a feed. You can set your watch by him!'

Rain began to fall while the christening party were eating; cold November rain coming down in slanted lines, pooling on the earth beneath the recently pruned roses and dripping from leafless trees. By the time it eased off night had fallen and the street lights and house lights had been switched on.

Rachel, in an armchair facing the big bay windows, thought of getting up to draw the curtains, and then decided that she couldn't be bothered. Tonight, passers-by were welcome to look in on the busy room if they so pleased.

She rested her head against the high back of the fireside chair and relaxed, for the first time that day. Alex, worn out by his big day, was sound asleep upstairs and Robbie, perched on the piano stool, was deep in conversation with Fiona, who sat on the floor, one elbow resting on his knee, her face uplifted to his and her hair loose around her shoulders. She looked, with her autumn-coloured skirt spread over the carpet around her, like a woodland nymph.

Cara, Flora and Doreen were all talking busily, their heads close together. Maggie, Kathleen and Chrissie formed a group of their own, while Murdo Ramsay, still deeply tanned from his time in Saudi, was discussing his new allotment with Angus. Or possibly he was grabbing yet another chance to boast about the book of soup recipes his wife was writing.

Just then Murdo glanced swiftly towards where Kathleen sat, and as though sensing his gaze, she looked over at him. They exchanged swift smiles before turning back to their companions. It wasn't the first time Rachel had noticed them exchanging quick glances; ever since Murdo's homecoming they had been behaving like newly-weds.

So much had happened over the past year; bad things as well as good, but all in all, the good well outweighed the bad. A year ago, Rachel hadn't even known half the people now in the room. A year ago she hadn't known that she had a sister, let alone a twin. She yawned, shifted into a more comfortable position, and then suddenly remembered the guinea pigs, no doubt forgotten by the

357

boys, waiting in the dark garden to be fed. With great reluctance, she dragged herself from the comfort of the armchair.

Upstairs, the whirr of trains rattling round a track came from the boys' room. Rachel put her head round the door. 'What about . . . ?' she began, but Danny, Fraser McNaughton and her sons were so absorbed in the train set that nobody heard or saw her. Deciding that it would be easier to feed the pets herself, she withdrew.

A glance into Fiona's room, illuminated by a night light, showed that Alex was sound asleep on his back, a fist curled on either side of his head, his lashes no more than soft shadows against his plump cheeks.

Rachel fetched a jacket before going downstairs to the kitchen. As she filled a jug with fresh water Angus said from the doorway, 'Now, what are you doing, woman? You should be with your guests, not working in here.'

'I'm just going to settle the guinea pigs down for the night.'

'I'll do that for you.' He had been leaning against the door frame; now he came towards her, one big hand outstretched to take the jug. The gold chain he always wore glinted against the solid pillar of his throat and he was smiling lazily down at her; the smile that, when they first met, had sent a tingle through her entire body.

Head slightly to one side, she studied him. He was undeniably attractive, in a Viking warrior sort of way, but the tingle was no longer there. He was Angus – a nice man, her children's much-loved uncle, her twin sister's adored husband, and Rachel's brother-in-law. But he just wasn't her type.

'It's all right,' she said easily. 'It won't take me a minute.'

And Angus, as though he knew just what she was thinking, said, 'Okay then,' and slowly drooped an eyelid over one green eye before heading back to the hall.

The rain had stopped. After the bright house lights, the garden was like a deep dark well, but in the winter months the hutch was situated against the rear wall of the house and so she didn't need to go far. In the glow from the kitchen window, she saw a dark shape stooped over the hutch.

'Martin?'

'I suddenly remembered the guinea pigs,' he said. 'So I thought I'd make sure they were fed.'

She smiled in the darkness at this man who was quite definitely, beyond any doubt, her type. 'Two minds with but a single thought,' she said. 'I brought water.'

'I've given them fresh water already, and fed them and put more straw in their sleeping quarters.' He dropped the waterproof cover down over the front of the hutch, saying, 'Just in case it gets colder.' Then, taking the jug from her, 'Come on, let's get inside.'

As they returned to the patio they met Flora and Doreen on their way out of the kitchen.

'Donald Peers,' Doreen was saying. 'Now *there* was a beautiful voice! Did you ever meet Donald Peers?'

'Yes I did; a very nice man. I've got a photo of him on the wall in my front hall.'

'We're just going outside for a minute, Rachel; Flora's gasping for a cigarette.'

'Are you sure? It's cold out there.'

'I'll smoke fast.' Flora fished in the pocket of her blue sequined jacket and drew out a cigarette case and lighter. 'You should come down to Largs some time, Doreen, to have a look at my photos.'

'You'd be better to keep them in a photo album. They gather dust hanging on walls and sitting on sideboards.'

'Not my problem,' Flora said airily. 'My Danny's a dab hand with a feather duster.'

'Now that,' Martin said as he and Rachel arrived in the kitchen to find Chrissie filling a glass from the cold-water tap, 'is something I never thought I'd see – Doreen and Flora getting chummy. Talk about chalk and cheese!'

'It's the theatrical connection that's done it.' Chrissie turned the tap off and drank thirstily, then said, 'Doreen used to be daft about film stars and singers and the like when she was younger.'

'Mum?' Rachel asked in disbelief.

'Oh yes, she was forever getting me to do wee stage acts with her – not that I was any use at it. I had two left feet, but she was a good dancer in her time.'

'I suppose I should make a cup of tea before everyone goes home,' Rachel said.

'I'll help you.'

'You go and enjoy yourself, Chrissie,' Martin said. 'We'll see to the tea.'

'Cara was thinking of having a second christening party,' Rachel ventured as Martin filled the kettle. 'She wants her own family to see Alex.'

He turned on the hot-water tap and reached for the washing-up liquid. 'I suppose we should say yes,' he said. 'It'll give Fiona and Robbie another chance to show off the baby. I'll wash the cups and you dry.' And then, after they had worked together in silence for a few minutes, 'Remember the days when the top tier of the wedding cake used to be kept for the christening?'

'Sometimes life throws things up in a different order, just to keep us on our toes.'

'Is that what it is? I thought it might be us – turning into old fogies,' he explained when she raised her eyebrows at him. 'You know, starting to say things like, "In my day it was different."'

'I don't think we've reached that stage yet.'

'We're grandparents,' he reminded her.

'But very young grandparents. Imagine Mum being daft about dancing and film stars when she was younger. We never really know all about other folk, do we?'

'No, we don't. He straightened, his hands dripping water and soapsuds back into the sink. 'Rachel, I'm still trying to make sense of everything that's happened.'

'I know.'

'It's not easy, for I don't like change. Never have.'

'I know.'

'I'm not the sort of person who can adapt quickly.'

'I know that too. It's one of the things I've always liked about you.'

'But you've managed to change.'

'Only because I had to. Like having to learn to swim because you've been thrown in at the deep end. And at least I know who I am now, thanks to Cara, and Flora – and you. And Fiona as well, I suppose.' Rachel picked up a cup and began to dry it carefully.

'I suppose if I was truthful, I'd admit to being scared. What does changing feel like?'

She smiled at him. 'Like trying on coats. When you find one that fits perfectly, everything else falls into place. Getting the right fit is the difficult bit.'

'Do you think I could find the right coat?'

'I know you could.'

He looked at her for a long moment, and then said, seriously, 'I'll work on it, Rachel, but it might take a while yet.'

'That's all right,' she said. 'I'm not going anywhere.'

He took the towel from her and dried his hands, then took a step towards her. 'Rachel, I . . .'

The back door opened and Doreen and Flora scuttled in on a blast of cold night air.

361

'Blimey, it's bloody freezing out there!' Flora said. 'I could do with a cup of tea!'

'The kettle's coming to the boil,' Rachel assured her.

'Good.' She headed for the living room's warmth, Doreen at her heels.

'Jack Buchanan,' Doreen said as the two of them went through the door. 'Now there's another lovely singer. Did you meet him?'

'Come on, Doreen, I'm not *that* old!'

Rachel and Martin, left alone in the kitchen, looked at each other.

'Tea, I think,' he said.

'Tea,' she agreed.

A Matter of Mischief

To Claire and Don Guinn

Chapter One

1775

A stone flew past Margaret Knox's cheek as she turned into the narrow lane from the Sneddon.

Another landed in one of the many puddles that made the lane an obstacle course whatever the weather, causing filthy water to splash over her good skirt.

She stopped short, clutching her small daughter's hand so tightly that Christian squeaked a protest. Only yards away two bodies were locked in fierce combat, staggering like an ungainly four-legged monster, rebounding from the slimy wall of one building to lurch across the few feet of space and collide with the slimy wall opposite.

Fights were commonplace in Paisley's slums. As often as not the combatants were clawing, scratching women, as dangerous as any man once they got the blood-lust. But these fighters were mere lads, one in his teens, the other scrawnier and several years younger.

The stones were being hurled by a ragged little girl, her thin face red and puffy with angry tears, her body racked at intervals with bouts of coughing. Although she threw hard her aim was poor. A few people stood at the close-mouths or leaned from windows, watching the struggle with vague interest. Some of the men egged the fighters on, but nobody did a thing to stop them.

Margaret hesitated. Her husband Gavin had warned her often enough to keep out of things that didn't concern her, but that didn't deter her, if she thought she could be of some use to someone.

A fight, though, was a different matter. It was a personal thing, an issue that had to be settled by the people concerned. Besides that, Margaret, on her way to one of the slums at the far end of the lane with some food for an old woman who lived alone, had four-year-old Christian to think of.

'Come home –' She tugged at her daughter's hand. 'We'll come back another time.'

Christian dragged back on the grip that would have whisked her away from the scene, her hazel eyes wide in her round little face.

'Leave him alone!' she screamed raucously as the smaller boy was tripped up and thrown with a teeth-jarring thud to the ground. Another stone sailed dangerously near to Margaret. The girl who had thrown it squatted in the dirt to rummage for more ammunition and, finding a stick, proceeded to beat the older boy about the shoulders whenever she got the chance.

'Christian –'

Even as Margaret spoke the small hand left hers and Christian sped down the lane to where the older boy was pinning his adversary face-down on the ground, holding him with one hand and both knees. His free hand gripped the neckerchief about the other lad's throat and began to twist.

The girl dropped her stick and hurled herself onto his back, pummelling at him with her two fists. He shook her off, and she rolled on the ground in a paroxysm of coughing before getting to her knees, ready to throw herself at him again.

Margaret's heart was in her mouth as she saw her first-born child, her only daughter, advance with determination and pick up the stick that had been dropped. She clutched at it two-handed, waiting her chance to use it.

The thought, 'What's Gavin going to say about this?' flared into Margaret's mind. He could be disapproving enough about her own refusal to conform to his picture of a surgeon's wife. He certainly wouldn't take kindly to the news that his daughter had been allowed to involve herself in a street brawl.

She pushed between two men without ceremony and caught Christian's arm, pulling her aside, almost tripping over a bundle that lay against a house wall. Just then a newcomer, an older girl with long black hair flying about her head, sped past her and rushed towards the warriors.

She pushed the other child back against the wall beside Margaret and thrust a small parcel into her arms before launching herself onto the older boy's back, hands locked about his chest in an attempt to throw him off balance.

The young victim had managed to turn his head sideways so that his features were no longer being ground into the mud. But the neckerchief was still biting into his throat, and the part of his face that Margaret could see was purpling, his visible eye bulging. The breath whistled painfully in his throat.

'Let him go, Walter Shaw!' the girl panted.

'I'll let him go when he begs me to!'

'He can't! You'll kill him!'

He ignored her, giving the scarf another twist, and bringing a horrible choking gurgle from his victim. The younger girl, still clutching the cloth-wrapped bundle that had been pushed into her arms, broke into panic-stricken sobs.

Christian made another bid to hurl herself into the fray, but her mother's hand caught her and held her back.

'Do something –' Margaret appealed to the watchers, but they were too intent on the struggle to want to spoil their own enjoyment.

Little enough happened to brighten their drab lives, and they weren't about to put a stop to a good fight.

The throttled boy's hands scrabbled at the ground, his nails scratching audibly on one of the big stones that had once causeyed the lane, but were now few and far between, mere islands in the mud.

The girl dug her knees into the youth's ribs, releasing her grip round his body so that she could grind the knuckles of her two fists into his ears as hard as she could.

With a yelp of pain he released his victim and spun round like a dog trying to free itself of a stone tied to its tail. The girl was catapulted into the air, landing on a causey-stone that caught her hard between the shoulder blades, forcing the breath from her.

The younger boy, sucking air into his tortured lungs,

tried to push himself upright as Margaret reached his side.

'Leave him be –' she said crisply as the younger girl, sobbing, 'Lachie – oh, Lachie –!' tried to hug him. 'Let him get some air, lassie!'

She set down the basket she had been carrying, steadied the boy as he swayed on his hands and knees, and gently massaged his heaving chest, noting as she did so that every rib could be easily counted beneath his thin torn shirt.

The terrible whistling sound in his throat eased, and his head came up at last. Margaret left the girl to help him to his feet as she turned her attention to the other two.

The boy had managed to pin the winded girl down. She struggled, but he had captured both her wrists in one large strong hand, forcing them to the ground above her head.

He was sitting back on his heels, grinning triumphantly down at her.

'Now, Mistress Islay – beg my pardon nicely.'

'No!' She kicked out at him, but only succeeded in freeing her legs, shamefully bare for lack of decent undergarments, from the folds of her skirt. He cast a swift look at them, and Margaret saw that his eyes were suddenly hot.

'Then I'll claim my forfeit –' he said, and the watching men sniggered as he moved to kneel astride his new victim, and bent to seek out her mouth with his own.

She struggled like a wildcat, twisting and writhing, trying to eel her way out from under him. Caught off guard, he almost lost his balance, clamping his hands about her shoulders in an effort to force her into submission.

Her head whipped round and her teeth found their mark in the soft mound just below his right thumb.

He howled and released her; then, as she clung to his hand like a terrier holding a rat, his other hand caught her a painful blow across the cheekbone and with a muffled cry of pain she let him go and fell back.

Clearly, someone must do something. Margaret looked about for the stick her daughter had been wielding a few minutes earlier, but before she could reach for it a newcomer forged a way through the watching crowd, tossing people to left and right. Then the youth was plucked from the ground by a hand the size of a leg of mutton hanging in the meat market.

It gripped him painfully by the ear. Its owner, a mountain of a woman with a face that looked as though it had been fashioned from dough and had never been finished off in the oven, shook her captive vigorously, and his howls increased.

'Brawlin' in the streets!' Glasgow Annie, unofficial queen of that part of Paisley's slums, spoke with the disgust of one easily able to forget her own brawling when it suited her. 'Brawlin' wi' a slip o' a lass!'

She released him, and he immediately nursed his bitten hand.

'It's bleedin'!' Panic gave a womanly squeak to his voice. 'Look what she's done to me!'

'Look what you near did to our Lachie!' The girl's voice shook with rage. 'He's just a wee laddie – nothing like as old as you are –'

Even in her distress, her voice was light and musical with tones that sang, rather than spoke, of the mountains and glens of the Highlands.

Paisley was used to such voices these days; they belonged to the displaced clansfolk who had been driven in their thousands from their homes in the thirty years since the great battle at Culloden, forced to leave the land of their birth, the ground that had been theirs by natural right for generations, to make way for the sheep and cattle that were bringing new, undreamed-of prosperity to the landowners.

Walter began to spit out a flood of abuse.

'That's enough,' Glasgow Annie ordered. 'One o' these fine days, Walter Shaw, it's me ye'll tangle wi' – no' a wee bairn or a defenceless lass. An' when that day comes –'

She moved in on him and he backed away nervously, blood dripping to the ground from his injured hand.

Rumour had it that years before, when she was a young girl in her native city, the slopes and valleys of Glasgow Annie's body had been a source of infinite pleasure to men. She had earned a fortune by selling her favours. But the fortune had been spent on drink, and the drink had turned sweet curves into unsurpassable mountains, a coquettish smile into a grimace, a saucy nature into a hot, quick temper.

Men of courage had been known to flee in terror from Glasgow Annie's wrath, and Walter was no exception.

'How – how am I to do my work at the looms with this hand now? Tell me that?' he whined self-pityingly. 'She's taken my livelihood from me, the besom!'

'Only yer livelihood?' Glasgow Annie simpered, a terrible sight to behold. 'Come tae Annie, my darlin', an' I'll relieve ye o' yer manhood as weel!'

Walter's face, pale with the shock of finding himself injured, flamed as the watchers gave a roar of delighted laughter.

The boy he had been warring with was still supported by the two girls who had fought so hard to save him. The older girl said something to him in their native Gaelic but he twisted away from her, his face sullen, muttering something in the same tongue.

Scarlet drops showered the girl's tattered dress as Walter's bleeding hand was flourished accusingly in her direction. 'As for you, Mistress Islay McInnes –' he rolled the title sneeringly on his tongue. 'I'll have plenty to tell Mister Todd about you! Give me the pirns I came for and let me out of this place!'

Margaret realised that the bundle she had almost fallen over when she snatched Christian out of danger was a bag of pirns bearing newly-spun yarn for the looms. Walter spotted it and snatched at it, lifting it carelessly, so that the opening hung down.

Islay McInnes cried out in anguished protest as some of the precious reels, the result of hours of labour at a spinning wheel, fell out into the mud.

'I'll tell him on you,' Walter babbled, retreating up the lane backwards, his injured hand pointed accusingly at the girl who had bitten him. 'He'll have the militia on the lot of you!'

Grinning, Glasgow Annie spun round, turning her back on him. With a gesture that might have looked coquettish fifteen years before, she flipped up her skirts and waggled her huge buttocks at Walter, who gave up all pretence at further bluster and ran, washed along the lane and around the corner by a wave of laughter.

Islay turned to the younger boy and girl, her face twisted in quick disgust and her arms spread as though trying to protect them from the coarse Lowlanders they were forced to live among.

'As for you, laddie –' Annie rounded on Lachie as soon as the older boy disappeared. 'I've telt ye afore – if ye must fight the likes of him, ye'll have tae learn tae cheat the way he does.'

His hand was still clasped to his sore throat. Above it his dark Highland eyes sparked anger and defiance at her.

Without a word he turned and marched in through the low door leading to one of the single-roomed houses in the street, his thin little back rigid with humiliation.

Islay, suddenly aware that her skirts were still twisted up around her slim bare legs, hurriedly shook the ragged folds into some semblance of decency.

Then she nodded to Margaret before she and the younger girl went into the house together.

The watchers, their entertainment over, began to drift away. Annie turned her attention to Margaret.

'Good day tae ye, Mistress Knox. Ye'll be on yer way tae see Granny Ferguson?' Her doughy face split into an ingratiating, gap-toothed grin, like a parody of a lady greeting visitors in her parlour.

'What was all that stramash about?'

Annie shrugged, a shrug that set up a corresponding wobble all the way from shoulders to ankles. Christian, fascinated, watched the rippling blouse and skirt.

'Ach, it's the Heilanders. They're too hot-blooded. Thon wee laddie's like a fightin' cock – Walter well knows that it takes only a word tae set the wee laddie goin'.' Annie said casually. Then she peered short-sightedly down over her huge breasts at Christian.

'Yer bairn's growin' fast,' she boomed.

The little girl stood, feet planted firmly in the mud, and looked up at her, head tilted to one side. Then she said thoughtfully, 'So are you. You're awful fat.'

'Christian Knox!' Margaret gasped, scandalised. Annie's face swelled, reddened, then a laugh that started somewhere deep in her massive chest broke forth with a bellow.

'Ach, away, Mistress Knox, I mind the day ye'd have said somethin' o' the same yersel' as a bairn. An' I mind the day,' she added, leering at Christian, 'When I wis as wee and bonny as you are, my pretty henny.'

'You must have eaten up all your porridge,' Christian suggested, and was hustled away by her mother to the accompaniment of another wheezy gobbet of laughter.

It took a lot to embarrass Margaret Knox, but even so her face was burning as she whisked her daughter in through the doorway of the hovel where Granny Ferguson huddled her stiff old bones close to a fire that was so poor it couldn't have offered warmth to a mouse.

As she put the food she had brought into the empty store cupboard, then sat for a while and let the old woman talk, Margaret's thoughts were elsewhere.

'What d'you know of the Highland family down the lane?' she asked suddenly.

Granny Ferguson, alone in the world since her only son, a weaver who had once worked for Margaret's father, had died of a lung disease, enjoyed a good gossip. 'The man's a sojer, somewhere over the water, and the eldest boy with him. The woman worked herself to death, poor soul, trying to keep the bairns. The older girl's a relation of theirs, and she does her best to look after the other two now. A kindly neighbour, she is – she looks in on me now and then, and never comes empty-handed, for all they've little enough themselves.'

Margaret took in the information thoughtfully. Later, when she and Christian were walking back along the lane, she paused outside the Highland family's door and rapped on the faded, gapped planks.

Chapter Two

The three people on the other side of the door stared at each other when they heard the summons. Morag's eyes were round with fear, and Lachie, obviously convinced that his tormentor had come back, began to get up, bristling like a small fighting cock.

Islay pushed him back into his chair. 'Stay where you are! Morag –'

She held out the rag she had been using to soothe the boy's sore throat, and her cousin, who had been spreading the muddy pirns over the table, wiped her hands hurriedly on her skirt then took the cloth and dipped it into the bowl of cold water as Islay opened the door.

The well-dressed woman who had helped Lachie stood outside, her little girl by her side.

'I've come to see if the laddie's recovered.'

Islay hesitated, then stepped back to admit entrance into the room, 'Will you walk in, mistress?' She heard the half-challenging note in her own voice. There weren't many respectable folk in Paisley who would have set foot in Jenny's Wynd, let alone in one of the houses. They were all afraid of catching some terrible illness, or being robbed. But this visitor only hesitated for a fraction of a second before stepping down into the single tiny room. The child followed, taking a firm fistful of her mother's figured silk gown.

Islay gave the caller time to accustom her eyes to the gloom and observe the uneven floor of beaten earth, the small glassless window half-covered by a piece of sacking to keep out wind and rain.

The few furnishings in the room consisted of a table, some stools, a couple of low beds and some shelving that had been roughly nailed together out of odds and ends of wood.

15

The spinning wheel stood by the fireplace, flanked by a basket of flax on one side and a basket of empty pirns, still awaiting the linen yarn the weavers needed for their work, on the other.

As she saw her Lowland home anew through the visitors' eyes Islay felt deep embarrassment wash over her. Then she lifted her chin high, and consoled herself with the thought that at least the place was as clean and neat as she could make it. It was no shame to her if she and the children were forced to live in conditions that they wouldn't have wished on their hens or pigs back home.

Courtesy demanded that she ask, 'Will you take some refreshment?'

Both Lachie and Morag stared, knowing full well that there was nothing to share, apart from water from the street well and the meagre store of day-old bread that Islay had just brought home, having earned it by scrubbing out the bakery.

She ignored them, her eyes on the visitor who said, mercifully, 'Thank you, but no. We took some tea with Mistress Ferguson.'

To cover her relief Islay took a straw from the hearth and held it to the poor fire; when it blossomed into flame she lit the crusie-lamp on one of the shelves. The flame smoked and flickered; the acrid smell of burning oil caught at the little girl's snub nose almost immediately, making her sneeze.

Lachie sat at the table, head bowed, one hand still caressing his throat gingerly.

'Are you all right, laddie?' the lady asked.

'I'll kill him!' he replied huskily, between gritted teeth.

'Lachie, that's not the way to speak before guests,' Islay reproved him in their own tongue. His dark head came up at once and his eyes blazed at her.

'Speak English! The Gaelic's dead to us now!'

His shame at being vanquished by the older boy then rescued by females made her want to cradle him in her arms and comfort him. He was still a child, when all was said and done – a child who had been forced into ill-fitting adulthood before his time, and tried too hard to carry his responsibilities like a man.

But she couldn't do that. Instead, she joined their visitor, who was examining the muddied pirns on the table.

'Were many wasted?'

'Enough.'

'Sixpence, at least, we've lost,' Morag said drearily, and Islay rounded on her.

'Hush, Morag!'

'He said he'd tell Mister Todd,' Morag went on as though she hadn't heard. 'What if –'

She stopped. She and Islay gazed at each other, so closely locked in their shared fear that the others were forgotten for the moment. What if Mister Todd, the weaver who held the purse-strings, decided that he didn't want the wild, trouble-making Highlanders to spin yarn for his looms any more? How would they survive then?

'Is it Jamie Todd you spin for?' the lady asked. 'I know him well. I'll tell him what –'

'We don't need to ask anyone to fight our battles for us,' Islay told her sharply, then added in a gentler voice. 'I've seen you in Jenny's Wynd before. Your man's Mister Knox, the surgeon, is he not?'

'My father makes folk well again.' The child ventured out from behind her mother's skirts to proffer the news proudly.

Islay swallowed. 'It's my place to tell Mister Todd what happened. I'll go and see him myself, in the morning.'

'But won't you let me –'

Islay's eyes, large with fear and determination, met and held Margaret Knox's.

'It's my place,' she said.

Chapter Three

Gavin Knox had been in Glasgow from mid-morning. Most of the time since he had kissed his wife good-bye and left his home had been spent amid the gore and noise and suffering of an operating room, and he looked tired and drawn when Margaret herself ran to welcome him in from the rain-swept doorstep.

Her heart turned over at first sight of him, as it always did. The practical side of Margaret's nature, the side that dominated her life – indeed, the side that she had thought made up her entire life before she met Gavin – was acutely embarrassed by the way she felt about him.

She was a 28-year-old woman, after all; mother to two children, mistress of her own house, and still, on two days of each week, a teacher to the pauper children in the Town House school-room. But just a glance from Gavin's clear hazel eyes, the touch of his hand, the joy of waking in the mornings and seeing his dark head on the pillow close by hers, made her feel like a girl in one of the romantic stories her lifelong friend Kate Miller enjoyed reading.

It gave her some consolation to know that she was not alone in her foolishness. Gavin, as sensible and level-headed a man as anyone would hope to meet, a surgeon respected the length and breadth of Glasgow as well as in Paisley, was as passionately in love with her as she was with him. Why this should be so, Margaret couldn't think. But it was, nevertheless, and she was oh, so glad of it!

'Father!' Christian, who had scorned their attempts to teach her to say 'Papa', came scudding from the kitchen and across the hall, her joyous voice raised so loudly in greeting that Margaret, afraid that small Daniel would be wakened, shushed her vigorously.

Gavin only had time to take his wife into a swift, light

18

embrace before the little girl was upon them, tugging at his
wide-skirted coat. With a glance that promised Margaret a
more appropriate greeting once they were alone he swung
his daughter up into his arms and carried her into the
parlour while Margaret went to the kitchen to see if Ellen
was managing the evening meal without help.

Gavin was sprawled in his favourite chair when she
returned to the parlour. His long legs, still booted,
stretched across the rug before the fire. He had unbuttoned
his waistcoat, and in his hand, its contents glowing like a
precious ruby in the firelight, was a glass of his favourite
claret.

Christian squatted on the rug by his feet, her voice
running on like one of the burns that rushed down from the
braes to join the river that flowed through Paisley.

Her grandfather, Duncan Montgomery, had been
known to say more than once that Christian had been born
with a busy tongue; she had certainly learned to speak early,
while her brother, a more solemn child, had only a fraction
of the vocabulary she had possessed at his age.

Margaret looked fondly at the little tableau before her,
then realised to her horror that Christian was saying, 'Then
we went to see Granny Ferguson –'

'It's time for bed, Christian,' she interrupted.

Gavin's eyes were closed; he looked tired. But now his lids
lifted and he smiled at his wife. 'And time, I hope, for
supper. What do we eat tonight?'

' – and there were all these folk in the lane –' Christian
pattered on like the rain that fell steadily outside.

'Beef, and broth made from the bones.'

Gavin yawned mightily. 'Good. I'll swear that the fowl
they gave me at the Infirmary had reached its ninetieth year
before they took mercy on it and wrung its neck.'

'Then Glasgow Annie picked him up and –'

'Daniel was too tired to wait up for you after all. He's been
in his bed this past hour, and asleep almost before the
coverlet was over him.'

'I'll look in on him and put on some fresh linen before I
eat. I feel as though I've been wearing these clothes for a
week, instead of a day.' Reluctantly, Gavin set his glass down

and got to his feet.

'Christian, come along to your bed.' Margaret held out her hand to her daughter. By tomorrow, she thought thankfully, Christian's tongue would be chattering about some new adventure and she would have forgotten the incident in the lane by the river.

Gavin had reached the door and opened it when Christian asked, her voice clear and bell-like, 'Why doesn't Glasgow Annie wear anything underneath her skirts?'

Gavin, on his way out of the door, stopped, pivoted on one heel, and fixed his daughter with a look that would have made anyone else quail. 'What did you say?'

Christian never quailed. She didn't know the meaning of fear. 'Why doesn't Glasgow Annie wear anything under her skirts?' she repeated.

Gavin's face flushed a dusky red. He threw a quick, puzzled look at his wife, read guilt in her blue eyes, and fixed his attention on Christian again.

'What makes you think that?' he asked, with deceptive gentleness.

'After the fight, when she'd pulled the big boy away from the other boy – before I even got a chance to hit him with my stick –' said Christian, suddenly recalling a grievance ' – she did this –'

To Margaret's horror she scrambled to her feet, turned her back on her parents, and whisked the skirt of her warm wool dress up in passable imitation of Annie's crude sexual gesture to Walter Shaw.

' – and everyone laughed, and the big boy ran away. And Annie didn't have anything on under her skirt. She's awful big. I told her she must have eaten all her porridge.'

'I think,' her father said, his voice still mild, but with a cutting edge of cold steel beneath it, 'that it's time you were in your bed, my lady.'

*

Supper was a silent affair. As she drew the curtains before sitting down at the table Margaret saw that the rain had gone and the late-summer evening was clear and calm. She took her seat opposite her husband and waited for the domestic storm to break.

Gavin, seemingly lost in thought, ate his way steadily through each course as it was laid before him.

When they went back to the parlour Margaret sat by the fire, her mending in her lap. Gavin paced the floor.

'You've been taking her down to these – these stinking hovels again!' he said at last. 'Down by the river, where it's alive with vermin and filth and disease –'

'It's never done me any harm, and I've been down there often enough in my life.'

'You've been fortunate. My daughter might not be.' His voice was low and intense, as it usually was when he was angry. Gavin rarely shouted. 'I told you before, Margaret, if you must go visiting the folk that live there, then do so alone. God knows I've no control whatsoever over your movements. I recognise and freely admit that. But I will not have my children exposed to danger.'

It was her turn to feel anger. She had been in the wrong, taking Christian with her, knowing that Gavin wouldn't approve. But even so his high-handed attitude incensed her. 'Gavin, you speak as though you birthed the children entirely on your own. They're mine as well as yours – perhaps more so, since I carried them and bore them.'

'All the more reason to cherish them and keep them safe from harm.'

'Christian's as strong as a – a horse!'

'Have you forgotten that we almost lost her to the croup before she completed her first year?'

Could she ever forget that? Margaret recalled, as vividly as though it had happened only a few hours ago, her anguish as she paced the floor with her first-born, watching the flushed little face, listening to the child's choked, gasping breath, something like the sound the young lad in the lane had made that very day as his tormentor drew the neckcloth tighter.

'Christian outgrew the croup! There's not been a thing wrong with her since!'

'If you must visit the slums, you're not to take her with you again. I mean it, Margaret. And if you won't listen to me, then by God,' said Gavin, his eyes bright with anger, 'I'll stop you from going as well, somehow – even if it means locking you into your bed-chamber when I'm not here to watch over you.'

'We can't make poverty and suffering stop happening just by turning our backs on them!'

'I know that,' he said with a contempt that sent a surge of colour to her face. 'I'm reminded of it every day I walk the wards in the infirmaries. I don't spend all my time caring for moneyed folk, you know – only part of it. I don't turn my back, Margaret. I thank the good Lord every day that I can protect my family from poverty and want and the suffering they bring. But I'll not have Christian exposed to it in any manner!'

There was a short, angry silence, then, 'I'm tired,' Gavin said stiffly. 'If you'll excuse me, I'll retire.'

She bowed her head in silent, formal assent, biting back the angry words that wanted to pour out.

Alone, she cleared the table, carried the used platters to the kitchen, and sent Ellen off to her bed, refusing the woman's offer of help. She needed to occupy her hands. That way she could block out the thoughts that seethed in her mind.

But later, as she sat by the parlour fire, with the house silent about her apart from the ticking of the clocks, the needle that was repairing a tear in one of Daniel's garments with swift, assured efficiency slowed and stopped.

Gavin had the right of it; she was sensible enough to admit that. Christian, despite her sturdy independence, wasn't much more than a baby. It was foolish to expose her to unnecessary peril. God knows there were dangers enough for her to navigate as she grew without her mother seeking out more.

But deep down in Margaret lay a fear that her children, born to privileges she herself, a weaver's daughter, had never known, might grow to accept unquestioningly the vast gulf between those with more than enough money and those with none.

Since her marriage she had met many rich people at gatherings and at dinner tables. Most of them displayed such indifference to the misfortunes of their fellow men that it made her skin crawl to be in their company. She couldn't bear the thought of Christian and Daniel growing up to be like those addle-pated, shallow puppets.

The needle went about its work again, then slowed and stopped as she recalled the other side of the coin – the Highland children in their damp, dark little room near the river. Vividly, she saw again the expression on Islay McInnes's face as she stared down at the ruined pirns.

The handsome clock in the hall struck the hour and Margaret gathered up her work and put it aside. It was time she was abed.

Contented snoring could be heard faintly from the rear of the house as she started to mount the stairs. Ellen was sound asleep in the little room off the kitchen. The children were also asleep in the room next to their parents' bedchamber – Christian snug beneath her coverlet, Daniel with arms outflung and hands loosely fisted above his head.

There was no sound from the bed she shared with Gavin. The fringe of light from her candle gave her a glimpse of him, eyes closed, lashes against his cheeks, dark hair tumbled over his forehead.

Margaret stripped her clothes off and put on her night-shift, cool and still smelling pleasantly of the fresh summer's day when it had been stretched over a bush in the back yard to dry.

She took off her lace cap and let her dark brown hair fall about her shoulders so that she could brush it out.

It vexed her that her hair, which had had a curl to it in childhood, had straightened over the years. Daniel had inherited her blue eyes and her straight, silky hair; fortunately, Christian had her father's thick tresses, with a vigorous wave in them.

The brush moved from crown to tip with an even, soothing rhythm. The mirror showed her candle-lit face, cloaked in the fall of long hair, as that of a pale, mysterious stranger.

The sight reminded her of a Hallowe'en party that her aunt Mary MacLeod had once held, and a game they had played that night. Each girl had to sit alone before a mirror, eating an apple and combing her hair. The tale was that she would see her future husband's face reflected in the mirror.

The face Margaret had seen in the glass on that long-ago night had belonged to her childhood friend William Todd, who had crept into the room to speak to her. Gavin had followed hard on William's heels, but she hadn't seen his reflection.

Gavin, however, was the man she had married, and William was dead now, drowned in the rain-swollen River Cart.

She missed him sorely. William had been her closest friend, the only person she had been able to confide in. She wished with all her heart that he had lived, instead of dying so young, and so cruelly.

She shivered, laid the brush down, and turned to blow out the candle. Its light picked out the gold flecks in Gavin's hazel eyes, wide open and studying her.

'How long have you been awake?'

'Long enough.' He pushed the bedclothes back, held out his hand to her. 'Come to bed, Margaret.'

She blew out the candle and walked bare-footed, with the assurance of one in familiar surroundings, across the night-black room to the bed.

Gavin's hand closed about her arm, drew her down beside him. He shifted so that she could nestle in the warm hollow his body had vacated, and gently pulled the covers over her.

'Of all the men you could have bewitched and tormented, Margaret Montgomery,' he whispered, 'why did you have to choose me?'

His body was hard and eager against hers. The quarrel was over. There would be others, no doubt – many others. That was part of marriage as far as Margaret and Gavin were concerned.

But always, there was the forgiving, the coming together again, the loving.

And pray God, Margaret thought as she let herself melt against him and felt the hard planes and angles of his face beneath her palm, may there always be the loving.

Chapter Four

Jamie Todd, normally the sunniest of men, was in an irritable mood. His mother, Kirsty Carmichael, had been summoned to the neighbouring town of Barrhead first thing that morning because of some domestic crisis in the home of Jamie's sister, Kate. Which meant that Jamie and his step-father, Billy Carmichael, had been obliged to make shift for themselves.

Two handless men in the one kitchen, particularly when one of them was old and stiff and clumsy with the rheumatics, and therefore given to dropping things, didn't make a good start to the day.

Furthermore, Kirsty's absence meant that she would not be spinning any yarn for the looms that morning.

At a time when work was scarce, Jamie's reputation was as good as his father's had been. He had eight looms under his care now, four in the High Street shop his father had worked before him and four in the shop he had taken over in Wellmeadow almost two years earlier.

They all worked on linen cloth, and they needed as much yarn as he could obtain for them. Although the Paisley weavers had built up a very good name for themselves a number of looms in the town were lying idle for lack of orders. Jamie worked his looms in partnership with his close friends Duncan and Robert Montgomery – a partnership that stood all three men in good stead. Even so, Jamie found it hard to keep all his looms employed. The fact of the matter was that in buying over the Wellmeadow shop he had taken on more responsibility than he could comfortably handle. But his nature wouldn't let him admit that to anybody, and so he worried over his financial obligations in silence.

Then, of course, there was that dolthead Walter Shaw – at

the door first thing that morning, with a hangdog look in the grey eyes that couldn't quite meet Jamie's, one hand bound in a grimy cloth, and less than the number of pirns he had gone out to collect from the spinsters the day before.

Jamie, his stomach uncomfortable after the makeshift breakfast he and Billy had managed to cook between them, his head buzzing with the list of all that he had to do that day, had boxed the young weaver's ears there and then on the doorstep, before the interested and amused gaze of the passers-by. Then he brusquely ordered the lad back to the loom shop, where he would have to spend the day making himself useful as best he could, fetching and carrying for the others while his own loom stood idle, the web Jamie had managed to contract for it half-finished.

Walter slouched off. Jamie thumped the door shut and stamped along the passage-way to the weaving shop. He had just reached it when the door-knocker made itself heard.

'I'll go,' one of the other men offered.

'Stay where you are. There's no point in bringing all the looms to a standstill. I can see that it's precious little work I'll get done this day!'

He tramped back along the passage and threw the door open, almost lifting it from its hinges in his irritation.

Islay had worked for most of the night in the crusie's flickering light while Lachie and Morag slept curled together in the wall bed. Towards dawn, with enough pirns filled to make up for those spoiled in the mud, she had joined the other two beneath the thin blanket, falling at once into an exhausted sleep haunted by uneasy dreams.

In the morning she carefully dressed herself in the best clothes she had, brushed out her long hair until it shone, and fastened it back beneath a threadbare lacy cap that had once, a long time ago, adorned the head of some well-to-do lady. Then, leaving what remained of the bread to make breakfast for Lachie and Morag, for there wasn't enough for three, she set off for the High Street with reluctant feet.

Her courage almost failed her when she saw that Jamie Todd himself stood at his street door haranguing Walter

Shaw, his rugged face angry beneath the thatch of blazing red hair.

As she watched, the master weaver aimed an open-handed blow at his employee's head, then stepped back and slammed the door shut.

Passing women and children gawped at the spectacle, then laughed. Walter, shoulders slumped in humiliation, turned away, and came face to face with Islay.

He flushed scarlet at the realisation that she had witnessed his humiliation, and glowered at her.

'Come to gloat, have you? Pleased with yourself at taking a man's livelihood from him?'

She glanced down at the bandage on his hand, then back to his face. 'I'm vexed, Walter. I didn't mean –'

'Damned Highlanders! Why did you have to come to Paisley and get under the feet of decent folk?' asked Walter, pushing roughly past her.

Miserably, she watched him go and then, with every muscle in her body poised to flee for her life if necessary, she rapped on the sturdy wooden door.

All too soon footsteps sounded on the stone passageway within, the door opened, and Jamie Todd was looking down at her.

'Aye?'

'Mist – M –' Her lips fluttered, then firmed. The fingers of her free hand twisted in the ragged folds of her skirt. She made a determined effort at the name, and this time it came out clearly. 'Mister T – Todd –'

'Aye, that's my name, lass. Well, state your business, for I've more to do than stand here all day.'

Her lips fluttered again, and were brought under control again. 'It was me that bit Walter.'

'Eh?'

'I b – bit Walter Shaw.' Then, as he said nothing, but continued to stare with bewildered incomprehension, she fisted her two hands before her over the handle of the basket she carried and said in a rush of outgoing breath. 'He was fighting with my kinsman Lachie so I bit him to make him let go. It's my fault he can't work and the pirns fell in the mire and –'

'You bit my weaver?' He seemed to be finding it hard to make sense of the situation.

'Aye. I'm mortally vexed, Mister Todd. It was wrong of me to injure his hand, and him working on the looms. But I had to make him let Lachie go, for he was throttling the laddie.'

'Lachie?'

'My cousin. He's only twelve, but Walter knows Lachie must fight him, being the man of the house, so he –'

'What's your name?'

Her tongue moistened her lips. She was still poised to run. 'Islay, sir. Islay McInnes.'

She held out the basket and Jamie Todd took it and glanced at its contents then back at her, his blue eyes puzzled.

'Where did you get them?'

'I spun them, in place of the ones that got spoiled yes – yesterday.'

'But – lassie, you must have been working all night!'

'I had to make up the number of pirns. Mister Todd, you'll – you'll not take the work away –?'

His jaw set truculently. 'I should, for what you've done to my weaver. But you can tell your mother that I'll overlook it this once. Just this once, mind.'

'My mother's dead –' Islay started to say, but to her horror tears of worry and exhaustion suddenly misted her eyes. Her mother had already been ailing when they were put out of their home. She had died soon afterwards, in the dark draughty corner of a barn.

Not a day went by without Islay recalling that terrible time. The mere thought of her dead mother at a time when her own courage was at a low ebb was too much.

She saw consternation and then embarrassment come into the face of the man who looked down at her. He began to say something, but Islay, beyond words now, turned and stumbled back along the footpath, anxious to get out of his sight before her tears won her over entirely.

It wasn't until much later, when she had sobbed her heart out in a quiet corner, that she realised that she had forgotten to claim payment for the pirns.

Chapter Five

On one side of the entrance passage of the Todds' High Street building was the big room that housed the looms; on the other was a smaller room where Billy Carmichael, Jamie's step-father, had plied his trade as a cobbler before the rheumatics put an end to his work.

Margaret had persuaded Jamie to let her move two small inkle looms in there, to enable some of the women from the Poors' Hospital where she taught to weave ribbons and earn a few coppers.

Before going to talk to him about the three children who lived in Jenny's Wynd she put her head round the door and had a swift word with the women working on the looms. Then she left them and opened the other door.

Weaving shops were always noisy. The babble of voices – for in Paisley, at least, the men gossiped just as much as the women – vied with the steady clack of the big looms. A pair of linnets chirrupped in a cage by the window. The room was large and, as always, it seemed to be lit by Jamie's mop of fiery red hair. He was working away at his loom and unusually silent, but a welcoming grin split his face when he looked up and saw her. Margaret and Jamie had always been close, even although she had refused to marry him years before.

She waited in the passage until he joined her. Then she asked, 'Jamie, d'you have a weaver called Walter Shaw?'

His face darkened. 'Aye, in the Wellmeadow weaving shop. Have you come to lecture me about him too?'

She raised puzzled brows.

'First I'd Walter at the door with a sorry tale about a wounded hand keeping him from his work, and pirns falling in the mud. Then a wee lassie from down by the river came with some nonsense about biting the man – biting him,

as if she was a dog! – and spoiling my pirns into the bargain.'
He shook his head. 'Then, if you please, she gave me pirns
she must have spun during the night, and ran away without
waiting for her money.'

'She's not a wee lassie, she's almost a grown woman. And
you must have said something to fright her if she ran from
you.' Swiftly Margaret gave her account of the scene down
by the river the day before.

'It must have been the younger girl who came to the door,
then, for she was only a child. And I said nothing to fright
her,' Jamie protested.

'You'll let the girl go on spinning yarn for you, won't you?
She's fair desperate for the money. And if you could mebbe
find work for the laddie –'

'But they're Highlanders, Margaret! Highlanders are all
fingers and thumbs when it comes to weaving, you know
that yourself.'

'Mebbe so, but they're decent enough folk, trying to earn
their bread like the rest of us.'

'Why should I go out of my way to help them? Highlanders cause nothing but trouble, and Walter can show you his
bandaged hand to prove it.'

'Yesterday's brawl was no fault of theirs! It was Walter's
doing, I'm sure of that.'

Jamie glowered down at her, but he could never resist
Margaret for long, and they both knew it. 'Aye – well – she
can go on spinning for me, if that'll please you,' he said at
last, reluctantly. 'The good Lord knows I need all the
spinsters I can get to keep the looms going.'

'And d'you think you might find some work for the boy?'

'I'll make no promises. But I'll go along to Jenny's Wynd
myself and have a word with them.'

'You'll find them in a miserable room, the poor souls.'
Then Margaret was struck by an idea. 'Jamie, isn't the
dwelling house above your loom shop in Wellmeadow
empty?'

'I'm planning on using it as a store.'

'Och, it's too good to waste as a store!'

But Jamie had had enough. 'Find somewhere else for
your Highlanders. I must get back to my loom,' he said

crisply. 'I've had too many interruptions today as it is. If you've got the time you might go on up and talk with Billy for a while. The man's lonely without my mother about the place.'

'Is she still at Barrhead?'

'Aye. Both Kate's bairns are down with some fever.'

'What is it?' Margaret asked sharply, and he shrugged.

'Nothing serious, from what I hear.'

'Run back to your loom, then – but think on what I'm asking you. I'll have a word with Billy.'

Margaret eased past him to where a flight of stone steps led up to the dwelling house above. There, she found a more sympathetic listener in Jamie's step-father.

'Jamie's not as hard as he makes out, lassie,' the old man said. 'He's got a lot of responsibility, what with eight looms to see to. And things arenae easy just now.'

'But Jamie's surely not having any trouble finding work. He's said nothing to me about it – or to my father, or I'd surely have heard.'

'He's not the sort who would.' Billy knocked his pipe out against the side of the kitchen fireplace.

'He needs a wife. If only Beth had lived –'

Her voice tailed off, and they were both silent for a moment, thinking of what might have been.

Shortly after he returned from the Army, Jamie had become betrothed to the young woman who worked as companion to Margaret's aunt, Mary MacLeod. But Beth, who wasn't strong, had died during an outbreak of pleurisy that swept through Paisley a few months before the wedding.

'If I could just think of the right person –'

'Now don't go black-footing, Margaret. Jamie wouldnae thank you for finding a wife for him. Better trust to Fate.'

'Mebbe,' Margaret agreed. But privately, she was of the opinion that Fate would be none the worse for a nudge in the right direction.

Chapter Six

Ellen ushered Margaret's young brother, Thomas Mont-gomery, into the tiny dining room while Margaret and Gavin were still at their evening meal.

The three Montgomery men, Duncan and his sons Robert and Thomas, were all alike; of stocky build and medium height, with dark hair and clear, honest blue eyes.

But whereas Duncan and Robert had strong, square faces, Thomas's was still round, overlaid with the rosy bloom of youth, despite the fact that he was now twenty-five years of age, and a qualified physician.

A bachelor, he still lived under his parents' roof. This, coupled with the fact that he was the youngest of the three Montgomery children, led his family to think of him at all times as 'wee Thomas', a habit that rankled deeply with him.

But there was nothing youthful about his face as he advanced into the room, brusquely refusing Margaret's invitation to share their evening meal.

'I'm not here as a guest. Gavin, I've need of your help.'

Margaret, who had heard that Kirsty had sent for Thomas to go to Barrhead that afternoon, felt a chill creep towards her heart.

'Kate —?' Her voice shook, and Gavin came to her, put his arm about her.

'Kate's well enough, but both the children are down with fever.' He looked at the couple before him, his eyes dark with the news he had to tell. 'It's the pox, Gavin. The serving-girl took it first, and she died two hours back.'

Margaret sensed the sudden tension in Gavin's body. His arm fell from her shoulders. 'I'll come at once,' he said, and went from the room.

Margaret and her brother looked at each other word-lessly. There was nothing to say.

The pox. The two words circled through her head in time to some macabre tune.

The pox. She had seen men, women and children fall victim to it in the Poors' Hospital. Most sufferers died but Margaret knew some who had survived.

There was Jockie Gray, who had been blinded and terribly disfigured by the disease. There was Mirren Tennant, a woman of Margaret's own age, who had been turned into a simpleton and now lived in the Poors' Hospital, roaming the rooms hour upon hour, keening to herself.

Few recovered fully – but some did, Margaret told herself, doubling her hands into fists, digging nails into palms, determined not to give up hope.

When Gavin came back, shrugging into his coat, his bag in one hand, she said, 'I'll come with you.'

Both men shook their heads, and Gavin said sharply, 'You must stay here, Margaret, and see to your own bairns.'

There was no sense in arguing. She knew, looking at their faces, that they had already shut her out, pushed her into the background. All at once they had become strangers to her, medical men with no need or time for anyone else.

She followed them to the front door, watched as they clambered into the carriage that had brought Thomas from Barrhead. When they had gone, rattling off through the gathering dusk, rounding a corner, passing from view, she went slowly back into the house to begin the long wait for Gavin's return.

As she lay alone in the darkness later she thought of the little family in Barrhead. Archie, easy-going and devoted to his wife and children; four-year-old John and three-year-old Alyson; laughing, lovely, red-haired Kate, who was eagerly awaiting the birth of her third child in a few months' time.

Margaret closed her eyes then opened them again hurriedly as pictures of smooth, formerly healthy skin covered with pustules imprinted themselves on the insides of her lids. She sought the comfort of the window's grey shape in the darkness of the room, and watched as it lightened, and dawn came.

*

Carriage wheels rattled to a standstill outside the gate a few hours later, as the birds were pouring out a joyous, full-throated welcome to the new day.

Margaret tossed a shawl about her shoulders and was at the front door by the time Gavin came wearily up the path.

She flew into his arms and he held her tightly, hungrily, burying his mouth in her hair, before holding her back so that he could look down at her.

'How are they?'

His face was haggard. 'The wee lad's gone, but I think Alyson'll recover now. Come inside – I'm in sore need of warmth, and some food.'

The kitchen was quiet and still warm from last night's fire. Its embers glowed dull red in the range and Margaret poked it into life again, refuelling it from the coal scuttle that was filled last thing every night.

Gavin slumped wearily into a chair by the table, staring at the wall, seeing pictures there that she couldn't see. That was just as well, she realised as she set bread and cheese and ale before him.

He ate hungrily, and persuaded her to share the ale with him. She wasn't fond of the liquid's bitter taste, but it helped to ease the painful block of ice that had formed in the very core of her being.

The kettle boiled and she made tea, asking at last, as they both sipped the hot liquid. 'How are Kate and Archie taking it?'

Gavin reached out and put his hand over hers. His fingers were warm; hers, she realised, were very cold. 'If – God forbid – you and I should be faced with such tragedy, Margaret, I pray we'll find the courage they've shown.'

'I should go to Barrhead.'

'Kirsty's there. And you've your own bairns to think of. You can't afford to bring the sickness home to them.'

He left his chair and came to her, holding her close.

'I'd do anything, Margaret – anything! – to find out how to put an end to bairns dying like that, almost before they've had a chance to live,' he said fiercely against her hair.

Then the door opened and Ellen, still tousled from her bed, stood looking at them in sleepy surprise.

*

Five minutes later Margaret sat on her tumbled bed and watched as her husband stripped his soiled clothes off, letting them lie where they fell. He washed quickly in the warm water he had brought from the kitchen, then dressed in clean clothes and tied his dark hair back with a broad ribbon. Gavin had always scorned wigs and powder, though many of his colleagues favoured them.

'Must you go to Glasgow today? You should get some rest.'

'I must. There's work to be done.' He drew her to her feet and kissed her, a hard, possessive kiss. 'I'll come home as soon as I can.'

At the front door he took her hands in his, raised them to his lips.

'Sometimes, Margaret,' he said against her fingers, 'It's only the thought of the three of you, well and happy and safe in this house, that keeps me from giving in to despair.'

Then he went, and she was alone once again.

Chapter Seven

Jamie Todd strode along the Sneddon, carrying in one hand a basket of flax to be spun into yarn for the linen weavers, in the other a bag of empty pirns, the wooden reels that the yarn was spun onto.

Above, the sky was leaden, weeping a thin drizzle of rain to add to the stinking puddles under Jamie's booted feet. His fiery head was the only splash of bright colour in the drab day.

The weather suited his mood. A few hours earlier he had watched his young nephew being hurriedly buried. His mother was still in Barrhead with Kate and the rest of her family.

A stray trickle of rainwater from a wet straw thatch found its way beneath Jamie's collar. He shivered, partly at its icy touch, partly because his thoughts were back in Barrhead with his sister.

It did a man no good to feel so useless in times of adversity. Jamie was used to taking life by the throat and shaking it; nobody could do that where illness and death were concerned.

He turned down Jenny's Wynd and stopped to survey the place, his nose wrinkled with disgust at the smell of soaked, rotting rubbish. Once, over a century before, the tiny houses had no doubt been adequate enough. Now dampness seeped into them from the River Cart, which ran past the bottom end of the lane, adding its own stink to the already over-laden air. Refuse lay piled against damp house walls, filthy water dripped from thatched roofs, windows gaped like empty eye sockets.

It was a wonder that every resident in the place hadn't fallen victim to the pox or one or other of the fevers and lung complaints that abounded in the town.

A few men lounged in a doorway; he asked where the McInnes family lived, and was directed to a house near the far end. The shrunken ill-fitting door was flimsy. Inside, a child was coughing; a harsh, wrenching sound. Jamie lifted his fist and thumped briskly on the door.

For a moment he thought that it was going to give way beneath his hand. No doubt the people inside would think that it was the militia that had come calling, he thought, and followed the commanding thump with a more sedate tap of the knuckles. Nothing happened. He was about to knock again when it opened.

Jamie peered into the dim oblong and saw the under-nourished child who had delivered the pirns and admitted to biting Walter Shaw.

*

Islay drew her breath in sharply as she recognised the caller. Then she stepped back, gripping the edge of the door so tightly that her fingernails almost sank into the soft, rotted wood. 'You'll come in, Mister Todd?'

The man hesitated, as though he would have preferred to stay outside, then stepped through the doorway, ducking his head beneath the lintel.

Then he gave an abrupt exclamation, stumbling and almost falling headlong into the room, because he hadn't realised that the sill of the door was several inches above the inner floor.

Instinctively, Islay caught at his elbow, releasing him as soon as he had recovered his balance.

Morag, sitting on a stool by the fire, coughed again, and Mister Todd stared at her, then at Islay.

'Are you the lassie who bit my weaver?'

'Aye, sir. Islay McInnes.'

'And what age might you be, Islay McInnes?'

'Sixteen years past.'

'Indeed?' There was no mistaking his surprise. 'I took you for –' He stopped, then added, 'So you're the oldest member of your household?'

'Aye, sir.'

Lachie, no doubt stung by the inference that there was no

man of the house, came from the corner of the room to stand by Islay's elbow.

'This'll be the laddie that fought with Walter?'

Lachie took a step forward. 'He started it!'

'You're no' big enough to take on the likes of him,' Mister Todd said sharply.

'I'm growing!'

'You'll not live long enough to grow if you behave like a fighting cock every time the mood comes over you.'

Islay could feel the boy's thin body tense with anger. She pressed his arm warningly and he subsided.

Jamie Todd swung his basket and bag onto the table. 'I brought more flax and pirns. And I brought the payment for the last lot, since you didnae see fit to wait for it.'

As the coins rattled on the wooden table Islay's hand moved forward of its own volition, but before her fingers touched the money she managed to check herself and drew back. There was no need to let this man see how desperately they needed his money.

'But mind – there's to be no more fighting.'

'I'm grateful to you, Mister Todd.'

'Prove it by working well and not bringing any more trouble on my head. Is there nobody – older – in the family who could care for you all?'

Her head tilted proudly. 'My uncle and cousin went to be soldiers.'

'Your uncle would have been better to stay home and see to his bairns.'

'He couldn't find any work here. He went while his wife was alive. He doesn't know we're alone now, for I've no way of contacting him.'

'There's little enough money to be made in the Army. I know, for I spent some years in it myself.'

His criticism wounded her, and a sharp answer was out before she could stop it. 'It's better than dying of a broken heart in a place like this.'

It was obvious that his patriotism was stung. 'There's nothing wrong with Paisley, if you're prepared to work hard and learn our ways!'

'I meant this house,' she said. 'But since you speak of

Paisley, Mister Todd, I'll remind you that it's your home, not ours. We had our own land, once. We had space to move and clean air to breathe, and the water in the burns was sweet and pure –'

'It sounds bonny enough, but you must just make the best of what you have now, and stop feeling sorry for yourselves.'

'We didn't leave our home from choice,' she told him firmly. Lachie moved protectively closer. 'We were forced out by the landowners. We did nothing wrong.'

'Islay –' Morag faltered nervously, aware that there was a quarrel brewing.

Islay touched her shoulder with a comforting gesture. 'It's all right, Morag, don't fret. I just want to tell you that we're not criminals to be punished, Mister Todd, or beggars to be tolerated or whipped out of the town. We don't ask for your pity, or expect it. We just want to make our own way, without causing or receiving trouble.'

Jamie Todd's face warmed, and she feared that she had gone too far. Cold sweat beaded her forehead. If he took back his money, she wouldn't be able to bear it. She'd go down on her knees to him first, cut out her tongue – anything rather than lose those few precious coins.

For a moment there was an awkward silence, then, 'I see that you've a sharp tongue in your head, lassie, to match your sharp teeth,' he said dryly. 'And the boy?'

'Lachie's twelve.'

'What d'you work at, Lachie?'

'I run errands, when someone's willing to take me on.'

'Morag and I do some cleaning,' Islay added. 'And there's the spinning –' Her voice trailed away. She wasn't certain, any more, of the spinning.

'Mmmm.' He hesitated, then said, 'I'm in need of a drawboy in one of my loom shops.'

For a moment they all stared at him, unable to believe their ears. 'I could do it,' Lachie said eagerly.

'It would mean working in my loomshop in Wellmeadow, beside Walter Shaw. I'll have no fighting among my workers, lad, I'll tell you that here and now.'

Lachie swallowed hard, then ducked his shaggy head in mingled submission and acceptance.

'Very well, then, come and see me in the Wellmeadow shop tomorrow morning.'

Mister Todd turned towards the door, fumbling for the latch. He couldn't find it in the gloom. Islay went to his side; her hand touched his lightly, moved on, found the latch, and opened the door.

He stepped into the lane, and would have walked away if Islay hadn't followed him and touched his arm.

'Well? What d'you want now?'

The drizzle had stopped and the sky had begun to clear. A watery sunbeam fell onto Islay's uplifted face, dazzling her.

'Mister Todd – we're grateful for your kindness. You'll not have cause to regret it.' Then, as he stared down at her in silence, she asked, 'Is there something amiss, Mister Todd?'

'No,' he said at last. 'I was just thinking – there's an empty dwelling house above the loom shop in Wellmeadow that might do you better than this place –'

*

As he walked back home Jamie cursed himself for a weak, loose-tongued fool. He had had no intention of doing as Margaret asked, and letting the Highlanders live in his empty house.

But there was something about the older girl's spirited determination to survive, something about her face when the sunlight fell on it in those last moments; it was too pale and too thin, that face, but its fragility only served to highlight her flawless skin, a covering for the delicate, exquisitely fine bones beneath it; the dark, long-lashed eyes under finely drawn brows; the rich blue-black sheen of her thick hair.

She was only a child, this Highland girl who had travelled all the way from the mountains and glens of her homeland to blossom to womanhood unnoticed in the slums of Paisley. Only a child, and yet –

Again, Jamie cursed himself. But what was done was done. For better or for worse, he had saddled himself with Islay McInnes and her kinfolk.

Chapter Eight

On the following morning Islay hurried along to Jamie Todd's weaving shop in Wellmeadow, telling herself over and over as she went that Mister Todd had no doubt changed his mind, or found a better use for the rooms he had spoken of.

Years of hoping, then having these hopes dashed, had taught her that she could rely on nobody. The people of her clan had trusted the lairds who owned the land, yet in the space of a breath the habits and rights of generations had been overturned to make way for cattle and wool-bearing sheep.

In her wanderings since then Islay had seen many promises go sour, many folk who had been kindly enough in the beginning tire of the burden of homeless Highlanders and turn away from them, sending them off on their journeying again. She had seen her parents and her aunt die, her uncle and cousin grow bitter through enforced idleness.

Jamie Todd would like as not be the same as the others – regretting his talk of empty rooms almost as soon as the words were out of his mouth.

Islay couldn't understand why the man had made the offer in the first place. She had a feeling that he couldn't understand it, either. Which made it all the more likely, she told herself, walking faster as though by reaching him quickly she could forestall it, for another change of mind.

She stumbled over a raised stone and almost fell against someone.

'Mind your feet, lassie,' the man said roughly, in a hurry himself, and passed by without giving heed to her apology.

She went on, paying more attention to the path now. Four years before, the Council had forbidden the townsfolk to toss their household refuse out of their street doors onto the path; now, each family had to keep its midden at the back of the house. So at least there was no longer any danger of the passer-by being tripped up by a pile of stinking rubbish extending from the house wall to the roadway. But the footpaths, particularly in the town's older wynds and streets, were still rough and muddy and treacherous underfoot.

Islay reached the loom shop without any further mishap. A pend, an open, arched passageway, ran from the street to the back yard. A door in the wall of the pend led to the weaving-shop; she timidly knocked, then went in.

The second of Jamie Todd's loom shops was large enough to accommodate two handlooms and two drawlooms. The intricate drawloom harness, reaching to the ceiling, dwarfed the others.

The room was a confused clutter of sound – the clack of the handlooms, the louder clatter and thump of the harness looms as the upper mechanism lifted to raise the warp threads, then fell back to lower them again, the musical skirl of the caged birds by the window, a sudden rich deep bellow as one of the weavers raised his voice in song.

Islay's eyes fell first on Lachie who, bare feet planted solidly on the earthen floor, was already working the harness, his small face intent on what he was doing. It was humid in the shop, and the sleeves of his over-large shirt had been rolled up to just below the shoulder.

Muscles corded on his scrawny arms as he pulled with all his might on the gut cords that lifted alternate groups of warp threads in an intricate and carefully-worked system, allowing the weaver to create a more elaborate pattern than the handlooms could ever achieve.

She was relieved to see that Lachie's weaver looked cheerful enough. She had heard stories of weavers who treated their drawboys cruelly, but at least the lad seemed to be working with a kindly man.

Jamie Todd was sitting on the side windowsill studying a sketch. He looked up as Islay went to stand before him.

For just a moment, as he recognised her, his jaw tightened and his blue eyes went dark. She felt her heart constrict, tensed herself for the dismissal that was sure to come.

Then he tossed the piece of paper down and rose, brushing past her, indicating with a movement of the head that she should follow him back into the pend.

As she did so she saw that Walter Shaw was working at one of the looms. The youth looked up, caught her eye, and ducked his head again quickly, faint colour staining his cheekbones.

'You've come to look at the dwelling house,' Mister Todd said almost coldly when they were outside, away from the noise.

'Aye, sir, if it's not too much trouble.'

'Now's as good a time as any, I suppose.' He led her through to the back and up a flight of wooden stairs fastened to the rear wall of the building.

Then he unlocked the door of the dwelling house and motioned her to go on ahead of him.

Islay stepped past him, and found Paradise on earth.

The first, and larger, of the two rooms was easily twice the size of the one room she shared with Lachie and Morag in Jenny's Wynd. The floor was good strong wooden timbers, sound and free from dampness.

The walls were of white-washed stone, and two glazed, deep-silled windows, one looking out over the busy street, the other to the back, provided ample light. The open fireplace had a hinged 'swee' to enable a kettle to be swung over the flames to heat, then swung out into the room for easy access. There was a wall-bed recess, and a door that stood ajar in the corner revealed a deep-shelved larder.

Tiptoe-ing, afraid to make a noise in case the spell broke, or she woke and found herself huddled in the bed in Jenny's Wynd, Islay pushed the inner door open and found herself in a smaller room, this one with a single window looking out onto the street.

An impatient clearing of the throat from outside reminded her that Jamie Todd was waiting. When she rejoined him he was at the outer door, looking down over the yard.

'There's work needing done down there –' He swept an arm out to indicate the over-grown area beneath. 'I'd expect you to tend it.'

'I could grow kale, and potatoes. And mebbe keep some bees – and some hens, if you'd not mind.'

'Do as you wish, as long as you look after things.' He started down the stairs.

'Mister Todd.'

He stopped, looked up at her with irritation darkening his face. 'Aye? You want the place, don't you?'

'Oh, I do! But – how much would the rent be?'

'No need to think about that.' He continued on his way. Islay stood her ground.

'But I do. I must.'

'Confound it, lassie, either take the house or stay in that stinking hutch you inhabit now! Don't go fretting me with talk of rent. Now – are you biding, or are you going?'

Her heart sank like a stone. She cast one last look at the roomy, light-filled interior of the house, then closed the door slowly. The click of the latch was like the tolling of a death-knell.

'I'm going.' She picked up her skirts and began to descend the stairs. 'Thank you for letting me see the rooms.'

'But – what's amiss with you now?'

'We cannot live here without paying you rent.'

'I don't want your money!'

'If we pay nothing, you can put us out whenever it pleases you. I've Lachie and Morag to think of – I couldn't let that happen to them.'

He gave her a sapphire-hard look, then asked abruptly, 'What d'you pay to the creature that cries himself a landlord to the place you live in now?'

When she named the sum, he gave a short angry laugh. 'I might have known it would be twice what the place is worth. Very well then, pay me the same.'

'It's not enough!'

'Can you afford more?'

'No, but – it's not enough, not for a place as fine as this.' She drew herself upright. 'We don't ask for charity, Mister Todd – or accept it.'

'You may not be a fool, but you're a nuisance,' said Jamie Todd in heartfelt tones. 'Listen to me. Pay me the same as you're paying in Jenny's Wynd, and in addition you can tend the yard and keep the weaving shop clean. In return, you'll have my oath on it that I'll not put you out on the streets. Will that satisfy your stiff-necked Highland pride?'

She considered, then nodded.

'Thank the Lord that's settled,' he said.

Then he went back to his weaving shop, and left her in possession of her new home.

*

Two days later she was down on her knees in the Well-meadow kitchen, singing softly as she scrubbed the kitchen floor, when a shadow darkened the open doorway and she looked up to see Mister Todd hesitating on the wooden landing.

She jumped to her feet, drying her hands on her sacking apron. 'Come in, sir.'

For a moment she thought that he was going to refuse, then he came slowly through the doorway, ducking his head beneath the lintel.

'Is the other lassie not helping you to prepare the place?'

'She's sorely troubled with her lungs today. I made her stay in bed.'

'Has she been ailing for long?'

'Since our first winter away from our own home.'

'Has a physician seen her? No, of course not,' he answered his own question.

'Physicians cost silver, Mister Todd.'

'I've a friend, Thomas Montgomery, who'd have a look at her. I'll speak to him.' Then he added, as Islay opened her mouth to argue, 'Or is your pride more important than the bairn's health?'

She flushed hotly and said nothing.

'That's settled, then.' He looked about the empty room. 'What are you going to do for furniture?'

'Mistress Knox came to Jenny's Wynd yesterday to see me. She has some pieces we can use, she says.'

'No doubt,' said Jamie Todd dryly, and left as suddenly as he had arrived.

Plunging the scrubbing brush back into the basin of

water, Islay puzzled over the man's strange blend of antagonism and kindness. It was almost as though Mister Todd was helping her family against his will.

It was as though Mister Todd was fighting an inner war with himself, and in some way that she couldn't fathom, Islay McInnes had become his battlefield.

Chapter Nine

'I'll go along today to see how the Highlanders are settling in. I knew I'd get Jamie to see things my way,' Margaret said with smug self-satisfaction.

Gavin, tying his stock about his throat, glanced at her reflection in the mirror. 'You always do.' His tone was mocking, but affectionate.

'Well, it's a mortal sin, letting two good rooms lie empty when the lanes down by the river are fair crammed with folk in need of a good roof over their heads and solid walls to keep the wet out.'

He turned away from the looking glass and picked up his jacket. 'I'd like to see these hovels pulled down. They're a disgrace to the name of Paisley. Most folk wouldn't keep their dogs in places like these.'

'My father would tell you – and so would my Aunt Mary – that it's up to the people down by the river to make something of their own lives, and not expect others to do it for them.'

Gavin grunted in reply. He and Margaret had fought many a battle with the older generation over that sore issue.

When the day's housework was done to her satisfaction Margaret left Ellen in charge of small Daniel and set off for the Wellmeadow house with Christian, who had clamoured to accompany her.

Islay greeted the two of them with a radiant smile. 'Morag, we've got a visitor,' she called, and her young cousin came shyly from the inner room.

Margaret stepped inside, casting a swift eye over the place. The house was spotless, and the pieces of furniture that she had managed to gather from all over the town were already in place.

'It looks grand!' She ran a hand over the back of a chair,

noting the high polish on all the woodwork, the gleaming black range, the fresh curtains at the window. 'You've been working hard.'

'We all have. You'll take some tea?' Islay asked, and this time Margaret was able to accept, and to sample some freshly-made scones. Christian was clamouring to be allowed to go into the back yard, and Morag timidly offered to take her.

When the two girls had gone out, Margaret asked, 'Is your cousin's health any better for the move?'

'I'm sure it is. Mister Todd asked a friend of his, a physician, to have a look at her.'

'That'll be Thomas Montgomery, my brother.'

'He says it was the damp house that caused the trouble, and that this place, and good food, will be the saving of her. I'm so grateful, Mistress Knox. I think another year in Jenny's Wynd would have been the death of Morag.'

'And how's your brother getting on with Walter?'

'Och, they're fine together. Walter's not a bad soul — laddies always enjoy fighting. Mister Todd's warned them both well — any trouble and they'll have to find another employer. And Lachie well knows,' the soft Highland voice added ' — that we can't afford to lose our new home.'

Margaret watched the girl as she moved about the room with the springing energy of youth. Happiness and freedom from anxiety had already brought about changes in Islay. Her long black hair was glossy, her eyes shone, her face had begun to fill out.

Her shabby, ill-fitting clothing had been replaced by a full-skirted dark red gown that Margaret had given her, with a white fichu over her shoulders, and a plain white linen cap sat neatly on her smooth dark hair.

Margaret, suddenly aware that she herself had left her youth behind and was now approaching her thirties, envied the natural grace of the girl's movements. One day in the not too distant future Islay McInnes was going to be a beautiful woman.

Someone knocked at the outer door. Islay opened it, and Margaret saw that Walter Shaw stood there.

'The surgeon's waiting downstairs for Mistress Knox.'

Margaret rose and went to the door. 'Tell him I'll be down directly.'

Walter ducked his head in answer, then lifted it and looked again at Islay before turning away. The intensity of his glance struck Margaret forcibly, but Islay didn't seem to notice it.

Perhaps, thought Margaret as the two of them began to descend the wooden stairs, the girl was still too young and naive to be aware of the attraction she held for the young weaver.

*

Islay's work was evident to Margaret as soon as she walked into the loom shop. It was accepted in Paisley that the drawboys should keep the machines clean and in good working condition, and sweep the floors each morning.

But some strange tradition that had subtly established itself said that drawboys didn't have to be responsible for the hearths. That was woman's work. As a result, the fireplaces in most of Paisley's loom shops, other than those with drawgirls, were messy, ash-ridden areas, tended now and then, with much grumbling, by the weavers' wives. Margaret had always felt that it was an unfair tradition.

In this loom shop, the fireplace that had always been an affront to a self-respecting housewife was clean and sweet, shining from the same vigorous polishing that Margaret had seen upstairs. She looked it over, and nodded in silent approval.

The drawloom Lachie worked at had stopped while the weaver untangled some yarn. As he went about his task, the man sneaked puzzled glances at Gavin and Lachie, who were over by the window.

Gavin was examining the boy's arm closely. Lachie looked worried, and bit his underlip as he looked down on the surgeon's bent head. Jamie, also puzzled, stood by. 'Margaret, here a minute –' Gavin called.

When she and Islay joined him he said absently, 'I thought I might find you here, so I looked in in the passing. See here –' He indicated a white puckered scar that marred the skin on Lachie's upper arm.

'Is there something wrong with Lachie?' Islay asked swiftly, her eyes large with apprehension.

'No – far from it. Tell Mistress Knox how you came by that scar, laddie.'

'It's –' Lachie, worried at finding himself the centre of so much attention, looked at his cousin for support, swallowed hard, then said, 'It's only the kindly pox, mistress.'

'The –?'

''Tis only the way to keep the pox at bay, that's all,' Islay's voice sang with relief. 'All the bairns at home have it done.'

'How did your physician go about it?' Gavin wanted to know, and the girl looked at him pityingly.

'Och, we'd no need of physicians. One of the old men had the way of it, and the womenfolk took their wee ones to him.'

Margaret listened, appalled, as the girl casually explained how the old man had used a sharp knife to ease a piece of the outer skin free, then rubbed the area with what he called the 'kindly pox', a substance obtained from diseased cattle. To her, it sounded barbaric. Gavin, however, paid rapt attention to every word, making Islay repeat one or two pieces of information.

'Didn't your arm bleed?'

'Not at all. He put a wee bit leaf over the place and it soon healed.'

'What happened next?'

'After that the fever comes, and the bairns have to be kept abed, away from everyone else, till they're better. It passes after a few days,' Islay said casually, and Margaret shivered.

'It's a wonder you didn't die of it!'

'Och, we never would. Nor the bad pox either. We can't catch that now.'

Then Jamie, not interested in the talk and impatiently aware of the time being lost in his weaving shop, curtly sent the young Highlanders back to their work, and Gavin and Margaret collected their daughter and took their leave.

After walking down the High Street they paused for a moment to rest before commencing the uphill climb to their home. The Cross offered a grand view of the busy stalls in the market place and the River Cart, with the Abbey ruins and the houses of the New Town sitting cheek by jowl on the opposite bank.

As she surveyed the scene Margaret was aware of a great feeling of contentment. The inkle loom she had had installed at the Poors' Hospital and the two other looms at the Todd's house were doing well. At the moment, unknown to Gavin, who would have disapproved, she was secretly looking out for a larger workshop so that she could bring in more of the ribbon-weaving looms and provide work for more of the Poors' Hospital women. When she had found it, Gavin would come round to the idea – she had no doubt of that.

Life was good, Margaret thought complacently, and put her hand on her husband's arm.

He didn't notice the caress. His face, she saw, had that closed pre-occupied look that she called his 'physician's face'.

After a moment Christian became restless, and the three of them turned their back on the Cross and continued their way home.

Chapter Ten

'No! I forbid it!'

'Margaret –'

'I'll not talk about it! How could you even think of doing such a thing to your own bairns, Gavin Knox!'

'Whose, then, if not my own?' Gavin asked in a maddeningly reasonable tone.

'How could you think of taking the knife to any child?'

'The Highlanders do it, and their bairns come to no grief.'

'The Highlanders –!' Margaret said, with Lowlander scorn for the folk who lived far from civilisation, and practised strange customs.

'Would you sooner see Christian and Daniel falling sick of the pox and dying as Kate's bairn died?'

'If they should fall sick it'll be God's will, and we'll do all we can to save them. But I'll not stand by and see it happen to them through your will!'

'I tell you I've spoken to a number of Highlanders over the past weeks, and so has Thomas. All their bairns've had the inoculation done. They're all healthy, Margaret.'

'So you and Thomas have decided that my wee ones should be made use of, have you?'

'It was nothing to do with your brother. He's no bairns of his own, and I have, so –'

'They're not just yours!' she rounded on him. 'I carried them and bore them. I nursed them and I've had the raising of them. You minded me yourself not four weeks past of the time we near lost Christian to the croup.'

'Now, Margaret –'

'You were sore vexed with me then for taking her down to the lanes by the river where the air's bad. And now –' Her voice broke with rage and she had to struggle to bring it under control again ' – now you and that heartless brother

52

of mine want to cut her arm and put poison into the wound and make her sicken and mebbe –'

'I want to save her from the pox!' he insisted. 'A surgeon's work should be to stop folk from falling sick as well as trying to cure them. And it's my idea, not Thomas's, so keep your tongue off him.'

There was a short angry silence. Gavin stood by the fireplace, Margaret by the window. The space of the parlour lay between them, the air so thick with emotion that she felt as though she could reach out and gather it up by the handful.

'The Highlanders have been keeping their children safe from the pox for years by the same methods,' he said at last, in his most reasonable voice. 'It's here, in the Lowlands, that we're putting our bairns in danger by being slow and stubborn.'

'Slow and stubborn, is it? It seems to me that you're more willing to put Christian and Daniel in danger than I am.'

'You're being unjust, Margaret. I might be able to save scores of children – hundreds, even – with this method. But how can I persuade folk to let me vaccinate their bairns when I don't vaccinate my own?'

'And if they take the pox?'

'They won't.'

'Only God knows that, Gavin. Only He's got the right to play with lives – not you, and not Thomas. If you cut one child, and that child falls sick and dies, you'll be guilty of murder.'

'And if a child that's been denied vaccination falls to the pox and dies?'

'It's the will of God.'

His laugh was chillingly bitter. 'What a Saviour He must be, to take wee bairns in such suffering.'

'You'll not blaspheme in my house, Gavin Knox!'

'Why, Margaret, I've never known you to be so pious,' he mocked her, and she doubled her hands into fists to prevent them from picking up the fine china bowl her Aunt Mary had given them for a wedding gift and bouncing it off his thick skull. Then he added, 'And it's my house, come to that.'

'Take care then, lest I leave you in it and go elsewhere.'

The words lay heavily between them. They had been spoken in thoughtless haste, but she knew by the sudden widening of his eyes, the almost inperceptible gasp as he drew his breath in sharply, that he believed her.

When he spoke again his voice was chillingly cold. 'What would you have me do, then? Vaccinate the children in the Poors' House?'

'No, of course not! They might be poor wee unwanted souls, but you've surely not fallen so low that you'd use them like beasts to suit your own purposes – in the name of progress!'

The barb struck home. He flushed a dark, angry red, then turned on his heel and left the room. Margaret, her fists pressed tightly to her thumping heart, heard the door of the small room that housed all Gavin's books and papers and medical apparatus close with a crisp controlled sound that seemed worse than a resounding slam.

After a long moment she went upstairs and into the children's room. Christian, the hoyden, lay on her side, the coverlet tucked beneath her chin, her long lashes neatly ranged on her cheeks, her mouth primly buttoned. Margaret wondered what sort of dreams kept her daughter so still and tidy during the night.

By contrast Daniel, a sturdy, sober little boy by day, lay on his back in a tangle of sheets, his pillow on the floor, his mouth open, his strongly defined black eyebrows, which were oddly mature and seemed to be waiting for the round baby face to 'grow into them' as though they were an over-large pair of britches, twitching now and then.

As Margaret tried to ease the pillow beneath his head he opened wide blue eyes, focused blearily on her face, and gave her a sudden sweet smile before sleep claimed him again. As it did so his arm flailed above his head and knocked the pillow back to the floor.

Margaret stood between the two cots, listening to her children's breathing. They were more dear to her than anything or anyone else, even Gavin.

Not for the first time, she thought wryly that motherhood was only a way of delivering up hostages to the Fates. She would never again be free to follow her own will. And Gavin knew it.

*

They spent the night apart, Margaret in their bed chamber, Gavin downstairs. By the time she woke in the big, lonely bed, dressed, and made her way to the lower floor her husband had broken his fast and left for Glasgow, where he was due to spend the day in one of the infirmaries.

He had left word with Ellen that he would be late home.

The day passed drearily for Margaret. She irritated Ellen and the children by insisting on turning out cupboards and washing all the linen. The house was thrown into a turmoil, and by the afternoon every bush in the garden was festooned with sheets and towels and Ellen was tight-lipped at the thought of the amount of ironing that would have to be done on the following day.

Finally, having polished and scrubbed until she was exhausted, Margaret took herself off to the Poors' House to visit some of her pupils in the sick-room, where they had been laid low by what Margaret sardonically called the 'poor fever'.

The name had first come to her when, as a young teacher in the Poors' House, she had heard the master and mistress dismissing a fever that was prevalent in the place as something that 'just happened' to the poor. Margaret, to mask her anger, had flippantly suggested that the fever was attributed to some chronic carelessness on the part of the paupers, and her suggestion had been considered seriously then agreed with, much to her surprise.

Now, years later, the 'poor fever' was still around. Every inmate of the House could be sure of falling prey to it at least once during their stay.

Afterwards, still restless, she called in on Kirsty, Jamie's mother. Kate was there with her small daughter. Although she looked well, with the bloom of a healthy pregnancy adding to her natural beauty, Kate's eyes were still dark with grief over the loss of her son.

'I know I've still got Alyson, and that the coming bairn'll help me to get over my loss, but somehow –' Her eyes filled with tears that she couldn't blink back, 'I know that there's nothing in the world that can bring John back to me. And it's knowing that that makes it so hard to stop missing him.'

Margaret was in a chastened mood when she left her friend. She wanted nothing more than to get back to her own two children, and to see Gavin smile lovingly at her again. Their quarrel had been one of the worst they had ever experienced in their stormy marriage, and she wanted it to be over and done with.

A lane led to Oakshawhill from a pend in the High Street, hard by the old almshouse. At the other end of the lane Margaret emerged onto a road that was quieter and cleaner than the town streets, flanked with large houses on each side.

The air was purer here, and heavy with the fragrance of the late summer roses in the big gardens.

She slowed her walk, inhaling the scent, letting her mind empty itself of all irritations. A pleasant September day was coming to a graceful end, and the retiring sun set the sky to the west ablaze with tongues of crimson and gold.

The house was pleasantly quiet as she let herself in and hung her cloak on its peg in the hall. The children would already be abed, and Ellen preparing the evening meal in the kitchen.

The parlour was flooded with golden evening sunlight that poured in through the west-facing windows. Dazzled, Margaret paused in the doorway, then as her vision became accustomed to the light she saw the tall figure standing by the fireplace.

'Gavin! I didn't think you'd be home. Oh – I'm so glad!'

He had been studying one of the ornaments on the mantelpiece. As he turned she ran into his arms, holding him close, burying her face in his chest.

For a terrible moment he stood passively within her embrace and she thought that the anger of the previous evening was still with him. Then to her relief his arms closed about her.

'We must never be harsh with each other again,' Margaret said fiercely into his chest. 'Never, never ag –'

She lifted her head, seeking his lips with her own, and the

words died in her throat.

The man who held her in his arms said, 'Forgive me, madam – I think there's a slight misunderstanding.'

Chapter Eleven

'Oh –!' Margaret drew back sharply, pulling away from him, retreating step by step in the direction of the door. Unfortunately the bell-pull was by the fireplace, close to his shoulder, and therefore out of her reach. But one hand moved behind her, feeling for the door-handle.

'Mistress Margaret Knox?' He made no attempt to follow her, but stood still, turning both hands palms-up in a gesture of good-will. 'Your maid-servant permitted me to come in and wait for you.'

Her finger-tips brushed the door-panel. 'Who are you?'

'If, as I suppose, you're Margaret, then I'm your brother by marriage. My name is Richard – Richard Knox.'

Her hand fell away from the door. 'Richard?'

'Has Gavin never spoken of me?' His broad shoulders lifted in a faint shrug; his mouth, so like Gavin's, twisted slightly. 'Perhaps not. We parted with bad feeling and we've not had contact with each other these six or seven years now. It would be like Gavin to cut me from his life entirely.'

Margaret moved back into the room. 'I knew that Gavin had a brother who left home and went abroad.'

'Who quarrelled with all and sundry and ran off, over the seas and far away,' he corrected her, smiling now. 'And they all said good riddance to him, I've no doubt, and assumed that damnation would overtake him. But the Devil chose to look after his own and so –' His hands moved again, this time to flick their finger-tips lightly against the satin lapels of his smart blue coat. ' – here I am, come to pay my respects to my brother and his wife. Unsure of my welcome, which turned out to be warmer than I had hoped.'

The amusement in his voice brought colour surging back to her face. 'The sun was shining in my eyes. I'd naturally expected to find my husband here.'

'A fortunate husband, to have such a loving wife.'

His voice had the same rich depths as Gavin's, but there was more of a drawl to it. Margaret recalled, tardily, that the man was a guest in her home.

'Gavin's in Glasgow, but I expect him back before long. Did Ellen not offer you any refreshment, Mister Knox?'

'Richard. She did indeed, but I chose to wait until I had company.'

She indicated the corner cupboard where Gavin kept the glasses and decanters. 'Please take whatever you'd like. I must just go and see that the supper's being attended to.'

He bowed, and she fled to the kitchen, demanding angrily as she burst in, 'Why did you not send word to me that we'd a visitor? Why did you not tell me in the hall?'

Ellen, sampling a pot of broth, screamed and let the ladle go. It splashed into the simmering mixture and droplets flew up to spatter the maid's face.

A few minutes later, while Margaret busily soothed the burns with a cloth wrung out in cold water, Ellen eyed her reproachfully.

'A body could die of a fright like that!'

'D'you think I should rap on my own kitchen door, now?'

'I mean, I didnae even know you were in the house at all,' Ellen grumbled. 'You must have come from outside like a mouse. I meant to catch you in the hall and tell you about your caller.'

Margaret thrust the cloth into the woman's hand and turned her own attention to the food cooking on the range.

'Well – I found him for myself. The master's brother, it seems. Is there enough to do four of us instead of three?'

'He's got an awful dark-coloured face for a Scotsman.'

'He's been in far countries.' Margaret peered and poked and stirred, her mind swiftly dividing a meal meant for three into a meal that would do four, her inner eye picturing the servings. 'We'll manage – if you and me don't eat much. Mind that, now. You can fill your belly with bread and bannocks for once. And if Mister Knox isn't home in another thirty minutes you'd best serve the supper anyway and he can have his later. Now – do I look all right?'

Ellen cast an eye over her mistress, and nodded. 'You

look fine. Will he be staying the night?'

Margaret tutted irritably. 'I never thought to ask about that. You'd best get the wee room upstairs ready, just in case.'

'Aye,' said Ellen, adding, as Margaret made for the door again, 'He's awful like the master, is he no'?'

'Not a bit of it,' said Margaret crushingly.

Richard Knox stood by the parlour window, gazing out. He turned to face her, the firelight striking a rich red glow from the glass in his hand. The sun had set and the room was dim enough for his teeth to gleam briefly as he smiled at her.

'You've no Jamaican rum in your cupboard.'

'Gavin never developed a taste for it.' Then, as Richard raised his brows, she added in her husband's defence, 'Claret and good Scots whisky seem to suit his palate well enough.'

'I built my fortune on rum. I shall see to it that he has a half-dozen bottles within the week.'

He watched in silence as she busied herself about the room, poking the fire, using a taper to light the lamps.

When she finally ran out of things to do and settled in her usual chair he came across the room and offered her a glass that had been waiting, unnoticed, on a small table nearby.

'I don't drink spirits.'

He seated himself in the chair opposite – Gavin's chair. 'And I hate to drink alone. It's claret, not whisky. Just a sip or two, while I tell you why I've suddenly arrived on my brother's doorstep out of the past.'

Margaret was not fond of liquor, but to her surprise the claret went down very well. As she sipped, relaxing into the cushions of her chair, Richard Knox talked about four years spent in Jamaica, a fifth in America's deep south, and a sixth among the cotton manufactures of Lancashire before he finally decided to return to the land of his birth.

Margaret studied him in a series of quick glances when his own gaze was elsewhere.

He was probably a little heavier about the shoulders than Gavin, but of the same height. His clothes were both elegant and expensive, and he wore them with stylish grace.

Gavin's taste ran to dark colours, but Richard was a peacock in a vivid blue full-skirted satin-faced coat with a foam of snowy white lace at his throat, a heavily embroidered bronze waistcoat, fawn britches and brown boots. There were silver buttons on the coat and silver buckles on the boots.

As Ellen had said, his ruggedly handsome face was brown, no doubt from the Jamaican sun. His eyes were green with hazel highlights, while Gavin's tended to hazel shot through with flashes of pure emerald.

His warm brown hair, touched here and there with gold as the lamplight fell on it, was lighter than his brother's, but of the same strong springy texture. She knew exactly how it would feel beneath her fingers. He wore it tied back, but allowed it to curl crisply round his forehead and temples.

Although she knew that Richard was considerably younger than Gavin, he had an air of great maturity about him. In this man, Gavin's naturally confident bearing had become a casual arrogance which she found intimidating, and yet exciting.

Knuckles tapped at the door. 'It's gone time and he's never home yet, so I've put the food on the table,' Ellen announced with as much style as she could summon.

Richard talked on while they ate, surrounding Margaret with word pictures of skies bluer than she had ever seen for herself, cool sea breezes setting exotic blossoms a-nod, hot sands as white as fresh-fallen snow, sparkling seas and brown-skinned peoples.

The man could have been a poet, she thought at one point, then took another look at him and realised that she was wrong. Richard Knox was too world-wise, too strong in character to be a dreamer. His natural role in life was that of a leader, in full control. She sensed something almost menacing about him. He would make a formidable enemy, she had no doubt of that.

But this evening he had set himself out to charm, enchant, and amuse his new-found sister-in-law. He succeeded admirably. Long after the meal was over they sat on at the table, and the first thing Gavin Knox heard when he let himself into the hall was the sound of his wife's laughter from the small dining room to his right.

Margaret looked up to see him standing in the doorway, one eyebrow raised as he glanced from her to their visitor, who had his back to the door.

She rose and went to him at once. 'Gavin, see who's come to visit with us.'

Richard got to his feet without haste, and turned. 'Well, brother?' he said, and waited, one hand resting lightly on the back of his chair.

Gavin, drawn and exhausted after a long day walking the wards, looked and then looked again, unable to believe his own eyes. 'Richard?'

'Richard!' Margaret confirmed, putting a hand on his arm to lead him into the room. With surprise, she realised that through the thick sleeve of his jacket she could feel his muscles suddenly tense. 'Such a surprise – I could scarce believe it myself, at first.'

'But that made your welcome no less warm,' Richard put in, and she flushed, then laughed with him.

A mixture of expressions flowed over her husband's face. Shock, bewilderment, and then, of all things, anger that was quickly suppressed and replaced with the polite, formal smile Gavin, with what she always thought of as the caution of the Borderer, reserved for first meeting with strangers. After a moment he moved forward, pulling free of her touch as he went, and held his hand out to his brother.

'Welcome home, Richard. I confess that I never thought we'd set eyes on each other again.'

'And I thought to find you well settled in Dumfries, physicking the folk there. I'd occasion to come back across the water a year ago. By the looks of things, now that there's trouble started in the Americas, I've come back for good.'

'Give me your coat – I'll go and tell Ellen you're ready for your supper now –' Margaret watched Gavin's long flexible surgeon's fingers flip buttons from buttonholes, then she bounced onto her tiptoes to help him ease the coat off. She hung it up in the hall, making a mental note to sponge and brush it first thing in the morning, before he left the house, then hurried to warn Ellen, dozing by the fire, that her master was home, and hungry.

Finally, she poured generous measures of whisky into two glasses. About to leave the room with a glass in each hand she hesitated, then went back to put glasses and decanter onto a small tray which she carried carefully across the square hall to the dining rom.

Gavin accepted his glass with a brief, pre-occupied smile, emptied it in two gulps, and refilled it. Ellen bustled in with a steaming bowl in one hand and a platter of bread in the other.

As Gavin began to eat hungrily and Richard resumed his account of his adventures Margaret sat down again and looked from one to the other of the brothers.

She herself had always felt that she had two families in her background – the Todds as well as the Montgomerys – and she had pitied Gavin's solitary state. His parents had both died while he was in Glasgow studying medicine, and he had made only casual mention of the brother who had left home.

Margaret, who had first met Gavin when her brother Thomas brought him to her parents' house, knew that it was the very solidarity of Thomas's family life that had caught and held the lonely young surgeon's interest, bringing him back to Paisley again and again until eventually love blossomed and he and Margaret had married.

He had welcomed fatherhood with open delight. At last he had his own family, and she took great pleasure in the knowledge that she had been the one to bring him such happiness.

But now that his brother, his own blood-kin was sitting in Gavin's home, his handsomely booted feet beneath Gavin's table, there was something wrong. Although her husband talked and smiled and even laughed on two occasions Margaret knew that in his mind he had set up a wall between himself and Richard.

'How did you know where to find me?'

Richard twirled the stem of his glass between his fingers. 'It was a most amazing happening. After making enough money in Jamaica to satisfy my immediate needs I decided to investigate the Americas. From there my new interest in cotton took me to the big manufactories in the North of England, then to Glasgow and the exporting business.'

'Did you never think to go to Dumfries?' Gavin's voice was sharp, and Richard shot him a sidelong glance from beneath lowered lids.

'I went, of course – only to find that our parents were long buried, the old house sold and nobody about the place who knew what had become of you, except that you were a surgeon and settled somewhere near Glasgow. I had it in mind to search for you, but before I could start in earnest my business brought me to Paisley, to a weaver called Duncan Montgomery. Imagine my surprise when it came out in the course of our talk that his daughter was wed to a surgeon from Dumfries with the same surname as myself, and that they lived not a mile from the weaving shop where I stood.'

'So you're interested in the Paisley cloth?'

Richard's vivid eyes tured to Margaret. 'I'm interested, dear sister, in anything that makes money. And there's silver to be had in every throw of a Paisley shuttle. I have access to a particularly good cotton thread spun in the English manufactories. I'm hoping that your father and others of his trade will agree to use it.'

'Would this thread suit the inkle looms as well?'

'Margaret –' Gavin warned.

'The inkle looms?'

'Small looms used for weaving tapes and ribbons. I have four in operation at the moment, and I hope to have more soon.'

Again, Gavin started to say something, but was interrupted by a betraying, jaw-cracking yawn.

Richard rose immediately. 'You've had a long day, and here I am, keeping you from your bed. I'll leave you now, and hope to call on you tomorrow.'

'Where will you go?'

'I've lodgings in Glasgow. I left my horse in stables at the foot of the hill, so I've not far to go.'

'Oh, but you must stay here, with us. We'll not hear of you lodging in Glasgow when your own kin lie not five miles distant. Will we, Gavin?'

There was a faint, almost imperceptible pause before Gavin came to stand by his wife. 'Margaret's right. You must stay here tonight, Richard. Your mount'll do well enough in the stables till morning.'

'And in the morning you can send to Glasgow for your things. If your business lies in Paisley, it makes sense for you to bide in the town. Ellen got the room ready hours ago,' Margaret said decisively, and Richard shrugged in submission, and smiled.

'I'd heard that Paisley folk are the most hospitable in the West of Scotland. Now I know it's true.'

'You were over-quick with your offer of hospitality,' Gavin said coolly when they were alone in the privacy of their bedchamber.

'But he's your kin – your own brother. Surely it's natural to offer him a room under your roof.' She lay in bed watching him undress.

His hand carefully smoothed the shirt he had laid over a chair. 'I'd have appreciated the chance to decide that for myself.'

'Gavin Knox, sometimes I can't make head nor tail of you!'

He said nothing, but blew the candle out.

The mattress moved slightly beneath Margaret as his big body settled beside her. She lay for a moment looking into the darkness, listening to his breathing. After five years of marriage, it still gave her a thrill of pleasure to know that she was sharing his bed, even if, as now, they weren't touching each other.

Into the darkness, she said, 'I like your brother.'

'Do you?' His voice was non-committal.

'What's amiss, Gavin?'

'Nothing's amiss,' he said, and a few minutes later he was asleep.

Chapter Twelve

'How many ribbon looms did you say you had?' Richard asked on the following morning, after Gavin had left the house.

Christian and Daniel had been charmed with him from the first moment they set eyes on him. For an hour their new uncle had played with them, before sending them out into the garden and seeking Margaret. He found her on her knees in the parlour, polishing table legs.

'Inkle looms?' She sat back on her heels, glad of a rest. 'Only four at the moment. The women from the Poors' House weave ribbons on them, to earn a little money. See –' she opened a drawer and brought sample of the work to him. He ran it through his strong fingers.

'Where d'you get the thread? And who buys the finished product?'

'The thread comes from some of our own spinsters. My father sells the ribbons along with the linen cloth made on the looms owned by himself and my brother Robert, and Jamie Todd.'

Richard handed the ribbon back. 'The Lancashire thread I have to offer would do very well on your looms. And I think I could find a market for it in the Americas and farther afield.'

'But we're at war with the Americas.'

Richard's eyes sparkled at her from beneath lazy lids. 'Women need cloth and ribbons, war or no war. There are ways. You only have a few of these looms, you said?'

'Two in the Poors' House, and another two in a room at one of Jamie's loom shops. I'd like fine to have more, for there's plenty of women would like the work. But it costs money to find the machinery and the premises.'

'As to money, I've more than enough to spare for a

venture that might bring in more again.' He got to his feet, took her hand, and drew her up beside him. 'Show me one of those looms, sister.'

'Now? But I've the housework to do, and the ironing to see to, and –'

'Let your servant do it,' said Richard with a casual arrogance that would have angered her in anyone else. But it was impossible to be angry with Richard.

'We'll take the children with us. This Jamie Todd – I seem to recall your father using his name too. Do they work together?'

'My father and my brother and Jamie have fourteen looms between them. My father sells the cloth that they make.'

'Indeed? Show me the looms you own in Jamie Todd's shop, then, for I've a mind to talk with him, too.'

*

They walked down the hill, the children scampering ahead, the two saddle-bags holding Richard's thread samples riding easily over his broad shoulder.

Margaret was pleasantly aware of the curious, sometimes covetous glances of the women who passed by. One or two who knew her well stopped them and managed to gain an introduction to Gavin's brother. In every case, Richard set them a-flutter and a-simper.

'I can't think why you never gained a wife during your travels,' she said dryly as they neared the High Street loom shop. 'Indeed, I can't think how you managed to avoid one.'

He grinned. 'A man travels easier without responsibilities.'

'You and Gavin are so like each other in looks, and yet so unlike each other in every other way.'

'He was born with his feet planted firmly on the ground,' Gavin's brother said. 'Whereas I, dear Margaret –'

'You were born with your head in the clouds?'

'Oh no, never that. I was born to succeed,' said Richard and then they were at the door, and the children were already racing each other up the stairs to Kirsty's kitchen.

Richard watched the inkle looms at work for some time, his eyes alight with interest.

He talked to the raw-boned, poverty-pale women who worked the looms; and as he did so Margaret noted with interest that there was no trace of the ruthlessness she had sometimes glimpsed beneath the surface. At that moment he was more like Gavin, gentle and courteous and reassuring, bringing pleasure-colour to the women's faces, making them laugh, listening with interest to what they had to say.

Standing back, content to watch and listen, Margaret decided that the man was even more of a puzzle than she had first thought.

Jamie was working at his own loom in the apartment on the other side of the passageway. He got up from the saytree – the weaver's bench – to shake hands with the newcomer. The men, much the same height and build, sized each other up swiftly before Richard turned away to give his full attention to the looms.

'I see it's hand-looms you have.'

'There are two draw-looms in my other shop.'

'Margaret tells me that you work with her father and brother, weaving linen cloth.'

'Aye. Between us we've eleven hand-looms and three draw-looms.'

'I've been spending a fair bit of time in Lancashire. They've found it of benefit to bring all their looms into big buildings in England, instead of having a few here and a few there.'

Jamie's blue eyes cooled slightly. 'I know all about the English manufactories. Here in Paisley we do fine as we are.'

'You don't produce as much cloth as the manufactories, though.'

'We produce as much as we need to.'

'Linen cloth. Have you not thought of turning to cotton yarn?'

'There's plenty Paisley weavers on it already. But there's still a market for the linen, and we're content.'

'Richard has some English cotton yarn, Jamie –' Margaret chimed in.

'I have – and I'd like fine for you to have a look at it.'

Jamie shook his red head. 'We do well enough as we are,' he said stubbornly, and cast an impatient look at his idle loom.

Margaret took the hint and removed Richard, leading him upstairs to meet Kirsty and Billy.

*

'He's a stubborn man, Jamie Todd,' Richard said thoughtfully, when they were outside again.

'He's cautious.'

'He doesn't look like a cautious man to me. More of an adventurer.'

'He has been, in his time. But now that he's got responsibilities it's a different matter.'

'Responsibilities?'

'Towards his mother and step-father – and his weavers, of course. The weaving trade's not doing so well at the moment. Billy thinks Jamie's worried about it.'

'All the more reason to try something new, surely?'

'All the more reason,' Margaret pointed out patiently, 'to be careful, and wary of change.'

'Not a bit of it. As to your father and brother – are they as cautious as he is?'

'More so, I'd say.'

'But you're adventurous, Margaret. You'd be willing to try my thread on your inkle looms, would you not?'

She had liked the look of the English cotton yarn, finer and smoother than anything the Paisley spinsters could produce. It would be ideal for the inkle looms.

'Yes, indeed I would. But then, I've less to lose than the others. My looms earn very little.'

'You said last night that you'd like more looms.'

'That would take money.'

'I have money. Find yourself a loom-shop, and the machines to fill it, and the women to work them. Could you do that?'

She stopped so abruptly that Christian and Daniel came trotting back to find out what was wrong. 'Of course I could do it! Oh, Richard – d'you mean it?'

He laughed down at her indulgently. 'Certainly.'

'But – how could I pay you back?'

'We'll draw out an agreement. A proper partnership. The decisions will be yours. All I ask is that you use my yarn, and give me the ribbon to sell where I think fit. I'll take a percentage of each sale, and we'll all make a profit.'

'I've no wish to make a profit, I just want the Poors' House women to earn some money.'

'You must earn some yourself, or else there'd be no sense to the venture,' he said firmly.

'Gavin won't be pleased. He's against me giving up any more of my time to the Poors' House and its concerns.'

'My brother,' said Richard, 'lacks imagination. Does he need to know the full extent of our plans?'

'Yes, of course he –' She hesitated. She had never deceived Gavin before, but perhaps it would be better for his own peace of mind if he knew little about this latest venture for the moment. 'Well – mebbe I'll wait until I've got the weaving shop and the machines before I say anything.'

And by then, she thought guiltily, it would be too late for Gavin to protest. The deed would be done.

By her side, Richard said lightly, 'You see? The matter is easily decided, after all.'

Then he added, 'And perhaps you can do something for me in return. Ask your father and brother – and Jamie Todd – if I might have a meeting with them, to show them the English thread and talk to them about my ideas for a cotton cloth.'

'It'll do no good, Richard.'

'Perhaps not. But I've found that everything is worth the try.'

Chapter Thirteen

The meeting Richard wanted took place in Jamie's Well-meadow shop two afternoons later, after work had finished for the day.

It had long been the custom in Paisley for the weavers to set their own hours. They always began work early in the morning, and in the winter they usually went on until dusk, sometimes lighting candles or crusies so that they could continue after dark.

In the summer they preferred to stop early in the afternoons – unless the web on their machines was urgently needed – to take advantage of the good weather. Some went bowling, others walked or fished or swam, went to the cock-fights or worked in their gardens, a good number had formed themselves into debating societies, and more than a few, in this town of weavers, spent their leisure time reading, or writing poetry.

Richard had a persuasive tongue, but even so, he found himself outnumbered. The Montgomerys, father and son, were representative of their trade – stolid, hard-working men, eminently practical, and cautious when it came to money matters. They eyed each other uneasily as Richard outlined his plans. When he had finished, Duncan was the first to speak, after a long and thoughtful silence.

'You're proposing that we should give over our looms to this English thread and grant you the right to sell the cloth wherever you should find the best market for it?'

'Aye, that's the shape of it.'

'Your thread's bonny enough, there's no denying that –' Robert's voice and manner of speech was uncannily like his father's ' – but man, we're content enough with the yarn our own spinsters provide.'

'Tell me this – d'you get a goodly supply of yarn?'

'We can always do with more,' Jamie admitted. 'If a spinster falls sick we're sometimes hard put to it to make up the yarn we need, it's true.'

'But we aye manage,' Duncan Montgomery said shortly. As the oldest of the three men, it had fallen to him to lead the partnership they had set up. He heartily disliked and mistrusted the thought of change.

'And you've no trouble in selling your cloth?'

'None. We sell to a warehouse in Glasgow. He offers us fair prices.'

'Fair, mebbe – but no harm in looking into prices elsewhere.'

'I'd not want to let the man down, after all these years.'

Richard gave a snort of laughter. 'Man, he'd let you down this very day if it suited him! Now listen to what I've got to offer –'

Skilfully, swiftly, he outlined his plan. The Montgomery and Todd looms would start using the cotton yarn he could provide, and turn the resulting cloth over to him. He would then sell it to England, Europe or the Americas – wherever he found the highest bidder.

The silence fell again after he'd finished, then Jamie said cautiously, 'It's worth thinking on, Duncan.'

The older man's blue eyes travelled uneasily from face to face. 'We'd not be able to go back to our present merchant if the scheme went wrong and we had to return to the linen cloth.'

'It won't go wrong!'

Duncan's clear gaze settled firmly on Richard. 'Laddie, I've been weaving since ever before you tasted your mother's milk, and I've seen many a good man reduced to poverty because he tried to fly too high.'

'If everyone thought as you do, Mister Montgomery,' said Richard silkily, with just a hint of impatience in his even tones, 'there'd be no need for your cloth, for we'd all be living in caves and wearing animal hides – and all too frightened to try anything new.'

Duncan let the veiled sarcasm slide from his broad shoulders. 'Mebbe so. But if everyone thought as you do, Mister Knox, we'd all be in a sorry pickle. It takes all sorts to make up the world.'

'How many looms would you need to make enough cloth?' Jamie asked.

'As many as I can get. But if need be I could start with six, or eight.'

'Then can we not put some of our machines over to the new thread and keep others on the linen? I'd be willing to use half of mine – one of your two, Robert, and two of yours, Duncan –'

There was an instant, adverse reaction from the Montgomerys. 'That's madness!' Duncan said angrily, and his son chimed in with, 'We'd not make enough of one cloth or the other, Jamie. It's all the machines or none of them as I see it.'

The red-headed weaver fingered the thread again, then took a deep breath. 'I'm for trying it.'

'Why, in God's name?'

'Because the linen industry's bound to come to an end, Robert. Mebbe the time's come for us to turn to cotton.'

'I'm not happy about the market,' Robert said, and his father nodded.

'What guarantee do we have that you'll be able to sell this cloth you want us to weave for you, Richard?'

'My word on it.'

The Montgomerys eyed each other, then Duncan shook his head. 'Laddie, you might be Gavin's brother, and a fine upstanding man, just as he is. I'm not doubting that for an instant, you understand. But cloth's not your trade. I'd need more of an assurance than that.'

'The best assurance would be to weave the cloth and let me prove that I can sell it – and bring you orders for more.'

'And in the meantime,' Duncan pointed out, 'we'd have lost our own merchant. If your fine promises came to nothing, what would happen to us then?'

From where Jamie sat on his saytree, swung round so that the intricate wooden loom was behind him, he could see over Richard's shoulder and through the window. His attention was caught by a movement in the yard outside. He shifted position slightly and saw that Islay McInnes was digging the over-grown, weed-infested kale bed, her sleeves rolled up to above her elbows, a long scarf looped over her dark head and about her throat.

The argument raged on about his head as he watched the girl work. Mention of his own name brought him back, finally, to the business in hand.

'What did you say?'

'I said, I think you're in favour of trying out the scheme,' Richard repeated.

'It's worth considering.' All at once Jamie wanted the meeting to be at an end. The weaving shop had become claustrophobic.

'And I think it would be madness, at this time, for us to consider a change,' Robert said bluntly, and his father nodded.

'No offence to you, Mister Knox, for I'm certain that your scheme has merit. Mebbe other weavers in the town would be interested in hearing about it. For ourselves – we'll go on as we have done, for it suits us well enough.'

Richard studied Jamie thoughtfully before asking, 'And you, Mister Todd – d'you agree with that?'

Jamie hesitated, then said, 'The three of us have always worked together. I have to go with what Duncan and Robert say.'

Richard shrugged, rose, picked up his three-cornered hat, and bowed, his handsome face stiff with disappointment.

'In that case, gentlemen, I must thank you for listening to me so courteously, and take my leave.'

'The plan had its merits,' Jamie said when he had gone.

'Mebbe, but it was all too full of hopes and possibilities for me,' Duncan's voice was heavy with disapproval.

'I still think we could have given over some of the looms to his new thread.'

But the Montgomerys were both adamant. 'It would have been too great a risk,' Robert said, and his father added, 'Best to stay as we are. Caution's a good watchword.'

When they were gone Jamie stepped out into the pend and closed the loom shop door behind him.

He hesitated, hearing Duncan's voice, which still carried some of the inflections of his native Ayrshire, say again in his head, 'Caution's a good watchword.'

But caution had never come easily to Jamie Todd. Indeed, in his present restless mood the word filled him with irritation.

He turned towards the street, heard behind him the clang of a spade striking a hidden stone, changed his mind, and walked through the pend and into the yard.

*

'Give me the spade – I'll see to it for you.'

Islay's thoughts had been far away, in the glens of her childhood. She jumped at the sound of Jamie's voice, and looked up to see him standing before her, one hand oustretched.

'Och, I can manage fine.' She used the force of both arms to drive the blade into the hard, root-matted ground, planted one shabby, booted foot on it to force it in further, and bent to lever up a sod of black earth.

'But it's a man's work. Can Lachie not do it for you?'

'He's gone to fetch a settle that was promised us. And I can do this sort of work as well as any man.' She retained her grip on the spade handle, and got on with the business in hand. After a moment she risked a peep at the piece of ground before her. It was empty. He had gone.

Then, at the sound of another blade thunking into the ground nearby, she lifted her head to see that he hadn't gone any further than the house wall, to pick up an old rusting spade that leaned there.

It had been far too heavy for her, but Jamie Todd's muscles drove it hard into the ground, up to where the wooden handle joined the blade, then levered a solid mass of soil and roots free easily, turning it over, splitting it with the blade so that the earth crumbled and the pale strangling roots were exposed to daylight.

Then he straightened up and grinned at her. 'Two can make lighter work of it.'

She smiled back, and they worked on together in companionable, contented silence.

Chapter Fourteen

'So you've come home for good, Mister Knox?'

Mary MacLeod, Margaret's aunt, handed a teacup to her guest. Richard, who had learned impeccable drawing-room manners from somewhere during his travels, passed the cup to Margaret.

'Perhaps. If the trouble in the Americas eases I'd like to go back there, at least for a while.'

Mary tutted. 'That's a sorry business.'

Richard took his cup and sat down. 'It is indeed. It's going to hit trade badly if it isn't brought to an end soon,' he agreed blandly.

Then, to Margaret's amusement he flinched back, almost slopping tea into his saucer, as his hostess barked, 'Man, it's not trade I'm fretting over, it's folk that used to be friends spilling each other's blood! Why men never seem able to put an end to an argument without turning to swords or guns is beyond me!'

'But – if we let the American colonies dictate to us –' Richard made a valiant effort to rally, and was vocally beaten back against the wall and pinned there.

'Tuts, give the matter a bit of thought, can't you? It's like raising a family,' said Mary, who never had, but who knew better than most how it should be done. 'There comes a time when you've to stand back and let your bairns go out into the world on their own. It's the same with colonies.'

'I fail to see –'

'Aye well, you're a man,' she excused him kindly. 'So of course you'll not be able to follow my way of thinking. But it seems to me that if you were to picture Britain as a woman, and the Americas as her great lump of a bairn –'

'With respect, ma'am, I still cannot see –'

Mary shook an admonishing finger. 'With respect, sir,

that's because you havenae the patience to listen when you're being told. If you were to picture Britain and the Americas as a woman and her bairn – as I was saying – then you'd see that it's pure foolishness to suppose that we can go on leading it by the hand – or through a ring in its nose, depending on the way you look at it,' said Mary, mixing motherhood, which she had never experienced, with the farmyard where she herself had been raised. Then, having swept magnificently up the final stretch to the winning line, leaving Richard to come in a very poor second, she said, 'Are you ready for more tea, Mister Knox?'

'Your aunt's a lady who follows very – convolvulated thinking,' he said ruefully when he and Margaret left the house together an hour later.

'There's nobody can keep up with Aunt Mary when she's in one of her moods – except perhaps Thomas, and he does it by agreeing with everything she says.'

'All the same, I like her exceedingly well. She's got a – an air about her that pleases me,' he said approvingly, then turned to business. 'How are you getting on with your search for an empty loom shop?'

'I think I might have found one in the New Town across the river. Near to the Poors' House, but not close enough for folk to find out too much about my business before I'm ready to tell them.'

'Your business venture is having more success than mine,' Richard's voice was a trifle grim. 'There's a good overseas market for cotton cloth, and to my mind the Paisley weavers are the men to tackle it. But your father's not an easy man to deal with. And where he leads, the other two follow.'

'My father worked for Jamie's when he first came to Paisley, and it seems only natural now that the Montgomerys and the Todds work together. Robert used to be more interested in change and progress; I mind him arguing often enough with my father when I was still at home. But now that he's older, with a family to care for, he's changed his tune.'

'Your friend Jamie Todd was more willing to follow my thinking in the matter – until the other two persuaded him to change his mind and see things their way.'

They had reached the Knox house. Margaret beamed up at Richard as he opened the gate and stood aside to let her pass. 'You'll just have to find other weavers to try out your yarn.'

'Oh, I will. There's no doubt of that. But after meeting you I'd set my heart on dealing with your fam –'

The words tailed away as they reached the front door and heard the uproar from inside.

'Mercy me, that's Daniel! What's happened to him?'

Margaret forgot all about Richard in her haste to get to her son. Daniel rarely cried, and this hysterical continuous screaming was something she had never heard from him before. He was in pain, and terrified, and in great need of her.

All thought of looms and progress vanished as she ran into the hallway. The screams came from upstairs.

She had crossed the square hall and her foot was on the bottom step of the staircase when the door of Gavin's small study opened and he came out. He was in his shirt-sleeves and his hair was tousled.

'Margaret –'

He caught her by the arms and stopped her when she wanted to run up to where her baby was still screaming and screaming. She turned on him wildly.

'Daniel – what's happened to Daniel? What's wrong with him?'

He tried to take her into his arms, but she fought him.

'Daniel's all right, I promise you. Nothing bad has happened to him. Listen to me, Margaret –'

'All right?' she screamed at him. 'Listen to the wee soul! How can you tell me he's all right, and him making a noise like that?'

'He's frightened, not hurt. Now just listen to what I'm trying to tell you,' he said insistently. But now she was looking past his sheltering arm to the open door of the study. Within, she could just see a part of her daughter's skirt.

'Christian?' Torn between her two children, blocked from the stairs by Gavin's body, she pushed past him and ran, as best she could since her joints suddenly seemed to be fashioned out of wood, to the door. She pushed it open.

Thomas, on his knees, in the act of wrapping a cloth about Christian's bared arm, looked up at his sister, his round face drawn with guilt. Christian beamed cheerfully.

'Look, Mother –' she boasted, pulling away from her uncle, drawing the bandage down and twisting her arm to show the small bloodless incision that had been made in her soft skin.

Margaret looked, and heard a roaring sound as her world tumbled about her.

'It didn't hurt,' the little girl prattled on. 'I didn't cry one single wee tear, and now Uncle Thomas is putting a bandage on me, just as if I was a soldier in the wars.'

Now Margaret understood what had been going on while she was out of the house and out of the way. Ignoring Thomas, she turned to her husband, who stood in the doorway.

Inside, she was screaming, and yet her voice came out flatly, quietly, 'You've given her the pox.'

'No, I've vaccinated her with cowpox to keep her safe, Margaret.'

'I told you!' Her voice began to shake. 'I told you, Gavin, that I'd not have my children used like this!'

His face was white. 'I had to do it, Margaret. I had to prove that it worked.'

'There's no danger,' Thomas said uncomfortably. 'They're quite safe.'

'Are they?'

Christian, aware that something was badly wrong, lost her broad, proud grin. She brushed past Margaret and went to stand by her father, slipping a hand into his. His fingers lay slack in her trusting grip.

'I said they could cut me, Mother. I wasn't frighted, not one wee bit.'

'Margaret, it was as much my fault as it was Gavin's.'

She ignored her daughter and her brother, and spoke only to Gavin.

'I told you I'd not have it!'

'We didn't think you'd be home till after it was all by.' Christian's tell-tale tongue rattled on; then, as her parents stared at each other, ignoring her, she tugged at Gavin's hand. 'I didn't cry, did I, Father? I was more brave than a soldier ever could be.'

He dragged his eyes from Margaret's at last, and smiled down at his daughter. 'Yes, you were very brave.'

With a trusting gesture that was beyond Margaret's comprehension at such a time, Christian lifted her arms to him and he stooped and gathered her up.

She nestled her dark head into the hollow beneath his chin and told Margaret complacently, 'Daniel wasn't like a soldier. He was like a baby. He cried and cried.'

The sound of her son's name brought Margaret out of her trance and into action. The little boy's terrified wails were still ringing the house. 'Daniel –'

'I tell you he's all right, Margaret!'

'How do you know?' she said furiously to her husband. 'How can you tell?'

For the second time she tried to push past him, and this time he stepped aside and let her go. Richard, hovering in the hall, was only a hazy figure to her as she sped up the stairs to the children's room.

The noise in there was indescribable. Ellen, with Daniel struggling and kicking in her arms, was pacing the floor. The little boy's face was puffed up, scarlet, tear-streaked, distorted with fear and pain and outrage.

'Oh, mistress, I'm that glad you're back –' The maid turned a flushed, frightened face to her mistress. And at last Daniel, his upper arm bandaged, was in Margaret's arms, close against her racing heart.

'Oh, my love, my wee birdie! Don't fret, I'm here, and I'll not let them touch you ever again –' she said over and over again into his silky dark hair as she carried him downstairs to where the three men waited in the hall with Christian, who was obviously puzzled by the to-do.

Margaret paused on the bottom step and held out her free hand to her daughter. 'Christian, come to me.'

Christian hesitated, glanced at her father for guidance. He, looking sick and white, put her down and gave her a gentle push forward.

The hall suddenly began to slide and surge around

Margaret. The hand that had been outstretched to Christian groped for a support and fastened on the carved polished newel post. Dizzily, she clutched at Daniel and wondered if she, who had never fainted in her life before, was about to make a fool of herself.

She saw all three men move towards her, but to her relief, for she could not have borne to be touched at that moment by either Gavin or Thomas, it was Richard who reached her first.

Carefully, gently, he steadied her within the circle of his arm until the hall stopped revolving and became its usual steady, unmoving self again.

Then he said, 'Come, Margaret –' and led her past the other two to the parlour.

At the door she turned, still within Richard's embrace. 'Christian –?'

Gavin, ashen to the lips, watched as Christian obediently went to her mother.

Margaret and her children, escorted by Richard, went into the parlour, and the door closed behind them.

Chapter Fifteen

A few hours later the children were settled in their cots; Christian puzzled, guilty without knowing why, but defiant, Daniel swollen-eyed, hiccupping, clinging to his mother's hand until sleep loosened his hot fingers.

Margaret sat on in their room, watching them, listening to Daniel's snuffling and gasping breaths.

Her eyes felt as though they were hot rough stones in her skull's sockets. Her hands moved restlessly in her lap all the time, even when she tried to lock the fingers together to still them.

She had sent Ellen to bed, and Richard, after making sure that Margaret wanted nothing more from him, had retired to his own room. Thomas, she supposed, had long since gone, though no doubt Gavin was somewhere in the house.

At last, when she was certain that both children slept soundly enough to be left, she rose and left the room silently, suddenly aware that she hadn't eaten or drunk anything since taking tea in Mary's parlour.

The kitchen was a warm peaceful haven. Margaret poured some ale into a cup, and ate some cheese and bannocks. She was draining the cup when she realised that she was no longer alone, and turned to see Gavin standing in the kitchen doorway, his eyes haunted.

'Margaret –'

She put the empty cup down, staring at him bleakly.

'The decision was mine, not Thomas's, so don't take your anger out on him. I needed assistance and he gave it. That's all.'

Carefully, ignoring him, she put the utensils she had used on the board by the stone sink and went by him, towards the door.

His hand caught her shoulder, whirling her round to face

him. 'For the love of God, woman, don't look at me as though I was the devil incarnate!'

'If anything happens to my bairns, Gavin Knox –'

'Nothing will happen.'

' – I'll kill you with my own bare hands,' she concluded, and saw by the sudden tightening of his jaw that he knew she meant what she said. At that moment she hated him, hated the man who had been the mainstay of her life, the father of her children, the guardian of her future and the reason for all her happiness during the past five years.

'Nothing will happen to them, I tell you!' He shook her slightly to add emphasis to the words. She stood within his grip, making no attempt to free herself, the hot coals of her eyes burning into him.

'Go away, Gavin. Go out of this house and leave me to see to my bairns in peace.'

'I can't go, even if I would. I must be here, with them. For a day or two – a week at most – they're going to have a fever. They'll have to be kept abed. I must stay with them.'

A panic-stricken wail from upstairs brought both their heads jerking round towards the open door.

'Daniel!' Margaret wrenched herself free of Gavin's hands and ran into the darkened hall and up the stairs, hearing Gavin close behind.

Daniel was sitting up in bed, scream after scream pouring out of his wide-open mouth. Christian, raised on one elbow, blinked like a baby owl as Margaret scooped the little boy into her arms.

The howls began to subside; then as Daniel, his head resting on her shoulder, opened his eyes and saw Gavin standing by the door, they redoubled. Margaret felt the small body in her arms curl into a ball as the child tried to burrow deeper into the safety of her body.

She turned to her husband so that the child's face was averted from him. 'Stay away from him, Gavin.'

'Daniel –' he said, taking a step into the room. But at the sound of his voice the little boy's wailing immediately increased until the room rang with ear-splitting shrieks. Christian clapped her hands over her ears, eyes screwed up tightly. Gavin shrugged helplessly and went out, closing the door quietly behind him.

'Daniel's being a baby,' Christian said.

'Hold your tongue!'

Christian's eyes, so like Gavin's, were hurt. Without a word she turned over in her bed and hunched her shoulders, her back to the room. Then she drew the coverlet right over her head, and said no more.

Margaret spent that night in Daniel's low narrow cot, cramped and uncomfortable, soothing him every time the nightmares wakened him again, waiting for the long hours of darkness to pass and give way to grey dawn.

*

She got very little sleep over the next week. As Gavin had predicted, both children developed a fever. Their arms, where he and Thomas had cut into the top layer of skin and deposited minute amounts of matter obtained from the pustules of cows sick with cow-pox, became swollen and painful. Even Christian, flushed and fretful and feeling very ill, stopped looking on the whole business as a game and wept and whined and fretted along with Daniel.

Margaret, convinced that both her children were going to die of the pox, was almost out of her mind with worry. She refused to leave the house, spending her days and nights with the two of them, sponging them down with cool water, coaxing them to swallow broth or gruel, watching over them as they slept, ever-vigilant for the first signs of the virulent disease to appear on their bodies.

People came and went – her mother, her Aunt Mary, Kirsty Todd. But she refused to let anyone else stay with the children. Ellen brought food to their room, and when they slept, Margaret dozed on a truckle bed the maidservant had brought in for her, waking with a start every time one of the children whimpered.

Much as she would have liked to insist that he go far away and leave them all to see to themselves, she had need of Gavin's help and advice. Christian, who worshipped her father and was firmly convinced that he could save her from all ills, gave herself up readily to his examinations and his treatments, but Daniel screamed and fled into

Margaret's arms every time Gavin tried to touch him.

Gavin looked as though he, too, was going without sleep. On the few occasions when she looked fully at him Margaret saw the man he would become when middle age reached out and claimed him. Once, glancing in a looking-glass during that terrible time, she saw the same indication of things to come in her own face. Her eyes had dulled and become sunken, her face was almost grey, her mouth was thinner, with a new downward droop at the corners.

Then one night the fever broke and in the morning, just as Gavin had predicted, both children were clear-eyed, hungry, and clamouring to go outside into the garden to play. The tender swellings on their arms had subsided, and when the bandages were taken off the small wounds had begun to dry and scab.

Gavin, his face radiant with relief, tried to take Margaret into his arms when the two of them met on the upstairs landing. He had shaved and changed into fresh clothing and his hair was neatly brushed and tied back.

'I told you they'd be fine.'

She drew away from him. 'But you'd no right to take the risk.'

'If I'd thought it was that much of a risk, I'd not have taken it.'

'Are you sure of that, Gavin?'

'What does that mean?'

'Mebbe being a surgeon's more important to you than being a father.' Then, as he flushed, she added dryly, 'I suppose you'll be persuading other folk to let you and Thomas cut their bairns now?'

'Aye, since it'll help to save them from worse harm. You can't deny, now, that it's safe. Listen to the two of them.'

The children, eating their porridge in their bed-chamber, were chattering to Ellen like a couple of magpies. A smile curved Margaret's mouth for the first time in a week as she heard them. But when Gavin reached out again to hold her she took another step back, shaking her head. She couldn't forget the horror of the past days. She couldn't yet find it in her heart to forgive him for his betrayal.

His face changed as he recognised the rejection in her

swift movement. 'You've surely more sense, Margaret, than to nurse your anger like a spoiled child.'

'I've more sense than to trust you ever again, Gavin Knox!'

Anger settled on his rugged features. He gave her a small, stiff bow and said tightly, 'Then behave as you wish. You always have. I must be in Glasgow for the rest of the day, for I've been too long away from my work.'

'Very well.' As she followed him downstairs Richard came out of the parlour.

'Ellen tells me that they're fully recovered – quite well again.'

'Aye, they're well.'

'I'm pleased to hear it,' he said, and took her hands, smiling down at her. 'Now we must set about putting you to rights. You look over-pale. Gavin, would you permit me to take the bairns and Margaret out for a carriage ride this afternoon?'

A muscle jerked in Gavin's jawline as he looked at Richard, still holding Margaret's hands.

'Aye, if the children are warmly wrapped up and don't catch a chill.'

'No fear of that. I'll take care of them. You'll not refuse me, Margaret, will you?'

'Indeed not.'

'I'll mebbe not be home until late tonight,' Gavin said abruptly, then he turned on his heel and left the house.

Chapter Sixteen

Early each morning Islay's eyes seemed to spring open of their own volition and she rose from her bed, luxuriously spacious now that she only had to share it with Morag, ready to begin a new day.

After waking Lachie and stirring the fire into life she prepared breakfast for herself and the boy, letting Morag lie abed a little longer.

Then Lachie went off to waken the other weavers and Islay made her way into the weaving shop to clean the fireplace and sweep the floor and give the linnets fresh seed and water and tend to the pinks that grew in pots on the deep window-sills, and make everything ready for the day's work.

In the few short weeks since moving from Jenny's Wynd she had grown to love the atmosphere of the weaving shop.

In the morning, before the men arrived, the looms waited quietly, the hand-looms squat and stolid, the harnesses of the two great draw-looms, with their intricate arrangement of pulleys and lashes, towering overhead in majestic splendour.

At that time of the day the only sound came from the caged birds, already trilling their music into the room. Later, as the men tramped in one by one, rubbing sleep from their eyes, the place took on another feeling altogether. The looms sprang eagerly to life, shuttles clacked to and fro like the tongues of gossips, the webs began to grow, the men talked and laughed and sang, giving the linnets competition – and in the space of a few minutes the shop took on its day apparel.

She liked the men who worked the Wellmeadow looms. They were a kindly group, even Walter Shaw, who wasn't nearly as bad as she had thought in the days when he used to come to Jenny's Wynd to fetch the pirns and taunt Lachie into fighting him.

Indeed, more than once Islay had turned her head suddenly to find him watching her as she went about her work. At first she had looked away again quickly, as embarrassed by the brief contact as he was. But of late Walter had taken to greeting her by name if she was still in the loom shop when he arrived. He had a nice smile, when he took the trouble to give it an airing.

Not as nice, though, as Jamie Todd's broad, blue-eyed grin. She looked forward to the days when he called in at the shop, although he scarcely had a word for her, other than a swift greeting.

When the place was as clean as she could make it and the men had arrived and started work she went back upstairs to where Morag was breaking her own fast before going off to the dress-making shop on the bridge, where Margaret Knox had managed to find work for her. Nothing too strenuous, Thomas Montgomery had said, and not long hours.

So Morag, who was to learn the dress-making trade, was excused an early start until such time as Thomas decided that she was strong enough to manage it.

Once Morag had gone Islay was free to see to her own housework before she went out to collect pirns for the loom shop. Then she settled down at her wheel and got on with her own spinning, with the steady thump of the looms below and the occasional faint sound of one or more voices raised in song to keep her company.

It was when she was bringing back the collected pirns that she first met Richard Knox. She was setting her loaded basket down to open the loom shop door when a voice said, as courteously as if she was a grand lady instead of just an ordinary lassie, 'Allow me, ma'am.'

The door whisked open, the basket was lifted as though it contained no weight at all, and Islay found herself looking into a pair of appreciative hazel eyes set in a pleasing, bronzed face.

'Thank you, sir, but I can manage well enough.'

'So can I.' He ignored her outstretched hand. 'I'm

looking for Mister Jamie Todd. Is he inside?'

'He'll be at his loom in the High Street weaving shop.'

'Ah.' He made no move to return the basket to her, or to take it inside. Instead, he leaned one shoulder comfortably against the wall. 'And who might you be?'

'Islay McInnes, sir. I live in the house above.'

'Do you indeed?' He sketched as graceful a bow as his burden would allow. 'And I am Richard Knox, at your service.'

'A relation of Mistress Margaret Knox?'

'Her husband's brother. You know Margaret?'

'She and I are – friends.' It might have been presumptuous of her, but all the same it gave her a great deal of pleasure to say the word aloud.

'Then it follows that you and I will be friends too, Mistress McInnes.'

'We're Mister Todd's lodgers – my cousins and myself,' she added breathlessly, for the sake of having something to say.

There was something disconcerting about the man's gaze. It wasn't improper, or objectionable. But nevertheless it troubled Islay. She ducked by him and stepped over the sill, saying over her shoulder, 'If you'll just bring the pirns in, sir –'

'The –?'

'The pirns. In the basket.'

'Ah –! Of course, ma'am.' He followed her into the shop, setting the basket down and watching as she transferred the filled pirns from it to the box used by the weavers. As she straightened up she caught a glimpse of Walter's eyes, heavy with resentment, fixed on the well-dressed visitor who stood watching her so attentively.

Richard Knox followed her as she went outside again. 'Have you more – pirns – to collect? If so, I would be happy to accompany you and help to carry them.'

'No more today. Now I've got my own wheel to attend to.'

'Some other time, then.' He sounded quite disappointed. 'The High Street weaving shop, you said?'

'Aye sir. Not far past Townhead. Anyone can tell you where it is.'

'I've already been there. I can find my way easily enough again.' To her astonishment he captured her hand and raised it to his lips. 'Goodbye, Mistress McInnes,' he said, and left her.

At the entrance to the pend he looked back and saw that she was still standing where he had left her, watching him. He raised one hand in a light salute, and disappeared from view.

Confused and flustered, Islay went upstairs, where she sat at her wheel for some time before starting work, her hands lying idle in her lap, one stroking the other, where the touch of Richard Knox's lips could still be clearly felt.

*

'The bairns might be right as rain again, but you're looking awful out of sorts yourself these days, Margaret.' Mary MacLeod peered at her niece. 'What's amiss?'

'Nothing.'

'Tush! It's that quarrel you had with Gavin, isn't it? Have you never made it up yet, the two of you?'

Then, when Margaret stayed stubbornly silent, her aunt went on, 'I'll grant you that he and Thomas behaved badly, but the bairns came to no harm, did they?'

'They might have died!'

'Tush – the sky might have fallen in on us yesterday. Bailie Menzies's wife might not have liked the new bonnet I made her,' said Mary, who still maintained her little millinery shop at the Sneddon, despite the fact that she had no need of its support. 'The world's full of things that might have happened. Gavin did what he thought best, the bairns are fine, and that's an end of it, surely.'

'D'you think so?'

'I never took you for a fool before, Margaret Knox.' Mary sighed, and gathered up her gloves. 'Well, I must go.'

Then she sat down again and glared at Margaret. 'All this nonsense between you and Gavin's addled my wits. I clean forgot why I came here in the first place.'

'Why?' Margaret asked dutifully, but with little interest.

'You know that Caroline Cameron's managed to find a man for that elderly daughter of hers at last?'

'No,' said Margaret, who had never cared for local gossip.

'Well, she has. A man who bides in Perth, with more money than sense if you ask me, though the lassie's pleasant enough. But she's got no conversation in her at all. Anyway, nothing would please Caroline but that she should hire the assembly rooms in the Saracen's Head Inn and hold a big gathering to show the man how well-set-up the Camerons are in Paisley.' She settled herself more comfortably in her chair and Margaret, aware that there was a pile of ironing awaiting her in the kitchen, wondered how long her aunt was going to take to tell her story.

'And, of course, it never occurred to her until the thing was settled that the Camerons don't know all that many folk in the town when it comes to it – being a family that likes to keep themselves to themselves. And most of the people they do know are so old they'd drop dead in a strathspey, let alone a reel. So Caroline came running to me in a panic and asked would I see to the gathering for her. Now, there's you and Gavin and Richard – he'll make a handsome addition to the festivities, and the Paisley women like to have their hearts set a-flutter now and again –'

Margaret moved in swift protest. 'Oh no, I don't think I could go to a gathering just now!'

'Of course you could. It's just what you and Gavin need. There's the two of you, and Robert and Annie, and Thomas, and Jamie. Kate's too near her time to be able to attend.'

Mary ticked off names on her beringed fingers, then tutted. 'Mercy me, there's not going to be enough women to go round. D'you know of anyone you could bring?'

Margaret, realising that there was no escape, put her mind to the problem. 'There's Islay McInnes.'

'Who's she?'

'One of the people living in Jamie's house at Wellmeadow.'

'A Highlander? How old is she? Is she bonny?'

'Sixteen years old. And she's very bonny. She's going to be a beautiful woman soon.'

'D'you tell me?' asked Mary with interest. 'Then she'll do. You can see to her for me, Margaret, for I've got enough to do. Besides, I don't know the lassie.'

'She might not want to come.'

'Of course she will. Don't take no for an answer – I never do,' said Mary.

At the front door she paused and fixed her niece with a firm blue eye. 'You've got a good man, Margaret, so mind and guard that quick tongue of yours. It'll not keep you warm at night, or give you loving when your spirits are low.'

'We'll be fine, Gavin and me.'

'Hmmmphh,' Mary snorted, and went.

Margaret's farewell smile vanished as soon as she had closed the door behind her aunt's upright back. She was beginning to wonder if things would ever be the same again between herself and Gavin.

Christian and Daniel were as well as ever, and yet the stubborn streak that had often proved to be more of a curse than a blessing in the past refused to let her forgive him, or forget the way he had risked their children's lives in order to prove a medical theory.

She bit her lip, and sighed; then she went to the kitchen to deal with the ironing.

*

'Me? Go to a gathering?' Islay's eyes were large and bright with panic. 'Oh, Mistress Knox, I couldn't!'

'Tush,' said Margaret, and winced when she realised how like her aunt she must sound. 'You can dance, can't you?'

'Yes of course, but – but I'm not gentry!'

'Neither am I. And neither are most of the folk who'll be there. It's time you met people, Islay. You're a young woman now.'

'I'd not know what to say to them!'

'As to that, you've no need to concern yourself. You could recite nursery rhymes in that lovely Highland voice of yours and folk would listen quite happily.'

'And I've nothing to wear –' Islay was tossing as many objections as she could find in the way, while Margaret caught and demolished them with an efficiency that had been inherited from her Aunt Mary rather than from her own placid, easy-going mother, Meg Montgomery.

'I've more than enough clothes for the two of us,' she said, lifting Daniel, who had begun to grizzle, onto her knee. Christian, who couldn't stay still for a minute, had gone down to the loom shop to see the linnets.

'And I won't know anyone there!'

'You'll not get to know them if you don't attend gatherings. You'll be with me and my husband, and his brother Richard. And my brother Robert and his wife Annie will be there. And my brother Thomas – you've met him. And there's Jamie of course. It's time you found out for yourself that the Paisley folk aren't so bad after all.'

The last name caught and held Islay's attention. She hadn't thought that Jamie Todd would be going to the gathering. Here was a chance to see him in a different setting, among his own folk. Here was an opportunity to try to unravel the enigma of this man who was, in turns, abrupt, aloof, kindly – but always remote, refusing to let Islay close enough to see what lay beneath the surface.

'Well? Will you come?'

Islay's mind was made up for her in the space of a few seconds.

'I'll come,' she said.

Chapter Seventeen

On the evening of the gathering Islay stood in the middle of Margaret Knox's bedchamber, revolving slowly, trying to take it all in at once – the polished, beautifully crafted furniture, the hangings at the windows, the carpet underfoot, the elegant long framed mirror.

'It's – it's so big!'

Margaret, laying the gowns she had selected out on the bed, looked round the familiar room in her turn, seeing it anew through her guest's eyes.

'I mind the first time I was in a fair-sized house.' She sat on the edge of the bed, her face soft with memories. 'It was on the day my Aunt Mary was wed, and we were in her new house, here on Oakshawhill. I'd been raised in a weavers' cottage, and I fair affronted my mother by saying out loud that it was wrong that some folk had so much space, when others had none at all. D'you know, Islay – for all that I've got a big house myself now, I still think the same.'

Then she blinked the past away, and laughed. 'But we're not here to talk – we must get ready, or the menfolk'll be girning their heads off.'

*

As she came downstairs behind Margaret, her stomach tense with excitment and fear and anticipation, Islay found herself looking for approval in Richard Knox's eyes, and finding it.

She knew as soon as he came forward and stood waiting for her to reach the hall that she would do, and her relief was so great that she gave him a dazzling smile.

Margaret had chosen a dress in deep rose pink trimmed with dove-grey for Islay. The tight-fitting bodice was cut low, but not immodestly so. Down the front panel foamed delicate bunches of grey ribbon.

The sleeves, tight to the elbow, ended in a series of grey, rose and pink layers that fell back from Islay's smoothly rounded arms when she raised her hands to her throat, where a small ruff in the same rose shade fitted neatly about her neck.

Her hair had been brushed until it was a sheet of night-black satin, and pinned at the back of her neat head, fastened there with a spray of pink rosebuds. It had been drawn back tightly from her face to allow her neat features and wide, thick-lashed dark eyes to be seen to best advantage.

Her work-roughened hands had been pampered and creamed and massaged, and the nails trimmed then polished with a soft cloth to make as much of them as was possible.

'I thought you'd never be ready,' Gavin said abruptly, taking his wife's arm.

'But you must admit,' said Margaret, in a gown the same deep clear blue as her eyes, 'that we're worth the waiting.'

Gavin smiled down on her, the first real smile she had seen on his face since the whole sorry vaccination business began.

'I'll admit it gladly. But I'm not so sure the coachman who's been kept waiting would agree with me, for it's cold outside.'

*

It was largely due to Mary's endeavours that the main assembly hall of the Saracen's Head Inn at Paisley Cross was filled almost to overflowing. As well as being a local businesswoman and the widow of one of the town's wealthiest and most respected textile manufacturers, Mary MacLeod had been popular, despite her outspoken manner, since the day she first arrived from her parents' farm in Beith, a beautiful and ambitious young woman. An invitation from Mary was looked on as more of a summons, and few had the courage, or the inclination, to defy her.

She stood now at the door with the Camerons and their daughter, a plain, awkward young woman not much younger than Margaret, pathetically grateful at having been rescued by marriage at the last minute. Her intended husband, a little younger than she was, but just as plain and awkward, hovered uneasily by her side.

Mary's eyes swept over Islay when they were introduced, and liked what they saw.

'Have a good time, lassie,' she instructed.

'I intend to see that she does, ma'am,' said Richard, magnificent in a loose plum-coloured coat and white ruffled shirt, with blue waistcoat and breeches. Like his brother, he wore his thick hair unadorned, tied back with a blue ribbon.

Mary, never one for feminine modesty, eyed him with the open admiration of a woman who appreciates a fine-looking man, 'I've no doubt you will, sir. But the lassie's here to meet folk, so I'll be grateful if you'll not take up every minute of her time yourself. And I'll be looking to you to claim my own hand for at least one dance.'

As they advanced into the crowded hall Islay saw an unpowdered red head almost at once. Jamie Todd, his back to the door, was deep in conversation with a group of men.

The evening was almost over by the time she and Jamie met. Earlier, she had caught his eye once or twice; on the first occasion he had clearly not recognised her, though he gave a courteous, formal bow in response to her tentative smile. The second time his brows had dipped in a puzzled frown, then lifted with startled recognition.

His red head had begun to forge its way towards her, then someone – there had been so many folk, apart from Richard himself – claimed her and led her onto the dance floor.

She had had no option but to go with her escort, and later she had seen Jamie join the dance with his own partner, a stranger to Islay.

Towards the end of the evening she escaped to a quiet corner behind a pillar for a moment's respite. As she smoothed the skirt of her lovely gown the rough skin on her fingers caught the soft material, reminding her, as she had been reminded every time Richard Knox took her hands in his during the dance, that however white and smooth her throat may be, her hands were those of a worker.

Islay bit her lip with humiliation. She had never had occasion to think of that before. After all, only the gentry could afford to have soft, smooth hands. But it would be nice to feel her fingers slide over beautiful materials instead of rasping over them, Islay thought longingly, wondering if Mistress Knox might be persuaded to tell her what oils or lotions she could make up to use on her red, rough skin. She was examining her fingers closely when Jamie Todd said from behind her, 'Islay?'

She turned, flushing guiltily as though caught in some wrong-doing. 'Mister Todd.'

'What's amiss?' Before she could put her hands behind her back he had taken them in his and was examining them, brows knotted. 'Have you hurt yourself?'

'No.' She tried to draw away from him, but he tightened his hold slightly.

'I thought when I first came on you that there must be something wrong with your hands.'

She squirmed uncomfortably under his glance, then confessed, 'I was just wishing that they were as soft as – as the other women's.'

He looked impatient. 'Who's been worrying you about such nonsense? Is it Richard Knox? I saw that you were dancing uncommonly often with him.'

'He said nothing! They were my own thoughts.'

'I didn't think that vanity was part of your nature.'

'It's just that –' She managed to reclaim the offending hands and put them out of sight, behind her back. 'I only wished –'

'You earn your living with your hands, as I do. Most of these women you see fit to envy –' he jerked his head towards the vivid, chattering throng on the other side of the row of pillars where they stood – 'expect others to do their work for them. I'd not want to be of their persuasion, and neither should you. Enjoy their company, by all means, for they're congenial folk, and decent enough. But never envy them. You're worth just as much as they are in the scale of things.'

His eyes touched briefly on her upswept hair, the tiny milky Scottish pearls Margaret had affixed to the small neat lobes of her ears, the rich stuff of the gown she wore, and he gave a short, half-apologetic laugh. 'You must forgive me my poor manners earlier. I didn't recognise you. You look so –' He paused, and she waited with rising hope. Would he say that she looked beautiful? Would he at least say that she looked pretty? 'Grown up,' he said, at last, and her hopes were dashed.

'Mistress Knox loaned me the dress. And it was she who invited me.'

'It was only right that she should. I should have thought to ask her to in the first place. Are you having a pleasant time?'

'Oh yes. Everyone's been very kind.'

'There's no reason why they shouldn't be.' His mouth twisted wryly. 'The Paisley folk aren't all ogres like myself.'

'You're not! You're –' She hesitated, then said lamely, 'You've been good to us, Mister Todd.'

He brushed the words aside with an impatient movement of the hand. 'Will you dance with me, Islay?'

It was one of the more sedate of the Scottish dances. Islay moved through the steps with confidence, for she had learned them as a youngster in the glens of her birth. Jamie danced competently, but without Richard Knox's natural sense of rhythm. Even so, his was a style that suited her, and she floated around the hall like a puff of thistledown, twirling and stepping, parting from him and rejoining him, putting her work-roughened hands into his without so much as a thought for the white smooth fingers she had been longing for so passionately.

At the end of the dance he offered her his arm, and led her over to where Margaret and Gavin were sitting. Before Islay could take her seat beside Margaret the musicians struck up again and Richard arrived to claim her for the next dance.

She hesitated, glancing at Jamie Todd, but he merely moved aside, so she put her hand into Richard's and let him lead her away.

*

Jamie watched the two of them take their places among the

dancers then said abruptly, 'Your brother seems to be very interested in Islay McInnes, Gavin. He's scarce allowed her to dance with anyone else all night.'

The surgeon shrugged. 'My brother's activities are none of my concern – and never were.'

'All the same, I gather from Islay that she's with your party tonight.'

'I invited her,' Margaret said. 'It's time the girl met some of the townsfolk. Richard's only making her welcome. Would you be happier to see her sitting alone and unwanted all evening, Jamie?'

'Of course not,' he said stiffly. 'But the man's much older than she is. Attention from a man of the world such as Richard could turn the child's head and set up all sorts of unhappiness.'

'Jamie's right, Margaret. Richard's altogether too aware of his own charm and the effect it can have on women.'

'Oh – tush!' Margaret glared at both men. 'I'm just grateful to him for making Islay's first evening in Paisley society so pleasant. And as for her being a child, Jamie – she's a woman now, as you've surely noticed for yourself.'

Jamie said nothing, but watched unsmilingly as the rose-pink gown and its attendant plum-coloured coat wove their way in and out of the dance.

Chapter Eighteen

Somehow, whether by design or by chance, Islay found that Jamie was her partner in the final dance of the evening.

'I'll walk back to Wellmeadow with you,' he offered as the music came to an end, adding, 'Or mebbe you'd prefer to travel by carriage with the rest of your party.'

She beamed up at him. 'No, indeed. It would be pleasant to walk in the night air.'

Richard was waiting at the edge of the dance-floor, holding the warm cloak that Margaret had loaned Islay. Jamie took it from him and put it about her shoulders. 'I'll escort Islay back to Wellmeadow.'

'That's not necessary. A carriage is waiting outside for us.'

The men loomed over Islay, one on either side. She put a hand on Richard's arm. 'I'd like to walk, truly.'

'Then it's my place to escort you.'

'It would take you out of your way, Mister Knox.'

'But —'

'Besides,' said Jamie with cool finality, 'Islay and I have to discuss some matters to do with the loom shop as we walk.'

Richard hesitated, then shrugged gracefully, kissed Islay's hand, and went off to join his brother and sister-in-law.

*

Although autumn had arrived the night was unseasonably cold. The chill struck home after the warmth of the Inn, and Islay drew the borrowed cloak close about her shoulders as she and Jamie walked through streets that fell quiet once they had left the bustle of departing guests about the Saracen's Head's doorway.

Now and again they passed a lighted window and heard sounds from within of a child crying, an adult coughing, men's voices raised in the lengthy debates that the Paisley weavers loved, whatever the subject. But most of the houses were dark, their inhabitants long a-bed.

Jamie said nothing, and Islay was happy enough to patter along by his side, her hand resting as lightly as a flower petal on his arm, letting her thoughts roam around the evening she had just spent, carefully listing and preserving each moment.

The rose pink dress rustled about her legs; tomorrow it must be carefully wrapped and taken back to Mistress Knox, but for tonight it was Islay's, and she relished the feel of it, the whisper of silk, the snug way the bodice cupped her breasts and fitted to her waist, the soft kiss of the flounces against her forearms as she moved.

In no time at all they had passed the house where Jamie lived. From there it was only a matter of minutes to the building in Wellmeadow.

When they reached it, Jamie paused and looked up at the night sky. Clouds had formed a thin veil before the moon, shutting out most of its clear cold light.

'Will you see to find your way up the stairs?'

'Yes, indeed.'

'In that case, I'll bid you goodnight.' Jamie Todd wasn't one to kiss a woman's hand, and Islay hadn't expected it of him.

She ducked her head in farewell and turned to go through the pend. Beneath the stone arch the place was as black as pitch, but she had walked it often enough to know just where to set her feet. Confidently, she moved into the dark area, angling slightly to the right as she neared the other end of the archway. The wooden staircase was just a few steps round the corner.

She was almost out of the pend when her foot struck against something soft and she stumbled.

Someone – or something – grunted, there was a scrabbling, then a hand closed about her ankle and she cried out in fright, taking a swift, involuntary step back, wrenching herself free but losing her balance in the process.

She staggered, and for a moment she felt herself falling

back, then one shoulder hit painfully off the far wall of the pend.

'Islay?' Jamie Todd called sharply from the street. The pend was suddenly filled with a flurry of sound as whoever had startled her fled towards the street and collided with Jamie as he came running in. There was a short scuffle, then Jamie said breathlessly, urgently, 'Islay – in God's name where are you?'

'Here. I'm here –' She put her hands out and almost at once felt them grasped in his.

'Are you hurt, lassie?'

'No –' But her voice trembled with shock, and so did her hands, still trapped in his. He put one arm about her and supported her weight easily.

'I'll take you up to the house.'

'No! I don't want to fright Morag and Lachie.'

'Then we'll go into the loom shop.'

He found the door without any trouble and half lifted Islay over the raised wooden sill and into the room. Then he lit the candle that was always kept on a shelf just inside the door.

In its glow the loom shop was a place of elongated shadows; the looms stood silent, unmoving guard round the pool of light that cupped Jamie and Islay. The place smelled faintly of the oil that was used on the machines.

Jamie held the candle up so that he could see Islay's face. 'Are you certain you're not hurt?'

'Just frightened. He caught my foot and I didn't know what was going to happen to me. Who was it?'

'Some drunken vagabond sheltering in the pend for the night. He'll not do that again in this town,' said Jamie savagely. 'I'm going to hand him over to the town watchmen, and tomorrow the magistrates'll run him out of the place.'

'No!'

He stared. 'The man's a danger to the community, Islay! You said yourself that he caught hold of you. There's no knowing what he might have done if I hadnae been there to hear you cry out!'

'He was probably just sheltering for the night. He'd have

got as much of a fright as I did, poor soul. Oh – don't hand him over to the militia – they'll like as not flog him before they run him out.' She shivered, remembering what it was like to have nowhere to sleep, no knowledge of where the next meal was coming from, the continual fear of being forced out of towns or villages with nowhere else to seek shelter.

'He probably deserves a good flogging.'

'That's a wicked thing to say!'

'God's teeth, lassie! The man gives you enough of a fright to stop your heart – and heaven only knows what other mischief he had in store for you – and you accuse me of being wicked just because I want to see him being taught a lesson? I'll never understand you Highlanders!'

That was the trouble, Islay thought wretchedly. Nobody in this town understood her people. And not being understood was almost as bad as being rejected altogether.

Then she suddenly thought of the gown and jumped to her feet, twisting round in an attempt to examine the back of the skirt. 'Mistress Knox's fine dress! I've mebbe dirtied it against the wall –'

'No matter if you have,' he said, 'As long as you're not hurt.'

Then he gave that wry smile she had seen on his lips before. 'Mebbe you'd have done better to accept a lift home in the carriage instead of trusting yourself to me. Now – I'd best bring in that ne'er-do-weel that's lying out in the pend.'

While he was gone Islay had time to reassure herself, at least by the candle's light, that the lovely dress seemed to be unharmed. Tomorrow morning she would have a better opportunity to study it in daylight.

Then Jamie was back, dragging with him a slightly built man who lolled in his grip, only half-recovered from the blow Jamie had dealt him. His head rolled on his chest, his feet stumbled as they tried to walk. He tripped over the sill of the door, and Jamie jerked him roughly inside, deposited him on the settle by the fireside, and went back to shut the door.

'Is he hurt bad?' Islay forgot her worries about the dress as she went to the settle.

'If he is it's no more than he deserves.'

She touched a limp hand. It stirred beneath her fingers and the man groaned.

'He's so cold!'

Jamie brought the candle over and set it down. Then he caught a fistful of the long, lank black hair that hung round the stranger's drooping head and jerked on it, pulling the man's head back and exposing a gaunt face, white beneath its grime. Dazed brown eyes blinked in the light, trying to focus.

Islay's own eyes opened wide in disbelief.

'Ross!'

'Eh?' asked Jamie blankly.

'Dear God! It's my cousin Ross MacInnes – Morag and Lachie's brother! Oh, Ross –!'

Her cousin's eyes cleared at the sound of his own name and he made an attempt to pull himself upright, shaking his head to clear it.

'Islay?' he asked wonderingly in the Gaelic.

'Yes, it's Islay. What are you doing here – where did you come from? Is my uncle with you?' The questions poured from her.

He put a hand to his face and probed his jaw, then winced and looked round, still groggy. 'Islay? How did you come to be here?'

'We live in the house above, now – Morag and Lachie and me.'

'They're safe, then?'

'They're safe – and well.'

'Mother?' He said the word reluctantly, as though he knew the answer already.

Islay took one of his hands in hers. 'She died some time back. I'm sorry, Ross.'

He was silent for a moment, then said, 'I thought she might be. Mebbe she's better off. Where is this place?'

'Jamie Todd's loom shop. Oh, Ross, I never thought to see you again! How did you know where to find us?'

He began to talk, haltingly at first, then more easily as his head cleared. Islay, sitting beside him, still clutching his hand, couldn't take her eyes from him. As far as Morag and

Lachie were concerned, she had never given up hope that Ross and her uncle would return; but in her own mind, she had never thought to see either of them again.

She was only dimly aware of Jamie Todd's presence. At first he leaned back against one of the looms, surveying the cousins, his hand absently stoking the wooden roller that held the yarn.

Then he began to prowl restlessly, and finally he came to stand before them, interrupting the flow of words.

'Islay – what in the world's going on? I can make neither head nor tail of your gibberish!'

It was only then that she realised that she and Ross had been speaking in their native tongue.

'He's out of the Army now, and he's walked all the way from London to find us. He went to Jenny's Wynd and someone told him Lachie worked here. He was sheltering in the pend until morning, waiting for Lachie to come to work.'

'What of his father?'

She bit her lip, then said, 'He knows no more about my uncle than I do.'

'Well –' said Jamie, at a loss. 'And now what do you plan to do with him?'

Ross dragged himself upright and stood by Islay, clutching with one hand at the back of the settle, swaying slightly from weakness and exhaustion.

As she glanced swiftly from one man to the other Islay's heart was wrenched with pity for her cousin. When she had last seen him Ross had been a strong, well-set-up young man.

But lack of nourishment and hard usage had turned him into a pathetic, shabbily dressed shadow of his former self.

Jamie, on the other hand, had never known what it was like to be destitute. Although his garb for the evening was much less elaborate than Richard's he looked, in his dark green jacket with silver buttons, and black britches, like nobility compared to her cousin.

Ross's eyes, as he faced the sturdy, well dressed man before him, were hostile. So, Islay noted with some dismay, were Jamie's.

'What d'you plan to do?' Jamie repeated.

'I must take him upstairs and give him some food, for a start. Come, Ross –' Islay said in the Gaelic, and put her arm about her cousin.

Jamie brushed her aside. 'I'll see to him. You go ahead with the candle.'

Ross drew back slightly, but Jamie ignored the movement, putting a strong arm about the other man and half carrying him out of the shop and up the stairs after Islay.

At the house door he hesitated, releasing Ross. 'Will you manage on your own now?'

'Yes. Thank you for your help, Jamie.'

'I'll see you in the morning,' said Jamie, and departed without a backward glance.

It was only then, as she watched him disappearing from the pool of candle-light, that Islay realised that during the excitement his first name had come to her tongue – as naturally as if she had always used it.

Chapter Nineteen

As Mary MacLeod had prophesied, the gathering at the Saracen's Head Inn had gone some way towards easing the situation between Margaret and Gavin.

For one thing, it had brought back memories to both of them of the time when Gavin formally invited Margaret to be his partner at a public dance there.

It was on that night that he had first kissed her, she thought as they walked into the hall with Islay and Richard. And giving Gavin a sidelong glance, she caught him doing the same to her. They smiled, then laughed together, and set out to enjoy the evening.

Later, much later, Gavin made love to her in the privacy of their bed-chamber and as she drifted off to sleep with his head pillowed on her shoulder and his bare arm wrapped about her, Margaret knew a sensation of deep, healing peace.

But trouble erupted only two days later, proving that the chasm set up by the original quarrel still existed, and had only been hidden for the moment beneath their new-found contentment with each other.

It started when Gavin, finding Margaret in the parlour, proposed that she and the children should ride out with him on his country rounds that day.

'We'll not have much more sunshine this year, and it's time the four of us had a day to ourselves.'

She bit her lip. 'I must go to the Poors' Hospital school-room this morning, then I've to see how the inkle looms are doing –'

'Och – confound the schoolroom and the inkle looms!' Gavin said with a sudden spurt of irritation. 'Margaret, I'll not have these folk at the Poors' Hospital taking up time you should be giving to me and to your own bairns. When was the last time we all were together properly? When are things going to go back to the way they should be in this house?'

She kept on folding the table-cloth in her hands, matching side to side precisely, smoothing each fold meticulously. 'There's nothing wrong with the way things are.'

'You can say that, when Richard's forever under my feet and I never seem to have a moment alone with you? When Daniel still draws away whenever I go near him, and cries out if I put a hand on him?'

'It was you that frighted Daniel, Gavin. You can't deny that.'

His voice sharpened. 'And you've encouraged him to keep that thought in his mind. You've made a baby of him again.'

He turned to the door, put a hand on the handle, said over his shoulder, 'You'll turn the lad into a timid wee creature frighted of its own shadow if you're not careful. It's high time I put a stop to it.'

'I scarce think you've the right to tell me how to treat my own bairns – not after what you did to them!'

He left the door and was across the room before she realised what his intentions were. The table covering fell to the floor as he caught her upper arms, his face dark with anger.

'Listen to me, Margaret. You didn't produce them entirely on your own, for all that you're such an able creature,' he said between clenched teeth. 'They're mine too, and what I did I did for love of them. Mebbe one day you'll come to see that for yourself. As for the Hospital and the inkle looms – I've stood by long enough, Margaret. Let someone else see to them for you from now on.'

'I'll not be ordered about like a servant!'

'You'll do as I –'

Gavin stopped short as the door opened. Richard stood on the threshold, looking from husband to wife.

'Still here, Gavin? I thought you'd gone long since.'

Gavin opened his hands and released Margaret as his brother advanced into the room.

'I've arranged to meet Jamie Todd later, but I'll walk down to the Hospital with you, Margaret. We'll mebbe have time to inspect the new loomshop first –' he added before she had the chance to stop him.

'What new loomshop?' Gavin asked swiftly, suspiciously, looking from one face to the other.

Margaret laid the neatly folded cloth on the table and smoothed it before turning to face him.

'Richard and I are setting up more inkle looms for the women in the hospital.'

Her husband's eyes were blazing agates. 'Richard may do so, if he wishes. But not you.'

'It's all been decided. We hope to move the looms in to the new weaving shop next week.'

'I forbid it, Margaret!'

Even if she had wanted to, there was no changing her mind after she heard that. 'And I've decided, Gavin.'

He rounded on Richard. 'This is all your doing!'

'Mine? Surely you, of all men, should know that nobody forces your wife to do anything against her will.'

'Get out of my house.'

'Gavin!'

'I may not hold any authority over you, Margaret. I may not even be allowed to be a father to my son. But by God, this is my house and I'll have my say as to who's welcome in it and who isn't!' Then he turned his attention back to his brother.

'You were never done causing trouble and mischief as a laddie, Richard, and you've not changed. But from henceforth you won't do it under this roof!'

'Gavin Knox, have you taken leave of your senses? Richard's done nothing to deserve this treatment!'

'Not yet, mebbe. But he will, Margaret, he will, if he's given the least chance for mischief.'

Richard's eyes had narrowed slightly, but his face was still and untroubled. 'I've done nothing to be ashamed of, Gavin, but since you –'

'Nothing? You call causing the death of your own mother nothing?'

Richard went white to the lips. 'You're lying!'

'Am I, Richard? You know the truth as well as I do! Always, from the moment of your birth, you were the centre of her universe. And what reward did you see fit to give her?' As the bitter words poured from Gavin in a torrent, Margaret, appalled, realised that they must have lain within him for years, rankling and festering.

'She had to lie for you, to protect you from the consequences of your mischief-making,' he raged. 'And you repaid her by running away – leaving her without a backward glance, never sending her word of your whereabouts. She sickened from that day. She died of a broken heart, Richard, and it was you who broke it!'

He stopped, and for a moment there was silence. Then Richard lifted one shoulder in a faint shrug and half-turned away. Gavin, maddened by the gesture, lunged across the short space of carpeted floor between them and caught at his brother's arm, spinning him round so that they faced each other.

Richard's hands came up in a self-protective move just as Margaret took hold of Gavin's arm and pulled him away from his brother.

'Gavin! For pity's sake, the man's a guest under our roof!'

As soon as he was released Richard stepped back, slipping his fingers distastefully over the crumpled material of his sleeve.

Gavin drew a long ragged breath then said coldly and steadily, 'I've told you – you're no longer welcome beneath my roof. If you're not out by the time I come home tonight I'll take you by the neck and run you out!'

Neither of them spoke until they heard the front door crash to behind Gavin. Margaret found that she was clutching tightly at the back of a chair, so tightly that the skin stretched over the knuckles of both hands was bone white.

Shakily, she released her grip and sat down.

'Richard –'

He shrugged again. 'Don't concern yourself, sister. Gavin was always given to sudden bursts of rage, as I recall. I shall easily find suitable lodgings in the town.'

'But all these accusations – are they true?'

'Oh, I doubt it. I'll not lose any sleep over them, I can assure you. Gavin always had a possessive love of our mother, as I recall. Clearly he needs to lay the blame for her death at someone's door. But never at his own. And, as the family scapegoat, I must accept any blame he chooses to cast.'

Margaret, remembering the white-hot rage in Gavin's face, began to shiver, though the room was warm enough. All at once the future, usually predictable and safe, was like a dark endless corridor, a fearsome place that she was afraid to enter.

'Richard –' she said. 'Oh, Richard – what's to become of us? What's to become of Gavin and me?'

Chapter Twenty

Gavin was right about one thing – winter was fast approaching and there wouldn't be many more lush warm late autumn days to come.

After she and Richard, accompanied by Christian and Daniel, had inspected and approved of the new loomshop, Margaret went back to the Poors' Hospital to conduct the morning class.

Her own children often attended the classes with her, working diligently on their slates, enjoying the novelty of being with the others.

Today, too pre-occupied to concentrate on the lesson, Margaret led her young charges out of the high-ceilinged cheerless school-room and into the fields by the river where they could run about and play in the sunshine.

On the way through the large entrance hall they encountered the hospital mistress. The woman's nostrils flared slightly with disapproval as she watched the young-sters scampering past her and out of the door, heading gleefully towards freedom; but she said nothing, acknow-ledging Margaret's greeting with a painfully manufactured smile.

Margaret had been the first ever teacher to be appointed to teach the pauper children, and she had done her work well over the years. The board of directors, Mary MacLeod among them, approved of her work in general, although there had been many clashes between them when their views on the treatment of the wretched, dependent inmates under their care were at variance with hers.

Now, of course, she enjoyed extra powers as the wife of a respected surgeon and the sister of a local physician, both known to have given their services, unpaid, to the hospital on numerous occasions.

She sat on a fallen tree and watched the children at play, their pinched little faces lifted to the sun, their under-nourished bodies seeming to fill out and blossom in its meagre autumnal warmth.

Beside these pauper children Christian and Daniel appeared to be both overfed and pampered, Margaret thought, and knew that she couldn't abandon the hospital inmates, no matter how much Gavin railed at her.

She bit her lip, recollecting his face earlier that day – the face of a stranger. He hadn't asked her to give up her work, he had demanded it. And Margaret Montgomery – not for the first time since her marriage Margaret fully understood and appreciated the Scots custom whereby a married woman was perfectly entitled to retain her own name instead of being obliged to use her husband's at all times, as in England – Margaret Montgomery, she repeated to herself defiantly, didn't take kindly to demands.

*

A carter had just finished loading bales of linen from Duncan Montgomery's loom shop later that day when Margaret and the children left her mother's house. The man, an old friend of her family's, gave her a nod, and on the impulse she asked, 'Are you going to the bleachfields?'

'I am that.'

'Will you take us up to the braes?'

His eyebrows climbed. 'Bless us, Maggie Montgomery, you're surely past the stage of riding on the bleachfield carts!'

'My bairns aren't.'

'You'll have to walk back.'

'I always did.' She lifted Daniel up, and deposited him on top of the bales. The man shrugged and swung Christian, squealing with excitement, to a seat beside her brother. Then as Margaret gathered up her skirts he gave her his hand and the past five years vanished like snow in the sun as she stepped, sure-footed, onto the cart to join her children.

When the three of them were settled in a nest among the bales the man clicked his tongue at his horse and the patient beast set off, the cart joggling and bumping along behind it.

Margaret wrapped her arms about the giggling children and for the first time in years savoured the pleasure of riding in the back of a linen cart, looking down on the pedestrians.

Now and again she waved to familiar faces among the folk on the footpath. Some, after their first puzzled stare, recognised her and laughed and waved back; others looked shocked. Margaret was thankful that she had left her mother safely out in the back garden, tending to her bees. She could just imagine what Meg Montgomery would have had to say about a grown woman, a wife and mother too, disporting herself on the back of a linen cart for all the town to see.

Jamie, coming out of the Wellmeadow pend as the cart drew level with him, didn't notice its occupants. His head was lowered, his eyes fixed on the ground.

'Hello, Jamie! Stop a minute –' Margaret appealed to the driver, who obediently reined in his horse as the red-headed man looked up.

'Margaret, now what are you up to?'

She laughed down at him and reached out her hand, 'We're off to the bleach-fields. Come with us, Jamie.'

'The bleach-fields – the bleach-fields –' Christian began to caper about on the linen bales, chanting, and Margaret locked a firm hold on her skirt and dragged her down again.

'Come on, Jamie!'

As the carter shook the reins and the vehicle began to move again Jamie made a sudden decision, caught at the tail of the cart, and swung himself up beside them.

'It's a while since you and me last used this form of transport,' he said breathlessly.

'Too long.' Margaret settled back against the bales, and gave herself over to enjoying the ride.

*

The driver stopped his horse about a mile beyond the town, just before it reached the bleach-fields. There, the linen would be stretched out on the ground, exposed to the sun and doused with pure burn water until it was bleached from its original coarse grey shade to as near white as was possible. 'Will this do you, Maggie?'

'It'll do me fine!'

Jamie got down and lifted the children to the ground. Then he reached his arms up to Margaret, who dropped lightly into them.

Christian and Daniel, drunk with the excitement of this most unexpected treat, were already racing over the short tufted grass, swerving in and out of the whin bushes. Margaret and Jamie, after a word of thanks to the carter, turned to follow the children as the cart moved away.

At first they walked in silence, each occupied with private thoughts. Then Jamie said abruptly, 'I've decided to throw in my lot with Richard Knox.'

'Use his cotton yarn to weave cloth for him?' She stared at him with astonishment and a little dismay. 'But what about my father, and Robert?'

He had the grace to look uncomfortable. 'Och, they're set on continuing with the linen yarn. Richard needed six or seven looms, and I thought that perhaps we could have spared that many between us. But Duncan and Robert are determined to keep all their machines on linen cloth. So, today I told him I'd turn my eight looms to cotton and weave his cloth for him.'

Margaret could scarcely believe it. Ever since her father had come to Paisley as a young, newly-wed man and been taken on by Peter Todd, Jamie's father, the Todds and Montgomerys had worked together. Jamie's move put an end to all of that; to Margaret, it represented more than just a change of cloth. It meant a split between the two families.

'Jamie –'

'I know, I know!' he said angrily. 'But it's time for a change, Margaret. The linen's not bringing in enough money. I've got seven weavers and two drawboys to think about, as well as Kirsty and Billy to support. I must think ahead!'

'But what if the new cloth doesn't sell? What if Richard's wrong when he says he's got a good market?'

'It'll have to sell, Margaret. That's the truth of it. If not – well, I'll give up the whole business and get out of the town.

We're at war in the Americas – I could go back to being a soldier.'

'You said you'd never do that!'

Jamie's hair seemed to flame belligerently. 'Is it only women that are entitled to change their minds?'

'Anyway, you're getting too old to fight.'

'I'm too old for many things,' he said bitterly. 'But not too old yet for soldiering. Not quite.'

She put a hand on his arm. 'Don't go, Jamie. Don't leave us again.'

'Lassie, if this cloth doesnae work, I must leave, before I'm laughed out of the town!'

Beneath her touch the muscles of his arm were corded and rock-hard with tension. 'There's more than the cloth troubling you, Jamie Todd. What's amiss?'

'Nothing,' he said, and pulled away from her, striding ahead as the ground suddenly dipped into a small hollow.

Margaret picked a grass head and began to strip it of its seeds as she followed. Ahead, the children's voices rang like bells in the clear cool air.

On the opposite side of the hollow Jamie slowed to let her catch up. But his face was still averted, and she knew better than to say any more about the cloth.

'How are the Highlanders coming along?' she asked instead. 'Have Lachie and Walter managed to keep their hands off each other?'

'Aye. They know what they'd get from me if they tried to make trouble in my loom shop.'

Margaret twirled the grass stem. 'I think there's more on Walter's mind than fighting. If you ask me, he's smitten with Islay.'

'Nonsense!'

'I'm telling you. A man never notices these things, but a woman does.'

'They scarce know each other.'

'What's that got to do with it? I saw the look on his face when she opened the door to him once, when I was visiting with her.'

'Walter?' He said the name as though she had just mentioned the most unlikely candidate possible for Islay's hand.

'Aye, Walter. He's a fine-looking laddie, and Islay's fast growing into a beautiful woman now that she's got enough to eat and she's wearing better than those poor rags she used to have. And they're both of marriageable age. She could do a lot worse than to settle for Walter.'

There was a pause, then, 'Islay's cousin's back from the Army,' Jamie said.

'Oh? I didn't know that. I must call on her. What's he like?'

'I can't take to him. For one thing, he persists in speaking in his own tongue – though he can probably speak English as well as the next man – and I can never tell what he's saying. For another, there's something in his eyes when he looks at me –' He stopped, and swiped irritably with his boot at a bush. 'I'll be glad when he's out of Paisley. It seems to me that he's of no use to Islay. But she fawns over him as if –' He stopped again, then finished, 'I don't care for him at all.'

Christian and Daniel, some distance in front of them as they walked back down to the town, reached the top of a slight slope and began to disappear from view. First Daniel's dark head, then Christian's, vanished from Margaret's sight. All that was left of them was the sound of their laughter carried back to her on a breeze.

Then she and Jamie topped the rise and saw that the children had thrown themselves down on the grass and were rolling down the hill, bumping from tussock to tussock, screaming with amusement as they went. Christian's skirts had wrapped themselves round her knees, and her legs kicked free.

'Times I wish,' said Jamie, grinning, 'that I was their age again.'

'Oh – so do I!'

He stopped, turned her round, and looked down into her face. For the second time that day a man held her shoulders, compelling her to look up at him.

But this time the face above hers was compassionate and concerned. It was his turn to ask, 'What's amiss, Margaret?'

If he had been anyone else she would probably have denied that anything was amiss. But she and Jamie had always had a special relationship. If he had had his way, they would have been man and wife. Margaret wondered, bleakly, if that might not have been a good idea after all.

'It's Gavin and me. Everything's gone wrong, Jamie, and I don't know what to do to make it right again.'

'I can't advise you, for I've no experience of marriage – nor likely to have now.'

'For goodness' sake, Jamie Todd!' She felt tears of self-pity prickle the backs of her eyes, and chased them away by forcing a mock frown. 'You're not as old as all that – there's plenty of good marriageable years in you yet. All you need to do is to find the right woman.'

He released her and they began to walk again. Below them, now, lay the town, blurred beneath a soft blue haze of smoke from its chimneys. The children had picked themselves up and were racing on.

'I'm not so sure about that,' said Jamie. 'Sometimes it seems to me, Margaret, that I've made a right confusion of being an adult.'

She slipped her fingers into his and gripped his hand tightly.

'Sometimes, Jamie, I think the same about myself,' said Margaret.

Chapter Twenty-One

By the time Gavin returned that night Richard Knox had found lodgings in St Mirin's Wynd, near to the Cross, and moved his belongings out of the Oakshawhill house.

Gavin made no comment about his brother, and neither did Margaret. When the children noisily wanted to know where Uncle Richard was, and when he was coming home, their father silenced them with a look that cowed Daniel completely and even caused Christian to find the sense to close her mouth.

Neither of them mentioned Richard in their father's hearing again.

The business over Richard not only re-opened the chasm between Margaret and Gavin, but made it all the wider.

She went about the work of setting up more inkle looms in the new weaving shop, and finding capable women from among the hospital inmates to take on the work. She attended to her Hospital duties and to her household duties, and made certain that Gavin could find nothing to complain of; and she did it all with an unhappy heart.

'Your mother's getting worried about you,' Mary MacLeod told her at last.

'There's nothing amiss with me.'

'Oh, you put a very good face on it – and so does Gavin. But Meg and me aren't daft altogether, Margaret. We can tell when a marriage has soured. Is it not time you and Gavin agreed to forget about this smallpox business?'

'It's nothing to do with that. It's the way he's treated Richard.'

'Margaret, you're the man's wife, not his owner. You'd not thank him if he interfered between you and Robert, or you and Thomas. Leave him and his brother be.'

'I'll not stand by and watch Richard ill-used and insulted!'

'It's not worrying him half as much as it's worrying you. I saw him in the town this morning, looking even more handsome than ever. For all that Paisley's air's damp, it seems to be doing Richard good. But then,' said Mary dryly, 'Richard's getting everything his own way these days.'

She was right. Richard Knox had come to Paisley in search of looms to weave his cotton yarn. He had them – and in addition he had some eight inkle looms using up the yarn he bought from the English manufactories, and turning out ribbons and tapes for him to export abroad from the Glasgow docks while he waited for the first consignment of cloth to roll off Jamie's looms.

He had found himself comfortable lodgings and taken on a manservant; during that winter he became a familiar sight, riding about the town on the fine chestnut horse he had bought for himself, his dour-faced servant riding behind him on a sturdy grey.

He was very popular with the local people, and much in demand at the flurry of gatherings and dinners that took place during the dark winter months.

Each time Margaret and Gavin encountered him at these social events Gavin was formally courteous, treating Richard as though he was a little-known acquaintance. His manner didn't seem to trouble his brother one bit.

Margaret, curious to see Islay's cousin, found time to visit the house above Jamie's loom shop. She wasn't long in Ross McInnes's company before she had decided that Jamie was right. There was something almost menacing about the youth, something that made it impossible to chatter with Islay in his company.

Normally Margaret would have felt a quick, warm sympathy for him, for he carried the stamp of someone who had seen and experienced a great deal of suffering. But Ross, embittered by his experiences, clearly didn't want anyone's sympathy.

When he spoke to Islay in the Gaelic before Margaret, the girl flushed and said sharply in English, 'Ross, you must speak the Lowlander tongue before our guest.'

His dark eyes rested briefly on Margaret, then moved away again. 'I said I'll away out for some fresh air.'

He picked up a carefully patched and darned jacket, gave Margaret a mocking bow, and left. Islay watched him go with troubled eyes.

'He's had a hard time,' she said apologetically as the clatter of his feet on the wooden stair died away. 'He should have gone to the Americas with the rest of the soldiers, but he was very ill, and like to die. They left him behind, and when he was well enough he walked here from London.'

'Does he have to go back to the Army when he's strong again?'

The girl shook her head. 'It seems not. Or he's made up his mind not to go. I don't know the truth of it. He's talking of going to Edinburgh to settle once he's well enough.'

'And leaving you alone again?'

Islay looked down at the hands twisting together in her lap, then up at Margaret. 'He wants us to go with him, all of us. He – he wants me to wed with him.'

'Oh? And what do you want, Islay?'

'I don't know. You've all been kind to us – you and Mister Todd, and the others. I like Paisley well enough. But Ross is set on leaving the place. He'd not settle here.'

'Islay, if you don't want to marry him you don't have to. He seems –' Margaret hesitated, searching for the right words, and the girl said swiftly:

'It's not his fault that he's bitter and suspicious. Bad things have happened to him. You should have seen Ross before – when we were all at home together. He was strong and able and willing. He was good at everything he turned his mind to.'

She smiled faintly, remembering. 'He was the best dancer and the fastest runner – and there wasn't a thing Ross couldn't do with the beasts. That's what he has in mind now – to work on the land, with mebbe a wee farm cottage for us all to live in. The way it would have been, if things hadn't changed for the worse for us.'

The smile faded, to be replaced by a sadness far beyond her years. 'But then we were thrown off our land, and there was all the hardship, and seeing folk sicken and die, one by one. The old ones and the littlest bairns, then the others. Not knowing where we were going to lay our heads, not knowing if we were going to eat, or be made welcome, or stoned. Not finding work, when we finally arrived in Paisley. Then the Army – so many things to change him.'

'Most of these things happened to you, too. And you've not let them turn you to bitterness.'

'But it's different for us, isn't it? Men take it badly if they can't look after their families. Men have their pride.'

'And you think women don't?' Margaret asked tartly.

The girl flashed her a sudden mature, sharing smile; a smile that bound them together, once and for ever, as friends and confidantes. 'Oh yes, women do – but we know how to temper our pride, don't we? It's something we have to learn early in life.'

As she was taking her leave, Margaret said again, 'You don't have to marry with Ross if you don't want to, Islay.'

'I'll see – when he's well enough to move on. I'll see.'

'Is there someone else?' Margaret thought of Walter Shaw, and was sure she had hit on the truth when sudden colour stained the girl's face.

'Who else would there be?'

'Nobody special – I just wondered,' said Margaret, and left.

*

When she had closed the door behind her guest Islay leaned her forehead against it for a moment. Margaret Knox's words echoed in her mind. 'Is there someone else?'

Fleetingly, she thought of a man with very blue eyes and a thatch of blazing red hair. A man of changing moods, a man she longed to know and understand. A man, she thought, her brow knotting with worry, Ross disliked. A man who returned that dislike, measure for cold measure.

Morag, returning from an errand, clattered up the wooden stairs and lifted the latch. Islay put all thought of Jamie Todd firmly from her mind and stepped aside to let her cousin in.

*

Towards the end of the year Gavin received an invitation to work in his home town of Dumfries for a short while with a surgeon he had known in his youth.

For the first time in many weeks his face was animated as he told Margaret his news. 'It was that man who decided me to take up medicine in the first place. I'd like fine to have the chance to work by his side.'

It pleased her to see him come to life again. 'Then you must certainly go.'

'Will you come with me – you and the bairns?'

'Gavin, where would we stay?'

'I could find a house to rent easily enough.'

'But I don't know anyone there,' she said in dismay. 'And it would be an awful upheaval, taking Ellen and the bairns all that way for a short while. At this time of year, too, when it's so cold and the weather's bad for travel –'

'Then leave them here. Ellen can look after them, and there's your Aunt Mary and your mother to help her. Come yourself.'

'Oh no, I couldn't leave them –'

Gavin's face was suddenly cold. 'You couldn't leave your looms and the Poors' House, you mean.'

'I don't mean that at all! See reason, Gavin – you'll be in the hospital most of the time. I'd be alone, in a place where I don't know anybody.'

'You'd meet folk. It's not just in Paisley that people are friendly. I was a stranger here myself at one time, but it didn't stop me from settling when you wanted to stay.'

'It was different for you. You didn't have a family, and you didn't have bairns –'

Gavin got up abruptly and made for the door. 'I'll go alone.' He threw the words over his shoulder.

'How long will you be gone?'

He stopped at the door and looked at her with angry eyes. 'I don't know. Does it matter?' he said, and walked out of the room.

*

Meg Montgomery eyed her daughter closely when Margaret walked into her kitchen and announced that Gavin was off to Dumfries.

'Should you not go with him?'

'It's not worth it for all the time he'll be away.' Margaret loosened her bonnet strings and put her cloak aside. 'I'd only have found myself in a strange town, with Gavin at the hospital all the time.'

'All the same, a woman's place is with her man. And the way things have been with you two –'

'The way things have been, a wee spell away from each other might be just what we're needing. Anyway, I'm busy with my new inkle looms.'

'I suppose you know what they're saying in the town –' Meg said unhappily. 'That Gavin and Richard had words, and Gavin put his own brother out of the house. It's a shaming thing, Margaret, to hear such talk of my daughter's man.'

'It's none of your concern, or mine, what falls between brothers.' Margaret unblushingly made use of Mary's words. 'Besides, who pays heed to the town gossips?'

'Plenty do. Specially where Richard Knox is concerned. That man's set the fox among the hens as far as your father's concerned, I can tell you.'

Margaret flapped an impatient hand. 'It's nothing to do with me. I've no wish to hear about it.'

Meg gave a loud sniff. 'You'll hear about it all right, if Duncan has his way of it.'

Almost as though husband and wife had pre-arranged it, the door opened and Duncan Montgomery walked in and caught the last few words.

'If I've my way of what?'

The women eyed each other before Margaret, realising that there was no getting out of it, said, 'We were talking about Richard Knox.'

Duncan's strong square face was normally cheerful. But at the mention of Richard's name it settled into dour lines. 'Him! That man's a trouble-maker!'

'He's a man of business, that's all.'

'Oh aye, I heard he'd got you on his side – against your own husband's wishes, too.'

She felt her anger begin to rise. 'I'm not on his side – he's helping me to set up the inkle looms I need, and we're using his cotton yarn. As for Gavin, that business is for him and me to settle between us.'

'I don't know what's possessed you, Margaret. And I don't know what's possessed Jamie Todd, agreeing to turn all his looms over to cotton weaving.'

'He thinks linen's on its way out. The man has a right to use his own looms in whatever way he thinks fit.' Then, as her parents said nothing, she pressed on, 'I don't know why you and Robert wouldn't agree to trying the yarn on some of your machines.'

'Richard Knox isn't a weaver, and never has been. He knows nothing of the looms. I'll not trust my livelihood to a man whose only interest is in buying and selling and making money for himself.'

'And for the weavers.'

'As to that, Robert and me'll wait and see what happens. The man's full of high notions and promises, but they've yet to be proved,' said Duncan darkly, and try as she might, Margaret could find no way of shifting him from his pessimistic view of Richard Knox's business in the town.

Chapter Twenty-Two

The old year had ended and 1776 had settled in before Ross McInnes was well enough to consider moving on, out of Paisley.

Islay had been in no hurry for him to make a full recovery. She dreaded the time when she must make a decision about her own future.

In some strange way she now felt more secure in the loomshop than in the house above. Each morning as Lachie scampered off along the dark empty streets to waken the weavers she looked forward to the time spent alone with the silent, waiting looms. There was a good feeling about the place, a sense of security and timeless peace.

All too soon Lachie would come hurrying back and begin squirming his thin, agile little body beneath the machines, cleaning out the threads and fluff and snails that sometimes found their way into the pits left in the floor to make room for the set of foot treadles.

Then the others arrived, yawning and sleepy-eyed, filling the place with their talk.

Islay usually found some excuse to loiter until the first weaver settled himself on his saytree, running his hands over his loom in the way that the weavers had, as though re-affirming the bond between man and machine. Eventually the man would press his foot down on a treadle and the loom would lumber into action, the harness that held the weft threads lifting to form the 'shed'.

The weaver would skilfully throw the yarn-loaded shuttle through the shed from one end to the other, the yarn stretching out behind it. The treadle was released, the harness fell back into place, the newly-thrown weft thread was firmly tapped into its place on the cloth with the weaver's 'pooking pin', and the day, for Islay had begun.

Although Jamie Todd's looms were no longer using linen yarn he found weavers willing to take all the yarn that his own spinsters had formerly spun for him, and so Islay's wheel was kept as busy as ever.

As she went about her housework, or settled at her wheel, Islay was continually aware of Ross's dark eyes fixed on her. He tended to follow her about the house, or hovered restlessly by the window if she had to go out, watching for her return. He himself rarely went further than the back yard.

With each day that passed, she sensed his growing restlessness. Finally, on a mild day in early February as he was sitting by the fire, watching her work at her wheel, he announced abruptly, 'It's time we were moving on.'

Islay's fingers tightened on the yarn, almost snagging it, then deliberately relaxed. 'Why should you want to move?'

'I told you,' he said impatiently. 'I'm going to find work on the land.'

'There are farms round here. No doubt you could find work on one of them.'

'No, not here. We're going to the other side of the country, by Edinburgh way.'

'But Ross, we've got a good house, and Lachie and Morag have work.'

'I can't settle in Paisley,' he said impatiently. 'I don't like the place.'

'You'd come to like it if you'd just give it some time.'

'We'd be better somewhere else – anywhere else,' he went on, without heeding her.

'When did you have it in mind to leave?'

'As soon as we can.' It was always 'we', she noticed, and felt her heart begin to thump.

'You're not well enough to travel yet.'

'I'm as well as I'll ever be. It's doing me no good to sit here day after day.' He got up and began to pace the floor, his lithe body jerky with his impatience to be out of the town.

'But Lachie and Morag have work now.'

'They'll find work elsewhere.'

'Ross, will you stop and think –'

'No!' He glared at her, his eyes stormy. 'I'm the man of the family – I decide what we do. And I've decided that we're leaving.'

'Lachie and Morag –'

' – will want to be where I am.'

It was true. The youngsters were overjoyed to have their brother back with them. They would follow him to the ends of the world without question, rather than be left behind.

'And you, Islay, you'll come with us?'

The words were shaped as a question, but a question that didn't need an answer. Ross took it for granted that she, too, would follow where he led.

The moment Islay had dreaded ever since his arrival had come. She stilled the wheel, studied it for a moment, head bent, then looked up at him.

It needed all her courage to say, 'No, Ross. I want to stay here.'

For a moment his jaw sagged in sheer astonishment. Then his mouth snapped shut and immediately opened again to say, 'Of course you'll come with us!'

'I don't want to go wandering again. I've found a home here. I like the folk. I want to stay.'

'I'm your kinsman. I must care for you – and you must do as I wish.'

'I can see to myself well enough.'

His eyes narrowed. 'Is it some man – is that it? Has some Paisley man got a hold of you?'

'Does there need to be a man? Can I not just decide to stay because I'm happy here?'

'But Islay, we'll marry – you and I.'

'No, Ross.'

'Yes! It was always known that we would, even when we were children!'

She twisted her hands together in her lap. 'That was when we thought we'd be living a different life. No doubt we'd have been wed by now, if things had gone on as before. But everything's changed now.'

'I've not changed, and neither have you. Islay –' He came to her, lifted her to her feet, his hands urgent on her. 'All the time I was soldiering, all the time I was making my way here, I had the thought that once I found you again we'd be wed, then we'd always be together – all of us.'

The desperation in his voice shook her to the centre of her soul. She was consumed by pity for him. But pity made poor soil for the long, strong roots of a good marriage.

'It was what our people wanted, Islay –'

'Our people are dead now,' she heard herself say stonily.

'It's what I want!'

'But not what I want. Not now. I can't marry with you, Ross.'

'Islay –' He pulled her roughly into his arms and kissed her. She submitted to his embrace, but when his hands began to fumble at the fastenings of her gown she tried to push him away, realising what his intentions were. Once he had taken her she would be his, with no right to refuse to marry him. 'No!'

'Islay!' He wrapped his arms about her, held her closer so that she was trapped within the circle of his embrace. She hadn't realised that he had gained so much strength. The spinning stool fell over as the two of them struggled silently, Ross intent on winning his own way by force if necessary, Islay determined that he should not.

She was losing ground, being forced step by step towards the wall-bed, when someone rapped at the door.

The sudden unexpected noise tore the cousins apart. They stared at each other, both breathless from the struggle. The angry colour that had flared in Ross's thin face suddenly fled, leaving him white and sick-looking, his eyes bright with terror. 'Who's that?'

'How should I know?' Hurriedly she pulled her gown straight and tucked in hair that had become unloosened from beneath her cap in the struggle, then went to open the door.

Jamie Todd stood outside. 'I'm going along to Maxwellton, Islay. If you've got some pirns ready I'll take them along for you.'

His eyes flickered over her, then beyond, narrowing as they settled on the overturned stool.

'Yes –' She tried to calm her breathing, certain that he must realise what had been going on. 'I'll fetch them for you.'

'Tell the interfering fool to go,' Ross said sulkily in Gaelic. She ignored him, going to where the basket of pirns lay. When she picked it up and turned, she saw that Jamie had stepped into the room and was waiting just inside the door.

Ross looked from the newcomer to Islay, then snatched up his jacket and went out, ducking his head as he passed the Paisley man, slamming the door behind him.

Jamie picked up the fallen stool and put it neatly back in its place. 'Is there something amiss?'

'No.' She held out the basket. For a moment she thought that he was going to persist in his questioning. But instead, to her relief, he took the basket and left.

*

Ross stayed away until it was almost dark and Islay was beginning to worry about him. He returned just in time for the evening meal and ate it in silence, not looking once in her direction. Immediately afterwards he retired to the inner room, where he was sleeping on a mattress supplied by Margaret Knox.

The household was accustomed to bedding early and rising early. Once the meal was over and the dishes cleaned and put away Lachie and Morag went to their beds; Islay, after spinning for a short while by candle-light, took off her blouse and skirt and cap, brushed her hair, then blew out the candle and slipped into the wall bed, falling asleep almost at once.

She was wakened by a draught of cold air as the bedclothes were lifted back.

'Wha –?' The sleepy question was cut short as a hand clamped over her mouth.

The mattress beneath her dipped under the weight of someone climbing into the bed, and Ross's voice hissed in her ear, 'Hold your tongue! D'you want to wake the lassie?'

Then his hand left her mouth as he settled in the bed beside her, his body clamped urgently against hers from shoulder to toes. Morag, always a heavy sleeper, stirred and mumbled something, then settled again.

'Ross! Leave me be, Ross –' She tried to fight off the marauding fingers that tore at the fastenings on her chemise but she was hampered by the blanket that covered her, and by her fear that her young cousin would waken and realise what was going on.

'Be still, will you!' he panted into her ear. There was a soft ripping sound as the material of the chemise gave beneath his strong, determined onslaught, and she felt his chilled hands cup the soft warmth of her breasts.

'No!' She put her own hands against his chest and tried to push him out of the bed, but he was spurred on by lust as well as a grim determination to bend her to his will, and too strong for her. His mouth found hers and claimed it just as his hands were busily claiming her body.

Now he had her half-pinned against the mattress, his thigh thrown across her hips so that she was prevented from moving freely.

Outrage at being used against her will gave way to fear as Islay realised that there was little she could do to stop her cousin, other than to scream at the top of her voice and waken Lachie and Morag. But she couldn't bring herself to rouse the youngsters, no matter what happened to her.

Ross chuckled breathlessly, as though reading her mind. The hem of her shift was dragged to her thighs, then his hand groped between her legs.

It seemed that there was little else to do but to stop struggling and let him have his way with her. But some part of Islay, the part that had kept her alive during the terrible time after the Clearances, refused to let it happen. She whipped her head round on the pillow and sank her teeth into his wrist, just as she had bitten Walter Shaw on the day he had tried to throttle Lachie.

Ross cursed sharply in English, a foul obscenity that had no place in his own language and must have been learned from his companions in the Army, then as Islay's teeth released him he balled his fist and hit her.

A burst of stars flared before her eyes and she struck out with clawed fingers, her nails finding and digging into the flesh of his cheek.

He cursed again and drew away sharply. But he was already on the edge of the bed, and with flailing limbs he fell out, landing on the floor with a bone-jarring thump.

Light as a startled deer, Islay sprang from the mattress, leaping over him and landing on the middle of the floor. Sure-footed even in the dark, she ran the few steps to the range, blessing the instinct for tidiness and order that caused her to put the heavy iron soup ladle away on the same hook each time she used it.

She whirled, moving her hand so that the dim glow from the range gleamed dully on the metal implement she held. 'Get back to your own bed and leave me be, Ross,' she whispered, 'or I'll –'

'Islay?' There was movement from the bed, and Morag sat up. Her voice was peevish and clogged with sleep.

'I – I'm just coming to bed. Go back to sleep, Morag.'

'I heard a noise –'

'I tripped over a stool in the dark.' Islay drew the torn chemise across her breasts, her other hand keeping a tight grip on the ladle. If she had to, she would use it. 'I'll be with you in a minute.'

Mercifully, Ross stayed where he was, out of the girl's sight. Now that her eyes were accustomed to the little light that the range provided Islay could see his eyes glittering at her from the floor like an animal's.

Morag sighed, turned her back on the room, and lay down again, curling into a ball and falling asleep at once.

Islay stepped to where her clothes had been placed over the back of a chair. She put the ladle quietly down on the table and began to dress hurriedly, ready to snatch the improvised weapon up at the first sign of movement.

'What are you doing?' her cousin's voice hissed out of the dark corner by the bed.

'I'm going outside, away from you.'

'You're not going to get the militia?' There was sudden terror in his voice.

'Not this time.' She fastened her skirt, picked up her woollen shawl. 'But if you ever touch me again, Ross McInnes, I will get them! I swear before God that I will!'

His sudden silence assured her that she had managed to cow him. Even so, she picked up the ladle again before letting herself silently out of the door and closing it behind her.

For a while she sat on the wooden stairs, huddled into herself, intending to stay there until morning came. But the cold quickly struck through her clothes. She got up, already stiff with the night chill, but hesitated with her hand on the latch. What if Ross tried again to get into her bed when she was asleep? What if he hadn't gone back to the room he shared with Lachie, but was waiting on the other side of the door, knowing that she must eventually return?

Slowly, she backed away from the door and went down the stairs into the inky black pend, fumbling along the wall until she found the door of the loom shop.

Although the fire had gone out long since the room seemed warm after the night's chill. Islay, afraid to light the candle in case the town watchmen saw the glow in the window and came to investigate, made her way slowly across the room, stumbling against the looms. Then she crouched over the grate, holding her hands close to the grey ashes in a search for the last vestiges of fire.

After a while she drew her shawl tightly about her shoulders and sat down on the saytree of one of the looms. The long narrow bench, made as part of the machine, was polished and shaped by many years of constant use, and comfortable enough.

Islay leaned her elbows on the beam directly before her and pillowed her head on her arms. Her face throbbed where Ross's fist had struck against her cheekbone. She recalled her cousin as he had been in the old days, her childhood companion, her friend, her protector.

In those days she had happily expected to join with Ross in marriage, to share a home with him, to bear his children. But not now, not now that hardship had embittered and warped him and brought him so low that he was prepared to treat her with as much respect as an indifferent farmer would show to the animals beneath his care.

Not now that she had ventured into the world, and had come to know a different life from that of the glens and mountains.

Not now that she had met with Jamie Todd.

The thought of Jamie comforted her. She held him close in her mind until finally, without realising it, she slept.

Chapter Twenty-Three

She wakened early in the morning to the tread of a man's boots on the footpath outside. Startled and confused, she stared for a moment at the angular grey outlines of the looms about her, and put wondering fingers to the side of her face, which felt strangely stiff and clumsy.

Then she winced as pain shot through her cheekbone, and remembered where she was, and why.

Almost crippled with cold, she made her way up to the house, to find everything as it should be – Morag sound asleep in the wall-bed, and no sign of Ross. Moving silently, Islay took her shawl off, put the ladle by the bed, where it was close at hand, and slipped beneath the coverlet fully dressed, trying to draw some warmth from Morag.

Five minutes later, hearing Lachie stir in the next room, she rose and put the ladle back on its accustomed hook, then tidied her hair and began to make his breakfast.

The boy's eyes widened when he saw her. 'What happened to you?'

She looked into the little mirror that hung on the wall, and saw that there was a swelling bruise high on her cheek, just below her left eye. 'I tripped over a stool in the dark last night and fell against the table.'

Lachie accepted the explanation. But later in the loom shop Walter Shaw eyed her sceptically when she gave her story.

'Are you certain?'

'I should know how I hurt my own face!'

'I'd not put it past that cousin of yours to lift his fist to you.'

'He'd never do that!'

Walter scowled and settled himself at his loom, the same loom Islay had pillowed her head on during the night. A change had come over him in the few months since the

Highland family had moved into the dwelling house above. He kept his tongue and his hands off Lachie – although Islay sometimes thought shrewdly that her young cousin wouldn't mind a good fight. Lachie had his elder brother's enthusiasm for the sport; it was an enthusiasm that was inbred in their race, and the reason why Highlanders made formidable and fearless soldiers. But at times such as the times they found themselves in, and in places such as Paisley, the lust for blood was out of place and more of a curse than a virtue.

Walter had become quite considerate towards Islay herself, helping her to carry well-water or pirns if he chanced to come across her in the street. Often, if she was working around the loom shop while the weavers were there, she looked up to see his eyes fixed on her. At first he had ducked his head with quick embarrassment when she met his gaze, but in the past few weeks, since Ross's arrival, he had smiled at her before turning his attention back at his work.

Now, when Islay had set the fire burning to her satisfaction and went out of the room with a bucket of ashes for the midden, Walter left his saytree and caught her at the door. 'I'll carry that for you.'

'It's the lassie's face that's bruised, no' her hands,' one of the other weavers said with a grin, but Walter, cheeks reddening, took the bucket from Islay's fingers and followed her out into the back yard.

The midden was over in the far corner, in an angle of the wall that shaped the back yard. Several times a year, when it grew too large to be manageable, a refuse cart came and took the assorted rubbish away. In the heat of summer the house windows in the town often had to be closed against the stench arising from these domestic middens; when that happened, the refuse carts were called more often than usual.

Walter tossed the ashes onto the heap with less care than Islay would have shown. A fine cloud of pale grey ash lifted into the air and was blown back in their faces by the cool moist breeze, setting the two of them coughing.

Islay briskly swept the worst of it off herself, took the pail

back, and was about to return to the loom shop when he
detained her with one hand on her arm.

'Islay, wait a minute.'

She stopped, her head still turned away from him so that
the bruise on her cheek was hidden. She wanted no more
questions about that – she had trouble enough without the
likes of Walter Shaw causing more.

But he had other things on his mind. 'Will you go walking
with me later, when the work's done?'

Sheer surprise brought her chin up swiftly. 'Walking with
you –?' she started to say, then she saw that a covering of
grey ash had landed on his brown hair and his eyebrows,
turning him prematurely into an old man. The sight was so
funny that she burst out laughing, wincing when the
movement hurt her bruised face.

Walter flushed scarlet under a fine speckling of ash, and
his brows drew together fiercely. 'What's so amusing about
that?' he asked stiffly.

She tried to sober herself. 'Nothing. It's just – oh, Walter,
you've gone grey!' And then she lapsed back into the
comfort of helpless laughter as he put a hand to his head
and brought it away to stare at the grey powder on his
fingers.

Then he looked up at the sky, completely mystified.

'It's the ash from the grate, you daft gommerel! You
threw it onto the midden against the wind. You should have
stood over there, and avoided it,' Islay managed to explain,
between giggles.

Gradually a smile broke over his face, developing into a
broad grin as he ran his hands vigorously through his hair,
surrounding them both with another, smaller cloud of
powder.

'Is that better?'

'Here, bend down –' She whisked a hand over his head,
restoring him to his own youthful colour again. 'That'll do –
but think what you're about next time you throw out the
ashes.'

'I will. You've not answered my question, Islay. Will you
come out walking with me?'

'Why me?'

'Because –' Walter floundered, then said, exasperated, 'Lassies are nae supposed to say that! Just tell me – will you or won't you?'

Something – not a sound, but a sixth sense – made her look up, to where Ross stood on the landing outside the dwelling-house door, watching the two of them. Both his fists gripped the flimsy wooden railing tightly.

Walter hadn't noticed him. 'Islay?'

'It's kind of you to ask, Walter, truly it is. But I – I can't.'

'Can't? What sort of an answer is that?' he began, aggrieved. Then seeing that her attention had left him completely he swivelled about and looked up, too, taking in the sight of Ross. 'Is it because of him?'

'No!' The way men took a refusal to mean that there must be another man in a girl's life infuriated her. 'I just don't want to go walking with you, Walter Shaw!' She thrust the pail back into his hand. 'I've got work to do, even if you haven't. Here – you can put that back by the grate for me.'

Then she walked away from the sight of his hurt expression and went up the stairs, brushing by Ross and stepping into the house, where Morag was up and dressed and preparing the morning meal.

The girl's mouth fell open at the sight of her cousin's swollen cheek.

'I fell against the table in the dark last night,' Islay snapped, forestalling the inevitable question.

Morag said nothing, but as Ross came into the room to sit sullenly at the table, she looked from one to the other, from Islay's bruised cheek to the scratches on Ross's gaunt white face, and for a moment her own small features held a knowing expression that was far older than her years.

*

Islay kept the kitchen knife close by her after that, leaving it on the table while she worked about the house, or sat at her spinning, and putting it beneath her pillow at nights. But Ross never again tried to lay a finger on her.

But the incident couldn't be forgotten. The air in the little house seemed to vibrate with Ross's smouldering anger and Islay's apprehension. She scarcely slept, and only toyed with her food. She stayed indoors as much as she could, sending Lachie and Morag out with the pirns, and rose early to make certain that her work in the loom shop each morning was over long before the weavers arrived, so that she didn't have to face Walter's resentment.

It was a relief when Ross told his brother and sister after supper a few nights later that they were about to leave the town.

Islay had thought that the youngsters might resent being uprooted as much as she herself did. But the two of them glowed at the prospect of being with Ross.

'Lachie, it means giving up your place as drawboy,' she said, and Ross shot an angry glance across the table at her, the fading red marks of her fingernails suddenly standing out against his skin like whip-lashes.

'He'll find other work. Paisley's not the only place in the world.'

'You'll come with us, Islay?' Morag asked, her eyes darkening with apprehension.

'If she's got any loyalty to the dead she will,' said Ross.

Islay swallowed hard and looked at the two children who had been her care and her support during the long lonely months of exile. 'I must stay here.'

This time the glance Ross shot at her was positively malevolent. Then he spread out his arms so that he embraced Morag on one side, and Lachie on the other. 'So it'll be just the three of us.'

'The three of us,' Lachie said enthusiastically, face alight at the thought of fresh adventures. Morag took a moment to ponder, then nodded slowly, her choice made.

'The three of us, Ross.'

But that night in bed, she snuggled up to Islay and put her thin arms about her neck. 'Please come with us.'

'I can't.'

Morag raised herself on one elbow, her face a pale glimmer, her soft straight hair tickling Islay's cheek. 'Is it because of Ross?'

'What makes you say that?'

There was a silence, then, 'I don't know,' said Morag, and lay down again with a sigh. After a moment her moth-wing whisper said in the darkness, 'I had a sort of dream – about you and Ross. It frighted me.'

'It was only a dream.'

'When I woke up you had a sore face, and so had he. Dreams can't do that, can they?'

'I told you – I fell against the table. Go to sleep, Morag.'

'He's kind, underneath,' Ross's sister said. 'And he wants you to come with us, Islay. I know he does.

Islay said nothing, and after a while she heard her cousin's breathing deepen and slow.

She put a hand beneath the pillow and felt the hard smooth knife handle against her fingers. Then she, too, fell asleep, comforted by the proximity of Morag's body.

Chapter Twenty-Four

Ross spent the next few days away from home, reappearing on the Saturday afternoon, just when Islay had begun to wonder if he was ever coming back.

He took Lachie and Morag away very early the next morning, loading their possessions onto a cart that arrived, apparently by prior arrangement, while the town was still asleep.

Islay, roused from her bed to make a meal for them before they left and prepare some food for the journey, hugged Morag tightly when the girl was ready for the journey.

'You'll take care, now, and not let the damp air get to your lungs?'

Morag, bright-eyed and pink-cheeked with excitement, and healthier than she had ever been since the days when they were thrust from their Highland homes, nodded vigorously. 'Don't worry about me, Islay. I'll be fine.'

'You'll look after her? She shouldn't sleep out in the open in weather like this.' Islay turned to Ross, who was impatient to be away.

'D'you think I'd neglect my own blood kin? There's folk I know along the way – houses where we can find shelter at nights until we get to our destination.' Then he said swiftly, urgently, 'Come with me, Islay. I need you by my side.'

For a moment the true Ross, the Ross she had trusted and loved, the Ross she had been ready and willing to marry, looked out of the pale thin face at her. For a moment, Islay wavered before she drew back, shaking her head. 'No, Ross. My destiny lies here, whatever it may be.'

His eyes turned to clear glass in an instant. 'Then may you rot along with the rest of this God-forsaken town,' he said with soft menace, and turned away, leaving her without another glance.

*

When the cart had rattled off into the gloom and she was alone again, Islay went back upstairs and surveyed the empty, silent house.

Then she rolled her sleeves up and began to give the place a thorough cleaning, unable to bear the prospect of sitting down and letting her thoughts take over.

Several times during the day she almost put her shawl on and went along to tell Jamie Todd that he had lost one of his drawboys. But, grieving as she was over the loss of the only family that was left to her, she couldn't face his anger. So she did nothing, and left the matter lying until the morrow.

The loom shop was scoured and the fire set very early on Monday morning. After that, Islay set off on Lachie's duties, tramping the streets in the cold grey dawn, hammering at doors until a sleepy, querulous voice from the other side of the panels or from an upper window assured her that the weaver was awake and about to get ready for his day's labours.

On her way back to the house she stopped a small boy who was out early on an errand of his own and gave him some money to take a message to Jamie Todd. Then she went home, made some food, forced herself to eat it, and sat down at her spinning wheel.

*

She had to wait almost until noon before he came tramping up the stairs and thundered his fist against the door. By that time she was in such a state of nervous anticipation that she couldn't trust herself to walk across the short space of floor between her stool and the door.

So she called out, 'It's on the latch –' and kept working as the door was thrust open and Jamie erupted into the room.

'What's this I hear? Is it true?'

'If you mean Lachie going off with Ross – aye, it is.'

'Without so much as a word? And me left without a drawboy? This is what comes,' said Jamie wrathfully, 'of putting my trust in Highlanders!'

She tried to speak, but couldn't. Instead, she slowed and stopped her wheel, and sat with bowed head, letting him spill out his justified anger on her.

'Oh, I was well warned at the time. You can't put faith in them, some said. They'll use you and leave when it suits them, others said. But daft fool that I am, I gave the laddie his chance, and emptied my store rooms so that the pack of you would have a place to live – and what's my reward? Eh?' he thundered as she still said nothing. Then he asked, with a sudden change of tone. 'Why aren't you with them?'

'I – I chose to stay.'

He stopped his pacing and stood before her, feet planted firmly on the floor. 'Speak up, lassie! I cannae hear a word when you mutter at the floor like that!'

She drew a deep ragged breath and lifted her face to meet his. 'I said – I chose to stay.'

He was no longer listening to her.

'In Heaven's name!' He grasped her shoulders, lifting her from her seat, making her stand before him. One hand took her by the chin and tilted her face to the light. She stood mute beneath his hands, although her heart fluttered at his touch.

'Who did this?'

'I fell against the table in the dark.' She had said it so often that she had begun to convince herself.

But Jamie Todd took more convincing than most.

'You fell against that scoundrel Ross McInnes's fist, more like. Is the rascal coming back? Because if he is I'll have a few words to say –'

'He's not coming back. None of them are coming back.'

'Then why did you not go with them?' he asked puzzled.

'I want to stay here.' Islay said, and felt her throat suddenly tighten. She closed her eyes against Jamie's look, but two tears, determined not to be held back, forced themselves beneath the lids and slid down her cheeks. All she wanted to do at that moment was to rest her head on his broad chest and know that at last she had found a home.

Someone walked in at the open door. Jamie's hands fell away from Islay, and she whirled, convinced for a panic-stricken moment that Ross had come back and that he and Jamie would have a confrontation there and then. But the newcomer was Margaret Knox.

The surgeon's wife took one look at Islay's tear-wet face and said crisply, 'Jamie Todd, what have you been doing to the lassie?'

'Me? It's not me that did this, that's for sure!'

He tried to take hold of Islay's face again and turn it to the light. She pulled away from his grasp as Margaret said, 'For goodness' sake – that's not a horse you're trying to harness, it's a lassie! Have some care!' Then, as her eyes fell on the large fading bruise, she went on, 'Mercy me! Was it Ross?'

'It was,' Jamie did the answering. 'And now the ne'er-do-weel's fled the town. I knew from the moment I saw him that he'd cause nothing but trouble. I'll not weep tears over his going, I can tell you.'

'What about the bairns?'

'Gone along with him, without a word of warning – and left me missing a drawboy, confound them!'

Islay dried her eyes on her apron and faced up to him. 'I'm sorry, Mister Todd, for what Lachie did. I'll move my things out of the house as soon as I can.'

'Eh?'

'Well, Jamie? Isn't that what you wanted – to get rid of the lot of them and get your nice store-room back?' Margaret asked with sarcastic sweetness.

'Of course it's not what I want!'

'Then why go on at the girl? It's not her fault if her kinfolk have left town without telling you. Does it mean nothing to you that she's shown her own gratitude by staying on – and taking the rough edge of your tongue into the bargain?'

A wave of crimson swept over the weaver's rugged face. He looked helplessly at Islay, then said, awkwardly, 'Lassie, I'd no intention of punishing you for your cousin's misdeeds. From the look of you, you've had punishment enough.'

'Just so. Now off you go and find yourself a new drawboy,' Margaret instructed him. 'I'll see what I can do to help Islay.'

When he had left them she said, 'Well now, Islay – what's to be done about you? Would you like me to make enquiries as to suitable employment in the town? My aunt, Mistress MacLeod, might be interested in taking on a new companion. I know she misses Beth sorely.'

'Thank you, but I'll manage fine between my work in the loom shop and my spinning wheel. There's only me to feed and clothe now, so I'll not need much.'

Margaret's eyebrows rose. 'You mean you're staying on here? I thought after the way Jamie behaved you'd want to get out of his way altogether and find somewhere else to live.'

Islay shook her head. 'Oh no,' she said. 'I've done with moving on and trying to make a new life for myself. I'm staying.'

Chapter Twenty-Five

Gavin Knox stayed in Dumfries for longer than he had originally planned. As February passed by and gave way to March Margaret missed him more and more. But her pride wouldn't allow her to admit that, to Gavin or to anyone else.

So she wrote formal little letters giving him news of the household and the town, and received equally formal little letters which, like hers, gave no indication whatever as to his true thoughts and feelings.

'He seems to be quite content, working with his old friend,' she said to Richard.

'Gavin was always a single-minded man,' his brother said easily from where he sprawled in Gavin's favourite chair. Today he was dressed in a sky-blue coat that contrasted with the dark winter clothes worn by the Paisley men. Richard, who had spent so many years in a warm climate, seemed quite impervious to the cold.

'He seems to be too preoccupied to think of returning home.' Margaret kept her voice light and brisk. 'As to that, I'm so busy myself that I've scarce noticed the time passing. I was thinking of asking Islay McInnes if she'd take on the task of visiting the inkle loom shop each day. I've more than enough to do with the school-room and this house to run.'

'Islay –?' He repeated the name thoughtfully. 'Is that not the pretty little girl who lives above Jamie Todd's weaving shop?'

'Yes. She's reliable, and sensible – and she could do with the extra money, I'm sure of that.'

He shrugged. 'Whatever you decide.'

'I'll call in on her the next time I'm at Wellmeadow – or mebbe I'll send word to her to come up here, then we can make a social visit of it.'

Richard got to his feet. 'I'm going to Wellmeadow myself

today. I'll ask her to call on you.'

'I'd be grateful. Are things going well with the new cotton cloth?'

He smiled down on her. 'Oh yes,' he said. 'Very well indeed.'

*

'It's an unlikely friendship, but it seems to be firm, for all that,' Richard said a few weeks later in Mary MacLeod's parlour.

'What makes you call it unlikely?'

He shrugged. 'Margaret's well-to-do, married to a surgeon. Islay McInnes is a nobody, rescued from a pauper's life.'

Mary gave an unladylike snort. She and Gavin's brother had become fast friends. Mary loved Richard's worldliness; Richard appreciated the older woman's honesty and knife-sharp wit.

'My dear man, you've got a lot to learn! Margaret's from common stock the same as Islay, or me – or you, if it comes to it. Oh, I'll grant you that your father was mebbe more of a gentleman than mine, but that makes no odds in Paisley. It's what you are that counts, not who birthed you.'

'Indeed, ma'am?'

'Aye – indeed, sir,' said Mary firmly, refusing to let his amused bating divert her. 'Of course Margaret and Islay have become friends – they're much alike, these two. They're both strong-minded and independent – and they're both lonely. Margaret because that man of hers seems set on staying away for as long as he can, first in Dumfries, and now in Edinburgh,' said Mary, a worried furrow appearing between her brows for a moment, 'and Islay because some pompous jumped-up nobody of a landlord in the Highlands knows no more than to treat folk like insects. I'm glad the lassie's found a good friend in Margaret.'

'Mmm.' Thoughtfully, Richard took a sip of the excellent rum he had presented to Mary. A bottle was kept in the corner cupboard specially for his visits. His hostess watched with indulgent approval as he rose and refilled his glass with the air of a man who felt completely at home.

'You know, a parlour's always the better of a man's presence. Thomas comes to visit me now and again, but like Gavin, he's too busy with his physicking and his visiting to call more than once a week.'

'You should marry again.'

'Oh – tush! I said I like to see a man in my parlour now and again. I didnae say that I'd care to have one around for all the hours in the day and night, getting under my feet and wanting to rule the roost,' she retorted. 'No, no, laddie, I'm happy enough as I am. But you could do worse than take your own advice. It's high time you found yourself a wife and settled down.'

Richard laughed. 'I manage very well as I am. I'm more interested in making money than in marriage.'

'Have you not made enough of that to do you?'

He lifted the glass, studied the colour of the liquid within it with satisfaction. 'I'll never make enough.'

'D'you say so? I hear the first of your new cloth's off the loom now.'

'Aye, the first shipment goes out in April. Jamie Todd made the right decision when he agreed to weave my yarn. He'll not regret it.'

'It's to be hoped not, for he's lost two good friends through it.'

'There's no quarrel between Jamie and the Montgomerys, surely? None that I'd heard of.'

'No quarrel, but a coolness. Duncan and Robert'll never forgive him for breaking away from them.'

Again, Mary's brow was furrowed for a moment, but Richard's eyes were clear and untroubled as they met hers.

'They had no contract. And I've as much time for loyalty as I have for marriage. Unless, of course, the loyalty's being shown to me.'

'Sometimes,' she said, looking at him with a mixture of affection and irritation, 'you make me think of a spider, Richard Knox. Europe and Jamaica and the Americas and Paisley, all woven into a web of your making. Tell me, have you ever had anything to do with slave-trading?'

'You think I'd stoop to that?'

'Of course I do. You're ruthless enough – and moneyed enough.'

'And you're a clever woman, Mary MacLeod.' He lifted his glass to her in laughing salute, then drained the last drop and put the empty glass on a table. 'Speaking of Jamie, I must go down to his loom shop now.'

Mary got up, moving a little stiffly and muttering a swift curse at the rheumatism that had caught her in its grasp that winter, for the first time. As she came to stand beside him a movement outside took her eye.

A slim, cloaked figure hurried along the footpath beyond Mary's small front garden, head bent against the March wind that swept down the length of the road.

'Islay McInnes,' Mary said. 'She'll be calling on Margaret, I expect.'

Richard picked up his tricorne hat. 'I think I might call on Margaret myself.'

'I thought you'd to go down the hill to see Jamie?'

'Eventually. I could escort Islay back down into the town. She's a bonny girl, is she not?'

'I'm surprised to hear you say so, her being a nobody.'

'But as you reminded me yourself, I'm from common stock too. There's no harm in friendship between commoners – is there?'

Mary surveyed him shrewdly, and he returned look for look. Finally she shook her head.

'There's no besting you, is there, Richard? Whiles I wonder why you've lingered so long in a dull town like Paisley.'

'You know why. I'm here on a matter of business.'

'It seems to me,' said Mary shrewdly, 'that you're here on a matter of mischief.'

Chapter Twenty-Six

It was late April before Gavin Knox finally returned home from his travels.

During the long weeks and months of his time away from her Margaret had pictured his homecoming over and over again. His favourite meal would be on the table, she herself would wear a new, becoming dress

She would go into his arms immediately, without allowing either of them time to set up barriers. She would, if she had to, tell him how sorry she was that there had ever been misunderstanding between them.

For some time now she had been patiently working on Daniel, talking to him about Gavin, reminding him of his love for his father. Now she was certain – well, almost certain – that the little boy had overcome the fear Gavin had instilled in him with his surgeon's knife.

But Fate tended to turn sullen when mere mortals tried to plan their own destinies. Instead of letting her know when he was coming home Gavin arrived unexpectedly, walking into the house one evening when Margaret was presiding over a dinner party made up of her parents, her Aunt Mary, her brothers Thomas and Robert, Robert's wife Annie, Kirsty and Billy Carmichael, Kate – returned to her usual slender beauty since her baby son had been safely delivered – Kate's husband Archie, Islay McInnes, Jamie Todd and Richard.

The gathering had been planned by Margaret and Mary, and was an attempt to reconcile Jamie, Duncan and Robert. It hadn't entirely worked, Margaret thought as the meal came to its close, for the three men had had very little to say for themselves, and had tended to avoid each other's eyes.

The other guests, however, were in light-hearted mood, particularly Richard and Mary.

When the door opened Margaret, seated at the head of the table, looked up, expecting to see Ellen marching in to chase them all into the parlour so that she could clear the plates away.

Instead, the doorway was filled by a tall, familiar figure, clothes rumpled by hours of travel, face pale with fatigue, hazel eyes darting with quick surprise round the crowded table – then cooling as they landed on Richard.

'Gavin!'

Everyone turned and gaped. Margaret, remembering her plans for his homecoming, ran round the table to him, her arms outstretched. That, at least, she could do. But he forestalled her, catching her hands in his before she could embrace him, bending to drop a light, chilly kiss on her forehead.

'Margaret. It seems that I've come home at a difficult time for you.'

'Of course you haven't!' She retained his hands, drawing him into the room, talking and talking in an attempt to cover up his coldness. 'It only means that we're all here to welcome you. Have you had any food?'

'Not since noon.'

'I'll fetch Ellen at once – I'm sure there'll be enough left. You should have let me know that you were coming –'

Thomas was on his feet, coming forward with hand outstretched and a broad welcoming grin on his round face. Mary followed, stretching up on tiptoe to kiss Gavin's cheek, and one by one the others followed, clamouring round him, drawing him back into the fold.

Faced with so much open affection Gavin began to thaw – until at last Richard got to his feet and came forward. 'Well, brother – you've become almost as travelled as I am.'

Gavin's face closed again, and he barely touched the hand his brother offered. 'Scarcely, Richard,' he said, and turned to Margaret, presenting his broad back to Richard. 'I'll eat in the kitchen, and join you all in the parlour presently, when I've had time to change my clothes. Where are the children?'

'In bed and asleep. You'll see them in the morning.'

His face was suddenly hungry with love – a hunger that she had hoped to see when his eyes first fell on her,

Margaret thought bleakly. 'I can't wait until tomorrow. I'll go up to them now.'

Before she could stop him he had turned on his heel and left the room. Panic seized her. If Daniel was to wake suddenly from sleep and see his father without benefit of the careful preparations she had planned –

'Mother, take everyone into the parlour. I'll see to Gavin and join you all there –'

She sped from the room, almost bumping into Ellen in the hallway.

'The master's home – put out food for him in the kitchen at once.'

'But there's little left. That lot ate everything I prepared.'

'Find something!' Margaret gathered up her skirts and ran up the stairs. By the time she reached the children's room he was there, candle in hand. Christian, with some sort of sixth sense, opened her eyes at once, leaping from sleep to wakefulness in one easy bound, and shot upright in bed, with a gleeful scream of, 'Father! It's Father!'

Daniel's small body gave a convulsive leap as he was startled out of a deep sleep. He, too, sat bolt upright, eyes staring, just as Gavin, dimly-seen in the flickering candle-light, bent over his bed, stooping down to embrace him and kiss him.

With a shrill animal-like scream of terror Daniel threw himself away from what he saw as a monstrous attacker. Caught up in the bed-coverings, he struggled in total panic, and rolled right off the other side of his narrow bed, landing on the floor with a thump.

Margaret reached him first, scooping him up, holding him tightly.

'It's all right, Daniel, you're all right!'

Recognising her voice, the little boy clutched at her and buried his face in her neck, his body trembling violently.

Christian, still whooping, 'It's Father, it's Father!' shot from her own bed to wrap her arms about Gavin's legs. He stroked her hair, his eyes fixed on his wife and son.

Margaret, half-strangled, looking at Gavin over Daniel's silky head, felt her heart sink as she saw the bewilderment and anger in his eyes.

The home-coming she had prayed for and planned so carefully had become a shambles. And Gavin's absence, it seemed, had done nothing to resolve the troubles that still threatened their future together.

*

When Gavin had put on fresh clean clothes and eaten in the kitchen he joined his wife and their guests in the parlour.

Thomas immediately drew him aside and started asking him about his work in Dumfries and Edinburgh. Margaret, glancing over at the two of them now and again, saw that Gavin was talking cheerfully, though every so often he would shoot a sidelong glance of pure dislike at Richard, who seemed quite unaware of it.

Gavin looked drawn and tired, she thought with compassion. Mary, insisting that she had come to enjoy herself, not listen to physicians talking about death and disease, tried to draw him into the general conversation. But once he and Thomas had been separated Gavin lapsed into silence, staring at the floor, giving brusque answers to any questions that were put to him.

He only became animated again when Kate asked him outright if he would go to Barrhead and vaccinate her children against the smallpox. Gavin agreed swiftly, casting a look of thinly veiled triumph at his wife.

Margaret was relieved when Kirsty and Billy rose to go, and started a general exodus. Richard went off into the hall, and came back with Islay's cloak. He tucked it carefully about her shoulders.

'I'll see you safely home.'

The girl flushed becomingly. 'But it would take you out of your way –'

'In that case I think I'll just take the evening air before I go back to my lodgings,' he said with an attractive, half-mocking and half serious smile, 'Will you grant me the pleasure of your company along the road, Mistress Islay?'

She laughed, and nodded.

Gavin stood beside Margaret at the front door, bidding their guests a courteous good night. When the last had gone and she was closing the door he left her side.

She went into the parlour to find him already there, pouring some whisky into a glass. Then he took up his favourite stance by the fire and said without wasting time on formalities, 'I thought I made it clear that my brother is not welcome beneath my roof?'

'While you're away from home the domestic responsibilities fall on my shoulders. This time you were gone for so long that I confess I'd begun to think of it as my roof – or, at least, ours.'

'Nevertheless –'

'I shall not invite Richard here when you're in residence, Gavin. But when you're away from home I shall do as I think fit.' Then she added, as his face tightened dangerously, 'Richard is my business partner, after all. I must offer him some hospitality when I'm in the position to do so.'

'Ah, yes, the inkle looms. How are they coming along?'

'Very well.'

'No doubt you'll soon be in a position to become completely independent. How gratifying that will be for you – and for Richard.'

'Gavin, I cannot understand why you bear such malice towards the man!'

'You know very well that he was responsible for my mother's death.'

'He didn't strike her down with his own hand. And you were away from home when she died, from what I heard. I fail to see how you can lay her death at his door with such confidence.'

'My mother,' said Gavin slowly and clearly, 'was a gentle woman, with no interest or concern in her life but her home and her husband and Richard – and myself.'

The final two words, Margaret noticed, were added on as an afterthought. He seemed to read her thoughts.

'She lost two children in early infancy after I was born, so naturally Richard was especially dear to her. He was a pretty child, with an endearing manner, whereas I was perhaps too solemn and serious. My mother worshipped him, but unfortunately Richard had a tendency to fall into every sort of mischief a small boy could find. As he grew, the mischief became more serious. He was – the cause of trouble among neighbours and friends on more than one occasion, and my parents were grievously upset when this happened.'

He drained his glass, and stared down at the final golden dregs. 'I did my best to talk to Richard, to reason with him, but it did no good. Finally, when I was in my first year at University, he – fathered a child on a young girl, the ward of my father's best friend. They weren't much more than children themselves, but even so, the girl was more than willing to marry my brother, and her guardian and my parents would have approved of the match.'

'But Richard didn't want it?'

'He didn't want it,' Gavin agreed. 'And it's not in Richard's nature to do anything against his own wishes. He ran away, and that was the last my parents ever heard of him.'

'So he has a child in Dumfries?'

'I've no doubt that he has at least one child somewhere in the world,' said Gavin dryly. 'But none in Dumfries. The girl died in childbirth, and her baby with her. Fortunately my mother never knew of that final tragedy, for she began to decline from the day he left. She passed away within a few months, still hoping to her last breath that she would hear from Richard. My father died not long after that. From heart trouble, his physician said. But I suspect that his heart stopped from shame.'

There was a long silence before he spoke again, with a bite in his voice. 'Now you know why I'll have nothing to do with him, and why I would prefer you to have nothing to do with him.'

'It's not a pretty story. I'll grant you – but Richard is still my business partner, and Jamie's. Even if I wished to have no more to do with him, it's not possible.'

'I see. I'll bid you good night, Margaret, for I must go to Glasgow tomorrow and it's getting late.'

'Gavin,' she said as he put his empty glass down and moved towards the door, 'why did you stay away for so long?'

He stopped, but didn't turn to look at her. 'There was a lot to be done, in Dumfries and then, as fortune would have it, in Edinburgh. I was needed.'

She got to her feet. 'And you thought that there was no need of you here?'

When he turned to her his eyes were hazel pools, so deep that she couldn't read them. 'You were always too independent to have need of any one person, Margaret. And it seems that your independence is growing, and therefore your need is diminishing.'

'I do need you.'

Gavin raised one eyebrow mockingly. 'Prove it, my dear,' he said. 'Give up the Poors' Hospital, give up the inkle looms.'

'I can't. I won't.'

'You see?' He inclined his head slightly. 'Good night.'

When she followed him upstairs some ten minutes later he seemed to be asleep. She moved around the bed-chamber quietly so as not to disturb him. Each time she glanced at the bed, his dark lashes were peaceful on his cheeks, his breathing unchanged.

She blew out the candle and slid between the sheets. His hand, strong and sure, closed about her shoulder, turning her to face him. His lips sought and found hers in the darkness.

He made love to her with stormy insensitive hunger, and she responded with a need and passion as strong as his.

Finally, sated and exhausted, they fell away from each other and slept in the tangled, dishevelled battleground of their marriage bed.

Margaret woke in the morning to find Gavin dressing swiftly.

'What time is it?

'Early. No need for you to rise yet.'

She lifted herself on one elbow. The sheets fell back from the upper half of her body and she saw him throw one burning glance at her breasts, naked as he had left them in the night, before he turned away. 'Gavin, must you go to the wards today?'

'Yes,' he said, and went out without looking back.

Chapter Twenty-Seven

Although Islay was living alone for the first time in her life there was little danger of her feeling lonely.

Her work in the loom shop and the house, together with the hours she put in at her spinning wheel each day, took up most of her time.

In addition, she crossed the bridge every afternoon to visit Margaret Knox's loom shop in the New Town, checking that the inkle looms were all in operation and that there was a good supply of yarn for them.

More yarn had to be ordered if it was needed, and she had to keep a tally of the amount of ribbon that was being woven.

She also paid a daily visit to the two inkle looms that were still housed across the passage from Jamie's High Street loom shop. Sometimes, especially if she had to order more yarn, she saw Jamie himself. But never for long. The red-headed weaver seemed to become more and more abrupt with her, and more incomprehensible.

Now that spring had arrived there was the garden to tend to as well as her other duties. She had expected that Ross would have been there to help her with the digging and the planting, but now there was nobody but herself to see to it.

Quite often, when the loom shop finished early for the day and Islay was working in the garden, Walter came through the pend to help her. He was a strong willing worker, and with his help she gradually gained control of the whole area.

Afterwards, she gave him ale and home-made oatcakes in her kitchen.

Jamie had never again worked alongside her as he had done that day in the autumn, although once or twice when she was away from the house in the lengthening evenings she came back to find a stretch of earth that had been waiting for the spade neatly turned over and ready for planting, or some weeding done.

When she asked Walter outright if he had done it the young man shook his head firmly. 'Not when you weren't there – there'd be no pleasure in that. I'd have to be daft to do the digging then.'

One day he plucked up the courage to ask her along to his house to take tea with his mother, a thin, over-worked woman with far too many children and little liking, Islay soon realised, for Highlanders.

Sometimes she and Walter walked out along the river bank, or over the moors – Islay's favourite walk because it reminded her a little of home.

And, of course, there was Richard Knox. He had taken to calling at the house if he happened to be at the Wellmeadow loom shop on business, sitting for a while in the pleasant warm kitchen, talking on and on as Islay worked at her wheel.

He was amusing and charming, she realised as her initial shyness wore off. He knew how to put folk at their ease, and he always treated her with courtesy.

Summer arrived unheralded and unexpectedly at the end of April. Islay woke to a soft quiet dawn that seemed to hold the promise of a warm fresh day out to her in cupped hands. She sang as she worked about the looms and the linnets, newly freed from their shrouding night-cloth, chirruped in answer.

The housework done, she went down to the yard and, for want of bushes to dry her washing on, stretched a piece of rope between the house wall and the wall at the back of the yard. Then she dragged out the fair-sized wooden tub she had found during earlier explorations in the ramshackle shed, and scrubbed it out.

It took some time to heat enough water for the tub, and several trips up and down the stairs, lugging the heavy big kettle.

But at last the tub was ready, and Islay knew great satisfaction as she deposited the last armful of washing into it and stripped off her stockings before hoisting her skirt and high-stepping in on top of the blankets.

As she worked her way round and round the tub, treading the washing down vigorously so that the winter's grime was forced out, warm water bubbled up between her toes. A cool breeze lapped pleasantly round her bare legs.

Treading blankets on a warm sunny day was one of the most pleasant occupations Islay could think of, and she sang as she worked, treading to a song she had learned from her mother as a small child.

Her singing came to a sudden stop when she revolved to face the pend and saw that Richard Knox, hat in hand, was standing on the rough flagstones watching her, a broad grin on his handsome face.

'Oh –' She stood facing him, confused and embarrassed, suddenly aware of her bare legs but unable to drop her skirts because then their hems would land in the water.

'A very pretty sight, Mistress Islay.' He bowed, then came forward. 'And a pleasant way of spending a warm afternoon. I'm tempted to join you.'

'I doubt if there would be room, Richard,' Jamie Todd said curtly, stepping from the shade of the pend. 'Islay, have you nothing better to do with your time than disport yourself in this fashion?'

He looked from Richard to Islay, taking in her kilted skirts, her flushed face framed by silky black hair that had loosened itself from the knot she had pinned on the top of her head before she set to work.

His eyes, she noted miserably, were a deep cold blue, with none of their usual sparkle. For a moment she quailed before those eyes, then she rallied, fingers gripping her skirt tightly.

'I'm only washing the blankets, Mister Todd. Would you have me leave them as they are, after a winter's use?'

'Of course he wouldn't – and nor would I,' said Richard smoothly.

'Surely they're done by now. You've been in that tub for near enough half an hour!'

Richard raised an amused brow. 'You've been keeping time, Jamie?'

The weaver's face flamed, and he took a step forward, holding out a hand. 'Come on out.'

Richard, too, held out his hand. Islay, unable to take both hands because it would mean letting her skirts dip into the water, hesitated, looking from one man to the other, wishing that she had never decided to wash the dratted blankets.

She was saved by the clatter of feet in the pend. Thomas Montgomery burst from its shadow.

'There you are, Islay – I've need of your help.'

'What's amiss?' It was Jamie who asked the question. But Thomas's eyes were on Richard as he gave the answer.

'It's Gavin. He's down with the pox. He fell sick in hospital in Glasgow yesterday.'

They stared at each other, sick at heart. It was Richard who spoke first. 'At least he's in the best place.'

'He was,' Thomas agreed grimly, 'before Margaret insisted on fetching him home.'

Richard's face paled. 'In the name of God, why? What about herself, and the children? What about the rest of the folk in the town?'

'As to that, nobody can go in or out of the house until the matter's resolved one way or the other,' Thomas said rapidly. 'The children and Ellen are with Aunt Mary. Margaret refuses to give a thought to her own safety. She's alone in the house with him, and determined to stay until –'

He broke off, then said directly to Islay this time, 'She can't nurse him all on her own. You've been protected against the pox. I thought you might help her.'

She was already scrambling from the tub unaided, heedless of how much slender bare leg she showed in the process. 'I'll go at once.'

'No!' Jamie said violently as she brushed past him to sit on the bottom step so that she could dry her feet and legs. 'No, I'll not allow it, Thomas. The lassie might sicken.'

'She's been vaccinated.'

'When she was a child! Who's to know if she's still protected? Islay –'

She finished drying her feet and began to draw her stockings on, aware with some part of her that Richard, for all his shocked silence, was watching her, and yet not caring about his gaze. 'I must go to Oakshawhill, Jamie.'

'I'll not allow it!'

'You've no right to stop me.' She finished putting on the second stocking and nodded to Thomas. 'I'll just fetch some things and close the range down. I'll not be a minute.'

When she came back down Richard had gone. Thomas and Jamie waited for her at the pend opening.

The weaver put a hand on her arm as she brushed past him. 'Islay, what if you fall sick?'

She looked up at him. 'There's nobody to care if I live or die now.'

'I'll not allow it!'

'What's amiss with you, man?' Thomas asked in angry amazement. 'You don't own the lassie – Margaret and Gavin need her help, and she's free to do as she pleases!'

Jamie's white teeth bit into his lower lip. the detaining hand fell from Islay's arm, and let her go.

Hurrying up the hill by Thomas's side, she realised that once again, in a moment of stress, she had used Jamie's Christian name.

And once again it had lain naturally on her tongue, as though it belonged there.

Chapter Twenty-Eight

On the night before summer came to Paisley Margaret had dreamed of the road that stretched from Glasgow.

Along that road, in her dream, came the smallpox in the form of a malevolent, horribly disfigured old man riding a black cart, whipping a black horse on in its mad gallop towards Paisley, getting nearer with every swift turn of the flaying hooves and iron-bound wheels.

She woke to the echoes of her own muffled scream. The room was in darkness, her body was damp with sweat, her heart hammering. She was alone, for Gavin had stayed in Glasgow for the past few days, with not enough time to come home at night.

Small-pox was rife in the area where his hospital stood, Margaret already knew that; but he and his colleagues had hopes of containing it.

It hadn't, as yet, reached as far as Paisley. The wizened, hideous old man in Margaret's dream hadn't galloped his black horse and cart along the road, between fields and hedges sprouting the summer's fresh green growth. But there was still time, she thought, collapsing back onto her pillows. It could still happen.

And despite what Gavin and Thomas had told her over and over again, despite the fact that Kate and Archie had had enough trust in the new method of vaccination to have it done to their older, surviving child, and would have it done to the new baby whenever Gavin considered the boy old enough to undergo the knife, Margaret feared for her own children. She got up, moving sure-footed in the dark, and crept into the next room, listening to their soft, even breathing.

Then she returned to bed, praying that the white puckered patch of skin on their chubby upper arms, the only reminder of the day Gavin had taken the knife to them, and had in doing so cut the bond between himself and Margaret, might after all turn out to be some sort of magic charm to keep Christian and Daniel safe.

The next morning the dream was forgotten – until mid-morning, when Thomas arrived at the Poors' Hospital in search of her, his face grim and haggard.

Margaret, in consultation with the Master and Mistress, emerged from the small office as her brother strode through the big front door.

'Margaret – I went to the house and Ellen said I might find you here –'

'What is it?' But she already knew; something had whispered a name to her as soon as she saw her brother's ashen face. 'It's Gavin, isn't it? He's been hurt – an accident –'

'No!' Thomas looked about the big bleak entrance hall, where some of the residents lingered, eyeing them inquisitively. 'There's been no accident. Is there not some private place where we can talk together?'

'The g – garden – ' Her lips were numbed, stumbling clumsily over the words. He cupped a hand round her elbow and they went swiftly down the corridor that led to the kitchens and the back door.

The walled garden at the rear of the Poors' Hospital was meant for vegetable beds only, so that kale and potatoes could be grown cheaply to help to feed the inmates. But a former master with imagination and a firm belief that even paupers could benefit from colour and beauty had managed to set aside a small corner for a few rose bushes and clumps of pansies and carnations.

Some men and youths were digging the kale beds; they paused for a moment in their work and looked at the man and woman who passed them and went towards the flower-beds, then returned to their task, leaving Thomas and Margaret in peace.

'Tell me!' she insisted, ready to take him by the shoulders and shake the news out of him. But when he did tell her, she would have given all she had in the world, all she held dear, except Gavin and Christian and Daniel, not to know.

'It's the pox, Margaret.'

There was a strange sound in her ears, as though she was standing down at the Cross, near where the river thundered over the small weir called the Hammills.

But she wasn't at the river, she was in the walled garden of the Poors' Hospital, and the flowers near her feet were undisturbed by any wind.

She realised, as Thomas gripped her shoulders and sat her down on a bench, and she saw his lips moving and knew he was speaking, that the noise was within her own head.

With that realisation it ebbed and died, and she could hear her brother's voice again.

'I got word last night to go up to Glasgow, to the infirmary,' he was saying. 'I've been with him all night. He asked me to tell you why – why he can't come home.'

'You saw him? Is it bad?' She remembered that Gavin had complained of a headache three evenings before. She remembered him grumbling about the cold on the following morning, how warm his lips had felt against her forehead when he kissed her. She remembered that he had gone out that day, the last time she had seen him, without breaking his fast, and she cursed herself for not realising then that he was ill.

But Gavin was never ill; he made sick folk better, as Christian was proud of boasting. He was a surgeon – sickness couldn't put its hands on him. Or so Margaret had always thought. Until now.

Thomas's final sentence hung in her mind, and finally she made sense of it. 'You've not brought him home?'

'He's got the pox, Margaret! How can he come home? He's in the infirmary, where he'll be looked after until – until –'

His eyes slid away from hers. He was too honest, and he knew that she was too shrewd, for reassuring lies to be mouthed or believed. But she wasn't thinking of that. She was recalling everything that she had heard about infirmaries from Gavin himself, and from Thomas.

The big rooms filled with folk, most dying. The women – drunken slatterns, many of them – who were paid to tend the patients as best they could. She had often thought that the sickroom in the building that loomed behind Thomas's shoulder as he stood before her was a dreary place, but from what she had heard it was far superior to anything that could be found in an infirmary for sick people.

'How bad is he?'

'There's no knowing as yet. The sickness is in its early stages.'

'Have you a carriage at the door?'

'No, I travelled on horseback.'

She was already on her feet, hurrying along the narrow earthen path towards the house.

'Then find a carriage – a cart – anything that'll take us to Glasgow.' She threw the words over her shoulder.

'Margaret, you're not thinking of going to the infirmary?'

She stopped, rounded on him so fiercely that he stepped back, away from her, and one foot sank into soft sticky earth. 'D'you think I'd stay in Paisley, safe and sound, when my man's mebbe dying only a few miles away?'

'I can't allow you –'

'Thomas!' Her voice ripped through his words. 'There's no 'let' about it! Either you'll help me or I'll go and find him on my own!'

She would have struck him to the ground if she'd had to, and he knew it. In thirty minutes they were in a small open two-wheeled gig, rattling over the bridge that spanned the River Cart. A few more minutes later the neatly laid out streets of the New Town were falling behind them, and they were on the road that led to Glasgow.

*

The infirmary where Gavin worked for part of each week was a large stone building that looked more like a prison than a house of recovery. People buzzed round it, swarming in and out of the great door like the bees inhabiting the skeps in Margaret's parents' back yard.

As the carriage drew up before the main door two men jogged past and into the building carrying the infirmary bed, a mobile cot enclosed with striped curtains to conceal the patient who had been too ill to travel to the infirmary unaided.

A twinge of horror took hold of Margaret as she saw the canopy, once boldy bright, now shabby, flutter its way through the door. She knew without being told that most folk who were admitted like that were already beyond recovery.

Gavin lay in a corner of a vast ground-floor ward. As Thomas led her towards him she only had eyes for her husband, and didn't notice the surroundings at all.

To her relief he looked much like his usual self, though feverish. He was in a restless sleep; a pattern of tiny scarlet spots overlaid his face and throat and hands.

'Are you certain it's the pox?'

'Aye, I'm certain. By tomorrow the pustules will have appeared.'

It hurt unbearably to see Gavin lying there, sick and helpless. She looked away, and was appalled by what she saw.

The ward was large, with cots all down the walls and in two lines along the middle of the room. Every one of them was occupied, and a smell of mingled sweat and vomit, blood and unclean skin and putrefaction, hung over the place like a thick blanket. The windows were tightly close and the room was stuffy, depending on the ever-open door for all its fresh air. Underlying the stench of sickness and suffering was another smell; it reminded Margaret of something, and after a moment her nose identified it as the stink of a midden heap, no doubt just outside the ward windows.

The narrow passageways between the rows of beds were crammed with people. Physicians worked over patients or conferred in twos and threes. Men and women and children, many of the men grim-faced and helpless, the women in tears, the children bewildered and terrified, crowded round cots that held friends or relatives.

Here and there a dog or a cat scavenged round people's feet or cowered under a bed. The women she had heard Thomas and Gavin talk of went to and fro, carrying jugs and bowls or with their arms filled with dirty, bloody sheets.

One of them brushed past Margaret; her grey hair hung in lank greasy ropes from beneath a cap that had once been white, her dress was crusted with dried blood and grime, and in her wake she left a smell of ancient sweat and alcohol.

Margaret felt her stomach move, and swallowed hard, turning back to her husband so that she needn't look any longer at his surroundings.

Now she saw that the pillow beneath his dark head was filthy and the blanket tissue thin and completely inadequate.

'I must take him home!'

Thomas stared. 'Margaret, see sense!'

'If he stays here he'll die.'

'If he goes home,' said Thomas with brutal candour, 'He'll likely die anyway, and you with him.'

'At least he'll die in comfort, in his own bed.'.

'For God's sake –!'

The sound of their quarrel roused Gavin. His lids fluttered and opened and his eyes, bright with fever, fixed on Thomas. Dry lips shaped themselves into a smile.

'You've –' His voice was hoarse, and he cleared his throat and tried again, ' – you've been to Paisley?'

Then his gaze travelled on and found Margaret. Immediately his face suffused with horror.

'No!' He pushed himself up on one elbow, shock giving him a surge of unexpected energy. 'Margaret, get away from here!'

'I will, as soon as I can. And you'll come with me.'

'No, I must stay – and you have to go! You should never have allowed her to come, Thomas,' he fretted weakly.

'I couldnae stop her,' her brother said wretchedly.

The surge of energy left Gavin and he fell back, coughing and gasping for breath. A jug stood on the floor by his cot; Thomas lifted it and supported Gavin's head so that he could drink from it.

Then Gavin collapsed onto his thin dirty pillow, his eyes anguished as they fixed on his wife's face again. 'You must go away from here!'

'We must both go away from here, Gavin.'

'I can't!'

Margaret drew a deep shaky breath, more afraid than she had ever been in her life. 'Then I'll stay and tend to you.'

'Margaret!' Both men spoke together, Thomas's voice sharp and horrified, Gavin's a weak groan.

'Look at the women that work here –' Thomas indicated the room with a sweep of his arm. 'You can't stay. You'd not be safe!'

She knew that. She knew that if she didn't die of the pox in this terrible place she'd like as not be robbed, perhaps even murdered. Or she would die of cold or hunger or sheer fright. But her mind was made up.

'I'll not leave Gavin. Either I stay with him here or I take him back to Paisley.'

'And spread the pox through the town?'

'I'll nurse him myself, and not let anybody else into the house. I'll send Ellen and the bairns away and put quicklime on the walls and wash the house with vinegar and spirits of camphor and –'

'And if you fall sick?' Thomas asked, despair in his voice.

'I'll not fall sick.' How she could prevent it she didn't know, but at that moment she was prepared to promise anything if she could just get Gavin out of this dreadful place. She reached for his hand; with a whimper of fear lest she be contaminated he tried to draw it away, but she captured it in both of hers. Its unnatural heat struck through her own skin and her fingertips felt the raised pattern of the rash.

'Gavin – I'm your wife. One way or the other, I'll not leave you,' she said. 'We'll not be put apart!'

'Unless it's by death itself,' her mind added, but she left the words unspoken.

'Margaret, see reason,' he whispered painfully. 'If anything should happen to you as well as me, what'll become of our bairns?'

She bent over him, and realised that he, too, was inflicted with the stench of decay. Even Gavin wasn't invincible, after all.

'They'll never be alone,' she said steadily, her eyes on his. 'They've got my mother and father, and Aunt Mary, and a host of folk to make sure of that. But I've only got you, Gavin. I'll not leave you to fight this battle on your own!'

Chapter Twenty-Nine

She won, as she knew she must.

She had anticipated a further struggle against the infirmary's authorities and the driver of their small carriage, but she was spared.

The wards were over-crowded with new patients coming in all the time and visitors anxious to see their sick friends and relatives; nobody had the time to worry over what was happening to Gavin.

Mercifully, the shivering which he had put down to the weather but had instead been the fore-runner of his illness had caused him to put on a long warm cloak when he left Oakshawhill. This, together with Thomas's wide-brimmed beaver hat, hid the tell-tale rash from sight.

The driver of the gig, only interested in receiving payment for his work once it was done, paid no attention as Margaret and Thomas half-carried Gavin from the building and, with difficulty, helped him into the open carriage.

As the vehicle began to move Margaret drew a deep breath and looked at her brother, seeing her own tension reflected in his round face.

Between them, as the carriage lurched and jolted towards Paisley, Gavin shivered and burned and muffled his groans in Margaret's shoulder.

*

When they reached Oakshawhill Thomas waited in the carriage with Gavin while Margaret ran into the house, shouting for Ellen.

'Is the house on fire?' the servant squawked, running to the hall, the rolling-pin still in her hand, a trail of flour sprinkling the floor behind her.

'Where are the bairns?'

'At Mistress MacLeod's house.'

Margaret snatched the rolling-pin from the woman's hand and dragged her upstairs. 'Listen to me, Ellen. Mister Knox is taken sick and I've brought him home.'

'Och, the poor soul! I'll put a hot brick in his bed this minute, and make him some of my –'

'I'll see to him.' She threw open the door of the children's room and hustled the maid inside. 'You must take some clothes for the bairns and for yourself and go along to Mistress MacLeod's house. And you must stay there until – until I tell you that you can all come home again.'

'But –' Sudden understanding dawned in the serving-woman's eyes, followed by fear. 'The sickness – is it –?'

'Never mind what it is, just do as I tell you! If you're not down in the parlour and ready to go in five minutes I'll – I'll turn you out of this house and never let you back in!'

And Margaret flew back downstairs to the parlour where she scrawled a hurried note to her aunt.

As she finished it she heard Ellen lumbering down the staircase, laden with her own and the children's belongings.

'Give this to Mistress MacLeod as soon as you get there. And remember – don't let Christian and Daniel come back until I say so. Keep your eyes fast on Christian, for she's stubborn, that one.'

'I'll take the letter and the clothes, but let me come back and help you.'

'No!' Margaret said sharply, then as the woman's eyes filled with sudden tears she added on a gentler note, 'The wee ones need you, Ellen. And I must know they're being cared for properly while I'm not able to see to them myself.'

Ellen had been a part of the Knox household since Margaret's marriage. She had known and loved the children from the first moment of their lives. Standing at the door, watching the woman scurry as fast as she could out of the gate and along the footpath without stopping to look at the waiting carriage, Margaret felt as though she had just seen everything that spelled security vanish from her life.

But there was no time to let her imagination have its way. She had work to do.

Between them, she and Thomas got Gavin inside and put him to bed.

'God, Margaret, my heart was in my mouth!' her brother said as they settled Gavin against the pillows. 'If that driver had known what was amiss with one of his passengers he'd have thrown the three of us out onto the roadside – d'you realise that?'

'Fortunate for us that he didn't realise it, then,' Margaret said tersely, too worried about Gavin to fret over what might have occurred.

While she heated bricks to combat the fever that now consumed the sick man Thomas went off to warn everyone to stay away from the house and to collect medicines and vinegar and spirits of camphor and quicklime to whitewash the walls of the bed-chamber.

When she had made Gavin as comfortable as she could Margaret removed everything that wasn't needed, rolling up the carpets and dragging them out onto the landing, then set to and scrubbed the floorboards with lye.

By the time a knock on the door announced her brother's return her hands were red, and felt as though a thousand needles were being stabbed into the skin.

Islay stepped through the door first. 'I can't take the pox, so I've come to help you,' she said, and Margaret felt unbidden tears of gratitude and relief fill her eyes. She and Gavin weren't going to have to face the fight alone after all.

By evening the three of them had fumigated the room where Gavin lay, as well as the other rooms on that floor. Margaret's back ached, and the sharp smell of the agents used to fumigate the room stung her throat and her eyes.

They fed Gavin, then he fell asleep, soothed by clean sheets and a soft pillow and hot bricks.

When Thomas had gone, promising to come back first thing in the morning, Islay insisted that Margaret should eat something.

'You're going to need all the strength you can get before this is over,' she said firmly, walking into the kitchen and taking charge as though she had worked in it for years.

Margaret sat at the table, watching the younger woman, trying to concentrate on her words. The thought that Gavin might die was an insistent, clamouring black horror that must be kept at bay.

Islay, turning to put a platter of oatcakes on the table, read the fear in her face. 'He's young enough yet, and strong,' she said gently in her soft musical voice. 'He'll be right.'

As she ate, Margaret blocked the darkness in her head by repeating over and over again to herself, 'He'll be right. He'll be right.'

Later in the evening as she washed Gavin and made him comfortable she noticed with a fresh pang of fear that the rash had now unmistakeably become a mass of tiny blisters, each filled with a drop of liquid.

His eyes opened and met hers. Recognition faintly coloured the blank stare and he smiled at her. Then his heavy lids closed, and he slept.

Despite the balmy promise of the day the evening had brought rain. It pattered softly against the ground outside as Margaret turned the lamp down so that it wouldn't disturb her patient, then curled up in a chair, a blanket over her shoulders, her eyes on Gavin's face.

*

The fever had dropped slightly by the time Thomas called the next day, but the pustules were more pronounced.

'He's escaped the truly virulent pox, thank God,' he said, low-voiced, and Islay nodded wisely.

'Aye, the pustules are separate, one from another. I've seen the pox in all its forms, and helped to nurse those struck down with it.'

Thomas shot her a look of swift admiration. 'There's little to do but wait, and try to ease his sufferings,' he said as he and Margaret went out of the sickroom, leaving Islay to watch over Gavin.

'How are the bairns?' She was hungry for news of them.

'They're well. Christian wants to come and nurse her father. She says she's protected against the pox now, so she'll not catch it.' He grinned, and Margaret summoned up a watery smile.

*

The days and nights dragged by, interludes of light and darkness without number. The room where Gavin lay had to be kept dim at all times because the light hurt his eyes. The fever eased, then returned. The pustules spread into his mouth, making speech impossible. They grew and crusted, causing unbearable irritation. Even in his weak state he was too strong for the two women: they found it hard to keep his fingernails from tearing and ripping at his face and body.

It was Islay who suggested that they bind his wrists to the bed-frame. Margaret looked at Gavin, tossing and moaning in the grip of a frenzied fever, then stared back at the girl in horror.

'It's such a cruel thing to do!'

Islay met her gaze levelly. 'It's that, or have him cruelly disfigured for the rest of his life. We'll use soft cloths to spare him as much as we can. D'you have some old bedding that I can tear into lengths?'

When Margaret fetched a sheet, fragrant with lavender, from the closet, it was Islay's turn to look horrified. 'It's far too good, Mistress Knox! Have you nothing that's ready to be torn up for rags?'

'For any favour, Islay, will you call me by my given name?' Margaret said wearily, and ripped at the sheet with all her strength, knowing a certain vicious satisfaction as the material gave beneath her hands. 'And what do I care about good sheets at a time like this?'

They bound his hands to the bed-frame, then settled down to spend hour after hour by his side, sponging his ravaged face and body with cold water in an attempt to ease the itching.

They slept when they could, one in the children's room next door, the other keeping watch in the big chair by Gavin's bed.

Occasionally Islay almost forced Margaret out of doors, sending her into the back-yard to breathe some fresh cool air as she paced the long narrow path between the vegetable beds. Sometimes the sky above was blue, sometimes cloudy, sometimes night-black, studded with stars or silvery with moonlight.

It was hard to believe that in the houses nearby people entertained and baked and washed and talked and laughed and played with their children and slept and lived contented, normal lives; and all the time this was happening, she and Islay were helping Gavin to fight for his life.

Margaret's parents were staunch church-goers, of the Baptist faith. She had attended church meetings with them from the time she was a small child, and still did. Gavin's lack of interest in religion was something that until then had irritated her, but she had accepted it as part of the being that was Gavin.

One night when she was standing in the quiet dark garden, his lack of faith suddenly frightened the wits out of her. What if, lacking intervention from God, Gavin was allowed to die? What if he died anyway, and his soul was denied peace in Heaven?

'Lord,' prayed Margaret in a panic, 'Forgive him for not believing, spare him for my sake, and for Christian's, and Daniel's.'

A sudden fear caught at her heart, sending her stumbling into the house and upstairs and into the bedroom; it was a fear of being left alone, and it only eased its grip on her when she heard Gavin's harsh breathing and saw his dark head move restlessly on the pillow and knew with relief that he was still alive and she wasn't a widow. Not yet.

Islay was carefully dripping water into Gavin's sore mouth. She looked up and smiled as Margaret went to stand by the bed. 'I think he's a little better tonight.'

'Aye –' said Margaret. 'Aye, I think so too.'

But she wasn't speaking the truth, and she doubted if Islay was, either.

*

Occasionally, glancing from a front window, Margaret saw Walter Shaw hovering on the opposite side of the street, watching the house. The first time she mentioned it to Islay the girl's pretty face bloomed rose-red, with annoyance rather than pleasure.

'At your age, it's surely pleasant to have an admirer. And Walter's a fine-looking young man.'

'Aye, but – but he's not my choice.'

'So you've already got your eye on someone?'

Islay said nothing for a moment, concentrating on dampening a cloth and wiping Gavin's face gently. They were seated at either side of the bed, talking in low voices and taking it in turns to cool his brow and his crusted, swollen lips with water. The sound of their talk seemed to soothe him.

'Mist – Margaret, would you say that a woman's best to marry for practical purposes, or in answer to her heart?'

Margaret, taken aback, couldn't think of an answer right away. The Highland girl, taking her silence for a reply, nodded sagely.

'You see? You were fortunate, you followed your heart and made a good marriage into the bargain.' She looked round the room. Even stripped of its furnishings it was a handsome apartment, with large graceful windows and a decorative ceiling.

'You've got everything a woman could want. You've been so fortunate.'

She had no way of knowing that each word struck Margaret like a stone. She had indeed had everything, and she had been ready – almost willing, if it came to the truth – to throw it away for a matter of stupid pride. If Gavin were to die without their quarrel being resolved once and for all, she thought – and shivered at the prospect.

'Nothing's ever as perfect as it looks,' she said, low-voiced.

'I know that. What I don't know is –' Islay leaned over the bed, her lovely face – a woman's face now, no longer a girl's – intent. 'What should I do? Should I be practical, or should I listen to the voice inside that tells me to try to get what I truly want, even though there seems little chance?'

'Little chance? Islay, I can't think of a single man in Paisley who'd be daft enough to turn away from you. You're kindly and able, and bonny, and young –'

Islay's face twisted with sudden pain. 'Too young, mebbe.'

'You mean the man you care for's older than you?' Sudden fear touched Margaret. She herself liked Richard, but all the same, if those tales Gavin had told of his brother were true he'd not make a wise choice for a vulnerable girl like Islay. 'It's not Richard Knox, is it?'

'No, of course not.' Islay sounded so surprised at the idea that Margaret was instantly reassured. 'How could the likes of me ever think to marry with the likes of him?'

'Then who else can it be, but –'

Margaret stopped short as a rosy flood of colour stained Islay's cheekbones. 'It's nobody – nobody that you'd know,' she said swiftly, then, 'But tell me, Margaret – what should I do?'

Gavin moaned slightly and turned his head on the pillow so that his face was towards Margaret. Light from the window landed fully on his features, cruelly showing the crusted, disfigured mask that overlaid his former good looks. Margaret rested her eyes on the diseased face, and loved it with all her heart.

'You must do as the voice tells you,' she said. 'Even if nothing comes of it – you must try.'

After that, she said nothing to Islay when she happened to look out of the windows and see Walter standing outside.

*

Gavin's disease ran its course, and Thomas was cautiously pleased with his patient's progress. The pustules crusted – and then the fever came back with frightening suddenness and Gavin tossed and raved and fought against the hands that tried to ease his suffering.

Thomas came to the house four or five times that day, and stayed for most of the night. Looking into his haggard face, Margaret felt her heart contract painfully.

'If he comes through this crisis, he'll live,' her brother said.

'But you think he's going to die,' she challenged flatly, and saw his eyes slide away from hers.

'There's no way of knowing for sure, Margaret.'

He left at dawn, promising to come back later. Islay insisted that Margaret, who had been by Gavin's side all night, should go to the kitchen to break her fast.

She sat at the table, staring at the food and drink that lay untouched before her. When Islay came into the room she jumped up, her eyes flaring.

'Is he —?'

'Margaret — I think you should go to him. I think we'd best send for Thomas.'

'How can we, when we can't leave the house?'

'Walter's across the road. I'll call to him from a window. You go to your man.'

Suddenly Margaret didn't want to go back into the bedroom she had shared with Gavin. She didn't want to see him draw his last breath. She wanted to stay in the warmth and comfort of the kitchen, to let the dying pass her by. But Islay's hand was on her arm, gently propelling her to her feet.

'I think,' the girl's soft Highland voice said, 'that he needs you to be with him.'

'Yes,' Margaret said, pushing back her panic and fear, forcing herself to straighten and walk out of the door towards the stairs, and Gavin, and the passing that would end all the living and the loving they had shared together. 'Yes.'

Slowly, she climbed the staircase.

Gavin's eyes, a smoky tawny yellow now that the worst of the fever was gone, were open. The skin of his face was stretched over his skull. His lips curved in the ghost of a smile as she went to the bedside.

She forced a smile in return, although her face felt as though it was frozen and she didn't know if her mouth had obeyed the instruction to turn up at the corners.

'Gavin —' Her voice was a whisper in her throat, and she coughed and tried again, fumbling for the right words, words that would comfort him and ease whatever was to come. 'Gavin, you're not to worry about anything. I'll manage fine, and I'll raise Christian and Daniel just the way you'd have done yourself. We'll be fine, the three of us. And — and —'

Her voice struggled and faltered and faded away. Islay was right. He needed her at this moment, just as she would have needed him if she had been the one to fall sick.

Only when her time came, he wouldn't be there. She would be alone. Gavin was going to leave her. She would be alone.

At that thought a sudden passionate anger surged into Margaret, shattering the stone wall that had encased her heart from the moment she accepted that he was going to die. The warmth of her rage sparkled along her veins, crackled in her sinews, brought a tingling to every part of her skin.

'No!' said Margaret. She straightened. There was no need to lean over him now, no fear that he wouldn't hear her voice. It was loud and clear, honed to razor sharpness by the anger that made her want to take him by the shoulders and shake him until he promised not to leave her.

'No!' she said again. 'We'll not be fine, Gavin Knox. We'll not be fine at all! You promised before God to be my husband and to – to care for me. And what sort of caring's this? I'll not let you turn your back on me and our bairns! It isn't near time yet for us to part, and well you know it! It's your duty to – to see that Christian and Daniel grow up. You know I'll do it wrong if I'm left to my own ways! You know what I'm like! How can you even think of going away and leaving – leaving –'

She stopped, hands fisted, then said with a passion that almost shook her apart. 'You can't! You're mine and I'll not let you die! You can't!'

'Margaret!' Islay came into the room, took Margaret by the shoulders, her lovely dark eyes shocked. 'You must calm yourself! You don't want him to go with harsh words in his ears, surely?'

'I do! Yes!' Margaret stormed. If she was going to be forced to live on alone and in misery then Gavin should know that it was his doing, and only his. She began to weep, great stormy sobs dredged up from the depths of her being. Then, angrily, she pulled away from Islay, dashing her arm across her eyes, drawing in a long shuddering breath and pressing her fists tightly to her mouth to force the tears back. The time for crying was later, when –

'Confound it, Margaret,' Gavin's voice croaked from the bed. She turned to see that the eyes still fixed on her had taken on a new, stronger lustre.

'Confound it,' he said again, and there was a faint ghost of laughter in his weak voice, 'I might have known that you'd even deprive a man of his right to die with dignity.'

Chapter Thirty

Islay walked home slowly, tired to the bone after days and nights without adequate sleep. The small bundle containing her possessions banged rhythmically against her thigh as she tramped along.

She had just turned into the familiar pend when the weaving shop door opened and Jamie stepped out to stand in her path.

It was almost too much of an effort to lift her head and look at him. For a long moment they considered each other; it seemed to her that his eyes moved from feature to feature then went on to map out the shape of her face as though he needed to convince himself that she was indeed Islay McInnes, his troublesome tenant.

Since he seemed disinclined to speak, she said, 'Mister Knox is making a good recovery.'

'So Thomas told me. And you, Islay, are you all right?'

'You needn't concern yourself – I'm not diseased. I'm not carrying the pox to endanger you all.'

He flushed angrily. 'That's not what I meant. You look bone tired.'

'Nursing a man as sick as Mister Knox was doesn't leave much time for sleep. I'm fine. If you're wanting me to clean out the loom shop I'll be down as soon as I've taken my things to the house.'

'God's teeth, but you must take me for an ogre of an employer! Go home, lassie, and sleep for as long as you need. The loom shop can wait for another few days,' he said explosively, and marched back in, slamming the door behind him.

As she emerged from the pend she saw that someone had dug and planted and tended the kale beds during her absence. The house had been dusted and swept, there was a good fire on, and the kettle sitting atop the range was gently puffing steam into the air.

Islay let her bundle drop to the floor and surveyed the room, quick tears stinging her eyes. She was home.

*

Within a week her routine had fallen into its usual pattern, and it was as though Gavin Knox's near-fatal illness had never happened to disrupt the still, placid pool of Islay's existence.

Jamie continued to avoid her, and Walter continued to ask her to go walking with him. If she refused he accepted her decision with a quiet resignation that made her feel so sorry for him that every now and then she accepted. He was good company, but not the company she would have chosen.

It wasn't long before Richard Knox began to find his way up the stairs to her kitchen at least once a week, as before. And then, one day not long after she returned from Margaret and Gavin's house, Jamie himself put in an unexpected appearance at the house door.

She stared, unable to believe her eyes, then stepped back to let him in. He stood in the middle of the room for a moment, looking round at the waxed furniture, the shining range, the twinkling windows and clean curtains.

'You've looked after the place well.'

'I like to keep it right. You'll take some ale?'

'No.' He sat down in one of the chairs that flanked the range. Islay took the other, drinking in the sight of him sitting at her hearth. She had often dreamed of it, but never thought to see it come true.

Jamie shifted in the chair as though finding it uncomfortable. For the first time she realised that his interest in the room was a ploy to avoid looking at her. Nervous apprehension fluttered in the pit of her stomach, and she folded her hands over her apron in a bid to control the strange and unpleasant sensation of panic-stricken butterfly wings deep within.

'Walter's been at me to pay him more wages,' he said abruptly.

'Aye?' For the life of her Islay couldn't see what concern it was of hers.

Jamie studied the cupboard, where her precious collection of crockery shone in ordered rows. 'He's of a mind to get wed. To you.'

'Me?' Her voice rose in an unbecoming squeak of pure shock.

Jamie ploughed on as though she had never spoken. 'I think it's a fine idea, myself. I hope you'll consider it wisely when he comes to speak to you about it.'

'But – why should I want to marry with Walter?'

'You've been walking out with him, have you not?'

'Aye, but not as his sweetheart!'

'Walter thinks otherwise.'

'Then he must change his way of thinking. I've no intention of wedding him!'

Jamie's brows lowered and met. 'Don't be a fool, lassie! You could do a lot worse than take Walter Shaw as a husband.'

'I'm not your possession, to be married where and when you think fit!' She got to her feet, glaring down at him.

'You're under my roof, and in my employ. And so you're my responsibility.'

'No need for you to think that!'

Now he rose to tower over her, his broad shoulders making the room look smaller.

'Have you heard anything from that rogue of a cousin of yours?'

'No. And I don't expect to, either.'

'So – you're alone in the world. And my responsibility, whether either of us likes it or not.'

'I can see to myself.'

'Aye, but can you? Richard Knox comes around this house more and more often.'

'He only calls to talk now and then.'

'And you like that, do you?'

His voice was scathing, and she felt her face turning warm. 'I find him pleasant enough. It little troubles me whether or not he comes or stays away.'

'Lassie, he's a man years older than you – far-travelled

into the bargain, and wise in the way of the world. It's not right for you to entertain him the way you do. If you'd a husband he'd look after you and – and protect you from the likes of Richard. It's not only him,' said Jamie, speaking now as though the words were being wrenched out of him. 'There's mebbe others that would show an interest in you if they could. Some men don't have the self-respect they should have, when it comes to women. You need to be protected –'

'When I feel the need to marry, I'll find my own man!'

'And like as not find the wrong one. Walter's –'

'I'll not wed with Walter!'

'I'll send him up to see you when his day's work's done,' he said obstinately. 'You can talk the matter out between you, face to face.'

The small insistent voice that had been clamouring within her, the voice she had told Margaret about, made itself heard to Islay. Margaret was right – she had to listen to it before it was too late and the voice was stilled for ever.

'Jamie –' She reached the door before he did and stood with her back against it, barring his way. 'Why are you doing this?'

'I told you. To protect you from the likes of Richard Knox.'

'Are you certain of that? Is it not to protect you from the likes of me?'

Jamie's eyes blazed in startled comprehension, then were swiftly masked. 'You're havering, lassie!'

'Am I, Jamie Todd? You're far-travelled yourself. You're near as worldly as Richard. You're some years older than I am. Look at me, Jamie – can you not see the truth for yourself? D'you not know that Walter isn't the man that I want!'

His face had gone so white that it was in startling contrast to the blazing sapphires that were his eyes. 'No –' he said hoarsely.

'Aye! You know it!'

'For God's sake, Islay!' He looked and sounded like a man in torment. 'I'm thirty-three years of age, and you're only a child!'

'A child? A minute ago you were all for marrying me off to Walter.'

'He's only a year older than you are! You need to be wed. You need to be looked after –'

'I don't need protecting against my own wanting.'

'You do. You're too young to realise what you're saying!'

'I'm a woman! Look at me, Jamie, and see that for yourself!'

She didn't stop to think what she was saying. She was fighting for her future as hard as Margaret Knox had fought for hers in the bed-chamber where Gavin hovered between life and death.

'No –' Jamie said again. 'No! It would be wrong!'

'The wrong lies in giving myself – or being given – against my will, d'you not see that? Jamie –' She reached out to him but he moved back, beyond her reach.

'Islay –!'

'You'd force me into a marriage I don't want? You'd do that to me?'

'It's the best way. The only way.'

The muscles along his firm jawline were corded and a fine film of perspiration gleamed on his forehead. His eyes, when they finally met and held hers, were implacable.

Slowly Islay stepped aside, leaving the door free. Jamie opened it, and looked back at her from the threshold.

'I'll send Walter up, as I said. I hope you'll see fit to tell him that you'll wed with him.'

She followed him onto the small landing. 'What if I refuse him?'

Jamie, already starting down the steps, turned to look up at her. His face was still marble-white, and set in harsh uncompromising lines.

'Then he may well find another wife. But Walter can't afford a cottage of his own and there's not enough room in his mother's house for him and a bride. I'd feel obliged to offer him this place. If you're wise, you'll take him, and provide yourself with a good man as well as a good home.'

Then he blundered off down the stairs without a backward glance, and she was alone.

*

As soon as she heard the news Margaret hurried to Wellmeadow. 'What's this I hear about you getting wed?' she asked as she walked into the kitchen.

'It's true.' Islay carefully poured boiling water onto tea-leaves then swung the kettle on its swee back over the range.

'To Walter Shaw?'

'Aye. The banns have been called for the first time. We'll marry in two weeks.'

'But Islay – what about the other man – the feelings you told me of, when Gavin was ill?'

Islay filled a cup and handed it to her guest. 'Och – that was just a silly lassie's fancy. Nothing at all.'

'No, it wasn't. And I've a good notion who you were talking about, too.'

'It was nobody –' Islay said sharply. 'Nobody at all!'

There was a short pause while Margaret considered her thoughtfully. Then the older woman said gently. 'Lassie, are you being pushed into this marriage against your own will?'

Islay lifted her head, smiled brightly. 'Of course not. Walter'll make a good husband. It's for the best.'

'Oh? And who was it said that to you?' Margaret asked dryly.

In answer, a small, genuine smile suddenly brightened Islay's pale face. 'Mistress MacLeod's already been here to offer to make me a new bonnet for the day.'

'That's my Aunt Mary for you – she doesn't consider that a bride's properly wed unless she's topped with a bonnet of her making. You'll let me and Gavin give you your wedding gown, of course.'

'Oh, Margaret, that would be too much!'

'After you helped to save his life? It's not near enough!'

'How is he?'

Margaret, easily diverted these days by the very mention of Gavin's name, experienced the sudden glow of pleasure that always warmed her whenever she saw or thought of him, ever since she almost lost him to the smallpox. It reminded her of their courting days.

'Oh, he's coming along well. The marks have almost left

him, apart from a scar he'll always carry on his chin to remind us.'

Islay's dark eyes searched Margaret's face. 'You look happier than I've ever seen you.'

Margaret blushed like a young girl. 'It's because I've been blessed with another chance. I wish you looked half as happy as I feel – nobody looking at the two of us would know that you were the bride, and not me.'

Islay's smile wavered, made a valiant attempt to brighten, then faded altogether. 'I'm content enough. Walter's a good man,' she said, in a voice that forbade any further argument.

Margaret paid heed to it, and said no more on the subject. When she was standing on the landing outside the house, preparing to take her leave, she hugged the Highland girl and said on an impulse, 'Islay – let Gavin and me hold a gathering for you in our house after the wedding. There's room for all of your friends, and his.'

The girl shook her head. 'There's no need. The wedding gown's more than enough. It's not as if I'm one of your family.'

'You are! You're part of both our families – the Todds as well as the Montgomerys. Nobody belongs to one without belonging to the other.'

'I'd as soon as leave things as we've planned them. We'll get married quietly then come back here, just the two of us.'

'Very well, if that's what you want. Now – I'll call for you tomorrow morning, and we'll go to my dressmaker to look at material for the wedding –'

Margaret's voice tailed off. Islay wasn't listening. Her eyes had slid beyond Margaret, her attention held by something in the yard below. Her face was almost gaunt, sharp-etched with hunger and loss.

Margaret turned and caught a glimpse of a fiery red head below as Jamie Todd, who had come into the yard to collect something, disappeared into the pend.

After she had left Islay, Margaret found some excuse to go into the weaving shop below to talk to Jamie. Walter was at his loom, singing cheerfully in a pleasant tenor voice as he worked. He shot her a shy smile as she stopped to congratulate him on his coming marriage.

In contrast to his young weaver Jamie looked quite ill. In his face Margaret saw the same despair, the same hopeless longing she had read in Islay's eyes.

Now she knew the truth; and she knew, too, that she had found it out too late.

Chapter Thirty-One

Islay wore a deep blue silk gown for her wedding day. The overdress was open from shoulders to waist to reveal a beribboned paler blue stomacher, and open again over a pale blue flounced underskirt.

The tight sleeves cascaded into layers of white lace at the elbows; the same lace also edged the neckline and the low bodice line of the dress.

Mary MacLeod, recognising the pointlessness of vying with her young client's natural beauty by giving her a fancy bonnet, had made one of natural straw in a simple milkmaid style, trimmed with ribbons in shades of blue to match the gown. Beneath it Islay's glossy black hair had been drawn away from her face and twisted into a knot at the back of her head.

Walter, too, looked his best. His straight brown hair had been well brushed for the occasion and tied back with a green ribbon. He was dressed in his finery – a green topcoat and brown britches fastened at the knee with silver buckles. There were silver buckles on his sturdy black shoes, and his calves were encased in brown hose.

His face shimmered with joy and pride as he led his bride to her wedding. But Margaret, who had gone with Gavin to witness the marriage, watched Islay with concern. The girl's face was pale, her eyes deep dark unfathomable pools. An occasional smile flickered nervously about her lips when she caught anyone looking at her, then faded and died.

'It's all wrong!' Margaret mourned in a whisper. Gavin laid his free hand restrainingly on the fingers clutching at his arm.

'Hush, Margaret – the lassie's old enough to go her own

way. There's nothing we can do to change things, no matter how much you might want to.'

*

Islay scarcely heard a word of the marriage service that bound her to Walter Shaw for the rest of their lives. She stood motionless within the wedding gown, beneath the lovely new bonnet, with no feeling that she was actually wearing them. It was as though they merely enclosed her.

Walter took her hand in his own warm strong clasp and slipped his ring onto her finger. It was over, she was wed; she had stepped through a door that led from one life to another and there was no turning back.

They walked to Wellmeadow alone after the small wedding party had dispersed; Islay with her hand through her husband's arm, Walter swaggering with pride as one well-wisher after another stopped them. He had been given a day off work for his marriage, and as they went through the pend the other weavers and the draw-boys swarmed out of the loomshop to greet them. Jamie wasn't among them.

When they finally climbed the stairs and went into the house Walter unbuttoned his coat and peeled it off, throwing it carelessly over the back of a chair. It half-sprawled to the floor as its owner dropped into one of the fireside chairs with a grunt of satisfaction.

'It's finally done, lass! Man and wife!'

'Aye, it's done.' She picked up his coat and put it away neatly. Then she took off her new bonnet and replaced it with a linen cap.

'You'll be ready for your meal.'

'I am that,' said Walter. 'Where are you going?'

She paused, her hand on the door leading to the inner room. 'To put on my working clothes.'

'No need to go in there. You're my wife now – have you forgotten?'

He was sitting upright now, his eyes suddenly intent on her. Heat was creeping into them. Islay swallowed convulsively, then said, 'I've not forgotten.'

Her hand fell away from the door and she moved back into the kitchen, reaching for her apron.

Walter got to his feet and took her by the shoulders as she finished tying the apron round her waist. 'Islay, you'll not regret marrying with me, lass. I'll look after you.'

His face was anxious, and absurdly young. All at once she felt years older than he was. 'I know you will, Walter. It'll be fine.'

He smiled. 'Aye, it'll be fine.' Then he bent to kiss her, his lips touching hers lightly at first, then increasing their pressure as his arms closed about her.

She submitted to the embrace, putting her own arms about him, telling herself firmly that he was her husband now, and she his wife. But as the kiss became fiercer and Walter's body began to tremble against hers, his hands moving with more and more urgency on her, she broke away. 'I'll – I'll see to the food,' she said, and turned to the range.

After they had eaten she cleared the table before picking up a bucket and going to the door.

'Where are you going now?'

'To fetch water from the well.'

He took the bucket from her. 'I'll do that. I'm the man of the house,' he said, and went out.

Alone, Islay tore off her apron and the pretty wedding gown and dressed in her working blouse and skirt, her hands trembling with haste.

After she had put her apron back on and hung the gown up in the press, letting her hands linger for a moment on the soft luxury of the silk, she looked about the kitchen that had been hers for some six months, and was hers no longer.

'I'm the man of the house –' Walter's words echoed in her head. Already his stamp was there; his good coat on the peg behind the door beside her cloak, the air in the room heavy with the smell of the pipe he had been smoking. The pipe itself lay on the range, the tobacco in its bowl dully glowing at her like a red eye within a deep black socket.

She took a deep breath and swung the swee away from the range, out into the room, so that she could tip hot water from the kettle into a bowl.

When he came back Walter glanced at her everyday clothes, but said nothing. Instead, he refilled the kettle before settling himself back into the fireside chair. He took off his shoes, picked up his pipe, and stretched his muscular legs across the rag rug, sighing with contentment.

'It's like a palace here. At home the place is full of bairns, and my mother screaming at them from morning to night. But here –' he looked around with an air of satisfaction, and settled his buttocks more firmly into the chair.

When she had finished washing the dishes Islay took her place opposite him, her sewing in her hands.

Walter reached across and lifted a handful of the light material she was working on. 'What is it?'

'A nightshift. I should have finished it yesterday, but I didn't have the time.'

'Is it for tonight?'

'Aye.'

He rubbed the ball of one thumb appreciatively over the cloth. 'It's bonny.'

Evening wore on and the room darkened until Islay could no longer see the tiny stitches she was taking in the hem of the new nightgown. She put down her work and rose. Walter reached out a long arm and caught at her skirt as she passed his chair.

'Where are you going now?'

It was the third time he had asked that in the short time they had been married. She began to feel as though her freedom had suddenly been taken from her. 'To light the lamp.'

'No need for that. It's surely time for us to go to bed now. I've to get up early in the morning.'

'I've not finished the shift. It only needs a few more minutes –'

'No need for the shift, either,' said Walter. 'Not tonight.'

He put his arms about her and his fingers fumbled at the strings of her apron. It fell to the floor between them and Walter's foot nudged it to one side as he began to unfasten the small buttons down the front of her blouse, squinting with concentration.

When the blouse, too, had been dropped to the floor and pushed aside he started working with the same dogged purpose on the ribbons that fastened her chemise. His breathing seemed loud in the quiet dimness of the room.

When Islay put her hands up to take over the work herself rather than submit to his clumsy ministrations he lifted his gaze briefly to her face and said, 'Don't!'

She dropped her hands and stood before him, feeling his fingers tremble against her skin; feeling that same tremor begin deep within herself, though she didn't know whether it was caused by nervousness or pleasurable anticipation, dread or excitement.

The chemise dropped away and Walter's hands took her breasts, claiming them as triumphantly as any explorer coming on hitherto undiscovered terrain. Fire darted through Islay as the touch of those masculine hands began to rouse her to stiff-nippled excitement.

Her own breath caught raggedly in her throat as Walter took time to unfasten the strings of her bonnet and toss it away. Then he loosed the knot of hair at the back of her head and let it fall in a black curtain about her naked shoulders.

'Your skin's like – like the softest silk that ever was,' he breathed, and bent to brush wondering lips over her throat and shoulders and, finally, down over her breasts.

Islay closed her eyes, bringing her hands up to busy themselves in his thick hair, loosening the ribbon that held it back. All at once she felt that everything was, after all, going to be all right. She could be happy with Walter; he would help her to forget Jamie.

He lifted her and carried her over to the bed and stripped her naked before tearing off his own clothes, scattering them all over the room in his urgency. He was more heavily built than she had thought, his chest and groin matted with crisp dark curls.

'Walter, let me gather up the clothes –'

'Leave them!' he ordered, then plunged down on top of her, burrowing and snatching, bruising soft tender skin and the flesh beneath, paying no heed to her gasps of pain.

It was then that Islay realised that in her new husband's eyes marriage was a taking by the man and a submitting by the woman. As far as he was concerned there was no question of sharing love. He didn't need or ask for her love

– only her body.

And he had every right to take that whenever and in whatever manner he chose.

Because to Walter Shaw and men like him that was what marriage meant.

Chapter Thirty-Two

Pride in his new marital state made Walter a possessive husband. He liked to know just where Islay was at each moment of the day, when he was at his loom and unable to be with her.

He scowled if any of the other weavers talked and joked with her. Soon she began to start her work in the weaving shop early so that she was free to leave before the other men arrived.

It was better that way, for then she didn't have to face Walter's resentment and his accusations that she had been altogether too friendly with this man or that, once his day's work was over and they were together again.

The words 'My wife –' which he liked to use whenever possible, began, in Islay's ears, to take on a leaden ring.

She saw little of Jamie during the first weeks of her marriage. He rarely came to the weaving shop, and if he had to it was usually in the afternoons, when the place was cleaned and the pirns delivered and Islay out of the way upstairs, working at her spinning wheel.

To her relief Richard Knox had the good sense and the courtesy to stay away now that she wore another man's ring on her finger.

A month after the wedding she was hanging out washing in the back yard when she happened to turn and catch a glimpse of red hair glowing within the pend's gloom. Her heart jumped, but she resolutely turned back to her task, determined not to indicate by a look or a word that she had seen him. It was possible – indeed, probable – that he hadn't seen her, after all.

After a moment footsteps sounded on the cobblestones then Jamie said, from just beside her, 'Good day to you, Islay.'

She turned, looking no higher than the top button of his waistcoat. 'Good day, Mister Todd.'

'Are you well?'

'Aye, sir.' She ducked her head in nervous acknowledgment, and went back to her work.

'Good. You look well,' said Jamie formally. 'Marriage agrees with you.'

Her fingers fumbled on the clothes-rope. A wooden peg fell from her grasp. She stooped swiftly to pick it up just as he did the same. For a brief moment in the fabric of time their fingers touched, and simultaneously withdrew from the contact as though they had each touched a burning coal.

'Is Walter treating you well?' Jamie asked, his voice suddenly losing its formality and becoming low and urgent.

'He's a good husband.' No sense in speaking about the pain of a body regularly violated because the man who took it had no knowledge of any other way to couple with a woman. Indeed, for all Islay knew that was the only way between men and women. It might be that she herself was in some way set apart from the rest of her sex. It might be that the thrill of desire she had known when Walter's hands first rested on her naked breasts, the desire she felt at that moment, close to Jamie Todd, wasn't normal in a woman.

And so she only repeated, as the two of them rose to their full heights again, 'He's a very good husband.'

'I'm pleased to hear it, for if he made you unhappy he'd have me to answer to,' said Jamie. Then he bowed and turned away, and strode back through the pend and out into the street beyond.

She stood motionless, her hands filled with wet clothes and pegs, looking after him; then she saw Walter's face swimming palely behind the glass panes of the weaving shop, and went back to her work.

*

'What was Mister Todd saying to you?' he wanted to know when they were at their evening meal.

'Nothing much. He asked if we were settling down well together.'

'And you told him that everything was fine.'

'Of course. What else is there to say?'

'He's a good man, Jamie Todd,' Walter said. 'I've a lot to thank him for. I've got work, when many a good weaver in Paisley has idle hands and an empty belly. I've got a fine wee house —'

His hand reached out across the table and captured Islay's. His face, as he surveyed her, was alight with pride and his own form of affection ' — and I've got you, Islay. Aye, there's a lot the two of us have to thank Jamie Todd for.'

*

His smiles changed to scowls when Mary MacLeod invited the newly-wed couple to a gathering in her home.

'What does the likes of us want to visit gentry in a grand house in Oakshawhill for?'

'Mistress MacLeod's not gentry, Walter — well, not real gentry.' Islay, who had been raised in a society where a man was judged by his own worth, not by his possessions, and where the clan chief and the poorest of his clansmen were judged to be on equal footing, found the Lowland obsession with class confusing. 'She's a kindly soul. And Margaret and Gavin'll be there. They're good friends of mine.'

'Well they're not friends of mine. They'd never have thought of inviting me to their fine houses if I wasnae married to you.'

'Och, Walter! They're all decent folk, with no airs and graces to them at all. Margaret Knox is a weaver's daughter, raised in a cottage herself.'

'That's as may be. Now she's a surgeon's wife, with servants and carriages and the Lord knows what else. I'm in no mind to go,' he said peevishly.

'But I can't go on my own.'

'I'd not let you. You'll stay home, with me.'

Dismayed, she put aside her knitting wires and went over to kneel by his chair. 'Walter, I want to go. We've been nowhere since the day we married, except to visit your mother. Can you not bring yourself to go, even just this once?'

Disarmed, he stroked her hair. 'Does it mean as much as that to you?'

'I want you to meet the folk that have been so good to me in the past.'

'Aye – well –' he said reluctantly. 'Mebbe we'll go – but if I don't care for them, it'll be the last time.'

'Oh, thank you, Walter!' She began to get up, but he held her where she was with one hand on her shoulder. The other hand, the one that had been stroking her hair, loosed it so that it fell softly about her face, like night-rain. Her hair, long and rich and glossy, fascinated Walter.

He gathered as much of it as he could in his fist and used it to draw her head back so that he could bend to kiss her lips and then her throat. His hand left her shoulder and travelled to her breast, and he slid from his chair and joined her on the floor, pushing her down until she lay beneath him.

*

She prayed, as they went along the High Street and through the pend that led to Oakshawhill, that he would enjoy himself, for she didn't want to have to give up her good friends. Then, as they neared Mary MacLeod's gate, the prayer slipped from her mind and she began to wonder if Jamie would be there tonight.

Margaret and Gavin were coming along the opposite way, from their own house. They waited by the gate for the Shaws and greeted Walter warmly. So did Mary, when she met them at the door.

'Most of the folk are here. Come along, lassies, and put your cloaks in my bed-chamber.'

Gavin, now fully recovered from his illness and with nothing to show for it except a gash of puckered, damaged skin that stretched from one corner of his mouth, cutting diagonally across his cheek to the lobe of his ear, put a friendly hand on Walter's arm.

'We'll go on into the parlour and get ourselves something to drink. I know where it's kept.'

'You always did, you rascal,' said Mary indulgently, and swept Margaret and Islay upstairs and into a large comfortable room.

'I'm right vexed with Jamie,' she confided as they went.

'He downright refused to come, and nothing I could say would move him. There's still a coolness between him and Duncan and Robert over this business of Richard. And Jamie felt that if they were going to be here he'd be better to stay away. That's not deterred Richard, of course. The bold man's down there in my parlour, chattering away to the Montgomerys, and not caring a hoot about the cold looks he's getting from them.'

Margaret put her cloak aside and went to the full-length mirror to see that her hair was neat. 'It's as well that I've won my battle with Gavin, or we'd not be here ourselves. He'll still not have Richard in our house, but at least he's willing to be civil to the man if we should chance to meet him elsewhere.'

'Men! You're looking bonny, Islay –' Mary circled her young guest, admiring the way her gown, the one she had worn on her wedding day, fell in graceful lines to the floor. Margaret turned from the mirror.

'You suit that colour. I've got a gown that might well do you, in much the same shade. D'you have time to come to the house tomorrow afternoon to have a look at it?'

'You've already given me too much –'

'Oh, tuts, lassie! The gown's just going to go to the moths if you don't take it, for it's no use at all to me. I've not been able to get into it since Daniel's birth. I don't know what's happened at all.'

'You're just getting older, Margaret,' her aunt said briskly, and earned herself a baleful glare. She disregarded it and went on sunnily, 'Now – shall we go down and join the others?'

*

Walter was ill at ease; Islay realised that as soon as she entered the room and saw him, glass in hand, standing stiffly to attention as Gavin Knox chatted amiably to him.

She went to him at once, sliding a hand into his to comfort him. His fingers closed on hers like a drowning man grasping at a plank of wood and some of the tension went out of his body.

But there were too many people in the room for it to be

possible for husband and wife to stay together all the time. Inevitably, as always happened at Paisley gatherings, the women gravitated to one side of the parlour while the men gravitated to the other.

The women chattered about recipes and babies and clothes and housework. The men talked on what, to them, were weightier matters. Weaving and politics and prices, the war in the Americas, which had attracted a number of unemployed young weavers to join the flag, and the proposals for a proper water supply for Paisley, a project that was dear to Gavin's and Thomas's hearts.

Glancing across at Walter now and again Islay saw that her husband, who had matured so swiftly in her eyes since their wedding day, seemed to have shrunk back into callow boyhood, talking only when a question was put directly to him, pulling nervously at the buttons on his good jacket – if he wasn't careful, she thought anxiously, he would twist them right off and embarrass himself even further – and drinking too quickly and too much.

Later, when refreshments were served, the two sexes began to mingle again, but before he could reach the safety of Islay's side Walter was swept off by Mary MacLeod, who bore down on him determined to do her duty as hostess and make him feel welcome.

Islay, on her own for a moment, was quickly joined by Richard Knox, his green gold-flecked eyes travelling over her with the confident skill of the connoisseur.

'Marriage agrees with you, my dear Islay,' he said, unconsciously using Jamie Todd's words. 'But not, alas with me. I regret that I can no longer call on you and enjoy the pretty picture you make working industriously at your wheel. Now I must content myself with recalling it from my imagination instead. If I was your husband, my dear, I think I should hire the best portrait painter in the land to capture you on canvas. Helen of Troy – or the Queen of Sheba might be a title better suited to your dark beauty – spinning her web to catch men's hearts.'

'I'm happy to say that my husband has more to do with his money, and so I'll be spared the ordeal, sir.'

'Ah yes – you threw yourself away on a young weaver,'

said Richard, turning to cast a disdainful eye on Walter. 'A lusty enough lad, I suppose. Does he pleasure you, Islay?'

She felt colour rise to her face. 'I don't know what you mean, Mister Knox.'

'Oh, you do.' Richard leaned close to breathe the words into her ear. 'You do, my dark beauty. If it should ever be that he no longer holds your interest, remember that I would be more than happy to offer my assistance.'

He turned away, leaving her furious and embarrassed. So this was part of marriage, was it? This assumption by other men that once a woman had lost her maidenhood she might be willing to spread her favours further than the marriage bed?

She wanted, at that moment, to scoop Walter from beneath the friendly hand Mary MacLeod had laid on his arm and depart for home. But he had been watching her, she knew. He had seen Richard talking to her. If she suddenly announced that she wanted to leave he would know that somehow Richard had offended her. And there was no knowing what Walter's pride might lead him to then.

She took a deep breath, pinned a smile on her face, and crossed the room to Margaret and Gavin.

Chapter Thirty-Three

As Islay had suspected, Walter didn't enjoy the evening at all. They were the first guests to leave, and they walked back to Wellmeadow in silence.

When at last they were in their own house he took her to bed immediately, and made frenzied love to her.

'You're mine, Islay,' he said into the darkness when at last he had rolled away from her and they lay side by side. 'You're mine – and from now on we don't need any fine folks in big houses!'

On the following afternoon Islay went to Oakshawhill, where she tried on the gown that Margaret had spoken of.

It was made of pale blue cotton, a simple but elegant dress cut on lines that made the most of Islay's full young breasts and small waist.

'It's even a little wide for you,' Margaret said enviously. 'You'll have to take it in here – and here.'

'That's easily done.' Islay stood before the looking-glass, turning first to one side then to the other to admire the sweep of the skirt. 'It's a bonny gown.'

'And I'm glad to see it worn again, for it was always one of my own favourites. I think you've lost some weight since your marriage day, Islay.' She began to help Islay out of the gown. 'Did Walter enjoy himself last night?'

'Aye, he –' Islay started to say, then stopped herself. She didn't have to lie to Margaret. 'No, if the truth be told. He felt like a – a fish out of water, and it vexed him.'

'I thought the poor lad was finding it all a burden.' Margaret took the blue gown to the bed and began to fold it while Islay pulled on her own brown dress. 'Men don't care for gatherings as much as women do. Gavin was the same in the early days of our marriage. But he soon got to know all the folk, and then he began to enjoy himself. So will Walter,

I'm certain. Why don't the two of you come along to our house one evening next week? Once he feels comfortable with us, we'll slip him into society without him even noticing –'

'No, Margaret. It's well meant, I know, and it's kind of you, but we'd best not.'

'But you're surely not going to come to gatherings alone and leave him at home?'

Strands of Islay's hair had been loosed from their place while she was trying on the gown. She released all of it, shook it down about her face, then began to twist it back into its knot with deft movements.

'I'm his wife now – I'll stay at home with him.'

'Oh,' said Margaret, then, 'Islay, are you happy?'

Sometimes it was necessary to lie, even to a close friend like Margaret Knox. 'Of course I am. Walter's a good husband.'

The knot was firmly in place again. She let her hands drop to her sides, turned to face Margaret, suddenly hungry for information, or perhaps reassurance that, unsatisfactory as her marriage was, it was like everyone else's. Even that would help in a way – although for the life of her Islay couldn't imagine a man like Gavin Knox using his wife as Walter used her.

'But it takes a bit of getting used to – marriage. Learning what a man's needs are. Learning –' she stumbled, trying to chose her words carefully. ' – learning not to mind if he –'

'Not to mind what?'

Islay had gone too far to draw back, although she felt her face flame as she asked, the words tumbling over each other in their haste to get out, 'Margaret, is it a sin for a woman to need – to want –' She put an impatient hand up to her mouth, then pulled it away to say, ' – to want to love as much as a man does?'

Margaret, too, was crimson. Islay had never thought it possible for Margaret Knox to blush so.

But the older woman's voice was clear and strong as she said, 'Of course it's not a sin! It's only natural, surely. We're flesh and blood the same as any man.'

'Oh –' Islay clasped her hands tightly together.

'Does Walter not – not understand that?'

'Oh yes. It was just that I wondered, that's all.' Islay swooped to the bed and caught up the folded gown. 'I must go.'

'Stay and take tea with me. The bairns haven't seen you for a while. And it's long enough since you and me had a proper talk.'

'I must go. Walter'll finish work soon, and he likes me to be at home, waiting for him.'

Islay almost fled out of the house and along the road, her mind a bubbling cauldron of thoughts. She wasn't sinful, or wicked, or out of the normal, and that knowledge was a great relief.

But on the other hand she had found out, once and for all, that there was indeed more to marriage than the relationship she and Walter shared. There was mutual caring and wanting and, perhaps, mutual satisfaction. But not for Islay Shaw.

Not for the first time in the past month Islay seemed to hear the faint clang of a prison door slamming shut in her mind.

*

That night when the children had gone to bed and Margaret and Gavin were alone in the parlour she said tentatively, 'Gavin, it's natural for women to enjoy bedding with a man, is it not?'

He looked at her in astonishment, then burst out laughing. 'After all the years we've been married, you ask me that?'

'Gavin!' Exasperated, she swiped at his head, and he parried the blow, seizing her wrist and drawing her down to sit on the arm of his chair. 'I'm asking your opinion as a medical man!'

'It's as well you told me that, for I've little experience of the matter as an ordinary man,' he said, a glimmer of mischief still sparkling in the depths of his eyes. Then he added, 'Though as an ordinary man I've no fault to find with my own experiences, ma'am.'

From where she sat it was possible – and pleasant – to rest

her cheek on the top of his head. His fingers caressed the inside of her wrist, and he lifted her hand to his lips and kissed the palm.

Gavin was in a very relaxed, contented mood. The two of them had just spent most of the evening playing with their children; at last the barriers Daniel had built between himself and his father were noticeably crumbling.

With a feeling of guilt Margaret recognised that the little boy's fear of his father wasn't due only to the day Gavin had cut his arm with a knife. It had been fostered and fed by the child's instinctive reaction to the hostility he had sensed from that day on between his parents.

Margaret blamed herself bitterly for that, and always would, even though her precious, beloved family had weathered the storm and found happiness again.

'As to your question,' Gavin was saying now, 'it's perfectly natural for a woman to benefit from loving as much as a man. Though I'll admit that often enough men insist on claiming all the benefit for themselves and treating their womenfolk as objects for their own pleasure. But why should you want to know my opinion on a matter like that?'

Margaret slid from the arm of the chair onto his knee, so that she could look into his face. 'Islay was here this afternoon.'

'I see. Margaret,' he said carefully after a moment, 'there's nothing you can do for Islay, you know that. Nobody can – or should – come between husband and wife.'

'I know, I know. But I just wish I could help her. If Jamie hadn't been so thick-headed Islay wouldn't be wed to Walter Shaw now!'

'She might be. Jamie didn't force them to wed. Walter's been hungering after Islay for some time, from what I heard. She even went out walking with him.'

'I wish I could –'

Gavin laid a finger on her lips. 'Hush now, Margaret. We've said enough on the subject, and it's closed.'

Then he recaptured her hand and kissed her palm once more, his lips setting up a thrill that ran along her arm to her heart.

'As for me – I'm content to just thank God that I have

what I have,' said Gavin, 'and leave it at that.'

*

At that very moment Walter was asking suspiciously, 'Where did you get that?'

Islay lifted her head and saw him standing before her, one finger stabbing at the gown she was stitching. 'From Margaret Knox. It doesn't fit her any more, so she thought it might do for me.'

He was scowling. 'I don't like to see my wife in rich folks' cast-offs.'

'It's not a cast-off; it's a perfectly good gown that's too tight for her now. It was kind of her to offer it to me.'

'Kind? You Highlanders,' said Walter with scorn, 'don't have the brains of hens!'

'Walter!'

'It sickened me last night, seeing them fussing over you as though you were a pet dog. And you taking it all without offence!'

'They're my friends –'

'Your friends? From now on,' he said, his voice thick, 'your friends are the folk I want to mingle with, not gentry! Not men like Richard Knox with his silk clothes and his fine horse and his purse full of money! What was he saying to you last night?'

She moistened her lips. 'He was only congratulating me on our marriage.'

Walter threw his head back and brayed with mirthless laughter. 'Was he, indeed? Telling you what a fool you had made of yourself, wedding a poor weaver, more like. Telling you that you'd have done better with the likes of him!'

He was near enough to the truth to frighten her. But she gripped the wooden arms of her chair and glared up at him. 'Don't be daft! A man like Richard Knox would never dream of marrying me!'

'No, but he'd be willing enough to take you to his bed and pay you well for your favours!'

Sheer anger brought her out of her chair so quickly that he backed a step or two. 'That's a wicked, evil thing to say, and I'm shamed that my own husband should speak such words to me, Walter Shaw!'

She stooped to pick up the gown. He caught at it, and for a moment they tussled ridiculously over it, glaring like two children disputing a game.

With a rending sound the gown tore. Islay cried out in dismay and let go to save it from further damage. With a sweep of the arm Walter threw it away from him and it landed on the hot range. As the acrid smell of burning cloth filled the kitchen he wheeled about and marched to the door, slamming it so hard behind him that she thought it was going to splinter at the hinges.

By the time she snatched the gown from the range it was too late. One sleeve had fallen against the bars of the glowing fire, and was striped with black singe-marks. The struggle had not only half-parted the skirt from the bodice; it had ripped some of the cloth as well. There was little that could be done now.

Islay sat down, the gown in her arms, and wept. But after a while she stopped. Tears couldn't save the bonny dress, or turn the clock back.

She dried her eyes and got on with her work, waiting for the sound of Walter's footsteps on the stairs.

When they finally came, the steps on the wooden staircase were slow and uncertain.

When the door opened and he came in she saw at once that he had been consoling himself in a howff.

He held onto the door-frame for a moment, squinting blearily at her as she sat by the fire in a pool of light from the lamp she had put on a shelf nearby. 'You should be in bed.'

'I was waiting for you, to make sure you were all right.'

He came in, letting the door swing to behind him, and took off his coat, dropping it on the floor. 'I'm f – fine,' he said in a slurred voice. 'I've spent the evening in the sort of house that suits me, with the s – sort of folk that suit me.'

He sat down in his usual chair with a thud and tried to take his shoes off. Islay closed the door and latched it against the night. Then she picked up his coat and hung it in its proper place before going to kneel before Walter to help him off with his shoes.

She felt his hand patting her head. 'You're a good wee w –
wife, Islay. I shouldn't have sh – shouted at you, lass.'

'Come on – come to bed.' She stood up, took his hand,
helped him to his feet. All at once his arms were about her,
holding her so close that she could almost feel her ribs
creaking in protest.

'It's just that – I wish I could give you all these things they
have, Islay,' said Walter into her ear, tears in his voice. 'I
wish I could give you a fine house, and bonny gowns, and –
and a carriage –'

She managed to free herself and stood back, taking his
hands in hers. 'I know, Walter. But I'm content enough with
the things we have.'

'I'm not – not when I see what they have,' he said,
suddenly resentful. 'Why should the likes of Ri –' his tongue
and lips shied at the name, and tried again, 'Ri – ch'd High
and Mighty Knox swagger about the town with his fine
clothes and his purse full of silver when de – decent
hard-working men like me have to make do with plain cloth
and a few pence?'

He was working himself into another rage. Talking
soothingly, she managed to lead him across the room to the
wall-bed. He collapsed onto it, then reached up and touched
her face.

'I'm going to look after you, Islay,' he said blearily, then
rolled over onto his face and fell asleep, spread-eagled over
the bed, still fully dressed.

Chapter Thirty-Four

A few weeks later Islay knew beyond any doubt that she was expecting Walter's child.

He received the news with surly resignation. 'It's the way of things, I suppose,' he said, and cast a look about the neat kitchen. 'At last we've got more room for our bairns than my mother ever had.'

Islay wasn't certain of her own reaction. Although she felt ill every morning she looked forward with happy anticipation to bearing a child of her own making. But Walter's reference to his mother, and the thought it conjured up of Mistress Shaw's tired thin bitter face and her noisy crowded kitchen, filled from wall to wall with the squalling, fighting, peevish brood she had borne, was depressing. Walter seemed to assume that that was now to be Islay's fate, too. It was a frightening prospect.

As time went by and she was forced to let out the seams of her clothes to accommodate her increasing waistline Walter became more and more sullen. As the eldest of his family, he had been the main bread-winner before his marriage. He still contributed money to his mother's house, and Islay watched and listened with dismay as he became more and more obsessed with the threat of poverty now that they had started their family.

'Och, we'll manage fine,' she tried to re-assure him day after day. 'We've got a nice wee house, and you're in employment. Now that the new cotton cloth's doing well there's no likelihood of you losing your place.'

'Aye, it's doing well – but little that means to the weavers who do the work,' he growled. 'Jamie Todd and that fine Mister Knox of yours are lining their pockets – but not a penny piece more do I get out of it.'

'You're paid good wages – enough to help your mother

and keep yourself and me and a bairn, with what I make from my spinning –'

'You'll not be able to go on doing that, though.'

'Walter, I'm bearing a child, not falling sick with the pox! I'll not be away from my wheel for long. And then there's the wee bit of money I make seeing to Margaret Knox's looms –'

He shifted restlessly in his chair and looked at her from beneath lowered brows. 'As to that, I think it's high time you put a stop to it.'

'Put a stop to it? But a moment since, you were fretting about not bringing in enough money!'

'I've no taste for living off my wife's earnings.'

'You know fine that in Paisley plenty of the women help to bring in the silver! There's nothing wrong with it. It's not as if the work's hard. All I have to do is visit the loom shops every day and see that there's enough yarn and that the finished ribbons are collected.'

'I don't like you working for the likes of Margaret Knox. You're my wife, not her servant!'

She realised, too late, that she should never have persuaded him to attend the gathering in Mary MacLeod's house. The sight of the prosperous Knox and Todd and Montgomery families had filled him with bitterness and resentment. There was nothing to be gained by reminding him that all these folk had worked hard for what they now had; Walter looked at them and saw only that they were wealthier than he was. And he despised them for it.

His resentment centred itself mainly on Richard Knox. Islay rarely saw the man herself, other than an occasional glimpse of him riding his fine chestnut horse along the street, tall and elegant in the saddle, with his dour manservant in close attendance astride his grey mount. But she knew whenever he had paid a visit to the loom shop downstairs, for on those evenings Walter was especially surly. Sometimes he would go out to a howff, coming back the worse for drink, muttering about Richard Knox and his high and mighty ways.

He returned from one of his evenings out later than usual, running up the outer stairs and erupting into the kitchen so fiercely that the door crashed back against the wall and the candle Islay had lit so that she could go on with her sewing guttered in the great draught of wind that accompanied Walter into the house.

She jumped to her feet, spilling the material she was working on to the floor. 'Walter, what's –'

'Hold your tongue, woman!' He slammed the door shut and leaned against it for a moment, his shoulders heaving as he dragged air into his lungs. When at last he turned, her hands flew to her mouth. His face, beneath an untidy thatch of wind-swept hair, was grey-white, apart from a splash of crimson all down one side, from temple to chin.

'You're hurt!'

He put his fingers to his cheek and brought them away sticky with congealing blood as Islay ran to fetch a rag and some water.

'Sit down and let me look at it. What happened to you?'

He let her lead him to a chair at the table. 'I was – making my way home when someone sprang at me out of the shadows.'

'Who was it?'

'How should I know? The brute felled me to the ground before I could turn round.'

His clothes were certainly muddy. It had been a wet late September day and there were plenty of puddles around that night. But somehow his story didn't ring true.

'But why would anyone try to attack you, Walter?'

'There's plenty of vagabonds and thieves about the streets. Who knows why they do what they do?'

'Surely they could see that you'd not be likely to have enough silver on you to make it worth whi –' She stopped, biting back a cry of pain as Walter's hand suddenly shot out and gripped her wrist, his fingers digging painfully into the soft tissue of her inner arm. The bowl of water tipped, splashing some of its contents on the table, then teetered before righting itself.

'Someone sprang out at me from the shadows and felled me to the ground – and that's all there is to it!' Walter said from between clenched teeth. 'D'you hear what I say, woman?

Then he released her arm and sat back, lifting his face for her ministration. 'Now – hold your tongue when I tell you to, and see to the wound.'

A dozen more questions hovered on Islay's lips, but she didn't dare ask them. A dozen chill fears tugged at the fringes of her mind, but she didn't dare admit them any further. She concentrated instead on gently cleansing his face and mopping at the fresh blood that still welled slowly from a nasty cut on his cheekbone. The flesh around it was already swelling and purpling. It looked as though Walter had indeed been hit by a stick; if the blow had landed a little higher, on his temple, he would have been knocked unconscious.

'Fetch the ale!'

'If I take this pad away from the cut it'll start bleeding ag –'

'I'll hold it! Just fetch the ale when you're told!'

She did, and poured it clumsily in her agitation, slopping some onto the table to join the water that had already been spilled there. She brought fresh cloths and mopped up the mess, then sat down by the fireplace again and picked up her sewing, not daring to look at Walter in case she sent him into another bout of anger.

He sat on at the table for some time, drinking steadily until the ale jug was emptied. Now and then, when the wind outside gusted and set something rattling, he jumped and looked sharply at the door.

Once he asked in a whisper, 'Can you hear someone coming up the stairs?'

'It's only the sound of the wind. Who'd come here at this hour of the night?'

'Go out and look,' he insisted fretfully.

Outside, she closed the door behind her and stood for a moment on the wooden landing. The wind caught at her skirts and pulled them tightly against her calves and thighs. The moon was hidden by low scudding clouds and the night was dark around and above and below her.

After a moment she went back inside to find Walter on his feet, still clasping the padded cloth to his face, watching the door warily. As she came in his free hand tightened on the back of a chair, for all the world as though he would have picked it up and used it as a weapon if necessary.

'Well?'

'There's nobody out there.'

He relaxed a little. 'How does it look now?'

She went to him and eased the cloth from his face. 'It's stopped bleeding, but it looks awful sore.'

'It'll do. Come to bed, Islay.'

That night he made no attempt to touch her, but lay still and wakeful by her side. Islay, too, stayed awake for a long time before falling asleep. She roused once, and knew at once that Walter was still awake, although when she whispered his name into the darkness he didn't answer. She slipped back into drowsy oblivion, and woke again to see a muted light dancing on the kitchen ceiling.

It went out even as she blinked sleepily at it, and the room was dark once more. Beside her Walter finally slept, breathing heavily. As Islay raised herself on one elbow the dim light danced once again on the ceiling and she realised that the noises she heard outside weren't caused by the wind, but by feet scraping against the wooden stairs outside.

With mounting alarm she realised that the light on the ceiling came from a lantern shining through the window. A man's voice muttered something as she slid out of bed, her heart hammering in her chest.

'Walter!'

He grunted, muttered something, but didn't waken, even when she seized his shoulder. But at the first thunderous blow on the door from a determined fist he shot up and out of the bed, twisting away from Islay's fingers, an oath ripping from him as his feet found the floor.

There was a steady rain of blows on the door now, and a man's voice bellowing, 'You in there – open this door in the King's name!'

'The militia!' All the fears that Islay had refused to face earlier flooded back. 'Walter –'

He pushed her away when she went to him, and cursed as he stumbled over a chair in the darkness. 'Don't open the door!'

'I must!' If she didn't, the soldiers would knock it down.

She found her way across the room and lifted the latch. The first man to burst in pushed her firmly aside and lifted his lantern to illuminate the room.

Walter, ashen-faced apart from the livid bruise, seized a sturdy chair by the back and swung it over his head as more men poured in. They were all clad in the smart uniforms and blue feathered bonnets of the Fusiliers quartered in the town to assist the Council to maintain law and order.

They were more than a match for Walter. Before he could as much as lash out with the chair it had been whisked from his hands and he was pinioned between two men.

Islay, cowering against the wall where she had been pushed, sick with fright, convinced that she was trapped in a nightmare and unable to will herself to waken, heard the sergeant say, 'Walter Shaw, I've been commanded to arrest you.'

'No!'

At the sound of her voice the man turned to Islay. His eyes took on a certain sympathy as they travelled over her frightened face. 'I'm sorry, lassie, but we must take your man to the cells.'

'I've done nothing!'

The officer's face was suddenly wiped clean of compassion as he turned back to Walter. 'You tried to rob an honest gentleman of this town.'

'I've not been out of this house all night! Ask my wife – she'll tell you!'

'D'ye tell me that?' The sergeant's fingers caught at Walter's chin and jerked his face savagely to one side so that the cut, bruised cheek was clearly seen. 'And is it your wee wife that did this to you, then?' Then he added, as the other men laughed. 'No sense in telling us any of your lies, Walter Shaw, for Mister Knox saw your face and told us where we might find you.'

'Richard Knox?'

'Aye, lassie, Richard Knox. Bring him along,' he ordered, and Walter, struggling every inch of the way, was dragged out of the house. Islay caught up her cloak and his jacket and made to follow him, but the sergeant's arm barred the way.

'No sense in you coming too, lass, for you'll not be allowed to see your man again until the morning.'

'Will you see that he gets this – and these –?' She darted about the room, gathering up Walter's clothes, and deposited them in the man's arms.

'Aye, I'll give them to him.'

'Will he –' Her voice failed her, and she had to try again. 'Will he be all right?'

'He tried to rob Mister Knox. You know yourself what the penalty might well be,' he said, and withdrew, closing the door quietly behind him.

The chair that Walter had used in his attempt to crush the soldiers' heads in was lying on its side. Islay set it on its legs again and sank down onto it, clutching her cloak tightly in her arms. She began to shiver, and soon she was shaking like a leaf in a gale, unable to stop.

She knew well enough what the penalty for such a crime was, if the court was satisfied that Walter was guilty. It was death by hanging.

Chapter Thirty-Five

'The fool! The stupid, addle-pated fool!' Jamie Todd raged, striding up and down the length of his mother's kitchen, unable to rest in his anger.

His red hair stood on end, his eyes blazed blue fire, and his hands fisted and unfisted themselves by his sides continually, as though itching to hold Walter Shaw's irresponsible neck in their grasp.

His mother, Kirsty, and step-father, Billy, watched him pace ceaselessly to and fro, but said nothing. They well knew that when Jamie was in one of his tempers he was best left to work himself out of it again.

He marched from door to window, swung about with a practised economy of movement reminiscent of his days as a soldier, and went on, 'And what's more, he's left me with an idle loom and nobody to finish the web in time!'

'Jamie Todd, you'll feel the back of my hand on your lug in just one minute!' Margaret Knox, the fourth person in the room, had no reservations about interrupting Jamie, rage or no rage. 'To the devil with your loom, man – what about poor Walter, lying in the Tolbooth at this very minute in fear of his life? And what about Islay, carrying his child and not knowing what's to become of her man?'

Jamie had the grace to look a trifle embarrassed. His pace slowed. 'I went to see Islay as soon as I heard,' he said defensively. 'But she wasn't in, and I'd no way of finding out where she was.'

'She spends nearly all her time now with Walter's mother – when she's not visiting the lad himself. Poor Mistress Shaw's near out of her mind with grief over what's to become of him, they say.'

'And Islay? How is she?'

'Doing bravely, as you'd expect of the lassie. The dear

Lord knows she's had enough worry in her life as it is without this coming along.'

Jamie's fists clenched again. 'What possessed the damned fool to try to rob Richard Knox?'

'We don't know that he did. According to him, he was set upon himself that night, in another part of the town entirely.'

'I'd not say it outside these four walls, but I don't believe him,' said Walter's employer, then returned to his own train of thought. 'But why did he do it? I pay him fair wages, I gave him a house to live in –'

'Some folk just naturally want more than they have,' Billy's deep, slow voice said, and Margaret nodded.

'You're right. But it'll do no good to Islay or Walter if we sit and argue over why he did it. The thing to do now is to get him freed.'

Jamie stared. 'You've little chance of that. He'll be fortunate if he escapes the gallows.'

'He didn't take a penny piece of Richard's money,' Margaret pointed out.

'Only because he was too ham-fisted to do the job properly,' Jamie said sourly.

'That's as mebbe. The thing is – Walter jumped out of the dark when Richard and his manservant were riding home, and tried to snatch at Richard's saddle-bag. But Richard struck him down with his whip and Walter ran off. So Walter didnae actually lay his hands on the money. It's only Richard's word against his – though that's small comfort to Walter, for folk are reluctant to disbelieve a well-set-up man like Richard.'

'The Sheriff Officer's a fair man,' Billy pointed out. 'He'll give both sides a hearing, and not be swayed by Richard Knox's wealth the way some might.'

'If Richard could be persuaded to change his mind about charging him, things would go easier for the laddie,' Kirsty suggested. 'Jamie, you know the man – you could talk to him, could you not?'

'He's my business partner, Mother! And it was one of my weavers who tried to rob him. How can I ask him to forgive the man and get him freed and sent home?'

'I doubt if you'd manage to make him change his mind in any case. I've already spoken to Richard, and he's set his heart on seeing Walter punished.'

Kirsty looked at Margaret with wide eyes. 'You're surely not saying the man wants to see Walter thrown into the jail – or even hanged – when he did no more than to try to snatch at the money?'

Margaret's teeth nibbled at her lower lip, then she nodded. 'He does. There's a side to Richard that none of us has seen before – except Gavin, and I found it hard to believe him when he first spoke to me of it a good while back. Mebbe it's because he spent all these years over the water, in countries where they practise cruelties we've never even heard of. As he sees it, Walter deserves to die for even thinking of laying a finger on Richard Knox, or anything belonging to Richard Knox.'

There was a stunned silence in the kitchen. Even Jamie had stopped his pacing, and was staring at Margaret.

'Sending another human soul to his death, just for the sake of hurt pride?' Kirsty said softly. 'It's cruel!'

'It is that.' Jamie shook his head. 'I'd not have thought it of him.'

'I tell you this – I'm shamed of Richard. I told him so to his face, but I might as well have poured water over a duck for all the notice he took of me. He's not a man to be over-troubled by his conscience,' Margaret said bleakly.

'Mebbe Gavin's the one who could make his brother listen to reason,' Billy suggested.

'He says he couldn't, and he'll not beg the man for any favours. So – I'm calling on all the influential folk I know in the town, to try to get some support for Walter when the sorry business comes to trial.' Margaret rose and picked up her cloak.

As she was going out of the door she turned and said, her eyes on Jamie. 'Islay's the one I'm heartsick for. If you ask me, she should never have married Walter in the first place.'

*

'My Walter should never have married you in the first

place!' Isa Shaw was saying to her daughter-in-law at that moment in her over-crowded tenement room.

Islay, preparing a meal for the hungry, noisy family, said nothing. The woman had said the same thing over and over again since the moment she heard about her son's arrest. She desperately needed to blame someone else for Walter's wrong-doing, and his wife was the natural culprit.

'I told my poor laddie from the beginning – Highlanders are a queer lot. We never mixed with them, and we shouldn't start,' the querulous voice went on. 'But he'd not heed me. He was set on taking you to wife – and what has he to show for it? Rotting in the Tolbooth, mebbe even –'

The words ended in a dry sob. Islay, who knew better than to try to comfort the woman, dipped a spoon into the simmering broth, blew on it to cool it, and put it to her lips. It was ready. She set out bowls on the table and, with an effort, lifted the heavy pot from the range and carried it to them. Nobody offered to help her; Walter's brothers and sisters crowded round their mother and watched her every movement with mistrustful eyes.

'You and your well-to-do friends, flaunting their wealth in my poor laddie's face, making him feel that he wasn't good enough –'

As Islay ladled the broth out she wondered with tired irony what the Lowlanders thought Highlanders did that made them different from other folk? She had heard of all the daft stories spread during the Jacobite disturbances about Highlanders eating babies and indulging in other barbaric practices.

Her own father had fought on Prince Charles Stuart's side, and she could think of nobody less likely to harm a baby – or anyone else – in any way than that silent, gentle man who had died of his sufferings before his natural lifespan was over.

'There's scarce enough food in this house for the bairns and me as it is, without feeding you as well.'

Mistress Shaw's voice broke into her thoughts. She and her children were beginning to gather round the table now that the broth was ready for them.

'I don't want any. I'm just going.' Islay took her cloak

from the nail on the street door. Her back ached, her head
ached, and she hadn't slept since Walter had been taken by
the militia two days earlier.

'I suppose you'll have to come and bide here, you and the
bairn both. The Lord only knows,' said Mistress Shaw, fresh
tears falling into her bowl, 'how I'm going to feed two more
mouths – and with no more silver from Walter to help me.'

'I'll not be a burden to you,' Islay said quietly.

Unfortunately the words, meant to reassure the woman,
only set her off on her journey of recrimination again. 'Not
be a burden? Not be a burden?' she screeched. 'It was you
put my boy in jail in the first place, you Highland besom –!'

*

It was a relief to escape from them all, away from the
crowded room where the air was thick and stale and sour
with hopeless bitterness.

As she tramped along to the Tolbooth in the hope of
being allowed to see Walter for a few minutes Islay swore to
herself that no matter what happened she would not go to
live with Mistress Shaw.

She would sooner birth her child in a ditch, and beg for its
bread through the towns and villages.

*

The Tolbooth stood at the corner of Waingaitend, near the
Cross. Its steeple housed six floors. The jailer's room was on
the ground floor, with the criminal cells, where Walter was
being held, above it. Then came the debtors' quarters, the
women prisoners' rooms, and finally the steeple area with
the clock, the tiny bell-ringers' room, and the bell itself.

The main building housed the sheriff court rooms where
cases were heard each Tuesday, a guardhouse, and a howff
where the jailer was entitled to add to his income by serving
porter and ale to the debtors and their visitors.

An open landing outside the court held the stocks and a
whipping post, which were rarely used. In Paisley, people
sentenced to be flogged for their crimes were usually taken
through the town at the back of a cart and whipped at
various stopping-points.

Walter was sharing a small cell with two other men. When the jailer admitted Islay the two strangers, squatting in the grimy straw and taking turns to throw a dice, looked up and ran their eyes avidly over her face and body.

Walter had been huddled in a corner, knees drawn up to his chin, staring into space. He scurried to the door, putting his hands through the bars and clutching at Islay feverishly. The other men looked at each other, shrugged, and went back to their gambling.

'You must get me out of here!'

Strangely, his brief imprisonment had made him look both older and younger. His face was grey and haggard, his hair lank, his eyes sunken. And yet there was something heart-breakingly childish and vulnerable about the bright panic in his eyes, the tremble to his mouth and chin, the terrified way his hands kept hold of her.

'I'm doing all I can – we all are. Mistress Knox and her husband, and –'

'Your fine friends trying to help me?' A sneer temporarily overcame the tremor. 'It's only for your sake!'

'What does it matter whose sake it's for, as long as they help us? Is your head all right, Walter?'

Margaret had persuaded her brother Thomas to visit the prison and tend to Walter's head. Islay, who had been afraid of what might happen to the wound if it was allowed to fester, was relieved to see that the bandage about her husband's head was reasonably clean and dry, with no trace of blood or seepage.

'It's well enough.'

'I've just come from your mother's house –'

But he didn't want to hear about his mother, or the rest of his family. The fear was back, his fingers tightening on her arms, and hurting her. 'Islay, don't leave me here. Get me out!'

'Mister Knox is determined to see you before the court.'

'You must speak to him, then!'

'How can I speak to him? What can I say?'

'Anything – just make him change his mind!'

'Margaret's already tried it, and he wouldn't listen to her.'

'You're younger – and prettier,' said Walter rapidly, in an

undertone. 'He likes you, Islay, you know that. You could persuade him. You could offer him – offer him anything he wants, Islay. Anything!'

Reading the meaning in his eyes, she suddenly felt sick. 'Walter –'

'Anything!' he insisted, his face alight with hope. 'You could make him change his mind. You'd know how to go about it, Islay –'

Chapter Thirty-Six

The words rang through her head all night as she tossed sleeplessly. She couldn't do as Walter asked, and yet she must do everything she could to save him.

The next morning after she had cleaned out the loomshop as usual she bathed carefully in a basin of water and brushed her hair until it gleamed. Then she put on her best day dress and walked to St Mirin's Wynd, to Richard Knox's lodgings.

Her heart was in her mouth, and she walked up and down, past the door several times before plucking up enough courage to go in and enquire for him.

He was still at home and had just finished breaking his fast when his manservant showed Islay into his comfortable parlour. The smell of food at this time of the morning set her stomach churning, but she forced the nausea back as Richard kissed her hand and ushered her to a seat.

He looked handsome and prosperous in a spotlessly white shirt with flounces at neck and wrist, buff-coloured breeches, knee-length brown leather boots, and a beautifully embroidered satin waistcoat in blues and reds and greens. Despite the care she had taken to dress for her visit Islay felt colourless and shabby beside him.

Richard nodded to his servant and the man gathered up the dishes from the table and seemed to slide from the room, closing the door noiselessly behind him.

'My dear Islay – a pleasant surprise, though surely it's scarcely proper in Paisley for a beautiful young woman to visit a bachelor in his quarters at this time of day.'

'I must speak with you, Mister Knox.'

His smile didn't waver, his eyes were as intent as ever, and yet in an instant a hardness seemed to overlay his features, as though someone had slid a piece of glass before them.

'If it's about that foolish lad you married, Islay, I must tell you that you're wasting your time and mine.'

'Please –'

He waved a hand to stop her, then turned to take a bottle-green jacket from the back of a chair. 'My dear, you're very pretty, and I've no quarrel with you. Indeed, if only you would permit me to shower you with silks and jewels and all the things that beauty like yours deserves I would do so with the greatest of pleasure. Perhaps – one day – but not now. Not until the matter between your husband and myself is settled to my satisfaction.'

'Mister Knox, can you feel no pity for Walter? You have so much, and he has so little –'

'Nevertheless, he should have been content with what he had,' Richard said, a steely edge to his voice. 'And he must learn his lesson. You're wasting your time, Islay. On such a worthless object, too. To tell you the truth, my dear, I wonder that you ever brought yourself to marry the man.'

The door opened on the last sentence.

The newcomer stepped forward as Islay rose from her chair and turned – to find herself being surveyed by a pair of startled blue eyes.

'What are you doing here?' Jamie Todd demanded to know.

'She's on an errand of mercy, in the name of her scoundrel of a husband. Henry –' Richard Knox said, and the manservant, who had ushered Jamie in and was still standing by the door, stepped forward to take the jacket from his master's hands and help him on with it.

'As to your business, Todd –?'

'As it happens, I'm on the same errand of mercy myself.'

'What? Another visitor come to plead Walter Shaw's case? I never knew that he had so many friends – or that there were so many gullible folk in the one town. Besides, Jamie Todd, you're my partner. I thought to find you, at least, on my side.'

'The man worked for me.' Jamie shot a sidelong glance at Islay, then said levelly, 'The man works for me.'

The correction, and the way he moved to stand by her side, comforted her. She wanted to lay her hand on his arm, to assure herself that he was really there, but she didn't dare.

'If indeed he was the man who tried to attack and rob you, then –'

'I can assure you –' There was steel beneath Richard Knox's silken tones, a flash of anger in his eyes. 'He was the man.'

' – then he made a fool of himself,' Jamie went on. 'He acted hastily and clumsily, but he's been injured and punished enough, surely. Tell the Sheriff that you've changed your mind, Knox, and let the poor wretch go free.'

The silk in Richard's voice was shredding now, the hard cold steel more apparent. 'He tried to rob me, and he must pay for his impertinence. As for you, Jamie, let me give you some sound advice. It would be foolish to make an enemy of the man who's given you the opportunity to make a very good living for yourself.'

'As to that, you need me and my weavers as much as I need you and your abilities.'

The two men faced each other angrily, then Richard shrugged and smoothed the lapels of his jacket.

Behind him, his manservant stood quietly to attention, his face as closed and cold as his master's. He looked, Islay thought, like a man capable of doing anything his employer might wish of him, without giving it a thought.

'You're right,' Richard said at last, and held out one hand to the side, palm up. His servant instantly put a silver-handled cane into it.

Richard transferred the cane to his other hand, held out his hand again, and received his tricorne hat.

'You're right, Jamie, but neither of us truly needs Walter Shaw, do we? I'm sorry, my dear –' he acknowledged Islay's presence with a slight, faultlessly elegant bow. ' – that I can't grant you your wish on this occasion. But please believe me when I say that I'm convinced that life holds more riches for you than your present husband could ever give to you. You'd be well advised to rid yourself of him – if I don't manage to do it for you. May I escort you down to the street?'

'I'm on my way to Wellmeadow. I'll escort Islay,' Jamie said icily, and put a hand beneath her elbow.

If it hadn't been for that firm grip she would never have managed to stumble down the stairs and out into the street again. The building was beginning to revolve around her ears, and Jamie had to half-carry her outside, where he propped her against the house wall and commanded, 'Breathe deeply.'

She did so, until Paisley stopped circling about her and settled down again.

Jamie regarded her anxiously. 'Can you walk, or shall I fetch a cart for you?'

'I can walk.' She pushed herself groggily away from the wall, and he took her arm in a strong grip again.

'I'll take you to my mother's house. She'll look after you.'

'No, I can –'

'Yes,' said Jamie, in a voice that forbade further argument. She realised as they set out that she didn't want to argue anyway, she just wanted, desperately, to be looked after.

'I don't know what possessed you to call on that man,' he said angrily from above her head.

She stopped and faced him, swaying. 'I must do all I can to help Walter.'

'You must care about him very much,' he said tonelessly.

'The choice isn't mine. He's my husband. It's my duty to save him.'

Their eyes locked, and it was Jamie who looked away first, taking her arm again and urging her forward.

'From what I've just seen and heard I'd say that only God can do that,' she heard him say as they went on. 'And even He might not be a match for Richard Knox.'

Neither of them spoke again until they arrived in his mother's kitchen. Then Kirsty Carmichael took charge, gathering Islay into her arms, settling her by the fireside, removing her cloak and bonnet and rubbing at her cold hands. Billy, moving stiffly, brought some hot tea and coaxed their visitor to sip at it. His lined gentle face was alight with sympathy.

'You'll stay with us until this sorry business is over – you will,' Kirsty insisted as Islay began to protest. 'There's a wee room, the one my daughter had. It'll do fine for you.'

'But my work – and my house –'

'Jamie'll see that everything's taken care of,' his mother said firmly. 'You should never have been left alone in the first place. I thought Isa Shaw would have – but there, she's a poor handless creature herself.'

Jamie hovered by the door for a moment until his mother said, 'Well, laddie, what are you standing there for? Go about your work, and leave Islay to me.'

Then he went, leaving Islay to Kirsty's ministrations.

Chapter Thirty-Seven

Walter Shaw's trial was held in October, soon after his arrest.

Richard's thirst for revenge led him to press for a charge of attempted murder as well as robbery, an accusation that was much more serious. But he failed, for Walter hadn't dealt one blow, and nobody knew whether or not he might have, given the opportunity.

He had been the only man injured in the struggle, and he hadn't succeeded in stealing one penny piece.

Much was made of this during the trial in the Sheriff Court. When all was said and done Walter was a Paisley man and Richard an incomer. Popular though Richard was the Paisley folk didn't like to be dictated to by a stranger, especially when it came to their jealously-prized rights as a Royal Burgh with a Royal charter that had been granted by King James IV almost three hundred years earlier.

The trial aroused a great deal of interest, and the court-room was packed with onlookers. They were evenly divided, Islay felt as she looked at the noisy public benches, between folk who genuinely wanted to see the young weaver absolved from blame and restored to freedom, and folk who secretly yearned for the excitement and spectacle of a public hanging. Executions were rare in Paisley, and greatly enjoyed on the few occasions when they took place.

A gusty murmur of sympathy swept through the court-room when Walter was led in, pale and somewhat shrunk in on himself, shambling between two jailers. The scar on his face was fading, but could still be seen as a purple weal.

'If Richard hadn't been so greedy for revenge he'd have tried to delay the trial until the wound healed,' Margaret Knox murmured by her side. 'It's still too clearly seen to aid Richard's case.'

Isa Shaw sat on the other side of the court from Islay, surrounded by her children and a clutch of neighbours. Every now and again she shot a malevolent look at her daughter-in-law, who was escorted by Mistress Margaret Knox and Mistress Mary MacLeod, both well-to-do townspeople.

Islay looked away from the woman and caught Walter's eye. She tried to smile, but he just stared pleadingly at her, dumbly begging her to do something – anything – to save him. She had never before felt so helpless.

Margaret's hand touched hers. 'You've gone as white as a sheet. D'you want to go outside for some fresh air?' her friend whispered.

Islay shook her head, and began to concentrate on what was going on before her as the trial began.

At first it looked as though nothing could save Walter. Richard Knox told the court confidently how a man he clearly recognised as Walter Shaw jumped out of the darkness one night as he and his manservant rode towards the stables.

Walter had caught at the saddle-bags slung before Richard – where, as everyone knew, the day's takings were – and had been beaten back by Richard's whip.

The horses, said Richard, had been terrified by the suddenness of the attack. They had to be calmed, and in the confusion Walter had managed to escape.

'You recognised the man who leapt out at you, Mister Knox?' asked the Sheriff.

'I saw him often enough when I visited the loomshop where he worked. And I met him on one occasion when we were both guests at Mistress MacLeod's house.'

As the manservant followed his master to the witness stand, and repeated Richard's story almost word for word, Walter clutched at the railing before him for support, his eyes fixed on Islay as though he was convinced that she was the only one who could save him.

'And you, my good fellow, have you accompanied your master into the weaving shop where the accused works?' asked the Sheriff.

The servant shuffled his feet uneasily and glanced at

Richard before saying, 'No, sir.'

'If you hadn't set eyes on him before, how did you know that your attacker was the man called Walter Shaw?'

A ripple ran through the crowded hall. From where she sat on Margaret's other side Islay could hear Mary MacLeod whisper to her niece, 'I shall invite the Sheriff to dine, and the shrewd man shall have my best French brandy!'

Again the manservant shuffled uncertainly, then said, 'Mister Knox told me who he was. But I saw enough of him to know that that's the scoundrel there,' he added hurriedly, pointing at Walter. Isa Shaw gave a squawk of mingled rage and despair, and was hushed by her friends.

One or two men came forward to testify that Walter had been in a howff with them, but they were fairly disreputable-looking, and it seemed clear to Islay that in the eyes of the Sheriff their evidence didn't count for much.

Then Thomas Montgomery rose and went forward. 'If it please the court, I have something to say.'

The Sheriff gave a brief nod. 'We're listening, Mister Montgomery.'

The young physician's testimony was brief and to the point. He, too, knew Walter Shaw and his wife, and knew that until the night of the attempted robbery there had not been the slightest stain on Walter's good name. He pointed out that he had treated the defendant for a fairly serious head wound while he was in prison, and that the two men who had been attacked had not been hurt in any way. He asked for the Sheriff's leniency to be shown towards the young man in the dock.

There was a stir as Thomas sat down and both Gavin Knox and Jamie Todd stood up abruptly at the same time to take his place. The Sheriff looked from one to the other, then motioned Gavin forward first. Islay glanced briefly at Richard and saw him staring from one man to the other, his face set and white with anger.

Margaret's fingers tightened on Islay's hand as her husband described Walter and herself as good friends of the family and gave his own testimony as to the weaver's good character. Then Jamie strode into the body of the court and spoke up for the accused man, describing him as a conscientious worker who had never before caused any trouble.

'And never will again, if the court can find it in its heart to be lenient on this occasion,' he said sturdily, half-speaking to the Sheriff, half-speaking to the rest of the courtroom. His blue eyes met and held Islay's as he concluded firmly and clearly, 'I'm prepared to take responsibility for his future behaviour, sir, if you grant him his freedom.'

'Indeed –' the Sheriff's voice was dry. 'I find it strange, Mister Todd, that you and Mister Knox should speak in defence of the accused, when one of you is in partnership with Mr Richard Knox and the other his own blood kin.'

Gavin came to his feet again. 'That's as may be, sir, but it seems to me that at times justice must come before blood bonds. And no doubt Mister Todd will say the same for business.'

Jamie's red head ducked in agreement.

'Your concern for justice does you both credit, gentlemen.' The Sheriff consulted the papers before him. 'The serious nature of the case – and robbery is a most serious business –' he added sharply, glaring at Walter. ' – is somewhat mitigated by the fact that no actual robbery took place, and nobody was hurt other than the man accused of the crime. In view of that, I am prepared to be more lenient than might otherwise have been the case.'

Richard Knox made the mistake of interrupting, jumping to his feet to ask furiously, 'Is this what passes for the law in Paisley, sir? That felon –' a finger stabbed mercilessly through the air in Walter's direction, ' – tried to rob and murder me and my manservant! Is this town so lackadaisical in its morals that honest men can't be safe in its streets?'

A low, ugly growl rose from the public benches. The Sheriff's thin face suddenly became a collection of sharp cold edges as he crashed his fist on the table before him.

'Mister Knox, you forget yourself, sir! Not a penny piece was taken from you. You were not hurt. You lost nothing but a little pride, you received no injury but a blow to your own self-esteem.'

'I demand that this man be punished severely!'

'Oh, Richard; Richard!' Mary MacLeod rebuked under

her breath. 'You've damned yourself now, my mannie!'

'You may demand all you like, Mister Knox. This is my court, under my jurisdiction.' The Sheriff said, then sat back, his cold gaze travelling over the faces before him.

Then he said, 'In view of the facts heard in this court, and in view of the pleas put forward by three of our own most eminent townspeople –' His glance brushed Richard Knox's livid, set face and moved on, ' – including Mister Todd's solemn undertaking that Walter Shaw shall never again have to be brought before me or any other court on any mischief whatsoever, I find that the case has not been proven to my complete satisfaction. The prisoner is therefore free to go; although –' Now the sharp, cold face was turned in Walter's direction, 'I warn you, my man, that if you should ever appear before this court or any other, your punishment will be harsh indeed.'

Richard Knox stood up so suddenly that his chair fell over. He swung round on his heel and strode out of the courtroom, his manservant trotting after him.

Mistress Isa Shaw dissolved into hysterics. The jailers assisted Walter from the dock, and left him to stand alone, dazed and uncomprehending.

Islay went to him; when she was a few yards away he suddenly woke from his trance and ran towards her, clutching her in his arms, burying his face in her neck.

Over his shoulder Islay saw Jamie Todd standing alone, watching the two of them. His face was impassive.

Chapter Thirty-Eight

After he gained his freedom Walter was quiet and subdued, leaving the house only to go down to the weaving shop each day.

In the evenings he was content to stay close to Islay, watching her as she worked at her sewing or plied her knitting wires, occasionally reaching out to touch her hand as though convincing himself that she was really there, and he was really home.

Richard Knox didn't come near the weaving shop, much to Walter's relief. Once he realised that the man wasn't going to appear he began to relax, and even went off to spend an hour in the howff with his friends one evening.

When he returned he was cheerful and confident, even inclined to boast a little about what had happened to him.

'He deserved to be robbed, that Richard Knox,' he said as he undressed for bed. 'He'd not miss a bag or two of silver – not him. And as for a knock on the head – it'd do no harm to let some light into his thick skull.'

'Walter, for God's sake!' Islay, already in bed, sat bolt upright and clutched the sheet to her in a panic. 'Stop that talk before someone hears you!'

He laughed. 'There's nobody to hear me except you.'

'You didn't talk like that in the howff, did you?'

'What d'you take me for – a fool?'

She didn't believe him. 'You heard what the Sheriff said – if you appear in court again it'll go hard with you.'

Walter blew out the lamp and slid into bed, his hands reaching out for her greedily. 'The wise thing, my lass,' he said into her ear, his breath hot and rapid against her neck, 'is not to be caught.'

Islay worried all the next day. It would only take a few careless words in the crowded howff, a pair of listening ears, a man willing to report the foolish boasts in return for a coin or two. And then the militia might be back for Walter. He had been released on a 'not proven' verdict. That meant that he could be arrested and tried again.

Part of his saving had been his obstinate refusal to admit to anyone, even himself, that he had indeed tried to rob Richard Knox. But fuddled with drink, in the midst of his friends, Walter could easily talk himself into a prison cell or a hangman's noose, she thought. Richard Knox would be only too happy to act on any further evidence he might receive.

When she tried to persuade Walter to stay at home in the evenings for a while longer, he refused.

'Promise me, then, that you'll not talk about – about what happened. Not a word.'

'Ach – women! Aye skiting at a man!' he grumbled, and went out.

The evening passed and the street outside fell silent, and still there was no sound of Walter's footsteps on the stairs. At last Islay laid her knitting aside and put on her cloak.

The street was dark, dotted here and there with lamplit windows. Hardly anyone was out now. She walked almost to Town Head, where Margaret's father's cottage and weaving shop stood. She would have liked to go on to High Street to ask for Jamie's help; but he had done enough for her. She couldn't go running to him every time she was worried.

She retraced her steps, walking now into the teeth of the chill night wind. The house was still empty when she went back to it. She drew her chair close to the range and huddled over the warmth, waiting.

A full hour went by before feet trod on the wooden stairs outside. Islay's head lifted sharply. It wasn't Walter's step – this was a heavier man, and one unused to negotiating these steps in the dark.

She ran to the door and threw it open. Then her knees buckled and she had to catch the side of the door-frame for support when the caller arrived on the top step and moved into the pool of light spilling from the room behind her.

It was the militia sergeant who had arrested Walter.

'My husband –' Islay's voice was weak with fear.

The man looked down on her, and this time his face was warm with sympathy.

'I'm sorry, lass.' He put his arm about her and almost carried her into the house. Then he put her into her chair and sat opposite her while he told her that Walter's body had just been found in a dark empty lane near the howff.

He had been killed by a knife wound in the back.

*

On the night before Walter's funeral Gavin Knox made his way to his brother's lodgings.

Richard was alone in his parlour, reclining comfortably in a chair by the fire, a half-filled glass in his hand. He didn't rise as Gavin was shown into the room, but indicated a chair on the other side of the fireplace.

'Here's a surprise – I never thought to see you calling on me. Henry, take Mister Knox's coat. You'll have a glass of rum with me, Gavin.'

Gavin shrugged his coat more firmly over his broad shoulders as he stepped away from the manservant's outstretched hands. 'I don't care for rum.'

'You have barbaric tastes,' Richard said easily. 'Whisky, then? Claret?'

'Nothing. I only want to offer you a word of advice. A private word of advice.' Gavin glanced significantly at the manservant and took up a stance in the middle of the rich thick carpet, booted feet firmly planted apart.

'Henry –' Richard flicked a hand at the man, who retired noiselessly. 'Now, brother, what sort of advice could you offer to me?' His tone implied clearly that he doubted that it could be of any value.

'Just this – if you care anything for your skin, you'll leave Paisley tomorrow. Tonight, if you can manage it.'

Richard raised a lazy eyebrow. 'Indeed? And why should I have cause to fear for my skin?'

'Because Walter Shaw's been done to death.'

'Walter Shaw,' said Richard, sitting bolt upright, his voice suddenly low and soft with hatred, 'should never have set himself up against me. That travesty of a court and that poor excuse for a Sheriff should never have let the wretch go.'

'Walter's case was found not proven by law!'

'He was guilty! And nobody,' said Richard Knox, 'lifts a hand against me or mine and escapes punishment. If this was Jamaica he would have been flogged and then executed for what he did to me, I can promise you that!'

Then the anger was wiped from his face and he relaxed again, smiling up at Gavin. 'Besides, anyone could have killed your friend – the town's rife with thieves and beggars.'

A muscle jumped in Gavin's jawline. 'Nobody could have mistaken him for a man of means and killed him for his wealth. When he was found the few pence he carried were still in his pocket, undisturbed. He had a few friends, but no enemies. You found a scoundrel willing to do your bidding for a price, and you killed Walter Shaw as surely as if your own hand had put the knife into his back.'

'Prove it.'

'I don't need to prove it, and neither do the folk who'll take revenge on you. I know it, they know it – all Paisley knows it.'

There was a short silence. Richard drained his glass, then said, 'If, as you say, the miserable creature had few friends, I've nothing to fear.'

'You still can't understand, can you?' Gavin asked contemptuously. 'You're so used to gaining what you want by using your own means, Richard. First with charm, and then with money and influence. You've forgotten what it's like to live in a tight-knit community like Paisley. Those folk look after their own, no matter who it may be. Walter was a weaver, and the weavers are the most powerful group of men in the town – and for many miles outside it too. He was born and bred in Paisley – and you can take my word for it that his murderers will be punished.'

Richard opened his mouth to speak, but it was Gavin's turn to command silence with a movement of the hand. 'Perhaps not by law,' he went on, 'For there's no proof. But I tell you this – the man who wielded the knife, the man who gave the order, and the man –' his eyes flickered to the door that had closed behind the manservant minutes earlier, ' –

who acted as go-between: they'll all be found and dealt with. Unless they have the good sense to leave. I expect the knife-man's already far away. Take my advice, Richard. Move to new pastures.'

'If I do, what happens then to your wife's business, built up with my money and my help? What happens to Jamie Todd's loom shops, dependent on my assistance?'

The muscle jumped again as Gavin fought to control his temper. 'Jamie must find his own feet. I'm quite certain that Duncan and Robert Montgomery'll come to his assistance, as he'd go to theirs if he was needed. They'll not let old grievances come between them once you're out of the way. As for Margaret –'

He slipped a hand into his thick coat and brought out a small bulky pouch. He tossed it down onto the table by his brother's side. It gave out the muffled ring of coinage. 'She's already decided that stay or go, she'll have no more to do with you. Here's the money you put into buying the inkle looms and renting the shop – and your fair share of the profits besides.'

Richard picked up the bag and opened it. Gavin watched as the money was counted and carefully stacked on the table.

'So it's goodbye, brother?'

'Aye, if you're wise. If you decide to stay I'll not lift a hand to aid you, and neither will any of the others.'

'Your candour does you credit,' Richard said dryly, and held out his hand.

Gavin looked at it, then turned on his heel and walked out, letting the door lie open behind him.

*

On the day of the funeral the rain poured endlessly from a grey cold sky. Standing at the graveside, watching Walter's coffin being lowered into the earth, Islay found it impossible to grasp the idea of widowhood.

While he was in prison she had forced herself to come to terms with the knowledge that she was almost certainly going to bear and raise their child alone – for ever if he was hanged; for a long time if the sentence was one of a term of imprisonment.

But once he was released everything had changed. Life was set to go as before – Walter and herself, their child, and, no doubt, many other children after that.

The suddenness of his final going was more than she could take in at the moment.

They were all present at the grave – Margaret and Gavin, Margaret's parents and brothers, Mary MacLeod, and Jamie, who stood by her side in the dripping, chilly graveyard. and, of course, Walter's mother and her brood of sons and daughters.

At one point during the sermon Islay looked up and met her mother-in-law's eyes across the open grave. The accusation in the older woman's gaze made her shrink back slightly against Jamie's shoulder.

No matter what happened, she wouldn't – she couldn't – become further involved with the woman.

When it was done she refused all the invitations that showered on her.

'I'd as soon go home,' she said to Kirsty, to Margaret, to Meg Montgomery and Mary MacLeod.

'I'll walk back with her,' Jamie said, and steered her away from the grave with a firm hand.

'What are you going to do now?' he asked as they went back through the rain-washed streets.

'There's little I can do but go on with my life as before. Unless –' sudden fear gripped her, ' – you want the house for another of your weavers –?'

His hand tightened spasmodically on her elbow and his voice was gruff when he said, 'What d'you take me for? You can stay in it for as long as you need it. As for Walter's mother, I've already arranged to give work to one of her other children to make up the money he paid into the house each week.'

They reached the weaving shop and went through the pend. Icy rain soaked Islay's clothes, probing to her very soul with numbingly chill fingers.

In the back yard she said firmly, 'I'll be fine on my lone now.'

'You're certain?'

'I'm certain.' All she wanted was to be alone, and to sleep for ever and ever.

She began to climb the stairs, holding the railing, dragging herself from stair to stair. Her body had become very heavy. The landing seemed to be far above, almost too far to reach.

Doggedly, she went on. Then her foot slipped on a worn, rain-greased step and a sharp stab of pain shot through her ankle as it twisted.

She fell clumsily, rolling and bouncing and sliding down the steps, landing in the yard with a jarring crash. The pain spread until it was everywhere.

Jamie's face, white with alarm, loomed over her. She heard him say, 'Sweet Jesus!' felt him lift her in his arms.

The last thing she heard before the pain drowned her entirely was his voice, urgently calling for help.

Chapter Thirty-Nine

Seventeen hundred and seventy-seven was three months old before Thomas and Gavin pronounced Islay well enough to leave Margaret Knox's house and return to Wellmeadow.

She had begun to despair, during the long cold winter, of ever feeling young and healthy again.

The strain of Walter's trial, then the shock of his sudden, violent death, immediately followed by her miscarriage and a bad bout of pneumonia, seemed to have turned her into a frail old woman, fit to do nothing but sit listlessly in Margaret's parlour.

It was only as the snow melted and the daffodils blazoned their gold trumpets in the gardens and the trees began to show umistakeable signs of soft green growth that her strength began to return; first of all in a trickle so slight that she scarcely noticed it, then in a steady flow that tingled through her muscles and tissue and bones and blood.

It was then, and only then, that she began to want to get back to her own house. For weeks and months she hadn't cared whether Jamie gave it to someone else or reclaimed it as a store. But one day she found herself wondering if it had a neglected look, and the next she began to hunger to see it.

By the time Thomas agreed to let her go home she was almost beside herself with impatience. Margaret and Gavin had been kindness itself, and their home a haven of comfort. But it wasn't where she belonged.

On the day she was to go back she stood in her little bedroom in the Knox house, surveyed herself in the mirror.

'I've aged.'

'You've matured,' Margaret said from behind her. 'And little wonder, for you've had to grow up quickly, Islay.'

The face that looked out of the mirror was thinner than

before, and sadly lacking in colour and animation. The eyes, huge and dark, dominated it. There was a new, firmer set to the mouth, though the hair was as rich and thick as ever.

She had lost weight; her body was elegantly slender now.

'I'm glad you decided to stop wearing mourning,' Margaret said. Islay's hands, white and smooth through months of idleness, fluttered like night-moths in the mirror, touching the dark red gown she wore, and the crisp white lace-edged fichu over her shoulders.

'There's little sense in wearing black for a year, to my mind. I'll mourn inside for Walter and the bairn all my life, no matter what colours I might flaunt on my body. He was so young to die, Walter. And my poor wee bairn never even had the chance to draw breath.'

'There are a lot of years ahead of you, Islay,' her friend said. 'You'll meet another man, and have other bairns.'

The face in the mirror was suddenly closed, the eyes hooded. 'No,' Islay said, as much to her reflection as to Margaret. 'No, I'll not meet any other man. At least, none I'll take for a husband.'

She should never have married Walter. If she hadn't he might be alive today, and wed to someone more suited to him. As for herself, she had learned from her fatal mistake. If she couldn't marry with Jamie Todd she would take no other man. And there was little chance of her ever becoming Jamie's wife.

An hour later, with a tremor of excited happiness, she walked through the pend and up the steps – treading carefully in memory of the terrible day of her fall – and opened the door of her home.

It was just as she had left it, dust-free and with the brass and crockery and iron range twinkling and shining at her. Someone had set a fire in the range, and the kettle was coming to the boil. Someone had brought in provisions and laid them on the table so that she could put them away herself, in the proper places.

She put her bag down, and advanced into the room, tears wet on her cheeks as the house met her and closed about her, holding her safe, welcoming her back.

'So you're home again?' Jamie said from the doorway.

She spun round, rubbing an impatient hand over her face to remove the signs of weakness. 'Aye, I'm home. Who did all this?'

'The womenfolk – my mother and Meg and Mary. You're certain you're well enough to leave Margaret's house?'

'I'm as well as I'll ever be. What I need now is to get back to work.'

'Your wheel's waiting for you.' He nodded to the corner, and she saw that there was a bag of flax by the wheel, and a box of empty pirns. 'As to the loom shop –'

'I'll start on it tomorrow morning, if that's all right with you.'

He shrugged, a slow lifting of his broad shoulders. 'Aye, that's fine.'

She studied him as he hesitated in the doorway. He too looked strained. Margaret had told her that after Richard Knox's sudden disappearance from Paisley Duncan and Robert Montgomery had welcomed Jamie back to their number, and now the High Street looms were weaving linen again. But the Wellmeadow machines were still on what was left of the cotton yarn, and Jamie was determinedly searching for a market for them.

'He's restless again,' Margaret said. 'Somehow he can't seem to get back to the life he knew before. I doubt Richard's left his mark on us all.'

She herself, with Gavin's reluctant blessing, had pressed forward with the ribbon-weaving business, finding a manufacturer willing to take the ribbons, and arranging to buy cotton yarn from an English supplier.

'You can bring your pirns downstairs when they're filled.' Jamie's voice broke into Islay's thoughts, and she coloured, realising that she had been staring at him. It was a habit she had got into during her illness – fixing her eyes on something or someone and drifting away into a trance. She must put a stop to it. 'I'll take them along to High Street myself when I go.'

'Are you working downstairs, then?'

'Aye.' He shifted from one foot to the other, then said awkwardly, 'I'm working the loom Walter used to have. I'm trying out a new cloth.'

'For Mister Montgomery?'

'No,' said Jamie, 'for myself.' And he went back downstairs and left her alone.

When she had hung her cloak neatly in its usual place she sat down at her wheel and took up a handful of flax, drawing out the beginnings of the thread between thumb and forefinger. Then she lifted an empty pirn from the box and rolled the thread around it before slipping the pirn into place.

She put her foot firmly on the treadle and set the wheel in motion, helping it with one hand. The wheel picked up speed, the pirn began to rotate, gathering the twisting yarn thread.

Islay's foot settled to the familiar soothing beat of the treadle, and she knew with a great, healing rush of happiness that she was home again.

*

The new cloth Jamie was working on occupied all his time over that summer. Often Islay's ears caught the faint beat of a single loom in the evenings, long after the other weavers had gone. Now and then, unable to sleep, she stood at the back window, and saw a golden rectangle of light splashed across the cobbles; light from the lamp he was working by.

She heard from Margaret that his attempts seemed to be doomed to failure. But Jamie refused to give up.

One night when she was preparing to go to bed, footsteps clattered up the wooden stairs and someone thundered on the door.

Islay's heart began to race. Memories of the night Walter had been arrested, and the night the sergeant had come to tell her of his death, blazed into her mind.

'Islay! Islay, are you there?'

'Jamie?' The paralysis that had gripped her muscles eased; she found the energy to cross the room, her fingers fumbling with the buttons of the blouse she had been unfastening, and lift the door-latch.

Jamie Todd stood outside, his face almost split in two by a great beaming grin.

'Islay, come and see this!'

'See what –' She didn't have time to finish the word. He caught her by the hand and whisked her out into the cool air, down the stairs and through the pend and into the weaving shop, her loosened, newly-brushed hair streaming behind her in the night air like black smoke.

They came to a breathless stop by the loom Walter had worked.

'There!' Jamie indicated the web on the loom, then lifted the lamp that sat close by and brought it nearer so that Islay could examine the cloth.

'It's –' her hand went out to touch the fine soft stuff, much finer than any material she had seen on those looms before. 'It's bonny! What yarn did you use?'

'Cotton!' The word burst from him triumphantly. 'Fine cotton – the last of the stuff Richard Knox supplied!'

'I've never seen such a cloth woven from cotton yarn before.'

His hand came to rest by hers, feeling the cloth with an expert's touch. 'And neither has anyone else in this town. It's as like muslin as you could find. D'you see what this means? I've done it, Islay – I've shown them all!'

'Oh, Jamie!' She was radiant with happiness for him. When he set the lamp down and began to dance around the looms, his red head flaming in the shadows hovering beyond the light's glow, she clapped a rhythm for him, laughing as she watched.

Finally he ran out of breath and staggered, almost falling against a loom. Islay put a steadying hand to his wrist.

'God save us, lassie, you're freezing cold!'

'It's little wonder. This place isn't warm, and you didn't even give me time to put a cloak on before you pulled me down here.'

'Och, I didn't think –'

She smiled up at him, still caught up in his happiness. 'It doesn't matter.'

'I must fetch Duncan – and Robert –'

'They'll be abed and asleep by this time!'

'So they will.' His face fell at the prospect of having to wait until morning to spread his news, then as she shivered he said, 'On you go – back upstairs with you.'

'Jamie, have you had your supper yet?'

'No. I wanted to get a good length of cloth on the machine before I stopped.'

'Come upstairs and I'll make something for you.' When he started to shake his head she said firmly, 'It's no bother – and anyway, your mother'll be away to her bed too, by this time. There'll be no food for you at home.'

He hesitated, then nodded.

Five minutes later the loom shop light had been extinguished and the two of them were in the warmth of the kitchen, with the door closed against the night and Islay busying herself at the range.

Jamie ate everything she put before him, and half emptied the ale jug, insisting that Islay had a drink as well, to 'wet the new cloth'. Then he dropped into the chair that had been Walter's and talked and talked while Islay sat opposite and listened.

The words meant nothing to her, for she knew little of weaving. It was enough to act as his audience, to see the joy in his face, hear the enthusiasm in his voice.

Time passed, and the rest of the town slept around them. But Islay and Jamie sat on in the lamplit room; for them, time had ceased to exist at all.

He finally interrupted himself with a yawn. 'God's truth, I've talked half the night away. I must go, and let you get to your bed. And tomorrow first thing I'll be out and about to spread the news that a new cloth's come to Paisley.'

'What about a market?'

'As to that, I think I'd be best to go down to England myself at once, to find a buyer. And I must find a manufactory willing to sell me more of the cotton yarn. Richard kept his business close, and I've no idea where he got the yarn he brought in.'

He rose, and took her hands in his. 'You're very patient, to listen to all this talk about cloth and yarn when you must be wearying for your bed.'

'I'm just proud to be the first to hear your news.'

'I wanted you to know,' he said simply. Then his grin died as his eyes rested on her uplifted face, framed in shining black hair. 'Somehow it was right that you should be the first to know,' said Jamie almost wonderingly, and released her hands so that he could cup her face gently between his big palms.

She stood beneath his touch, afraid to move or to say anything in case she broke the spell that curled about the two of them and took them into its fragile golden grasp.

At last, moving with agonising slowness, Jamie bent and brushed her mouth with his.

'You're so beautiful, Islay. The sight of you could wrench a man's heart from his body –' he said.

Then suddenly she was locked in his embrace, and his mouth was hard and hungry on hers, and there was no longer any need for her to worry.

'Islay?' he whispered against her throat when at last the kiss was ended. She ran her fingers through his hair; it was rich and thick beneath her hands as she had always imagined it to be.

'Stay with me, Jamie,' she murmured in reply, and he lifted her easily into his arms and carried her to the bed before moving to put the light out.

Then he came back to her, and Islay learned that being loved by the right man could indeed be a sweet and tender thing, a giving and taking, a wanting and sharing, an ecstasy beyond anything her imagination had ever dreamed of.

*

When she awoke early next morning Jamie had already gone from her side, stealing away while she slept. She stretched her naked limbs luxuriously across the width of the bed and smiled at the ceiling.

At last she had truly become a woman, blessed with a woman's understanding and knowledge.

She turned her face towards the window and smiled again, nursing her newfound secret.

*

The next day the Wellmeadow loom shop was filled with interested, excited weavers, and there was little chance of Islay seeing Jamie.

She was content to go about her work, listening to the

tramp of feet in the pend below and the buzz of deep male voices in the loom shop, while in the house above she sat spinning her yarn, dreaming her dreams, waiting for him to come to her.

But he didn't come, not even at night when the weaving shop was closed.

The next day one of the weavers told her that Jamie had gone off to England with a sample of the new cloth.

Gradually, Islay's feeling of wellbeing and contentment began to fray and tear and fall apart. She began to realise that the pain of being denied Paradise completely was as nothing to the agony of being allowed a glimpse inside the gates, then being turned away.

A full ten days dragged by before Jamie Todd returned from England and called on Islay, and offered her marriage.

And was turned down.

Chapter Forty

'But why?' Jamie demanded, stamping up and down Islay's kitchen like a bad-tempered captain on his quarter-deck. 'In God's name why?'

'Because I'll not be obligated to you or any man.'

'Obligated? I'm talking about marriage – about offering you my name and my protection, woman! Not about obligations!'

'I can manage fine on my own,' Islay said stonily, staring down at the hands clasped tightly in her lap.

'Mebbe so, but you must see that you'd be the better for a husband. Damn it, Islay, I don't blame you for being vexed at the way I never came near you after – after –'

'I wasnae vexed.'

'The truth of the matter is,' said Jamie miserably, 'I felt black ashamed of what I'd done. I couldnae look you in the face.'

'There was no need to think that. You didn't take me against my will.'

'Aye, but even so – Islay, we must get wed now, d'you not see that?'

'I see no reason why.'

Jamie ran a hand through his fiery hair, then said, 'I must go back to Lancashire tomorrow, to see about getting a good supply of that yarn. I'll be gone for a good few weeks, but mebbe that's just as well, for it'll give you a chance to consider. I'll call on you as soon as I get back –'

'I'll not give you a different answer.'

'You're determined, then? You'll not accept my offer?'

'No, Jamie.'

There was a short silence, then, 'Confound all women!' said Jamie, and slammed out of the house.

Islay closed the wildly swinging door behind him and sat

down at the kitchen table, folding her hands on its well-scrubbed surface.

After a moment the tears began to splash onto her interlocked fingers, one after the other, slowly at first, then falling faster and faster.

*

Jamie Todd returned to Paisley two weeks later, earlier than he had expected. When he walked into his mother's kitchen, glowing with good health and good humour, full of the news of his successful foray among the English manufactories, Margaret Knox was there, paying a visit to Kirsty.

'Jamie, you'll walk part of the way home with me?' she asked when she was about to leave, and he nodded willingly.

'Don't stay away too long, now. Your meal's almost ready,' Kirsty instructed as the two of them left the house.

'Five minutes only, for I'm starved,' Jamie promised.

Margaret laid a hand on his arm as they reached the bottom of the stairs. 'Come into the back yard for a minute, Jamie. Once we're seen on the street one man after another'll be stopping us to ask how you fared in England, and I want to talk to you in peace.'

He raised an eyebrow, but followed her through the back door of the passage.

It was a golden, mellow early October day. The bushes were festooned with Kirsty's washing, drying in the sun. The apple tree was still heavy with fruit waiting to be picked and the bees that lived in the skeps at the foot of the garden busily gathered nectar from the flowers that edged the long narrow path.

Margaret walked almost to the end of the garden, then turned to look up at Jamie. 'Now then,' she demanded briskly, 'what was it you said to Islay before you went away?'

His jaw dropped. He coloured to the roots of his hair, then said belligerently, 'So – she went running off to confide in you, did she? Then I hope you got more sense out of her than I did!'

'She did nothing of the sort! Islay's not the lassie to confide in anyone, more's the pity. But she's been out of sorts ever since you left the town, and it's easy to tell by the look that comes into her eye whenever your name's mentioned that you're the cause of the trouble. So what did you say to her?'

'Damn it, Margaret, I only offered her marriage.'

It was Margaret's turn to stare. 'You did that? And what was her answer?'

'She refused me. And now,' said Jamie, thoroughly bewildered, 'I've got you flyting on at me. What have I done – just tell me that?'

'Just a minute,' Margaret ordered. 'I can't make head nor tail of this business. Why should Islay refuse you when she's been heartsick for you since before she wed with Walter?'

'Heartsick? Her? Your imagination's running away with you. She cares not a jot for me – and I care nothing for her!'

'In that case why did you ask her to be your wife?'

His feet shuffled uncomfortably on the beaten earth path between the kale-beds. He moved away a step or two and began to fiddle with a red-currant bush.

Margaret waited, and finally he said, low-voiced, not looking at her. 'I – I lay with the lassie.'

'Did you, now? Against her own will, was it?'

'No, but even so – it was wrong of me. But when I went back to her and offered to right the wrong by marrying her – she near bit my nose off!'

'You great daft lummock!' Light was beginning to dawn on Margaret. 'Of course she'd refuse an offer like that!'

'Why? I'd be a good husband, a dutiful husband –'

'Och, Jamie! That's not enough for the likes of Islay! What woman would want a man who only offers her his hand out of guilt? Did you not think to tell the lassie you loved her?'

'Love?' Jamie crimsoned again. 'Margaret, for any favour!'

'Aye, Jamie Todd, love! It's a condition of the heart and the head that means a lot to women – though little enough to some men, it seems,' Margaret said scathingly. 'Islay sets great store by it, and I don't blame her. The lassie's already made one loveless marriage, and think of the heartbreak that caused her. She's not about to take on another man just because he feels obliged to offer her marriage.'

'Mind your own business, Margaret Knox!' Jamie said explosively and began to march towards the back door.

'Where are you going?'

'To eat my meal!'

'Jamie –' She caught up with him in the passageway, tugging on his good brown coat with little regard for the material or the stitching. 'Islay's leaving Paisley.'

'What?' He stopped short, one foot already on the stairs leading to the house. 'When?'

'Soon.'

'Where's she going?'

'I've no notion – and neither has she. But she's made up her mind – and once she hears you're home she'll no doubt go all the sooner. For any favour, man!' Margaret caught hold of his lapels and shook him again. 'Can you not see that if you let her go you'll neither of you ever be happy again?'

There was anguish in his face. 'Margaret, I'm thirty-four years old. I'm too old for Islay – I knew from the start that it was foolish of me to let myself care for her!'

'Tush, what does age have to do with it? D'you think Islay cares a whit for the years between the two of you? Not her! And your own father was near forty when he met and married with Kirsty, and fathered you! Did you never think on that?'

He stared down at her, wide-eyed. 'No, I never did,' he said slowly.

'Then think on it now, before it's too late!'

The delicious aroma of meat cooked to perfection drifted down from the house above as the kitchen door opened. Kirsty's voice skirled down the stairs.

'Jamie, are you there?'

He hesitated, glanced towards the sound of his mother's voice, then said tersely to Margaret, 'Tell her I have to see Islay first. And I don't know which of the two of us faces the harder task, Margaret Knox – you or me.'

Then he was plunging along the passageway, into the street, and away.

'I think,' murmured Margaret dryly, 'that it'll be me.'

And she gathered up her skirts and began to climb the stairs to face Kirsty's wrath.

Chapter Forty-One

The big wooden tub had been dragged out and filled with warm water. The bedclothes were carried downstairs and put into it then Islay, hot and tired from her exertions, kilted her skirts and climbed in to tread the blankets.

She was splashing busily when well-shod feet rattled hurriedly through the pend and Jamie almost exploded into the yard, his hair blazing round his face.

He caught the railing, began to bound up the stairs three at a time, then saw the tub and the small figure in it, and came skidding back down again.

At the sight of him Islay had lost her grip on her skirts. They dropped into the water, and were hastily gathered up again as Jamie came to a standstill before the tub and glared at her accusingly. Because she was standing high on the blankets their eyes were on a level.

'Jamie – you're back early, surely?'

'You're going away!'

'Who told you?'

'Margaret.'

'She'd no right to say anything. She knew I didn't want anyone to know.'

'Aye, but she's devious, is Margaret Knox. You should have got her to swear on the good Book,' he said tersely, then repeated, 'You're going away!'

'Aye, I am.'

'Where?'

She tilted her chin. 'I've not decided yet. There are other towns in Scotland besides Paisley – I'll find somewhere.'

'But why?'

'Because it's best that I go.'

'I'll be the judge of that.'

She stamped her foot, sending up a spout of warm dirty

soapy water. It splashed his good fawn breeches, and he moved back a hasty step. 'You? I'm not beholden to you!'

'You are! I let you stay in my house. I gave you work.'

'And I'm grateful, Mister Todd! What's wrong – did I not say it often enough?'

'If you were grateful you'd have agreed to marry me when I made the offer!'

His voice had begun to get louder. Windows opened here and there and interested, neatly-capped heads appeared.

'The offer – aye, that's just what it was. Like an offer to buy the apple after you'd bitten into it!'

'By God,' said Jamie, startled. 'You've got a straight way of putting things, Islay.'

'I'm a Highlander. We don't know any better.'

'And I'm a Lowlander. Mebbe I don't know any better than to be clumsy and – and – oh confound it, Islay,' said Jamie, 'I thought you'd have known, that night, how I felt about you. But in the cold light of the next morning I was – angry and shamed of myself.'

'I've already told you, I was as much to blame as you.'

'I was shamed to face you again,' he went on, paying no attention. 'I thought –' Then he took a deep breath, and said, 'The truth of the matter is, Islay, I want you for my wife. I – I love you, lass.'

She stood in the cooling water and stared at him. Her face was flushed, her hair had come half undone from its knot and hung in strands to the shoulders of her plain workdress. A wisp fell against her cheek and she reached up without conscious thought to pin it up again.

'Leave it,' said Jamie huskily. 'You look beautiful as you are.'

The hand fell back to her skirt, but still she couldn't find any words for him.

'Did you hear what I said?' he asked, driven to distraction by her silence. 'I love you, Islay Shaw. If you must know, I've been out of my mind with love and wanting since I first set eyes on you.'

Then he said impatiently, 'Och – Islay!' and strode forward to scoop her out of the tub and into his arms. His good coat and breeches were soaked in an instant as she struggled against him.

'Jamie, I'm all wet – you'll ruin your clothes!'

'I don't care,' said Jamie, and kissed her. 'Islay, will you be my wife?'

'But –'

'Will you?'

'Yes,' she said, then tried to fend off another kiss, and failed.

A shrill voice corkscrewed through the warm air from one of the over-looking windows. 'Jamie Todd – what are you up to with that lassie?'

He swung round in a circle, still holding Islay close, and laughed to see the heads now filling almost every window. Burdened though he was, he managed to sketch a clumsy bow in the direction of the notorious gossip who had called out to him.

'I'm making an honest woman of her, Mistress Gibson!' he called back, and there was a skirl of laughter and exclamations from the other women.

'Jamie!'

'Wheesht, Islay, I know fine what I'm doing,' he said, and kissed her again before making for the stairs. 'Maggie Gibson's the best known gossip in this part of the town. That old wag-tongue'll have the whole of Paisley told within an hour. And once that happens you'll not be able to change your mind and turn me down again.'

'I'll never do that – never!'

Islay put her arms about his neck as he carried her up the stairs and into the house, her dark head close to his red curls.

Later, she thought happily, she would tell him the news. She had known, even on the morning after their night together, that such loving must bear fruit. And she had been right.

Later, she would tell him that she was already carrying his child.

But not just yet.

Later.